THE GOODE GIRLS

A DELICIOUS INTRODUCTION

KERRIGAN BYRNE

0 9 8 7 6 5 4 3 2 1

Published by Oliver Heber Books

SEDUCING A STRANGER

A GOODE GIRLS ROMANCE

FOREWORD

Chief Inspector Carlton Morley is and *always* will be a part of my Victorian Rebel series.

However, my publisher and I realized very quickly that Prudence and Morley's story doesn't go at the end of a series, because it is a new beginning. The Goode Girls are written in the world of the Victorian Rebels—and those heroes feature prominently—but the stories are ultimately about this remarkable family and these women who find love despite being scandalous, flawed, outrageous, unique, or daring to want what society tells them they shouldn't.

To that end, A DARK AND STORMY KNIGHT became SEDUCING A STRANGER.

I hope you enjoy the series I wrote to celebrate the fact that we shouldn't have to be good girls to do great things.

PROLOGUE

LONDON, AUTUMN 1855

The devil's breath was a persistent cold prickle on Cutter Morley's neck. He'd awoken with a start in the wee hours of the morning, propped up against the doorway to St. Dismas where he'd taken refuge. Vicar Applewhite had fallen ill, and so the rectory was locked against vagrants today. More's the pity. He'd not been able to scrape together enough money to afford a flea-bitten room for the night, but the fact that his twin, Caroline, hadn't met him in the abbey courtyard meant she'd found a roof to sleep beneath.

Or a protector willing to allow her into the warmth of his bed for a pound of flesh.

She wasn't a prostitute. Never that. She was just... desperate. They both were.

But not for long. He'd a plan—one he'd implement just as soon as he was old enough, or rather, as soon as he looked old enough.

He was so close. Just one or two more winters. One or two more inches. No one was right sure of their ages... maybe thirteen or fifteen. Probably not older, but his recollection of the first handful of years was cagey so he couldn't be sure.

They'd no papers.

The slick of oily disquiet Caroline's new sometimes profession wrought within him was a mild hum compared to the symphony of peril and impending doom sawing at his nerves.

It haunted him as he set off from Spitalfields to Shoreditch, increasing with every step until he lifted his grimy hand to swat at the itch and smooth the hair at his hackles back against his neck. He had a hard-enough time staying warm with only the moth-eaten jacket he'd filched from a rubbish heap, but something about this day frosted the marrow in his bones.

He thought to lose the disquieting demon in the Chinese tent city, hoping it could be distracted by inhabitants of the cloyingly fragrant opium dens just as easily as he was drawn by the sizzles and aromas of food cooked in the out-of-doors. His gut twisted with longing, but he found no opportunity to filch a breakfast. People were extra wary today. Perhaps they, too, felt whatever portent hung in the air.

He wandered through throngs of peculiar and elegant Jews, his ear cocked to the lyrical Crimean accents of those escaping the violence in Russia, Prussia or the Ukraine. He thought their industrious bustle would perhaps chase away this unfathomable sense of bereavement. But alas, he made it all the way down Leman Street with the healthy sense that calamity watched him from the shadows of the palsied, rotten buildings, waiting to strike.

It wasn't a matter of if, but when. Or… no… perhaps it had already happened. The thing. The terrible thing. And the world held its breath waiting to suffer some awful consequence.

Turning down Common Doss Street, he loped up to number three, a ramshackle place mortared with more mold than grout.

Mrs. Jane Blackwell land-lorded over the only seven rooms free from vermin. At least, vermin other than that of the human variety. In Whitechapel, vermin were as inescapable as the toxic yellow fogs belched up by the Thames and thickened with soot from the refineries.

Cutter didn't need an invitation to shoulder into the doorway of the Blackwell common house, he'd been doing it since he was a lad.

The sharp smell of lye cut through the noise and stench wafting from men and women of dubious nocturnal vocations who had already begun drinking beer for the day at half noon. It drew him to the back of the house where a square of garden was connected by several alleys cobbled with grime. Clad in a dark frock and a soiled apron, Mrs. Blackwell stirred laundry over a boiling pot.

"More discarded bastards in these sheets than in all of Notting Hill," she muttered with a grimace. "I'm charging Forest extra if he's going to wank all over me linens, bloody pervert."

She glanced up when Cutter ambled over, her marble-black eyes crinkling with a good-humor quite lacking round these parts. In a place where most humans were anything but humane, where corruption was the only legitimate business and vice the only escape, Jane Blackwell was a warm, if rough-handed oasis of compassion.

Cutter would have given his right eye for a mum like her, or any mother really. She was a crass and vulgar woman, but he knew nothing else. She'd inherited these rooms from her father back before the pernicious poverty had taken over Whitechapel so completely, and an addiction to gin rounded out her inheritance. Or rather, drained it.

On top of her rents, she could charge tuppence a week more for her laundry services, and when she was of a mind to be dry, the money kept her and her son, Dorian, in luxuries like meat, cheese, and sometimes milk.

No wonder the lucky bugger was so tall and broad when they'd only dipped their toes into their teen years.

So long as Mrs. Blackwell kept her broken teeth—courtesy of Dorian's missing father— behind her lips, she was still a handsome woman. Her night-hued hair remained free of grey, and curled from beneath her cap in the steam of her laundry. She'd clutched Cutter to her breasts from time to time in a fit of sodden sadness or effervescent good spirits, and he'd be lying if he said he didn't enjoy it. He enjoyed it twice when he got to rib Dorian about it until his best mate blushed and boxed him one.

"I'm going to marry your mum," he'd taunt before dancing away. "Then I'll raise ya proper."

"Sod off," Dorian would reply irritably.

"Don't worry, I won't make you call me Da."

"I'll call you worse than that, you poxy cock."

At the thought of future scuffs, Cutter directed a half-grin at her, the one he knew made his cheek dimple, and he hefted what little sparkle he had left into his eyes. It was the first time he'd felt close to warm all day.

"Hullo," he greeted. "Did Caroline breakfast here?"

"I ain't seen her, Cutter," Jane greeted with a noticeable slur and a lack of any T's whatsoever.

He reached for the back of his neck and rubbed once again, even though little needles of gooseflesh stabbed at every inch of his skin by now.

"Dorian about?" he asked.

"In the kitchen fleecing doxies out of their hard-won earnings wif his dice last I checked." She swiped at her forehead with the back of her wrist and wrinkled her nose at him. "I've a mind to boil your wee arse in my pot next, ya noxious goblin. I can smell you from here."

Cutter's testing sniff of his own person was interrupted by a strong arm around his neck as he was pulled in for a grapple choke that might have resembled a boisterous hug if one was feeling generous.

"Oi! I think you smell awright." Dorian's voice seemed to deepen by the day, though Cutter's had changed over a year ago, much to Blackwell's competitive consternation. "I've heard there's a dead body or some such washed up at Hangman's Dock." His mate's dark eyes gleamed with a greedy sort of mischief. "Wot say we go and work the crowd?"

Working the crowd was their language for relieving the distracted onlookers of their watches, coin, and pocketbooks.

"Maybe later." Cutter rubbed at his chest as the dread that had dogged at him now bared its teeth and struck, wrenching at his heart with an icy pain.

Pain meant weakness. And one never showed weakness here, not even in the presence of those he knew the best. He always covered his pain with humor if not indifference.

"Your mum just offered to bathe me." Cutter waggled suggestive brows and summoned a cheeky smile from lord-knew-where. "Now toddle off, son."

A hot rag hit him square in the face, eliciting a very unmanly squeak of surprise.

"Wash your face, you little deviant, and then both of you make yourselves scarce, I've work to do!" Jane's bellow was softened with a wink, and Cutter gave himself a half-hearted scrub before he tossed the soiled rag back to the laundry pile and threw Jane another smile.

This she returned with a curse and a shake of her head.

He'd felt this strange sort of veneration for her since the first time Dorian had brought him and Caroline around. She'd allowed them to curl up in the kitchens and sleep like dogs by the stove in the winter and eat whatever crusts they'd helped clean from the tables. The next morning she'd sent them to Wapping High Street with strong warm tea in their bellies and a few pointers on how to beg.

"You're two golden-haired angels, inn't ya?" She'd tugged their noses fondly. "You'll empty more pockets than a naughty peep show, eyes that big and blue. 'Specially you, darlin'." She'd pinched at shy Caroline's pale cheeks and tugged at her golden ringlets.

And so they had. For years, Cutter and Caroline worked the streets of London, his sister drawing upon the kindness of those who would stop to offer a coin, while he learned to divest them of the rest with a pick of the pocket and a nimble getaway.

Sometimes they'd be caught, and Cutter would take the beating meant for them both. Those were often their most profitable weeks, as he could use the pitiable bruises and abrasions to solicit more charity.

This kept them fed until they'd passed their first decade and were no longer young and wretched enough to pity. People began to solicit them rather than offer them kindness, and eventually Cutter learned to answer the beatings he received with violence of his own.

Because he lacked the brawn of other boys, he relied on reflexes more advanced than most, and he'd mastered a slingshot as well as his sleight of hand, earning him the moniker, "Deadeye."

It was that name the streetwalkers of Whitechapel squawked as he tumbled into the common room with Dorian, loping toward the front entrance.

"Bugger me at both ends, you ladies ever seen an angel and a devil so 'andsome?" A girl they ironically called "Dark Sally," jabbed at one of her friends, who gathered at the long-planked table nursing sharp beer and waiting for darkness so they might ply their trade.

Cutter knew instantly he was the angel, as Dorian's wealth of shiny, black hair and sharp, satirical features made the comparison bloody obvious.

"I don't see no ladies here." The older plump prostitute named Bess gave an overloud bark of laughter before peering over at the boys. "I've swived plenty of devils in my day, but I'd bonk an angel with pretty eyes like that for free." She reached out an almost masculine hand to Cutter. "Come over here, darling, and let's see what you're packing."

Cutter didn't raise his eyes from the floorboards as his cheeks burned. "Any you seen Caro?"

"Look! Someone who still blushes in this shitehole," crowed yet another woman. "I'll bet you a pence he's a virgin."

"Caroline, you seen her or not?" he asked again.

Bosoms bounced as shrugs passed around the table, though it was Dark Sally who spoke. "She took up with an old watchmaker last I heard." She turned to Bess. "Remember the one, had an orange to share and it weren't even Christmas."

"I'd do right sick things for an orange," muttered a girl he didn't recognize. "Little bitch swiped him up before anyone got the chance at him."

"Careful, you," Bess threw a soiled handkerchief across the table. "That little bitch is his sister."

"I like virgins," sighed a thin, waspish woman around her sip of beer. "They 'aven't learnt to be cruel yet, and it's over quick enough. Right grateful they are." She sized Cutter up with a look that made him squirm.

"At that age, they'll pay you for another go in five minutes!" said Bess.

"And, what they lack in skill they make up for in eagerness," added another.

Dark Sally's eyes turned from kind to malevolent as she speared the boys with a hatred they weren't yet old enough to understand or to have earned. "Don't no man 'round here bother with skill," she sneered. "They'll grow to be no different."

A roar of laughter followed the lads out into the yard as they escaped the loud and bawdy women only to be swallowed by the crowded din of the streets.

A bitter autumn wind reached icy fingers through their threadbare clothes, and Cutter snapped the collar of his jacket higher, though it did little good. He rubbed at the back of his neck, and again at the empty ache in his chest.

Something was fucking wrong. Off. Missing.

"Fleas at you again?" Dorian ribbed.

"No, I just..." Cutter could think of nothing to describe what he was experiencing. "I'm cold is all."

"Where's the coat you got from the Ladies' Aid Society this spring?" Dorian asked, shoving his hands into his pockets. "That jacket you've on wouldn't warm a fleeced sheep."

"The sleeves barely came past me elbows anymore," he answered, giving his newly elongated limbs a wry stretch. "Besides, Caroline's was swiped from a doss house while back, so I gave it her."

Dorian nodded.

A tepid humiliation lodged next to the demon dogging Cutter, and he glanced over at Dorian to suss his friend's thoughts. "Caro's not like them whores in there," he rushed to explain. "She's just...well she won't let me spend me rifleman money on a room while it's still above freezing, so she does what she's got to."

"I know." Dorian gave a sober nod, his shoulders hunching forward a little more. "She wants out as bad as we do."

"Maybe worse."

"We've almost enough, Cutter." A thread of steel hardened his friend's voice and worked at his jaw as he looked so far ahead, he might squint into the future. "I bet our haul today will cover at least one of us."

"But we go together," Cutter reiterated.

"Together," Dorian nodded, and they knocked their forearms.

A few months past, Cutter had hatched a scheme on the day

the royals had paraded through High Street to celebrate the betrothal of a princess.

Dazzled by the accompanying regimentals in their crimson coats and rifles, he'd decided that in the space of a year, he and Dorian would be tall enough to lie about their ages and join Her Majesty's Army whereupon they'd be paid a penny a day. Enough to keep Caroline in rooms, and even send her to the regimental school. Enough to get medicine for Jane Blackwell's deteriorating health.

Enough to buy a future that didn't end in an early grave or worse, prison.

But that took papers...documents of birth they didn't have, and forging papers took money. So, they all kept whatever savings they could scrimp together in a tin hidden in Dorian's wall, waiting for the day they'd have enough.

"All's we have to do is evade the coppers until then." Dorian shoved his chin toward a pair on their beat, cudgels already out though there was no disturbance. "They'll give you nickel in Newgate for just about anything these days."

"You'll still marry her, won't you?" Cutter's soft question was almost lost to the din. "Even after the watchmaker. Even after—"

A rough punch landed on his shoulder. "'Course I will, you toad. Caro's me first kiss and everything, and...we all gotta do what needs doing to survive."

Dorian less than some, Cutter didn't say.

Because it wasn't his fault he had a mum, a roof over his head, or at least one or two guaranteed meals a day. Besides, Dorian and Mrs. Blackwell were generous whenever they could be.

"Maybe, if I'm going to marry Caroline, Mum would let her sleep in my corner with me."

Cutter's head snapped up as he speared Dorian with a glare.

"Not like that." Dorian lifted his hands in a defensive

gesture. "I won't touch her or nothing. Just… so she wouldn't have to sleep somewhere else. With…anyone else."

Cutter had to swallow around a thickening throat before he could reply.

"You would do that?"

"'Course. We're family." Dorian shrugged him off. "I'd ask for you both if Mum didn't rent out every inch of space we own at a premium."

"It's all right. I can fend for meself."

They skipped, dodged, and slithered through the masses toward the docks, answering the calls of the other street lads, most of whom either feared or venerated them. Dorian, because he was strong as a cart horse with a punishing temper to match, and Cutter because of his aforementioned dead eyed aim and his sharp fists.

Cutter threw them convivial retorts out of habit alone. For some reason, the worse he felt the more stalwart he was at maintaining a pretense of normality.

If anyone knew you were down, they'd kick you for it.

So he did his best to conceal the devil of dread riding him today.

They arrived at Hangman's Dock the same time the coroner's cart did, so they had to act quickly before the police scattered the crowd.

"Look," Cutter pointed above. "There's a landlord charging a fee to get a glimpse from his fire escape. I'll wager there's at least a handful of shillings in that box."

"He's our mark." Dorian made a quick assessment of the buildings and boathouses above the river. "Think you can climb that drainpipe there, and get to the roof above him? I'll create a diversion and lead them away while you swipe what you can from the box."

"I'll swipe the whole bloody box, see if I don't." Cutter nodded and spit in his hands before raking them through the dry bank silt and rubbing them together. They'd just have to get to the other side of the crowd and then, he'd grasp the drainpipe, shimmy hand over hand until he'd scaled the two stories, and scoot onto the roof poised to drop into the spot the blighter would abandon once he tore off after Dorian.

This was one of his favorite ruses.

Cutter didn't care about the corpse. Hell, he'd seen his fill of death after the last typhus epidemic raged through the East End, what was one bloated river find?

Boring, was what.

He followed his friend as they shouldered and shoved and jostled as many people as they could, their enterprising hands dipping into every place and coming up with coin more often than not.

When they broke through to the front and took a breath, they each fished out their finds and shared a grin when they counted almost two shillings' worth between them, more than a day's wages around these parts. Today might make them rich, if they played it right.

They were about to scamper around the half-circled arc to dive back into the other side toward the building when the entire crowd made a collective gasp and took a step back, leaving them strangely exposed.

He barely heard the disbelieving whispers, so intent was he on his mission.

"She's in shreds...

"What sort of animal...?"

"...no more than a child..."

Cutter turned his back on the river and made to dive back into the safety of the throng when Dorian's hand clutched his wrist with an iron grip.

He said nothing, but he didn't have to.

The demon that had haunted him all day now roared.

It scratched and clawed and cut deep enough to sever a

15

limb. That was truly what it felt like. Something had been cut out of him. Off of him. Something vital and dear. Gone.

Amputated.

He already knew before he turned to look.

Before he saw the strands of identical golden hair sullied with river filth waving like soft reeds in the little dam created by a concrete dock. Before he registered the red abrasions at her wrists and bare ankles, or the ridiculous pattern of last spring's coat, the one he'd given her, only one arm haphazardly shoved into the sleeve.

Before it dawned on him that even such polluted water was never so red.

The coin in Cutter's hands fell to the earth. He stepped on them as he lunged forward, her name released to the sky by the devil who'd stalked him. Surely it had to be. Because no human creature could have made such an inhuman scream.

Caroline.

CHAPTER 1

LONDON, 1880, TWENTY-FIVE YEARS LATER

*P*rudence no longer desired to be good.

Or, rather, to be *a* Goode.

It was why she stood at the gate to Miss Henrietta's School for Cultured Young Ladies at midnight, her chest heaving and her resolve crumbling. She'd come all this way. And she wanted this. Didn't she?

Just one last night of freedom. One night of her own making. Her own choosing.

One night of pleasure before her father foisted her off on the highest-ranking noble desperate enough to have her at nine and twenty.

Three months. *Three months* until her life was irreparably ruined, and she'd have to love, honor, and obey the most notorious spirit-swilling, mistress-having, loud-mouthed, and fractious idiot in all Blighty.

George Hamby-Forsyth, the sixth Earl of Sutherland.

He'd marry her because she'd an obscene enough dowry to cover his debts and still maintain a generation or two.

Not because he loved her.

God, what a fool she'd been!

For the umpteenth time, the tragedy of her gullible nature slapped her until her cheeks burned. Had it only been yesterday she'd found out her happy engagement was a farce? That everyone around her knew she would be wretched and humiliated, and still expected her to go through with it?

That the two people closest to her in the world hadn't loved her enough to tell her.

The scene forever tormented her, illuminated just as clearly as it had been in the brightness of the late afternoon sun the day before. Every decision she'd made a perfect mix of timing and luck until she'd stumbled upon her own tragedy.

Pru had been pleasantly exhausted after spending a day with the seamstresses for her extensively fine wedding trousseau. Her sister Honoria had accompanied her, along with their oldest friend and neighbor, Mrs. Amanda Brighton of the Farley-Downs Brightons.

"Do let's go to Hyde Park," Pru had gestured expansively toward the park in question, shaking Amanda's arm in her eagerness. "I'm dying to sweep by Rotten Row and take a few turns on Oberon."

"I'm game for it." Honoria, her eldest—already married—sister, had lifted her nose and squinted into the distance where the horse track colloquially known as *Rotten Row* bustled with the empire's aristocracy, both human and equine.

Amanda was more Honoria's age than Pru's—which was three years older—but she and Amanda shared a blithe and energetic nature that made them natural mischief-makers and thereby the swiftest of friends.

Honoria, though a beauty, was born to be a dreary proper matron, and fulfilled her vocation with dreadful aplomb.

"I wouldn't at all mind examining the new stags on the market," Amanda said with a sprightly grin lifting her myriad of freckles. She tucked one arm into Pru's and the other into Honoria's, and nearly dragged them both toward the square.

Prudence's ride along the row had been every bit as exhilarating and satisfying as she'd imagined. Friends and acquaintances had called out their hearty congratulations, which had produced the sort of smile that she felt with her entire self.

It'd dimmed when she'd a brief encounter with Lady Jessica Morton, who was the reason everyone had called her "Pru*dunce*" in finishing school. But even her spinster nemesis had gritted out her felicitations. Had Jessica's smile been on a dog, it would have been called a snarl, and Prudence had to fight a spurt of victorious wickedness.

Jealousy was such an unflattering color.

Oh, it wasn't her best quality, this, but it *had* felt indescribably good to "win," for lack of a better word. Her entire life, she'd come in second. Second eldest and second prettiest of the four so-called, "Goode girls."

Second married, as well.

But to an Earl! And not just *any* Earl, but one of the most marriageable bachelors in the realm. Her happy engagement was delicious any day but became pure truffled pleasure when trotted out in front of Jessica.

Bidding a cheerful farewell to the retreating back of her childhood antagonist, Pru had handed Oberon to one of the grooms, and set off to meet the ladies for tea.

Bouncing her riding crop off her thigh in high spirits, Pru had searched for them, eager to share her bit of gossip about her conversation with Jessica.

She found Honoria and Amanda on a bench with their heads together. They admired a group of smartly dressed young men prancing about on thoroughbreds and sipped thin glasses of lemonade that sweated in the summer heat.

She was about to call out to them when she fumbled her riding crop and dropped it, kicking it behind a tree.

Cursing her constant clumsiness, she scampered after it,

and was still stooping to retrieve it when Amanda had said, "How bold of Lady Jessica to approach Pru in public."

Honoria retrieved a compact mirror from her reticule and checked the hue of her perfect lips, the pallor of her dewy skin, and tucked a stray dark hair back beneath her hat before snapping it shut. "I detest Jessica Morton. She tormented Pru endlessly in school."

Amanda made a sour face, as if her lemonade had suddenly become too tart. "I'd thought her affair with Pru's fiancé concluded, but now I'm not so certain."

Honoria's excessively pretty features pinched into a frown of disapproval. "George and Jessica? Are you quite certain?"

Heedless of her new wine velvet riding jacket, Prudence had pressed her back to the tree, less a furtive move than a collapse. She needed something to hold her up.

George...*Her George*...and Jessica Morton?

When? Why? And how? And how many times? And... *When?*

Certainly, she'd never assumed he'd been a saint, not with his roguish good looks, but now that they were to marry, she'd thought he'd have no need for other women.

That she'd be enough.

That their love would contain all the passion he'd require.

Amanda swatted at an insect with the fan previously hanging from her white-gloved wrist. "I heard about it at the Prescott Ball, Maureen Broadwell and Jessica Morton complained that Sutherland is a base and venal lover. She said, and I quote, 'That man can read a woman's body like a blind man can read music.'"

Honoria's breath hitched on her sip of lemonade and she hid a series of delicate coughs behind her handkerchief.

Pru swallowed back her own sob. The Prescott Ball had been only a fortnight ago. George had been her escort...and these women had been discussing him in such a manner as he waltzed her on the tops of clouds.

"Poor Pru," Amanda tutted, waiting for Honoria to finish her coughing fit before adding, "Don't you find it a bit disgusting how many bastards Pru's dowry will keep up once George has his hands on all her money?" She sighed, then shrugged it off as if it were no more disappointing than a broken fingernail.

Bastards?

Pru had tugged at the high neck of her gown, fighting for breath.

All she'd ever wanted was children.

To tuck chubby little limbs into bed. Kiss scraped knees and tears. She wanted to hear the peals of laughter when their strong daddy would toss them in the air and allow them to climb on his back.

George had been that man in her dreams. So dashing and virile.

He already had children?

Honoria had leaned forward, looking intently toward the track as if searching for Prudence's form. "Poor Pru, indeed. George has convinced everyone that he loves her. Even William…even me. I suppose we should tell her."

William Mosby, Viscount Woodhaven, was George's closest compatriot, and Honoria's husband.

Now that Pru thought about it, Honoria hadn't seemed particularly pleased with the betrothal, and she'd always assumed it was because Pru was marrying an Earl when William was merely a Viscount, and thereby his social inferior.

She'd been so absurdly blind.

Amanda let out a disenchanted sigh. "Pru needs to learn how the world works, eventually. That it's not all ponies and balls and butterfly nets."

Honoria sucked her lip between her teeth, a gesture she

made whenever she was conflicted. "Though, I'd hate to ruin her wedding for her, and it's not as if she can break the engagement now. I should have warned her off George ages ago, but William expressly forbade it."

Amanda nodded, smoothing the creases from her cream gown. "It's kind of us, I think, to maintain her frivolous naiveté for a bit longer."

"Yes. Kind." Honoria's famous composure crumpled for the slightest moment, uncovering the features of a woman beset by abject misery. "She's a lifetime to be disappointed by a husband."

Pru clapped two hands over her mouth to keep from saying anything. From screaming in the middle of the bustling park loud and long enough for all of London's elite to hear. She couldn't face them yet. She couldn't sort through her hurt and anger and humiliation enough to land on a single thing to say.

Frivolous naiveté? Was this *really* what they thought of her? Her best friend and her elder sister? Honoria... the woman she'd idolized for the whole of her life. The bastion of feminine perfection against which she'd been measured. The loveliest debutante to grace Her Majesty's halls in decades.

And Amanda? The naughty sprite who'd collected all her secrets and her sorrows. Who'd bounced and giggled through life with nary a care.

"Speaking of disappointing husbands...mine will be back in town tomorrow night," Amanda distracted Pru by saying. "And so, I think *that* one with the muscular legs will be my next acquisition." Amanda pointed in the direction of the riders, and Pru blinked through gathering tears in confusion.

Her friend had never expressed a great interest in horseflesh, and her husband was more interested in estate acquisitions than equine. He owned half of Cheshire.

"I've always admired your taste," Honoria said approvingly.

Amanda leaned in closer. "Lady Westlawn told me he

brought her to completion twice in one night. *In fact*, he was so skilled, she gave him one of her coveted diamonds." The sound Amanda made was laced with enough licentiousness to bring about a biblical plague.

Pru gaped. They weren't speculating about horseflesh at all. But the men astride!

"To the Stags of St. James." Amanda lifted her lemonade for a "cheers" in the fashion of a bawdy sailor at a public house. "Are you certain you won't try one?"

Honoria clinked her glass with Amanda's but set it down at her elbow. "As tempted as I am, William has me on a tight leash."

"That doesn't mean you can't come and look," Amanda offered. "That's nothing more than window-shopping, really."

"No. I suppose it doesn't." Honoria stood and drifted toward the Row, a trailing Amanda in her wake.

Pru couldn't stand any more. She'd fled home and immediately begged her father to break their engagement.

He'd blustered through his stately beard. "You and your sisters are beautiful enough to tempt men away from their mistresses, Pru. I dare say Honoria did, and you're almost her equal." He patted her head with the sort of fond deference he showed his hounds. "Sutherland is an Earl, a vital man of true English blue blood and the...passions and tempers to match."

"But, Papa," she'd sobbed. "He'll humiliate me. He'll make me a laughingstock."

"Nonsense. Sutherland has always been a discreet man. This marriage is your duty to your family, so don't let your doddle-headed fancies of romance get in the way of that, do you hear me? You will say nothing of this to Sutherland and when he next comes to court you, you'll keep a civil tongue in your head, or I'll not be responsible for what I do!"

A distraught and sodden Pru had then taken her shattered

soul to her mother, asking her to mend it. Begging her to intervene.

"It is the practice of men to have mistresses, dear. And you'll find it's a blessing in the end..." With that crisp reply, she'd nailed the coffin shut on any hope Pru had of reclaiming a sense of herself.

Something had hardened in her then. A fist of rebellious anger clenched around the last glowing shard of her heart.

The very next day, she had called upon Lady Westlawn and not-so-discreetly inquired about the Stags of St. James.

Which was how she'd ended up here. At the garden gate to Miss Henrietta's School for Cultured Young Ladies.

St. James, she was told, was not a reference to the park or buildings, but to the patron saint of riding.

Of all the vulgar things.

As she stared at the gate, Pru gathered her resolve. She wouldn't be like George. Nor would she be like Amanda. Once she'd taken a wedding vow, she'd keep it, regardless of what George decided to do. And if any children resulted from their marriage, she'd teach them to do the same.

One deceit did not merit another.

But tonight, she'd take a lover. A man who was nothing like the Earl of Sutherland in all his dark, brutish glory.

She'd claim a night of pleasure for her very own. One night she controlled with her desires and whims, and where *her* satisfaction was the object of the deed.

Because from what she'd heard, she'd live without it for the rest of her life.

Pru pulled the hood of her cloak down to shadow her face from the gaslights perched atop the wrought iron gate and tapped on the third bar three times.

A footman melted from the shadows, a pretty lad, barely old enough to shave.

He gave her a curt nod. "Do you have an appointment, madam?"

What had Lady Westlawn told her to say if she hadn't made prior arrangements at Hyde Park? Oh yes.

"I'm here to peruse the night-blooming jasmine."

The gate swung open on silent hinges and she took in a shaking breath. Thresholds, she'd heard were dangerous. Places of in-between, where fairy folk and demons could meddle with the living.

Or so superstitious ancestors once believed.

Tonight, she could believe it. Out on this street, she'd done nothing to speak of. She was no one of great importance. Prudence Goode. A second daughter of second-rate nobility.

A virgin.

To cross this threshold, was to be forever altered. Did a night like this always seem so monumental? Did the specter of fate seem to hover above every woman's head upon making such a decision?

Something intangible drifted above the lamplight but below the stars. Something sentient and dark. Perhaps a bit dangerous and wrathful, though she somehow wasn't afraid.

Destiny was on the other side of that gate, it told her. More than her virginity would be taken tonight.

No. Prudence shook her head. No, not destiny. What whimsical tripe.

She wasn't here to court fate…only fantasy.

It took two tries to swallow her nerves before she picked up her skirts, stepped over the threshold, and lost her breath to a marvel.

For a moment, she wondered if she had, indeed, been snatched by the Fae.

The gardens at Miss Henrietta's School for Cultured Young Ladies might have been a fairy patch. Strings of beads and ribbon flowed from curious shaped hedges and foreign willows with lush, wilting limbs. They glimmered and sparkled in the dim lamplight along lustrous cobbles, illuminating paths to dark places.

More importantly, they created concealing shadows, some of which were already full of revelry. The grounds were vast for the city, and the manor house glowed gaily on the other side of the garden.

She was not to approach the house, she was told. The ironically named school for cultured young ladies was anything but. Miss Henrietta's was one of London's most exclusive and expensive brothels where *men* took their pleasure among a menagerie of women.

The Stags of St. James, however, made discreet house calls.

And in the summer on certain clear nights…they rutted out-of-doors.

Except, Prudence realized as she ventured onto the grounds, the out-of-doors was not so rustic as one might assume. The gardens at Versailles might weep for the luxury here, and if one wanted to find a place to feel ensconced in privacy, one needn't look too far.

"Approach any stag you like, madam, so long as he is not engaged by another," the young footman startled her by appearing at her elbow. She'd quite forgotten he was there. He leaned down to whisper, "They'll lock horns for the likes of *you.*"

"Who—who would you recommend?" she murmured, instantly regretting the ridiculous question.

The footman didn't even break his perfect form. He might have been engaged by a Duke, not a derelict debutant looking to debauch herself.

"Adam is in the orchard, seeking his Eve," he proffered, gesturing toward a copse of trees, as if he directed her to pluck an apple, rather than the original sin. "Let's see…Daniel is bound in his den in anticipation of devouring, if you are feeling the role of lioness tonight." He pointed at a dark shadow in a glass enclosure covered by ivy.

"There's Goliath, the barbarian who might be tamed by the right gentle hand. Or David, if you prefer someone...younger. More eager."

Prudence stopped, suddenly seized by indecision and a not little fear of lightning, even on such a clear and cloudless night. "I'm sorry but are all of the—er—stags given religious names?" she queried. "Seems rather blasphemous, doesn't it?"

He gave her a mockingly chiding look. "Go to a church if you want to judge, Madam, we're all here to commit a cardinal sin, maybe several."

A decent point, that. She nodded and mumbled an apology, suddenly feeling very itchy and out of her element.

With a jovial wink that told her all was forgiven, he bowed. "If you're feeling indecisive, I encourage you to take a turn around the garden, let it dazzle your senses, and see what entices your...vigor."

That seemed like an excellent idea. She'd come here for a thing. An experience. Why the devil hadn't it occurred to her that what she was coming here for...was a person?

A man.

A man of her own choosing.

How very novel. She'd only ever thought to be chosen. Women were always waiting, hoping to be picked or plucked by the right man. Selected like a trinket in a shop, to be taken home and trotted out at expensive gatherings.

Tonight, she was the shopper. She would pick the man she wanted and pay him to do what she desired.

But who? Did she want David or Goliath, Adam or Daniel?

A hero or a heretic.

A saint or a sinner...

Venturing deeper into the fairy garden, she allowed her senses to take it all in. The gentle breeze ruffling at the ribbons and drapes of chiffon and silk along the path. The slight sound of running water in the distance. A giggle from that dark corner. A groan from that Bedouin tent over there.

She refused to look too far into the dark, and so she kept her eyes often skyward, up to the stars.

Which was why she never saw the dark shadow crouched behind a hedgerow by the fountain.

CHAPTER 2

hief Inspector Carlton Morley stalked his latest villain from the putrid slag pots of industrial East London all the way to Mayfair. Three young men had been slaughtered, and no one had connected their murders until today.

Until him.

The victims had been from several different boroughs of London and none of them had known each other, but their deaths were identical. No one had noticed the connection until the files had made their way to his desk, because detective inspectors from differing stations rarely had cause to collaborate with each other.

But they all answered to him.

The cases had been closed. Deemed unsolvable or without enough evidence to proceed through lawful means.

But Morley had other means at his disposal... and there were many forms of law and justice. The Queen's Justice. The law of the land. Divine justice. The laws of nature.

And the justice of the streets. The laws of which were unwritten but universally heeded.

The laws of the land were necessary to uphold, and he'd devoted his entire career to doing so.

But the laws of the streets afforded him the means to mete out justice where the system had failed.

And they'd failed these murdered men. Strapping, handsome lads, well-liked by their families and communities, all employed among the working class. And yet none of them seemed to be struggling to get by. Each of them lived above their station, kept family members fed and comfortable in clean and respectable dwellings on pittance a day.

The question was how?

The answer had led him here.

Miss Henrietta's School for Cultured Young Ladies, of all the unimaginable places.

And since he'd obtained the information that'd led him here by means not strictly legal, he couldn't very well walk through the front door, let alone obtain a warrant.

So, he'd taken to the dark, as he'd done with alarming frequency these days, disguising himself every now and again with a simple black mask he'd had lying around from one of the Duchess of Trenwyth's multitude of endless charity functions.

His view to the garden was impeded by impenetrable hedges or stockades of ivy around wrought iron, if not a full stone wall on the west side. He ultimately decided to circumvent the locked gate by scaling a nearby wych elm. He balanced out on a limb until he feared it would no longer hold his weight, and vaulted over the gate, expertly avoiding impalement on the iron spikes.

Morley landed in silence among the shadows and kept to them as he stalked along the circumference of the property. He waited and watched, his entire body attuned to danger, to a possible threat. A villain or a murderer.

A couple strode nearby, and he melded with the dark as a

tall and elegantly handsome man bent to whisper something scandalous into the ear of a woman ten years his senior and two stone his heft.

She tutted, flirted, and then her companion swept her into his embrace, pressing her against the column of a gazebo. He kissed her passionately before he grappled with the latch of a small outbuilding and shoved her inside.

What the devil?

A tree branch snapped around the corner of a hedge. Morley drew his knife, took two readying breaths, and burst from around the corner, dropping into a fighting stance.

Only from this angle could he have seen the gagged and blindfolded woman beneath the tree, holding its lower branches for purchase as a man brutally thrust into her from behind.

Something in the muffled sounds she made froze him in place. They were yips and mewls of encouragement. Unmistakable in their ardor.

Bemused, Morley sheathed his knife and blinked rather doggedly at the fornicating couple until the man noticed him and made an impatient gesture for him to go.

His hips never lost their rhythm.

The woman was enjoying herself, but the gentleman checked his watch as though... he kept track of the time?

Morley backed away, turning to the garden and seeing it for what it truly was.

If someone had told him he'd already died and gone to Elysium, he might have believed them. For this resembled something of a pagan paradise. Friction and fornication hinted at everywhere, if not flagrantly happening.

No one *exactly* fucked in the open, but neither was a gazebo, a sheer tent, a hedge maze or a copse of carefully placed trees considered a proper place for a romp.

Even the air was sweeter here, whispering of lilacs and

gardenias rather than the singular smells of the city. The garden sparkled like the very stars might visit to watch the debauchery. It was a dream crafted by honey-hued lighting and fluttering fabrics.

Of all the bastardly bacchanalian bullshit.

Morley retreated to a borderline pornographic fountain and crouched behind a hedgerow, grateful that the sound of the water covered the thinly veiled noises of carnal revelry.

A small mercy that, because his body was beginning to forget how exhausted he was and respond to the wickedness of the atmosphere.

It was how they got you, these places. Inundated one with sex and fantasy until instinct took over and a man forgot who he was. Became a needful, terrible creature, one led around by his cock rather than his reason, until he found his pocketbook emptied by his own weaknesses.

A brothel. He grimaced. He'd broken into a brothel of all places whilst searching for a killer. He must have taken a very wrong direction, or he'd stumbled upon another humungous clue.

Either way, he couldn't exactly begin an interrogation at— he looked at his watch—half one in the morning. Tucking the watch away, he scrubbed at his face with both hands before adjusting the mask over his eyes.

God's blood but he was tired.

He'd been waylaid on his way here by a contingent of the High Street Gang, who'd taken one look at his darkly elegant attire and decided he was an easy mark.

He'd kicked nine shades of shit out of four men and had left them tied to the corner for the next copper on his beat to find.

With a note, of course, as was courteous.

He'd broken up a domestic brawl that'd spilled out onto the streets, and gave a boy on the cusp of manhood a pence to sleep beneath a different roof than his ham-fisted father.

A man on Wapping High Street had mistaken a charwoman for a nightwalker and had been about to force his attentions upon her when Morley had picked up a palm-sized stone, and made a spinning slingshot of his cravat. The rock to the temple had felled the attacker, and Morley didn't stay to check if he was even alive. He'd shrugged off the woman's cries of gratitude and had been on his way.

He was no hero. These were just things he did, sweeping up small crimes while he chased nightmares through the night.

Back when he'd attempted to sleep, he'd been tortured by them. Eventually, those nightmares had seeped into the daylight, following him from the dark until they filled every corner of every room. Shades and specters. The ghosts of those he'd killed, of those who'd endeavored to kill him. Of the souls he'd failed to save and the monsters who'd escaped justice.

For decades they'd haunted him, tormented him endlessly each time he dared close his eyes. Until he'd done something about it.

He *became* the thing from which nightmares ran.

He rid the night of monsters, so he could continue to be the man he was during the day without sinking into a miasma of slow and indelible madness. He was both the system of justice and the shadow of it.

Because the shadow could do what the system could not.

Because he still had a dead-eye, sharp fists, and even sharper blades.

Because he'd sold his soul to a demon for justice years ago, and every subsequent sin merely deepened the fathomless pit into which he'd been thrown.

Every time he'd thought he'd hit the bottom, he realized he was still falling.

That the depths could always be deeper. That the night could always be darker. That the world could always be colder.

That honor didn't seem to mean much anymore, and he

continued to fight a war that might have always been lost and for a cause that was nothing more than an illusion.

He'd been fighting for so long. For so many endless years, and for what? These days, every victory felt as though it made as much difference as a teardrop to the Thames.

And still he hunted, because what else could he do? Collect a wage until the inevitable forages of time and regret came for him as they did for everyone else?

A snap of a whip and a snarl came from the glasshouse covered in ivy. Morley squinted over at it, watching the shadows take shape, illuminated by one dim lantern inside.

If he wasn't mistaken, a woman rode a man, but not his hips...Morley squinted...his face. Her pleasure sounds filtered through the fountain to him, hot and demanding.

They reverberated down his spine and landed in his loins.

God, it had been too long since he—

Another astonished sound broke his intent concentration, this one behind him. From his crouching position, he turned his neck to watch a woman's windmilling arms fail to balance her before she crashed down upon him like a felled tree, toppling them both to the grass.

Morley swam in a sea of skirts and petticoats, taking a slap to the jaw for his troubles, though he was fairly certain she hadn't meant to strike him.

The woman draped across his lap writhed and wriggled, apparently as surprised as he. He attempted to gather her up as one might a child, one arm behind her shoulders and the other beneath her knees, but she didn't seem capable of holding still enough for him to manage.

"Upon my word," she exclaimed from behind mountains of silk. "I'm frightfully sorry! Are you hurt?"

Morley opened his mouth to assure her he was unharmed, but she didn't wait for a reply.

Her next sentence was spoken in one breath. "I'm forever

ungainly, clumsy, my sisters call me, and in a place such as this it's rather impossible not to look everywhere at once and I was honestly attempting to look nowhere at all and you're rather dark—" She finally crested her skirts and wrestled them beneath her arms to look at him. She took a breath to amend... "No, not dark. Dazzling."

Morley blinked down at her, suddenly wishing he'd ever thought to steal a moment from crime reports and newspapers to crack the spine on a book of verse.

Because the woman in his arms was a poem, and he hadn't the words to describe her.

His hold of her became suddenly very careful. Delicate, like one would hold a teacup in a lady's parlor rather than the tin mugs at the Yard.

"Oh," she said breathlessly, as if discovering clarity. "It's you. You're who I've come looking for."

Even through his building confusion, some strange part of him was *as glad* she'd—quite literally—stumbled upon him as she seemed to be.

He shook his head, trying to dislodge the sensation.

As Morley always did when out about his nocturnal business, he adopted a bit of his childhood cockney accent. "Do I know you?"

The lanterns painted the shadows of her ridiculously long eyelashes across cheeks that could have been chiseled from the whitest of Roman marble. Those lashes fringed wide, dark eyes two sizes too large for her delicate features. The effect intensified her dramatic expression as she seemed to take him in with identical wonder.

"Yes, you'll do rather nicely, I think," she breathed, apropos of nothing. Her voice, alternately husky and sweet, seemed incongruous with this place. There was temptation in it, but no sin. Innocence, but also desire.

She leaned forward on his lap, and he became very aware

that he held her like a man held his bride when crossing the threshold.

The thought terrified him, and yet he couldn't seem to let her go.

"Which one are you?" she asked as though to herself as she conducted a thorough examination of his features. "I can't think of any biblical hero you'd resemble...and none with a mask, besides. I like a bit of mystery."

He cocked his head at that. Biblical? This was all lunacy. He neither knew this woman nor did he want to. If she was a prostitute, she was a bloody good one, but he was no customer. He should lift her to her feet and send her on her way. He'd work to do and—

The soft scrape of her fingers against his shadow beard froze him in place. She watched her own hand with a dazed, almost unfocused gaze as she discovered the line of his jaw with a featherlight touch before cupping it in her small palm.

The tender curiosity demonstrated in the motion unstitched something hard within him.

"No..." she whispered. "No, you're no hero."

He could do little else than hold his breath, his every sense hanging upon her next words. What would be her verdict, he wondered? Would she compliment or condemn him?

"You're an angel, aren't you? An archangel, perhaps. Or a fallen one? A warrior..." she decided. "But... for which side?"

"I'm no angel," he warned. "I'm nothing but a shadow." Morley hated to disappoint the fanciful woman, hated to dispel whatever magic she was weaving through him with her touch. But it was better he told the truth. Better for them both.

"How ridiculous of me, I beg your pardon. I'd like to say that I've been caught up in all this fantasy, but it'd be a lie. I'm like this all the time." At this she gave the ghost of a giggle, and the sound was more pleasant than the rush of the fountain beneath which they'd fallen. "You're a very solid shadow, sir, if

I may say so." Her gaze finally focused to resolute. "How much?"

He frowned. "How much?"

"How much?" she encouraged meaningfully with a thrust of her sharp chin. "For you? The—er, footman told me to select any one of the Stags of St. James who were not previously engaged. And I've decided upon you. I want to make love to you—or rather, I want you to make love to me. But only i-if you don't have other women—er—plans. I mean, that is, prior engagements."

"Prior engagements?" he echoed.

Her hopeful features fell into a petulant pout. "Did someone already make an appointment at Hyde Park for tonight?"

"No," he said carefully, wondering what to do next.

She brightened immediately. "Excellent. Then...tell me how this works. I've never...hired a man to make love to me before. And I confess I'm ignorant of how else to proceed rather than plainly. So, would you do me the kindness—er—the honor?"

Morley blinked down at her as three things had just become inexorably clear to him.

The first was this woman talked incessantly when nervous, and her babble was oddly endearing.

Second, she was from a wealthy family, likely blue-blooded and likely married.

And tertiary...he'd lived probably nearly forty years and had never met a woman he'd so keenly desired to fuck.

A hunger awakened within him with all the ferocity of a hibernating beast. It had teeth and claws and tore his decency to shreds before going to work on his restraint. His heart kicked at his ribs, which restricted in turn, relieving him of breath.

He was a moral man, goddammit. Lawful and without prejudice or vice. He'd lived as a veritable monk for more years than he cared to admit, and there was good reason for it. He should bloody well stand up and take his leave of her. Right now.

Except, what if she didn't go home? What if she lingered in search of a different stag?

That wasn't going to bloody happen. He wouldn't let it.

He could throw her over his shoulder and return her to her father. Her husband. Or whatever woebegone individual had the responsibility for her safekeeping.

He made to do just that when another variable struck him.

What if she returned tomorrow night? What if she took her pleasure with another man?

What if... he missed his chance?

The hungry demon within him snarled at this, raked his claws and expelled scalding fire through his veins like a hell-spawned dragon until Morley had to force himself to inhale and expel a protracted breath.

He was no kind of man to consider such a proposition. He was neither starving for coin nor lacking in romantic prospects.

No, this was ludicrous. Nothing more than a flattering fantasy.

He opened his mouth, preparing a gentle rejection. "What do you want me to do to you?"

His lips slammed shut. The question had ricocheted through his mind since the moment she'd asked him to name his price. But it'd been the *last* thing he'd expected to escape his lips.

Blotches of color stained her pale cheeks, but she didn't look away. "I-I'd like you to do...whatever it is women pay you for the most often." She reached into her hooded pelisse and retrieved a satchel of coins. "The skill you're most proud of. The thing that makes them come to you on a night like this."

Morley didn't know what women *paid* for sexually, but he knew enough about people to reply. "A bird like you knows her mind. She don't come looking for a man like me 'less she has some idea of what she intends to get from the encounter."

What the bloody hell was he saying? He wasn't even considering this... so why—

She made a wry sound. Half laugh, half gasp, as she reached up to smooth at the collar of his shirt, which had bent when he'd torn off his cravat. Something in the nervous gesture touched him. Something that had begun to unstitch him the moment she'd fallen, and now was quickly unraveling.

"My fiancé. He's a selfish lover. I don't think he'd ever..." She trailed away for a moment, before imparting information about a man Morley hoped to never meet, lest he murder the bastard. "I found out that he—well, he's not faithful. And understand he doesn't have to be—that most men of my class aren't. But *I* will be. If I take a vow of marriage, I shan't break it, but I've said no vows yet." She tilted her head to look back up at him, a defiant little furrow appearing beneath her dramatically arched brows. "He does not own me *yet*."

Tears colored her voice, though none had fallen, and something inside Morley twisted. Pain did not sit comfortably on features such as hers. She'd a visage that glowed with an inner light, even in the sinful dimness of this lusty place.

She didn't belong here in the dark, committing sins on the ground. Hers was a face for the sun. She was a spoiled woman experiencing her first heartbreak. Learning her first terrible truth about the world of men in which she lived.

She didn't know the first thing about pain.

And yet...the courageous way she fought her threatening emotion, tied him up in knots.

Christ, this shouldn't be happening. That he was even entertaining such an idea was lunacy. This woman was obviously an emotional disaster he didn't need and there was a killer to find.

And yet...she was warm and fragrant, and they were

surrounded by sensual indiscretions, the sounds of which glided through this infernal glade with increasing intensity. She smelled like a delicacy waiting to be devoured and his mouth would not cease watering.

So he held her, his cock hard as a diamond, and Lord save him if her eyes were not dilated black with passion. He knew he could give her what her fiancé would not, and that knowledge ate him up inside.

Inflamed as his body was, as hungry as the demon within him seemed to be, he gave one last feeble resistance.

"Making love to me won't make nights with him any easier," he warned.

"I know," she whispered, dropping the coin purse on the ground next to him so she could trace the hollows beneath his cheekbones with those soft, questing fingers, angling down toward his lips.

Morley's terse mouth softened involuntarily as her featherlight touch sensitized the rim of his upper lip as she charted whatever curve she found there.

"I—overheard tell that there are those of you who can bring a woman to completion with—with your mouth. I find I'd—very much like to know how that feels. And then... I'd like you to..." Her lashes swept down again as she battled with her own breath for a moment. "Lady Westlawn told me that some of you could make a woman come for you more than once..."

Morley swallowed twice before he could bring himself to cede defeat.

Of all the injustices and indignities he'd encountered in his long, lonely life, the one chewing at his soul was the idea that either of them would live one more night without knowing what it felt like for her to orgasm against his tongue.

And then again against his cock.

Though he cradled her as one would an invalid or a child,

his fingers curled around her limbs as the hunger tore through him, spilling hot and victorious through his veins.

Sweet Christ but he was going to devour her.

And she knew it as well as he did.

He saw it in the slight widening of her eyes, in the parting of her lips. In the way her body stiffened a little, and then slackened, settling into his arms with a sigh of submission.

That sigh was his ultimate undoing.

He lowered his head, lifting her to meet him. He didn't so much kiss her as consumed her, his searching, burning mouth parting the pliant pillows of her lips, delving into the honeyed depths he found there.

If this was Elysium, then she was ambrosia. And with her in his arms, he felt like a god.

He broke the kiss before long to cast about for a place for them to go.

"The fountain," she panted, sliding her hands to lock behind his neck so she could pull him back down to her mouth, her eyes homed in on his lips.

"You'll be exposed," he pointed out, realizing how ridiculous he sounded even as he said it. But now that he'd decided to have her, he was jealous that even the stars would have the chance to see her beauty, let alone anyone who should happen by.

"Only to you," she whispered, sliding out of his grasp and lifting herself to perch on the wide stone ledge.

The path with the row of dim lamps ended at the far side of the Italian style stone, leaving their side of the fountain cast in shadow. He could barely make out her features, but she must have been able to see him plainly enough.

She might have been a sea goddess commanding the stone deities behind her to spout her element into the night, anointing her wealth of carefully arranged dark hair with little gems of mist.

"I'm... I don't know if I can bring myself to disrobe," she said in a small voice.

"I'll do it." He lifted onto his knees and reached for her, but she intercepted his hands with hers, lacing thin fingers with his own.

"I mean to say, I'm too reticent to do this in the altogether."

She wanted to keep her fine silk dress on... and he'd be goddamned if he didn't find that oddly arousing.

And helpful. His lust had teeth, and something told him that if he were to unwrap this woman, he wouldn't last long enough to fuck her well.

She was too beautiful, her scent too alluring, and that look on her face. That coy mix of vulnerable vixen was going to drive him beyond all control.

God help him, he was doing this. With her. *To* her. A part of him knew he'd live to regret it, and he couldn't bring himself to care.

A hard life had turned him into a hard man. Harder and colder with every lonely year that passed. And all he did was work and fight. Work to keep the hard man from becoming an evil one, and fight the evil he recognized in others. Fight to keep it from devouring his city, as it had his family.

And here was someone soft. Soft and...beleaguered by a familiar loneliness. Asking for him to share a few moments of pleasure.

He was too soul-weary to resist such an enticing bargain.

Releasing his hands, she curled her fingers in her lap, bunching her skirts and lifting the powder blue hem to uncover lace boots and stark white stockings.

It was an invitation not to be denied.

Morley plunged his hands beneath the folds and frills, drawing them up shapely, silk-covered calves until he reached her knees. He parted them, filling the space he made with his body.

With her sitting up on the ledge, and him on his knees, their faces aligned. He claimed her lips once again, marveling that there was a mouth on this earth that tasted like hers.

He delved into the warmth, a velvet intrusion. A parody of what he would do to her elsewhere. Her little, warm tongue made gentle slides against his, tentatively testing his restraint.

Finding the edge of it.

A fire of anticipation immolated in his loins, and he suddenly ached to taste every part of her. To rip her dress open and see if she was as pale as the night suggested. If iridescent veins adorned her breasts and the thin, tender skin on the inside of her thighs. He wanted to mark her with little bites of his teeth, to show the man who had never pleased her that someone was able and oh so willing.

He hitched her skirts higher, hands venturing from her knees up her thighs, finding curious frills, silk garters bedecked with lace and little bows attached with delicate stitches.

His hands played there, plucking at things and testing textures while he savored her mouth for as long as his inflamed body would allow.

Her hands didn't remain idle.

They rested on the buttons of his coat, releasing them with jerky, uncertain motions until she could wrench it open and slide her hands inside. She explored the width and breadth of him until her arms locked around him.

The uncertain tenderness in the embrace was too much for him to bear.

Morley broke the kiss, pulling back to assess her. To watch her widening eyes as his fingers threaded higher, following the silken expanse of flesh until he met the barrier of her thin cotton drawers.

She tucked her lips between her teeth and trembled, but didn't look away.

"Tell me again what you want." He hardly recognized his voice, the dark, growling street accent, the insolence and lust.

She gave a delicate swallow before answering. "I-I can't say it."

"You want me to kiss you?" he prodded, covering her mound. "Here?"

She gave a little jump, and her knees clamped his hips, as if they might have closed had his body not impeded it.

"Yes," she replied with a bashful whisper.

Feminine heat radiated from beneath the thin barrier of her undergarment, and Morley leaned in to lift her hips and draw it down to her ankles.

He wanted to kiss her again. He never wanted to stop kissing her, and because of that, he didn't allow himself to do so.

Kissing her was dangerous. As was the sweet detention of her arms.

A man could find himself a willing prisoner of such shackles, and he hadn't the inclination. He hadn't expected such sweetness. Hadn't been prepared for the answering emotion evoked in his body.

Best he keep this carnal.

Lowering himself down, he ducked his head beneath her skirts. His shoulders widened her legs and she leaned back, giving him the sense she'd rested her hands on the stone.

In the pure black beneath her skirts, he used his other senses to guide him.

He breathed in the scent of her. Fresh floral soap, feminine musk, and something that reminded him of ripe, summer berries.

He stilled for a moment, just feeling the sensation of what he'd cupped in his hand. The slight tickle of soft hair. Warm, pliant flesh, which parted in a seam of liquid heat.

He separated her folds with a slow slide of his finger, and she clenched around him with surprisingly strong legs.

"Already so wet," he murmured, delighted.

"Er—should I—?"

"Should has nothing to do with this." He pressed his shoulders forward, fighting the reflexive tightening of her trembling thighs. "Relax."

She gave a tremulous sigh, but then she obeyed, her thighs going slack and her heels returning to the ground.

He moved his finger then, wondering if any woman had been quite so soft, so small, so incredibly hot. He allowed himself a gentle, caressing exploration as he pressed a worshipful kiss to her thigh.

She was highly responsive, this woman. She twitched and tightened to his every motion, her breath hitching over little catches in her throat. His finger drew from the well that sprang from the center of her and painted gentle wet swirls on the little nub of engorged flesh.

Christ, she was so ready.

He wouldn't even have to work for it.

Unable to wait any longer, he lowered his lips to hover above the very core of her.

"Whatever I do, do not scream," he warned.

In an instant she was tense again. "S-scream?"

But he did not answer her question.

Because he'd parted her sex with one long, powerful lick.

CHAPTER 3

*P*ru screamed.

Or, at least, she threw her head back and opened her mouth, but somehow her throat closed over the sound, releasing a choked whimper instead.

Dear God. This was *happening*. The most beautiful man she'd ever seen up close was now beneath her skirts.

Licking her.

There.

One of her hands clamped over her mouth, trying to contain the scandal of it all, the pure, wet, unadulterated wickedness.

A sound from beneath the silk of her skirts and petticoats filtered through the night. A growl, or a groan, she couldn't tell.

She couldn't listen. She could only feel.

After that first sinuous lick, he paused. His breath a warm devastation against her sensitized flesh. His shoulders wide against thighs that had never parted before tonight. Beneath skirts that had never lifted.

She bit into her finger, forcing herself not to ruin the moment with incessant, anxious questions.

Was he uncomfortable under there? Did he have one taste and decide against more? Was she different than other women, or boring and the same? Better or worse? Did he want to stop? She'd understand, of course. Perhaps she hadn't prepared properly. She'd bathed and used the finest perfumes and lotions, but what if such an act took a preparation she'd not thought of?

He was doing his job, she reminded herself. This was his vocation... and people often found parts of their jobs distasteful.

And did them regardless.

But the very idea painted her entire self with mortification. Because, dash it all, despite her intentions in coming here, she couldn't help but want to please him. Because that was who she was. She wanted him to like what he was doing to her.

She wanted him to like... her. This masked man whose name she did not know. Whose eyes were as wintry as the Arctic and hot as blue flame.

And he didn't. He hated her. She knew it. She'd read him all wrong and now that he'd tasted her, he was trying to figure out a way to extricate himself from the situation without causing either of them humiliation.

Too late for that. She should just—

"Get rid of him."

"What?" Prudence realized her hand had muffled the question, but her skirts muffled his words so they might be not even having a conversation at all.

He shoved the ruffles and gathers of her skirt up to lift his head and spear her with a look of such brutality, such carnal dominance, she flinched. God he was... almost frightening. Even with his smartly contained golden hair, a stubbled jaw a few shades darker, and his regal demeanor, had she met him on the street she'd have been terrified of him.

He still held her thighs open, and the absurdity of their positions drenched her in unease.

47

And other things.

"Your fiancé. Get rid of him," he ordered.

"B-but—"

"If there is a man on this planet who would prefer another woman to you...to this..." he thrummed a rough-skinned thumb over her slick and aching sex, eliciting a soft whimper from her. "He doesn't deserve it. He shouldn't be allowed to reproduce. Moreover, he should be shot. Drawn and quartered, and wiped from memory."

Even as he growled the savage words, Pru felt herself take a breath of relief. He was being kind, of course he was. But the sentiment was appreciated.

Necessary, even.

All her boldness seemed to have deserted her and she suddenly felt like what she was. A hapless maiden who knew nothing of men. Of the world.

Who was at the mercy of this stark stranger, spread before him, waiting for him to dine upon her.

Lapping up his compliments like a starving animal.

It occurred to her to thank him for his kindness, but her words were lost as he bent back to her, this time pressing a reverent kiss to her sex.

Unable to stand the wicked view, Prudence tossed her skirt back over his head.

His chuckle was a sinful vibration against her, and it tightened something low in her belly. A warning of what was to come.

She gasped as he pressed his lips into her, delving through her folds with slow, languid licks.

He unlocked her with his lips. Undid her with his tongue as he stroked and slipped over the swollen, aching core of her, eliciting pleasure she'd never known existed. She'd the sense that he savored this as she did, which was ridiculous. He did this every night. To every sort of woman.

No wonder they gave him diamonds. He'd been at it all of two seconds and she'd have handed him her entire dowry had he requested it.

And maybe her heart.

She closed her eyes, escaping from the whispers of guilt and shame her upbringing instilled in her. Focusing instead upon the tactile sensations of the moment. The soft, almost intangible coolness of the fountain's mist kissing her upturned face like snowflakes in the summer.

A miracle. Just like his tongue.

The tendrils of pleasure elicited by his ministrations diffused through her blood, and then seemed to be called back to her core by a tightening low in her belly. A harbinger of happening. A pulsing, pounding, throbbing thing that rushed at her from a great distance.

Something she was afraid to miss and equally frightened of being run over by. Like a train or a stampede of wild horses.

"Oh," she fretted breathlessly. "Oh, dear. I—I think I—"

He lifted his lips from her... stealing the sensation away to her utter consternation and relief.

"Don't think," he ordered in the voice of a man quite used to giving orders.

"Don't stop," she begged, her hand blindly reaching for the head hidden beneath her skirts.

He made a low sound of amusement, breathing a cool stream of air against her overheated flesh. He whispered something she didn't quite catch and was too overwrought to clarify.

But she thought she heard the word "forever" before his tongue returned to flicker against the little button of pure sensation.

His touch was eternally light. Barely there, even, but it infused her with such an electric pulse her entire body tightened and jerked with it, as if he'd plugged her into one of Edison's own machines.

She arched and bent with such strength she feared she might snap her spine in two, and he rewarded her by sucking that little bead of flesh into his warm mouth, rolling it gently with his tongue.

A raw sound escaped her, and she returned her hand over her mouth, leaving the other to support her against the stone ledge, all she had keeping her from diving backward into the water.

The wave crashed over her before she even realized it had formed upon the horizon. A crest of such unimaginable, inconceivable euphoria dismantled everything she knew about herself.

She came apart in his hands, against his mouth, and hoped to never again be found.

This was bliss. Rapture. Heaven. And a bit of the other place, too. Because once she'd begun to tumble into the grips of ecstasy, she already understood it was fleeting. That it would inevitably end, lest she die from the intensity of it.

For surely nothing like this could last.

Inevitably his mouth softened, gentled, and returned her back to herself. A self she wasn't certain what to do with. She was a weak, trembling, overwrought mess, and she couldn't seem to remember her own name let alone consider what to do next.

So she sat and breathed, because such was the extent of her functional capacity.

She'd expected pleasure… but not that.

Not her unaccountable unraveling.

He left her, sliding from beneath her skirts, and used one of the many ruffles of her petticoats to wipe his mouth before he rested back on his haunches so that they might take the measure of one another.

She couldn't see much of his body, as he was dressed in all black and the night was a moonless one. The lamps filtered through the fountain and cast the shadows of water against his skin. Like a mirage of tears. An entire ocean of them.

They bled down his stark cheekbones creating hollows beneath, and the effect somehow caused her heart to swell in her chest.

"You look... as if you are in pain," she ventured, doing her best to lift her boneless arms to reach for him.

"I'm hard as fucking marble." A crass, almost cruel admission, one that brought her body back to astonishing life.

"Bloody hell," he panted, running the back of his hand over his mouth again as if to rid it of her flavor. Stopping in the middle of the motion, he curled his fingers into a fist and bit down on his knuckle. Composing himself just long enough to command, "Stop looking at me like that, woman, or I won't be responsible for what I do next."

Little trills of danger thrummed through her veins. Something primitive and ancient in this garden of delights. Something as old as the first stories, when a man found a woman who tempted him to sin.

The stories had always offended Prudence as she'd obediently sat in church, listening to holy men blame Eve for everything. For the knowledge of good and evil and the ability to bear fruit. For life, itself.

And for temptation.

Why would God, in all his infinite wisdom imbue them with these forces of nature so powerful, there was barely the sentience to deny them? Didn't it make sense that a more pagan deity was responsible? Perhaps one with golden hair and electric eyes. With savagely beautiful features and an expression of half hunger, half wrath.

Eve was not tempted by the devil, but by the power of the very impulses already inside of her. She'd been in Eden, much as Pru was now, and had stared across at a man who'd looked at her just like that, infusing her with power and fire and subtle submission.

How could she have possibly denied him? How could she have denied herself?

Prudence slid from the fountain to her knees before him, little more than a puddle of pleasure and need. Her hands explored him a little, tested the mounds of muscle beneath his coat before slipping it up over his shoulders and down his corded arms.

He was hard and she was soft. He was stone and she was water.

Wet, ready.

Willing.

He watched her as she came to him, his eyes strangely wary and uncertain. His skin pulled taut over the shape of his bones.

The moment she freed his arms from his coat, he took over. He draped it on the moss before guiding her to it and following her down.

He kissed her gently, and she tasted a lingering essence of herself.

It tasted like sin. Reminded her of where he'd taken her. Someplace like paradise.

She opened her legs to welcome the lean intrusion of his hips and he took every inch of ground she ceded.

He distracted her with soft, probing kisses as he reached down between them. Lifting her skirts to her waist, fumbling with his trousers.

No romantic words punctuated his kisses and none were needed. Though his desire was rough and apparent, his mouth was gentle and endlessly restless. He dragged his lips up her jaw, breathing in great gasps, as if he could lock her scent in his chest. He pressed them to her temples, her eyebrows, her lids and the tip of her nose.

Prudence kept her eyes closed, under the guise of appreciating his attentions. All the while preparing to give him what George no longer deserved.

Her virginity.

She didn't tell him. She couldn't say why, exactly. Maybe because he treated her in this moment like no one else had. Like someone whose need and knowledge matched his. Someone who could take what he was about to give her with all its primal desire and no little bit of masculine anger, and provide him a little of the pleasure she'd only just experienced.

Lord knew, he'd earned it.

He returned his mouth to hers just as his fingers stole into her cleft once again, sliding against even more abundant moisture than before.

She squirmed a little, anxious and anticipatory. Wanting him to stop. Wanting him to get on with it. Not knowing what to say or do other than to cling to him.

Yes. That was it. She reared up, wrapping her arms around his trunk, and buried her face against his neck. She breathed him in, a scent like cedar and stringent soap and perhaps a bit of creosote, as if he'd been in a trainyard recently.

Her breath warmed and moistened the scant space between their skin, and she inhaled greedily as his arms locked around her.

"Please," she whispered.

He stole her next words with a strong thrust.

Prudence bit her lip so hard she tasted blood. She'd expected pain. Or maybe pleasure. But not this unbearably magnificent medley of the two.

Her intimate muscles were not exactly as welcoming as she wished them to be at first, but after the initial thrust, they seemed to clench at him. Pulling him inside.

He'd claimed to be hard, but she realized she'd never truly had an idea of what that word meant. He was like heated steel inside of her, over her, around her. He was everywhere she wasn't and also where she was.

He was her entire world, and yet still a stranger. He blocked out the sky and the breeze and the darkness, her lonely pain and her fears for the future. Reducing her entire frame of existence down to this.

To the place where they joined.

She suddenly wished for daylight. For a filter of illumination through which she could appreciate his nude form. She wished she'd seen exactly what it was he'd pressed inside of her. But for now, all she had was this. Darkness and experience.

And what an experience it was.

With a dark growl, he withdrew slow and deliberate. He held her to him like a coveted treasure as he curled his back to sting into her again. And then again.

Each gliding, slick thrust was easier to bear than the last, easing the way for the pleasure he began to pump from his body into hers, chasing away the lingering shadows of pain.

He made dark, needful, animal sounds. She reveled in the catches of his breath and the sheer wonder in the wordless questions he kissed into her mouth.

He took pleasure as he gave it, and she thought, that was what lovers ought to do.

For he felt like a lover, even though love had nothing to do with what they did here in the dark on the earth.

It was more like a rite. A swiftly intensifying, carnal ritual. One blessed by witches who would have burned once upon a time. As she was burning now, immolating as he thrust pure liquid heat into her with increasing brutality.

She pulled away from his arms, not because she wanted space but because she wanted to see what gathered between them. Because that celestial tide of pleasure was threatening to separate her from herself once again, and she had to make sure this time she was not alone.

That he came with her.

Come. This is why it was referred to as coming. Because no one quite stayed where they were, inside of themselves, inside of each other.

They came, and went, somewhere else entirely.

She looked up at him and instantly noticed that he was closer to that place, that he was afraid he'd leave without her.

His features were a mask of exquisite torment, more beautiful than any piece of art she'd ever seen. She gasped up at him with every motion, as he thrust her into the ground. Her legs widened, strained. Her body seized, and he barked out a harsh sound.

He reached between them and with three magical strokes of his finger, he brought the pleasure crashing into her and sent them both careening into the night.

They came together.

Locked in some paroxysm of bliss that might have looked like a contortion of pain. Neither of them seemed capable of sound, only straining, taut and impossible motion.

Her entire body pulsed around long, liquid warmth he buried deep into her womb, and *God* if that didn't heighten the entire experience.

She returned to herself before he did, it seemed, her body slackening to the earth as his still thrummed with spasms of pleasure. It seemed to drop him suddenly, and he collapsed over her. Not with his full weight, but with a delicious heaviness that compressed her into a puddle of pleasant affection.

He rooted around in the pool of ruined ringlets at the nape of her neck, breathing deeply, pressing reverent kisses to the sensitive skin. She fought the shrugging giggle as long as she could, but alas her ticklish neck broke the moment.

He rolled to the side, sliding away and arranging himself back into his trousers before she had the presence of mind to peek.

A consummate professional, he was.

They lay next to each other beneath the stars for an eternity, or maybe only a moment. Their breaths synchronized as they deepened and slowed.

A drowsy sense of satisfaction stole over her limbs, and Prudence was the first to roll to her side, acutely aware of the slick aftermath left against her thighs.

He was still far away, she realized. Somewhere in the night above them, unable to return back to the troubles of life below.

She understood a little, she thought. Morning would bring no pleasure to her, especially not after trust had been broken by those she'd once considered closest to her. But her sadness felt like a phantom next to what sort of bleak emotion settled on his features, and she thought to dispel it with a compliment.

"Whatever you charge, sir, it's not enough." She sighed contentedly. "You are a master of your craft."

"Never enough..." he murmured, his eyes still somewhat unfocused, his chest still struggling a bit for breath.

It made sense, she thought, he'd done all the work. She'd just lain there and enjoyed herself.

Feeling at a loss herself, she pushed herself up on her hip like a depiction of a mermaid, legs stretched out to the side. How did one conclude such an interaction? And why didn't she want to?

It wasn't an interaction, was it? But a transaction.

And yet she felt an odd sense of attachment to him now. Was this normal? She could ask, but something told her the question would drive him away.

"Are you cold?" She gathered his coat from beneath her and did her best to brush off errant blades of grass.

He finally glanced over at her, then at his jacket, as if seeing it for the first time. "No. But thank you." He sat up and took it from her, donning it deliberately. "Are *you* all right?" He asked the question as if he dreaded the answer, but his features didn't at all convey what his voice had.

She wished she could identify his expression, but it was a certain kind of inaccessible. Pleasant, but arch. Remote, but attentive. Intense, but polite.

Very carefully so. As if he was suddenly wary or mistrustful of her.

Had she done something wrong?

"Never better." She summoned her most dazzling smile, wishing she had the strength to open her lids past half-mast. That she didn't suddenly want to cry, not because she was sad, but because something powerful had just happened and her emotions hadn't been prepared for it.

"Do you ever—that is—do you care about the women with whom you've spent the night?" she ventured. "Romantically, I mean?"

His gaze flicked away from her, and he stared at the gate, as if hoping the exit would draw closer.

"I don't allow myself the luxury of romance," he answered, and Pru believed she'd never heard anything more honest. Or more depressing.

"Do you ever want to, in spite of yourself?" She was a sentimental fool, but something within her burned to know.

He shook his head adamantly. "Terrible things happen to those I care about."

His answer piqued both her curiosity and her compassion, but he stood before she could reply, and reached down to help her up.

He lifted her with such surprising strength. He was neither overly tall nor was he more than elegantly wide. But rather superbly fit, his every inch hardened with well-used muscle.

She'd first-rate knowledge of that.

"Is it gauche of me to express gratitude?" she asked. "Other than remuneration, that is."

His face softened and the glaciers of his eyes melted behind his mask, his gaze touched every part of her face. "Is your coach nearby? How are you getting home?"

"I'll manage, thank you." A part of her deflated. Of course, he was gently telling her it was time to go. Bless him, for keeping up at least the appearance of concern. "What are you called?"

A sad smile touched his lips as he lifted a lock of her hair that'd escaped its coiffure. He tucked it back in place, smoothing it down with such a tender motion, her throat ached. "It doesn't matter. I'm just a shadow."

Bending down, he retrieved her drawers from where they lay discarded by the fountain and turned to give her privacy. She turned as well, bending to step into them.

"But what if I—" She almost toppled when trying to step into the second leg of the garment and had to steady herself before going on. "What if I'd like to find you again?"

"You won't, I'm afraid."

She drew her underthings up over her stockings and garters. Glad that they'd absorb the dampness that lingered there, until she was able to return home. Wriggling into them, she dropped her skirts and petticoats and smoothed them down her thighs.

Thighs that had just been spread for him. For the man who didn't want to tell her his name.

She whirled back around. "I'm Pru—"

He was already gone.

CHAPTER 4

hree Months Later

"Congratulations, Morley, you're famous!" Millie LeCour lowered the periodical she read from across the carriage and wriggled dark brows at him. "They're calling you the *Knight of Shadows*." She leaned deeper into Detective Inspector Christopher Argent's side so she could show him what she read. "Sufficiently ominous, don't you think, darling?"

"Terrifying," he replied with his distinct brand of prosaic nonchalance. He didn't spare the paper a glance, but he tilted his head to inhale the very nearness of Millie before pressing a careful kiss into her coiffed dark hair.

Morley's grim mood darkened to thunderous. "Bloody journalists," he muttered, hoping his companions would believe the papers solely responsible for his ire.

And not their nuzzling nonsense.

It'd never much bothered him before that night with— No. *No*, he didn't allow himself to dwell on that. To transpose sylphlike features over Millie's bold ones, if only because she shared the slight build and black hair of the woman who haunted his dreams.

Because he'd almost convinced himself the most memorable night of his life had been exactly that. A dream. A strange fabrication of fancy. A hallucination induced by exhaustion, an overtaxed psyche, and vacuous lack of sex.

"Oh, I realize you two men are of the opinion it's sensational and absurd," Millie continued. "But if you think about it, a villain setting out to commit a crime might think twice if he's worried about running afoul of the *Knight of Shadows.*" Reaching up, the celebrated actress smoothed an errant auburn forelock away from Argent's soulless eyes. She touched him with the absent fondness of a longtime lover and Morley had to look away from them both. He sought refuge out the window in the bustle and unaccountable brightness of a late-summer London morning.

"And don't be too sore at the writers," she prodded Morley. "Anyone in my profession would commit *murder* for that sort of free press."

He'd committed murder for it too...

The Knight of Shadows. Another farce. Another mantle he'd thrown over his own shoulders almost purely on accident. One night, ages ago, Chief Inspector Carlton Morley had been denied legal entrance to a brothel where he knew evil men sold young, desperate foundlings to disgusting clientele.

He'd a suspicion the Justice involved in his denial was a customer.

The voices of every victimized child he'd ever known had torn through him. Dorian, Ash, Argent, Lorelai, Farah...

Caroline.

He could not abide it. *Would not* allow it. Not anymore. Not in his city and especially not within his own departments of Justice.

His questionable decision fortified by more brandy than he'd like to admit, he'd tied a mask over his eyes, and broke out the tools of a trade he'd long since deserted.

And a boy he'd long since buried.

He thought he'd left Cutter Morley in the grave he'd dug, but neither was it Sir Carlton Morley who'd shot every pimp in the brothel dead before sending the youths to refuge at St. Dismas Church in Whitechapel.

That night something had eased within him. A sense of helplessness he knew every police officer carried around with him.

The shackles the law locked upon its enforcers were both right and necessary. And yet, they created certain loopholes that became leashes whereby a lawman might be forced to watch an atrocity happen without being able to take recourse.

After years of fighting, of watching the system of which he was a part of, fail so many, mainly those unfortunates believed by most to reside beneath notice, he could stand by no longer.

He was the knighted war hero Chief Inspector because he had to be, and he'd become the Knight of Shadows because London had needed him to be.

How many bodies were there now? The pedophile watch-maker on Drury Lane. The murdering rapist in Knights-bridge. A maniacal doctor who performed gruesome experiments on his immigrant patients, often resulting in disfigurement or death. Two brothers who'd taken everything from their infirmed aunt and moved into her house, effectively keeping her prisoner whilst they spent her meager income.

He'd meant to merely evict them, but one of the men had pulled a pistol on him. And well...Morley's dead-eye had done the job for him.

Then there'd been—

"The public so loves a memorable sobriquet." Millie interrupted his thoughts.

"The public are idiots," Argent reminded her.

"A public you *both* protect, I might remind you." Millie

smacked him square in the chest, and Argent smirked down at her.

"If you ever hit me and I find out about it..." He tonelessly poked fun at her petite stature and feeble strength.

Though, Morley supposed, most anyone seemed diminutive next to the ginger giant.

"Think of everyone we know with anointed designations they never thought to give themselves," Millie ticked their connections off on her fingers. "The Rook, The Demon Highlander. The Blackheart of Ben More, The King of the London Underworld, though I suppose those two only count as one..." She trailed off and turned to her husband. "How did you escape without a moniker?"

Argent gave a rather Gallic shift of his shoulder. "If an assassin becomes famous enough to be recognized, it's time for him to retire."

"I'm glad you did," Millie said with feeling. Though the man hadn't retired because of any sort of infamy, but because he'd met his match. Her. The woman he'd been hired to kill, and instead fell in love with.

Morley supposed he should be concerned about how many people were privy to his nocturnal identity by now. Argent had guessed that Morley had begun to spend his nights as a vigilante before he admitted it, only because he and the former assassin were once after the same villain on the same night.

And what Argent knew, Millie knew also.

Morley had confided it to his childhood best mate, now known as the Rook, which meant his wife, Lorelai, knew. And probably also the Blackwells, Dorian and Farah.

The press had begun to follow his exploits but, as Morley had predicted, the descriptions of him scraped from the recollections of villains and survivors were notoriously unreliable, lost in the miasma of misinformation that was the London press.

They all remembered a mask covering the upper quadrant of his face and the fact that he often wore a hat.

He wore many hats. Both figuratively and literally.

Morley sighed before admonishing Millie. "You of all people know better than to believe what you read in the papers. I don't do half the good they credit me. Or, rather, this bollocks Knight of Shadows doesn't."

"The fact they've guessed you're a knight means it is possibly getting dangerous out there for you," Argent warned.

"I think the title is a coincidence." Millie waved a dismissive hand. "With that mask on, he could be anyone. The public has merely distinguished him by merit of his service on their behalf. Though everyone's *dying* to know. I saw an advert for him in the lonely-hearts column just yesterday." She turned to Morley, pursing her lips playfully. "If you're interested, a Miss Matilda Westernra is just nineteen and wants you to know you've touched her virtuous heart. I dare say stolen it."

"That's disgusting, I'm twice her age." Morley shifted in his seat. "Besides, I've no interest in touching or stealing hearts, lonely or otherwise."

"If you don't wish to touch her heart, I'd wager she'd let you touch her—"

Millie scowled at her husband. "Christopher, if you finish that sentence, so help me."

"What? I was going to say virtue."

"Like hell you were."

Morley realized it spoke to the esteem in which Argent held him that he was allowed such an unfettered view into the man's personal life. Even though Argent worked for Morley, only a fool would consider himself Argent's boss.

And Morley was no fool.

Except, it seemed, when it came to women.

"Knight of Shadows." Argent grunted in a manner a kind man might have called a laugh.

A fit of hysterics for the terse giant.

"Sod off," Morley muttered, as their carriage pulled alongside Holy Trinity Cathedral, and the footman opened the door.

Five years hence, if anyone had told Morley he'd be sharing a carriage with Christopher Argent, the Blackheart of Ben More's former right-hand assassin, he'd have laughed at them.

Or punched them.

But here they were, climbing the stairs on a perfectly good workday to attend a rather mandatory society wedding.

"How'd you get roped into this?" Morley queried out of the side of his mouth. "I wasn't aware you knew the couple."

"I don't," Argent said, looking around rather mystified. "Millie had me try on a new frock coat she'd had made for me, and suddenly I had some place to wear it."

Morley chuckled at that, but then Argent shrugged. "Actually, I think…she knows the bride, Prudence Goode, through her sisters who volunteer at the Duchess of Trenwyth's Ladies' Aid Society." Argent lifted his chin to the door where the father of the bride stood to shake hands. "When Millie realized their father was your immediate superior, and therefore mine, she said we both had a reason to attend."

Morley and Argent shared a look of chagrin. The second daughter of Commissioner Clarence Goode, Baron of Cresthaven, was marrying some Earl from somewhere, and if Morley was absent from the festivities, as he longed to be, he'd hear no end of it. Attendance was expected of him. And Carlton Morley always did what was *expected*.

So that his sins were never *suspected*.

As he mounted the stairs to the chapel, a raven cackled from where it clung to the stone banister, taunting him and twitching its wings.

A raven on a wedding day. Wasn't there some wives' tale about ravens being harbingers of death or doom or some such?

He paused, staring at it intently, transfixed by the brilliance of its feathers. Brilliant, he thought, because while the bird was black, it reflected the entire spectrum in the sun with a glossy iridescence.

Just like *her* hair had done when the lamplight had shone through the water...

He shook his head, trying to dislodge the thought.

Most of the time he was glad he didn't know her name. Because then she'd become too real. He couldn't shrug that night off as some fantastical dream that'd happened to someone else.

Other times, he longed for her to be something other than a pronoun.

Her.

Blinking, he turned from the blasted creature, taking the stairs two at a time to catch up to his compatriots.

He had to stop this lunacy. To cease searching for her in every slim, raven-haired woman of passable good looks he saw on the streets. Or the park. Or Scotland Yard. Or in a bloody church.

The city was full of dark-haired beauties, it seemed, and that fact had threatened to drive him mad.

One night, when he'd been unable to stand his longing, when his body had screamed for release and his every sense was overwhelmed by the memory of her, he'd gone to Miss Henrietta's School for Cultured Young Ladies, and had lurked near the fountain.

If only to prove to himself it had actually happened.

He'd touched the smooth stone of the fountain ledge where she'd perched and lifted her skirts and the mere sight of her shapely calves had driven him past all reason.

He swore he could still taste her, summer berries and female desire. He'd waited for her, his raven-haired miracle, and she'd not come.

Not that he was surprised. He'd told her she wouldn't find him again.

And he'd meant it.

Morley rubbed a hand over his face, scrubbing at a smooth jaw where she'd once found it stubbled, wanting to wipe her from memory.

The Commissioner had disappeared into the church as he'd dawdled in reverie, and he'd missed the entire reason he'd attended this blasted wedding to begin with. To be seen by Goode, and thereby make his excuses to leave.

This had to fucking stop, this...obsession with her.

The entire affair had been a mistake. He'd never in his adult life done anything so ridiculous. So dangerous.

So...marvelous.

He hadn't been himself that night. He'd been stretched at the end of a long-frayed rope. His will weakened by exhaustion and a seemingly futile struggle between him and the entire world. Between the two parts of himself. He'd been weak, there was no gentler word for it. Weakness wasn't something he allowed, in himself or those who worked for him.

This had to stop. He whispered a solemn vow then and there to never look another dark-haired maiden in the eye. Never search for her sharp jaw and arched brows, or her delicate ears with elfin tips.

What would he do if he found her, anyway? She thought him a prostitute or, if she were a clever woman, she'd have worked out that he was the so-called Knight of Shadows because of his mask. Because he hadn't taken her money. Because if she'd asked at Miss Henrietta's or approached any of the Stags of St. James, they'd tell her he wasn't among their ranks.

Either way, she'd a secret that could crush him in the telling of it—not that she'd come out smelling of roses.

Even so.

It was better to stuff the entire misadventure into the past and forget it. Forget *her*.

The church bells tolled the hour, or maybe the event, as Morley stepped into the already uncomfortably warm church. The organ music ground at his nerves, and he hoped to sit next to a large woman with a very busy fan, so he might not expire from the heat. How long was this bloody thing supposed to last? Did he have to go to the soirée after? If he made certain Commissioner Goode saw him at the ceremony, he could pretend he was lost in the crowd later.

"Sir. *Sir*." Someone clutched at his jacket, and he whirled to find a white-faced reverend at his elbow. "Sir Morley? Chief Inspector Carlton Morley?" the short, rotund old man whispered his name and title as if it were an illicit secret.

"Yes?"

"You *must* come with me. Oh God in heaven. Never in my life..." The Vicar's words trailed away as he furtively skipped his gaze over the guests now trying to step around them since they'd stopped in the middle of the aisle.

Instantly on alert, Morley glanced over at Argent, who made a baffled gesture.

"*Please*." The Vicar's pallor was alarming. "Don't make a scene."

Argent stepped forward. "Should I accompany—?"

"No! Only Sir Morley." The reverend was tugging on his jacket now, dragging him toward the back of the chapel like a recalcitrant child might his dawdling nanny.

"We'll find our seat and save you one," Millie offered, tugging her husband in the opposite direction.

Morley followed the frantic priest down an empty stone hall with vibrant purple carpets. "Lord Goode and the Viscount Woodhaven sent me to find you right away. There's been a— Well, the groom. The *bride*. Oh my God, of all the nightmares. So much blood."

When Morley entered the sitting room, he froze.

Not because of the blood, though it *was* everywhere. Soaking into the floral carpet, spreading past it onto the grey stone floor. Coloring the bodice of the bride's cream dress in a dappled spray. Saturating her hem and train where she stood, paralyzed, in the puddle draining from a man's neck. The dripping knife still clutched in her trembling, blood-drenched hands.

The fucking priest had been right.

Of all the nightmares...

It was *her*.

CHAPTER 5

$\mathcal{P}$rudence was locked in a chamber of red.

She drowned in it. It filled her lungs so she couldn't breathe. Her ears so she couldn't hear. She could even taste it, or could she? Metal stained her tongue, but her mouth was as dry as sandpaper. Her throat wouldn't allow her to swallow. She choked on her gall and grief.

William was yelling. He'd found her like this. Poor William. She'd never liked Honoria's husband because of this tendency of his...always making such a ruckus.

"You bloody viper. You lunatic!" the Viscount accused. "How could you kill him? In a church of all places?"

"I-I couldn't!"

Well, that wasn't strictly true, now was it? She *could* have cheerfully murdered him many times over the past three months.

"I didn't," she amended. *She hadn't.*

Pru looked down at her hands. Back at George. Over at William's purple, puffy complexion, then down at her fiancé.

The blood wasn't pumping anymore but draining slowly. Staining her dress. Everything and everywhere. The pool spread; the blood followed her as she stumbled back a few steps. A train of condemnation.

Oh God. She was going to be sick.

Except had nothing left to throw up, not since she'd emptied her stomach this morning.

"Prudence, don't you *dare* move! What have you done?"

When had her father come in? She should be relieved, shouldn't she? He'd know what to do.

She lifted the knife to show him. Someone had stuck it into the place George's shoulder had met his neck. This long, long, *long* knife. All the way in. Why would they do that? Where had they gone?

It was so cold. *So cold.* And it had been so warm before in the crowded church. Warm enough to complain about it. They were both screaming at her. Making so much noise they could almost be heard over the bells. Wedding bells. *Her* wedding bells.

It all clamored so loudly it was deafening, and yet also very far away. Bells and bellows. Her father shouting questions. William calling her every sort of name.

Prudence tried to speak, but her throat wouldn't allow it. Her tongue was stuck. Too dry.

Why was she still holding the knife? Why couldn't her fingers uncurl?

George. What happened to you? She stared down at him, unable to blink. His long body remained face down where he'd landed. His skin no longer ruddy from drink, but white. Whiter than hers, even.

Poor George. He'd been merry this morning. Insufferable and already drunk. And now...

The door opened. A man entered.

And the pandemonium stopped.

Everyone obeyed his command for silence and, for the first

time, Pru's throat relaxed enough to allow a full breath. The sick sense of impending doom released the band around her ribs and her stomach stopped threatening to jump into her esophagus.

Everything would be all right. *He* was here now. Even though the world was upside down, he would know how to put it right.

Except... who was he?

She couldn't look away from the blood.

"*Prudence*," her father barked, as if he'd been saying her name for a long time. "This is Chief Inspector Sir Carlton Morley. You tell him *everything*, do I make myself clear?"

"I don't...want to hold this anymore," she whimpered, unable to peel her fingers from around the knife. God it was so big. It had been stuck in George's muscles.

She moaned.

"Let me have the knife, Miss Goode." A deep, cultured voice came closer, and a hand covered with a white handkerchief relieved her of the weapon. She'd never been more grateful for anything in her life.

"That's one of our daggers!" Reverend Bentham exclaimed. "It's a holy relic."

"It's evidence, I'm afraid," the Chief Inspector said. "You can request it back once this affair is settled."

That word. *Affair.* It made her want to cry.

Gaining some strength, Prudence lifted her head and lost what was left of her breath.

Those eyes.

They had once been liquid for her behind a mask. They had watched her come apart.

He'd made her come.

Chief Inspector? There must be some mistake. He was...a stag. No, not that. A shadow. Or he had been on a night nearly three months ago.

Pru gaped at him, dumbfounded, searching a face she'd committed to every corner of her memory.

He was at once the same and yet vastly altered. His hair a shade lighter than gold in the gleam of the noon sun through the windowpane. His suit a somber grey. His jaw sharp, clean-shaven and locked at a dangerous angle.

Her lover had been rumpled and dark, his hair the color of honey, or so she'd thought on a moonless night. He'd emanated sex and menace. Hard hunger and brutal masculinity.

The Chief Inspector was all starch and serenity. A dapper, terse, and proper gentleman clad in a fine cut jacket with an infinite supply of decorum.

But that strong jaw. The sinfully handsome features cut sharp as crystal and then blunted with the whisper of ruthlessness. All of this slashed clean through with a sardonic mouth.

It *was* him.

She was sure of it… wasn't she? No one else had eyes so light, so incredibly elemental. Like the color of lightning over the Baltic Sea.

Those eyes bored into her now. Flat, merciless, and unsympathetic. He regarded her as if she were the last person *alive* he wanted to see.

As if she were lower than the earth upon which they'd sinned.

If she'd any hope that this man would be her ally, it was dashed upon the rocky shards of his glare.

"What happened here?" he asked her evenly.

Pru felt her face crumple with confusion. He didn't sound like himself. Where was the accent from before? Rough and low-born.

She'd have recognized *that* accent anywhere.

This man spoke like his betters. Was she going mad, perhaps? Was her desperation and shock so prescient that she'd summoned a memory and layered it over reality?

"Prudence, you answer him," her father barked.

"I-I was waiting for Father to gather me for the ceremony," she recounted, wanting to appease him. *Needing* to explain. It was so important he didn't think she had anything to do with this. No one would *really* believe that she would commit murder, would they? "There was a knock on my door and a note pushed under," she continued. "The note was from George." She pointed at the dead man at her feet and immediately wished she hadn't looked down.

Oh God. She'd thought the wedding was the worst thing that would happen to her today. She'd never been so wrong in her life.

How did so much blood belong in one body? How would she ever forget the sight of it? She doubted she could even look at her own veins the same way.

"Look at me," the inspector ordered. "What did the note say?"

"That he had to see me. That he had to apologize."

"Apologize," he echoed. "Had you reason to be angry with the Earl of Sutherland?"

Her brow furrowed and she cast an accusatory look at him. "You *know* I did."

"How would *he* know?" her father demanded. "You've never been introduced."

A glint of warning frosted the inspector's eyes impossibly colder. *Don't.* It warned. *Don't ruin us both.*

"I meant…" Pru turned to her father. "*Y-you* did. I told you George was unfaithful, and you insisted I marry him regardless."

Her father, a powerful man with the build of a baker who enjoyed his own work, put up his hands against Morley's attention. Such large hands for such fine white gloves. "It was little more than wild oats," he defended George. "And Prudence has

73

always been a romantic, fanciful creature. I wasn't about to see her future ruined by rumor."

"It *wasn't* rumor," she argued, even though everything inside of herself told her not to. "Everyone knows George had bastards. He conducted a very public affair with Lady Jessica Morton. And yet you insisted I invite her to the wedding."

Why was she having this discussion covered in blood? When all she wanted to do was flee. Or fling herself into the inspector's arms.

She knew how strong they were. How capable they'd be of carrying the weight threatening to drag her beneath the surface of an ocean of despair and desperation.

She had to tell him—

"And so, you came to meet him before the ceremony," the Chief Inspector prompted very gently, as if he were talking to a child. "You came to receive his apology. Then what? What did he say to make you angry?"

She shook her head with such vehemence her eyes couldn't keep up. The beautiful Chief Inspector became a golden blur. "*Nothing*! He said nothing. I opened the door and he was... like this." She gestured to George's body, unable to look down again. "Blood poured everywhere, the knife was already in his neck. He was rolling on the floor trying to pull it out, so I ran to him and tried to help. I was thinking if he took it out, it would bleed that much more. That maybe he should keep it in. I was trying to hold it."

"Nonsense, you'd put it there!" her brother-in-law accused, jabbing his finger toward her. William's features were purple with rage, his thinning ashen hair stuck out in disarray. He wasn't a large man, but he was tall, imposing. And not for the first time, Pru wanted to shrink away from him.

How did Honoria stand him?

"I was *trying* to *stop* the bleeding." She turned to Morley, beseeching him. "I know it was silly, I don't know why I thought I could. But I had to try, didn't I? He was *dying*. And finally, he dislodged the knife and blood sprayed…" She held out her arms to show him. "And he was gone."

"That's not what it looked like when I came in," William hissed through his disorganized teeth. "She was pushing the knife into his struggling body. He was thrashing about and she was sliding it into his neck."

"I never!"

"If the Earl took the knife out of his own neck, how did you come to be holding it?" The Chief Inspector held his hand up against further comment from William while he assessed her from deep set narrowed eyes.

His suspicion lancing through her like a spear thrown by an Olympian.

Don't you remember me? she wanted to ask him. In the middle of this lake of blood. All she wanted was to go to him. He had to understand why—

"Honoria told me you hated him," William continued after an embarrassingly wet sniff. Was he crying? Of course he was, his best friend had just been killed.

Shouldn't *she* be crying? She felt tears somewhere, a threat to her distant future when she wasn't so numb. So cold and confused.

William continued his relentless assault. "She told me that you wept yourself to sleep last night at the thought of being his wife."

Yes, she'd wept plenty over the past few months. Perhaps she was empty now. Honoria had been right, but why had she told her husband? Why did it seem like her sister continuously betrayed her?

Prudence shook her head again, fearing she looked like a lunatic. "I don't *know*. I must have taken it from him. But, I didn't do this. I didn't kill him. I needed him! If I had the will or the stomach for murder, I would have poisoned him. I would have been clever. I certainly wouldn't have waited for my *wedding day*. I wouldn't have gotten all this blood on my dress..."

"Your dress is the least of your problems, you conniving bitch!" William lunged forward and Morley caught him.

"That's enough out of you." Morley's voice was hard as he flattened his forearm against William's neck and shoved him against the wall. He jabbed his finger within a breath of William's eye. "You leave this room and walk one door over to the right. There, you will *sit* and *wait* for me, do I make myself clear?"

William nodded, his anger turning to fear in the face of such authority.

That dealt with, Morley turned to her father. "Sir, I understand this is delicate, that the suspect is your daughter, but you're aware you'll have to be excused from this room, as you cannot be an impartial part of this inquest or this arrest."

Arrest? He was going to arrest her?

Her father ran a trembling hand through his shock of white hair. "I'm going for our solicitor."

Morley nodded. "I think that's best."

Her father's shaking hand followed the length of his beard to his sternum. "For the sake of our department, Morley. Our reputation. If you take her to the Yard, I want it done quietly, do you hear me? I will not be humiliated more than needs be. Her innocence will be proven quickly enough."

Tears finally pricked her eyes. Her father. Her stern, distant, self-aggrandizing father believed her at least. Believed *in* her.

Morley glared over at her, but this time his gaze lifted no further than the blood on her pearlescent gown. "That remains to be seen."

Pru wanted to bury her head in her hands and cry. She almost did. But remembered the blood in time. She might have lost what was left of her wits if she'd smeared it on her face.

Morley stepped to her father and put a hand on his elbow. "She'll be taken quietly. You have my word. You should inform the guests of the death, but not the murder... none of the details need be made public. And I think you'll need to control your son-in-law."

"Honoria will see to that," her father stated with absolute faith.

Honoria controlled everything she possibly could.

Her father turned to Pru and she locked eyes with the man she'd desperately tried to please her entire life.

And she saw what broke her heart.

Doubt.

He might claim to believe her, but he didn't in his heart.

"What am I going to tell your mother?"

He left before she could answer, taking the hand-wringing reverend with him.

And they were alone.

Pru looked down, locking her knees to keep from going to him. From prostrating herself in front of this stranger.

So much blood.

She'd been so proud of this dress. She'd loved it. And now... it was all she could do not to rip the blasted thing off and throw it in the fireplace.

They stared at each other for a silent eternity, and when she could bear it no longer, she took a step forward.

"Prudence Goode," he stated blandly. "I'm arresting you under the suspicion of the murder of George Hamby-Forsyth, Earl of Sutherland."

"It's *you*. I know it's you. I've been looking everywhere since that night—"

"I told you to leave him," he said furiously, stabbing a finger at the body of her would-be husband. "I *ordered* you that night, and here you are."

"I know." Her miserable heart shriveled away from him.

77

"Did you do it?" he asked, his eyes snapping with constrained anger. "Did you kill him?"

"No! I just told you what happened. He was already—"

He held a hand up, turning half away as if he couldn't stand to look at her before he gathered himself and faced her with a greater sense of calm.

"Tell me the truth," he said with more restraint. "And this could be one more secret between us. Tell me now and I'll do everything in my power to keep you from the gallows..."

Pru stared at him incredulously. *He didn't believe her.* He truly didn't think she was innocent. Her heart dropped like a stone. This man... this stranger who knew her more intimately than anyone in the world. This dream lover who'd treated her with more care than anyone in her life...

He thought she was a murderer.

"I won't go to the gallows," she said stoically. "I don't need your help."

"Like hell—"

"They won't hang a woman in my condition." Her hand went to her waist. *This* had been her secret. Not the murder.

His mouth opened soundlessly, and his fists curled shut as he stared at her for a multitude of shocked moments. "You're...pregnant?"

"Yes," she whispered. "And the child is yours."

CHAPTER 6

$\mathcal{M}$orley retreated to his office on the third floor of Scotland Yard and stared at nothing for the space of an entire hour. His mind churned almost as sickeningly as his stomach.

Disbelief warred with distrust over acres of despair within him. And within that bleak, vast landscape a tiny pinprick of light pierced him.

A child? *His* child?

Had he ever dared to hope for such a miracle?

Did he believe her...about any of it?

How often had he fantasized about finding her? This goddess he'd met in the night. How many times had he wondered if he'd passed beneath her window without even knowing?

And, once again, she'd exploded into his life.

Covered in blood. Quite probably a murderer. And carrying a baby...

Christ, could this situation get any worse?

A sound drew his attention to the door, and Morley looked

up to see the most vicious, notorious pirate since Blackbeard saunter in with his hat tilted at a jaunty angle.

The man had come up with him in the East End as Dorian Blackwell, but a brush with death and a bout of amnesia had shucked the identity from him. Since they'd parted after Caroline's death, he had been christened The Rook on his pirate ship, but had recently married and subsequently shucked his murderous moniker for a brand-new one. Ashton Weatherstoke, the erstwhile Earl of Southbourne.

Known to his friends simply as *Ash*.

"Can you believe that wedding?" Ash tugged at the collar he wore impossibly high to cover the scars left by the lye meant to dissolve his body in the mass grave he'd crawled out of twenty odd years ago.

Morley stood to shake his hand, grateful for a friendly face on this, the rottenest moment of his adult life. They'd come so far from their days as street rats together, but some things never changed, like the man's impossible sardonic wit.

"I wasn't aware you were invited," Morley said. "I didn't see you there."

Ash smirked. "Oh, I was and declined the boring invitation, but it's all over London in the space of three hours. An Earl falling over dead at his own wedding? Whispers of foul play? What a bloody debacle, eh, Cutter?"

Morley lunged past his friend and slammed his door closed, whirling on the unfashionably tanned and brawny man who wore a smart suit as loosely as his devil-may-care smirk.

"I told you never to call me that," he snarled.

The smile widened to that of a shark's. "It's your name, isn't it?" He held up his hands against the onslaught of irritation burning from Morley's glare. "I'm sorry, I've tried, but I can't call you *Carlton* with a straight face." These last words were strained through a chuckle as if to elucidate his point.

"Call me Morley, then, everyone else does." He returned to

his desk to straighten the papers he'd upset in his haste, arranging them into tidy piles. One in need of signatures. One in need of written correspondence. One in need of dissemination to his clerk as signatures and replies had already been made.

Amidst all the chaos, he needed order. He needed it to think. To decide what to do next.

He needed to control the outcome.

What he *didn't* need was interruptions, even in the form of just-discovered long-lost best mates with murderous reputations of their own.

"Debacle," he muttered. "Doesn't even begin to describe what happened this morning." Looking up, he leaned on his desk with both fists, too agitated to sit down. What word could he possibly use? Catastrophe? Disaster? Nothing seemed quite strong enough.

Three stories below where they stood, a lone woman was locked in a secret cell.

A murderer? A mother?

His lover.

What to do with her was his only pressing concern.

"Is there a reason for your visit, Dorian?" he asked shortly.

"I told *you* never to call me *that*," the pirate sent him a black look that might have had a lesser man begging his pardon. Or his mercy.

Both of which he famously lacked.

"It's your name, isn't it?" Morley shot back the man's own words.

"Touché." Hard, obsidian eyes softened by scant degrees as Ash wandered about his spacious office. He read the commendations on the walls, looked at his certificate of knighthood, his army medals, a broken bayonet, a bullet that had been dug out of his thigh in Afghanistan displayed in a shadow box made by his regiment.

Catalogues of a life they were supposed to have lived together. A life that was stolen from them by the vagaries of fate.

The black eyes softened to something more filial and familiar. "Speaking of the man who took my name when I was presumed dead, Dorian is about to join us for a chat."

"Come the fuck again?" Morley straightened. "The Blackheart of Ben More, King of the London Underworld is coming here? To my *office in the middle of the day*?" His jaw locked against the rest of the sentence, hissing the last of these through clenched teeth.

"Former King of the so on and so forth. He's reformed, remember?"

"Allegedly," Morley muttered.

Ash waved him off. "It's a central location for us to meet, and we've information for you and Detective Inspector Argent to investigate in both your *vocational capacities*." He bucked his brows rather meaningfully.

Morley rubbed at the tension tightening at the base of his neck. "The last time the Blackheart of Ben More was in these walls, I tied him to a chair and beat him within an inch of his life."

"That isn't *exactly* how I remember it." As if summoned by his title, the subject of their conversation let himself into Morley's office with nary a knock and left the door wide open behind him as he stopped abreast of Ash, his very own doppelganger.

Morley's fingers still itched to throttle the man often. Or, like now, punch the vaguely superior expression from his features and blacken the obsidian eye that wasn't covered by the eyepatch.

But alas, he could not. Morley and the so-called Blackheart of Ben More had established a truce recently—well, a ceasefire —for the sake of the man they both called brother.

The real Dorian Blackwell—now Ash—and an orphan named Dougan Mackenzie had been locked in Newgate Prison together as boys. Because of their similar looks, black hair, and dark-as-the-devil eyes, they'd been christened the Blackheart Brothers in Newgate, and the infamous moniker had followed them through a menagerie of miseries and misdeeds.

Upon Dorian's supposed death in prison, Dougan Mackenzie, who was serving a life sentence for the murder of a pedophile, assumed Dorian Blackwell's identity and release date.

He lived as Dorian Blackwell for two decades, as the reigning King of the London Underworld, whilst the real Dorian, having crawled out of a mass grave with no memory, lived as the Rook, King of the High Seas.

However, when Ash reclaimed his memory, he saw no great need to reclaim his name from his good friend, as his life with Lorelai Weatherstoke was the epitome of his happy ending.

When all was said and done, both Ash and Dorian decided to live with names they'd adopted instead of the ones they'd been born with.

Only Morley and Argent were the wiser. And all the more befuddled for it.

However, since Morley also lived under an assumed name, he could hardly cast aspersions.

People in glass houses and all that.

Dorian strode up alongside Ash with his hands resting comfortably in his pockets. He bumped the pirate with his elbow in a show of camaraderie. An extraordinary thing, as Dorian famously hated to be touched by all but his wife, Farah.

Though the Blackheart Brothers looked much alike as young men, time had separated them somewhat. Standing side by side as they were, it was easy to tell them apart. Ash wore his hair close-cropped, and his skin was swarthy and weathered by years at sea. The grooves branching from his eyes and the brackets of his mouth were carved deeper into features more savage than Dorian's pale, satirical visage.

Despite his eyepatch, Dorian remained as handsome as the very devil. He displayed more spirit and mirth than his piratical counterpart, wore his hair down to his collar, and outweighed Ash by perhaps half a stone.

"Here's trouble," Dorian greeted Argent with a slap to the shoulder as the amber-haired man strode in holding a coffee and a paper.

Argent cast his previous employer a congenial nod. *He* at least, turned to shut the door behind him, cutting their conclave of reprobates off from an increasingly curious detective branch.

"Christ, almighty," Morley said by way of salutation. "I've no time for trouble if you've brought it to my doorstep. Not today."

"Well, considering the exsanguinated Earl you've cooling in your morgue, I'd say we've arrived in the nick of time," Ash went to the window and opened the drapes onto Whitehall Place, uncovering an unfettered view of the spires of Parliament. "We'd meant to discuss Commissioner Goode with you after the wedding, but it seems that needs must."

Morley's lips compressed. "What about him?"

"Something is rotten in the State of Denmark," Dorian quoted significantly. "And the closer we come to the Yard, the more it stinks to high heaven."

"Out with it, both of you," Morley barked. "I don't have time for your cryptic dramatics today."

"No time for corruption in your own department?" Ash's black brow arched, and he speared Morley with a meaningful look.

"We've information that the ironically named 'Goode' needs a bit of moral direction," Dorian informed him with no small amount of smugness. "Who did we think of but your august self, Morley? This place is your life and your wife, and the shadows of justice your mistress. Goode's the perfect man to ruin, especially for your career. You could rise and take his place."

Morley shook his head, rejecting the very idea. On today of all days? Could he not escape the name Goode? "Why would I do such a thing? What have you heard?"

Ash turned from the window. The light reflected off the lye burn scars that crawled up his neck and clawed at his jaw. When he spoke, it was with a great deal less inflection than his more demonstrative counterpart. "Goode's nobility was built hundreds of years ago on the import of lumber to our little island, but I have it on good authority that his shipping company is smuggling more than just wood. There's a plant being hailed in the Americas as the new drug of the century."

"The coca plant," Morley nodded. "I've heard of it. It's not exactly illegal to ship it here, and it's widely used therapeutically."

Dorian made a disgusted noise. "It is illegal if the substance isn't declared at customs, and if it's not being delivered to doctors, but instead distributed to obsessed ghouls by coppers who are little better than bookies handing out beatings if they're not paid on time."

Morley looked from Dorian's one good eye, to Ash, and then to Argent, who studied the dark-haired men intently from where he held up the far wall with his leaning shoulders. "You're *sure* of this?" he asked.

Ash nodded. "I'm certain the plants are coming from his ships. Though where it's being refined into cocaine, I couldn't tell you."

"And *I'm* certain the drug is being leaked onto the streets by your officers," Dorian insisted. "In the poor and rich boroughs alike."

"How certain?" Morley pressed.

"As sure as we are that you've nothing to do with it," Ash said. "And we've all the evidence you need to open up further investigation. However, since this man is your only superior, and you've no quiet way to investigate your own officers, I'd suggest the Knight of Shadows conduct the inquiry."

The Knight of Shadows. Did he want to be the sort of man who policed his own?

Was he truly so ignorant about what the Commissioner might be doing behind his back?

Morley stared at the three men who stood in front of his desk. Three men who'd once been three boys beaten down by the very laws that were supposed to protect them. They'd forged a bond together as teens in Newgate Prison that nothing on this earth could pull asunder.

Morley's own path had taken him on an entirely different road. A road that became a line between them. A line as tangible as the desk behind which he stood.

Alone.

They'd always stand together, those three. And no matter how much they trusted him, Morley never saw the insides of those prison walls and would thereby forever stay on the outside of their coterie.

On the other side of the line.

He'd been fine with that because his life had become one of order and regimentation where theirs were chaos and anarchy.

Cutter had followed the laws of the streets once.

But Carlton could not. He didn't exist without boundaries. He wanted the boundaries drawn in no uncertain terms so he could see exactly which parameters he was supposed to work within. He was a man forged in the meat grinder of war and then polished by the police force.

Except lately, the lines had been blurred by the Knight of Shadows. And he'd leapt over one particular line so far, he couldn't see it anymore.

And the consequences were about to be cataclysmic.

He lowered himself into his high-backed leather chair. The legs of which no longer felt so dense and steady. As if he could topple from his throne at any time. "I hear what you're saying, and I agree that this demands further investigation. But...there is a complication in regards to me."

"Do tell." Dorian's eye sharpened, and he was instantly rapt. "You are a famously uncomplicated man."

Morley let that go for now. "I've become a bit..." He cast about for the right word. Embroiled? Consumed? Obsessed? Entangled? "*Involved* with Commissioner Goode's daughter."

Argent perked to that. "Which one? Doesn't he have several?"

Morley swallowed, knowing that once this was out in the open, he could never take it back. It would be painful to endure their reactions, but possibly worth it if they could help him see through his pall to a course of action.

"The one whose wedding was interrupted by a murder," he muttered.

"Swift work, Morley," Ash exclaimed. "That was only what, three *minutes* ago?"

"Hours—"

Ash didn't appear to listen. "She's not *technically* a widow, so you don't have to wait the requisite year—"

Morley interjected. "No, you idiot, it was before today. Three months before."

Dorian gave an exaggerated gasp and clutched at his lapels, adopting an overwrought conservative, blustery affect. "An *affair*, Morley? A Chief Inspector and a knight of the realm. How utterly reprehensible."

"Morally derelict, I dare say," Ash added with a lopsided grin.

"Quite right," Dorian thumped him. "What *will* they think at church?"

Morley didn't even have it in him to rise to their japes as he buried his head in his hands. "It's worse than that, I'm afraid. I've locked her in one of the cells downstairs."

A protracted silence caused him to look up, but he didn't find the astonishment he'd expected.

In fact, these hard men with terrible reputations seemed to be fighting back almost proud smiles. "If I'm honest, Morley, a bit of kidnapping is no insurmountable impediment," Ash shrugged. "Show us a man in this room who hasn't had to lock his lady-love in some form of prison before she'd consent to be his wife."

"It was a Scottish castle for me," Dorian said with no little nostalgia.

"I'll see your Scottish tower, and raise you a pirate ship," Ash bragged.

"Closet," the monosyllabic Argent added.

Each of them shared a chuckle and, not for the first time, Morley was hit by a wave of sympathy for their wives.

"What happened?" Ash asked Morley, after wiping his smile from his lips with the back of his hand.

Morley pressed two fingers to each temple and worked in circles. He was about to regret this, but he needed to confess. To purge the sin that'd been weighing on him for so many weeks.

Because it'd been so long since he'd been so lost.

"Have any of you heard of the Stags of St. James?"

Ash and Argent shook their heads, but Dorian nodded. "Noble women pay fortunes for their sexual services. Madame Regina, who runs my brothel, suggested we recruit a few from Henrietta Thistledown."

Morley cleared a gather of shame from his throat. "Well, I was out one night, just about three months ago…"

"Being a vigilante?" Dorain asked.

Investigating," he corrected.

"No one else investigates with a mask, but do go on."

Once again, he let that go. "My *investigation* of some murdered men took me to Miss Henrietta's, where they'd worked as stags. I was in the garden and Miss Goode sort of... mistook me for..." He couldn't bring himself to say the bloody word.

Ash's mouth fell open. "*A prostitute?*"

"Is she blind?" Dorian's nose wrinkled as he raked him with a disbelieving glare.

Morley sat back in his chair, cursing himself for saying a damned word to any of them.

It was Argent who leaned forward, his expression fascinated. "And?"

"And...we..." Morley flicked his hand out in a gesture that could have meant anything.

"Holy fucking Christ, you didn't," Dorian shook his head as if begging him to deny it and hoping he wouldn't.

"I need to sit down." Argent groped for the chair across from his desk and settled his hulking frame into it.

"I need a drink." Ash went to the sideboard next to the door.

Dorian stayed where he was, staring at Morley. "*You* deflowered a Baron's daughter, no, a Commissioner's daughter —*your boss's daughter*—before her wedding and got *her* to pay *you* for it? Christ, Morley, I've misjudged you all this time. Color me bloody impressed."

"Don't," Morley warned.

"Oh, don't be cross." Dorian waved his leather-gloved hand at him. "I'm certain you did it *properly* and *thoroughly* as you do everything else and then made up for it with piles of guilt and self-flagellation and sleepless nights and all that rubbish."

Morley crossed his arms. "I'm not discussing this with you further." He never flagellated himself, bastard didn't know what he was talking about.

89

Ash stepped forward, a drink in hand. "Don't heed Dorian. Pearls before swine and all that."

Dorian feigned outrage. "Speak for yourself, *I'm* not the one rolling in the dirt with betrothed debutants."

They all looked at Morley and lost their battle with mirth.

"I didn't know who she was at the time," Morley explained darkly. "Or I'd never have touched her."

Ash came behind the desk where Morley sat, and put a glass in front of him. He leaned a hip on the edge and poured Morley a healthy snifter from his own decanter before patting him on the shoulder. "I, for one, am delighted," he said, encouraging him to drink. "You were living like a monk, and let's be honest, you never were very good with women."

"A monk?" Dorian scoffed. "I was worried he was a bloody eunuch."

"Or had a terrible predilection," Ash added.

"That wouldn't bother me so much," Argent cut in, declining a drink with a wave of his hand as he sipped his coffee. "I never trust a man without a dark side."

Dorian's shoulder leaned against the wall and he crossed one foot in front of the other, a cruel gleam in his dark eye. "All this time I worried you took no other lovers because you were still in love with my wife."

"*Enough.*" Morley tossed his whisky back and slammed the empty glass onto the table with a bang loud enough to be heard by the occupants of the floor below them.

For a man who didn't believe in miracles, he knew he was witnessing one now as they all blinked at him in blessed silence.

Wouldn't last long, he thought bitterly.

They'd been taciturn villains all, before their women had made them happy.

Happy men never seemed to tire of conversation.

Except Argent, who only spoke when words were absolutely required.

"So angry, Morley," Dorian tutted. "Struck a nerve?"

Ash tossed a disapproving look over his shoulder at Dorian. "A low blow, Dorian, even for you. We are all of us angry men. It is that anger that drives the best of us to succeed."

"*Au contraire, mon frère,*" the Blackheart of Ben More twisted an imaginary villainous mustache, ever unrepentant. "Cunning. Cunning is how we do what needs done."

"This isn't a bloody lark, it's my *life*," Morley grit out from between clenched teeth. "She's seen me as the Knight of Shadows. We engaged in a scandalous affair for a night. And now she's down there having quite likely murdered her fiancé and desperate to tell anyone who would listen my secrets."

"Does she recognize you as the Knight of Shadows?" Argent speared him with a serious gaze.

Morley nodded, feeling distinctly defeated.

"There's more to this, isn't there," Argent stated dryly, narrowing his verdant eyes. "Something you're not telling us."

Morley's head snapped up. There was no way for Argent to know, but the bastard was an infuriating genius when it came to reading other people.

"Is she blackmailing you or something?" the taciturn detective inquired.

Morley shook his head. "Worse. She's claiming I impregnated her that night."

At that, all sense of joviality drained from the room as the enormity of the situation pressed the very air into something heavy and dark.

For all their differences, all four of them had something very much in common.

They'd grown up without paternal care. Their fathers had abandoned them at best and tried to murder them at worst.

"Do you have any reason to believe her?" Dorian asked.

"Have you seen proof of her condition or is she simply desperate to save her neck?"

"She hired a prostitute," Ash said carefully. "So, there's the possibility the father of her child could have been any number of men."

Morley thought on that, and then violently rejected that notion, voicing the fear he'd had for some weeks now. "I'm not certain she'd ever truly had a lover before me."

All the men suddenly seemed uncomfortable, but it was Dorian who said, "Well... I mean... there's an uncomplicated way to tell."

"Not... the way we... Holy Christ I don't *know*." Morley buried his hands in his hair and pulled.

"I'm afraid to ask, and yet I find myself anxious to find out," Argent said as if this surprised him.

Morley sorely wished he could be anywhere else. He couldn't very well admit that he was so bloody ravenous that he might not have noticed the physical barrier of her virginity.

That her arms were so sweet. Her body so tight, yet welcoming. Her moans might have been pleasure or pain, but her words were nothing but encouraging.

He proceeded carefully. "She wasn't...experienced, but neither did I notice a... physical impediment. She wasn't the shy, wilting flower, obviously, she approached me. But, neither was she a vixen. She'd found out about the Earl of Sutherland's infidelity and was angry at his selfishness. She wanted a lover of her own."

He didn't want to give them more. To say how adorable she'd been. And so damnably desirable he'd been on the verge of orgasm the minute they'd kissed. He'd been beneath her skirts as he feasted her to completion and was unable to tell if she were shocked or expectant. Nervous or experienced.

And yet. He'd known it was her first climax. She'd left no doubt about that.

"She made it sound like her intended was a selfish lover," he defended himself to no one in particular at this point. "But I can't say for certain now that she knew this firsthand. And she never went back to Miss Henrietta's. I paid to be informed the moment she did. So the chances of her hiring another lover are slim."

Though, if he thought about it... she could entice any man with the crook of her finger.

"Why go through with marriage to the blighter, then, if he was unfaithful?" Ash wondered aloud.

"Strictly speaking, she didn't," Argent reminded them over his coffee cup. "She was found with her fingers around the hilt of the dagger that killed him."

"Red-handed, as it were." Morley huffed a sigh between his compressed lips. "Why would she do it? Why would she do *any* of it?"

Ash shrugged, as if it really was of little consequence. "It's not for us to understand the mysterious minds of women."

"Or people in general," Argent agreed.

"Perhaps she agreed to marry him because she didn't want her child to grow up a bastard," Dorian, the bastard born of a ruthless Marquess, put this to them without a hint of his earlier levity.

"It's a probability." Morley felt his lip lift above his teeth in a snarl. "Or she wanted my child to be the next Earl of Sutherland."

"Can you blame her?" Argent had a distinct gift for finding the practicalities in an emotionally charged situation. "This pregnancy makes her *less* likely to kill the man who would lift her out of this bind, not more. She'd have been a pariah to her family and society if the child had been born without the luxury of a name. It's extraordinary what women will give up for their children..." Argent trailed off, staring at the blank wall.

"Unless Sutherland found out and threatened to destroy her with the secret," Morley theorized.

"Cutter," Ash said the name written on no documents and spoken by no one in the world but the unlucky few who'd known him decades ago.

Their eyes met, and suddenly Ash wasn't a pirate king, or the Rook, but that black-eyed boy. The one with whom he roamed the streets and threw fists and stole food and created impossible futures.

"Congratulations, Cutter." Ash's lips lifted into the ghost of a smile, his dark eyes softening to something almost tender. "You're going to be a father."

The weight of that word knocked the wind from him. A *father*. He'd given up that dream years ago.

"What are you going to do about it?" Dorian, the besotted father of two children gave him perhaps the first look of commiseration he'd ever received from the man.

Morley stood and shouldered past them all, retrieving his jacket from where he'd hung it on the rack. "My job."

CHAPTER 7

"*I* *didn't* kill him."

It was the first thing the woman said when Morley descended the stairs to the private interrogation cell in the basement of Number Four Whitehall Place with a bucket of warm water and stringent soap.

Prudence. Her name was Prudence Goode. He knew that now.

This chamber had, decades past, been used for little better than inquisition-like torture. Though the walls had been cleaned and scrubbed by a million different char maids, Morley could still smell the blood. It hung like condemnation in the air, flavoring it metallic and spicing it with mold and despair. He'd given Dorian the famous beating here. He'd used it to hide traitors for the Home Office and other high-profile criminals.

In the middle of the grey stone, *she* stood like a soiled white lily unlucky enough to adorn a battlefield.

Rumpled and bloodstained.

A tug in his chest had him clearing his throat. She was so sweet to look upon. So lovely and small and concerningly pale.

He'd thought he'd met enough conniving criminals, both

95

men and women, to not be moved by seemingly innocent features. And yet, here he was, fighting the knight-errant inside him that desired to sweep her away from all of this and lock her in a tower where she would be safe.

Where she would be *his*.

"A clean frock has been sent for," he told her, pulling a tri-legged stool from the corner to perch in front of the bench upon which she sat.

The manacles on her wrists weren't secured to anything, she could have moved around easily. But she remained still, pressing her hands into her belly, as if holding on to what was inside.

A motherly gesture to be sure.

He sat close enough to watch her every expression intently, but far enough not to crowd her.

Far enough not to reach out, as he absurdly ached to do.

She'd been astonishingly fair-skinned the night they'd met. But today, even the slash of pink beneath her cheekbones had disappeared. Her lips retained no color. She seemed thinner now, less robust and vivacious.

This room did that to a person.

So did murder.

When she looked up, he made another astonishing discovery. He'd thought her eyes dark like Dorian's or Ash's, but he'd been mistaken.

They were the color of the sky before night descended. A deep, soulful midnight blue.

They widened at him, drenched with misery and fear.

"I *didn't* kill him," she repeated, her voice husky with unshed tears and the cold of this place.

Morley had made a profession of being lied to and could spot a crook with hound-like accuracy. It took him no time to suss out the merit of a man.

But women... What confounding creatures they were.

He read the truth on her open face. And it seemed so improbable. So unlikely.

That he now doubted his ability to interpret anything at all.

Morley set the bucket between them and remained quiet as he divested himself of his jacket and rolled his sleeves up his forearms. He placed a stool in front of her and crouched upon it. Next, he took the soaking cloth from the steaming water and scrubbed it with the sharp-smelling soap before reaching out, his palm up.

She stared at him for a long moment, the braid that had made a crown for her veil wilting dejectedly to one side. "Did you hear me?" she asked. "I said—"

"I heard you." He kept his hand extended until she slowly peeled her arms from the protection of her middle toward him. The blood on her hands was no longer fresh, and some of it had peeled away from the soft white flesh of her fingers. Elsewhere, it had dried into darker, less crimson colors.

He draped the warm, wet cloth over them both and let it soak away the evidence.

"There are reasons to kill, Miss Goode." His voice echoed softly from the stones around them, and he endeavored to keep his intonation gentle.

She blinked over at him and his heart wilted…or grew…he couldn't exactly tell. He'd forgotten he had one for so long that these tremors inside of his chest could have meant any number of things.

"Perhaps Sutherland hurt or molested you?" he prompted. "Threatened you or… or the child?" He swallowed. A child. *His* child.

He'd have killed the man himself, were that the case.

She shook her head violently. "He was a cad, a liar, and a rogue, but George was never physically cruel. Despite my anger, I didn't wish him dead."

"You *were* jealous." He took the soiled cloth and dipped it back into the bucket, before tending to only one hand, wiping between her small, elegant fingers and around her fingernails. It felt intimate, somehow, what he did for her. But he had no intention of that. He only wanted to be kind. "You were jealous enough to… to come to me that night. Perhaps that jealousy became hysteria after so long, a rage fed by the rigors of pregnancy."

She tried to jerk her hand out of his grip, but he held fast.

"You're seriously suggesting that I was hysterical enough on my wedding day to stab George with a relic in a church where I was certain to be found out?"

He pulled her forward, closer, capturing her gaze with his. "I'm trying to give you a defense."

"I don't *need* a defense," she said through her teeth. "I need someone to believe me. And do you know what else I need? A *husband.* I needed George's protection for the child you and I made together. Because you left me that night. You left me without even a *name.*"

Her accusation split him open like a blade. Left him raw and wounded.

Because she was right. Had she a way to contact him, she mightn't have had to stay betrothed to Sutherland.

"That is counted among the many misdeeds I committed that night," he acquiesced with a heavy breath as he released her one hand and reached for the other. For a moment, the only sounds in the dank room were the drops of water into the bucket and their uneven breaths.

"I know who you are." Her whispered words fractured around him, barraging him from all sides.

He looked up at her sharply.

Her eyes stayed locked on where the skin of her hand emerged from beneath the blood.

"I worked it out while I was reading the paper some weeks past. You were no Stag of St. James. You told me you were a shadow. In fact, I believe you are the Knight of Shadows."

"You're clever," was all he replied.

"I've been trying to figure all this time why the much-touted savior of the city, this moral vigilante with a reputation for protecting innocence, would relieve me of my own."

She still wouldn't look at him. And he didn't blame her.

Her narrow nostrils flared with breath, and the hand in his trembled.

She was afraid.

"I only accepted what you freely offered." It was the truth. Not a defense. He was a blackguard for doing so. A moral reprobate and a scoundrel and the worst kind of bastard. But he didn't steal her virginity. He didn't take her. He claimed the prize she handed him wrapped in such a lovely beribboned package. He'd given, too. He gave her pleasure. He gave her gentility and deference.

He gave her a child.

Shit.

"Under false pretenses." She finally speared him with a wounded, accusatory gaze. "You let me think pleasure was your vocation. Everything about you that night was a lie, even your voice, your accent. *God.* I dishonored myself with a man known to my father. Did you know who I was?"

"*No*," he stated firmly, dipping his cloth back into the bucket and running it between her fingers. "You know we've never met, and you'll forgive me if I don't keep up on society weddings, even that of my superior."

"Then…why?"

Her question stilled his hand, and this time it was he that could not meet her gaze.

"Why did you make love to me?" she pressed.

He'd been asking himself the same question for weeks.

"I didn't make love to you, I fucked you. I did it because you asked me to." He'd done it because she'd possessed something few women did. An indefinable allure that made him forget anything resembling reason or thought of consequence.

He'd done it because he'd been hungry and desperate for so many things in his life, but no privation had torn at him with such strength until she'd offered herself as a banquet.

She flinched as though he slapped her, and he instantly regretted his harsh words. But he'd be damned if he'd take them back. If he'd allow her to think she had any kind of sexual thrall over him now. Or any power at all.

Because the precedent had to be set if this was going to work.

Morley remained silent. Waiting for her next move. He expected her to make demands. To use that night as blackmail and threaten to tell her father.

"I wanted so desperately to find you," she murmured, as if in disbelief. "And here you were all this time, a charlatan charading as a gentleman."

She didn't know the half of it.

"A gentleman is nothing *but* a charade," he said stiffly, returning to his vocation of scrubbing her hand.

"I beg your pardon?"

"The million rules a gentleman lives by, or ladies for that matter, it's nothing but pretense, is it not? A construct to hide who we truly are. What we think. What we want. We are naught but artificial beasts."

"No..." Her little nose scrunched as if he'd stymied her. "Our rules of civility separate us from the beasts."

"Nonsense. The rules give us a pretty cage for our beasts to hide in. And let people like your lot put yourselves above the rest of humanity. It's a way to identify who thinks they are made better than others by happenstance of birth and rigorous training." He made a wry, bitter sound. "Well, any man can train himself. Just look at me."

"What do you mean?" She finally pulled her hand out of his grasp, the soap making her clean skin slippery.

He meant to show her exactly who he was. Exactly what she was about to get herself into. "I come from nothing. Lower than nothing. That accent you say was a farce, it is the one I was born with. I used to speak like any other street rat out there, and high-born folk would kick me in the gutters." He gestured to the wall, beyond which a bustling city scurried with unwanted children. "But I trained myself to act like them. To look and speak and dress like them. And now... I police them all. The entire city. And one of their own will be my wife."

She put her hands to her eyes. "Tell me you are not engaged."

He dropped the cloth into the bucket and stood. "Don't be obtuse, I obviously meant you."

"What? Absolutely not!"

An anger welled within him, one as ancient as he felt. The anger of every unwanted child. Every unrequited love. Every rejected, low-born git made to feel not good enough. "I don't see that you have a choice," he said in a slow, even tone. "If you're pregnant with my child. I will raise that child, and that's the end of it. In any case, it's the best way of getting you out of this predicament."

She sat on the cot with her hands in her lap, clenched and white-knuckled. "My father... he will never approve."

"Oh, he will now." Morley would make certain of it.

"But..." She held up the manacles surrounding her wrists.

"We'll get to that," Morley said darkly as he lifted the bucket of soiled water and stalked away from her.

One catastrophe at a time.

CHAPTER 8

Shackles came in many forms, Prudence decided. She was given a choice between two, and no matter which shackles she chose, they were until death.

They'd each left their marks on her body.

As she sat in her parlor—no, Morley's parlor—her fingers idly traced the disappearing circles of irritation on her wrists where she'd been cuffed earlier and hauled into a private arraignment in front of a judge who'd lifted her confinement. He'd done this only after the Chief Inspector had promised a staggering amount of cash for her surety before he drove her to the registrar to trade her cuffs for a ring.

Despite everything, it had been Morley who'd looked as if he were bound for the gallows. He'd stiffly spoken their vows and signed paperwork before ushering her to his astonishingly handsome terrace in Mayfair.

Where Prudence's family had been waiting.

Pru stared at the ring. The symbol of eternity. This day had been a bloody eternity.

They all had traded awkward conversation through an uncomfortable dinner where, thank heavens, her younger twin sisters, Felicity and Mercy, were sprightly enough at nineteen to chat incessantly when heavy silences threatened to descend.

After a sumptuous but abbreviated three courses, the ladies had been asked to withdraw to the parlor so the men could talk.

They'd been talking for entirely too long.

Prudence glared at the door. Her father and husband were discussing, nay, *deciding* her future somewhere beyond. Shouldn't she at least be there? Shouldn't she have a say?

A lump of dread had lodged within her throat, and try as she might, she could not swallow it.

She mustn't be surprised. When had she ever wielded power over her own life?

Especially when it came to marriage.

It wasn't as though Sutherland had been her first proposal. She'd offers from Barons, foreign leaders and dignitaries, a Viscount, and even an American magnate she'd liked once.

But her father had rebuffed them all, holding out for an offer that never seemed to come until, somehow, she'd found herself firmly on the shelf.

It was Honoria, herself, who'd long-ago suggested an alignment with George. Honoria's husband, William, was both besotted with and devoted to her. Woodhaven and Sutherland were great friends, and he very much wanted his best friend married to his wife's sister, even if he had to press the man into the arrangement.

George had so much as admitted it. "I never thought to have a wife. Sorry you'll be stuck with me, old thing, as I'm terribly certain I'll make a horrendous husband." He chucked her on the chin, and everyone had laughed as though life would be a lark.

But in reality, they'd been laughing at her. Poor Prudence. She'd be stuck at home while her husband spent her fortune on other women. He'd gamble everything away and she'd nothing to say about it.

But at least her child would have a name.

The irony of it all was, being a wife and mother was all Pru had ever desired. She'd no great need to be an accomplished and influential noble matron, nor a modern single woman with progressive sensibilities. She left that to women possessed of better and bolder minds than she.

Her hours were happily spent enjoying simple pleasures. Riding fine horses on beautiful days and reading fine books on dreary ones. Shopping with her sisters. Paying calls on friends. Attending interesting lectures, diverting theater productions, and breathtaking musical venues.

She didn't dream of an important life, just a happy one. One with a handsome man who loved her, and healthy children to do them credit and fill their lives with joy.

And now, it seemed, one mistake in a fairy garden precipitated a lifetime of misery, scandal, and, at least for the moment, immediate imprisonment in her husband's home until everything was decided by men who knew better.

It was enough to crush her.

"Did you hear me, Prudence?" Baroness Charlotte Goode's shrill question broke her of trying to stare through a solid door.

Pru put her fingers to her aching temples, suddenly overcome by exhaustion. "I'm sorry, Mother, what were you saying?"

Pursing her lips, Lady Goode clutched a dazzling shawl around her diminutive shoulders and shivered. "I was wondering at the dark fireplace, dear. One would worry if your new husband can afford to warm the house."

Considering the sum Morley had paid for her freedom without blinking, Pru very much doubted the man had trouble keeping the household. Though, there did seem to be an alarming lack of staff for such a grand, sizeable home.

"It's still warm, Mother," she said with a droll breath, doing her best not to roll her eyes.

"He likely didn't want us overheating, Mama," Felicity defended from where she perched on a delicate couch overlooking the lovely cobbled street. Even in the dim gaslights of the late evening, her coiffure glinted like spun gold.

Mercy, never one to sit still for long, handed her mother a glass. "Drink this sherry, it'll warm you."

The Baroness took the drink, her shrewd dark eyes touched everything from the golden sconces to the muted sage and cream furniture of the sparsely decorated parlor. "You'll have to engage my decorator, of course. You can't be expected to live in such barren conditions. The house is nearly empty and old enough to be decrepit. I mean, look at the panes in the windows, they're positively melting. And only three courses for your wedding meal? It's as if—"

"It's as if I were released from prison for murder only this morning to be saved by a man who would give me the protection of his position," Prudence said sharply, her voice elevating in octaves and decibels with each word. "It's as if he had scant hours to plot the entire affair and endless things to consider, the least of which are the courses of a *farcical* celebration."

Her mother gave an indignant gasp. "I thought we all agreed *not* to mention—"

"Oh, don't let's antagonize her, Mama." Mercy moved to Pru's side at once and sank next to her. She gathered up both her hands and kissed them. "Poor Pru, it's been an upsetting couple of days."

Prudence attempted to summon a wan smile for her younger sister and wasn't up to the task. Her nerves felt like they'd been stretched on the rack and were screaming for release.

Upsetting... the word couldn't touch a description for the last forty-eight hours.

"I rather like Sir Morley," Felicity remarked, daring a glass of sherry of her own. "He's so...well he's such a..." Her wide eyes narrowed as she searched for the right word, tapping her chin with a burgundy-gloved finger. "Well so many men are either elegant, or handsome, or extremely masculine, but the Chief Inspector somehow manages all three."

Pru blinked at her sister. Leave it to ever-romantic Felicity to describe her husband perfectly.

It was what had attracted her to him that night. He'd been a savage in a bespoke suit. A beast burdened by sartorial elegance. The dichotomy never ceased to fascinate her.

Mercy patted her hand. "And your new home is lovely, Pru. Everything is so fine and well-preserved."

"Indeed, our rooms in town look like closets in comparison," Felicity added encouragingly.

Mercy nodded. "People are paying large sums on the market for these spacious grand old places. I'll bet that chandelier is imported and at least a hundred years old."

"How many times do I have to tell you *not* to discuss money in public, Mercy?" their mother lamented. "And our rooms in town might not be so large, but they've a fashionable address."

"This is Mayfair, Mama, every address is fashionable," Felicity said with a droll sigh.

The twins shared a wince with Pru, who returned Mercy's fond squeeze.

She'd always admired young Mercy's enterprising wit and busy mind. It was as though her trains of thought were numerous and confounding as those running through Trafalgar station, and branched in just as many directions.

Whereas Felicity's notions were a bit less weighty and more idealistic, their mode of transport a hot-air balloon drifting upon the whims of a strong wind.

Either way, they were each darling girls dressed in gem-bright silks and forever the fair counterparts to Prudence and Honoria's dark looks and darker deeds.

Before she could reply, footsteps clomped down the hall before the parlor door burst open containing the storm cloud that was her father. The dark blue eyes they'd all inherited from him glinted with displeasure from his mottled features.

"We're going," he stated shortly.

They all stood.

"Is everything all right?" her mother queried anxiously.

The Baron pinned Prudence with a scathing look as he announced through his teeth, "Everything is settled."

Morley stood in the door looking both resolute and enigmatic. He watched the tableau with a vague disinterest. Removed from it all.

Remote.

Would she ever be able to reach him?

Felicity and Mercy embraced, kissed, and congratulated Pru, each wearing identical looks of pity and concern.

"We've left a trunk of your things for you from your wedding trousseau," Felicity said. "Come around for the rest when you can."

Her mother curtsied to Morley and her father shook his hand, each of them maintaining the barest façade of civility.

Her husband's manners remained impeccable and his expression impenetrable. His spine straight and tall as he looked each of them right in the eye.

They left with barely a word for Prudence.

She swallowed as a lump of hurt lodged above that of the ever-present dread aching in her throat.

Would it ever be comfortable to breathe again?

Morley stood between her and the door, his wide back expanding with deep breaths, as if he were bracing himself for something unpleasant.

Like turning to inspect his unwanted wife.

The short-cropped hair at his nape did little to hide a red flush on his neck and a trickle of sweat that ran into the collar of his evening suit. It was the only indication that he even suffered an emotion or two.

When she could no longer stand it, Pru asked, "What happened between you and Father? How on earth did you get him to agree—?"

He finally turned, and it was all she could do not to take a step back, so abrupt was the movement. Military in its precision.

"You don't have to worry about that."

"This is my future, of course I must worry about it."

Rather than look at her, his stare remained fixed on a distant point down the hall. "It's settled to both of our satisfactions...or neither. Now, follow me," he said as he swept past her.

What about her satisfaction? she wanted to ask. *Didn't that matter at all anymore?*

The old Pru would have said something. But fear lurked in the Prudence who'd spent the night in a jail cell. One that feared that if she displeased this new husband of hers, he'd toss her right back in the cuffs.

She trailed him as he led her through a long hall with stunning antique scroll paneling but devoid of portraiture or art.

"I'm glad you both agreed, I'm just bewildered is all," she rambled. "My father is a stubborn man...not easily convinced of anything. And the very fact that he suffered through dinner without making a scene is nothing less than miraculous."

"Suffered?" Morley's disdainful sniff echoed in the empty hall. "I'm certain it causes him no end of suffering that his newest son-in-law is beneath him socially. Sitting at my lowly table must have been a torment for you all. I commend you for containing your disappointment."

"No! Not at all," she rushed, before ceding the falsehood.

Her father, and especially her mother, were devastated more by the loss of Sutherland's earldom than the man, himself. And to have him replaced with a man of the working class, even a knight, was little compensation. "What I mean to say is that we're attempting something highly irregular. It'll take a miracle for society not to discover that I married two days after my wedding to poor George was interrupted by his murder and that I gave birth not six or so months after—"

He paused, and she nearly ran into the back of him.

"I would take it as a kindness if we mentioned the former Earl of Sutherland as little as possible in this house." His chin touched his shoulder, but he didn't exactly look back at her. A chill had been added to his endlessly civil tenor. "If *ever*."

"Surely that's impossible while I'm still under suspicion." She stepped closer to him. Close enough to put her hand on his back if she wanted. "Is that how you convinced my father to be agreeable? By offering to protect me from—"

"Your father is being investigated by the Yard for smuggling illicit substances into the country through his many shipping companies. He is aware of your pregnancy, and he concedes that marriage to me is the thing that could very well save your life and his reputation. If you want the honest truth, I resorted to little better than blackmail to gain his word and his silence." He paused. "Let's not pretend I have his blessing." He turned the corner at the end of the hall and began to conquer the stairway up to the second floor.

Pru stood there for a stunned moment. "Smuggling?" She roused herself and trotted after him, lifting her skirts to climb after him. "Are you the one conducting the investigation against him?"

"I cannot discuss it."

"Not even with me?"

At the top of the stairs he finally looked back to level a droll look down his sharp nose. His eyes were like two silver ingots glowing from the shadows covering the rest of his features.

"*Especially* with you."

He disappeared from the stairwell and Pru crested the steps to turn and chase him down the corridor.

"The green parlor downstairs is for your particular use." He both spoke and walked in short clips. "But I will leave the running of the house to you. Decorate and arrange it how you like. I've a cook, a maid of all work, and a footman, but I'm certain you'll require additional staff. Hire them at your leisure."

A naturally curious person, Prudence ached to open each of the doors they passed, but she didn't dare. "Surely you don't have my dowry yet," she remarked.

He stopped, having come to the end of the hall. "Surely *you* don't think I need it," he threw a perturbed glance over his shoulder. "I've quite enough to keep a wife. Even a high-born one. I should think that's evidenced by my estate."

She'd offended him. She hadn't meant to, but despite his very fine house in an expensive part of town, and the sum he'd forfeited for surety, she hadn't any true ideas what his finances were like. "I didn't mean to imply…"

"You needn't worry. Your dowry is yours to do with as you wish. I don't require it and I won't touch it." He said this like her money was diseased, before he swept open an arched door. "Your room."

Pru had to brush past him to step inside, and she hesitated to appreciate the scent of cedarwood and soap wafting from his warm, virile body. She prolonged a blink as she remembered that scent. Remembered burrowing her face into his neck and gasping in great lungs full of it.

Even now, it provoked her exhausted body into a state of unnatural awareness.

When she opened her eyes, she marveled.

This wasn't a simple chamber, but a veritable suite. She'd a wardrobe at home smaller than the gilded fireplace, and everything else was to scale.

Like the rest of the house, the room was devoid of extraneous furnishings. However, the bed was half again as big as anything she'd slept in and angled toward windows that stretched from the ceiling to the floor.

Unlike the antique, leaded panes of downstairs, these had been installed recently, and the whole of the vast city spread out beyond in a tableau of dazzling light and spires.

"Your trunks are at the foot of the bed," he informed her. "Until a lady's maid has been procured for you, Lucy, the maid of all work, will tend to your needs. Unfortunately, she is with her ailing uncle until tomorrow afternoon. So you might need to call upon—"

"It's all right. I'll manage." She turned around, clasping her hands in front of her, doing her best not to look at the bed.

He seemed to be avoiding it as well.

Lord, how different this interaction was from the last night they'd spent together. Would they ever find that sort of warmth again? Would he ever look at her with that all-consuming heat threatening to turn her into a pile of ash and need?

She watched him stride around the outskirts of her room, inspecting the view as if he'd never seen it before. Avoiding her as if she carried the plague rather than his child.

Perhaps he needed his mask.

"If you pull on these cords, the heavy drapes will fall and block out the sunlight if you are prone to sleeping late." He demonstrated by tugging on a tasseled cord releasing one of the cobalt velvet panels. "This one next to it secures the drape back in place without needing to tie."

"How clever," she murmured.

"I thought so." His hands clasped behind his back in a regimental pose and they stood like that, staring at each other for longer than was comfortable.

It struck her in that moment how little she knew this man. How little she understood him.

He stood like a soldier, but wore white-tie finery. Just today he'd been a blackmailer *and* a bridegroom. He was a Chief Inspector. A vigilante. A knight. Her lover. A husband.

Her husband. One who had certain rights. One to which she had certain marital duties.

Despite herself. Despite everything, a little flutter of excitement spread through her belly.

"Well." Morley cleared his throat and skirted nearly the entire room to avoid her in a controlled dash for the door. "Good evening to you."

"Good evening?" She parroted his words back to him as a question. Wasn't this their wedding night? "Where are you going? That is…are you…coming back?"

He stopped in the doorframe, his wide shoulders heaving with a long breath before he slowly made an about-face to regard her with a strange and vigilant wariness. "Only a base creature would expect you submit to the marriage bed after such a traumatizing few days." His expression turned hesitant. "You don't know me very well, but I assure you, I am not a man who is prone to—the kind of behavior I demonstrated upon the night we met."

The realization that he was being considerate warmed Pru a little. "It seems that night was out of character for us both."

His eyes skittered away. "Yes. A hard-won lesson of our mutual folly."

Something about that statement tempted her to argue but she could find no words. "I appreciate your consideration, and you're correct. I don't know you at all…" Pru fiddled with her wedding ring as she took a tentative step forward, latching on to an idea. "Perhaps you could stay for a while. We could talk.

We could...become acquainted. I don't relish the idea of being alo—"

He retreated a step to hers, shaking his head decisively. "I've work to do."

Pru frowned. "Work? You mean... as the Knight of Shadows?"

"Among other things." His features locked down and everything about him became as hard as granite, including his voice. "You do realize if you utter a word about the so-called Knight of Shadows, the house of cards I've managed to build around you will collapse entirely. Any notions of ruining me will only lead to your own damnation."

Perhaps *this* was why he'd been so cold. So distant. He thought she might reveal his secrets to the world, thereby ruining his life. He hadn't cause to know otherwise, it wasn't as though they'd a relationship built on trust.

"I'd never," Pru vowed. "You have my word."

She tried not to let it hurt her feelings that her word didn't seem to allay him in the slightest. "Very good." He gave her a stiff nod that might have been a bow, and his weight shifted to take a step away.

"Wait!" she called, evoking the brackets of a deepening frown.

"What else is it, Miss Goode? I did not lie when I said I had duties to attend."

The irritation in his voice stung her sinuses with the threat of overwhelming emotion. She turned from him, grateful to have a reason. He'd called her Miss Goode, as if he'd forgotten that she'd taken his name.

"My buttons," she croaked huskily. "They're in the back and if I haven't a lady's maid... I can't reach them."

She waited in the silence with bated breath until, finally, the creak of the floorboards announced his approach.

Prudence tightened her fists in her skirts and forced

herself to be still as his fingers found the top button of her plaid, high-necked gown and released it. Gooseflesh poured over her and a little tremor spilled down her spine as he was unable to avoid brushing the upswept hair at the nape of her neck.

She closed her eyes again, swamped with an overwhelming longing. Gods, she wanted him to hold her.

No, not exactly. Not *him*. Not this wary creature of starchy reticence and wary silence. But *him*. The Knight of Shadows. She'd never felt as safe and marvelous as she had in his arms. Clutched to him. Pinned beneath him. Clenched around him.

Was he gone from her forever?

Had he ever truly existed at all?

She listened for his breath, and realized he held it.

The buttons gave way beneath his deft motions and she couldn't seem to summon words until he'd made it below her shoulder blade. Then everything she was thinking burst out of her like a sneeze.

"It's only that I have so many questions and so many fears that I feel I will die if I don't know *something*. Can't you understand how that feels? Is my life in London over? My reputation ruined? Does everyone think me capable of murder? What about George's funeral, I'll be expected to attend, won't I? Unless everyone thinks I killed him, then... Oh God. And what about you? Everyone will think—"

"People will think what I tell them to think," he said in a voice only a fraction less even and measured than his hands upon her buttons. "Only a trusted few know of your arrest last night and even fewer your release. The reverend has been silenced. Honoria and William have been sent away. Your fiancé had blessed little in the way of family, and his earldom is passed to some distant Scottish cousin who is happy not to ask too many questions. As for my part, I'm investigating the matter thoroughly, though Argent is officially handling the murder inquest for the sake of records, and a more secretive man you've never met."

She'd have to take his word on that. "What about the press? An Earl dying at his own wedding is an enormous story. All the people in attendance…someone will figure out where I am and what we've done."

His sigh was a warm tickle on her neck. "For now, they're chasing Honoria and William across the continent, thinking you are absconded to Italy to grieve and escape the horror of it."

She chewed on the inside of her lip. "Even still…there's bound to be a scandal. The truth will come out eventually."

"What troubles you the most?" he asked disapprovingly, having undone enough of her buttons to make the bodice of her dress sag. "Scandal? Or the truth?"

"I fear the consequences of what we've done," she said, holding her bodice to her chest before turning to look at him. "I don't want to raise a child under such a shadow."

The brow he notched was a few shades darker than his fair hair, and Pru realized her error. He *was* a shadow. The Knight of Shadows, in fact.

"As a man who has braved many a scandal, I care not what is said behind silk fans." He waved her worries away. "You've a bedroom rather than a cell. And no one as of yet calling for your blood. Until the inquest is over, it's best you remain out of the public eye so that I might protect you as well as I can. Those are the only answers I can give you for now."

Bereft, shaky, and utterly exhausted, Prudence gathered the last bit of strength she had to square her shoulders and ask, "Promise me you'll search with everything you have. Promise me you'll look elsewhere than in your own house for the killer."

"I promise I will look where the investigation leads."

A desolate disappointment pressed upon her with a tangible

weight, curling her shoulders forward as if they could keep his words from piercing her heart. "Do you believe me...husband? Do you believe that I am innocent?"

His gaze became intent, searching, and then frustratingly opaque. "I believe you were right when you said that the truth will come out."

Pru successfully fought off crumpling until he'd turned his back.

"Good night, Miss—" he paused then, catching himself this second time. "Good night."

When the door closed behind him, Prudence limped to the bed as if a herd of horses had trod on her feet, suddenly hurting everywhere.

She collapsed onto the counterpane and released the tears she'd been too numb to cry since this nightmare began. They broke upon her like the tide, threatening to pull her under their current of despair.

She should have wept for a dead man. For the loss of her parents' respect and her freedom. For the horror of her utter ruin and the fear of being unable to lift her head in society ever again.

But she wept, because her husband couldn't bring himself to say her name.

CHAPTER 9

*M*orley didn't think his wife was dangerous solely because he wanted her. She was dangerous because he wanted to believe her.

He emerged from the underground tunnels into Whitechapel, searching for trouble. Aching for it. His muscles rippled beneath his skin. Ready. Oh, so ready. He felt hot and cold all at once. He needed to hit something. To maim. To pound.

Fucking unfortunate word, that.

Also…relevant.

He'd wanted to pound into *her* everything he'd denied himself for the past three months. To thrust and thrust and thrust until he lost himself to the bliss he knew he'd find in her body.

What harm could it do now?

She'd almost seemed like she'd wanted it. Hadn't she? No. *No.* Surely, he'd imagined the expectation in her eyes.

The invitation.

Leaving her like that, with her dress half hanging off her shoulders, was one of the most difficult things he'd ever done.

God! Just uncovering her neck to the top of her corset—the mere sight of her shoulder blades had driven him mad with lust.

For a stranger. For a possible murderer.

For his wife.

He was a beast on a short leash tonight. *His wedding night.* He'd used every ounce of civility he could feign on this difficult, exhausting day and now he could set free his wrath on the dregs of the city. Tonight, he was on the hunt for a singular criminal. A particular crime.

And he knew just where to find it.

He passed plenty of illegal acts. Bordellos, gambling hells, gin peddlers, thieves, and all sorts up to every kind of sin.

This was his genesis, and might very well be his end. This putrid place where the shadows were full of danger and the pallid streetlamps only illuminated unpleasant truths. He slid between them like a cat, avoiding detection as even desperate, waifish fiends and daring prostitutes shrank from his shade.

He heard the name whispered behind his back upon occasion.

Is that him? The Knight of Shadows?

The police beat was easy to avoid, he'd been doing it for decades. He knew their routes, and their times.

Hell, he knew most of their names.

What he needed to discover, was which ones sold cocaine to the innocent and weak.

The deeper he drove himself into the squalid darkness of Dorset Street, the more layers of himself peeled away. He shucked off Carlton Morley. His stringent mannerisms and his staunch courteousness. He even yearned to be rid of the ridiculous mask and moniker of the vigilante.

Tonight, he felt like someone else. Someone he thought he'd buried long ago.

Cutter.

As he lurked through the thoroughfares he'd once owned as Cutter 'Deadeye' Morley, he felt a piece of his puzzle click into place.

For three bloody months he'd been turning a problem over in his mind, chewing it with as much success as he would a rock. Breaking against it. Grinding himself down.

Who was the man who'd made the ballocks decision to fuck a stranger in a garden?

Carlton Morley? Or the Knight of Shadows?

He'd needed to come here to find the answer.

It all made perfect sense now. He'd been so visceral that night. So raw and filled with every emotion he'd never allowed himself. Anger and lust and need and pain. He'd been so fucking hungry. Hungry for a kind of sustenance he'd never had.

He'd been...

Cutter.

Cutter had fucked her because he wanted to. Because she was a bit of beauty and warmth he'd never allowed himself. The thief who'd never had parents to speak of, who'd learned his morals from whores and cutpurses. Who'd committed murder for the sake of revenge.

And reveled in it.

He covered up the murder in his past, and if he found out that she'd been the woman to stick that dagger into the Earl of Sutherland's throat...he'd be tempted to cover that up too.

Because despite everything she may or may not be... he still wanted her.

Could she sense it, somehow?

Was it because they had killing in common? Like begets like, after all, and if Prudence Goode was the woman he feared she was, had she selected him because her dark soul recognized his?

Even as the suspicion lanced him with horror, his gut

violently rejected it. She was a stranger, an enigma to him, but his instinct was to believe her.

To trust her!

Trust was not an emotion with which he was familiar.

What did he know about her, really? That she was both bold and amenable. Her eyes were kind and her mouth wicked. She'd a temper, but was as levelheaded as anyone could expect under the circumstances. She succumbed to logic just as easily as lust.

She might have killed a man in cold blood.

What sort of mother would a woman like that make?

A rueful sound echoed off the damp walls of a dank alley he all but slithered down. The irony of his hypocrisy both irritated and amused him.

The father of this child was Cutter fucking Morley.

And that was both why he'd married her and why he hadn't touched her. No matter how her shape enticed him. Regardless of how the memories of her creamy thighs and silken intimate flesh tormented him. Despite the urge he had to throw caution to the wind and plunge his hands into her luxuriant hair and trail his mouth over every delectable inch of her—sampling summer berries and soft flesh...

His leather gloves creaked against the tightening of his fists.

He. Couldn't. Touch. Her. Not until he found out if she'd *innocent* blood on her hands.

There were reasons to kill. He kept reminding her of that because *if* she was found to be guilty, he wanted—he needed—a reason to save her.

Because the life inside her womb *was* innocent. Pure and untainted by the ugliness of this world. Of these streets. And he'd be goddamned if he wouldn't do everything in his mortal power to keep it that way.

Six months. He had six months to investigate the death of

Sutherland and the shipments of illicit substances sweeping the streets.

He felt like a man standing before a tryptic of mirrors, seeing a separate reflection in each. One, the methodical Chief Inspector. The next, a vengeful vigilante. And the third… a boy with a terrible secret and a broken heart.

To reconcile himself. He needed to shatter the third mirror.

Two shades broke from the lamplight of a rotten pub moving toward the alley in between, stealing his focus. Morley trailed them, melting from shadow to shadow like death, himself.

He moved when they moved. Waited when they waited, pressing himself against the corner of a building, listening to their excitement. Catching it with rampant kicks of his heart in his chest as the blue uniform of a London Metropolitan Policeman absorbed the light as he strode toward them, waving a walking stick.

This was what he'd come to see. An exchange of illicit substances. This… was where his trail to the very source began.

Morley waited for the men to pass the Copper his money. He waited until they checked the purity of the substance he handed back to them. He waited until they damned themselves.

Moving slowly, he cracked his fingers and reveled in what was to come. Three criminals. One in his uniform wielding a nightstick.

There would be pain. And he needed the pain. To inflict it. To endure it. To escape.

Yes. He'd put an end to Cutter very soon. But first…he'd use every weapon in his arsenal. He'd cut out the truth if he had to. The sooner the better.

Because as much as he trusted no one, he trusted himself least of all…

To keep his hands off his wife.

CHAPTER 10

$\mathcal{I}$f it was the last thing she ever did, Pru was going to get behind the two locked doors in her house.

She'd been staring at them for a week. Or, rather, they had been staring at her.

They'd a somewhat strange relationship now, she and the doors. They greeted her every day on the way down to breakfast, beckoning to her with their iron latches and symmetrical arches. A cream-colored obsession, they were, and if she didn't get behind them today, she'd give in to the madness waiting in the periphery of her thoughts. Threatening to engulf her and drag her to perdition.

She couldn't exactly say why it bothered her so much. Why she spent so long in front of them when there were so many diverting rooms to occupy her. The first floor alone contained the large drawing room, the dining room, and a morning room attached to the well-tended back gardens through which the modest stable and carriage house hunkered in a cozy stone corner. She'd found a small library, in which she rejoiced, connected to her spacious parlor on the second floor, along with a couple handsome unused guest rooms, and her husband's study.

The third story was where she slept, and only four doors graced the long hall. One was her bedroom and dressing room, obviously, and the other a washroom.

She needn't the deductive powers of a Scotland Yard detective to suss out that her husband slept behind one of the locked doors.

In theory, at least.

Nighttime was when her body reminded her she carried his child with bouts of vicious nausea. So, when she lay awake staring at the canopy, doing her best to contain the retching, she'd often hear the clip of his shoes on the floorboards as he returned home from occasional nocturnal adventures as the Knight of Shadows.

Pru would lie awake and listen to him putter about behind the locked doors. Sometimes it sounded as though he'd brought his enemies home to grapple with them in the middle of the night and she'd burn to know what he was about.

He'd be gone before she awoke.

She never saw him. They never spoke. But she knew her husband kept apprised of her. That the staff, meager as it was, updated him on her well-being.

After a particularly restless night where she'd vomited until the wee hours, she'd been presented an effervescent drink by the thin, birdlike cook at the lonely breakfast table.

"From the master," the woman had told her. "To settle your ills."

She'd not even been able to stomach her usual breakfast of toast that morning, but the moment the ginger ale had fizzed its way down her throat and spread relief in her belly, she'd thanked the stars for him.

The gesture, tiny as it was, had touched her.

He cared.

More likely about the baby rather than her, but even so. She wasn't surprised, per se. She remembered his deference the night they'd been lovers. The tempering of his strength. The tenderness of his touch. The attentiveness to her pleasure.

To dwell on it now would drive her deeper toward madness.

A tray had appeared in her parlor, and upon it she found little treasures almost every morning. A furniture catalogue. A card of information for a staff employment company. Clothing patterns and collections for infants from which she could order.

She'd never had to send for her things from her father's house, workmen had simply arrived and collected her. She'd gone to her parents' house in her husband's fine carriage, finding them conspicuously absent, and had gathered what belonged to her.

And a few things that didn't.

They'd moved and unpacked her entire life without her having to so much as lift a finger.

Chief Inspector Sir Carlton Morley did just about everything around the house...

Except sleep. Or eat. Or live.

She might as well reside in a crypt for all the interaction she had. Ester, Lucy, and the footman, Bart, were polite but disinclined to break the barrier between mistress of the house and staff, regardless of her clumsy attempts. They treated her with careful suspicion, and in the moments they weren't aware of her regard, open disapproval.

Mercy and Felicity had sent word that they were only allowed to call around once per week.

There'd been no word from Honoria. And Pru had not spoken to Amanda since that day in Hyde Park. All her other acquaintances assumed she'd escaped her despair to Italy.

But no. It was right here. Screaming at her through the silence and loneliness that pressed her down from all sides as she stood between two locked doors.

Dammit. She'd had enough.

Prudence waited until Ester had gone out to the market, and went below stairs to pilfer the master set of keys from their hook in the pantry. She'd done this before, on day three, and discovered that none of the master keys matched the locks for the two mysterious doors.

Morley probably kept them upon his person.

The master set did, however, grant her access to his office.

Out of respect for her husband, she'd not disturbed the room past a curious peek that day. What if he somehow discovered that she'd snooped? She'd no desire to incur his wrath.

Today she was past caring. She needed a diversion. She needed to *know*.

It took her an hour and a half of rifling through his office to find what she'd somehow suspected would be there. He was so tidy for a man, so orderly, so comprehensively methodical. If he thought of everything, then he'd keep in the house just exactly what she'd been searching for.

Spare keys.

They'd been tucked into a file of legal papers in a drawer marked "security."

Clever.

They burned her palm as she raced back up the stairs. Her heart trilled in her chest like a captured sparrow as she stood in front of both doors.

She selected the left one first. Inhaling a bracing breath, she slid the key in the lock and turned it, unlatching the door.

Upon first glance she was disappointed. She hadn't really known what to expect, but in her more fanciful moments she might have conjured a lair befitting the so-called Knight of Shadows. Uniforms maybe. Weapons. Masks and the like.

Unsurprisingly, it was nothing more than an immaculate bedroom. Even the dust motes that'd danced across her open windows didn't seem to dare venture into his space. The bedclothes had not a wrinkle. The shaving implements gleamed in a row on the curio as if they'd been shined with the silver.

But the faint scent of shaving soap clung to the air as the opaque water in the bowl had yet to be refreshed. That and other aromas drew her deeper into the room as if she'd been summoned by a spell. Cedar and fresh linen.

And that masculine spice that was distinctively *him*.

The rustle of her skirts disrupted the almost mausoleum-like silence as she drifted to a high-backed chair where a dressing gown had been neatly draped but obviously discarded after use.

Lucy hadn't laundered it yet or changed the pitcher, which meant that Morley, the master of the house, had straightened his own bed and shined his own shaving accoutrements.

What a bemusing man.

Unable to stop herself, Prudence lifted the robe to her face and inhaled. Since her pregnancy, she seemed to have the nose of a bloodhound. She'd never forget the warm, wild scent of him. It taunted her now, surrounded by his things as she was.

It might be the only appetizing aroma she'd encountered for weeks.

Belatedly, she looked around the room and noticed something amiss. The paper on the walls was decidedly feminine, little forget-me-nots wrapped in ribbons. There was no view on this side of the house, and the space was decidedly smaller than her chamber at the end of the hall.

Her sound of wonderment snagged the air as the robe slipped from her fingers back to the chair.

He'd surrendered the master suite to her. The room with

the best view, the largest bed, and the most comfortable furnishings.

An awfully considerate gesture, for a man who couldn't bring himself to share a meal with her, let alone a conversation.

It first occurred to her to offer the gesture back to him. To tell him she didn't want it, that she'd take the smaller room so he could once again enjoy his own accommodations.

If he'd only come home.

She'd have to figure out how to offer without him finding out she'd snooped.

Heaving a morose sigh, Pru left and locked his room, burning with curiosity about the next door. She fumbled with the key twice before opening it, and when she finally managed, she stood in the doorway for several moments while tears stung behind her eyes.

The room was in disarray. A lovely chaos. The entrails of packing crates were strewn about their treasures as if the unpacking had been interrupted.

This was what her husband had been wrestling with the past few nights.

Floating inside, Prudence touched each one as if it were made of the most fragile glass.

A wicker cradle. An expensive-looking perambulator. Delicate furniture ready to store tiny things. Soft blankets and cushions. Cunning toys.

Her breath hitched as she stopped in front of a fine-crafted rocking chair. The piece, itself, was lovely but what had her transfixed was the simple little doll placed just so on the velvet cushion.

Pru couldn't say why she used infinite care to retrieve it. The doll was neither fragile nor costly. The body little more than soft fabric stuffed with batting and covered in a white eyelet lace dress. The round head fit in the palm of her hand, the face painted somewhat catawampus, and the hair comprised of soft strings of lose gold yarn tied with blue ribbons.

No, the doll wasn't at all extraordinary.

But the thought of the man she'd married. The intense, mercurial knight selecting it for this room... now that was... that was...rather a marvelous image.

Smoothing her fingers through the strings of yarn she wondered, what if their child bore his golden locks? Or the impossible silver-blue of his eyes?

Little butterflies erupted in her belly, this time not at all precipitating sickness. This person they'd created... would sleep here, God willing. Would fill this house with commotion, and maybe a little cheer.

Lord knew they all needed an injection of that.

As Prudence spun in a circle for a moment, taking in the soft butter yellows, muted pinks, and periwinkles of the room, some of the weight pressing upon her fell away. Morley might not be ready to be any kind of husband, but he was preparing to be a father.

And, it seemed to her, relishing the venture.

But, why lock this room away from her?

A dark thought landed in her stomach, crushing the butterflies beneath a stone. What if he meant to raise this child without her? What if—

A ruckus interrupted the stillness of the house. Doors shutting, heavy footsteps on the wood floors downstairs. The scurry from elsewhere as Lucy and Bart rushed to attention.

Of all the days for her husband to come home before tea!

Prudence abandoned the doll to its perch and flew out of the room, locking it behind her. She raced down the first flight of stairs, but it became instantly obvious that she wouldn't have time to return any of the keys. Masculine voices filtered closer to the base of the stairwell.

"Bloody traffic," Morley's growl echoed up to the second floor. "Has the Earl of Northwalk arrived yet?"

"Not yet, sir," Bart replied.

"Good. Bastard is just as insufferably punctual as I am, which means I have to make a point of being early."

Pru suppressed a little flutter of panic. An Earl? Coming here? Now?

Northwalk, the title itched at her memory. Something so familiar and yet, she was certain they ran in higher circles than her family.

"I finally abandoned my coach to jog here. The rain soaked through my jacket. If I've time, I'll go upstairs for another."

Panicking, Prudence shoved the keys behind a potted plant beneath a window, and did her very best to affect a glide as she descended the final stairs to the main floor, hoping to cut him off.

Conversation seized as both men looked up at her appearance.

Pru faltered halfway down.

Why did he have to be so unspeakably handsome?

Why did he have to be so categorically inaccessible?

A week's time had almost blunted the reality of his imposing, vital allure in her memory. She'd almost forgotten the very sight of him threatened to steal every breath from her lungs and every thought from her head.

Her husband's gaze swept over her. An arrested expression tightened the casual one he'd been wearing for Bart, his eyes flaring with something intense and ephemeral.

Before she had cause to hope, his features shuttered with the immediacy of a shop locking down for a long absence.

Bart had only just taken his employer's hat and coat, draping the later damp garment over his arm. He turned and bowed to her low enough to show the round bald spot on his pate. "My lady," he addressed her diffidently.

"Good afternoon." She shook herself from her thrall and summoned what she hoped was a convincing smile. "I'd no idea it'd begun to rai—"

He'd already swept through to the corridor to hang his master's things, apparently feeling no great need to await her reply.

Pru battled with an acute misery that warred for sovereignty with shame. She was such an unwanted stranger here. This didn't feel like her house.

Nor did it feel like her life.

And the man at the foot of the stairs wore more of a mask now than he ever did as the Knight of Shadows.

He just looked at her with those alert, assessing eyes. She'd begun to feel that even his silence was an investigative technique. A weapon he used against her.

An effective weapon, at that.

Because she felt wounded. Bruised.

But then, everything about him was weaponized. The smooth, composed movements of his powerful limbs, hinting at a controlled brutality. The precisely cut layers of his hair, the perfectly pressed creases of his suit, and the carefully manicured elegance of his hands.

Hands that could manipulate just as much pain as pleasure from a person.

There were men who radiated menace, danger, or violence. But her husband hid all that and reserves of so much more behind the cool, placid lake of his façade.

He was the danger you never saw coming until it was too late.

"You're...home," she observed, cringing at the daft bloody obviousness of her statement.

He addressed her with a curt nod, his eyes breaking away from her for the first time, allowing her to breathe. "I was just informing Bart I've a meeting best conducted here rather than the office."

"An Earl, I heard."

His mouth twisted ruefully. "A courtesy title, but yes."

"Is there anything I can do to help?" She hoped she didn't sound as pathetically eager as she felt.

"Not especial—" he looked sharply toward the door and cursed under his breath, his expression turning pained.

Pru hurried down the remainder of the stairs. "What is it?"

"He didn't come alone." Agitated, he took three steps away from her and thrust his fingers through his hair, smoothing it back. "I'm in no bloody mood."

"Did he bring his solicitor?" Pru guessed, wondering if he meant to interrogate the man without one.

"Worse." A beleaguered breath hissed out of his throat. "He brought his wife."

Pru brightened at the prospect of female company. She was acquainted with very few Countesses and even if the woman were difficult, she likely couldn't hold a candle to Prudence's own mother.

"I'm quite finished," she declared. "I can entertain the Countess while you conduct your interview."

A frown pinched his brow. "Finished with what?"

"No," she laughed. "I've attended finishing school with excellent marks. I know how to receive someone of her station."

"Oh." Surprisingly, his frown deepened. "Well that will be of little consequence to Farah."

An instinctive little needle of discomfort pricked her. Farah? Not Lady Northwalk?

The bell chimed and Bart materialized from behind them to answer.

Her husband faced the door with the grim determination a battle general might face an onslaught of marauders. "I suppose it would be cruel not to tell you that Farah used to work as a clerk at Scotland Yard. I've known her for nigh on a decade."

"Why would it be cruel to—?"

"Because Blackwell is certain to mention that I asked her to be my wife."

CHAPTER 11

"**C**arlton Morley, you unforgivable rogue!" An angelic beauty with a coronet of silver-blond ringlets swept into their grand entry in an energetic flounce of mauve silk. "When Dorian told me you'd taken a wife, and under which circumstances, I nearly collapsed."

Pru stood blinking at the uncommonly lovely woman in open-mouthed dismay as Morley stepped forward to receive her light kiss on the cheek.

They knew the circumstances of their marriage? All of them?

Even Miss Henrietta's garden?

"You forget I know better," Morley replied in a voice infused with a charm he'd never bothered to apply with Pru. "You've never fainted in your life."

The appearance of Farah's husband had Prudence forcing herself to unclench her fists. She'd have to accept his hand, and it wouldn't do to have her palms bleeding from where her nails had dug.

"This is my...wife, Prudence Good- er Morley." He said the word wife as if it tasted strange in his mouth. "Prudence, might

I introduce Lady Farah Blackwell, Countess Northwalk, and her husband, Dorian, the Earl."

"Technically my son is the Earl," Blackwell said. "I've titles enough, and I actually earned all of them."

Of course! Prudence recognized him now. This was Dorian Blackwell, the Blackheart of Ben More. Who could care to be an Earl when you were once the King of the London Underworld?

The man was monstrous large and dark as a fiend. Despite the eyepatch, his gaze was keen and rapt, as he assessed her with undue intensity.

Pru thought she saw something like a comprehending approval in his smirk.

"Lady Morley," Dorian Blackwell greeted as if he'd never before thought to utter those words together. He bent over her knuckles and pressed a kiss to the air above them, never touching the skin. "It's been the cause of much speculation between Farah and me as to what prompted Morley to so hastily take a wife." In an inappropriate show of public affection, he straightened to put his arm around his Countess, and rested his hand low on her waist just above her bustle as if it belonged there. "I think the mystery has been solved, my love."

Farah turned her saintly smile upon Prudence. "You're a beautiful woman on any day, Lady Morley, but in that lilac gown you're a vision. Utterly glowing with maternal beauty."

Glowing? Surely not. She'd been losing weight because of her inability to digest food. She was pale, wan, and her eyes sunken with dark circles beneath. She felt more like a shade than an actual person.

They were being kind, of course.

She had to pinch herself to stop gawking like an open-mouthed carp. "I-I thank you, my lady, my lord. What an honor to greet you both."

An honor, and a horror.

The Blackwells were a sight unto themselves. He, dark as a demon with a demonic air of handsome ferocity, and she his unfettered radiant counterpart. It was plain as day Dorian Blackwell adored his wife.

The question was, did Farah return his affections? Or did she still covet Morley?

How could she not? Blackwell was a compelling man, if not specifically handsome, and he'd an air of vital masculinity few possessed, however he was a shadow in Morley's golden presence.

At least where Pru was concerned.

She looked to Morley, who wore an expression of one in a dentist's lobby awaiting a particularly unpleasant procedure.

The question was what? Did he not want the woman who owned his heart to meet the woman who now lay claim to his name?

The very thought was like a punch to the ribs, taking the wind from her lungs as well as her sails.

She didn't know which would have been crueler, for him to tell her or not... she might have been tempted to like the Countess had she not known her husband had once desired her.

That he'd wished to share a home and children with her.

Had they kissed, she wondered.

Prudence had kissed a few men in her two seasons out, enough to know that kissing Morley was an experience that eclipsed all else.

"Carlton, allow me to purloin your wife whilst you and Dorian conduct your affairs. I'm dying to know her."

Carlton? Even Pru, herself, wasn't on such intimate terms with him. Moreover, every time she tried to pin the name upon him in her mind, it refused to stick.

"Lady Morley?" Farah Blackwell didn't wait for her husband's reply. "Let's retire to your preferred rooms."

"O-of course. This way, Lady Northwalk." She gestured toward the stairs to her second-floor parlor.

"You'll call me Farah, of course, all my friends do."

They weren't friends, but Prudence nodded as she turned to lead the Countess away. She moved as if quicksand sucked at her feet, a sense of doom washing over her as she climbed the staircase. This woman in her wake, would she be cruel or kind once they were alone?

Farah Blackwell knew who she was, and the circumstances of her marriage.

Did that mean her husband truly trusted these people? Or that their secret was already out and they were trying to control the damage?

Either way, brittle though she felt, she was determined to face this woman with dignity and aplomb befitting the Queen of England, let alone a knight's bride.

Farah couldn't have astonished her more the moment the parlor door had shut behind them. She turned and swept her up into a desperate, but gentle embrace and held her there.

"Oh, you poor dear, what a nightmare you've been through. When Dorian told me the extent of the situation, I haven't been able to sleep but for worrying over you." She pulled back for a moment just to look at her. "I hope you don't mind the intrusion of a stranger, but I just had to see for myself if you are all right. Knowing Carlton, he's bungled the entire thing, stashed you here, and thrown himself into his work."

Pru swallowed a lump of alternating emotions. Gratitude and jealously. "You certainly know my husband well."

A wry smile brought dimples to the woman's cheeks as Farah pulled her over by the rain-streaked window. "I see you are aware of our former attachment," she said, her grey eyes soft with understanding. "Then you must know how short and dispassionate it was. And how very long ago. I mean, my lands,

I was still in my twenties." She waved it all away. "Ancient history all but forgotten."

Pru wasn't certain what to say. She was tormented by the memories of her husband's very physical all-consuming passion. Was Farah being kind again? Or dishonest?

Or had they truly not suited?

"It's nothing, my lady, should I ring for some tea?"

"I'd rather you sit. I'm not certain how long we'll be staying, and I have a rather lot to say."

Carefully, Pru perched across from her on the emerald settee and gestured for her to go on.

Farah's manner was soft and somber as she leaned forward to say, "I worked as a clerk at Scotland Yard for a handful of years. I have known every sort of criminal, and my share of murderers, and I am convinced you are not one."

Pru let out a shaky breath. "How can you be so convinced?"

"Well it makes no sense, does it? A woman in your condition doing away with the one man who can provide her the protection of his name on her wedding day. Found with the dagger in her hands and no story of defense?" Farah tutted and shook her head. "Furthermore, I've lived with a man whose life was ruined when he was wrongfully accused. There's a very singular helpless fury in that. I sense it torments you, as well."

"I wish you'd convince my—" Prudence caught herself in time. "Well, everyone else."

Farah gave a short chuckle "They're men, darling. Adorable idiots to the last. I'm sorry to say but your methodical husband will take incontrovertible proof to convince him, but it seems to me that he's intent upon finding it."

Was he?

"Listen." Farah gathered up her hands. "I know you'll feel isolated in the coming months, and that I cannot abide. I want you to call upon me for support in regard to all things. Be it men, marriage, motherhood… or Morley. I worked for the man for years, I am aware of his faults and flaws as well as his heroic qualities, of which there are many. I've birthed two lovely, healthy children of my own and I've been through—well, not what you are—but enough that I feel I can be sympathetic to your plight."

Pru didn't know what to say, or even how to feel. It was all too wonderful. Too wonderful to be true?

"How…incredibly kind of you."

"Also, I hope you don't find me too forward, but I've secured you an appointment with my doctor who specializes in the care of expecting mothers. He's the absolute best in his field, and he works closely with a local midwife, where they both tend to you *and* rely on each other's expertise. I'd never trust my feminine health to anyone else. All of my nearest and dearest friends are patients."

A little glow bloomed in the cockles of Pru's heart. Here she'd been so ill. So afraid. So incredibly alone, and had all the time in the world to go mad with questions and anxieties over the impending arrival of a child.

She gave the hands around hers a responding squeeze. "Farah," she tested the name. "I thank you. Truly. Anytime you would like to be so forward, I heartily encourage you."

"Splendid!" the Countess beamed. "Next week you're to come with me to the Duchess of Trenwyth's to meet with our Ladies' Aid Society. Let's see, Lorelai, Countess Southbourne will be there. Millie LeCour."

"The actress?" Pru marveled.

"Yes! She and her beau, Christopher Argent, live next to Trenwyth where Imogen, I mean, Her Grace, resides. Oh, Samantha and Mena are coming in from Scotland. You'll have to excuse Samantha, as she's American." Farah said this as if it explained everything. "The Countess of Cursing, we call her, but once you get to know her you will be as in love with her as we all are. Mena is a delight. Never will you find a warmer

Marchioness. In fact, she'll likely adopt you as she can't have children and will certainly angle to be godmother to Morley's child, as she is to all of ours. Devotion is her exper—"

Pru pulled her hands away. So many names, so many titles. It was all so much. "I'm sorry, but I'm afraid I won't be able to attend. I...I'm supposed to be in hiding, for lack of a better term. Besides, surely you agree I don't *belong* in this society. I've no title nor prescience to bring. I'm the second-born daughter to a Baron, is all. I'm merely Chief Inspector Morley's wife."

For the first time, Farah's mouth compressed with displeasure as her eyes gleamed. "My dear, no one is *just* Morley's wife. He's had a hand in everyone's fate in that room. He's saved more than lives, he's saved souls. I mean, there isn't time to regale you here, but I feel that you should come so we can all tell you the sort of husband you're blessed with. Morley is and has always been a remarkable man. We've all speculated and even schemed to get him a wife. I'm unutterably glad he's found you."

Grief threatened to bubble over in her chest in the form of a sob. "If you know of our situation, then you know this is not a love match."

Farah suddenly became very serious. "May I call you Prudence?"

"Pru, please."

"Pru... you've done what I was certain no woman in the world could do."

"What's that?"

"You've distracted Carlton Morley from his unimpeachable principles. I think, in time, you'll come to know what a Sisyphean feat that was."

Pru shook her head, unable to understand.

Farah seemed to debate something internally, then said, "Morley and I had a working relationship for longer than five years, and a flirtatious companionship. It took him those five

139

years to drum up the nerve to kiss me. You felled him in five minutes! You, my dear, are the temptation he needs. You will force some happiness upon him, I think, and it's the only way, as he will fight you tooth and nail. But he is the best of men, he deserves every happiness."

Prudence didn't allow herself to close her eyes, because every time she did, she saw her husband's lips on Farah Blackwell's.

And she desperately wanted to like the woman.

"Why didn't you marry him?" The question surprised Pru more than it did Farah, it seemed. "I mean, when he asked you. What made you refuse?"

Farah gave a nonchalant shrug, her expression rather wistful. "My heart always belonged to Dorian. It's as simple as that. He never had a chance. I never once regretted my decision, but I won't hide from you the fact that I will always be fond of Carlton. That I respect and admire him. Everyone does. Even my husband, who was once on the wrong side of the law. For all Carlton postures, he's an exceedingly fair and understanding man. He's not without his own past, you know."

That intrigued her. "What past?"

Serious conversation preceded boots as the men climbed the stairs, announcing their inevitable invasion of the parlor.

"I will leave that for him to tell you," Farah said mysteriously.

This time it was Prudence who reached out and clung to Farah's hand as if it were a lifeline. "I don't know that he will...I don't know him at all. I'm so lost. Please, if you have any information. Any insight...I..."

Farah regarded her indecisively. "I promised I will, and I shall impart to you everything I can. Come to us next week. You'll learn all that we know, I vow—"

It was Blackwell who barged in first. "What ho, wife? We've the unfortunate need to leave now to meet my brothers' train. I've brought the second carriage to contain either Ravencroft's shoulders or Gavin's ego. I'll allow them to fight over it."

Pru gawked at the man. If Blackwell thought Ravencroft large, the man must be a giant.

He bowed to Pru. "It was an unmitigated pleasure to meet you, Lady Morley. Please call upon us for the smallest thing."

"Thank you."

Farah gave her another impulsive hug before releasing her with a blustery noise. "The smallest thing. I *really* mean it."

They saw themselves out, and took a whirlwind with them.

Prudence watched her husband peer at the empty door-frame as though contemplating the emptiness he found there.

Did he also note the easy way Blackwell put his possessive hand on his wife's waist? How he walked in deference to her. His every muscle seeming attuned to her movements, her protection, her needs.

Did it make him envious? Or melancholy, like her.

Eventually, he flicked a glance at her as if surprised to still find her there.

"It was very kind of the Countess to come," she ventured. "She was…very solicitous. Gave me the name of a good doctor."

He gave the illusion of a nod. "Farah is a good woman," he said carefully.

As opposed to herself?

Pru stared at him, doing her best not to appreciate how the cut of his vest hugged his narrow waist, flattering the width of his chest and shoulders, the breadth of his back.

A back she'd once clung to in spasms of bliss.

Her fingers curled at the memory.

He was right *there*. So close to her. She could reach out to him and touch the body that'd once rode her like an untamed stallion, wild and rhythmic and powerful.

His lips had tasted the most secret parts of her. His eyes had burned with lust. His features softened with worship. Tightened with pleasure. Tortured with hunger.

And now?

Nothing. He was so remote. So empty. Bleak.

Where are you? She wanted to shout. To throw things. To rant and rave at him until he bloody cracked the mountain of ice between them. *Who are you? What have you done with my lover?*

He turned abruptly, as if he'd heard her silent screams. But the question in his eyes quickly flickered out, replaced by that infuriating civility.

"It's a chilly night," he said. "I've had a bath sent to your room."

So thoughtful. The ponce. "Thank you," she gritted out.

He nodded, looked as if he might say something else, and then thought the better of it. "Good evening."

He left her in her puddle of her own frustrated loneliness, possibly to pine for the woman who'd gotten away.

CHAPTER 12

*M*orley let himself into the nursery and shut the door, leaning against it for several breaths.

With all he had on his mind, one simple fact existed in the world, crowding out all others.

His wife bathed only paces away. She'd lowered that soft body into the steaming copper tub and slicked soap across creamy, unblemished, aristocratic skin. Her breasts would lift above the water as she washed her luxuriant hair. Her thighs would relax apart, her hands perhaps finding their way between them to…

The bundle he'd clutched in his hand crumpled beneath the clench of his fist, and the product inside provided a much-needed distraction.

He tore the package open with uncharacteristic lack of ceremony, and went to the rocking chair, crouching to place the intricately carved train engine next to the doll.

He fantasized about the train given locomotion by a chubby little hand. A boy, perhaps. But maybe a girl. He and Caroline had spent hours playing trains with some charity toys they'd found at the church once.

So long as he capitulated to Caroline's demand that the conductors fell in love with the women they'd rescued from the marauding bandits, then she was a fair hand at the battle, itself. Just as bloodthirsty as any outlaw.

He touched the gold of the doll's hair and took a moment to keenly miss the girl with whom he'd shared a womb. She'd be an aunt now, probably a mother, too. They'd each be forty in a year, or so he thought. No one had ever told them their precise birthday, but he'd pieced it together as well as he could.

Caroline.

How different the landscape of so many lives would be if she'd lived.

Morley might have still been a rifleman in the army, but it was unlikely he would ever have considered the beat at The London Metropolitan Police.

So many others would have carved a different story in the book of fate if not for the choices he'd made.

Perhaps their lives were arguably better for the path Caroline's death put him on, but what he never expressed to his friends was that, in his darkest moments, he'd have taken it all away from them just to have her back. To give her the chance at life. To leave him any kind of family.

So he wouldn't have spent the past twenty odd years so acutely alone.

Perhaps, he'd often reasoned, if she'd been there, he'd not be so bloody broken.

He'd become the man he pretended to be. A better man.

Today, this moment, was the first time he shrank from that thought.

If it had all gone differently, he might have married young. He might have even sired children.

But not *this* child.

Not whomever quickened within the womb of his lovely wife.

His hand went to his heart to contain an extra little thump at the thought.

Children were born every day. Thousands upon thousands of them. It was no great happening or miracle. But he couldn't shake the feeling his entire life had led up to this. *This* child.

If Caroline had lived, this child might never have come to be.

And, for the first time, while he still mourned her loss, he couldn't bring himself to wish as he had before.

Beset by a complicated amalgamation of regret and love, shame and anticipation, he pushed himself to his feet and set about tidying up the disorderly packing material in the nursery.

It seemed impossible that his wife's scent lingered even here, but he tasted it in the air. Berries. Sweetest in the late summer. She'd forever remind him of breakfast. His favorite meal until he'd feasted upon her—

Slamming a crate shut, he realized he couldn't be only a wall away from where she bathed without going mad. He retreated to his study, intent upon getting some work done.

By God. She was in here too. The walls might as well have been smeared with marmalade. She permeated every corner of his thoughts, and now there was nowhere in his house to escape her.

Slumping into his office chair he dropped his head onto his palm and rubbed at a blooming headache. God he was tired again. He'd not slept for longer than three hours for... well, he couldn't remember how long.

And it didn't seem that would change in the near future.

Blackwell and he had conceived of a plan to concentrate their investigative efforts on the Wapping docks. His interrogation of the crooked officer the other night had been the first link in a supply line of narcotics, and other smuggled goods, that was more twisted and dangerous than the web of the most venomous spider. Morley, or rather the Knight of Shadows, had been spinning his own webs, beating answers out of countless men. Throwing them to what police he'd known still operated aboveboard.

Or, in some of the cases where he'd been forced to defend himself... throwing their corpses into the river.

All fingers pointed to the Commissioner, Baron Clarence Goode.

His bloody father-in-law.

However, the shipments had dried up entirely. Abruptly, in fact. And because of this, crime wars brewed in the gambling dens and rookeries of the underworld, and Morley couldn't be certain the city was ready for what was about to hit it.

Or how many casualties the impact would leave behind.

Christ. He was just one man. Who could he trust to—?

A few heavy, staggering sounds reverberated on the ceiling above him before a great, thunderous crash drove him to his feet.

The master bedroom. *His wife!*

Feeling as though he'd been kicked in the chest by an unruly horse, he took the stairs three at a time, sprinting down the hall until he exploded through the door, shearing the latch.

His very shaken, very *nude* wife was attempting to pull herself into a sitting position from where she'd sprawled on her back, using a toppled marble table to stabilize her.

He lunged forward. "Don't move," he barked in the same commanding voice he'd used on countless criminals.

She'd already frozen when he'd burst in, but his words had the opposite effect, sending her scrambling to find something with which to cover herself. "Oh, bother," she groaned. "I-I don't... I'm all right. I just need—need a towel. Please. *Please* go."

"Don't be foolish," he admonished as he hit his knees next to her, his hands hovering over the slick, lithe lines of her prone form, searching for injuries. "What the bloody hell happened?" he demanded. "Did you hit your head? Is anything broken? Can you move all your limbs? No, never mind, don't try to move. I'm calling for a doctor. Bart?" he bellowed. "Where the bloody hell is he? Did no one hear you fall hard enough to shake the house? *Bart!*"

"*No!*" She seized his shirt when he would have risen with one desperate claw, keeping the other arm ineffectually over her breasts. "I don't want anyone to see me!"

"If he sees you, I'll replace his eyes with hot coals. I'm calling him to send him for the doctor."

"I don't need a doctor. I am perfectly well, I simply—"

"You don't get to make that decision, a slip like this is serious, especially in your condition! Must you fall so bloody often? I order you to take more care with your footing!"

He put his hands on both her shoulders to keep her still as she tried again to sit up. His grip slid as her still-slippery limbs flailed in a wild attempt to fight him off.

After a few slick and ineffectual endeavors, he succeeded in pinning her arms at her sides, leaving her gleaming body completely bared to him.

He resolutely examined *only* her eyes, as he leaned above her. They held no indication of the clouds one noted with a head wound. In fact, they sparked with dark azure tempests that would make Calypso proud.

"I didn't slip, exactly," she protested with a mulish expression.

"No? Then tell me how, *exactly*, you came to be on the floor."

Long, dark lashes swept down over damp cheeks flushed with heat. "I... finished my bath, stood, and stepped out of the tub to reach for the towel. By the time I had one foot on the ground I was overwhelmed by extreme vertigo and thought to steady myself on the table." A confused frown pinched between her brow as she looked over at the fallen furniture . "I must have fainted, because the next thing I knew I was on my back staring up at the ceiling."

"I suspect you're truly addled if you think *anything* you just imparted to me makes me feel a modicum of comfort," he gritted through his teeth. "You and the child *must* be all right; do you understand me? You lie here. I will get a doctor. And he will examine you thoroughly. That is the end of this ridiculous discussion."

He would have said more, but all the words had compressed the air out of his lungs, and he couldn't seem to fill them. His hands trembled where they shackled her arms and the legs he knelt on felt too unsteady to hold their position for long.

It had been *years* since his body showed such obvious signs of terror. Maybe since his very first battle when bullets missed him so narrowly, he could *hear* them sing by his ear.

Lord, but she was a weakness.

Instead of arguing, she lifted her palms to his chest, this time in careful conciliation. Her expression softened, warmed, and something pooled in her eyes that evoked inappropriate memories of the last time he'd held her beneath him.

"I'm not being reckless, you know. I often feel faint after a hot bath, and because our child is possessed of a finicky appetite, I haven't been eating as I should. Certainly, that's the cause of this spell." Her lovely features gathered into a twist of self-effacing mortification. "I dare say I crumpled rather than fell, and landed on my back, not my stomach."

His heart kicked beneath her hand, and he grappled with fierce and foreign emotion that stole his ability to speak.

"Is it your aim for the doctor to examine me in a shivering, naked puddle on the floor?" she asked with an arch of her brow.

Morley's jaw slammed shut. Now was *not* the time to notice her nudity. This was quite possibly a medical crisis.

He refused to glance down at her breasts.

He glanced.

He refused to look.

He looked.

Well he refused to appreciate.

Goddammit.

Lunging to his feet, he snatched the towel from the stand and returned to her, averting his eyes as he covered the more scandalous parts of her before crouching down again. "I'm going to carry you to the bed," he warned.

"I'm quite capable of—ooph!"

He scooped her from the floor and hauled her against his chest as her bare legs dangled over his arm. The towel covered the front of her, but there was nothing between her skin and his hands as he hauled her to the bed and sat her down gingerly.

"Sir?" Bart called from the end of the hall. "What's happened?"

Morley released her and strode to the door to keep the footman from venturing into the room and seeing anything he ought not to.

Likely saving the footman's life.

"My wife has fainted and taken a fall; I need you to send for the doctor."

Bart's eyes went round with worry in his moonlike face. "Right away, sir." He scurried back in the other direction.

Morley shut the door, and when he turned around, his knees nearly buckled from beneath him at the sight of his wife levered over her chest of drawers, her arm frantically fishing within.

She still clutched a towel to the front of her, but she currently faced away from him. Revealing. Everything.

Morley's mouth went dry as lust punched him low in the

belly with such savagery, he felt slightly ill. His body responded violently to a sight he'd never forget.

Her ripe bare arse and thighs created a perfect heart shape to frame the shadow of the cove between her legs.

Sweet Christ just when he didn't think he'd anything left in him to break.

Snatching up a nightdress, she straightened and pulled it over her head and down her body, all the while still flailing to find the openings for the arms and neck.

He went to her in swift strides. The moment he put his hands on her, she stilled, allowing him to guide her arms into their sleeves and unbutton the high collar enough to permit her dark head to pop through.

Something about helping her into her gown settled him, as well. His breaths calmed, though his cock did not, but he no longer felt as if his heart tried to escape by way of his throat.

She reached up to push the tangles of her hair away from her face, but he beat her to it, smoothing the damp tendrils from her cheeks and elegant neck.

She regarded him with a lost, rather unsure expression that tugged at his heart.

"For future reference, you're being neither prudent nor good," he said in a voice suddenly made of silk.

Her lip quirked. "For future reference, my name has always been a lamentable irony."

She attempted a good-humored smile, but it never took. She only succeeded in looking exhausted and alluring, and very young.

Too young for him, probably.

Good Lord, he didn't even know his wife's age. He knew next to nothing about her. Her health. Her skills, her strengths, her flaws. Her life before this.

Before him.

Though he'd had her in a garden, he'd never even seen her naked before tonight.

Certainly, he'd fantasized about it to an obsessive degree, but nothing had been able to prepare him for the perfection of her. Generous breasts, dramatic curves, and an arse so delectable he ached to—

"You really should be lying down," he said with brusque efficiency, closing the door firmly on those thoughts.

Her face fell. "I needed to dry and dress. I'm not about to meet the doctor in the altogether, am I? Also, my hair will dry in clumps of snarls if I don't brush it."

He gently but firmly steered her toward the bed. "I will tend to you."

She kept any remonstration to herself as she allowed him to tuck the bedclothes around her lap. Her eyes tracked him as he retrieved her silver hairbrush from her vanity and brought it to her. "Allow me to—"

She snatched the brush from him. "No need, I've a tender head and it takes a delicate touch."

Better she do it, then. His hands still shook, and his emotions seemed to be taking wild, pendulum-like swings. His feelings for her, he realized, were not gentle. But ardent.

Violent even.

It was why he stayed away. Something volatile hung in the air whenever she was near, and volatility wasn't something he allowed himself.

Lord, but it felt as though he were an abandoned tangle of yarn only just discovered by a sharp-nailed woman intent upon unraveling him.

Morley perched on the foot of the bed, bending his knee so he could face her. "Do you still feel ill?" he asked as she began to run the brush through her damp hair, starting at the ends and working her way up.

"I haven't been for a few days beyond mild bouts of nausea."

She flicked him a shy look from beneath her lashes. "Thank you for the ginger ale. I've been sipping it when I feel poorly."

He shifted uncomfortably. "Yes. Well. I read about it somewhere."

He'd read anything he could get his hands on, actually. Books on pregnancy and childbirth. Doctor's pamphlets and periodicals. Everything. If he was going to be a father, he'd be the most knowledgeable father in the kingdom.

She fell into a contemplative silence, her entire being focused on the task of her hair.

Morley watched her alertly, examining her for signs of... well, of anything out of the ordinary. Not that he exactly knew what to look for. Bleeding, he supposed. Another loss of consciousness. Confusion. Pain.

Charming little mannerisms became apparent under such close scrutiny. She'd one very expressive left eyebrow, while the right one never so much as arched. Her left hand was the dominant one, as well. She'd a freckle beneath her right eye. Just the one. And a little scar behind her jaw on the right side. She slept in a great deal of ruffles.

And when she brushed her hair, she laced her fingers through the section to test for snarls in very rhythmic, graceful gestures.

The inky swath draped over the shoulder of her white nightgown, waving in places and framing her face with little tendrils that beckoned to be touched.

Lord she was lovely.

And she was his.

He'd never seen her like this. Even pale and fresh-scrubbed, damp and unadorned, she remained a beacon of beauty. The kind of siren that would dash a man like him on the rocks.

And still, he'd go willingly.

A strange, unidentifiable emotion stole over him. Not peace, exactly, never that, but a loose-limbed mesmerism he would akin to that of a cobra being charmed by a clever instrument. He couldn't look away. Nothing else existed. Just the woman in his bed and the gentle motions of her grooming. The air was warm and moist from her bath, and he breathed in the summer scent of her soap as his heart slowed and his lids grew heavy.

They sat in silence for a moment, or maybe an eternity, him content to do little else but drink in the sight of her.

"Do you still love her?"

The question manifested in the air between them, surely, as he'd barely noticed her lips move.

Morley started a little, sitting up straighter, uncertain if he heard her correctly as his mind had been quite pleasantly—extraordinarily—empty. "Pardon?"

She kept her gaze firmly focused on the gathering sheen of her smooth, glossy, untangled hair. And yet she kept brushing. "The Countess, Farah, do you love her still?"

"No." The promptness of his answer surprised even him.

She flicked him a fleeting glance. "You can tell me without fear of reprisal," she urged. "I'm in no position to cast aspersions, and I can't imagine you lived like a monk before we—before our nuptials."

The irony was he'd done exactly that for some time now. He'd a few wild years during and after the war but…if one was to describe his romantic exploits of late.

Monk was apropos.

Until her.

"I hold Farah in high esteem," he answered. "But that is all."

"She returns your esteem." An inscrutable emotion darkened her features for a moment, and she abandoned her brush to the nightstand with a sigh.

"I don't know if I ever loved her." Morley couldn't tell what compelled him to explain, but the words escaped him in a torrent of truth. "I was of the opinion that she and I suited, is all. We worked easily together, and we enjoyed each other's company. We attended events and she liked to eat at the same establishments I do. I thought..." He'd thought she'd fill this empty house with something other than silence. He'd wanted someone to come home to. To share a life and all the beautiful, terrible things therein. "I thought love might grow between us. She's a good woman. Someone I'd grown to trust, respect, and admire."

The wobble of her chin belied her hard-won stoicism and she nodded slowly as if she did her best to digest his words.

"Unlike me."

I never wanted her like I want you.

He almost said it. The words tripped to the edge of his lips like a reckless man about to jump to his death. Farah was never a danger to him, but neither had she been a joy. He'd desired her, as she was lovely, and he was a man. But she'd never tempted him anywhere close to the line he'd leapt over for Prudence. He'd never ached in her absence nor did he fear the power she had over him.

For there was none.

Whereas now...

"Was your meeting with Blackwell about me?" she queried, her gaze pinched and worried as it finally met his.

"You know I can't discuss—"

"You can't discuss what? My case? My life? You realize this is my innocence to prove and if I knew what was happening, I might have a chance to help."

"It simply isn't—"

"How would you fare, husband, under similar conditions? Locked in this infernal house with nothing to do but worry about the future. Treated like everyone's terrible secret. It's cruel." Her voice became ragged on the last words, and her eyes shimmered with unshed tears.

Morley had felt pity in his life. Shame, regret, sympathy. But not this strange amalgamation of all of it.

"You're not a prisoner here," he soothed. "But it's safer for you if you're out of sight until things...settle. I thought we agreed it's the right thing."

She made a noise of irritation and scrubbed at her eyes to erase a forthcoming storm.

Hesitantly, Morley reached out and placed his hand on her ankle over the counterpane. Her bones were so delicate, so small beneath his hands.

"I sympathize," was all he could think to say. "In your circumstances I'd likely go mad."

She blinked at him, and her face relaxed a bit, some of the frustration draining into acceptance. "Then...why must I be left in the dark?"

"Because that is where I need you," he answered more vehemently than he'd meant to.

At her pained flinch, the explanation burst from him like a geyser. "Don't you understand? I cannot stand to be in the same room with you—*wait*." He held up his hand against her unspoken pain as her eyes went owl round. "That is, I cannot be in your presence *and* possessed of my wits at the same time. You're like...a tune in my head I cannot rid myself of. A torrent, or a whirlwind, spinning me until I cannot see my way forward. I can't have that now. I need to be objective. Unemotional."

"Unemotional?" she echoed slowly.

"Especially when the stakes are so high. When I want—" He caught himself just in time.

To see that she'd stopped breathing, her stare rapt and absorbed.

He'd said too much.

"When you want what?" she whispered.

"I meant to say...when the outcome has such a monumental

effect on the life and future of everyone." He slid closer toward her and she moved her legs to give him room. Leaning forward, his hand drifted toward her until it fit over her abdomen. "Of the three of us."

She covered his hand with her own, and Morley suddenly found himself a prisoner.

His shackles silk rather than steel.

Even through her nightgown and the bedclothes, he could fell that her firm stomach had a barely discernable curve to it.

They each let out an identical breath, wondering at the life beneath their hands.

"Somehow I'm going to prove to you that I'm innocent," she declared with the resolution of a royal. "If I do that, would I be worthy of you then?"

Awash in a tide of foreign and frustrating sentimentality, Morley pulled away from her, unable to stand the intimacy and not take it further. "This isn't about that."

"It is to me."

He threaded his fingers through his hair, yearning to believe her. If only so he wouldn't have to face the dark part of him whispering that her innocence mattered not.

That he'd fall for her, regardless.

"Please, let's not talk of this now. I'm too...where in God's name is the doctor?"

"I assure you, I'm well. The table took the hardest tumble, I all but glided to the floor."

He turned his back on her, going behind the screen to lift the table back to its position. The furniture was a heavy piece, the top pure marble.

Gads, what if she'd pulled it over on top of her?

Suddenly he was very aware how dangerous a home could be to a woman and child.

"You don't have to stay, you know," she said, arranging the

covers in a prim display. "It's dark. You may go about your... your work as the Knight of Shadows."

He took the watch chain from his vest and checked it. "There's no chance of me leaving tonight."

"I don't know how many times I have to tell you, there's hardly a reason to fret," she insisted.

"Oh? And from what distinguished institution did you get your medical degree, Doctor Morley?" He scowled at her. "I just found my *wife* crumpled on the floor; if that's not a time to fret, I can think of none better. So you will submit to an examination or—"

"Or what?" she asked around a wry smile. "You'll have me thrown in jail?"

That surprised a sharp snort of mirth from him. "Don't tempt me."

A red-faced Bart arrived with the doctor, a beakish gentleman with a gentle manner, interrupting further conversation between them.

Morley hovered as his wife was examined, palpated, and interrogated all in time for the doctor to declare that she and the child were likely in little to no danger of miscarriage. After advice was given and a draught administered, Morley left his wife's side long enough to pay the man and walk him out.

He stopped to fortify himself with several scorching swallows of Ravencroft Scotch before returning to her room.

Only to find her sleeping peacefully.

Her dark hair flared on the pillow, shining like a phantom halo of ebony around her delicate features. Her hand was draped next to her cheek, relaxed into a little cup, as if he might give her something precious.

A stark pang of yearning pierced him as the smooth side of his bed beckoned to him. Here she was, a strange and seductive fantasy sleeping the sleep of the innocent.

And she was his.

A dark desire welled within him with such ferocity he shuddered with it. He wanted to own her. To claim her, body and soul. To plant himself inside of her and pleasure her until she was mindless, until she was boneless, replete with satisfaction.

He wanted to feed her from his hands. To nourish her and the life within. He wanted to buy her things to adorn her loveliness. Gems and ribbons, silk and precious metals. A storm of errant whims and desires swirled and eddied within him until he felt as though his flesh could no longer contain the strength of it.

He. Wanted. Her.

He wanted…everything.

"Don't tempt me," he whispered once more.

He'd meant it in jest before, but now it was a plea.

She was nothing but a temptation. One he couldn't resist for much longer. One that could bring his entire world down upon him.

And still he'd use the last of his bloody, broken remains to shelter her.

CHAPTER 13

$\mathcal{L}$ess than a handful of days later, it'd taken Prudence and Mercy the better part of three hours to comb over their father's study, library, and personal belongings before they had finally stumbled upon the documents she'd been searching for.

Mercy was the perfect partner to rely upon for this assignment. She was fleet-footed, quick-witted, and always up for an adventure. Or, as she'd dubbed their vocation, a *caper*, a word she'd claimed to have purloined from the detective novels she was almost never without.

"Do you really feel like this will help clear your name, Pru?" Mercy worried. "I don't see what father's business could possibly have had to do with Sutherland's death."

"Probably nothing," Prudence agreed, carefully filing the papers away in a case. "But if I can provide my husband means with which to further his investigation into the illegal goods being smuggled into the city—to find the truth about father—I think it'll go a long way to establish trust between us."

Mercy sobered, a glimmer of doubt reaching through her

eyes. "Pru...what if the truth is that our father is guilty? It would kill poor Mama. And...the rest of us would be ruined."

Prudence had abandoned the briefcase to gather her sister close. "Don't think I haven't thought of that," she soothed. "Our father is many things, but he is a principled, law-abiding man. I'm hoping the truth clears the Goode name. And, in the unlikely event my husband somehow uncovers his guilt..."

Mercy stepped away, smoothing her smart plaid frock and adjusting her hair. "Like Detective Inspector Aloysius Frost says in his fourth novel, *The Cheapside Strangler*, 'When the guilty escape justice, it is denied the innocent, as well.'" She wistfully locked the briefcase and handed it to her. "No matter how this plays out, Felicity and I will survive it. I mean...what's the worst that could happen? We're denied a season and end up as spinsters?" She shrugged. "Considering what you and Honoria are up against...I can't say either of us are aching to be wed."

Pru could have cried, but instead she kissed Mercy on the cheek and rushed to Number Four Whitehall Place.

She navigated the chaos of the infamous Scotland Yard with her briefcase clutched in hand, asking solicitous clerks, and a few gruff policemen, how to find the Chief Inspector's office.

Several minutes and four stories later, she stood in the hall adjacent him, admiring her husband at work.

Prudence felt rather like an explorer on a safari, watching a magnificent beast in his native habitat.

Unlike the holding cells and general rank pandemonium of the first and second floors—or the secrets in the basement, one of which she had recently been—men of all sorts and sizes crammed around desks here on the fourth. They filled the room with the bustle of the more intricate and intellectual side of crime enforcement.

Men with important titles retained the line of offices along the wall, and Morley's was the grandest.

He propped the door open to accommodate the tide of active lawmen marching about like worker ants. At the moment, he scanned documents of two uniformed officers standing at attention as if in front of a brigadier general. Oddly enough, he appeared more comfortable and casual than she'd ever seen him. His shirt brilliant white, and cravat tight as ever, but he'd shucked his jacket as a concession to comfort in the crowded and close air of the top floor.

Absorbed as he was, he didn't seem to notice the distress of the officers when he reached for his pen, crossed something out, and corrected it in the margin. The younger one, a brawny but baby-faced chap, blinked several times as if he might dissolve into tears as his comrade's shoulders slumped.

Prudence sympathized.

Another man in a somber suit and expensive hat barged into his office and Morley held up a finger, silencing him immediately without looking up.

Upon finishing, he signed the paperwork at the bottom and handed it back to the officers. "This was excellent. You're both to be commended."

The exaltation of the men brought a pleased smile to her lips as she took a moment to enjoy a triumph some might call trivial but was one she would give a limb for.

The approval of her husband.

Retrieving the papers, the officers nearly skipped out of his office and bowled her over as they turned the corner.

"Begging your pardon," the young one breathed, unable to contain his brilliant smile.

She nodded and pardoned him, genuinely happy for the lad as he marched away.

Her husband now conversed more discreetly with the new man who, she assumed, was a detective inspector as he wore no uniform.

She took the rare opportunity to study him in a candid moment.

Chief Inspector Sir Carlton Morley. This man was as different from the Knight of Shadows as chalk from cheese. He would never deign to rendezvous with a woman in a garden beneath the early summer night sky. Not this exemplar with a tidy desk, an army of officers, and sober, restrained manners. He was more machine than man. A cog that couldn't stop spinning lest the entire apparatus break down.

How strange that this was her spouse. This leader of men. This workhorse with a tireless back and fiendish reserves of strength and endurance.

Except. Did no one else note the grooves deepening in branches from his eyes, or the brackets of strain about his mouth? How could they not realize how isolated he was? How exhausted?

If he directed the force by day, and was a force unto himself at night... when did he rest? He'd no hobbies to speak of. He expressed no desires nor particular joys. She'd found nothing in their house to suggest any to her. No periodicals about riding or hounds. No cigars or much alcohol to speak of. Not even sporting outfits or antique weaponry.

His identity, both his identities, were dedicated to justice.

It was why the truth mattered so much to him. He'd devoted his life to it.

The conversation with his subordinate ended efficiently, and the detective was given his marching orders.

The veritable giant of a man glanced down at where she hovered just beyond the doorway as he left, and his astonishing russet mustache parted in a yellow-toothed smile filled with appreciative charm.

"Can I 'elp you, miss?"

She smoothed her hand down the front of her cobalt silk gown and touched her glove to the absurd little cap that sat atop her coiffure. "I'm next in line for the Chief Inspector, I believe."

"Lucky 'im," The detective gave a cheeky wink and swept his arm toward the door.

It was in that moment she noticed the floor had become much quieter than before as she felt more than a few speculative gazes following her.

This didn't exactly surprise her, as she was the only woman in sight.

Bobbing a quick curtsy, she stepped into the doorway.

Morley didn't seem to register who she was at first glance, but then he started in his chair as he gaped back up at her.

She imagined a ripple of pleasure in the liquid blue of his eyes before a frown furrowed his brow and deepened the grooves beside his mouth.

No. The glaciers of his gaze made it astoundingly clear he was distinctly displeased to find her here.

Both hands splayed on his desk as if he had to keep an eye on them. "Prudence. What are you doing here? Did you come through the front?"

Right. While he was an asset to her, she was only a liability to him. But she worked so hard to change that and had to bring the fruit of her labors straightaway.

Hurrying into his office, she took one of the leather chairs in front of his desk without being offered. "I found something, and I couldn't wait a moment longer to give it to you," she revealed, unable to contain her enthusiasm as she handed him the briefcase she'd been clutching. "The registers from my father's shipping company. Well, one of the triplicate copies on carbon paper. You're looking for evidence of smuggling, are you not? I believe, if you cross-reference it with the shipping records from the docks you'll find what you need to condemn or exonerate—"

He held up a hand for her silence, and something in the

gesture drove her heart to jump into her stomach as he regarded her as one would a troubling puzzle.

"You realize..." he hesitated. "Prudence, where did you get these?"

"From the safe in his study," she said. "Felicity came out with me this morning to attend an appointment and then Mercy helped to search—"

"Have you considered what would happen if your father is convicted of a crime?" he flicked a careful look to his office door, but it seemed no one lurked close enough to listen. "If he is guilty, he'll be thrown in prison. Are you ready to facilitate that?"

Prudence had felt the weight of that since the moment he'd informed her of his suspicions toward her family. "My father is in a position of power, and I'd not have him exploit that at the expense of the health of the people he's sworn to protect. These documents have the ability to exonerate him just as easily as condemn him. I'm ready to facilitate you finding the truth, as soon as possible."

She'd the suspicion his silence was more intense than contemplative as he considered the briefcase for a protracted moment before spearing her with a look so full of possible meaning, her heart leapt from her stomach to her throat.

"If he is guilty..." she preempted his response. "Might you have mercy on him for the sake of my sisters?"

His lips compressed into a tight line. "The law is justice, and justice doesn't often reside with mercy."

"Yes, but...you have made yourself more than the law, have you not? You conduct half your life in darkness."

Again, he checked the open door, his jaw tightening as he tilted his head in a warning gesture. "Let's not discuss that here."

"I'm not asking you to overlook a crime," she said with a furtive lean toward him. "Only to allow my sisters and my mother to retain their money and property should he be sent away." She pressed her hands together in a supplicant gesture. "I'm asking you to show them the mercy you've shown me."

"You're different," he said with a terse annunciation.

"Why?"

"You know why." He shoved back from the desk and stood. "Besides, that sort of decision would be up to a judge." Pacing the length of the window behind him he glared at the briefcase. "I didn't know you were going to your father's house today. You shouldn't have procured this, it's too dangerous. What if you'd been caught?"

"No one else was home." She wrinkled her nose. "My father isn't the most scrupulous of men, but he wouldn't hurt me."

"You don't know what men will do when threatened," he lectured. "And you can't understand how you've complicated things. To procure evidence like this, I must go through the proper channels. If anything is to hold up in court then—"

She stood also, his reaction to her gesture crushing any exuberance she'd felt. "*You* forget I've been a Commissioner's daughter for as long as I can remember. Why do you think I didn't bring you the original copies? Surely you could come up with a reason for a warrant, and then procure the real thing."

At that, he froze, regarding her as if he'd never seen her before. "Yes. I suppose I could." His gaze warmed to something that looked like admiration as he drifted around his desk. "Forgive me..." He paused, suddenly distracted as his notice drifted over her, lingering at the swells of her breasts hugged by her fine high-necked gown, the curves of her hips accentuated by gathers of silk.

She'd dressed for him. To please him. And she found a giddy satisfaction that her endeavor had been successful.

"You didn't have to bring them all this way," he said in a voice roughened with a darker, more primitive emotion. "This isn't an agreeable atmosphere for you. You could have given it to me at home."

She shrugged and looked around curiously. "I wasn't worried about being recognized, as I've never been here before, and I was already in town at the doctor's so—"

"The doctor?" He tensed. "Are you all right? Is the child—did something happen? You sit and rest." He grasped her shoulders and pressed her back into the chair before striding to the doorframe. "Dunleavy, get my wife something to drink, and if it's that swill that passes for tea on the sideboard, I'll demote you."

Prudence twisted in her chair in time to see the lumbering man with the red mustache pop his head around the doorjamb to gape at her. "That was...I mean...you've a wife?"

One look at the wrath on his boss's face, and the big man scampered away, reminding her of a dog needing to find purchase on a smooth marble floor.

Prudence stood again. "Nothing is amiss. I had an appointment with Lady Northwalk's doctor and midwife, that's all."

"Yes, but *why*?" he demanded, his muscles bunched with agitation.

"Well, it is common to be checked by doctors regularly when in my condition."

His lips twisted with grim approbation. "You didn't *inform* me of any appointment you had with a doctor."

"Why would I? Men don't usually bother with such matters."

"When have I ever given you the impression I'm like most other men?"

"Here you are, Mrs. Morley! I found you some of the good stuff fresh-brewed by that fancy ponce DI Calhoun." Dunleavy appeared with a clattering porcelain tea set on a tray that looked patently ridiculous in his mallet-sized hands. He walked like a man on a tightrope, his tongue out in concentration.

"Swiped it right out from under 'is nose afore he had a chance to taste it."

"I don't mean to conscript someone's tea," Pru protested.

"'E were right chuffed when I told him who it were for."

"It's Lady Morley," her husband corrected with a sharp edge as he relieved the man of his tray and set it on the edge of his desk before pouring her a cup.

"Right, right, and a fine lady you are!" Dunleavy looked back and forth from her to his boss with a smile so wide it shoved his apple cheeks so high his eyes half closed. "Sir and Lady Morley, as I live and breathe! 'Andsomest couple in the whole of the city, I'd wager. I don't know why we always just assumed ya were a bachelor, din't we, Sampson?"

A little fellow poked his head around the mountain of a man, his checkered wool suit hanging on him like it would a spindle of limbs.

"We always just assumed," he agreed in a voice as reedy as he was.

"No wonder the Chief Inspector din't tell us of ya, my lady," Dunleavy went on, swiping off his hat. "You're much too young and beautiful for the likes of 'im, in'nt ya?"

"You're too kind. I'm Prudence Morley, it's a thorough pleasure to meet you both." She extended her hand to them, receiving their deferential accolades as she enjoyed using her new surname in her introduction more than she'd expected.

Suddenly the two of them were three, and then four, the company in the office multiplying exponentially until Prudence felt as if she'd been introduced to every detective, sergeant, constable, and clerk on the entire floor.

Unsurprisingly, no one recognized her as Prudence Goode. Her picture never made it next to George's in the papers, as she wasn't high enough in rank to be a socialite nor low enough to be in their social class. Nor would these working men have aught to do with her father who held his offices in a separate government building.

To them, she was Prudence Morley, and her pedigree meant nothing past the man at her side. Didn't bother her one bit.

"Your husband's been keeping you secret, all to himself," a stout man of dusky complexion tattled.

She lifted her brows across at Morley, who seemed to be grappling with the storm of his temper before he allowed himself to speak.

"Should I be offended?" she queried with a mischievous smirk.

"Not at all!" Dunleavy hurried to his defense. "He's a jealous man, I think. Didn't want the likes of us 'round the likes of you, can't say's we blame 'im."

"Oh," she drew out the word playfully. "A bunch of scoundrels, I see."

"He keeps us in line, don't you, Guv?" Sampson prodded Morley with a boney elbow.

"Not very well, apparently," her husband grumped. "Don't you lot have work to do?"

She put a hand on Dunleavey's arm, noting that more of the men crowded around the office, unable to squeeze themselves in, but wanting a look. "Tell me, Mr. Dunleavy, is my husband a monstrous, iron-fisted curmudgeon?"

"Naw," Dunleavy blushed and bristled his whiskers in a shy gesture. "He's as fair as they come."

"Fairest iron-fist in the land," someone called from the back. "Now convince 'im we need a raise, Lady Morley."

And uproarious laugh swept through the gathering, and she couldn't help but be swept along with it in their joviality.

"You've a husband to be proud of, but you already know that, don't you?" Sampson beamed.

She couldn't help but study him, enjoying his rare moment of discomfiture. "Of course. He's a paragon."

His expression shifted from irate to rueful as he held her gaze. One might almost believe them a couple now...sharing secrets with their eyes.

"Still holds the record on murder nabs, if you don't mind me saying," another crowed.

"I don't at all mind!" She glowed at them. "You know Carlton, he's such an enigma. Not at all prone to bragging. I want to hear everything."

Despite his protestations, she was inundated by his praise. Did she know he'd shot a man threatening his own mother at greater than fifty paces? He'd not only nabbed the thief of the Wordston Emerald, but recovered the gem and returned it to his owner. He heroically pulled fourteen men out of the rubble when the Fenians bombed the Yard some years ago. If they were to be believed, he'd had single-handedly reformed the Blackheart of Ben More.

"All right, that's quite enough out of you lot!" Morley shouldered past his men to widen the door in a not-so-subtle invitation to leave. His skin darkened to crimson at the collar and the color began to creep into his cheeks. "Lady Morley was just departing. She needs her rest."

Never had she seen such a crowd deflate so rapidly.

"You'll visit us again?" Dunleavy asked.

"Of course."

"Can't believe you kept 'er such a mystery, Chief Inspector. Next, you'll be telling us you 'ave an entire brood we've never met."

"Not yet." Unable to contain her smile, Pru placed a hand on her stomach as it still maintained the illusion of slender beneath her corset. "But I've been to see the doctor today, and he's confident that before spring..."

The men gasped and crowed, chuffed, and chuckled with enough enthusiasm to do any cadre of grandmothers proud. They took her hands and kissed them, and many of them moved to give Morley a grand slap on the back or an energetic handshake in congratulations of his virility.

Prudence couldn't remember the last time she'd enjoyed herself so thoroughly. There were words one didn't say in the aristocracy. Things one didn't even express. Babies were announced on paper and then hinted at as a "happy event" or "new addition" until the woman went into confinement. Isolated as if her pregnancy was a shame.

But not so here. She was celebrated. And so was the father-to-be.

She looked over at him, suddenly overwhelmed with something that very much felt like joy.

His thunderous expression had morphed to more thunderstruck than anything. As if he'd stepped into some world adjacent to the one in which he usually resided, and couldn't make heads nor tails of it. He accepted the shakes and slaps and hearty compliments, looking around uncomfortably as if he didn't know where to put them.

One thing became instantly, and heartbreakingly clear to Pru. Her husband's subordinates didn't just venerate and admire him…

They loved him.

Because he was a good man and a great leader. Someone who not just commanded respect but deserved it. He put wrong things right every day. He took care of so many details at home, she was certain he was just as thorough in his business, if not more so. No task was too menial or too difficult. He did what must be done without compunction or even complaint.

Prudence knew enough about the world of men to realize that was a very extraordinary thing.

A virtue to respect. A man to venerate.

He shredded his own soul and sacrificed his own health and

happiness for countless Londoners who would never even know to whom they should be grateful.

How many women had the honor of sharing the life of a great man? A man who would leave his mark on the world and not have to sing his own praises because others did so. How many could claim to be honored to walk next to her husband?

To share a child with him.

She had to blink away a misting of emotion as the wonderment flowed through her.

Morley's forehead furrowed in concern as he caught her overwrought expression and was at her side in a moment, gripping her elbow to support her. "I'll walk you out," he murmured before addressing the room at large. "And I don't want to see anyone on this floor. You're either on the streets hard at work, or on your way home for the evening, is that clear?"

The men hopped to obey him, but not without jibes and whispers and merriment.

Morley pulled her off to the left toward the door to the back stairs. "I am your husband," he hissed.

"Yes…" was her slow reply. "That's been quite established."

He turned her to face him. "You mustn't keep important things like this from me."

Her eyes worked from side to side, searching for his meaning. "Like…like what?"

"You went to the bloody doctor, Prudence," he said in an exasperated whisper, drawing her through a hidden door and into an alcove full of dusty boxes. "I should have been there!"

Oh, they were picking up where they'd left off. "I-I didn't think you'd want to."

He sent her a bruised look as he resumed his pacing. "What…what sort of monster do you think I am?"

"The male sort of monster. Men never attend these things. It's up to the purview of the mother to—"

171

"If there is medical news about my wife and child, I'll bloody well be the first to know it." He rubbed at his forehead and then flung his hand out as if hurling away stress. "I will never understand aristocrats. The distance squeamish men keep from their families for the sake of propriety. It's patently ridiculous."

She let out a short sound. "I could not be more astonished at you."

"What do you mean?"

"You are either being obtuse or cruel," she accused. "Which is it?"

"Cruel? I've been nothing but deferential to you."

"I don't want your deference. I want you. Home. We've been married a fortnight and I've set eyes upon you perhaps thrice in all that time. You maintain a distance that surpasses the very idea of propriety. When in the past two weeks would I have possibly had the chance to tell you about this appointment?"

His shoulders fell a little and his chin dipped, reminding her of a chastised boy.

"You could have…left me a note," he muttered.

"A note, he says!" She gestured to the boxes as if they'd still an audience. "Is that what our lives are going to be? The polite passing of notes?" She extracted an imaginary pen from her bodice and dabbed it on her tongue. "Dear Carlton," she began. "Or should I call you Mr. Morley? Yes, I believe I should, that's more proper." She drew two strikes through her imaginary note. "I know we have not seen each other in several months, but I'm leaving this note to inform you that I've gone into my labors with our child. Please attend at your earliest convenience. All my kindest regards, Prudence Agatha Morley."

She shot him a glare as she signed her imaginary name with a flourish.

"You've quite made your point." He crossed his arms and leaned against the windowsill. "Your middle name is Agatha?"

"Argh!" She threw up her hands before reaching for the door, intent upon leaving.

He gripped her arm, whirling her around. "This is *me*, Prudence," he growled. "This is who I am. Paperwork and late nights. Responsibility and distance, this is—"

She stepped closer to him, her face lifted in challenge. "You're *wrong*. That isn't you, at all."

"You don't know the first thing—"

"You forget, husband, I've met you already. That night in the garden."

His eyes flared that quicksilver spark. "*That* was not me. That was—"

"If you say *a mistake*, I will slap you." She raised her hand in warning. "You were more yourself that night than I think you'd been in some time before, and *certainly* since. You were stripped of all this stalwart artifice. Bare and vulnerable. And yes, dark and angry." Her hand landed on his cheek, but only with caressing care. "And you needed me just as much as I needed you. And I think...I think you still do."

His chest expanded with short, rapid breaths as he held himself as straight and taut as a marble statue. His jaw, however, leaned slightly into her hand like a beast searching for comfort.

"You were so wonderful with me on my very first night," she remembered. "So gentle."

"Not bloody gentle enough," he bemoaned.

"You were perfect. *We* were perfect."

He regarded her warily. "Are we...not in the middle of a row?"

Her breath hitched with amusement. Farah was right, men were adorable idiots.

"I'm your *wife*, Carlton." She'd never called him that before. Not to his face. "For better or worse, our fates are tied together. I might not be what you envisioned, but...I'm *here*."

She glided closer, until her breasts pressed against his chest, her body molding to his. "It's permissible to need me. To want me. If we have nothing else, we have *that* night. We have *this* child. And this…attraction between us. One that might, in time dare I hope, turn to affection?"

She lifted on to the tips of her toes to glide a soft kiss against his jaw.

"Prudence," he growled.

"You're so tired. So *tense*." She pulled his head closer, whispering her breath over his neck, allowing her suggestions to glide into his ear. "Let me ease you, husband," she urged. "Further than that. Let me *please* you. After all you've done for me—"

His head whipped back. "I'd never expect—not as payment—"

"I know," her fingers caressed the close-cropped down of fine hair at his nape, urging him back toward her. Aching for his kiss. "That is why I offer. I want you, husband. Through everything, that's never changed. Given the chance, I would make a myriad of different choices over the past three months, but not that one. I cannot bring myself to regret giving myself to you…having you…does that make me unforgivably wicked in your eyes?"

"No." She sensed the tempest within him, the battle of his dual nature, and identified the precise moment one of the factions beat back the other.

With a foul curse, he closed his hand around her wrist and pulled her after him as he veritably slammed open the door to their alcove, and another to the stairwell. He silently marched her down one flight of stairs, through two more doors in another chaotic office full of typewriters and noise, and then veered her into a long, deserted hallway.

She trotted to keep up as he swept her to the end of the hall and shouldered open an old door swollen with disuse. In an incredible dance of fluid motion, he tugged her inside, firmly shut the door, threw the lock, and pulled her into his arms to crush his mouth to hers.

All pretense of the civilized Chief Inspector melted away beneath the heat exploding between them. His hands were suddenly everywhere. His lips were no longer compressed into their tight, laconic lines. They molded to hers with a wild, wet consummation that surpassed anything she'd ever imagined.

He'd once again succumbed to the starving, carnal beast that lurked inside him. One locked away in a cavern so deep it was as if he attempted to bury it forever.

But anyone knew that a predator denied sustenance became the most dangerous of creatures. Prudence realized that she somehow possessed the key to the dungeon where he kept that beast.

And she'd hoped that once she'd let it lose, it would devour her.

True to his nature, he didn't let her down.

Her body melted against and around him while he kissed her as if he could make up for every absent night and every empty morning. Beneath the fervency of his embrace, a heart-rending sweetness existed. A sort of awestruck marvel that moved her to the very marrow of her bones.

This was something he couldn't express with words, she understood. Not yet.

Perhaps not ever.

Though there was no chance of him releasing her, she still clung to him, her fingers digging into the convex muscles of his back, reveling in the mounds of strength she found there.

His tongue didn't wait for invitation, sweeping into her mouth in drugging, silken strokes. He moaned against her lips and she breathed it in, relishing the honest pleasure in the sound.

The ragged need.

He crowded her backwards, never breaking the seal of their kiss. His hands cinched her waist and lifted her onto a desk, or a table, she couldn't be sure. Only once he'd secured her there, did he allow his restless lips to venture elsewhere. He dragged them across her cheek, rooting into the sensitive hollow of her throat, nipping at the soft lobe of her ear as he pressed her knees open to fill the space with his hips.

This was how he would have her next, she realized. Here. Now.

He was going to take her again. To consummate their marriage.

In the scant moment she was allowed to absorb her dim surroundings, she identified the skeletons of shelves and boxes as some sort of ill-used storage room lit only by a grimy window.

Something about the illicitness of their setting sent excitement and anticipation surging through her. The only sound in the room was the rasp of her dress as he gathered it up in desperate fistfuls, and the tiny explosions of their rapid breaths.

She was frustrated by the layers of his clothing, as well. Whatever clay composed him, the very essence of him called to her. Arrested her every sense. She wanted to see him. To score his skin. To smell and touch and taste.

His rough hands snagged on her stockings as he pressed forward, urging her legs further apart to accommodate him. His fingers were both strong and gentle as they charted her inner thigh. Breathing seemed to become more of a struggle for him as he found the edges of her stockings and her garters.

When he tugged at the ribbon on her drawers, the curse he emitted drew fire from her blood and a flood from her loins. The desperate, crude word from lips such as his was indescribably erotic as it vibrated against her skin.

His fingers grazed her heat, producing a gasp between

them. Prudence clawed at his shoulders and the short layers at his nape as he found the soft, turgid flesh already swollen and damp with desire.

"Yes," the word escaped on a jagged breath and her body moved sinuously, her hips curling forward, seeking the forbidden pleasure of his intimate caress.

He angled back just enough to look down at her. His face half exposed to the grey light, and half in darkness. The dangerous glint in his eye caused her to catch her breath before the slick movement of his fingers forced her to release it on a whimpering plea.

He watched her like a man witnessing a miracle or mapping the very cosmos, his features a mask of reverent awe and blasphemous lust.

"So wet," he breathed, his thumb circling the aperture of aching flesh above her opening.

She couldn't answer.

He didn't need her to.

As he evoked thrills of molten pleasure in her womb with the relentless pressure of his thumb, his finger slid through the ruffles of flesh protecting the entrance to her body, probing gently before sliding inside.

The electric delight of the intrusion drew from her throat a desperate sound she'd not known herself humanly capable of making.

"So tight," he ground out as though in agony.

She wanted to say something. To entice and encourage him. To praise and plead with him. But every time she opened her mouth, only a mewl or a moan would escape as she suffered instant and excruciating rapture at the mercy of his clever fingers.

He covered her mouth with his, swallowing the sounds as her pleasure intensified into a surge of throbbing beats as wild as primitive drums. Her hands clawed at him, her thighs clenched as spasms of bliss assaulted her, driving against her like the unrelenting waves of a violent storm. She was helpless to do anything but ride his hand, emitting strangled sobs, as her release drenched his fingers.

She was too pleasured to be scandalized by their wickedness. Too captive of her passions to be worried about discovery. She existed only in this moment. In this place where he dismantled the woman she was and rebuilt someone new. A creature of desire and darkness, suffused with only one need.

Him. This. *Them.*

He didn't bring her down gently this time, didn't take the time to soothe or distract her with drugging, lavish kisses, or to croon sweet words against her flushed skin. His hand left her only for a moment as his hips levered away.

And then it was there. Thick and hot and pulsing.

The crown of his cock brushed her sex and she bloomed like a garden of summer roses. She'd yet to regain her breath before he thrust forward, filling her with a sensation so infinitely wonderful, it unstitched her at her very core.

The sound he made could not have been less human. It was both dark and divine. Tormented and victorious.

Through the haze of frenzy and desire, Prudence recognized this for what it was. Her husband was claiming her. Possessing her with demanding aggression and fierce, primal need.

Finally.

He paused only at the hilt, grinding his hips to hers as if testing her depths. Even stretched to the limits of her physical capacity, Prudence welcomed every inch of him. Wishing she could take him deeper, that they could truly meld into one.

The moment lasted but the space of a breath before instinct seized them both. She quivered with delight as he withdrew and filled her again and again with relentless, almost vicious, thrusts. His eyes were glazed pools of silver and shadow. His jaw clenched. His body a bunched, lithe machine of muscle, wrath, and unspent passion.

He was the most beautiful thing she'd ever seen.

"Again," he commanded tightly.

She shook her head, unable to express her lack of comprehension verbally.

His hand plunged beneath her skirts, stroking her where their bodies joined until it found the source of her intimate bliss once more. "I want to feel you...around me. Coming. Clenching..." His thrusts deepened, his muscles straining tighter as he thrummed at her with slick, masterful motions. "I...need..."

Without preamble, Prudence shattered into shards of pleasure. She flew apart, her soul rending from a body unused to and unready for such pure, electrifying ecstasy. Her head fell back on her shoulders, exposing her neck. He latched onto it like a fiend, laving and sucking and nipping at the tender flesh there until his own body suffused with a paroxysm of wracking shudders. He buried himself inside her as he climaxed, coating her womb with warm jets of his seed. His body locked inside her as wave after wave seemed to curl his spine, drawing raw, low, harsh sounds from somewhere deeper than his chest.

Perhaps, from his soul.

Eventually, his forehead fell against hers, and they stayed like that for an eternity, sharing breath and heat and a relieved sort of peace that had eluded them for months.

Sex with him was nothing like she remembered, and everything she'd wanted.

Perhaps it was different every time.

Oh, she hoped so...was it wicked of her to want to do it again when he remained inside of her?

Smoothing a featherlight caress down the soft cotton shirt covering his arms, she gave him an affectionate nudge with her nose.

That was all the encouragement he needed to gather her closer, lowering his head to kiss and kiss and kiss her until she thought she was in danger of another swoon. He took his tender time with her now, his lips pulling and tugging at hers. Exploring and soothing, nibbling and sampling as he allowed her to caress his jaw, the intricate fibers of his finely tailored vest, and wrap around to the silken panel on the back.

"One of these days," she whispered, "we'll make love in a bed."

He released a breathy sound of mirth, but still seemed unable to summon words.

Heartened, she nuzzled him. "Do you know what I think?" she asked rhetorically. "I think, if we tried a little, that we could make a go at love."

He pulled back from her. Out of her.

Prudence wanted to cry, to clutch at him, to plead with him not to retreat back behind his damnable façade. What had she been thinking speaking her mind out loud? She should have known better than to ruin the moment with sentiment. Not with a heart as fortified as his.

This had been her lifelong problem. She was never just happy with what people deigned to allow her.

She always demanded more.

His expression became guarded as he swiftly rearranged himself and righted her as well. "If I've learned anything from watching the successful relationships in my life, it's that love takes trust. And that, we do not yet have."

Though his words stung, she had to accept the veracity of them. "Friendship then... comradery at least?"

When he didn't reply immediately, she reached for him, feeling him slip through her fingers like the fine silt at the beach.

"This isn't nothing is it? It isn't empty." She tugged at him, needing him back against her, if only for a moment. "Because it doesn't feel empty to me."

When she worried he'd resist her, he didn't. He rested his temple against hers and took in a deep breath, as if he could lock the scent of her in his lungs. "This...isn't nothing," he ceded. "That is what makes it dangerous."

Pru did her best not to beam. It was something to him. She was something. Something she could work with. Could expand upon.

"Well...that's a start, isn't it?"

He nodded carefully. "You could say it's a start."

She kissed him and wriggled until he stepped back to help her down so she could smooth at her dress and hair. "Now that we've established that, I'll leave you to examine the evidence I've brought you. Perhaps if I can help you prove me innocent of murder, you'll think me worthy of your heart."

CHAPTER 14

*M*orley couldn't believe he was thinking of fucking his wife in church.

It wasn't even her fault. Quite the opposite, in fact.

She dressed as modest as a nun and adopted the visage of a saint for nobody's benefit as they occupied the front pew and no one but him could see her.

He'd not even had to mention that her Sunday best wouldn't do for a parish in Whitechapel. She'd emerged from her room wearing a gold and green striped high-necked morning gown that might have been the simplest in her trousseau. Her hair was pulled back into an uncomplicated braided knot and her hat and veil were suitably staid. Still she was the most superbly dressed woman in the congregation.

And the most desirable.

The sermon had nothing to do with the pleasures of the flesh, or the sins of seduction. Indeed, it was a rather sedate ecclesiastical exploration of personal generosity that'd set his libido to humming like the ceaseless vibrations of bumblebee wings. Not overshadowing things per se, but always there on the periphery, waiting to strike at the most inopportune time.

Perhaps that word, generosity, was the impetus for decidedly less room in his trousers.

If the last couple of days had taught him anything, it was that he'd a generous wife. One with a generous mouth, generous curves, and an adventurous spirit. Her appetite for food had returned with a surge and, along with it, other appetites demanded to be indulged.

He had only to reach for her and she was there, her arms winding around him with a tempting smile. She read his need like a sage, intuiting if he felt wild or languorous, deviant or tender. She denied him nothing and brought ideas of her own to their lovemaking that both astonished and thrilled him.

He looked over to where her gloved hands were folded primly in her lap over the placid tones of her skirt.

Last night those hands had been miraculously wicked. She'd insisted upon undressing him in the lamplight of her chamber. Purred with appreciation as she explored every inch of his skin with her elegant, wandering fingers. Her rather innocent delight gave way to illicit desire, and by the time she'd made her way below his waist he'd been nothing but a cauldron of boiling lust, his nerves in absolute anarchy. She'd requested to stroke him to completion, as she was curious about the male sexual experience and couldn't concentrate on it when she was also being pleasured.

A request he would have been an imbecile to deny.

He'd returned the favor, of course, his sense of gratitude and chivalry not allowing him to stop until she'd shuddered with exhaustion and begged him for mercy.

God, how he'd enjoyed their play, but he hadn't actually been inside her last night.

He missed her.

He'd missed her when he'd left her bed to prowl her father's warehouses at the docks. He'd missed her when he'd fallen into his own bed after only removing his jacket and shoes.

He missed her now, even as she sat next to him, her arm rubbing his occasionally, creating sparks between them he was surprised other parishioners couldn't see.

This was what he'd feared all along.

Attachment. Sentiment. Bloody befuddlement.

Before he'd discovered the truth.

As the organ played the closing hymn and her clear, sweet voice mingled with that of the congregation, Morley sat quietly, chewing on his thoughts. Pondering his misgivings rather than any forms of grace.

At first, when he'd thought her a weakness simply because his body responded to her, the situation still seemed somehow manageable. Now, he didn't just want her.

He...*liked* her. Dash it all.

As they stood in the back of the line waiting to file out of the church, she slipped her arm through his and tilted her head to gift him with a winsome smile.

She was like a spring garden against the grey stone. Vibrant and lush. Full of sunlight and sometimes rain. Always inviting, shamelessly flaunting her blossoming beauty, tempting him with pink petals of—

Goddamn and blast, could he not think about her naked for two bloody minutes?

Catching his scowl, she tugged at his arm and said, "Don't let's be grumpy, it's too beautiful a day."

"I'm not grumpy," he argued, grimacing at the ironic note of irritation in his voice.

"Hungry, then? I know I'm famished." She pressed a glove to her stomach, a gesture becoming more familiar the further along she became.

He wasn't particularly hungry, not for food, at any rate. But it suddenly became imperative that he provide her sustenance.

Over the past fortnight, his cook had given up on satisfying Prudence's increasingly obscure gastronomic whims. Which was just as well because his wife, being of the upper classes, had never much had the opportunity to sample London's culinary delights. Ladies were not allowed by some ballocks code of superior conduct to eat in public houses or dine at restaurants or clubs.

The working class, however, rarely shared such compunctions.

Morley found himself often hurrying home from Scotland Yard at the day's end, eager to garner a report of just what madcap craving would decide their supper. As soon as his carriage pulled into the mews, she'd sweep out in her pelisse and hat, and announce something like, "Your child is demanding salt. And onions, I think. Just mouthfuls of flavor and sauce."

"Onions, you say?"

"Mmhmm." She'd nodded rapturously. "And cracking large chunks of succulent meat."

"My child is an unapologetic carnivore?" he'd asked with a lifted brow.

She'd cocked her head and looked up to the side as if listening, before revealing. "Undetermined...I believe that last requirement is all mine."

That conversation had prompted him to drive her to Manwaring Street, where East Indian bazaars and spice markets magically unfurled with the dawn alongside eateries serving flavorful curries and savory meats and cheeses roasted in tandoori ovens.

They'd eaten with their hands, sprawled on cushions like ancient royalty whilst tucked away in a quarter of a city where they might have been any avant-garde couple. After, she'd insisted upon a constitutional back through the evening market where she'd purchased a pair of earrings and wildly impractical shoes.

The next night had called for cabbage and fish of all things, so he'd introduced her to Russian cuisine. The night after that, she'd given the rather innocuous request for lamb, however the precedent had been set. Morley had whisked her to a Greek establishment where lively men had danced to rousing music, delighting her to no end.

It alarmed him how much enjoyment he gleaned from these outings of theirs. How, for entire hours, he'd forget everything that threatened their future happiness and lose himself in nothing more extraordinary than a conversation.

His wife held little in the way of personal prejudices and was endlessly curious about, and appreciative of, the traditions and people he introduced her to. She'd a rare gift for observation, carefully and cannily picking out the subtleties and nuances of culture whilst doing her best to not offend. She never remarked upon the perceived class of the neighborhoods to which he'd taken her, nor did she make anyone she met feel like less than the most interesting person with which she'd ever held a conversation.

All of her attention was absorbed by whomever was speaking, and he noticed she'd the kind and genuine way about her that garnered them little extras of gratitude wherever they went.

It was why he'd dared to bring her to St. Dismas. Because this was the floor upon which he and Caroline had often slept in the winter. In the borough that'd whelped him and abandoned him.

He'd not been to the parish since before his wedding, and he knew Vicar Applewhite would be bereft he'd not been invited to the wedding.

They'd almost made their way down the aisle as the old blind priest stopped to bid every family a personal farewell, and to cover his anxiety, Morley leaned down to ask Prudence, "What does the little fiend crave for luncheon, I wonder?"

She made a pensive sound. "Do you remember three days

ago when we sampled those sautéed Chinese noodles?" She swallowed before continuing, and he'd the notion she'd salivated.

"I do."

"Something *like* that, but not exactly that."

Instead of clarifying, he allowed her to work through the conundrum, having learned that she'd arrive at a specific flavor and texture eventually, and his job would then be to provide it.

"Butter," she finally announced. "There must be butter. And... maybe cheese."

"Pasta?"

Her mouth fell open and her eyes twinkled like sunlight on the South Sea. "Pasta," she breathed. "Ingenious suggestion."

"Angelo's on the Strand, it is," he decided, realizing that his own stomach grumbled emptily at the thought. "Francesco serves this white wine and butter dish with garlic and scallions—"

She grasped his arm with undue dramatics. "Cease tormenting me or I'll expire before we arrive."

He adopted a sly, teasing smile. "I suppose you don't want to hear about the fresh loaves of—"

"Morley?" Vicar Applewhite turned his face in their direction, the tufts of his hair sticking out in a riot of copper-grey as his grin unfurled a gather of teeth yellowed with age. "Morley, my boy, that you?"

Morley took the blindly offered hand and pressed an envelope into it. "Vicar," he said. "I'm sorry I'm late this month. There's extra in there. Just have Thomas count it out and he can take some home to Lettie and Harry, as I know they've likely covered expenses in my absence."

"You know them well." The envelope disappeared into voluminous robes with the swiftness that bordered on sleight of hand. "I'm sure you had good reason and...well, you're not beholden to our upkeep."

"You know I am," Morley murmured, very aware of how still his wife had become as she watched the exchange with interest. "But I do have reason. I'd like to introduce you to…my wife, Prudence Morley."

Out of sheer habit, she curtsied to the blind man. "How do you do, Vicar Applewhite? I was very moved by your words today."

The Vicar's features lit with an almost childlike radiance of unadulterated glee. "Oh my God! My happy day! I've had many prayers go unheeded, Lady Morley, and I'd given up on this rascal hitching himself to anyone ages ago." Before she could reply, he turned back to Carlton. "I heard we'd a new voice in the congregation. Like that of an angel. Pure and sweet and good. What a blessing. What a blessing! Praise be."

Disconcerted and embarrassed by the man's effusive emotion, Morley pressed his cold hand to the back of his heating neck. It'd become concerningly evident to him that his marital status—or lack thereof—had been more disturbing to those in his sphere than he'd ever have guessed. And among those who claimed to care for him, they unanimously approved of his selection of spouse.

"We'd stay and visit…" he began uncomfortably.

"No, no, I've tea with the Brintons as soon as they call around to collect me, but you must visit soon. You must tell me everything." He turned to Prudence, both hands reaching for her.

She took them in her gloved fingers, squeezing fondly as if they'd known each other for a lifetime.

"There always seems to be plenty of demons in this world of ours. And not enough angels. I'm glad our Cutter's found his own."

Morley excused them and hurried her to the main thoroughfare, hoping she'd not caught the old man's slip of the tongue. He hired them a hackney, as he rarely brought his own carriage to this part of the city, and lifted her in, instructing the driver to deposit them at Angelo's.

She swayed silently on the overwrought springs of the cab as she subjected him to a thorough study before saying, "My sisters and I were raised by borderline zealots, as evidenced by our virtuous names. However, I wouldn't have thought you a religious man."

He looked out of the window at their dismal surroundings, hardening his heart against every over-thin waif or shifty-eyed reprobate. "I don't know that I am," he said honestly. "But others believe with such confounding fervency, don't they? I attend to observe them, I think. To learn what they love. Or what they fear. To watch the rapture on their faces and wonder what it must be like. To believe in something so vast. So absolute. To trust..." He broke off for a moment, returning his entire attentions on her. "To trust...in anything."

He found no condemnation in her, but an infinite sadness. "You do not go there to find grace? To find God?"

He made a caustic noise. "I've never understood the words. But, I think, I go there in case He might find me. If I'm standing in the right place. Maybe an answer to all this madness will fall on my head." He gestured to the city and the world beyond it.

To his surprise, a laugh bubbled from her, warming the moment. "Considering how much sinning we've been doing lately, you might do to fear a bolt of lightning instead."

In spite of himself, he chuckled along with her. "I'm not familiar with all credences and commandments but I'm fairly certain we've not been sinning since we married."

"I don't know," she said from beneath coy lashes. "It feels rather wicked to me."

If this had been his coach, he'd have gathered her to him and shown her the meaning of the word wicked.

"St. Dismas." She tested the name. "The penitent thief."

He shifted in his seat.

Smoothing at her skirts, she smiled to herself. "I confess I'd initially assumed you took me to this church so no one would recognize us, but now...I think I understand."

He shook his head, wishing he'd never taken her there at all. What had he been thinking? That he'd wanted to reveal the part of himself he blamed for her debauchment? Had he wanted to see if she'd hold a handkerchief to shield her nose against the stench of the wells and pumps he used to draw his drinking water from? If she'd shy away from the hard-working class and earnest people that lived in poverty alongside the criminal element?

If so, it was an unfair test. Although, one she'd passed with perfect marks.

"There's nothing to understand," he informed her with as much dispassion as he could. "I attend St. Dismas monthly. I'm their patron, you see. Applewhite shelters and tends to many of the hungry and naked children in this part of the city. One of the few true Christians I've ever known. I finance his mission to take some of Whitechapel's unwanted boys and help them find a direction. A trade. A means of survival."

"Because—"

"Because crime and violence are born of poverty and cruelty," he explained. "The more means a man has to provide survival for himself and his kin, the less likely he is to succumb to vice or villainy."

"And because the Vicar once did the same for you?" Her gaze, as her assessment, was frank and open, and Morley wanted to shrink from it.

This was what he'd come here to tell her. Whom he'd come to introduce her to.

So why now did he hesitate?

Because he'd always had the upper hand in this relationship, he realized. It wasn't comfortable to give her something she could wield against him.

Across from him, the daylight slanted into slick iridescent blues glimmering from the absolute darkness of her hair. "You told me once that you'd grown up with the accent you used as the Knight of Shadows," she said. "The same accent the Vicar has, and everyone here."

"So I did."

"Farah mentioned you had secrets...and the Vicar, he called you Cutter."

His heart erupted into chaos as he watched her braid the strings of his past together without him saying a word.

"Is that your name? Cutter. Are you the penitent thief?"

He retreated back toward the window, watching as the years fell away between that time and this. A blond boy stood on a corner with his black-haired friend, assessing which pockets would be full. Which punters would be easily fleeced.

"It's who I was," he admitted reluctantly, staring into the hard, hard eyes of that boy in his past. Eyes that'd seen nothing but oppression and desperation, set into a face that only knew the touch of another human being as a quick box to the ears or a heavy punch to the face. A body thinned with ever-present hunger and strengthened by hardship and labor.

Deadeye.

"I was a pickpocket and thief bound for a prison cell until one night..." He hesitated as the boy on the street corner lifted his finger to his cracked lips to hush him.

Don't tell her. Don't trust her.

But...what if she could understand where he'd come from? What he'd lost.

What he'd done.

What if his admission repulsed and terrified her? What if she told? She'd have the final secret. One that could rip his entire life to shreds and dump him right back into the gutter.

If he didn't hang for it.

"One night...the Vicar took me in and gave me a place to

191

stay when I had none," he explained lamely, vaulting over the most important parts. "He was the one who nudged me to reinvent myself through documents I'd receive when joining Her Majesty's Regiment. And upon my return from war, he handed me the paper wherein there was an advertisement for men of my physical build and prowess to wear the uniform of the London Metropolitan Police." He sent her what he hoped was an unconvincing smile. "The rest, as they say, is history."

"That was truly wonderful of him," she murmured, extrapolating what she could from his vague memoir. "And so you repay him for his kindness with a monthly stipend?"

Morley seized upon the opportunity to distract her from the entire conversation.

"I give him the entirety of my salary as Chief Inspector," he revealed.

She visibly blanched, her mouth falling open as she gaped at him as if he'd ripped off his skin to reveal a demon. "But... but...how do you...?" Good breeding caused her to shy away from conversations about money. To know a man's work, even one's husband, might be considered vulgar. He pinpointed the moment she made peace with that vulgarity.

"I always wondered how you, even on a Chief Inspector's salary, could afford such a lofty address," she said. "Even my father has mentioned his government pay wouldn't cover food for our horses, let alone our houses. He's always implied our money comes from his land and shipping company."

His lips compressed ruefully. He was still looking into where exactly her father's wealth came from.

"Then...what about you, husband?" It was her turn to stare out the window. "If you were raised in these gutters and went straight from the army to the police, then how did you amass enough of a fortune to speak for me, without a need for my dowry? Dare I ask if you are a thief still? If the money you pay to the church is penance?"

"Actually," he said, becoming rather amused. "I suppose I did thieve a bit when making my fortune."

She did her best not to look appalled, and almost pulled it off. "You didn't!"

"Don't fret, I only stole information."

She leaned forward as if entranced. "Tell me."

"Once I was back from the army, I would be asked to go to exhibitions by my former regimental officers so they could place bets on me."

"What sort of exhibitions?"

"Shooting ones, mostly."

"Shooting ones? Why?"

He gave her the short answer. "Because I was a rifleman in corps."

Her eyes narrowed to slits as she tilted her delicate chin in assessment. "You must have been a rather incredible rifleman if you were asked to compete in exhibitions."

"Tolerably good."

"Oh come now, you'd have to be more than tolerable if they—"

"They called me *Deadeye*. It doesn't matter." He felt his neck heating again as he rushed past to avoid her comments or questions. "At one such event, I overheard my Captain discussing an investment scheme with an American by the name of Elijah Wolfe, a ruthless and unscrupulous miner who was drumming up funds to reopen his dying town's defunct iron mines. He was able to find no support whatsoever and I could smell his desperation. But despite all that, there was something about him..."

"Did you save a grateful noble from being fleeced by this unscrupulous American Wolfe?" she guessed.

He emitted a low sound of amusement. "I gave Eli everything I'd won on the exhibitions for a ten percent share. It was barely enough to keep his mine open for a month, let alone pay the workers."

Her eyes went round as saucers. "You made your fortune in iron?"

"No," he said wryly. "The mine is still defunct, as it only took a month to exhaust it. However, another mineral often resides where iron is found. A great deal less of it, worth a great deal more."

"Really?" she asked. "What is that?"

He caught her hand and gently squeezed the tip of her glove from the long middle finger, sliding the garment from her creamy skin. Holding up her knuckles, he kissed the ring on her finger.

"Gold."

CHAPTER 15

$\mathcal{P}$rudence barely tasted her pasta. Instead she chewed on a puzzle, determined to uncover just what secret her husband was keeping from her.

She studied him across a private garden table behind what was possibly the most charming Italian café in the city, and contemplated everything he'd been in his exceptional life.

An urchin, a thief, a crack shot rifleman, an exhibitionist, a knighted war hero, an officer of the law, a vigilante, *and* a venture capitalist with interest in an American gold mine worth a fortune.

And, quite possibly, a liar.

Not about the gold, which was both startling, fascinating, and wonderful. But about what came before.

His childhood.

He'd left something out of that story, she was certain of it. As he'd spoken of his time at St. Dismas, she could feel him jumping over the graves of long-buried emotions, ripping up their headstones to pretend they'd never existed at all.

What a complicated man she'd married. Possessed of dichotomy between a heart capable of such unequaled valor, gallantry, and courage tied to a mind bedeviled by skepticism, enigma, and for lack of a gentler word, fear.

It was a word he would toss away and spit upon if she accused him of it. But if she boiled the amalgamation of his wariness, mysteriousness, and protectiveness down to a reduction as thick as the wonderful sauce anointing her pasta. She was certain she would find fear the main ingredient.

Not a fear of death or danger. His nocturnal vocation was evidence of uncommon bravery in the face of death.

So, what terrified this bold and daring knight? What drove him to hide himself, his past, in the shadows?

What had been done to him?

Or…what had he done?

"You're not eating," he prompted over a sip of his coffee. "If it's not to your taste, we can go elsewhere."

Jostled from her thoughts, Prudence picked up her utensils again and crafted herself an especially delicious bite. "No, it's marvelous. I was just lost in thought."

"Oh? About what?" He ate like he did everything else, she noticed, with correct and decisive efficiency. He'd been served a dish of pasta stuffed with meats, cheeses, and savory herbs in a voluminous red sauce, whereas she'd instantly selected the butter and white wine reduction over Capelli d'Angelo.

"I was thinking you're the one who needs to eat more," she said.

"I'm consuming a veritable mountain of food right now." He gestured to his plate. "In fact, if we keep this up, I'll need to have my trousers refitted."

Hardly. He was filling out a little, but the extra portions seemed to simply fuel the production of muscle rather than storing anywhere unsightly. "Yes, but, before I started prevailing upon you to take me to all these wondrous places, it was the perception around the house that because of your punishing schedule, you're woefully undernourished. Beyond that, you barely sleep."

She'd noted that in the past week his skin had gained a bit more color, and his cheeks filled from rather gaunt to merely sharp. He'd been eating better, but the smudges beneath his eyes remained, and the lines of constant strain, of ever-readiness, still etched into the chiseled handsomeness of his features.

His utensils stilled in his pasta and he stared down at the food with a queer little smile that vanished as quickly as it appeared. "I've heard officers complain for years about their wives nagging them to stay home more often. To take better care of their health."

She bristled a little until he graced her with a look so tender, she might have melted into a puddle beneath her chair.

"I always envied them." The glint in his eye dazzled her more than the sunlight fragmenting off the spray from the little garden fountain. Their round table was large enough to hold their meals, but only just, and it precipitated them sitting in such a way that their knees often brushed. An embarrassment of hyacinth, calendulas, and lilac blossoms cosseted them from the din of diners inside, creating a lavish, intimate oasis of their own in the middle of the world's largest city.

"Well, Lady Morley," he said around a circumspect bite of bread. "My lack of slumber is entirely your fault. Before you tempted me to your bed at all hours, I'll have you know I managed quite well to wedge sleep into my schedule."

"I suppose I shall lock you out of my bedchamber, then," she sighed as if it were a great shame. "If only because I care for your health."

He nudged her knee in challenge. "Don't you dare."

She laughed flirtatiously before a note of uncertainty pricked at her. "I know you live two very important lives but...

would you possibly consider…devoting a few nights to staying at home?" she ventured.

You could sleep with me, she didn't say. Because he hadn't yet. He would leave her in the night, beholden to his self-proclaimed duties as the Knight of Shadows. Upon his return, he'd sleep in the room down the hall from her. Her breath trembled in her throat enough that she had to tug on the high neck of her gown. "I know I don't have the right to make undue demands, but once the baby comes—"

"Say no more." He reached over and caught at the hand still fluttering at her chest, caressing a gentle thumb over her knuckles. "I've been thinking the very same—"

"*Mi scusi, Signore Morley, mi scusi!*" The proprietor, Francesco, weighted down by a magnificent mustache, a round belly, and a Sunday newspaper labored over to their table. "*Il giornale! Il giornale! È così brutto quello che dice! Non ci credo!*" He turned to her. "I do not believe."

A dawning frown overtook all semblance of her husband's good humor as he snatched the paper from the restaurateur and scanned it. Storms gathered in his eyes and thunder in his expression as he crushed it in his fist.

"Thank you, Francesco," he said, his teeth never separating as his lip curled into a silent snarl.

"Of course…" The man shot her a look of pity and scurried inside, not wanting to witness Pru's reaction to what she knew was going to happen. She wished she could follow him. Her heart became like a sparrow in a cage, flittering around her ribs as though searching for escape.

They'd drawn upon the luxury of luck for far too long. Eventually, the story would have to break. The truth was always going to come out, and with it a few lies as well, to flavor the story with delicious scandal.

She wanted to read it, but her eyes refused to focus. Not only did she blink back the threat of overwhelming tears, but also a creeping darkness at her periphery. She felt as though she'd been the victim of a blow to the head, and couldn't seem to shake the accompanying disorientation.

She caught the unmistakable word in the title of the article. MURDER.

"What? What do they say? Do they think I—"

"It'll be all right," he soothed, instinctively tucking the paper behind him.

"Tell me what they wrote," she implored him.

He hesitated for a moment, before exhaling defeat. "It's been released to the press that Sutherland was stabbed and that you were in the room with him. The article mentions his past... infidelities and your possible reaction to them."

"They've given me a motive." She lifted her hand to her face, just to make sure she was still in possession of one, as it'd suddenly gone quite numb. "That can't be all," she fretted. "How did Mr. Francesco know to bring you the paper, does it mention our marriage?"

His features became ever more grim. "Thankfully, no."

"Then..."

He produced the paper and folded it so she could see. "Your portrait, I'm afraid."

"Oh, dear God." She looked down at the likeness, touched by a cold, cold horror. "What a rude sketch! It doesn't even look like me."

"Not perfectly, but enough that Francesco stitched it together."

"What am I going to do?" she cried, unable to stop the words she didn't want to read from jumping out at her. "They've made me out to be a villainess. They've all but made the adjudicator's case for him."

"We're prepared for this," he said, attempting to calm her. "However, I think it's best we go home."

"But...I'm supposed to go to the Duchess of Trenwyth's

Ladies' Aid Society gathering with Farah today." She looked down at her plate of cooling pasta disconsolately. She wasn't finished, but she'd lost her appetite.

"I'd rather you didn't." He gave his lips and hands one last wipe with his linen before tossing it on the table. "The damned vulture who wrote this, and any other press, will be looking for you. It's best you stay out of the public eye for a bit, until we get this sorted."

"I see the logic in that," she said, her insides twisting with desperation. "Wouldn't that prove the journalist's point? I'll be hiding in disgrace. I'll look guilty."

Beyond that, she *couldn't* go back to the way it was before, back to only having their quiet staff and dust motes for company. Back to sheer silence and distance from the one man who'd begun to mean so much to her. "How close is this to getting sorted, would you say?"

She'd avoided pressing him about it too much. The past several almost carefree, passionate nights had heralded a new epoch in their relationship, and she'd convinced herself that he'd all but forgotten about his suspicion. That he believed she didn't have blood on her hands.

That he was looking to exonerate her.

His face became a cool mask of careful emptiness. "I've a church full of suspects in Sutherland's case, and we're working through them as fast as we are able, starting with those closest at the time of the murder. Lord and Lady Woodhaven, your father, the Vicar, and spreading out from there. I'm even looking at Adrian McKendrick, the new Earl of Sutherland."

She nodded, scanning the paper again and again. "What about Father?"

"My searches of your father's warehouses and interests have borne some rather rotten fruit, I'm afraid," he admitted reluctantly, examining her for a reaction. "I've found registers of shipments from ports where the plant is believed to be indigenous. Shipments that bear Sutherland's name and signature. This intimates that your fiancé might have been in league with your father...and if that's the case, we'll need to add the Commissioner to the very short list of lead suspects in his murder."

"What?" She jerked entirely upright, dropping the paper into her food. "George wasn't a businessman, he thought trade and shipping were, frankly, beneath him."

"And so he certainly did," he agreed. "But impoverished nobility are being forced to consider all manner of desperate means whereby to buttress their dwindling fortunes. Could Sutherland have been one of them?"

Stymied, she shook her head. "I never thought to ask. But I had reason to believe he was after my dowry when I heard that he'd several illegitimate children to support."

"Disgraceful bastard," he said beneath his breath.

She knew they shouldn't speak ill of the dead, but she couldn't bring herself to disagree.

Do you really think he and my father were...dear God. This just keeps getting worse, doesn't it?" With trembling hands, she rescued the paper from her plate, and stared down at the words that damned her, possibly for the rest of her life. "How did they get this information?"

He shook his head. "I thought we'd plugged all possible leaks," he muttered. "The reverend, perhaps? He'd a jolt of conscience?"

"I suppose...but it's unlikely. Like you, my family have been patrons for years. He christened us all. What about anyone at the Yard? The judge? The registrar who married us?"

He made a fervent gesture in the negative. "I called in a bevy of favors that you wouldn't believe if I told you," he said. "They all knew that hellfire would be preferable to the wrath I'd rain down upon their heads if they spoke out."

"What about Honoria's husband, William?" she whispered.

"He *loved* George and he was…was so *angry* with me. So certain I'd done it." A band reached around her chest and tugged, forcing a rather forceful exhale. The same pressure cinched at her head in a vise-like grip at her throbbing temples. "If William thinks I got away with murder, he might be using popular opinion to force your hand. To make me pay." She could say no more, her lungs had compressed the ability of breath completely away from her.

"Your bloody family," he gritted out, looking as if he might hurl the table in a fit of temper.

The dam she'd built to stem the current of her emotion crumbled, overwhelming her entire being with a desolate flood of emotion. As a last stopgap, she pressed both of her hands over her mouth to contain the cries, but she still couldn't seem to manage. They erupted from her as hot tears spilled in veritable rivers down her cheeks.

He was at her side in a moment. Gathering her to him in a bundle of bereft limbs and hiccupping sobs. His chest was hard and steady as the rock of Gibraltar as the tides of her pain broke upon it.

"I'm sorry, sweetheart," he crooned, his hands doing a tender dance of comfort up and down her spine as he tucked her head beneath his chin. "There now. All will be well. You're not in any more danger than you were before. Not with me to protect you."

She clung to him, listening to his words as they rumbled in his chest, grasping onto them like a life preserver thrown to her before she drowned beneath her despair.

"There, darling." He pressed his mouth to her brow. "You weep as you like. I have you."

Yes. He had her. She was utterly his.

Could she claim the same tenure?

"I-I'm not weeping," she declared, as an order to herself to cease more than anything.

"Of course not, dear," he said solicitously.

"I mean. I d-don't ever," she said around hitches of breath. "I'm-I'm not a hysterical p-person. But I can't seem to s-stop. I —I—" She hiccupped loudly and could feel his smile against her hair.

"Sweetheart," he rumbled. "Not only are you going through what is likely the most difficult trial of your life, you're also with child." He pulled her back so he could look down at her with infinite tenderness, before brushing at her sodden cheeks with his thumb. "I should not have said that about your family," he repeated. "I was…aggravated by your distress, that's all."

"You've every right to curse them. I'm disenchanted with them as well. Here I thought them almost too righteous, and it turns out the entire lot could be crooked but for the twins." Her chin wobbled as a new wave of gloom assaulted her enough to push away from him. "God, how you must regret me. I've brought such chaos to your orderly life. Surely you wish we'd never—"

He caught her, pulling her back into the protective circle of his arms, this time having produced a handkerchief. "Stop it," he ordered against her temple as he pressed little kisses of consolation there. "Don't think like that."

"How can I not when—"

He distracted her by looping the handkerchief over his finger and tracing the corners of her mouth where the tears had run, then along her jaw, beside her nose, and gently across her cheeks. He feathered cool, wine-scented kisses across her swollen eyelids and against her heated forehead.

"Would it make you feel better to know my family would put yours to shame?" he asked, injecting a bit of levity into his voice.

She gave a delicate sniff, and then a heartier one. "A little," she admitted as he surrendered the handkerchief to her so she could blow her nose. "You've never spoken of your family," she realized, with no little amount of chagrin. She'd never inquired about them. "Where do they live?"

"They don't," he answered in an even, nonchalant tone that asked for no pity. "My mother died not long after our births, and my father drank himself to death a handful of years thereafter, but not before making life miserable for my sister and me."

She lifted her chin to look at him, finding his expression distorted by her watery confusion. "You have a sister?"

"I do. I...did. A twin. Caroline."

"A twin," she breathed, her heart softened by the way he'd said her name, and then skewered by the use of the past tense. She tried to imagine Mercy without Felicity—or vice versa— and her eyes threatened to summon a storm the likes of which they'd not yet seen. "Can you tell me...what happened to her?"

He looked down at her for a long time, and she met his gaze with silent encouragement. This was like the doors in their home. This was what he'd kept locked away from her, this pain shimmering in his eyes, radiating from his body and fragmenting his soul.

After an eternity, his lips parted and he revealed to her what she understood he'd not been prepared to impart in the carriage.

She stood in the circle of his arms as he took a sledgehammer to the shards of her already broken heart. He told her about two children shivering on the cold cobbles, stealing their food and necessary supplies. Of hoping his sister would marry his best mate. Of his desperation and disappointment when she'd turned to the profession of so many to provide for herself what he, an ignorant thief, could not.

He recounted the violent day of Caroline's death in vague and broken detail, though whether for her benefit or his, she couldn't be sure. His eyes remained dry. Distant. As if he recounted the horrible tale of someone else's sister's cruel murder.

Pru was a puddle of emotion again when he ran out of words. The story didn't even exactly seem over and yet he just...stopped abruptly.

Much like Caroline's life had, before it had truly begun.

This time, when she buried her face against his chest, she plunged her arms around his waist, holding him close to her, wishing to impart all the solace she possibly could.

He stood still for a moment, stiff and unsure, before heaving out a kept breath, and dropping his cheek to rest on her hair.

He relaxed against her, allowing her to take some of his weight as they propped each other up, creating a creature of more strength for the sharing of their collective burdens.

"To think," she said. "You could have drowned in that pain. Could have let it own you. But you chose to rise, instead, to become this...this miraculous, extraordinary man—"

Abruptly, he drew back, lifting a finger to press against her lips lest she say anything kinder. His eyes were still shuttered, opaque with uncertainty bordering on anxiety. As if he still hadn't come to a decision. "I didn't tell you to gain your sympathy nor your admiration," he said before casting a furtive glance around the garden, finding only bees noisily eavesdropping on the last blossoms of lavender before autumn stole their bloom.

"I told you because I want you to know that...you're not the only one in this marriage with damning secrets."

Prudence shook her head, not understanding. "I have no secre—"

"I killed him." The confession hung in the air like a cold blade, waiting to slice them apart. "The man who hurt my sister, who looked into her eyes as they dulled and died. I found him, I cut his throat, and watched as his blood soaked my hands." He released her then, stepping away to show her his rough palms as if the stain remained. "He was a watchmaker, some nobody, who liked to hurt women. Girls. Who thought they deserved it." His voice broke for a moment, and he looked away, not in agony, but apparent disgust for a human he'd helped out of this world and into the next.

"Dorian was nabbed for theft that night, which provided me a getaway, and I showed up on Vicar Applewhite's doorstep. He granted me sanctuary. He washed the blood from my hands, much as I did for you the day I proposed."

"My God." Prudence stood as if her shoes had been welded to the cobbles. Her husband had just confessed a murder to her. The Chief Inspector of Scotland Yard. He'd killed the man who'd raped and murdered his sister in cold blood.

So why wasn't she horrified? Or angry? Why did she still want to take him—and that grubby, starving adolescent he'd been—and rock him in her arms until she'd soothed away that pain? Confounded as she was by the truth, it took her a moment to process his next sentence.

"I revealed this to you as an olive branch," he said earnestly. "No, a commiseration. We're not so different, you and me. You see, revenge isn't only a human trait, but a universal one. Justice is our society's way to punish crimes, but when there is no justice, it's natural to seek vengeance—"

She jerked away from him so violently, his hands were still outstretched as she retreated a few steps to the corner of the garden.

"Yes, we *are* different," she insisted, her trembling intensifying again, but for an entirely different reason than before. "We are *absolutely* different."

He stared at her, his head cocked to the side in almost doglike befuddlement.

"You avenged your sister's death, and I do not think I condemn you for that. But I..." She clasped both her hands to her chest. "*I did not.* I'm innocent of any and all crimes but the one you and I perpetrated together in that garden."

She wanted to cry again, but, it seemed, she'd been wrung out of tears. Now, all she had left was a raw and open wound where her heart used to reside, one that ached and stung with every breath. "The fact that you still think I'm guilty is more disappointing than the condemnation of every paper and person in the whole of the empire. Don't you see?" She shook her head, knowing that, even now, her husband's mind, his heart, was closed to her. "I could face all this, every last individual I know and love turning their backs on me, if I could only hope that you believed me."

He stepped forward, reaching for her until she held up a hand against him.

"What I'm telling you, Prudence, is that it doesn't matter what I believe," he said fiercely, gesturing with fervent, sharp swipes of his hand. "It doesn't matter what happened in that room, I'm taking your side. Come what may, you have every tool at my disposal, every cent to my name, and every ounce of my power, influence, and expertise. I will get you out of this, you have my word."

"And I thank you for that, but does it not destroy you to do so? Should you not only take up my defense if I am worthy of it? You don't *know* that I'm innocent."

"And I don't bloody care!" he roared. "I'm telling you, dammit, that I would do anything for you. Do you understand? I would take responsibility on my own shoulders if I thought it would help. I would bring back the bastard and kill him, myself. I would commit perjury for you, Prudence, hell I'm afraid I'd commit murder if you asked me—"

"But I *wouldn't.* I. Would. Never!" She threw her arms up and turned away from him, pacing toward the fountain, wishing the sound of the water didn't bring up memories of the night they'd met. "All I ask, is that you find out who killed George and clear my name."

She felt him behind her, a looming shadow of conflicted torment. "Why are you angry?" he asked in a hoarse and ragged whisper.

"Because you don't trust me," she told the fountain, unable to look at him. "I'm sorry but you can't imagine how frustrating that is."

"Please," he beseeched her. "Try to understand, Prudence. I want you. I…am fond of you. Christ, you're the mother of my child and I believe we're building something of a life here. But in my line of work, it matters not what you believe. It matters what you can prove. The feelings I have for you would already influence the outcome of any investigation, and that's a liability I've decided to live with."

"How altruistic of you." With his every word, the wound in her heart began to stitch together. Not with a balming comfort, but with glacial sort of frigidity. She'd begun to erect her own fortifications, it seemed, so she didn't bleed out entirely right here in the middle of the midday meal.

And still he went on. "Try to appreciate the chance I took becoming your spouse. A woman I'd met only once in a reckless encounter. One with a knife in her hand and the blood of her would-be husband soaking her. Had we never met before. Had we not…" He trailed away with a brutal noise. "I have to look at the evidence, Prudence, and when it's all laid out in front of me, there is only one conclusion to be drawn from it."

"That I'm a murderer." She spun on him, her fists clenched at her sides. "Is that why you don't sleep in my bed? Why you lock the door to your rooms and to the nursery? To keep yourself safe from me, your mad, murderer of a wife?"

He made a helpless gesture as his eyes darted away. "Come now, that isn't fair. I can't rightly say…"

"Then wrongly say!" she spat. "You're afraid I might, what,

sneak into your rooms and murder you in your sleep?"

"Not afraid, per se. I just felt it necessary to maintain a certain amount of distance."

"Ugh!" Picking up her skirts, she fled around the fountain, hurtling herself toward the door. It was all too much. The scandal, his revelations, confessions, hypocrisy, and concessions. Every emotion she'd ever named swirled within her until she felt as though she might detonate into a million plumes of volcanic ash. "I can't look at you."

His footsteps followed her. "Where do you think you are going?"

"To Trenwyth's."

"Wait." He seized her wrist, his grip careful but firm. "It's not safe. I thought we'd agreed you weren't—"

"You agreed!" She whirled on him, turning the full force of a mounting rage against him. "You've done nothing but make decisions for me since the beginning. And I've been so solicitous, haven't I? Because I needed to be grateful. Because I needed you to trust me. To help me. To save me. Because something awoke in me the night we met, and I fell a little in love with you then. The very moment I landed in your arms." She swiped at angry new tears as she twisted her wrist out of his grasp.

"But you've taught me that love is not possible without trust, and trust is not possible without proof, so..." She made a frustrated gesture before returning her hands to clench at her sides. "Here we are. I'm leaving now so you can be about your work. Go, Chief Inspector Carlton Morley, go find my measure."

"Prudence—" He lifted his hands, but she swept away from his reach.

"Don't," was all she said as she retreated through the door to escape in a hansom.

He didn't.

CHAPTER 16

I fell a little in love with you.

Her words haunted Morley as he followed Pru's hackney to the Duke of Trenwyth's spectacular white stone Belgravia mansion, and watched from a discreet distance as she went inside. They plagued him for several restless hours as he endeavored to focus on something, anything else. No amount of training, paperwork, reading, or investigation could silence the admission.

In love.

Every document he examined blurred beneath the image of the abysmal wells of pain in her eyes. The wounded expression that'd precipitated her anger. Wounds he'd carelessly, selfishly inflicted.

What a fool he'd been, having such a conversation after the disaster with the article. She was disconsolate, and he'd been awash in his own recollected grief and loss to handle that moment with the aplomb it had called for. He'd spoken in haste and had said every wrong thing he possibly could have.

If marriage had a dunce cap, he'd be in the corner for weeks, his nose against the wall.

Agitated, he attempted any number of pastimes, wishing to calm the need to crawl out of his own skin. Crawl on his knees to her and beg her forgiveness.

He watched every minute go by, aching for her to return. Wishing she'd not sought comfort elsewhere, but also recognizing her need for a separation from him.

She was in one of the safest places in the city apart from home, among the wives of the most dangerous and protective men he could think of besides himself.

An eternal evening gave way to nightfall, and when he could stand it no longer, Morley punched his fists into the sleeves of his jacket, and struck out on foot toward Belgravia, keeping his eye on the traffic for her.

Trenwyth's imposing house was ablaze with light as Morley chanced to meet his prodigal best mate striding up the walk for, presumably, the same reason. To escort his Countess home.

Ash, Lord Southbourne, put his cane to his hat and saluted him with a piratical grin. "Look at us, Morley," he commiserated with a devilish tone. "As boys, did you ever in a million years dream we'd claim the West End as our neighborhood, casually fetching our high-born wives to take back to our manor houses to swive them like the common perverts we are?"

"Never in a million years." Morley couldn't even bring himself to pretend to enjoy the Earl of Southbourne's charismatic irreverence. He very much doubted this night would go in that direction with his own high-born wife.

He didn't merit it.

"I saw the papers today, Cutter," Ash said, sweeping him with an observant look bordering with as much filial concern as the shark-eyed pirate could muster. "How is she? How goes the investigation?"

Seeing no point in correcting the man regarding his name,

Morley lifted his hand to the back of his tense neck and squeezed, trying to summon an answer.

He was saved from doing so by the doors being nearly yanked from their hinges, revealing a frowning Farah Blackwell backlit by enough lanterns to give the impression of a heraldic halo of an archangel.

Apparently, one on the warpath.

"Carlton Morley, you incomparable *idiot*," she declared, planting her fists on the hips of her violet gown.

Morley winced. He might have known the women would rally against him.

It was what he deserved.

"Oh my," Ash turned to him, his dark brows crawling up his forehead in surprise, and no little amount of delight. "I'm dying to hear this."

"You told your pregnant wife you thought she might try to murder you in your sleep?" she nearly shrieked.

Ash gasped, pressing his hand to his chest. "Morley!"

Standing a few steps on the landing beneath where Farah seethed down at him, Morley squinted up, thinking that her words sounded a bit slurred and her eyes over bright.

"No!" he said reflexively, and then realized he was wrong. "That is, I didn't deny—"

"I have never been so disappointed in someone in my entire *life*," Farah scolded.

"I know your husband, Lady Blackwell," Ash jested. "I very much doubt that."

Emitting a cavernous sigh, Morley nodded, intent upon taking his lashes. "Invite me in, Farah, and I'll make amends."

"I think not!" she snapped. "You'll stand out there where you belong and explain yourself, or you'll turn right around and go home."

"But..." He looked to Ash for help, and found only avid, ill-concealed enjoyment. "This isn't even your residence. Is Lady Trenwyth in there?"

She held out her hand against him with the judgement of St. Peter, himself. "You do not want to cross paths with the women in that house right now, Morley, as you are speaking to the only one who feels a modicum of compassion for you at the moment."

"Don't go in there, old boy," Ash said out of the side of his mouth. "There are plenty of banisters from which to lynch you. Best you run and change your name…again."

Shoulders slumping, Morley climbed the last few stairs to stand at least eye level with his accuser. "Let me preface this with the fact that I realize I handled the situation poorly."

"Understatement, but go on." Farah narrowed her eyes.

He turned to Ash. "Do you remember what Caroline looked like?"

The man's lashes swept down. "Yes, but I don't know what that has to do with—"

"Face like a fucking saint, she had," Morley pressed on. "Eyes wide enough to contain all the innocence in the entire world."

Ash's lip twitched at a fond memory. "Yes, and the brilliant girl could steal bacon from a bloodhound and get away with it."

"*Precisely.*" Morley turned back to Farah to elucidate. "My wife is the loveliest creature I may ever have the opportunity to envision in my lifetime. She's radiant and sweet-natured and wise and I enjoy nothing so much as her presence. But, doesn't that make for the perfect swindler? How can she ask me to trust her when I don't know her?"

Farah's brow crimped with concern as she contemplated his words. "You've lived with her for weeks. Surely you have *some* idea of her character now."

"Do we ever really know anyone?" he asked as defensiveness spilled over into ire. "I've arrested criminals who've been married for decades, to the absolute astonishment of their spouses. Besides, I'm not one of you idle rich with nothing better to do than lounge and travel and revel in each other. I'm kept rather busy tasked with the safety of the city and all, and then I've an entirely different vocation in the evenings. When have I possibly had the time—"

"Oh please," Ash snorted with distinctive derision. "I've killed men who've tried to feed me half the horseshit you just did, Morley."

"*Make* the time," Farah interjected firmly. "For both your sakes. Because I've met your wife all but twice and I'd take the stand to profess her innocence tomorrow. Not only that, but it's patently clear she might be the loneliest woman I have ever known."

Morley jerked, taken aback. "What do you mean?"

Farah regarded him with rank skepticism. "Do I have to spell it out for you?"

"Pretend I'm an idiot."

A chortle erupted from the man at his side. "Why the need for pretense?"

Forgetting her indignation, or maybe just taking immense pity on him, Farah glided over and placed her hand on arms he hadn't realized he'd crossed.

"Morley, she's lost her entire family and reputation to this scandal. Her father might be a criminal. Her fiancé died in front of her. Her sisters are hardly allowed to speak to her. She was deceived by her best friend and her elder sister. And then... her *husband* abandons her in a strange home with nothing but stress to occupy her thoughts while she's pregnant with his child. A stranger's child. And a stranger you seem determined to remain. How can you make it impossible to get to know each other, and then punish her for it?"

Sufficiently chastised, he hung his head. "I always wanted to be a husband, but I think I waited so long because a part of me knew I'd mangle it."

"Oh, ballocks." In a rare show of the affection they once shared, Ash bumped his shoulder with his own. "You are the best of us, Morley. Always were. But you're prioritizing doing the right thing in front of being a good man, and thereby getting in your own way. That's all."

"She loves you, I think," Farah said.

Morley's head snapped up to catch her dimples appearing in a knowing smile. "I don't believe a woman can be as hurt by mere words unless she's opened her heart to that pain."

It was the second time the word had been uttered tonight. A word he never before dared to contemplate.

"And we loved her too," she finished, patting his arm. "I'm glad you came, now home to your wife. She's desperate to hear from you."

At her words he went instantly alert. "Go home? I'm here to *take* her home."

Doubt clouded Farah's soft grey eyes. "Morley...she left nigh an hour ago."

He seized her shoulders, panic landing like a stone in his gut, squeezing the blood from his veins. "An hour? Did you see her leave? Which way did she turn? Did she hire a hansom?"

"I confess I was busy with other details when she said good-bye." Anxiety crept into her eyes as well. "Do you have any reason to think she's in danger?"

He wanted to say no, but something didn't allow it. "She's fainted once already and what with the investigation into her father...the story in the papers today...I don't know. I sense peril."

Next to him, Ash's rangy frame tensed beneath his fine suit. "Those aren't instincts you should ignore, Cutter. Go back to your house, tear it apart, I'll look around here and we'll rally if she's not found immediately."

"I'll ask Dorian," Farah said, visibly shaken. "He disappeared some time ago; I think he's hiding with Trenwyth."

Morley clapped Ash on the shoulder before he launched himself from the landing and down the stairs to the road. He ran the mile home flat out with lung-bursting speed. He juked about pedestrians and dove behind and around carriages to the stunned approbation of many a driver.

He didn't care. Nothing mattered. He would tear the city apart. Hell, he'd burn it to the ground to find her. He'd dismantle every brick. Scorch every spire. Everything that'd ever mattered to him fell away in her absence, exposing exactly what she'd become to him in this short amount of time.

Did he fear for his unborn child? Of course, he did. But it was *her* name echoing in every footfall. Prudence. His wife. His woman.

As he rounded the corner to his own street, he allowed himself to slow at the sight of a familiar coach idling in front of the golden brick terraces. He felt the fear leach out of him with each panting breath when he found his wife standing on their porch, staring at him as if he were a wolf loose in the middle of town.

"Morley," Dorian Blackwell greeted him from the carriage window with the seemingly disembodied head and conceited smile of a Cheshire cat. "I've just spent the most entertaining hour with your lovely wife."

The adrenaline still surging through him mixed with a knee-weakening sense of relief as Morley tried to lock eyes with Prudence. Instead of allowing it, she gave him her back to let herself in the house, closing the door behind her with a fatal click.

Morley fell on Blackwell like a rabid dog. "Where the fuck have the two of you been for an hour? I just came from Trenwyth Place, where Farah is looking for you. If I didn't know how absolute your devotion to your wife is, I'd pull you out of that carriage and beat you to death for being alone with mine."

To his surprise, Blackwell's smile widened as he held up his hands. "Hardly alone, I conducted my sisters-in-law, Lady Ravencroft and Lady Thorne, to the Savoy where they are staying while in town from Scotland. I informed Farah thusly before we left."

The very plausible explanation stole the wind from his sails. "Yes, well…she did not mark you."

"We'll blame that on her third glass of wine," Blackwell chuckled fondly.

Morley scowled, rippling with displeasure. "Why didn't you drop Prudence here first? This is rather out of your way."

"It was upon her request." Blackwell's one uncovered eye flicked a meaning-laden glance toward the ominously closed door. "If I'm honest, she wasn't in any great haste to go home."

Morley stood on his walk feeling like the war banner of a defeated army. Trampled. Torn asunder. And rather pointless anymore. He nodded his thanks to Blackwell, not feeling capable of forming kind words. "You might want to hurry back and tell Ash and your wife all is well," he muttered.

"Certainly." After a hesitation, Blackwell leaned out the window. "I know killers, Morley. I am one. You are one. We can sense each other, I think. Surely you already know she is not."

The moment when the truth collided inside of him felt as though a thunderbolt had reached out of the sky and touched him. He suddenly knew what to do. He knew what to say.

Blackwell continued, "If you want my advice—"

"I don't." Morley pulled an abrupt about-face, and marched up the stairs to his home, hoping his wife hadn't locked him out for good.

217

CHAPTER 17

*P*rudence had known he'd follow her. That he'd have much to say. She didn't bother readying for bed as she felt no great need to confront him in a state of undress.

She felt vulnerable enough.

An acid taste crawled up the back of her throat, as she perched on the very edge of the mattress and laced her own fingers together in a painful clench at the sound of his footsteps coming down the hall.

She regretted how she'd acted before. Even after the Ladies' Aid Society had supported and encouraged her position...she still wished she'd have not lost her temper.

She hadn't exactly meant to tell the Ladies' Aid Society matrons her story, but Farah Blackwell had taken one look at her upon arrival and swept her into a circle of the warmest and most extraordinary women, who all demanded to know what was wrong so they could help.

Once she'd recounted everything in various shades of detail, Pru became surprised at just how eventful the past three or so months had been. No *wonder* she felt as deflated as a collapsed souffle. No wonder she'd been so unaccountably upset this afternoon.

Shame oiled her insides as she thought about the intimacy of the confession Morley had shared before their row. His sister was a protected and painful secret. His avenging of her death a susceptible concession for a man such as he.

He'd handed her the power to destroy him, and she'd whipped him with it.

After her ire had cooled...she'd had to admit he'd made some salient points. Even though the points skewered her through with injustice and agonizing distress.

She knew they needed to have a discussion, that she needed to make concessions just as much as he did. However, she couldn't bring herself to do it tonight. Not now, when she felt as though her entire being, both inside and out, was just one taut, brittle nerve flayed open and exposed.

Though she expected it, she still jumped at his gentle knock.

Closing her eyes against the dread, she silently pled. *Please, I can take no more. Not tonight.*

The door opened, and she knew she should stand and face him, that she should gather up her reserves of strength and determination, notch her chin high, and meet him will for strong will until they overcame their problem.

But, everything at the moment seemed as insurmountable as Mount Kilimanjaro. Producing tears would be a chore, let alone peeling herself off the bed.

She tensed as he neared, her eyes unable to lift above the carpet as she focused on steeling what was left of herself for this. For him.

He stood in front of her for a fraught and silent moment, and when she couldn't bring herself to lift her head, he did something that took her breath.

He knelt like a penitent on the carpet before her, reached out, and covered her clenched hands with his own. The contact thawed her frigid fingers, unleashing tendrils of warmth that radiated up her arms to ignite the tiniest glow of hope into her shivering heart.

"I'm going to tell you something, Prudence, and I don't require a response. In fact..." he hesitated. "It would be better if you just let me bungle through it, as we both know I will."

She swallowed in reply, staring down at his large hands. At once so masculine and elegant, so capable and so brutal.

His voice was paradoxically decisive and uncertain, but it lacked the harshness of before. It contained a hoarse note too tame for desperation and too bleak for nonchalance.

Composure, it seemed, eluded them both.

"Deceit has been a relentless part of my entire life," he began, dousing a bit of her hopes. Tempting her to curl in upon herself like a salted snail.

But she didn't move.

And he didn't stop.

"The only things I remember of my parents, are the lies they used to hurt each other with. When my father died, Caroline and I survived only through dishonest means. Everything we had could be taken by a craftier thief, a better con artist. It was the game we learned to play on the streets. After she...after I..." He broke off, filling his chest with an endless inhale as he pressed his thumbs into the grip of her fists as if he could likewise penetrate her closed heart.

Prudence relaxed her grip incrementally, doing her best to allow her insides to mirror the action. To open. To hear him.

"My parents never documented our birth, so I had no papers. I read the name Carlton off an advertisement for the Carlton Football Club posted on the building next to the military office where I joined up." He made a rueful noise, shaking his head at the younger man. "Another lie I told, one I thought would have no consequences because I fully intended to die in some hole on another continent somewhere. I never thought

I'd live to see England again. Instead, I shot a swath through entire countries. Killing for an empire that fabricates false-hoods and misrepresentations to the world as if words like humanity and honor do not exist in the face of progress and expansion. And then..."

He turned her hands palm up to caress the delicate lines there with his thumbs as he continued. "I became a police offi-cer, of all things. And I implore you to find me a vocation wherein someone is confronted with more deception. Not only do criminals lie to me for every kind of reason, but regular, frightened, generally honest people do as well, merely for what I am and the authority I wield. My subordinates consistently report errors and embellishments, and many of them, appar-ently, use the uniform for criminal enterprise."

He crept closer on his knees, powerful thighs bunching and straining against his trousers as he entreated her to hear him. "So much of my day-to-day life is spent unraveling untruths and investigating inaccuracies. I see them everywhere, and because of that, I think I've come to expect them from everyone."

"I understand," she murmured, as a sense of sympathy infil-trated her gloom. Such a life was not easy, such a mindset awfully arduous and burdensome. "You're telling me this is why you are unable to trust."

He gathered her hands to his chest as he brought their gazes even. Anchoring them against his pounding heart, he placed a fingertip beneath her jaw, nudging her to look up at him. Something shone in his gaze she'd never marked before. A gentle contrition. The glimmer of vulnerability. "Sweetheart. I'm telling you why I've been a fool. An unmitigated bastard. Prudence...I'm sorry."

She would have sworn her heart ceased beating if not for the thrumming in her ears. Had she heard him correctly? Or was she fantasizing this?

Had she fainted again?

Her gaze flew to his, searching for signs that she was truly going mad.

"You…don't have to—"

"I do," he insisted, his visage claimed by an emotion both desolate and resolute. "The truth is, I don't know you like a man should know his wife, but that is my failing, not yours. Beyond that, I think you are an honest person, possessed of integrity I've only ever pretended to have."

She stalled, blinking over at him in wonder. "You do?"

His features softened as he regarded her with such infinite tenderness, she felt as though it might melt her completely. "Yes. You're so open and vulnerable. You tell me everything you're thinking. You tell me what you want, and what you feel and what you know to be true. Hell, that very first night, your shocking candidness was the first thing that drew me to you. From the beginning of it all…I've been inclined to believe every word from your mouth."

The mouth he referred to fell open in abject incredulity. "Then…why?"

"Because everyone—literally *everyone* else—is a liar, including me, and with that, I have made my peace. But Prudence," he brushed his thumb up her jaw, his eyes touching her face everywhere, searching for something. "You are the one person who can truly betray me, do you understand?"

She tilted her neck, pulling away from his distracting touch to shake her head with incomprehension.

"You're going to make me say it," he realized wryly, giving the impression of a boy squirming beneath a scolding adult's insistence he explain himself. The electric blue of his eyes disappeared as he hid his expression behind his lids. "You are the epitome of every desire or dream I've conceived of since before I can remember, and that is a very specific kind of torment. An unparalleled beauty, a superb lover, a woman of grace and kindness and intellect whom I can only respect and admire. A fantasy in the flesh, here in my house. With *my* name."

He lifted his empty hand to swipe it through his hair. "Christ, sometimes I have to just stand in the hall and stare at the door you sleep behind because I cannot believe my luck, my undeserved good fortune. You are *here*. You are real. And so is our child."

A sob escaped her. Not one adorned by tears, but disbelief. "But..." She didn't even know where to start. A part of her had awakened at his words, the part made of need and love and hope and happiness. "But...only this morning you thought that I—You said—"

"I know what I said." His jaw tightened before he continued, his brow crimping with earnest anguish. "Trust is not a word I understand. Faith is a foreign concept to me. Despite that, my instincts have screamed at me to trust you." His gaze cast down as his jaw worked over powerful emotion.

"And then that insidious voice inside of me warns that if I *did* believe you, and then discovered you lied? That you'd somehow swindled me, possibly the most incredulous man alive. Well...I've survived any number of disappointments, treacheries, and sorrows. But I don't see the way back from that. You could break me, Prudence, don't you see? It's why I've been pushing you so hard. Why I almost needed you to be guilty, so the terrible truth—if it was a truth—would be out. So it was safe to fall for you because you were just as dishonest as the entire world. Just as deceitful as me."

Prudence yearned to say so many things. To ask so many questions. To soothe him and set his churning mind at rest, but now that he'd begun, his torrent of words tumbled out in escape, like the freed captives of a heavily fortified prison.

Her hand stayed against his heart hammering beneath the hard muscle of his chest as he released his grip to tenderly cradle her face in his palms. The spark of warmth he'd ignited within her bloomed to an incandescent radiance, reanimating the spirit within her.

"I meant what I said earlier," he whispered, his gaze searching hers, beseeching her. "Even though I was being an inconsiderate ass when I said it. I don't care about scandal in the paper but for the fact that it distresses you. I'll send anyone to the devil before they hurt you. I am a knight. A man with a code. A warrior with a creed. I vow, from this moment onward to be *your* knight, wife. Someone who is honor bound to protect your name, your life, and your soul. I swear to you, that before this child is born, the world will know who did this. And they will know you didn't." His voice grew in fervency until he finished with the one thing she'd yearned to hear. "They will believe you, as I believe you."

His words eroded any thought of erecting barricades between them. Her next sob was filled with joy as she flung her arms around his neck, pulled him toward her body, and brought his lips down to receive her kiss.

The kiss that contained her heart.

She was lost. She'd been lost to him since the moment she'd tumbled into his lap. A fated fall, she realized, as if destiny had pushed her over.

And he'd caught her, as he ever would.

The moment tilted from overly emotional to intensely erotic in the space of an instant as he gathered her close and crawled up onto the bed, pulling her beneath him.

He was a remarkably self-contained man, her husband... until he wasn't.

His kisses began as soft as prayers and then built in power and demand as his grip on his own control became less tenuous. Hot glides of his tongue became deep, mating dances with her answering passions.

She melted beneath him, and he filled her spaces with the force of his ardor.

A voice inside urged her to let go of the brittle, desperate edge she'd been clinging to, realizing it was safe. She wouldn't fall. No, she'd join him here, to dance among the clouds.

His kiss contained so many things they'd still left unsaid. So many parts of his fractured being. He was at once the Knight of Shadows. A man possessed of unmerciful darkness, devouring her with breath-stealing intensity. And so, too, was he the Chief Inspector, assessing and observant as he brushed his lips across hers, creating delicious friction with his mouth, evoking an ache in her sex that demanded satisfaction.

And maybe the thief was here with her, threatening to steal her heart, even the parts of it she was still afraid to give. There was the sense of marvelous reverence in his touch, a bit of disbelief that belonged to the youth he'd been, the one unused to any kindness or affection.

Though she felt a fervency in him, he lingered over her mouth, kissing her with slow, languorous efficiency and tantalizing promise.

For the first time, he kissed her as if he should be doing nothing else. As if his mind was empty of naught but this moment. And the next. As if they were immortals who might go on kissing for a hundred years and never tire of it.

And, indeed, she wished it were so.

If ever there was a moment in need of prolonging, it was this one.

And yet...a pressure built within her that urged her legs apart so he could settle his big body between them. The barrel of his erection ground against her between the impediments of their clothing, and she was suddenly anxious to be rid of them.

She wanted all of his skin next to hers. All of his heat and his need and his sex.

As if reading her mind, he broke the kiss, lifting away from her only to tackle the placket of tiny buttons that stretched from her chin to her waist.

He made it to her clavicles before ripping the garment open, and lowering back to swallow her faint protestations with more distracting kisses.

"I'll buy you a dozen bodices," he whispered against her mouth. "If you only let me tear them from you each night."

Appeased, she let him unwrap her like a present, releasing this strap, undoing that ribbon, unclasping a hook. His mouth explored every inch he uncovered as if finding it for the first time.

Her chemise caught beneath her swollen, tender breasts as he dragged it up, and she felt them pop free with a little bounce before he swiped it over her head and tossed it somewhere on the floor.

"You are so beautiful," he groaned.

"So are you," she replied with breathless candor.

His smile was touched with chagrin as, instead of reaching for her breasts, he lifted his fingers to her hair, deftly searching the plait for pins, pulling them from a head she hadn't known was aching until the pressure had ceased.

He returned to kissing her with new depth and untried angles as his fingers wended through the braid, unspooling it softly until her hair fell in soft waves down her bare back.

Questing fingers slid up her spine, thrilling her to the core and mingling a shivering chill with the answering heat of need.

No longer willing to stay dormant, Prudence slid her arms around him, sinking her fingers into the heavy, lambent locks of his neatly trimmed hair before lowering them to tug at his collar.

His fingers lifted to help, and their hands tangled in a newfound haste to divest each other of the trappings of their garments.

Once they'd wrestled themselves naked, he climbed up her

body like a cat, laying her back beneath him as he pressed a muscled thigh dusted with golden hair between her legs.

They spoke in smiles and sighs as she tested the taut ridges of muscle at his ribs, and down over his corrugated abdomen to reach for the hard and tender flesh below. She still marveled at how silky the skin of his sex was, pulled canvas tight and pulsing with blood and lust. It was hot velvet poured over steel, and she loved nothing more than the moment it fit inside her. As if he'd always been made for her. The key to her lock.

A apropos metaphor, as whenever he'd finished with her, she became quite unlatched. Undone. Open.

He began to chart a course with his lips down her body, pulling his sex from her grasp with a plaintive moan. A little moisture lingered on her fingertips, and she knew by now that meant his arousal had reached a peak. That he approached a point of no return.

His golden head bent over her breast to release a steaming breath against the puckered peak. He browsed at the nipple with only his lips, laved at it with a barely there lick of his tongue.

Moaning her encouragement, Pru squirmed beneath the attentions, not too far gone to be touched by his conscientiousness. Her breasts had been unabatingly tender before, and he was the kind of man who didn't forget that.

One who always cared about her pleasure and her comfort.

He didn't use his teeth until he nuzzled into the valley between them, nipping at the skin and then soothing it with a velvety lick.

In the light of the lamp on her dresser table, he became a silhouette of sin, his powerful body hunkered over hers as if protecting his next meal.

And a meal, she was certain to become.

He swiped his tongue across his lips, making them glisten

before he dipped his head to press a butterfly-soft kiss to the delicate swell of her belly.

The sight of it touched her eyes with the burn of emotion to rival that of the heat of desire. It was him that put this child inside of her. This act. This bit of miracle of making allowed mere mortals, the culmination of which one might call a glimpse of divinity.

"Mine," he growled possessively. The tickle of his breath against her bare stomach set every hair on her body to vibrating in awareness. Her muscles coiled with need, and her knees fell further apart, inviting his kiss to the throbbing center of her.

Offering herself.

His hands smoothed up her taut thighs as he nuzzled into the soft, fleecy curls, inhaling deeply.

"Christ, you're perfect," he breathed against her sex, causing an intimate spasm of anticipation.

His tongue split her in one upward stroke.

He kissed her there as he'd done her mouth, with feverish ardor. His tongue slow and long, hot and hard as it tangled with the satin of her intimate flesh. Sliding forward, withdrawing, slipping in and about as she writhed beneath him.

Struggling to breathe, Pru reached for him, lacing her fingers in his hair as he nibbled and tugged with his lips, explored with his tongue as if he couldn't decide which part tasted the best.

And then he was there, at the tight, clenching opening of her body, delving against it, entering her in shallow thrusts that sensitized her so exceedingly, her hips came off the bed in a sinuous arch.

Unable to contain herself, she chased the pleasure of his mouth in lithe, supple movements. She trembled and strained, danced and bucked, until he was forced to seize her hips and pin her down, so he could thoroughly dismantle her by enclosing his mouth over the stiff, tender bud.

Euphoria suffused her in spasms of delight as the culmination of desire broke over her in wave after wet wave of release. She wanted to thank every pagan god of sex and sin, and she rather thought the rhythmic, ecstatic sounds she made might have paid sufficient tribute as he wrung from her a bliss she'd never before reached.

Only once he was certain she'd been sufficiently brought back to earth, did he leave her with one last naughty kiss before wiping the gloss of her from his mouth with the back of his hand.

His features were taut with a particular wickedness as he kneeled up between her parted thighs and gazed down at her exposed sex with the reverence of a man at the end of a grail quest.

Suddenly shy, she went to close her knees to hide the still-pulsing flesh from his view. He stopped her by shaping his hand over her mons, stroking it gently, dipping inside to wet his fingers, then spreading her nectar on the jut of his sex.

He lifted to retrieve a pillow, and effortlessly maneuvered her to slide it beneath her hips, tilting them upward.

Leaning over her, he caught himself on his elbows as he slid the head of his shaft along the slick cleft, lodging against her entrance.

His eyes burned down into hers, as he fed her his cock inch after pulsing inch until he'd embedded himself so deep, she felt the stirrings of a new pleasure. Of a glory left untapped.

Something unfurled as he seated inside her. Something previously dormant and unaccountably sweet. They'd been lovers a handful of ecstatic times now, and each time had been incredible in its own right.

But this. This connection...it reached beyond the physical. She could feel his heartbeat, but in her own chest. The cavern of his loneliness and the space she took up inside it, making it smaller.

His gaze became incredulous, and he gasped out her name as if unsure of what was happening.

"I know," she whispered, drawing her hands down the splendor of his skin. "I feel it too."

The uneven struggle of his breathing called to her, and she twined her arms about him, pulling him in for a searing kiss. Tasting her pleasure on his lips. The essence of his skill and her unending desire for him.

Then he moved.

He set a deep, primal rhythm, angling into her with maddening proficiency. She felt the heavy weight of him inside her, against her, over and around her, cocooning her body with his.

Though her limbs felt liquid with the torpor that followed such a consuming climax, she couldn't bring herself to remain still beneath him. She lifted her knees to his sides, wrapping her legs around his pistoning hips.

His cock touched something inside of her, eliciting an instant pleasure so keen, it bordered on pain. She arched toward it. Or maybe away, feeling as though he'd thrust a rod of lightning against her spine and the currents lifted her into thunderclouds where a storm shook her asunder.

She was dimly aware of his own breath catching before a sound ripped from him, something like a growl snagging on velvet as his muscles built upon themselves. Tightening. Trembling. Seizing. Before the warm rush of his release spread inside of her.

It took her a while to find her way back from the stars. Her husband, as was his way, took care of everything. He washed her, then himself, pausing at the lamp to turn down the light, melting the shadows down the walls until they were only encased in a dim amber glow.

He settled them both beneath the coverlet, resting his shoulders against a pile of pillows, and pulling her to lean back against his chest so he could rest his chin on her head and twine his arms around her. Big hands encased her tightening belly, and he idly stroked her as she lazed in the aftermath. Their limbs entwined and the fine down on his legs tickled her bottom, but she was too spent to care.

Prudence tuned to the aftershocks of their joining, the twitches and throbs of her body, the resonant beats of her heart. She loved the scent of them, the bloom of sweat and heat and come, subtle and alluring. Tempting and erotic.

He'd never held her like this before. He'd…never stayed.

Lanced with a sudden anxiety, she swallowed. "If you're going to leave, you'd better go now." She injected a teasing note into her voice. "I'll be cross if you wake me later."

"I would stay…" he hesitated. "If you'd have me."

"What about the Knight of Shadows?" she protested, angling her head to look up at him. "Doesn't he have somewhere to be?"

His hands coasted up her ribs and gently palmed the weights of her breasts, testing the thin, silky skin beneath. "He's exactly where he should be."

She relaxed against him, her heart swelling until it felt two times too large for its chamber. This was bliss. This moment. Were she a cat, she'd be purring.

"I'm going to be a better husband to you," he murmured, his voice full of self-approbation as he curled around her as if he could create a buffer of skin and muscle and blood from the rest of the world.

Nestling deeper against him, she turned to press a kiss to his jaw, feeling the tug of sleep against her lids. "You already are."

CHAPTER 18

hat they needed was a honeymoon, Morley decided.

He'd eschewed the very idea at first—no—that wasn't right. He'd never even *entertained* the notion for obvious reasons.

But now...

Now he'd lost all ability to focus on his work.

Reports needed briefing, men required orders and permissions, warrants begged approval to go to the courts. He had half a dozen active crime scenes in this borough, alone, and an iron worker's strike waiting to happen right on London Bridge.

He signed the correct papers, assigned the appropriate investigators, listened as best he could to debriefings and such. But now, as he waded through reports, he realized he'd read the same paragraph going on fifteen times now.

He wanted to just send it all to the devil and climb back into bed with his wife.

He'd been late to work for the first time in fifteen years this morning, because he'd lost track of time just watching her sleep.

Though he usually kept the blinds pulled dark and tight,

Prudence preferred to sleep with them thrown open so she would appreciate the light as it played across the city, and wake to the sunshine beckoning her out of bed.

He balked at the idea, at first, but then he'd woken to the pillars of dawn painting the lavish dark waves of her hair with the beautiful iridescence of a raven's wing as it trailed across the white silk of the pillow. She might have been some mythical heroine of a fairy tale, locked away in a torpor spell, awaiting him to slay her dragons and kiss her awake.

He might have done it, too, if little smudges of shadow hadn't lurked beneath her fluttering eyes. Her breaths had been so soft and deep, her onyx lashes a stark contrast over cheeks paler than he liked.

Instead, he propped himself on his elbow and simply studied her in a rare, unguarded moment. It only seemed fair. She'd stripped him bare, laid him wide open and dangerously close to defenseless. The intimacy he felt forming between them, the bond that wove between his ribs and hers, stitching their ticking hearts together, was made of some stronger material than the steel and ice he'd encased around his heart.

Something magical, probably, if one believed in that sort of ridiculous thing.

Which he didn't.

And yet, when had he ever slept so well? When had he ever been on the precipice of such a sheer and infinite ledge, and felt so safe?

She really did sleep the sleep of the innocent. Even after all the wicked things they'd done together.

And the ones he still wanted to do.

Christ, they'd need weeks. Perhaps longer. Honeymoons made so much sense now.

He could take her to Antigua to swim in a warm ocean as blue as her eyes. Or maybe closer, somewhere continental? They could cosset themselves in the far north beneath ceilings of glass, watching the Northern Lights snap overhead as he made love to her on soft furs like a Viking lord. Or they could visit a Moroccan spice market or Turkish bazaar and sleep beneath lattices of flowing silk with air spiced with exotic blossoms.

He'd let her decide, of course. He didn't care.

For the first time in...maybe ever...the idea of doing a bit of nothing actually appealed to him. So long as it was with her. He would lounge like an Olympian, feeding his goddess any ambrosia she desired. Learning her, consuming her. Mind, body, and soul.

"Wherever your mind is, I want to be there too."

Morley jolted back to the present to see a smirking Christopher Argent lounging against his office doorframe.

"You're not invited," he said irritably.

"Ah." A sly understanding sparked in the man's clear eyes. "Speaking of your wife. A messenger boy came to deliver this. She's gone to her sister's to help pack some things."

Morley snatched it from his hand, his ire spilling over to impatience. "You read it?"

"It was on a card, not in an envelope," Argent remonstrated, not a man used to defending himself. "How could I help myself?"

"Unscrupulous cretin." Morley's words had no heat as he looked at his name scrawled in flawless feminine script.

Argent's shoulder lifted. "I've been called worse." He stalled, lifting his hand to his jaw to rub at some tension there. "Morley...the murder case you handed over to me some months back, the Stags of St. James..."

He looked up at the uncertain note in Argent's voice before he'd been able to read the note. The Stags of St. James...a case growing colder by the day.

The very investigation that'd started this entire thing.

"What about it?"

Stoic features arranged themselves carefully, as if Argent knew he was treading on unstable ground. "I interviewed a man recently who intimated one of the Stags of St. James had regularly lain with a high-born, dark-haired beauty. He said she was a, and I quote, 'Good girl.'"

Good girl...as in...*Goode* girl?

Morley went very still, carefully examining the effect the information had on him.

It wasn't his Goode girl. He knew that. He trusted that. His wife had told him it had been a discussion between her friend and her elder sister that'd sent her looking for a stag in the first place.

"Prudence has a sister with dark hair," he said. "She's married, but could have used her maiden name for such purposes. She and her husband, William Mosby, the Viscount Woodhaven, were sent to Italy by the Baron."

Agent's brows made a slow decent as he pondered this. "How does a Baron send a Viscount to Italy, one wonders? Even if he is a son-in-law, I can't see a man like Woodhaven being easily told what to do."

"*Impoverished* Viscount," Morley clarified, rifling through some papers to find the slim file he'd made of Woodhaven on a whim. "Honoria's dowry and monthly upkeep is all that keeps them afloat, I've gathered."

"Honoria?" Argent echoed, his voice sharp as a blade in the close office. "If she's in Italy...how can your wife be meeting her at a row house in Gloucester Square?"

Morley's skin flushed hot, though his blood felt like ice in his veins as he looked down to scan his wife's hastily scrawled message.

Darling,

My sister has sent a carriage and request for my help. It seems Honoria is ill-treated by William, and has decided to leave him. I'll be at her residence at Gloucester Square to help her pack and figure out a new temporary living situation. I don't imagine I'll be late for dinner, though I warn you we might have a third guest at, what I've come to view as, our rather sacred suppers. I apologize in advance.

Yours,

Prudence

His thumb brushed over the word *Darling* before he stood, buttoned his jacket, and retrieved his hat. A slick of unease oozed between his ribs and he knew in his gut that he needed to go to his wife.

Puzzled by the strength of the instinct over such a trivial note, he stopped to inform Argent. "Their stay on the continent wasn't supposed to be indefinite, however..." He rubbed at a queer weight lodged beneath his sternum. "Something's not right."

It was all he needed to say to receive a grim nod from Argent. "I'm accompanying you to Gloucester Square, obviously."

They arrived a miraculous half hour later, after galloping through the streets as if the whole of London was Rotten Row.

The house was handsome, but not what one would expect of a Viscount, and Morley could only imagine what a blowhard like Woodhaven thought of his diminished circumstances.

Morley unceremoniously shoved past a sputtering butler intent upon denying them entrance, and found Honoria in a dimly lit drawing room, squinting down at a book with a glass of wine in her hand.

It wasn't even half one in the afternoon.

Dark, raptor-keen eyes lifted, advertising that the woman was not yet in her cups.

"Chief Inspector," she greeted blithely before snapping the book closed and gathering the voluminous, cream-colored skirts of her dress to stand.

Morley was given to understand it was widely accepted that Honoria was the great beauty of the Goode daughters, but he couldn't bring himself to agree. There was a sharpness to the symmetry of her features that he'd never prefer to look upon. Too many pointed angles and dramatic lines. He much preferred his wife's pleasant, ethereal comeliness.

"Do come in. I haven't been able to properly meet dear Prudence's husband. Please," she gestured to a piece of furniture that must have been expensive half a century prior, "sit down and I'll ring for tea."

"Where is Prudence?" he queried, eschewing her civil offer. His hand couldn't seem to release the door latch. He wouldn't relax until he set eyes on his wife.

"Certainly not here." Her features were smooth and cool as tempered glass.

Morley's heart stalled. "Then where? Where did the carriage take her?"

The only outward sign of a response was the slight tilt of her head. "Are you telling me you have...lost my sister, Chief Inspector? Because I assure you the last place she would be likely to venture is this...woebegone house."

"If not lost." He shoved the card at her. "Then she's been taken."

"I'll search the house," Argent said, neglecting to ask for permission as he began opening every door down the hall of the first floor.

Honoria scanned the note two full times, her composure crumbling like the walls of an ancient fortress ruin. "Dear God." She covered her mouth as eyes brimming with moisture flew to his. "William forged this note. I swear it. If she is in one of our carriages then...he has her."

"Woodhaven," Morley said, feeling his muscles harden at the uttered name. He never liked the man's reaction to Prudence, but he'd dismissed it as the lunacy of grief. A brief investigation of him had him dismissing the man as a coddled milksop dining out on his family's ancient name. If he'd returned from

Italy so soon, could he intend to take revenge on the woman he blamed for his best mate's death?

"He was so angry, about so many things," Honoria revealed in a horrified whisper. "But I didn't think he'd—" Unable to finish the thought, she rushed forward. "Please. Come with me. I might know where they are."

A cold blade of dread slid between his ribs, threatening his own poise. "Would he hurt her because of Sutherland?"

She caught her lips between her teeth as if biting them could hold back tears. "If I had to guess, it has something to do with me."

"What do you have to do with it?"

"My husband is an obsessive man, Chief Inspector," she said, revealing the shadows that haunted the façade of serenity as she stepped past him to reach for her shawl in the front entry. "He is vindictive and manipulative. The only thing that controls him, is his need to control me. His need to *make* me love him. Make me…God. You can't know what life with him is like."

"If he has touched a hair on Prudence's head, you won't have to worry about living with him anymore," Morley said darkly. "Where have they gone?"

"William told me he and some partners of one of his investment schemes had business at the Chariton's Dock in Southwark."

Morley didn't know the place. He thought he knew every inch of this city, but that dock didn't even ring a bell.

"There's an old flour storage warehouse there. My father bought it years ago, but he's done nothing with it. I know William's been working out of it. I can show you where it is."

"How many men would he have with him?" Argent asked from where he glided down the hall. "Would these partners be armed, perchance?"

The question drew her eyes wide with panic, but she shook

her head. "I-I don't know. I rarely mark my husband when he's discussing business. You have to understand, he's never had one of his ventures succeed." Her brows knit together. "But this one, it's been profitable. He's not been able to keep himself from throwing the income in my face but...I don't have the details."

"I'm going." Morley rushed back toward the door.

"So am I." Honoria dogged him down the steps and onto the front walk before he turned and seized her by the shoulders.

His grip gentled when he felt her tense and flinch.

"You're staying here," he fought to keep his voice gentle against the rising tide of his own urgency.

"She's my *sister*. Besides, you just said you don't know where it is."

Argent jogged down the stairs after them. "We might need backup if these associates are as shady as they are likely to be. I'll go for Dorian and Ash."

"Very good." Morley angled himself in the opposite direction, lamenting how much city lay between Southwark and Mayfair. "I'll meet you at the docks."

Argent stopped him with a hand on his arm. "Is that wise? To go alone?"

"I don't give a dusty fuck if it's wise," he growled. "It's what is happening."

The large man assessed him with that cold, cold gaze of his. "Are you good, Morley? Where is your rage?"

"What sort of question is that?" he asked impatiently.

"An important one," Argent insisted in that monotonous way of his. "Where is it? Because I can't see it. Is the fury deep or is it close to the surface? Can you make the decisions that have to be made? Because that is your wife and unborn child. What if you arrive to find the worst—?"

"Don't," Morley snarled, wrenching his arm away and shoving his finger in the assassin's brutal face. They stood like that for a moment, Morley's breath sawing in and out of his chest. "Just...*don't*."

It didn't bear consideration. It would be the loss that shattered him completely.

Morley glanced at his reflection in the window. He didn't look like himself. Harsh. Mean. Drawn tight and locked down. His eyes gone flat.

Dead.

"I'm going to get my wife," he said. "You do what you will, I'll do what I must."

Argent nodded, leaving him with his departing words. "Wait for us, Morley. Don't let your fury endanger her life. I made that mistake once and Millie paid for it with blood."

Morley leapt onto his horse and reached down to pull Honoria up behind him.

"I didn't know she was with child," Honoria said into his ear. "Is it...George's?"

"It's mine," he growled, gathering up his reins. "Now, I'm going to ride like hell," he warned. "Can you hold on?"

"Like hell is the only way we Goode Girls ride," she said, her voice flinty with an admirable strength.

Morley spurred his horse out into the square, astonishing society matrons and bustling errand staff as he went.

Where *was* his rage? What emotion lived in him now?

Fury was often hot. A constant companion of masculine brutality he assumed every man carried within him.

But not now. *This* emotion was stark. Unutterably bleak. An icy chill that echoed through a vast yawning abyss opening in his chest. This was what caused men to summon demons and sacrifice virgins. This rage. This power. This need to crush and consume. This desperate hope to stop all things beyond his control if only to protect that which was most precious.

Men like Argent. They owned their darkness. They wore it on their skin. He'd always had to hide his behind a badge of gold. Or a black mask. He had to pretend the darkness wasn't there. Waiting. Breeding. Growing.

His was patient fury. A glowing ember of ever-present wrath.

And now, that fury was about to be unleashed.

CHAPTER 19

*P*rudence wondered if the fact that she carried a child made her more or less likely to survive her brother-in-law's madness.

It was the most awful thing she'd ever had to contemplate.

He'd shoved her in the corner of a long warehouse with a labyrinth of wooden crates haphazardly strewn about the moldy stone floor. Crates he and his four comrades were now frantically prying apart with crowbars, flinging the lids, and diving into as if they might contain the holy grail.

The afternoon was grey, but abundant windows filtered light into the two-story warehouse that was little more than an open floor free of landings or offices. One wide wooden gate would open right onto the docks where steam-powered boats unloaded their goods for storage and dissemination out of the wide bay facing Water Street. From the skeleton of a silo taking up nearly the entire street-side entrance and the strange, layered architecture of the roof, Prudence thought maybe this had once been a place to store grain or flour.

Impossible to tell now.

She'd suffered the bulk of her paralyzing panic in the

carriage, where William had shoved a pistol in her face and screamed at the driver to ride on. Her saving grace was that he had done a horrible job of tying her wrists and ankles.

Thank God.

Taking advantage of their distraction, she worked frantically on the bonds. The ones at her hands were loosening, of that she had no doubt, she just had to keep at it.

It was the only thing that gave her hope. The one reason she kept a tenuous hold on her sanity.

Because once she was free, she'd have to figure out her next step...

How to get past five men with pistols tucked into vest holsters or waistbands when she had no weapon at all.

One thing at a time.

At least he wouldn't get away with it, she thought. If the worst happened...her husband would miss her at dinner, and he'd come looking. He'd *know* who had her.

Morley...a well of longing surged inside with such visceral desperation, it escaped on a sob.

William straightened from another fruitless search, slicking his thinning hair back from a sweating brow as he speared her with a pinched glare. A gentleman of leisure like him was unused to such strenuous exertion. Especially one as soft and bloated as he.

"Your fucking husband," he sniped, as if reading where her thoughts had just been lingering. "Gave the order for old Goode to send me abroad without so much as a by-your-leave. Just to save your narrow hide." Thin lips parted in a leer so chock-full of disgust, she could barely look at him. "What did he think, that I would take orders from him? A *nobody?*"

She wanted to tell him that her husband wasn't a nobody. That he was more advantageous a spouse than a dozen viscounts or even a hundred dukes.

She held her temper, for the sake of her child.

"He thought you'd help your family in crisis," she said evenly, trying to keep him calm. "William, if this is about Geor—"

"*This family*, so uppity for such low rank." He shook his head and began to wedge his crowbar into the next waist-high crate. "I've done my part for this family, merely by elevating it from the slums of mediocrity."

He threw his body weight down on the crowbar and tipped the lid aside before wading into the shavings of protective packaging. "Why do they even allow Barons to keep titles, anyhow?" he said as though muttering to himself. "They're hardly needed these days, it's not the Middle Ages. And your father, debasing himself with this shipping venture to make his fortunes, only to remain so miserly with his stipends." His lip curled in disgust. "A tighter bankbook doesn't exist in Christendom. *Where is it!*" In a shocking explosion of temper, he pushed over an entire crate. Prudence cringed away as it splintered, spilling an array of silks that unspooled in a riot of color.

"What are you looking for?" she asked, hoping to keep him talking as the knot at her right hand *finally* gave enough for her to slip through it, rendering the other one useless.

Still, she kept her hands behind her back.

"Payment for the risk I took," he snarled. "Payback! I've a barge waiting at the end of the dock, and we'll be out to sea before we're missed with a crate full of cash."

"If this is about money…"

"Of course, it's about money!" he roared "Every bloody thing is about money these days. Birth and titles and blue blood mean nothing anymore in this churning, blasphemous machine that is our nation now. What happened to the nobility?"

She leveled him her coolest stare. "Are you acting nobly now, William?"

"Don't question me, you sanctimonious cow." He struck her

with the back of his hand, wrenching her neck to the side. Pain singed her cheek and brought tears to her eyes.

An explosion shattered the very next moment.

Prudence managed to look back in time to see one of the men nearest a window drop to the crate he'd been bent over.

Missing the top of his head.

She covered her open mouth with both of her hands to contain the scream bubbling up from inside of her. It escaped as a raw, strangled sound.

Another crack resounded through the warehouse, shattering the window beside where a grizzled man reached for his weapon.

The bullet sheared through his neck.

Pandemonium erupted outside the warehouse as day laborers and dock workers scattered at the unmistakable sounds of a rifle.

Prudence was sorry for their fright, even as her chest expanded with elated, overjoyed relief.

He was here. Her Knight of Shadows.

He'd come for her.

William dropped the crowbar and drew his pistol as he and the two remaining men scrambled to find from which shadow the gunman fired.

"Don't fucking stand at the windows, you bloody imbeciles!" he screeched.

The hired thugs took longer than was wise to recover after the initial volley, and Morley was able to clip the wing of a third man before they scrambled to take cover behind the very crates they'd been searching.

A deafening barrage of bullets pinged everywhere from the floor to the few skylights above. Prudence dropped to her knees, covering her head with her hands as slivers of splintered wood rained down on her.

Eventually, they ran out.

Her heart skipped several beats in the eerie silence that followed.

Had they gotten him? Had they shot the man she loved? Her one hope at salvation?

Right when happiness was in their grasp?

The sound of glass breaking behind them stole their attention to the far end of the warehouse by the loading bay. One more man dropped to his death before the echoes of the gun blast finished rebounding in her head.

"William," she hissed, tucking her legs beneath her so she could loosen the rope around her boots. "Let me go now, or this will end very badly for you." Her foot popped free on the last syllable, roughening it with strain.

He opened the cylinder of his pistol and shoved his shaking hand in his vest pocket, extracting two bullets and angling them into the chambers. "Do you *really* think it's wise to threaten me?"

"I'm not threatening you, I'm warning you," she cried. "My husband was a long-distance rifleman in the army. He's going to shoot every man in this room. He's *going* to *kill* you."

"Not before I kill you."

Prudence spied the crowbar he'd dropped next to a container and lunged for it, hoping to get it before he had the chance to reload that gun.

He surged up, caught her by the hair, and wrenched her back against him, using her as a human shield.

The cold kiss of the pistol against her temple matched the metallic taste of fear in her mouth.

"Either we both get out of this alive. Or neither of us will," he yelled to the unseen gunman before whispering to her. "Not that you deserve to live."

He dragged her so his back was against the stone wall, clutching her to his front with an arm locked around her neck.

Any tighter and she'd choke.

"I didn't kill George," she panted, both hands pulling at his arm to keep her throat from being compressed. "I swear. There's no reason to hurt me."

"I've known that all along, you idiot cunt. Who do you think plunged the knife through his neck?"

Shock sent Prudence's limbs completely slack.

It made sense. William had found her. He'd been so keen to point the finger at her.

Because it got him off, scot-free.

"He was…your—your closest friend!" she cried.

"The friend who fucked my wife." Hatred dropped like acid from his words.

"*What?*"

"Don't be too sore at Honoria," he said in a voice as dry as sawdust. "She had her scruples. When I told her I was going to set up a match between you and George, she protested most ferociously. Until finally I sussed out why. She was bending over for him at least three times a month. It disgusted and disturbed her, to think of her lover fucking her sister."

Prudence fought for breath, her panic flaring to a fever pitch as they neared the doors out to the docks. Honoria? And George? The betrayal of her sister sliced through her worse than any pain George might have caused her.

"I told her if you ever found out about them, I'd ruin you in a way she hadn't yet conceived of. And she knew me well enough to believe me."

"But, I've done nothing to you," Pru said in a broken voice.

He'd finally made it to the far corner of the warehouse, and he dared to peek up to see if he could open the door without a hand blowing off.

The air remained still but for the clamor outside. "All wars have collateral damage, I'm afraid." His voice echoed off the cold stone walls. "Besides, you deserve it now. That bloody husband of yours has been getting in my way. Confiscating my goods. Arresting my brokers and interrupting my supply chain all to clear your name."

"The cocaine," she realized aloud. "You were smuggling it in my father's ships?"

He let out a long-suffering sigh. "I care not for the stuff," he said. "I was going to boil the frog slowly, establish the vulgar shipments to smuggle in goods, make a tidy fortune. Then, tip off the police so the Baron would be arrested. George too, as I forged his name on the papers. And I'd walk away with your father's wealth as well."

"But you killed him instead? On our wedding day?"

He made a noise of derision. "Did you know, by the time you were to marry, George was actually besotted with you? That he was thinking of trying at being a decent man. That's when I knew, he didn't get to claim happiness. None of them get to. And I ended him. Now open the fucking door."

She reached out and fumbled with the latch, her fingers weak and cold from lack of blood. *Wait*, she paused. "None of whom?"

"The men my slag of a wife fucked beneath my own roof!" he roared.

Prudence froze. "The Stags of St. James," she whispered.

"Whores!" Panic and rage, it seemed, was making him maniacal. "My wife paid *whores*. They defamed her. They turned her into a creature of vile lusts and tempted her to stray. Men like them, like George, cunning and handsome and charismatic."

"So you...murdered them?"

"If only to make *her* pay twice. Thrice, even. She had bruises where no one can see. She has wounds that will never heal. I made sure of it. But still she wouldn't keep to *my* bed. She didn't obey me. She didn't fear me! And so, she forced my hand. I've put every man who touched my wife into the ground. As a warning to her...she has no ground to run to, not even after we make our getaway. I'll come for her. I will—"

"Why not take me now?" The door swung open, and the gun ground into Prudence's head with devastating force.

At the sound of Honoria's voice, William cinched his arm so tight, little stars danced in Prudence's periphery as she fought for breath.

Honoria stood at the doorway draped in gingham and cream silk, her features almost serene in their perfection. Her beauty a beacon in the chaos of blood, bodies, and broken glass.

Prudence clawed at William's arm, trying to warn her sister, to scream her name.

Honoria only shook her head. "William. Is all this really necessary? Could you not have just taken me with you today, instead?"

"Honoria," he choked out, his hold slackening a little. "You came."

"Of course I did," she said with a coy roll of her eyes. "You're my husband. Do you think I would have let you get away?"

The sound he made was pure anguish and abject joy.

It disgusted Pru, who couldn't help but search the doorway for another shadow. For the man who could come put an end to the horror.

He was here. He'd already leveled the entire field. But... where was he now? What could he do?

"Go, Honoria," Pru pleaded. "He's mad."

Her sister never broke eye contact with her husband. "He knows exactly what he's doing. He always does, don't you, husband?" She held a hand out, the elegant fingers steady and coaxing. "Now let us leave here, together."

"The money," he said, in the voice of a plaintive boy. "It's not in the blasted crate it was supposed to be in. I haven't found it yet."

"Because I seized it last night."

At the sound of Morley's seemingly disembodied voice, William cocked the pistol at Prudence's temple, drawing a shameful whimper from her.

No, Morley hadn't seized the money. He'd been with her all night. Why was he lying? Why would he upset the man with the gun to her head?

"Don't you dare, Inspector," William crowed. "I'm taking the boat and crossing the channel. These two are my tickets out of Blighty, do you understand?"

"That is where you're wrong," said the shadows. "You're not taking one more step."

"Or what, eh? Do you want me to paint the floor with her brains?"

"William, no," Honoria pleaded, her façade of composure cracking. "She's pregnant. I *know* you wouldn't kill a child."

"It seems I picked the wrong sister," a disgusted William hissed in her ear. "Honoria's dry and barren as the Sahara, and frigid as the Arctic."

"Only toward you," she said in a voice gone flat as death. "I made certain your seed never took root, but none of my other lovers found me cold."

William's entire body tensed, and for a moment, Prudence knew it was over. Time slowed to a fraction of its pace, and the greatest regret she could muster in her last moment was that she wouldn't get to see her beloved husband's face before the end.

A tear escaped her as she squeezed her eyes shut.

He jerked, and a shot detonated, the pain lancing the side of her head with a searing agony she'd not expected to feel before the end. Another shot blasted. And another.

The weight of his arm around her throat immediately released and she screamed in a long breath.

I'm...alive, was her first thought. But the pain...had she even been shot?

More puzzled than shocked, Pru opened her eyes in time to witness the immediate aftermath.

William's gun was no longer aimed at her head, but forward, before his hand went slack and the weapon clattered to the ground.

Honoria's eyes swung to hers and they held for a moment as the only sound Prudence could hear was the air screaming with one insufferable monosyllabic note.

The pain was only in her ear, because the pistol had discharged next to it.

A starburst of red appeared on Honoria's buttercream bodice right above her heart.

They both stared down at the bullet wound in her sister's chest as William's body slumped to the ground, a puddle of blood rushing beneath her boots.

Her husband had killed him, but not before William had taken a shot at his own wife.

Prudence's scream echoed from far away as she launched herself forward, hoping to catch her sister before the woman's buckling legs failed her.

CHAPTER 20

Dorian Blackwell swooped inside, catching Honoria in his arms as she slumped forward.

Prudence panicked at the dire look he gave her as he lifted Honoria with a grunt and swept her from the warehouse, out onto the planked unloading dock.

Prudence scrambled after them, daylight blinding her as she seized her sister's hand and brought it to her cheek.

"Honoria! No. Oh, please. Can you hear me?" she cried as Blackwell gingerly settled her sister down flat on the planks of the dock and ripped her petticoats to create a bandage. He shoved it into Prudence's hands and guided her to press down on the bullet wound with brutal pressure.

"Keep this here," he ordered before he surged to his feet and left them. "Don't move."

Pru couldn't imagine how terrible the pain of a bullet was, but Honoria's eyes merely fluttered, her features draining from pale to a ghostly shade.

"Don't go. Don't go," Pru pleaded with her sister. "Not when you're finally safe. Finally rid of him."

Honoria's dark eyes opened and caught hers for a

moment, flooded with some awful emotion she couldn't identify. Her lips moved, but the pressure and ringing in Prudence's ears still impeded her from hearing such breathy tones.

"I can't hear you. Dammit. I can't hear you," she lamented.

Honoria's bloodless lips moved more deliberately, her porcelain features pinched with pain. "I'm sorry. I should have told you...I...was afraid..."

"Shh. Shh. Shh." Prudence wanted to smooth her hair, but she dared not let up on the pressure of her wound. "Honoria, I didn't know what he was. What he was doing to you. No wonder you strayed. I'm not angry about George. Please don't blame yourself. Just—Just be well."

"I love you," her sister murmured through her tears, and Prudence was glad to note enough of her hearing had returned that she could make out the words. "We don't say any of that, do we? We Goodes. But I do. I love you."

"I love you too," Pru said, tears leaking from the tip of her nose. "I will for a long time so don't start saying that like you mean goodbye."

"You are a wonderful sister. And I...I'm not..."

Prudence looked up at the almost-deserted docks, noting some brave souls began to push themselves away from the places behind which they'd taken shelter. "Send for an ambulance!" she shrieked at them.

"I've done one better," Dorian said, leading men back toward them. They set down two poles and spread a canvas material between them, presumably erecting a makeshift stretcher. "There's a sawbones not two streets over I've used for a decade to dig bullets out of men who don't want questions asked at hospitals."

"Absolutely not!"

Despite her near-hysteria, his features softened as he regarded her. "Lady Morley, I've seen a lot of wounds like this.

It's unlikely to be fatal if we get her immediate care and cleaning. Allow me to—"

"I will allow you *nothing*," she threw her body over her sister's, bracing her weight on her hands. "You will get an ambulance and she will be taken to a hospital, not some underworld sawbones. I'll not have it!"

Blackwell made a sound of impatient consternation. "Where is your husband, I wonder?"

"He was *supposed* to wait for us." The man she recognized as Millie LeCour's husband, Argent, peered into the doorway and took stock of the significant carnage inside. "He didn't leave aught for us to do but clean up the corpses." If she didn't know better, she'd have thought he sounded plaintive.

As if he were looking forward to the violence.

"I suggest you get to it then." A voice from above drew their notice, and they all looked to the roof of the warehouse where Morley stood against the slate grey sky.

Of course. He hadn't been shooting in through the windows. At least not the ones on the ground floor. He'd somehow scaled the building to the second or third floors and shot down through the smaller portals above. He'd have had to navigate the sharp angle of the roof and steady himself on precarious perches to shoot from such angles at such distances into the dimness.

His skill was nothing short of miraculous.

Morley dropped his rifle down to Argent, and then deftly levered himself over the edge of the roof, controlling his drop with only the strength of his arms until his feet were far enough from the ground to drop into a crouch.

He scanned the area, his gaze skipping right over Prudence as he stood and adjusted his cravat that had gone only slightly askew through the entire ordeal.

"Morley," Blackwell held up his hands helplessly, though he

was no longer armed. "You know Conleith; he's more than an adequate surgeon."

"Titus Conleith?" Morley's sharp jaw hitched as he stalked toward them with the predatory grace of a jungle cat. "That Irish devil dug more bullets out of more soldiers than any man alive. He could do it blindfolded."

Prudence didn't budge, something inside her had snapped. "This is no battlefield surgeon's tent," she hissed. "This is my *sister* and—"

"Titus Conleith?" Honoria astonished them all by breathing out the name in a ragged sob. She clutched at Prudence with clawlike fingers. "Take me to him," she begged. "Take me to him, *now*. You must let them, Pru," she said, her eyes over-flowing with desperate tears. "You must."

Pru peered down at her, trying to remember the last time she'd seen Honoria cry. "Are you certain?"

Honoria's eyes were wild and extra dark in a face drawing paler by the moment. "I—I need him. Please, Pru, let me up. Let them take me."

Scampering back, Prudence felt herself being lifted to her feet by strong arms and anchored to her husband's side as Blackwell and the men gingerly boosted her sister onto their makeshift stretcher and navigated the docks back toward the road.

"I should go with her," she fretted, her legs suddenly feeling like they'd lost their bones.

She'd never liked William. She'd never been very close to her sister; Honoria had always made it impossible. Was it any wonder she'd been so aloof? So alone. She'd been locked in a private hell inside her own home.

Married to a monster.

"You are going *nowhere*." Her husband still refused to look down at her, his mouth compressed into a tight hyphen as he sized up a few of the dock workers looking on in slack-jawed amazement.

"You," he ordered, pointing to a steely-eyed laborer in his fifties. "Go to M Division on Blackman Street. Ask for Sgt. Catesby and a contingent of men to secure the docks."

"Sir." The man touched his cap and hopped too, as men tended to do when Morley gave an order.

"Argent." He turned to where the heavy-built man in a sharp auburn suit was examining the rifle in his hands. "Send our men round to the Commissioner Goode's residence in case Viscount Woodhaven had any thugs making mischief there. Then, I want Detective Inspectors Sean O'Mara and Roman Rathbone to tear through any of the Baron's warehouses to find the missing crates with the contraband Woodhaven was looking for."

Argent gave a sardonic two-fingered salute and sauntered off.

"The rest of you, this dock is closed until further notice, clear off."

A few laborers, obviously unhappy about the loss of a day's wages, looked as if they'd argue. Others, perhaps the ones who'd witnessed Morley's capabilities on the roof, dragged them away without making eye contact.

Her husband was not a man in the habit of repeating himself.

That handled, he hauled Prudence with him as he strode for the river-side corner of the warehouse beyond which steam barges and various pleasure boats churned the river with their relentless traffic.

The moment they turned the corner, she gasped to find herself immediately trapped between a rock wall and a hard place—the hard place being her husband's body.

His hands were everywhere as a torrent of curses spilled from his lips. "Jesus Christ, Prudence. Did he hurt you?"

His fingers searched her face as if he were a blind man, his thumb hovering over her cheek where William had struck her. His glacial eyes flared with unnerving intensity he visibly struggled to contain.

Drowning in the unspoken but not invisible tension between them, she opened her mouth to speak, but nothing emerged. No words came forth to express the sheer incalculable emotion sweeping through her in knee-weakening waves.

An emotion she could now identify but didn't have the courage to express.

"I'm—we're—all right," she finally assured in a voice much wobblier than she'd intended.

"Well, I'm bloody not!" he burst, pushing away from her to rake shaking hands through his hair. "Never," he said with a hostile glare. "Never will you put yourself in danger for the sake of another, is that clear?"

"But...she's my sister. Surely you can appreciate the importance of that. You put your life on the line for people every day." She kept her voice even, soft, appreciating the volatility simmering through the heavy musculature of his shoulders and arms, heaving his chest into swells of uneven breaths. "Every night," she added meaningfully.

"I'm well aware of my hypocrisy, Prudence," he snapped. "But it doesn't fucking matter. You can't—I won't bloody—God! I'm not built for this." He paced three steps away, and then returned as if ricocheting off an invisible wall.

His words lanced through her, and she went taut with fear, grateful for the wall behind her, holding her up. "For...for what?" she asked in a watery breath, wondering if everything was about to change.

If she was about to lose him.

"For loving you, goddammit," he said with an almost savage antipathy. "I have to fight the image of that bastard's gun against your temple every time I close my eyes. For the rest of my damnable life. I have to relive the agony of possibly losing you. Of losing both of you."

"Oh…" she breathed, her heart giving a few extra thumps.

"It'll drive me mad," he ranted. "This unholy, unhealthy need I have to bask in your presence. This possession—no—this *obsession*. How am I supposed to run London's entire police force when I'm so consumed by you?"

"I—"

He wasn't finished by half. "I'm tempted to haul you to work with me and throw you in the cell, just so I can be certain of your safety. What sort of lunatic does that make me? Do you think that I could have survived this had it turned out differently?" He gestured to himself with sharp, wild arms. "And all of this right after last night. Right when I have everything I want in my grasp, *everything*. If he'd have—" His voice broke and he covered it with a rough sort of growl. "I swear, I've never felt fear like that before, Prudence. I've had you for a blink of time in my life, and yet, I'd have eaten a bullet before facing the rest of my years without you." He turned to her, his face mottled and the tips of his ears red as he nigh trembled with unspent emotion. "Now," he demanded. "What do you have to say for yourself?"

Prudence wondered if he could see the radiance in her heart shining through her eyes. If he knew how every word of his dressing-down had fallen like a Byronic poem on her ears. She wondered if she could ever have anything to say that could mean so much, because all she could come up with was, "I—I love you, too."

He blinked, his features gone perfectly blank.

Then, he seized her in a lightning fast motion, buried his hands in her dark hair, and slanted his mouth over hers, kissing her with a desperate ferocity.

Prudence surrendered to the kiss instantly. She understood

now, what his coldness out on the docks had meant. The reason he wouldn't look at her.

He had to make sure everything was taken care of before the fissures in his composure cracked, and then shattered. He'd just killed five men with five bullets. He'd climbed a three-story warehouse and, stealthily as a cat, he'd put his deadeye to use.

When the warmth between them kindled into heat, he tore his mouth away, apparently aware of their surroundings.

He put his forehead on hers and they shared desperate breaths as he smoothed his hands down her arms to her waist, splaying his palms on her middle. "I shouldn't have admonished you," he admitted in a voice laced with regret. "Especially not after the trauma you've had. Christ, all I want is to wipe this day from your memory. To erase the bruise forming on your cheek. To coddle and cosset you. It's damned unsettling." His brow wrinkled with chagrin.

She nudged him with her nose. "I want to remember this day forever. I will look back on this as the day you saved my life and freed my sister from the clutches of an evil man." She smiled, winding her arms around his neck as she clutched him close. "I'll remember this as the day you said you loved me."

His arms stole around her, bringing her fully against him, as if he couldn't hold her close enough for his liking. "I promise you, Prudence, I'll say it every day for the rest of our lives together."

Though she was still weak-limbed from the panic and strain of her ordeal, she thrilled with a sense of fulfillment and belonging. As if his love strengthened her, lacing threads of steel in the silken feminine fabric of her being. Nothing would tear them apart. Not lies nor doubt. Not villains nor adversaries nor their own wounded hearts.

Drawing back, she looked up into his dear, dear face, and

thought she might have seen something of the same sentiment lurking in the silver-blue brilliance of his gaze.

"Did you hear?" she asked, hope and pain catching in her throat. "Did you hear William confess to George's murder? And to the Stags of St. James?"

"I did, sweetheart." He flicked his gaze to the side, shadows reclaiming some of his brilliance. "I could grovel at your feet for a decade and it wouldn't assuage my guilt."

She reached up and traced the fine divot in his chin with a fingertip. "I would say it's not necessary," she shrugged. "But if groveling is what will placate your conscience, far be it for me to stop you."

He huffed the ghost of a chuckle against her hair as his arms tightened. "All right, my little minx of a wife...I'll admit I'm new to groveling. How does one go about it?"

She took a full minute to pretend to consider. Not to punish him, per se, but to enjoy the circle of his protective embrace. To feel their heartbeats synchronize as she pressed her head against his strong shoulder. To nest in the one place she'd truly felt alive. And at home.

From the first night she'd given herself to him, a stranger.

"I imagine foot rubs are excellent groveling techniques," she ventured.

"I imagine you're right."

"And long Sunday mornings in bed."

"Now," he tutted. "That's a reward, not a punishment."

"I suppose, groveling is neither of our strong suits." She buried a smile in his shirt. "I want to reward you."

"You are my greatest prize," he said, stiffening a little as the chaos of emergency sirens and the clattering of horse hooves against the planks shook the docks beneath their feet.

She pulled from his embrace with a weary sigh, drawing her hand down his arm to lace her fingers with his. "This life of yours, it will always be thus, I gather." She gestured to the warehouse full of chaos, the advancing lawmen, the curious milling crowds. "Whether you're the Chief Inspector or the Knight of Shadows."

His eyes glimmered with concern, a frown pinching his brow as he looked toward the approaching tide as if he would send them away. "You deserve more than—"

She turned him to face her. "If I'd have you promise me anything, it's this. I know you are a hero to many, but you are only husband to me. I will not be your mistress while the law is your wife, and your children will not be bastards. I cannot live in an empty house and sleep in an empty bed and love a man who has been drained empty by the demands of this city."

"I know," he said.

"That being said, I'm proud of what you do," she soothed. "Of who you are, and I'd not change that. I will send you out that door every day. But you must come home to me. I must hold you and love you and make love to you. You must eat properly, and rest appropriately, and find a bloody hobby, do you understand? Something that wastes time, but you enjoy for no reason."

His smile tilted over to a perplexed grimace. "A hobby?"

She just shook her head. "We'll have that row later."

He seemed to accept this with a Gallic sort of sobriety as he turned toward the streets. "I can send Farah and the ladies to come get you. You don't have to face all this."

The offer was tempting, but she shook her head, looping her arm through his. "We'll face it all together."

Just like they would everything from now on.

As a family.

EPILOGUE

FOUR MONTHS LATER

*M*orley lounged in bed with his cheek against his wife's creamy shoulder, gazing down at the mountain of her belly. He was only half listening as she, stretched on her back and naked beneath the sheets, read a Knight of Shadows penny dreadful aloud, stopping to giggle at a particularly unbelievable passage.

This Knight of Shadows business was certainly getting out of hand, but luckily, he'd recruited a few promising men to take up the occasional mantle. It was interesting to hear the conflicting reports of criminals and civilians alike who'd a chance meeting. Sometimes he was average height, lean, fair-haired and agile. Other times, a dark-skinned mountain of a man, able to meld with the shadows. He was a youth, or mature. Spoke with an exotic accent, an Irish one, or his own on Tuesdays and every other Friday.

He'd kept his word and it hadn't been difficult for a moment. Their quiet nights together soothed his soul and excited everything that made him a man.

They made ceaseless love in increasingly creative positions, as her stomach became an impediment. Then they'd talk, or laugh, or read until one of them, usually her, drifted to sleep.

Tonight, she seemed unusually restless and uncomfortable, so they'd mounted pillows beneath her knees and he'd promised to suffer while she amused herself with one of the new rash of novels written about his exploits.

Rain tapped on the windows, casting the shadows of rivulets upon the bed. The optical effect lulled him as did the lively rendition of his wife's voice.

"Oh, dear," she mocked. "The Knight of Shadows is about to sweep the damsel onto the rooftops and debauch her! Listen to this…"

He levered up, clasping his hands on both sides of her belly as if it had sprouted ears. "I beg you to spare innocent ears," he teased. "That can hardly be appropriate!"

She threw the book at him, missing on purpose. "Neither are the things you say when you're making love to me."

He cast her a chastised, wretched look. "Touché." Leaning down, he gathered the sheets away from her breast, and then swept them down her belly so he could lay his ear against it and close his eyes.

He loved to listen for the little one, and tonight a slight nudge pushed back against the pressure of his cheek.

His breath caught, and Pru's did, as well, her hand reaching down to sift and stroke the strands of his hair.

"I was thinking…" she murmured dreamily. "If one of them is a girl…we could name her Caroline. Or does that cause you pain?"

He opened his eyes, an ache bloomed in his chest both bitter and exquisitely sweet. "It hurts to remember, but it would be worse to forget," he told her honestly.

Honesty had become their default communication, and because of it, they flourished.

"Her loss has become a part of me. I'll never forget her. But she is a part of the past I can reconcile. With this. With you. And I'd love to give her name to our child. To allow her the childhood she never had…"

"I'm glad you feel that way," she gifted him a beatific smile, and his heart glowed.

Then stalled.

"Wait." He sat up and looked down into her eyes with a frantically pulsating heart. "Did you just say *them*…?"

Her face shone up at him, incandescent with maternal pride.

"I must have done," she said, pulling him back to collapse against her in bewildered amazement. "Because we're having twins."

COURTING TROUBLE

PROLOGUE

CHARITON'S DOCK, SOUTHWARK, LONDON,
1880

*A*s Honoria's blood pooled onto the dock from the bullet wound, she felt oddly relieved.

She was ready to die.

Marriage to William Mosby, the Viscount Woodhaven, had first stripped her of any innocence she'd had left. Then of her joy. Her confidence. And finally, her decency.

To slake her unceasing misery—or perhaps in defiance of her tyrant of a husband—she'd taken a handful of lovers over the years. One of those lovers, George Hamby-Forsyth, the Earl of Sutherland, had offered to marry her younger sister Prudence when Honoria had ended their affair.

William had forbidden Nora to tell Prudence about her previous affair. He'd threatened to ruin her sister and to visit tortures upon her she hadn't yet conceived of.

So she'd obeyed him.

She obeyed him!

How could she have been so stupid? So utterly selfish and blind? Her life was *already* a torment, and the ultimate torture was a marriage to the wrong man.

If Nora knew anything, it was that.

William had used her father's shipping company to smuggle cocaine into the country. He had sought out her lovers and murdered them, framing Prudence for the deed.

Her sister might have hanged if not for the protection of her new husband, Chief Inspector Carlton Morley.

As Morley closed in on him, William had baited Prudence to use as a hostage to escape the city. But first, he'd stopped at her father's Southwark warehouse to tear through stacks of crates, apparently searching for one full of money he'd had delivered.

Nora stood helpless as William held a gun to her precious younger sister's head.

Morley perched above on the warehouse roof, aiming his rifle at William, his shot frustrated as the bastard used Pru as a human shield.

All this could have been avoided if she'd not been a selfish coward.

Honoria often read that people heard a rushing in their ears or felt their hearts pounding against their rib cages before they did something reckless or heroic.

But facing the consequences of her actions, of her husband's treachery, tore her heart out of her chest. So, it didn't beat faster. Her blood didn't rush around.

She felt—numb. Detached. As if she no longer inhabited her body.

As if she'd died long ago.

And maybe she had.

Taking a breath, Honoria had stepped into the doorway and faced the man she hated most in this world. She'd taken in his thinning ashen hair, yellowed teeth, and expanding paunch, the consequence of a life devoted to vice and villainy. It was as if his viciousness and malevolence was beginning to seep from the insides and corrupt his physical body.

He'd taken the gun from her sister's temple, and shot her, instead.

As she fell, she watched Morley avenge his wife, putting William down for good with one shot from his powerful rifle.

Somehow, Nora had made it outside…and was looking up at the sky when she heard Prudence scream her name. Then her dear sister's face was hovering above her, dark eyes wild with fear.

With her last breaths, Nora tried to make things right. "I'm sorry. I should have told you…I…was afraid…"

"Shh. Shh. Shh," Prudence soothed. "I didn't know what he was. What he was doing to you. No wonder you strayed. I'm not angry about George. Please don't blame yourself. Just—"

"I love you." Nora forced the words through the burning pain. "We don't say any of that, do we? We Goodes. But I do. I love you."

"I love you too," Pru sobbed, tears leaking from the tip of her nose. "I will for a long time, so don't start saying that like you mean goodbye."

"You are a wonderful sister. And I…I'm not…"

She began to fade then, unable to feel the warmth of the afternoon sun, even though it still alighted on her face.

And then she heard *his* name.

Titus Conleith.

It brought her back to life, if only for a moment. She clawed at Prudence, begging for him. Pleading. Knowing it was too late.

Yes, she deserved to die, and worse.

Because long ago, she'd broken a boy. A beautiful boy with a true heart and a pure soul.

That sin had been unforgivable.

And she'd spent the last decade paying the price.

THE COAL BOY
LONDON, NOVEMBER 1865

itus Conleith had often fantasized about seeing Honoria Goode naked.

He'd been in an excruciating kind of love with her since he was a lad of ten. Now that he was undoubtedly a *man* at fourteen, his love had shifted.

Matured, he dared wager.

What he felt for her was a soft sort of reverence, a kind of awestruck incredulity at the sight of her each day. It was simply hard to believe a creature like her existed. That she moved about on this earth. In the house in which he *lived*.

That she was three years his senior at seventeen years of age was irrelevant, as was the fact that she stood three inches above him, more in her lace boots with the delicate heels. It mattered not that there existed no reality in which he could even approach her. That he could dare address her.

The idea of being with her in any capacity was so far beyond comprehension, it didn't bear consideration. He was the household boy-of-all-work for her father, Clarence Goode, the Baron of Cresthaven. Lower, even, than the chambermaid.

He swept chimneys and fetched things, mucked stables and cleaned up after dogs that ate better than he did.

When he and Honoria shared a room, he was beneath her feet, sometimes quite literally.

One of his favorite memories was perhaps a year prior when she'd scheduled to ride her horse in the country paddock and no mounting block could be found. Titus had been called to lace his hands together so Honoria might use them as a step up into her saddle.

He'd seen the top of her boot that day, and a flash of the lily-white stocking over her calf as he'd presumed to help slide her foot into the stirrup.

It was the first time she'd truly looked at him. The first time their eyes locked, as the sun had haloed around her midnight curls like one of those chipped, expensive paintings of the Madonna that hung in the Baron's gallery.

In that moment, her features had been just as full of grace.

"You're bleeding," she'd remarked, flicking her gaze to a shallow wound on the flesh of his palm where a splinter on a shovel handle had gouged deep enough to draw blood. Her boot had ground a bit of dirt into the wound.

And he'd barely felt the pain.

Titus had balled his fist and hid it behind his back, lowering his gaze. "Inn't nothing, miss."

Reaching into her pocket, she'd drawn out a pressed white handkerchief and dangled it in front of him. "I didn't see it, or I'd not have—"

"Honoria!" her mother had reprimanded, eyeing him reprovingly as she trotted her own mare between them, obliging him to leap back lest he be trampled. "To dawdle with them is an unkindness, as you oblige them to interaction they are not trained for. Really, you know better."

Honoria hadn't said a word, nor did she look back as she'd obediently cantered away at her mother's side.

But he'd retrieved her handkerchief from where it'd floated to the ground in her wake.

From that day on, it was her image painted on the backs of his eyelids when he closed them at night. Even when the scent of rose water had faded from his treasure.

Today, two of the three maids in the household had been too ill to work, and so the harried housekeeper tasked Titus with hauling the kindling into the east wing of the Mayfair manse to lay and light the fires before the family roused.

He'd done the master's first, then the mistress's, and had skipped Honoria's room for the nursery where the seven-year-old twins, Mercy and Felicity, slept.

Felicity had been huddled in bed, her golden head bent over a book as she squinted in the early morning gloom. The sweet-natured girl had given him a shy little wave as he tiptoed in and lit her a warm fire.

Against the mores of propriety, she'd thanked him in a whisper, and blushed when he'd given her a two-fingered salute before shutting the door behind him with a barely audible click. After tending to the hearths of the governess and the second-eldest Goode sister, Prudence, Titus finally found himself at Honoria's door.

He peered about the hall guiltily before admonishing himself for being ridiculous.

He was supposed to be here. It wouldn't do to squander this stroke of luck and not take any opportunity he could to be near her.

Alone.

Balancing the burden of kindling against his side with one arm, he reached for the latch of her doorway, then paused, examining his hands with disgust. He flexed knuckles stained black from shoveling and hauling coal into the burner of the huge stove that heated steam for the first two floors of the estate. Filth from the stables and the gardens embedded beneath his fingernails and settled in the creases and calluses of his palm.

A familiar mortification welled within his chest as he smoothed the hand over his shirt, hoping to buff some of the dirt off like an apple before trying the latch and peering around the door.

Titus loved that—unlike the rest of her family—Honoria slept with all her drapes tied open and the window nearest the honeysuckle vines cracked to allow the scent of the gardens to waft inside. It didn't seem to matter the season or the weather, he'd look up to her window to find it thusly open.

Sometimes he would sing while he worked outside. If he were lucky, the sound would draw her to the window, or at least he fancied it did, when she gazed out over the gardens.

Like the sun, he couldn't look at her for too long.

And she barely ever glanced at him.

Titus told himself if she closed the casement against the sound, he'd never utter another note.

But she hadn't.

It was as if she couldn't bear to be completely shut in. As if she couldn't bring herself to draw the drapes and close the world out.

On this morning, the November chill matched the slate grey of the predawn skies visible through her corner windows. Fingers of ice stole through his vest and thin shirt, prompting him to hurry and warm the room for her.

Shivering inside, he held his breath as he eased the door closed behind him, taking extra care against waking her as she'd been drawn and quiet for a few days and often complained of headaches.

In the dimness, she was little more than a slim outline beneath a mountain of arabesque silk bedclothes, curled with her back to him. Her braid an inky swath against the clean white pillow.

She occupied the second grandest bedroom, her being the eldest and all. The ceiling was tall enough to boast a crystal chandelier that matched the smaller sconces flanking her headboard. More than one wardrobe stood sentinel against the white wainscoting, containing her plethora of garments and gowns, each to be worn at different times of the day or for varied soirees, teas, and other such events unimaginable to someone like him.

She favored gem-bright hues over pastels, and silks over cottons and velvets. With her wealth of ebony hair and eyes so dark it was hard to distinguish pupil from iris, every cut and color flattered her endlessly.

But Titus knew red was her favorite. She wore it most often in every conceivable shade.

In the stillness of the morning, he could hear that her breaths were erratic and uneven, as if she were running in a dream, or struggling with some unseen foe.

On carpets as plush as hers, his feet made no sound as he tiptoed past the foot of a bed so cavernous that it would have swallowed his humble cot in the loft above the mews, three times over.

Was she having a nightmare?

Would it be a kindness to wake her?

Perhaps. But he'd expect to be summarily dismissed for even presuming to do such a thing.

He dawdled over the fire, laying the most perfect blaze ever constructed. Once the flames crackled and popped cheerfully in the hearth, he lingered still, content to simply share the air she breathed.

"Is it burning?"

Her hoarse words nearly startled him out of his own skin.

Titus jumped to his feet, upsetting his kindling basket, and dropping the poker on the stones with a thunderous clatter.

"The—the fire, miss? Aye. It's burning proper now. It'll

warm your bones and no mistake." Compared to her high-born dialect, his Yorkshire accent sounded like ripe gibberish, even to his own ears.

"It's burning me," she complained tightly, the words terse and graveled as if her throat closed over them.

"Miss?" His heart pounded as he approached her side of the bed, then sank at what he found.

Her braid was a tangle, escaped tendrils matted to her slick forehead and temples as if she'd done battle with it all night. Lines of pain crimped her brow and pinched the skin beside her lips thin and white.

She wasn't simply curled against the cold but, more accurately, around herself. As if to protect her torso from pain. Though beads of sweat gathered at her hairline and her upper lip, she shivered intermittently.

It was her eyes, though, that terrified him. Open, but fixed on nothing, not even noting his approach.

"Miss Goode?" he whispered. "Can you—can you hear me?"

Suddenly her limbs became restless as she arched and flailed weakly, shoving her bedcovers away from her body, revealing that she'd clawed her nightdress off sometime during the night.

Honoria Goode was pale in the most normal of circumstances, but her lithe nude limbs were nearly indistinguishable from the white sheets, but for the feverish red flush creeping up her torso, over her breasts, and toward her clavicles.

"It's burning my skin," she croaked, levering herself up on shaking arms. "Everywhere. Put it out, boy, *please.*"

Boy. Later, the word would pierce him like a lance.

She made a plaintive sound that sliced his guts open, and made to roll off the bed.

"No, miss. You're with fever. Lie still. I'll wake the house." Without thinking, he reached for her shoulders, meaning to keep her in place.

She stunned him by collapsing back to the pillow in a heap of bliss at his touch. "Yes," she sighed, clutching at his hands. "So cold. So...better."

The winter air was frigid and damp this morning and laying the fires had done next to nothing to slake the bone-deep chill from his fingers and toes.

Her skin did, indeed, feel as hot as any flame beneath his palms, leeching whatever comforting cold his hands could offer as she warmed him in kind.

Panic trilled through him, seizing his limbs. As an uneducated boy, he knew very little, but he understood the danger she was in all too well. She *was* burning from the inside out, and if something wasn't done, she'd become just another ghost to haunt the void in his heart where his loved ones used to live.

Snatching up her sheets, he carefully swaddled her enough to keep her from doing herself any harm, before tearing out of the room.

He rang every bell, roused every adult from their beds with frantic intensity. The Baron immediately sent him for their doctor, Preston Alcott. Not wanting to waste the time it took for the old stable master to saddle a horse, Titus ran the several blocks to the doctor's, arriving just as his lungs threatened to burst from the frigid coal-stained air.

Doctor Alcott was still punching his arms into his coat as Titus dragged him down his front stoop in a groggy heap of limbs, and shoved him into a hansom. To save time, he relayed all the details of his interaction with Honoria, noting her feverish behavior, appearance, and answering supplemental questions, such as what she'd had to eat the night before and where she'd traveled to in the past couple of days.

"You are a rather observant lad," the doctor remarked, peering over the rims of his spectacles. It was difficult to distinguish beneath the man's curly russet beard if he was being complimentary or condemning, until Alcott said, "Would that my nurses would be half as detailed as you."

Even though it wasn't his place, upon their arrival, Titus trailed the doctor up the grand staircase and lurked in the hallway, near an oriental vase almost as tall as he was, doing his best to blend with the shadows.

Through Honoria's open door, he watched helplessly as Mrs. Mcgillicutty, the housekeeper, ran a cool cloth over Honoria's face and throat. The Goodes hovered behind her, as if nursing their firstborn was still so beneath them, they needed a servant to do it.

Honoria laid on her back, mummified by her sheets, her lids only half-open now.

Titus thought he might be sick. She'd become so colorless, he might have thought her dead already, but for the slight, rapid rise and fall of her chest.

The doctor shooed them all aside and took only minutes of examination to render the grave verdict. "Baron and Lady Cresthaven, Mrs. Mcgillicutty, have any of you previously suffered from typhoid fever?"

Honoria's mother, an older copy of her dark-haired daughters, recoiled from her bedside. "Certainly not, Doctor. That is an affliction of the impoverished and squalid."

If the doctor had any opinions on her reaction, he kept them to himself. "If that is the case, then I'm going to have to ask you to leave this room. Indeed, it would be safer if you took your remaining children and staff elsewhere until..."

"Until Honoria recovers?" the Baron prompted through his wealth of a mustache.

The doctor gazed down at Honoria with a soft expression bordering on grief.

Titus wanted to scream. To kick at the priceless vase beside him and glory in the destruction, if only to see something as shattered as his heart might be.

"I knew she shouldn't have been allowed to attend Lady Carmichaels's philanthropic event," the Baroness shrilled. "I've always maintained nothing good can come of venturing below Clairview Street."

"Is there anyone else in your house feeling ill, Lady Cresthaven?" the doctor asked as he opened his arms in a gesture meant to shuffle them all toward the door.

"Not that I'm aware of," she answered as she hurried from her daughter's side as if swept up in Alcott's net.

"Two maids," Mrs. Mcgillicutty said around her mistress. "They took to their beds ill last night."

The doctor heaved a long-suffering sigh as they approached the threshold. "Contrary to popular belief, typhoid contamination can happen to the food and drink of anyone at any time. It is true and regrettable that more of this contamination is rampant in the poorer communities, where sanitation is woefully inadequate, but this is a pathogen that does not discriminate based on status."

"Quite so," the Baron agreed in the imperious tone he used when he felt threatened or out of his depth. "We'll leave for the Savoy immediately. Charlotte, get your things."

"I'll need someone to draw your daughter a cool bath and help me lift her into it," the doctor said, his droll intonation never changing. "If you'd inquire through the household about anyone who has been inflicted with typhoid fever in the past—"

"I have done, Doctor." Titus stepped out of the shadows, startling both of the Goodes. "It took my parents and my sister."

Before that moment, Titus hadn't known someone could appear both relieved and grim, but Alcott managed it.

"Absolutely not!" Charlotte Goode was not a large woman, but her staff often complained her voice could reach an octave that could shatter glass and offend dogs. "I'm not having my eldest, the jewel of our family, *handled* by the boy who shovels our coal and horse manure. This is most distressing; Honoria was invited to the Princess's garden party next week as the Viscount Clairmont's special guest!"

Titus lowered his eyes. Not out of respect for the woman, but so she wouldn't see the flames of his rage licking into his eyes.

At this, the doctor actually stomped his foot against the floor, silencing everyone. "Madam, your daughter barely has a chance of lasting the week, and the longer you and your family reside beneath this roof, the more danger your other children are in. Do I make myself clear?"

The Baron, famously pragmatic to the point of ruthlessness, took his wife by the shoulders and steered her away. "We're going," he said.

Without a backward glance at his firstborn.

TIED WITH A BOW

*D*octor Alcott took all of two seconds to dismiss the frantic bustle of the Baron's household, and yanked Titus into Honoria's bedroom before shutting them in. "Where is the bathroom?"

Titus pointed to a door through which the adjoining bathroom also shared a door with the nursery on the other side.

"Does the tub have a tap directly to it, or is it necessary to haul water from the kitchens?"

"It's a pump tap, sir, but I've only just started the boiler and that only pipes hot water to the kitchens and the first floor."

"That's sufficient." The doctor divested himself of his suit coat and abandoned it to a chair before undoing the links on his cuffs. "Now I need you to fill the bath with cool water, not cold, do you understand? We need to combat that fever, but if the water is freezing, it'll cause her to shiver and raise her temperature."

"I'll go to the kitchens and have them boil a pan just to make sure it inn't icy."

The man reached into his medical bag and extracted an opaque lump. "First, young man, you will take this antiseptic soap and scrub your hands until even the dirt from beneath your fingernails is gone."

"Yes, sir."

It took a veritable eternity for the water to boil, but it seemed he needed every moment of that to scrub the perpetual filth from his hands. Once his skin was pink and raw with nary a speck, he filled two buckets as full as he could carry and hauled the boiling-hot water up the stairs.

The Baron and his wife swept by him on their way down. "We mustn't let on it's typhoid," he was saying as his wife plunged her hands into an ermine muff.

"You're right, of course," the Baroness agreed. "What assumptions would people make about our household? Perhaps influenza would be more apropos?"

"Yes, capital suggestion."

Titus firmly squelched the impulse to dump the scalding water over the Goodes' collective heads, and raced to the bathroom, his arms aching from the load. He instantly threw the lock against the nursery as he heard the high-pitched, fearful questions the young twins barraged their governess with on the other side of the door. He plugged the tub's drain and turned the tap. Cringing at the frigidity of the water, he balanced the temperature as best he could.

That done, he returned to Honoria's room in time to see the doctor, clad only in his trousers and shirtsleeves rolled to the elbows, bending over a nude Honoria with his hands upon her stomach, spanning above her belly button.

Even in her catatonic state, she produced a whimper of distress that fell silent when the doctor's hands moved lower, his fingers digging into the flesh above her hip bone, on the line where her pale skin met a whorl of ebony hair.

An instantaneous primal rage surged through Titus at the sight. With an animalistic sound he'd never made before, Titus lunged around the bed and shoved the doctor away from her.

Alcott stumbled into the nightstand, upsetting a music box and her favorite hairbrush.

Titus threw the bedclothes back over Nora, snarling at the doctor as he placed his body as a shield against the much larger man. "You keep your fucking filthy hands from her."

Rather than becoming guilty or defensive, the doctor's shock flared into irritation, and then, as he examined Titus, it melted into comprehension. He adjusted his spectacles and advanced a few steps. "Listen to me, lad. I am a man, yes, and she is a lady. But in this room, I am *only* a doctor. To me, this is the body of a dying human. I must examine her."

Titus narrowed his eyes in suspicion, wondering if this man took him for a dupe. "You don't have to touch her... *there*. Not so close to—"

Alcott interrupted him crisply. "Though I am convinced of my initial diagnosis, I would do her a disservice if I didn't rule out all other possibilities. Internally, many maladies can produce these symptoms, and therefore palpating the stomach will often help me make certain she is not in other danger. You have an organ, the appendix, right here." He indicated low to the right of his torso, almost to his groin. "If it becomes swollen or perforated, it will spread fever and infection through the blood. If this were the case with Miss Goode, an immediate operation would be required, or she'd be dead before noon."

Noon? Titus swallowed around a dry lump, peering over his shoulder at her lovely face made waxen by a sheen of sweat.

"Your protection of her is commendable. But it is my duty to keep this girl alive," the doctor prodded, venturing even closer now. "That obligation takes precedence in my thoughts and my deeds, over anything so banal as modesty, as it must in yours now while you help me get her into the bath. Do you think you are capable of that?"

Titus nodded, even as a fist of dread and pain knotted in his stomach.

The doctor reached out and patted his shoulder. "Good. Now help me get the sheet beneath her and we'll use it as a sort of sling."

She fought them as they lowered her—sheet and all—into the bath, before suddenly settling into it with a sigh of surrender. After a few fraught moments, her breath seemed to come easier. The wrinkles of pain in her forehead smoothed out a little as her onyx lashes relaxed down over her flushed cheeks.

Alcott, his movements crisp and efficient, abandoned the room, only to return to administer a tincture she seemed to have trouble swallowing.

"What's that?" Titus queried, eyeing the bottle with interest.

"Thymol. Better known as thyme camphor. It has anti-pathogenic properties that will attack the bacteria in her stomach, giving her greater chance of survival."

"The doctor gave us all naphthalene," Titus remembered. "It helped with the fever, but...then they all got so much worse." The memory thrummed a chord of despondency in his chest with such a pulsating ache, he had to press his hand to his sternum to quiet it.

Alcott snorted derisively, his skin mottling beneath his beard. "Naphthalene is more a poison than a medicine, and while it's less expensive and more readily available, it is also little better than shoving mothballs into your family's mouth and calling it a cure. I'd very much like a word with this so-called physician."

Would that Titus had known before. He could have perhaps asked for this...thymol. "I don't know why I didn't get so sick as them. I did everything I could for their fevers. Yarrow tea and cold ginger. I couldn't lift them into a bath, I was a boy then, but I kept cold compresses on their heads and camphor and mustard on their chests."

Alcott's features arranged themselves with such compassion, Titus couldn't look at him without a prick of tears threatening behind his eyes. "You did admirably, lad. Sometimes, despite our best efforts, death wins the battle and we doctors are defeated."

To assuage both his curiosity and his inescapable anxiety, Titus questioned the doctor about bacteria, pathogens, medications, dosages, appendixes—and any other organs that might arbitrarily perforate—until Alcott deemed that Honoria had spent long enough in the water.

It was difficult to maintain the sort of clinical distance Doctor Alcott seemed capable of as they maneuvered her back to the bed, and dried and dressed her in a clean night rail. Titus did his best to avoid looking where he ought not to, touching her bare skin as little as possible.

But he knew his fingertips wouldn't forget the feel of her, even though it dishonored them both to remember.

The doctor left her in Titus's care while he went to administer thymol and instruction to the maids, both of whom were afflicted with the same malady but not advanced with high fevers or this worrisome torpor.

Once alone, Titus retrieved the hairbrush and, with trembling hands and exacting thoroughness, undid the matted mess that had become her braid. He smoothed the damp strands and fanned them over the pillow as he gently worked out the tangles. The texture was like silk against his rough skin, and he allowed himself to indulge in the pleasure of the drying strands sifting in the divots between his fingers. Then, he plaited it as he sometimes did the horses' tails when they had to be moved *en masse* to the country.

He even tied the end with a ribbon of burgundy, thinking she might approve.

His efforts, of course, were nothing so masterful as Honoria's maid's, but he was examining the finished product with something like satisfaction when the appearance of Doctor Alcott at his side gave him a start.

The doctor, a man of maybe forty years, was looking down at him from eyes still pink with exhaustion, as if he'd not slept before being roused so early. "We'll leave her to slumber until her next dose of thymol. Here, I'll draw the drapes against the morning."

"No." Titus stood, reaching out a staying hand for the doctor. "She prefers the windows and drapes open. She likes the breeze from the garden, even in the winter."

The doctor nodded approvingly. "It's my opinion fresh air is best for an ailing patient." He moved to put a hand on her forehead and take her pulse, seeming encouraged by the results. That finished, he turned to Titus, assessing him with eyes much too shrewd and piercing for a boy used to living his life largely unseen.

"She means something to you, boy?"

She meant *everything* to him. But of course, he could not say that.

"Titus."

"Pardon?"

"My name is Titus Conleith."

The doctor gave a curt nod. "Irish?"

"My father was, but my mum was from Yorkshire, where they worked the factories. We were sent here when my dad was elevated to a foreman in a steel company. But the well was bad, and typhoid took them all three months later."

Alcott made a sound that might have been sympathetic. "And how'd you come to be employed in the household of a Baron?"

Titus shrugged, increasingly uncomfortable beneath the older man's interrogation. "I saved old Mr. Fick, the stable master, from being crushed by a runaway carriage one time. He gave me the job here to keep me from having to go back to the workhouse, as his joints are getting too rheumatic to do what he used to. Besides, no orphanage would take in a boy old enough to make trouble."

"I see. Have you any schooling?"

Titus eyed him warily. "I have some numbers and letters. What's it to you?"

"You've a good mind for what I do. A good stomach for it, as well. I've a surgery off Basil Street, in Knightsbridge. Do you know where that is?"

"Aye."

He clasped his hands behind his back, looking suddenly regimental. "If Mr. Fick can spare you a few nights a week, I want you to visit me there. We can talk about your future."

"I will," Titus vowed, something sparking inside of him that his worry for Honoria wouldn't allow to ignite into full hope.

The three days he sat at her side were both the best and worst of his life.

He told her tales about the horses' antics as he melted chips of ice into her mouth. He monitored her for spikes of fever and kept her cool with damp cloths and linens packed with ice. The doctor even let him dose her with the thymol and look after most of her necessities when the maids took a turn for the worse.

He begged her to live.

All the while, he crooned the Irish tune his father used to sing to his mother on the nights when they drank a bit too much ale and danced a reel like young lovers, across their dingy old floor.

Black is the color of my true love's hair,
Her lips are like some roses fair,
She's the sweetest smile and the gentlest hands,
I love the ground whereon she stands.

. . .

HE BARELY ATE OR SLEPT UNTIL THE FOURTH NIGHT, AFTER SHE'D swallowed several spoonsful of beef bone broth, the deep sounds of her easier breaths lulling him to nap in the chair by her bed. Alcott had roused him with the good news that her fever had broken, and had then ordered him to wash and change clothing and sleep in the guest room nearby.

A commotion woke him thirteen hours later. Without thinking, Titus lurched out of bed and scrambled down the hall. Skidding to a halt, he narrowly avoided crashing into the Baron's back.

Every soul in the Goode family gathered around Honoria's bed, blocking her from view. Prudence, Felicity, and Mercy all chattered at the same time, and it was the happy sound of their cadence that told him he had nothing to fear.

Titus squelched a spurt of possession, stopping just short of shoving in and around them to see what was going on. This moment didn't belong to them, it belonged to him.

She belonged to him.

"Young Mr. Conleith, there you are." Doctor Alcott, a tall man, stood at the head of the bed next to his patient, who was still blocked from Titus's view. "Miss Goode, you and your family owe this young lad a debt of gratitude. It is largely due to his tireless efforts that you survived."

They all turned to look at him, clearing the visual pathway to her.

With an ecstatic elation, Titus drank in the sight of Honoria sitting up on her own. She was still ashen and wan, her eyes heavy-lidded and her lips without color.

And yet, the most beautiful sight he'd laid his eyes upon.

Her fingers worried at the burgundy ribbon in her hair, stroking it as if drawing comfort from it.

Was it his imagination, or did a dash of peach color her cheeks at the sight of him?

He already knew he was red as a beet, swamped in the blush now creeping up his collar.

"Thank you," she whispered.

Every word he knew crowded in his throat, choking off a reply.

"Yes," the Baron chuffed, taking his shoulder and firmly steering him backwards. "Expect our gratitude in remuneration, boy. I'll call for you to come to my office tomorrow to discuss the details. There's a good lad."

The door shut in his face, and he stared at it for an incomprehensible moment. From the other side, the Baroness's voice grated as she asked the doctor if Honoria might be well enough to attend the garden party at the palace three days hence.

Titus dropped his head against the door and closed his eyes.

She'd looked right at him. Had *seen* him for the first time. Did she remember any of the previous days? Had she heard anything he'd said to her? Sung to her?

She'd thanked him.

And he'd said nothing. His one chance to actually speak to her and he'd choked.

And then he'd been shut out like the inconvenience he was. To them, the Goodes, he was still a nobody. Nothing. They would never think about him after today unless the dog shat upon the carpets and someone needed to clean it up.

Would she? Would she come to him? Had she noticed him, truly? Not as a servant or a savior but as himself...

One question haunted him as he dragged his feet down the hallway, back to the mews, his hand curling over the memory of her skin.

Would he ever get to touch her again?

FOUR YEARS LATER

"*I* do believe someone is dead beneath your greenhouse," Amanda Pettifer said with no real concern as she pulled the curtain back from the carriage window. "That's quite a structure for merely a Baron's home. Why, it's as long as your stable walls."

Honoria Goode didn't miss Amanda's latent jab at their rank. As the daughter of a viscount, she needed, upon occasion, to put them in their place. It wasn't the most pleasant virtue for a friend to have, but neither was it uncommon among their class.

"Let me see!" Prudence lunged over Amanda's lap to peer out the carriage window as they clopped in beneath the mews. "Holy Moses! You're right. A man's legs are sticking out from beneath as if the structure landed right on him. What if he drowned in that puddle of muck he's in? Someone should do something, Nora! Oh...no...wait. The legs are moving. All is well. At least, I *think* it is."

"I'm glad our welcome party isn't a corpse." Secretly pleased that her sister Pru still used the nickname she'd gleaned at finishing school, Nora marked her page and closed her book.

She'd never liked the name Honoria. It was stolid and plain, belonging more to a nun or a suffragist than a debutante. Nora sounded much more sophisticated, she thought. Tidier, even.

Though Amanda Pettifer was Nora's age at twenty, she and Prudence—almost three years their junior at seventeen—were thick as thieves. Likely, because they both shared a penchant for mischief and misbehavior.

They'd all bundled into the carriage from the Green Street Station, anxious to arrive home. Nora's coming out ball was in three days, and there was so much to be done. She couldn't help but become almost overwrought with anxiety at the thought.

The carriage trundled to a stop in their Mayfair courtyard as she swept aside the curtains to see what all the hullabaloo was about.

Along the wall of their extensive stables, tucked into the square behind their grand row house, Mrs. Fick's glass and wrought-iron greenhouse glinted with the colors of the setting sun.

Indeed, sprawled in a shallow mud puddle from a pit dug beneath the foundation, were two long male legs clad in filthy trousers. As the girls all watched, the legs bent and splayed indecently as mud-caked hands appeared and clasped the underside of the structure. Then, with a serpentine struggle, the entire body of a man shimmied on his back from beneath.

Before sitting up, he reached back under and retrieved several work tools.

"Good lord, Nora, he's all but naked," Prudence gasped.

The young man hauled himself to his feet and smoothed his muddy hair before scraping some of the muck from his torso and flicking it onto the ground.

Amanda's buttercream lace fan snapped open with a frenetic rip. "My," she exclaimed huskily. "He's built exactly like that statue of Ares in the Louvre."

Nora barely heard their remarks, so arrested was she by the sight of him.

Amanda had the right of it. His figure could have been sculpted by the hands of a master. His jaw chiseled granite and his smooth sinewy torso shaped from marble. He was long-limbed and slender, his shoulders round and his arms corded with lean muscle. The flat discs of his chest gave way to grooved ribs and an abdomen so defined she could count the individual muscles, six in all.

She'd never seen a man like this in the flesh. Sculptors were a talented lot, to be sure, but they worked in clay and stone. A cold, lifeless modality in comparison. It could not begin to capture the jaw-dropping glint of golden skin. The line of intriguing hair disappearing into his trousers. Nor the peaks and shadows created by the grooves of muscle as he moved and flexed beneath the disappearing sunlight.

The moment the footman opened the door, Amanda accepted his hand and all but leapt out of the carriage to whistle at the workman. "You seem to have lost your clothing, sir," she taunted.

His head snapped up as Prudence followed Amanda out of the carriage and tittered, "Mr. Fick will have to turn the garden hose on you, before all that mud dries you into a statue."

"Let it dry, I say." Amanda made a show of leering over at him, assessing him from head to toe. "Store him in a museum. I'd pay admittance to see that work of art *regularly*."

"Amanda! What if someone heard you?" Prudence put a lace-gloved hand over her friend's unruly mouth, though they were both giggling uncontrollably.

"What do I care?" Amanda grappled her hand away and flounced toward the door, her cream ruffled skirts fanning out behind her. "I'm to marry a short, pudgy lord who owns half of Cheshire, but I will always be an appreciator of excellent artisan workmanship. They don't make men like that in our class, do they? More's the pity."

Nora was about to deliver a sharp word of reprimand when Mr. Fick, the spindly, white-haired stable master tossed a balled-up cotton shirt at the lad, hitting him square in the chest. "Oi! Titus! Make yourself decent; you're offending the ladies!"

"He *really* isn't," Amanda said huskily.

Turning, the kindly Mr. Fick bowed as Nora was the last to step down from the carriage. "Miss Goode, Miss Goode, Miss Pettifer, welcome back."

"Thank you, Mr. Fick, it's lovely to see you!" Prudence greeted with all her usual cheer.

Nora couldn't bring herself to speak, gaping as she was in slack-jawed amazement.

That was Titus Conleith?

He touched the shirt as little as possible as he held it away from his mud-covered skin. Shifting restlessly, his features arranged themselves into an uncomfortable frown that lanced Nora through with mortification.

"Pardon me, ladies. Mr. Fick, I'll test the piping to see if the water pressure is returned." His voice was deep and graveled, the register low enough that Nora had to strain to hear it. He barely gave them a curt nod, opened the door, and escaped into the long greenhouse.

"Let's go and surprise Mama and the Pater," Prudence crowed, peeling her hat away from the onyx curls that matched Nora's own. "Then I'll show Amanda to her room and hopefully supper will be ready soon. I'm positively faint with hunger. Are you coming, Nora?"

"In a moment," she replied, barely noticing the girls' giggling retreat.

Between the rows and shelves of vegetables, herbs, spices, and flowers tended by Mrs. Fick's magical green thumb, she could catch glimpses of Titus through the panes of glass as he drifted deeper into the greenhouse.

"Watch your pretty shoes, there, miss." Mr. Fick motioned to the puddle nearly large enough to be a pond. "We installed irrigation pipes into the greenhouse last week, and already one of them sprung a leak. Titus's been at fixing it all day. Knowing you, you'll be wanting to greet the horses before the people," he said affectionately. "I think old Cleo is back there waiting for you."

That drew a genuine smile from her. She did, indeed, prefer horses to people in almost all cases. "Yes, thank you."

He blinked over at the greenhouse, then cast the retreating girls a look of veiled disapproval before taking himself off toward the servants' entrance.

Nora waited for him to disappear inside before skirting the puddle, lifting the hem of her powder blue gown, and hopping onto the landing of the greenhouse to slip inside.

Moist air fragrant with loamy soil and herbs suffused Nora's lungs. She breathed it in, longing for the country. The sound of running water drew her past strawberries and asparagus, basil, rosemary, coriander, thyme, even a tomato vine struggling to find the sun.

Toward the rear of the structure, fresh flowers bared themselves shamelessly, overgrowing the pathway and impeding her view. Nora had to lift a few fern fronds to duck beneath them.

She found Titus surrounded by a bevy of hanging plants, bent over a drain as he scrubbed the dirt from his hair and back with the pump Mrs. Fick used to water her plants.

"Leak is patched, I'm sure of it, Mr. Fick," he said, shaking his hair like a dog. "Whoever installed that pipe must have been drunk or blind." He dropped the hose to the drain and ran his hands over his face, swiping water and grit away from his eyes. "Will you hand over my shirt?"

Even after his many years in the city, he had not lost those lovely long vowels of Yorkshire.

Nora retrieved his nearly white shirt from where it splayed over a bush that had been clipped ruthlessly short, and held it over to him. She had the odd desire to keep it captive, or do something ridiculous, like hold it to her nose and test the scent. "Here you are."

He didn't straighten so much as jump, his wet hair releasing a little arc of spray that barely missed her. It was the color of dark sand after the lap of a wave had been called out to sea, and it hung to his eyes in spiked gathers that dripped onto his skin.

The effect made his symmetrical features more powerful, somehow, causing the bones to etch dramatic angles that she knew would become even more stark and compelling when he was an older man.

He slicked his hair back with frantic motions before running his hand over his eyes and face once more, as if clearing the water from them would dissolve her from his sight.

The movements did things to the muscles of his arms and chest, that transfixed her into a mute sort of appreciation that should have shamed them both. He was cold, she noted. His nipples pebbled and gooseflesh chased across his skin.

What a constitution one must have, to bathe with the irrigation hose, the water pumped from frigid wells and aquifers.

"Honoria." Her name manifested in a throaty whisper, then he winced. "That is, Miss Goode." Instead of stepping closer, he bent at the waist and snatched the shirt hanging from her lax fingers.

She'd almost dropped it whilst gawking.

"My friends call me Nora," she said inanely before cursing herself for a ninny. He'd not be allowed to address her thusly. They were not friends because they were not equals.

He threaded his arms into his shirt without even bothering

to dry himself, heedless, it seemed, of the fact that his trousers were still filthy, thus rendering a clean shirt obsolete.

Propriety dictated, however, that he protect his modesty—and more importantly hers—before his own meager wardrobe.

He didn't look at her as he fumbled with the buttons, his eyes cast down at the drain. "Is there something I can do for you?"

She shook her head, suddenly feeling silly and...oddly short. The last time she'd seen him, she'd looked down at him. Now, he could likely rest his chin on top of her head.

Nora did her best to stammer out what she had come to say. "Y-you are owed an apology. Amanda and Pru—well, I suppose we all were being disrespectful just now by staring and carrying on. I'm sorry if we embarrassed you. It's only that, we've had an arduous journey back from a terrible few years at finishing school and we're all feeling a bit spirited. I suppose, what with the ball upcoming and such..." She trailed away, knowing she was babbling, and realizing how weak and awful her excuses made her sound.

She could cheerfully murder Amanda right now.

And then, perhaps not, because she had a reason to be alone. With him. She had the image of his musculature etched into her memory to take out and appreciate at her own leisure.

Titus Conleith.

She didn't used to think the grand name suited him when he was a small and skinny boy with huge, hungry golden eyes. His gaze had always reminded her of Ramses, their German shepherd puppy, when he begged at the kitchen door for scraps.

But, like Ramses, Titus was no pup now. Though his eyes were still hungry.

Piercing but evasive.

"Anyway," she said, stroking at the leaf of a dangling ivy plant, if only to have something to fidget with. "I hope you're not cross. Most young ladies are unused to the sight of... well..." She gestured in his general direction, lamenting the disappearance of his smooth chest as he buttoned toward his neck.

"I'm not cross, miss."

She could feel her brow crimping with worry. It was impossible to tell from the tone of his voice if he was merely being polite. Perhaps he felt as though he could not convey his affrontedness because her father was his employer. She disliked that thought immensely.

"It wasn't well done of us to stare, let alone for anyone to make a comment. It was uncouth and rude and—"

"You can stare." His eyes met hers then, the golden gaze intense and inescapable, though his sober features never changed from intractable. "I wouldn't stop you."

The way he was looking at her now, made her very aware of the cinch of her corset and how little air she was allowing into her lungs.

She did stare, then, rather dumbly, trying to dissect the meaning beneath his words. He wouldn't stop her because he *could* not? Because she was his superior? Or he would not stop her... because he desired her to look at him?

Because he wanted her to appreciate what she saw?

Because she had.

She *did*.

The air thickened between them, taking on the muffled, expectant quality of the atmosphere right before a thunderstorm. The hairs on her body lifted, shivered, as if anticipating a lightning strike.

"Nora!" Mercy's screech broke the spell of the moment as her little sister exploded into the greenhouse. "Nora, you're home!" The gangly, golden-haired girl barreled into her, cinching small, surprisingly strong arms about her waist in a breath-stealing hug.

Felicity, Mercy's twin, wasn't far behind, though she waited patiently for her turn. "Hullo, Titus," she said, adjusting her spectacles as if looking at him blinded her a little.

Nora understood the feeling.

"Oi, Miss Felicity." His voice softened when he spoke to her sister, and the effect was something like velvet rasping over silk.

"I've almost finished *Chemistry, Meteorology, and the Production of Vapour,*" Felicity announced. "If I return it this evening before you go, might you ask Doctor Alcott for another?"

Doctor Alcott? Nora wondered. Were they still in touch after—?

"Have you now, with those big words and everything?" Titus's eyes crinkled at the edges in a most alluring way when he smiled. "Clever girl, you are. I think Alcott has one on alchemical preservation I could bring you. It is all about mummies."

"I *love* mummies." Felicity blushed to the roots of her blond hair, and Nora realized that whenever the word *clever* was used regarding Felicity in their household, it wasn't complimentary. One would be pressed to find a volume that wasn't religious or political in nature. The Goode girls were not allowed vulgar modern literature. In fact, she should hide her novel before she went inside.

At the thought of returning home, another long-held anxiety floated to the surface like a poorly weighted drowning victim. Per her father's insistence, her ball gown wasn't cut to style. High necks were for everyday gowns, and evening wear went so far as to slide below the shoulders.

And yet hers was buttoned to the chin.

Everyone was going to laugh.

Suddenly a memory blew across her mind like an autumnal gust.

Titus. His hands at her neck, doing or... undoing buttons.

Her buttons... brushing soft, cool cloths over her neck and chest.

She swallowed, her fingers lifting to tug at her lace collar.

Mercy released her waist only to seize hold of her hand. "Papa sent us to fetch you, Nora. After you meet with him, you *must* come and have tea with us in the nursery. I've written a play and Pru said she'll be the boy but only today as you'll be too busy with your blasted ball after that."

"Don't let nanny hear you say blast," Nora warned, too charmed to truly scold her beloved sister.

"There's kissing in the play," Felicity said with a scandalized look up at Titus. "But we put our hands over our mouths."

"Come on." Mercy tugged. "Do hurry!"

"Good afternoon, Titus," Felicity said with a prim curtsy.

He nodded his head at them each in turn. "And a good afternoon to you, Miss Felicity, Miss Mercy." He bowed to them both with all the starched sobriety of a general before turning to her and inclining his head. "Miss Goode."

As Nora allowed herself to be towed to the house by two cherubic ten-year-old tugboats, she couldn't help but notice he'd called her *Miss Goode*. As he should have...and yet...

He'd enjoyed a bit of familiarity with the girls. Why not her? Could she insist he call her Nora? What would the word sound like now that his voice had altered so profoundly?

It was all she could think about for the rest of the day.

THE BALL

*N*ora hated every moment she shared with Michael Leventhorpe, the heir to the Marquess of Blandbury. He was not only a fool, but a bully and a rake.

She didn't like him.

She didn't want him.

And she was left with *no choice* but to marry him.

Which was why he'd been allowed to conduct her away from the stifling ball, out onto the balcony. He swept her to the darkest corner, where the stone columns of the banister overlooked the garden. The pathway was dimly lit for the occasion by decorative antique braziers that brought to mind Shakespeare's London.

Though most of the girls considered Blandbury handsome, nay, the catch of the season, Nora categorically disagreed. He was a big buffoon of a man, sporting and solid with pale hair and skin so white she could see some of the blue veins beneath the skin of his eyes. For some reason, she could stare at little else, all the while berating herself for being too critical of appearance.

She would never have given Blandbury a second glance if it hadn't been for her father's welcome home three days prior, delivered with a stern edict that'd stolen any light from her heart.

Clarence Goode, Baron Cresthaven, had always cowed her. But never so much as when she was made to stand before the desk he'd mounted on a massive dais in his study, simply so he could look down at people as if from behind the Queen's Bench in court. He was a veritable force of nature, tall and broad, but not in the way that Titus had become. Not with that lean strength and effortless grace. Her father was a rotund man with the dimensions of a whiskey barrel and the hands of a cooper, rather than a nobleman.

He had stared down at her with a disapproval she hadn't yet earned, regarding her with an assessment any ewe at auction might still find insulting.

"Every man wishes for a boy to take on his legacy," he'd begun, stroking at his impressive mustache as if delivering a homily of great import. "Since your mother and I were not so blessed with an heir, that doesn't change the nature of the necessity. Were you a son, you'd be groomed to take over my title and my company. I'd apprentice you to the shipping trade and school you in politics so you would be a pinnacle of the Tories." His eyes had taken on a dreamy cast then, as if this was a pleasant fiction he visited often in daydreams.

Nora hadn't been able to contain a sneeze, and the sound brought his disapproving gaze squarely back to her. He made it immediately clear her sinuses were not the only part of her body he currently found offensive. "As you are a woman, you haven't the constitution nor the intellect for such matters, but that doesn't mean you don't have a duty to uphold to your family as firstborn."

Nora hadn't known what to say to that, so she kept her own

council. Brevity wasn't among her father's repertoire, so she settled in for a lengthy diatribe.

"If our legacy is to advance, then you must marry well, as you know. I am spending a veritable fortune on this upcoming ball to put you out in society, and it is incumbent upon you to make a match in your first season, to make way for Prudence. You and your sister shouldn't be coming out so close together, but I suppose that couldn't be helped what with the entire year it took you to gain your strength after your contracting that dastardly fever."

He said this as if fevers were an affliction of the morally degenerate, and indeed, they'd treated her as such for quite some time after her illness.

Perhaps if she hadn't collapsed at the garden party she'd been forced to attend at Buckingham Palace, against the doctor's wishes, she'd have not been so thusly berated.

Her father continued, picking up a pen and opening a folder to study its contents as if the conversation was not important enough to keep his complete attention. "With your charm and beauty, and your competitive dowry, you could snag a Duke if you set your cap to one. There being a marked shortage of marriageable Dukes, I've been talking to the Marquess of Blandbury regarding his son, Michael. It is understood between his father and me, that you will have a proposal at next month's end after no fewer than four social outings with him."

At that, her stomach had lurched, and she'd had to stabilize herself by gripping the high-backed chair she had not been invited to sit in. "But, Papa...how can I be all but promised before I've even had a chance to—"

He stood then, startling her into silence. "You've always been an amenable girl, Honoria. Something I've admired in you. Don't let us disappoint now." He'd moved to the window to stare out over his view of the West End. "With the Marquess as an ally, I could finally clinch the support of the Home Secretary and get my hands on the Metropolitan Police Commissioner position. That done, I'd run the most powerful organized force in the Empire that isn't military."

And that's what it was all about to him.

Power. Prestige. Clout.

She'd be bargained away so her father could play at having a force of minions that would make him feel as though the city belonged to him.

And her buyer was *this* incomparable idiot who hadn't so much as allowed her a word in edgewise for going on ten minutes now.

Nora took in a breath as deep as her constricting peach gown would allow, and tried to listen to what the braggart was saying. Something about what he and his awful society of Oxford friends did to prank the unsuspecting acquaintances of their parents.

He talked too loudly with irritating animation, his eyes alight with self-satisfaction. "You see, it's not stealing, what we do. It's merely a lark. We don't take jewels or silver, because what's the fun in that? We all have plenty of our own, and often such items won't be missed for days or weeks. However, the lads and I pilfer small portraits or love letters, bank notices or diaries. You know, things that are impossible to replace. Then, we sit back and watch the mayhem ensue. One time, Lady Birmingham sacked her entire household!"

He brayed with laughter while Nora's insides twisted.

"That's…horrible," she gasped.

"Nah." He waved his hand in front of his face as if batting away her rebuke. "It's harmless mostly."

"Not if people are losing their positions. That's how they make their living. How they feed their families."

He rolled his eyes. "They'll find another. Who wants to be a servant, anyhow?"

She stared at him, aghast, before finding her voice. "I'm sure no one fantasizes about a life in servitude, but as you're aware, it's a vocation of distinction to work in a noble house. Not to mention a far sight better for many than the dangerous work at the factories, and—"

"Oh, *please* don't tell me you're one of those people in the *ton* who fancy themselves a *liberal*," he sneered, leaning his hip on the banister.

"I don't know what I am," she replied honestly. "I merely fail to see how being so unkind is considered entertaining."

Rather than allow her rebuke to riffle him, he leaned closer, his pale blue eyes darkening with lurid notions. "I'd be kind to you, if you'd let me."

Suddenly she was very aware that her side of the railing abutted a wall, and that no one could see them out here unless they came through the doors and turned in their direction. "Oh. Well that's—"

He leaned closer. "I'd be downright generous...if you'd return the favor."

She cleared a gather of nerves from her throat. "I can't possibly know what you mean."

His lip quirked, but not in the direction she thought it would. "Don't play coy. Not with me. If we're to be married, then everything is permissible." His step toward her felt like an advance, and she retreated in kind, bumping into the wall behind her.

"Are we not supposed to see each other four more times than this?" she reminded him, feeling very cornered. She glanced to the side, meaning to slip away from the wall and dash back inside where they might find someone lingering in the hall if they were lucky. "We've only just met."

He leaned in to brace one hand next to her head, cutting off her path of escape. "I've danced with you twice. Our engagement is all but announced."

Her thoughts began to race, pinging about like a trapped bird looking for escape but doing nothing but crashing into walls. "But I—wouldn't it do to wait until—?"

He didn't kiss her so much as he smashed his mouth to hers with such force, their teeth met. As she opened her lips to protest, his tongue punched past them, filling her entire mouth and causing her to gag.

His lips were wet and salty, still flavored of the fish they'd had at the banquet, which caused her own meal to rise up her esophagus in revolt.

She broke the kiss by wrenching her head to the side, and he followed her, pressing his mouth to her cheek, breathing hot air against her flesh as he sought to reclaim the kiss.

His weight was crushing, and it seemed as if all the air available to her in the world was his moist, fetid inescapable breath.

"I don't think we should," she said weakly.

"Who gives a damn about should?" he said against her skin, his hands resting on her hips. "This moment is ours, Nora. You're the most beautiful catch of the season and you're *mine*."

She *hated* the way he said that word. The possession in it disgusted her, and still she did her best to remain calm. She'd actually been taught in finishing school how to possibly discourage such advances. What had they said? When men are ruled by their baser natures, appeal to their higher intellect. Remind them they are better.

"We're not engaged, Michael," she said in a beseeching whisper. "If I were caught like this, I'd be ruined."

He scoffed. "I'd still marry you. My father needs your dowry for his estate. Make me a happy man now, and I'll make you a marchioness."

"Please," she whispered. "Don't—"

His mouth caught hers again, cutting off her words. His tongue invaded as tears sprung to her eyes. Hands roamed up and down her waist, his hips pressing her to the side, forcing her against the banister until it bit into her thigh.

Panic gripped her, clawing at her skin. What were her options? To allow him to do this to her or to make a reputation-shredding scene. He was going to be her husband... but how far did he expect to go tonight?

Was this what intimacy was going to be like with him? Forever?

A soft, low growl emanated from the shadows.

And then Michael was gone.

In the time it took for her to gasp a breath into her starving lungs, Titus Conleith had thrown the future Marquess of Blandbury onto the ground and imprisoned him there by grinding his heel against the man's jaw.

In different circumstances, Nora might have found the sight of the boy's cheek squished between Titus's shoe and the ground rather humorous as his body flopped about.

But at the moment, she was too distressed and astonished to ever imagine laughing again.

"Miss Goode said no," Titus informed him with a lethal calm she found more terrifying than if he'd snarled or roared.

"All right. All right, man. Let me up!" Blandbury's voice cracked when Titus's heel ground his face further into the flagstone. His golden eyes glittered with a dangerous intent, as if he considered popping the man's entire head like a ripe melon.

"No." Nora rushed forward and took his arm. "Please don't. Not tonight; it would ruin everything."

His features became still as stone, but a conflagration blazed in those tiger eyes.

It could have blistered her skin if he stared at her for long.

However, at her behest, he took his shoe off the boy's jaw

and even lifted Blandbury to his feet, going so far as to brush a smudge off his dinner jacket.

The lord's features mottled with rage. "You're only a *footman*? You dare to put your hands on me?"

Titus appeared unaffected, bringing his nose level with her aggressor's. "You put your hands where they didn't belong first, remember. That deserved an answer."

This time, it was Michael who took a step in retreat. "It is *you* who'll answer for this, the both of you!" He smoothed down his mussed hair and pulled at the lapels of his jacket with anxious, jerky movements as he backed toward the door. "The engagement is off, you hear me? A complete and utter fantasy, thinking to marry so far beneath me. I'll ruin you." He jabbed a finger at Titus, who'd positioned himself in between the furious lord and Nora. "And *you*. You'll be stricken from every decent household in the Empire. You'll die of some god-awful lung disease in the factories. Or worse, the workhouse."

"Marquess of Blandbury?" Clad in a footman's livery, Titus lifted a white-gloved hand to tap his chin as if recalling a memory. "Isn't it well understood that your father is dying of cancer?"

Michael's complexion deepened from mottled to purple. "You don't deserve to say his bloody name you—"

Titus's head cocked to the side. "Is it cancer, though? Or syphilis? What would they think, the Tories, about a man who can't abstain from syphilitic whores? What would the papers say?"

At that, Michael blanched, and Nora was again repelled by a man whose skin was so reactive to his every emotion. "How do you—where did you find out?"

"What matters is what I'll do with the information. Which is nothing if you apologize to Miss Goode, go to the washroom to sort yourself out, and—after thanking the Baron and his wife for their hospitality—get the fuck out of this house.

Because you're right about one thing..." Titus prowled forward, his arm bent behind his back in the posture of a solicitous footman, which made his words land with all the more gravitas as they slid into the night. "There's no *hope* of a wedding, but I know they can arrange a funeral even without a body."

Nora watched with queer, horrific fascination as Michael struggled to breathe. He just stood there, saying nothing until Titus feinted a threatening lunge forward.

"I'm sorry!" he cried. "I—I apologize. I shan't touch you again."

Nora didn't forgive him, of course, but she nodded, if only to release him from their company so he could scamper down the hall.

Once he'd gone, she was seized by a bout of intense vertigo, feeling as if the floor beneath her had become a small sea craft tossed by waves. She collapsed onto a stone bench, not certain her legs could take her weight for much longer.

The repercussions of this would be dire. Her father was going to be *so* angry, and that frightened her a little, but not so much as the tongue just shoved down her throat.

Repulsed by the memory, Nora wiped at her mouth with the back of her glove. Only when it came away damp did she realize tears now streaked down her cheeks in hot rivulets.

A handkerchief was pressed into her fingers, and she looked up to see Titus staring down at her with that alarmingly indecipherable gaze.

"Thank you," she managed.

Swallowing, she scooted over and gathered some of the ruffles of her dress to make space for him on the bench.

He took it, folding himself carefully next to her, making no move to touch her as she turned away to wipe her tears and dab at her nose.

"Did he hurt you?" The question was low. Dark. And it made her turn to look at him.

"No, not really. I'm not crying about that."

He nodded before his gaze lowered. "If the violence frightened you, I—"

"*No.*" She put her hand on his arm to stop that thought from forming, and he became instantly rigid beneath her touch. "No, you were wonderful. I don't know what I would have done. What I would have allowed him to do because I was too afraid or embarrassed to stop him."

"Allowed him to do..." Titus didn't finish the thought. He just stared at her hand on his arm as his brows drew together.

"How could *I* have stopped him without ruining everything?" she rushed to explain. "My father would have been furious with me. My reputation ruined. Any chances of a good marriage, to him or otherwise, completely dashed. My—my entire life would have been over. He knew he had put me in that position, I think. That I was truly helpless, because I'd gone with him into the dark. How could I have been so *thoughtless?*" She hit her own knee with the hand that clutched the handkerchief.

A frustrated mélange of emotions welled up inside of her. Resentment. Fear. Animosity. For Michael. For her parents. For the entire dastardly world.

For herself.

"That was—" Her breath hitched on a raw sob. She began to shake with the power of her reaction. "That was my first kiss."

She buried her face into the handkerchief, thinking it felt warm and familiar as she allowed a few more tears to fall. She'd taught herself to cry quietly from early on, and to regain her composure in an instant, forcing it all down beneath a façade of serenity before anyone could ascertain a weakness with which to whip her.

And she might have composed herself now, if a large, gentle hand hadn't splayed on her back and stayed there.

Titus didn't babble meaningless words. Nor did he caress her or crush her to him. He asked no questions and gave no encouragements. He offered comfort merely by being there, by letting her be and allowing her to feel what she needed to feel without the fear of reproof.

It must have been why she curled toward him, tucking her head against his shoulder, breathing in the cedar-sweet smell of his collar and neck. She could think of no other reason to do what was so utterly out of character. Something about the silent strength of him—something she fancied she glimpsed in that alert, opaque gaze of his—drew her toward him like a viper mesmerized by an exotic flute.

His arm cradled her against his side, the other reaching toward her face as he looked down at her with those extraordinary eyes. He'd taken off his gloves, she noted, as his fingers lifted toward her cheek. He hesitated before he touched her, as if waiting for permission.

Nora's lashes swept down, causing more tears to fall as she turned her face into his awaiting palm.

He thumbed away the drops with skin so rough it abraded hers, but still she buried her cheek deeper against his hand, seeking the warmth and strength she found there, tempered by utter gentility and something else she couldn't begin to define.

For the first time in her short life, Nora felt as if the pressure of the entire sky wasn't doing its utmost to crush her into the ground. This boy had strength enough in his shoulders to bear the burden that was *her* for a moment.

And he seemed willing enough.

She couldn't say how long they stayed like that before something restless stirred inside of her. Something that wanted more of him. Of this.

"Titus?" she whispered.

"Yes, Miss Goode?"

"Will you call me Nora? My friends all call me Nora."

He paused. "If I took such liberties, I'd lose my position here."

It was odd, him saying that, when they found themselves in such an intimate posture. But, of course. How stupid of her to forget. She wasn't the only one constrained by her station. "I only meant when we're alone."

His breath hitched then, as if something agitated him. "We...should not be alone."

Wanting to soothe him in kind, Nora placed her hand over the one he held to her cheek, the softness of her gloved fingertips snagging over his coarse knuckles.

Beneath her, his shoulder lifted and fell with quickening breaths, and the warmth of his exhales brushed her skin, lightly scented of dessert flavored by port.

The staff wasn't supposed to nip at the food, but she'd always supposed they did, and she was glad he'd had a taste.

He deserved every pleasure.

Suddenly she wanted to know more about him. "How did you know about the Marquess of Blandbury?"

"Doctor Alcott," he said simply.

"You must see him often if you know such intimate things about his patients and swap books from his library."

He shifted a little, as if talking about himself made him uncomfortable. "I work for him four evenings a week and every other Saturday."

"On top of your duties here?"

He nodded.

What a keen mind he must have. She rather appreciated that. "I think it's lovely of you to lend them to Felicity." A smile worked its way through her prior distress, at the thought of her sister's eyes, made unnaturally large by her spectacles, as she stared adoringly up at Titus. "I think she rather fancies you."

He made a sound in his chest that landed somewhere between amusement and embarrassment, but he made no reply.

She laced her fingers in between his as if she needed to hold onto something in order to make her next confession. "Sometimes I have vague wisps of dreams, or maybe memories, of those days I spent with the fever."

He tensed, and she had the impression that if her hand hadn't held his to her cheek, he would have retracted it.

"I think you were feeding me, singing me lullabies..." Unsure of what was prompting her to behave this way, she turned her face against his skin until her lips grazed the meat of his palm. "Bathing me."

He drew away then, his breath sawing in and out of him with true effort as he turned his back to her. "Don't remember," he rasped.

She couldn't tell if he meant *he* didn't remember, or if he was ordering *her* not to recall. But she *did*. Bits and pieces. She wondered sometimes, how much of it had been real. If he'd taken cooling sponges to her bare skin. If he'd lowered her naked body into baths and then tenderly arranged soft nightgowns over her.

She couldn't help but allow her thoughts to linger on the intimacy of that.

"I didn't ever thank you properly," she said, pressing her hand to his shoulder. "They whisked me off so quickly to that health clinic in Switzerland, and then to finishing school after that. But... I've thought of you often."

So very often.

He said nothing. Did nothing. Just breathed, or at least fought to do so.

Had he thought of her? She wanted to ask. Did she linger in his mind as he did in hers, like the sweet furloughs of the past?

A reassuring memory through a miasma of distress and expectation?

"Titus," she breathed, her own heartbeat gaining strength, pressing against her ribs. "Titus, look at me."

His chin touched his shoulder, and she reached out to encourage him to swivel his entire body to face her on the bench.

"I want to thank you," she said, bracketing his tense jaw with both her silk-gloved hands, searching his uniquely handsome face and finding what she hoped for.

Hope and hunger.

"Thank you for *everything*," she whispered. "For then. For tonight. And...for *this*." Following a reckless, unrelenting longing, she pulled his head lower so her lips could press to his.

She found his mouth harder than she'd expected.

Sweeter, too.

They sat like that for a moment, their lips locked and still, as if waiting for the night to catch its breath, because neither of them seemed to be able to.

Then, his mouth became pliant over hers, before he nudged gently forward.

Moving his lips in subtle, whispering sweeps, he took control of the kiss without even seeming to know he'd done it, drugging her with motions that were as languid as they were astonished.

As certain as they were untried.

His hands drew up her arms, but instead of taking liberties, they settled at the band of skin where the hem of her gloves ended above her elbow but below her sleeve. His thumb stroked lightly there, testing the softness, and eliciting more erotic sensation than she'd thought existed.

She'd somehow known it would be like this. That *he* would be like this. Something inside of her had sensed his need, not strictly by the way he looked at her. But in the way he avoided looking.

As if he didn't allow himself to want her.

She was a woman aware of her beauty. One who was reminded of it by nearly everyone she met. Usually, selfishly, she wished it were not her defining feature.

Except now.

Because she wanted nothing so much as his desire. The nature of it called to something deep within her. Something as incontrovertible as it was primitive.

And she could do nothing but answer.

When his tongue searched the seam of her lips with a questioning lick, she tentatively opened to him, but not too far. He hovered softly, before venturing into her mouth with the flavor of sweet cream and buttery cake. Not rich like the soufflé they'd had for dessert, but no less delicious.

He didn't stroke or demand, he merely explored and retreated before daring to do it again.

The taste of him ignited an unbearable ache deep within her that, if fed, would become dangerous for them both.

Suddenly Nora was very aware she'd been gone from her own ball for far too long. That she'd be missed, and people would come looking.

Especially since Michael would have returned and, hopefully, been frightened enough by Titus's threat, to make his excuses and leave.

Lord, she wished she could stay here. That she could kiss him all night and all the nights after. Indeed, she couldn't summon the strength to break away.

Seeming to sense this, he reluctantly broke the seal of their mouths, returning to soften the blow with a couple of short, soft tugs with his lips.

She emitted a sigh as he pulled back, thinking he might just be the loveliest being on this earth. A strange and silent crea-ture, as dangerous as he was docile.

"You taste like icing," she murmured. Feeling abruptly shy and ridiculous, she wanted to pluck the words back before they reached him.

"Cake," he explained in that deliberate way of his. "It's my birthday."

"Oh! I had no idea."

"Why would you?"

The words weren't meant to sound like a rebuke, she knew, but she felt it all the same. Why would she know such things about someone so beneath her?

"Well, happy birthday, Titus Conleith," she said, summoning a smile that drew his gaze to her lips. "How old are you now?"

"Seventeen."

Her eyebrows drew up at that. As tall as he'd become, as wise as the soul behind his gaze was, it was easy to forget he remained three years her junior.

"You should get back," he said, echoing her earlier thoughts. Releasing her, he let out a shaky breath, retrieved his gloves, and stood.

Nora felt his absence with a keen sort of ache that almost shamed her. She wasn't a woman of such need. She didn't form attachments, nor did she entertain impossible notions. So... what was this between them?

"I'll go in ahead to make sure that bastard is gone," he offered, pulling the white gloves on to hide the rough fingers he'd only just caressed her with. Ones that would offend any woman in that ballroom.

But not her.

"Of course. Thank you and... Goodnight, Titus."

He gazed down at her a breathless moment, and she almost thought he might reach down, haul her to her feet, and kiss her wits right out of her.

And perhaps more.

Instead he balled his fist at his side and strode away from her, but not before the night breeze carried his words over his shoulder.

"Goodnight... Nora."

Sniffling, Nora looked down at the handkerchief in her hand and gasped at the initials she found embroidered there.

They were hers.

She'd offered him this very handkerchief years ago in the paddock.

He'd kept it all these years.

CRUEL TO BE KIND

*G*oodnight, Nora.

He said it nearly every evening for three blissful months, and it never ceased to vibrate through her with a warm incandescence.

Titus Conleith had been not only her most lovely secret, but also a revelation.

Was it always like this, she wondered, falling in love? It was as if the world—nay—the entire *cosmos* had shifted to make way for the two of them to revel in each other.

And no one seemed to notice.

Or, rather, they'd been too rapt to pay heed to anyone else.

Her father had been not only furious but befuddled by the abject silence emanating from the direction of the Marquess of Blandbury, the man claimed to be inaccessible due to his health. Despite that, or perhaps because of it, the Baron had barely spoken a word to her, presumably moving on to more important matters now that Parliament had resumed session.

Nora still attended balls and soirees, fittings and functions as any dutiful debutante should, but whenever she had a moment to herself, it belonged to Titus, as well.

He'd become the groom she took to assist and accompany on her long, rollicking rides across Rotten Row in Hyde Park. They'd fly over the golden ground of the horse track, their heads low and their hearts racing in time to the hooves of their mounts.

She watched him covertly as they walked the park to cool the animals. How tall and fine he looked astride the bay steed, even among lords more turned out than he.

Titus didn't require a brilliant suit to stand out. To stand above. He did it merely by existing. When he trotted by, men made way for him, and women turned to look at him.

More frequently to gape and admire.

He wore no top hat, as he was no gentleman, though sometimes he'd set a wool cap against the sun or inclement weather. More often, he'd comb his fingers through locks as rich as Spanish chocolate, and they'd settle in the most perfect sweep back from his forehead.

Nora always overheard a dreamy sigh or two added to hers when he thusly contained a mane tousled by a spirited ride.

Extraordinarily, he seemed to be unaware of his effect.

He never flirted with the women who would try to capture his attentions; indeed, he was invariably aloof whilst managing to remain deferential. It was as though he used his politeness to keep people at a distance whilst still retaining their good opinion.

No small skill, that.

His was an honest, uncomplicated confidence. He'd a smooth way of moving about the world in which he existed, with the ease of someone who was born with a certain sense of self-possession. He never asked for anyone's respect or permission because he required neither.

He was who he was. He did what he must, and the rest of the time, he did what he liked.

And dared anyone to stop him. Or maybe he just realized no one would dare try.

There was something so refreshing about that. So unsophisticated and natural.

Nora basked in it. She rolled herself up in his atmosphere like it was a warm blanket, and she wished for nothing more than to stay within the shelter of his blindingly handsome smile for the rest of her days.

He escorted her on picnics, often with Pru or the twins in tow, and they'd all have impassioned discussions. She'd been delighted to discover that beneath all his solemnity he was possessed of a dry humor and a sharp wit that ignited with a quick tinder. He'd regale them about what he learned with Dr. Alcott, and she and Felicity would needle him for the gorier details, most of which he was loath to share. She loved how impassioned and animated he became when he spoke of medicine, his face alight with interest.

She loved that, in him, she had found a genuine companion. A true friend.

But most of all, she looked forward to evenings like this one, where, after his work with Dr. Alcott had finished, he'd scale the trellis to her balcony and slip into her bedroom.

Nora would leave a lantern lit and sit in wait, every hair on her body vibrating with anticipation. She'd brush out her curls until they glimmered, and smooth her skin with cream, touching a tiny bit of rose water behind her ears.

And when he would pause in the door like he did now, as if he needed a moment of stillness to take in the sight of her, she positively thrummed with feminine delight.

He didn't need to tell her she was beautiful; she could see it in the way those golden eyes ignited with a molten flame before he came to her. Before his hands sifted through the waves of her hair, setting every nerve of her body alight with sensation.

Though he'd fiercely protected her virtue, even from himself, he was all wickedness when he touched her like this.

When their lips met, she forgot that her feelings for him were forbidden.

When his hands skimmed across her skin, the coarse fibers of his fingertips snagging on the softness of her, she allowed herself a small sense of wonder. A tiny ember of hope.

She lost herself in the discovery of the peaks and planes of his topography. And she found herself in the reflection of worship with which he touched her.

Each night he came to her unlocked a new depth of passion. At first, it'd been chaste kisses and broad smiles. Then the kisses had become wilder, the caresses bolder.

More intimate.

Her nightdress began to disappear, and so did his trousers.

She learned the shape of his need. He learned the depths of her desire. And together, with breathless astonishment, they'd discovered the pleasure of which the human body was capable.

Tonight was different, though. Something more primitive lurked beneath his caress. A base and carnal urgency that called to everything that made her a woman.

He was no longer learning. *He knew.*

He no longer sought. *He claimed.*

Nora found herself beneath him, felt her legs open so he might settle between as she stretched with a liquid, boneless languor brought on by thorough attentions.

His movements and kisses had been so entirely masculine. Fervent. Arduous.

Possessive.

This new dynamic from him had excited her with such ferocity it had almost frightened her.

Because she wanted to claim him as well.

She wanted ownership of the heart that, even now, felt as though it were locked away in some hollow place. Sometimes, when he seemed very far away, she wanted to rip him open and lay him bare. If only to understand what constantly remained out of her reach.

Was this love? This desperate, wanton need? This endless curiosity?

This relentless infatuation?

As he hovered above her, this man who was barely not a boy, she smoothed a dark forelock away from his face, and smiled as it fell right back in place.

His arms trembled. His eyes burned with need. With the question. With a flame that matched the one burning in her heart.

She wrapped her body around him, welcoming him in.

Not a word was said in the darkness, as their virtue was relinquished to the other. They communicated in sighs and hitches of breath. They spoke with their fingertips and their features, the language that was created the moment one human had ever desired another. And though there was a flash of pain, there was pleasure, too.

And Nora knew he would forever own her body, heart, and soul.

THE NEXT MORNING

*N*ora decided to forgo a ride in Hyde Park, as she twinged and ached in secret places. The need to see Titus was overwhelming today; not only did her physical body feel a bit raw, but so did her soul. His quiet eyes would soothe her as they always did. His voice would lend her the reassurance she needed. It was silly, she knew, this desire to be certain that now that he'd had her body, his heart was still true.

She tried to find him in the stables, if only to tell him not to bother saddling her horse and to suggest a stroll, instead, to somewhere neither of them would be recognized.

They might even walk arm in arm like a true couple and discuss things that were not so idle. Like their dreams for the future.

Finding the stables empty of all but the horses, she mounted the narrow steps to his room above the mews, overlooking the hubbub of the street. Often, she would find him there poring over a medical text, and she'd have to distract him with soft kisses to his neck before convincing him to do something frivolous with her.

She knocked on his door before depressing the latch. "Titus? You're not still sleeping, are you? I thought we might—"

"Honoria."

That one word pinned her boots to the shabby wood floor as her father stood like a titan in the middle of the room, advertising just how small and sparce it truly was.

Glacial blue eyes speared her with such abject condemnation, her legs threatened to give way.

"So it's true," he spat, reading the guilt that must have splashed across her face with a fiery crimson hue. "Really, Honoria, your behavior is beyond the pale."

"Where is he?" she gasped, taking in the empty cot and the one scarred trunk now open and devoid of all personal effects.

"He's been thrown onto the streets like the rubbish he is." His boots made such a terrible thunder against the rickety wooden loft floor as he moved to the window to survey Mayfair, as if to make certain Titus was not still out there.

Nora's heart did a swan dive into her stomach as tears pricked her eyes. He was already gone? She knew that she stood on the precipice of a life-altering cataclysm, and she did her best to rein in her thoughts, which bucked and galloped like a panicked horse. Now was not the time to be irrational or overwrought. Clarence Goode did not react well to emotion or sentiment. He needed her to be logical. Amiable. Measured. Disciplined.

She took a deep breath. "Allow me to explain what is—"

"There is only one plausible explanation when a boy is climbing down from your balcony in the wee hours of the morning," he said with a lethal calm, though his jowls trembled with a barely leashed anger. "A *son* dallying with the help is understandable, I've done it myself from time to time, but you *know* better!"

He whirled away from the window to stab an accusatory finger at her. "A woman's worth is her virtue, as it says in the

Good Book. And I don't care to know how far you've carried on with this boy, but you've shamed me, Honoria, and you've disgraced yourself. I can barely stand to look at you."

She swallowed the disgust his words brought forth in her, and squared her chin against him. "I have not dallied with Titus, Father, I truly care for him. I-I love him. He's honest and kind and he's endlessly good. He saved my life."

"That doesn't mean he gets to help himself to your body! I'd rather you had succumbed to fever than to a coal boy."

She stepped forward, clasping her hands together in front of her wounded heart. "You don't mean that."

"Don't I?" he fumed.

"Titus has done much more for our family and our household than shoveling coal. He is going to be a doctor, like Alcott, who you consider your friend and social equal. He can make a good living. He could be part of our family."

He slammed the lid of the trunk closed hard enough to splinter it, causing her to jump. "Wake. *Up*. You stupid girl. Alcott is the fifth son of a very fortunate Viscount. Considering a street urchin like yours would ruin us all. Would you do that to your sisters? Would you soil Pru's chances at happiness? I'll have a hard enough time offloading the twins, what with Mercy's relentless mouth and Felicity's ridiculous mind. *You* will love whom I tell you to love, and that's the end of it!"

"I will not!" Though lanced with guilt at the thought of her sisters surviving a scandal she'd created, she likewise shook with temper and fear, longing and loss. She'd never stood up to her father before. To anyone really. She'd been born biddable, but *this* she could not abide. "I'm of age, Father, I'll leave with him. We'll go far away and we'll make it on our own. You'll never have to see me again. No one ever need know what I've done. You can make up whatever fiction you wish. Tell people I'm dead if that helps the situation."

He stunned her by throwing his head back and barking out

a harsh and mirthless laugh, before striding to her and grasping her by the arm. "If you do anything of the sort, I'll ruin that boy until he *wishes* he were dead. Do you hear me?" He shook her for emphasis, and she let out a gasp of pain as his fingers bit into her arm. "I'll make certain he can find no work in this city. *Worse.* I'll have him thrown into Newgate for molesting you. I have friends in the police and on the Queen's Bench. You know what happens to lads handsome as he is, in prison?"

Her eyes widened. "You wouldn't."

"Furthermore, I'll send you to Bedlam for being a disobedient wretch. They'll shave off your pretty hair and electrocute you into submission. Is that what you want?" He stood over her like a wrathful god, eyes flashing with condemnation. His hair and beard, once handsomely fair, now threaded with shocks of silver, added to the effect.

A terror Nora had never known gripped her. This was her father, a man known to be as extravagant as he was insouciant. Certainly, he'd never been a warm parent, but she'd not thought him capable of such dire, horrid cruelty.

"Answer carefully, Honoria," he spat. "Your next words will determine both of your futures. I can make certain that loving you will be the worst thing that ever happened to that boy."

She had to swallow over a lump of fear cutting off her available supply of air. "What—what do you want me to do?"

"I want you to never see him again. And I want you out of this house so I don't have to be reminded of your ungrateful wretchedness daily."

That was a blessing, she thought. She couldn't wait to leave.

"You'll marry William Mosby, Viscount Woodhaven, at the month's end. I'll post the bans this morning."

"Woodhaven?" Her breath hitched on the word as she shrank from him.

"Yes, the Cresthaven and Woodhaven titles were created by Richard III some four hundred years ago. Our families fought for the Yorks together. We're distant cousins. This would be an excellent match, under the circumstances."

Nora had danced with William Mosby at a function some months ago. There'd been a neediness in their interaction she didn't at all like. A strange sense of possession. Something frenetic and frankly, sinister.

"I'll have to rely on Pru's sweet nature and secondary beauty to secure someone higher than an Earl," he groused as if to himself.

"But, *Papa*," she pleaded.

"I won't hear it." He released her with a rough shove toward the door. "Get out of my sight. The next time I lay eyes on you will be at your wedding."

* * *

HONORIA DIDN'T SLEEP FOR DAYS. SHE SAT ON THE EDGE OF HER bed, staring at her balcony door, knowing beyond the shadow of a doubt that Titus would find a way to her.

On the fourth night, the latch clicked at one in the morning, revealing a Titus who looked as haunted and haggard as she felt.

It took every ounce of her self-possession not to fling herself into his arms.

"Nora," he breathed as he tumbled into her room, reaching for her. "Nora, are you all right?"

She stood and shoved his hands away from her, turning her back to him so she didn't have to look. "You need to go, Titus. You need to *go* and not ever darken my door again."

"No. Don't speak like that." His fingers gripped her arms and pulled her shoulder blades against his solid chest as he buried his cheek into her hair.

She wanted nothing so much as to turn into his embrace,

which was why she kept her back as straight as steel, her every muscle coiled with tension.

Lord, but she was cold. It felt as though ice ran through her veins rather than blood.

How could she do this?

"Come away with me, Nora," he implored, his hand cupping at her cheek and nudging to turn her toward him. "I know you're frightened, but we can be together."

"I don't see how," she mourned, soaking in his touch, in the hope his voice conveyed. Hope she was about to shatter.

"I've secured a position in Doctor Alcott's service," he told her urgently. "Next year I'm taking the medical exams. I've rooms to stay in and a steady income. We've a future, Nora. Just pack a case and we'll leave now."

"How could you even consider a future like that would appeal to me?" she bit out, her pain at least grating through her throat to lend her voice a harsh rasp that could have been convincing as cruelty.

His fingers tightened, and she was glad she didn't have to face him just yet, as she could feel him resist the astonished implication that it might not just be her father that would keep them apart.

"What are you saying?" he asked carefully.

"You think I want to live in a dingy room over Doctor Alcott's surgery?" she asked, summoning all the starched, imperious snobbery her upbringing had imparted to her. "You want me to malinger there while you earn pennies and ignore me for your studies? You want me to raise babies and scrub floors and cook your dinner whilst you toil away?"

She would have done it. Anything to be freed of this gilded prison. Of the walls that closed in nightly and the cage of her parents' strictures and expectations.

She would have done anything but destroy him.

His hands fell away from her and the lack of warmth

against her skin stung like the most unrelenting winter's wind. "I—I know it's not what you were raised to want."

God, she could feel him searching, could sense the frantic scrambles of his thoughts as he tried to catch up with a situation that was unraveling in a way he never expected. She wanted to hold him. To tell him what was in her heart. In her soul. To make him understand what they were both up against.

But she knew him. Knew he would fight for her because he was so noble. So true.

He was the man she wanted. A future with him was exactly what she desired.

"You wouldn't have to serve me, Nora," he said gently. "I would keep you fed. I would keep you happy. If you'd just give me a little time, I'd find a way to keep some semblance of the life you—"

"Stop!" She whirled on him, hiding her sob with a slap to his cheek. "You don't get to keep me at all."

The expression in his eyes pierced her with more pain than any she could inflict on him. The sheer bewilderment laced with betrayal. The pain.

And then, the hardening of his features as he began to believe...

He'd never know. He'd never understand what this took from her. She might be stomping on his heart, but she was rending her very soul from her skin and casting it into the abyss. She was killing herself in slow increments, knowing that the years ahead would be nothing but torture. That she would be the shell of a woman, haunting a body that no longer belonged to her.

Because her heart would be wherever he was.

"It was me who had you sacked," she lied. "Our dalliance was a bit of fun, to be sure, but I always credited you with enough sense to know nothing would come of it. And when we were found out due to your recklessness, it became more of a bother than it was a diversion. And so, I think it best we end things here."

To her astonishment, he didn't give up. "Nora, this isn't you! Tell me what's happened."

"I'm getting married."

Her words had more effect on him than her physical slap. He flinched, then froze, his body becoming unnaturally still.

"That's right." She notched her chin up higher. "I'm going to be a Viscountess, a small comfort, seeing as how you lost me a Marquess."

His expression became thunderous. "You were glad when I stopped that—"

"Was I?" She shrugged. "Perhaps I didn't feel ready then, to be a wife. But now..." Her gaze fell upon the bed where they'd made the sweetest love, so enraptured with each other it was easy to believe that no one else in the world existed. That they could overcome anything.

What fools they'd been.

And now they'd pay for it. She'd pay the most dearly.

His sharp intake of breath told her that her dagger had met its mark. That her sharp words had sawed through the invisible chord that seemed to link them together no matter where in the world they stood. All she had to do was make certain the link was severed forever.

That she smothered all hope.

"Don't make a fool of yourself by doing something so pathetic as begging, Titus," she said with all the frost threatening to harden her from the inside out. She was surprised she couldn't see her breath as she uttered the cruel words she'd learned from her father. "I can no longer stand the sight of you."

He stood looking at her as if she'd shot him, his features a mélange of denial and rage, before they, too, smoothed out into the cool lake of unrippled inscrutability she was used to.

"Goodnight, Nora," he said crisply before he strode to her door.

As she watched him go, she remembered wondering before if that sparkling, incandescent obsession, that cocoon of bliss and warmth in which they'd been ensconced, had been what true love felt like.

And here was her answer.

No.

This was love.

Sacrifice. Regret. Pain.

Love, the purest love, was diving into the lake of brimstone and hellfire, and drowning in it willingly, if only to gain freedom for the one who owned your heart.

Titus would have the opportunity to go to medical college. He'd heal people and find fulfillment and satisfaction in the worthy life he built, free of a powerful enemy like her father. He'd—no doubt—find a girl who loved him and could provide him with fat, cooing babies and happy chaos.

The idea stole her breath, it was so painful.

This was love.

And she was one raw, bleeding wound he could never heal.

A SAWBONES IN SOUTHWARK

London, 1880

"*I*f you don't hold still, I'm going to have to restrain you," Dr. Titus Conleith warned.

"Sorry, guv," said Mr. Ludlow, the dock worker currently perched on his table, gesticulating wildly for a man with sutures only half stitched. "But I just never seen any'fing like it, 'ave I? Sir Carlton Morley, the *bloody* Chief Inspector of Scotland *bloody* Yard, crawling about on a Southwark warehouse roof. Like a fucking spider he was, shooting his rifle into the windows. Glass shattered everywhere, and as I looks up, one sticks me right in me bloody 'ead."

"Morley, did this, you say?" he asked. "Here in Southwark?"

"As I live and breathe," Ludlow vowed.

Titus had met Carlton Morley when they served together in the second Anglo-Afghan war. He'd picked a bullet from the Chief Inspector's thigh once upon a time, and in the years since, they'd shared a bachelor's meal out at their club now and again.

They sometimes reminisced over how they had lost

331

Kandahar and what a blood-soaked ordeal it had been. Then they'd taken Kabul, which had been even worse.

Often in the throes of haunted insobriety, they'd share a hackney to their respective homes and part, only to do it again the next time their schedules permitted.

An unceasingly decent bloke was Morley.

These days, Titus avoided the chief inspector as the man had recently married none other than Prudence Goode under rather scandalous circumstances.

For such a large city, London was certainly a small world.

It brought Titus no little amount of pleasure that the Baron of Cresthaven's second daughter went to a man like Morley, who had been raised in a Whitechapel gutter.

He'd someday have to get the story from the horse's mouth, when he could trust himself to sit across from his old friend and keep from inquiring about—

As he always did, Titus firmly redirected his thoughts away from Morley's new sister-in-law.

Nora.

"What I would have given to stay," the man sighed, leaning in conspiratorially. "As Dorian Blackwell, his *own self,* showed up just as I was being drug 'ere by me mate, Stodgy Tim. It seemed to me like he and Morley 'us after the same poor ponce in the warehouse."

"You don't say." Titus tugged the suture clamps tight to make certain that if Ludlow moved again, they'd make him uncomfortable. He absorbed himself with stitching the wound so as not to reveal the odd amalgamation of tensions swirling within him.

The Chief Inspector of Scotland Yard and the king of the London underworld after the same enemy? There were certain to be casualties. He knew Morley from the army. He knew Blackwell from the streets.

How they knew each other was anyone's guess.

By right of their professions, alone, they were natural adversaries.

Titus worried for Prudence. A fondness for all four of the Goode girls had developed during his tenure at Cresthaven. He truly hoped that Pru—a child he remembered as sweet and mischievous—was unharmed. That Ludlow had the story completely wrong.

Was a war between the police and the underworld here at his doorstep?

The very thought curdled his stomach. How the streets would run red with blood if Blackwell and Morley truly went to battle. There weren't enough surgeons in the Empire to clean up after such a nightmare.

Titus exchanged a meaningful glance with his nurse, a battleax in her thirties by the name of Euphemia Higgins. Effie's hands were almost as large as his, and twice as gentle. She could just as easily carry a two-hundred-pound man as she could swaddle a newborn, and he'd follow her level head into a battle before most officers he'd served with. Beneath her nurse's cap and frizzy blond hair, was a brain with enviable computation capabilities. Were *she* the one with a medical degree from Cambridge, she'd rule the world and then some.

"So, you're not certain if anyone else was wounded?" he asked Mr. Ludlow with increasing urgency.

Any chance at a reply was squelched by a commotion outside.

Most people who called at Titus Conleith's Southwark Surgery door also lurked on death's doorstep. Therefore, patients or their loved ones rarely knocked politely. They pounded and screamed. Begged for help. Sometimes, they begged for death. He'd treated people who bled or leaked from every possible orifice, starting at the eyes and concluding at the other end.

Having his door splintered at the hinges with one kick, however, was entirely new.

A good surgeon trained himself not to startle. Titus had been educated with explosions rocking the earth beneath him, and bullets whizzing past his ears, so he was—luckily for Mr. Ludlow—more imperturbable than most.

"The door was unlocked," he blithely reproached Dorian Blackwell, the Black Heart of Ben More, whose boots thundered like the devil's on the rickety old floors of the clinic.

Doors didn't close to a man like him.

Not even Newgate could hold Blackwell, or so the story went. His suit, hair, and one eye were as dark as his heart, the other eye covered by a patch that almost hid the evidence of a vicious slash from his brow to his nose. The scar made his grim expression sinister as he surveyed the surgery with a critical frown.

"Someone's been shot, Conleith. Which table?"

Titus relinquished Ludlow's final sutures to Nurse Higgins, before marching past the one other empty examination table to pull back the curtains of the clinic's makeshift operation room. He'd done everything from delivering babies to removing ruptured spleens and appendixes here. Though, he usually dug bullets out of criminals after dark, and it was barely five in the evening.

"Tell me Morley's not on your heels, Blackwell," he demanded, glad to be one of the few men in the world tall enough to glare *down* at the Black Heart of Ben More as he marched past him to the sink to ruthlessly scrub his hands. "If there's a clash between the law and the underworld in my surgery, then you can find someone *else* to stitch up your army of reprobates and degenerates in the middle of the night; do I make myself clear?"

Blackwell, who had killed men for lesser offenses, merely held up his hands in a gesture of good will. "I forgot how fast news travels in these parts. I imagine Morley will be along shortly, but not for the reason you fear."

"Oh? Enlighten me." Nearly finished stripping the skin from his hands, Titus moved up his wrist and forearms with the stringent suds.

More footsteps clomped up the few stairs from the street into his surgery, these weighted down by the burden of a stretcher. As he stood at the sink, Titus's back was to the door, and Blackwell's bulky shoulders blocked any view he might have had.

"Where do we put her?" a rough voice inquired.

Her?

Titus froze, his hand at his elbow, his breath caught in his throat.

"Operating table at the back," Higgins directed in her starched Cockney accent.

"Is—is it Pru—Morley's wife?" he asked, after clearing dread out of his throat.

"No, Prudence is unharmed. She was kidnapped by her own brother-in-law, who used her as a hostage to not only escape the police, but some rather ruthless cocaine smugglers, even by my standards." Blackwell examined him oddly as Titus rinsed his hands. "The villain shot his own wife before Morley eviscerated him with frankly astonishing rifleman skills."

Nurse Higgins—the marvelous creature—had finished Ludlow's stitches in record time and left Mr. Ludlow to bandage his own wound so she could scrub her hands and retrieve the sterilized surgical instruments from the carbolic acid.

Suddenly Titus didn't want to turn to look. Not because he was bothered by blood…

But because he'd finally processed the information Blackwell had just imparted.

Prudence Morley—originally Prudence Goode—only had

one brother-in-law. William Mosby, the Viscount Woodhaven, who'd just shot his own wife before falling victim to Morley's rifle.

His own wife.

The room tilted as Titus turned to find his worst nightmare on his operating table.

Nora.

FROM THE VEIN

*T*itus's hands had never been so unsteady during a procedure.

Never had he barked orders so terribly at Higgins as he sheared Nora's blood-soaked gown from her alarmingly pale, unconscious body. Nor had he growled commands so fiercely at a man as dangerous as Blackwell, to wash his hands and prepare to help.

Never had he prayed to every saint his father had believed in with such dire fervency as when he searched for an exit wound. Nor given such thanks when he found one.

The bullet had gone through her, but the sheer amount of blood pouring from her shoulder meant the situation was increasingly dire.

"Her pulse and breaths are thready," Higgins informed him, timing them with her watch. "I shouldn't like to use the anesthesia."

"Nor I, but this amount of blood tells me an axillary vein may have been nicked, and if I get in there to repair it and she moves in the slightest…"

He couldn't say it. He couldn't even consider the prospect

that the only woman he ever loved and hated would bleed to death on his own table.

By his own hand.

For the first time in his career, Titus's choices were truly untenable. Like most doctors, he'd learned to accept early on that his profession was merely a way to delay death, not to defeat it.

But, regardless of what Alcott had taught him at such an early age, *she* could never be just a dying body.

Because death wasn't an option.

"I'll meticulously count every breath, Doctor," Higgins said in a gentle manner he'd never heard her use before, as she placed the anesthesia mask over Nora's mouth and nose. "She'll get through this."

Nora. Nora. Her name became the rhythm of his heartbeat as he delved into the intricate sinew of her shoulder. He had to irrigate away alarming amounts of blood to find the correct vein, and then to clamp and stitch it.

Fate aligned with his expertise, as every surgeon knew that each body was made up of similar constructions that could also be as vast and varied in their particular assembly as stars in the sky. Miraculous good fortune deemed that the vein was easily found and that the nick was small, or she'd have expired before they could have loaded her in the carriage.

Titus didn't breathe as he released the clamp, until he saw that he'd repaired the damage.

His relief was such that her name escaped him on a whisper, and he fought to keep the starch in his knees.

Nora.

He wasn't aware he'd been sweating until Higgins passed a cloth over his forehead and upper lip, firmly planting him into the present.

No, he reminded himself. Not *Nora*. Not to him.

Lady Honoria Mosby, Viscountess Woodhaven.

Now that the vein had been repaired, he still had to work on the other tissue and sinew surrounding the wound.

A tremor coursed through him as he looked down at her torso, bare but for where a strip of cloth placed by Higgins covered her breasts. *God*, she'd always been a small and fragile creature, but now her bones seemed like that of a sparrow's. The years hollowed out her cheeks, and dark shadows smudged beneath her eyes. Her features were still magnificent, though, and razor sharp. Her lashes black fans against porcelain skin made ashen from the loss of blood.

She was still the most beautiful woman he'd ever laid his eyes upon.

Still.

Always.

Which was why he'd resolved long ago to never fucking lay eyes upon her again.

But here they were.

In the stormy chaos of life, Titus prided himself on being a smooth lake of glass. Reflective and serene.

But right now, his thoughts spun like a tornado, flinging debris at him that he couldn't seem to avoid.

"Distract me, Blackwell," he ordered as he handed the man the clamp to discard, and selected other instruments.

The Black Heart of Ben More—who had assisted in a few late-night surgeries for lack of a nurse—had returned from the sink where he'd removed his coat, rolled up his shirtsleeves, and scrubbed his own hands. He looked at Titus askance. "I rather assumed you'd need to focus."

"It's difficult to explain, but often distraction helps me to concentrate." Titus bent over her, triple-checking his work on her vein before stitching the other sinew. He wished like hell her color wasn't so grey and her breath wasn't so shallow. That he didn't suddenly feel like that helpless boy of fourteen scrambling to save her precious life for the first time. "Since my other nurse, Miss Michaels, isn't here to assist nor read to me, that responsibility falls to you."

"You wish me to…read to you?"

"No, dammit, just—talk to me. I don't know. Tell me what the devil happened."

Blackwell looked as if he might argue, but something in Titus's countenance must have convinced him because he sighed and relented. "It's a rather sordid tale, but from what I gather, her husband was—if you'll pardon my technical language, Higgins—a fucking lunatic."

Higgins, a woman used to every curse word in the Queen's English, asked, "Why shoot his own wife, the poor lamb?"

"On a bit of a killing spree, her husband was," Dorian said with a grim sarcasm. "Do you remember the Earl of Sutherland, the one who Prudence was supposed to marry before she supposedly murdered him?"

Titus gave a curt nod. "I remember reading that in the papers…didn't believe it for a moment."

"Well, come to find out, Woodhaven killed Sutherland and a handful of other men who were reportedly Stags of St. James."

Titus wondered at Nurse Higgins's astonished gasp until she clarified. "You mean… the male prostitutes?" She whispered the last word, appropriately scandalized.

"Just so." Blackwell nodded.

"Was he…were they lovers of his?"

"Apparently not," Dorian answered blithely. "It was a revenge killing, you see. Woodhaven systematically murdered anyone who shared his wife's bed."

Titus dropped his suture clamps with an embarrassingly loud clatter, effectively putting a stop to all conversation. He took a precious breath to compose himself before directing Blackwell where to find another sterile instrument.

He didn't make mistakes like this. He *couldn't*. Not when the stakes were so high.

Nora had taken her husband's best friend to her bed? She'd paid men—a *handful* of men—for sex?

How the years had changed her. Or perhaps they hadn't...

She'd been a stranger to him the night she'd sent him away; perhaps that was when she'd truly been revealed to him.

Clean clamps appeared in his hand, and he immediately went back to work, muttering to Blackwell out of the side of his mouth. "If you ever tire of a life of crime, you'd have an excellent career as a nurse ahead of you."

Blackwell's chortle was nearly mirthless. "Well now, I'm almost completely legitimate these days. I've an angel of a wife and two cherubic miscreants with my name. One might even call me respectable."

"If you find me that one, I'll find you a liar," Titus jested, grateful to the man for helping to release some of the tension.

Higgins, however, had to satisfy her bottomless curiosity. "If her husband was a murderer, then, what's this I heard about cocaine?"

"Apparently, Woodhaven was using his father-in-law's shipping company to smuggle the drug into the city, and some corrupt police officers to deal to the public," Blackwell answered.

Titus's brow crimped as he tried to work out the angle of a lunatic. "Why smuggle? It's not as if cocaine is illegal. Many of my associates use it as medicine."

From beside him, Blackwell made a derisive sound. "And you don't?"

Titus shook his head, then steadied himself over a more complicated stitch. "I don't like the side effects. Nor the addictive properties. There are more effective treatments that have been more thoroughly studied."

"I approve," Blackwell announced. "I predict that, like opium, more ill will come of it than good. However, it is addic-

341

tive, inexpensive, and abundant on the black market. Men are making fortunes."

"Did Woodhaven?"

Titus had the sense that Dorian shrugged, but he couldn't look over just now to check.

"I believe he was beginning to, though no one knows how deep his cocaine smuggling reaches, and he'll never tell, seeing as how they're scraping his teeth off the wall of the warehouse where Morley's bullet planted them."

Titus dared a glance at Nora's face, glad it was currently covered by the anesthesia mask. "Do they suspect she had anything to do with it?"

Blackwell hesitated. "That I don't know. Whatever she's done, she was bloody brave, trading her life for her sister's at the warehouse."

Suddenly, it occurred to Titus to ask about the Black Heart of Ben More's involvement in all this. "Was he smuggling for you?"

Blackwell's incensed gasp was too overdone to be serious. "He was smuggling for the Fauves, I'll have you know. Something of a rival, once upon a time."

"The Fauves?" Titus searched his extremely limited French vocabulary. "Beasts?"

"Wild beasts, technically." He felt more than watched Blackwell roll his eyes. "Fucking smugglers with delusions of grandeur."

"Did they ever have children?" Titus didn't know the question was about to leave his lips until it materialized.

"How should I know? I don't socialize with Fauves."

"No, I mean she and Woodhaven."

"Evidently not," Blackwell said with no small amount of pity. "With no heir, she effectively has nothing. Perhaps a stipend, if her father is kind."

He knew that bastard was anything but kind.

Not wanting to hear any more, Titus worked in silence for a while as he looked down at her, wondering what tomorrow would bring in either of their lives.

He could feel Dorian's eyes on him with a niggling prickle long before the man spoke. "Before she lost consciousness, she acted like she knew you. She—*begged* us to bring her here. Demanded it."

God. He didn't want to know that. He didn't want to feel the extra beats that information threaded into his heart.

"I—worked in the Goode household as a lad," he said by way of explanation.

"Did you know her well?" Blackwell ventured.

The question caused an explosion of rage and wrath to tumble through his chest. He wasn't *this* man. He didn't have *these* feelings. He'd ruthlessly stuffed any sort of sentiment he had for her down into the deepest recesses of that clear, glass lake. Somewhere in the reeds and the shadows that no one could dredge up. That was where she lived. He'd never even looked twice at a dark-haired woman.

In fact, his current lover was a buxom girl with generous breasts, copper-gold hair, and a giving mouth.

Nora—Lady Woodhaven.

She was ancient history. And yet something stirred within him. An echo of intensity he'd suffered on her behalf as a boy. Did he know her well? He'd thought so.

And then she'd proven him wrong.

Blackwell inspected his work with an appreciative sound. "Did she mean something to you?" he prodded.

Titus speared him with a look so sharp, it could have drawn blood.

Blackwell's brow arched. "Say no more."

IN THE LIGHT OF DAY

P lease don't hate me.

Nora had made the silent appeal so many times in the past couple of days, it'd become a prayer. A chant. Both an invocation and a benediction.

At first, she'd not said it out loud because she was incapable of speech. A miasma of agonies occasionally intercepted by a sweet, dreamy numbness, had taken days from her. She'd swam in a lake of her own shame and sorrow, drowning in the dark of her unconscious, plagued by dreams and memories of blood and cruelty and fear.

She'd surface from the dark to a world of white. White-hot pain lanced through her chest and arm, whilst blinding-white fluttering veils obscured the world from view.

Then, Titus would appear—a miracle haloed by all that purity—frowning down at her from features older and more brutal than she remembered. She would drink in the sight of him like a condemned soul would their last glance of salvation, fingers twitching with the need to smooth that frown from his dignified brow.

She knew her limbs were incapable; to move would only

cause her pain, so she'd simply gaze at him and try to remember how her dry, swollen tongue worked.

In these brief moments of semi-lucidity, she would catalogue the changes wrought in this Titus from the one who resided in her precious memory.

His hair had darkened to a rich umber, though that unruly forelock still wanted to rest above his eye. The crests of his cheeks stood out in stark relief from features once angled by youth and now squared by maturity. His eyes, though etched with a few more lines than before, were still the color of brilliant sunlight through a glass of young whiskey. Light enough to glimmer golden against skin kissed by a foreign sun.

His lips moved, and the rumble of his voice would transfix her so utterly, the words fluttered in her mouth like a riot of butterflies disturbed by a predator.

Don't hate me.

She'd try so hard to say it, until a prick in her arm would drag her away from him. Back to that place where vivid dreams would first seduce her, then lash at her as they turned into nightmares.

Sometimes when she surfaced, other dear faces would hover above her in the white. Prudence, her features like a younger, fuller mirror of her own, the space between her eyebrows a furrow of worry. She spoke of forgiveness and love, and wiped away the tears that leaked from Nora's eyes into her hair.

Felicity's emotion would fog her spectacles, so she'd keep her thoughts to herself, deciding instead to read aloud, her gentle voice a soothing melody in the chaos of Nora's unruly dreams.

Mercy would often take her hand, squeezing too tightly as she bade her—commanded her—to recover. To win whatever battle she must in order to return to them.

Sometimes a stern-looking woman with a corona of fair,

disobedient hair would startle her awake, only to pacify her with unexpected gentility whilst she took care of necessities.

In those moments, Nora would become certain that she'd merely dreamed Titus and her beloved sisters into existence, and she was really trapped in some strange sort of purgatory, awaiting her sentencing to hell.

Just as she began to despair that the floating void would keep her forever, Titus's voice breached the haze with a new clarity as he held a genial conversation in her periphery.

When Nora surfaced, she was both delighted and dismayed to discover that she was herself. Her vision swam, her body was unnaturally heavy, and her shoulder throbbed like the very devil, but not so urgently as her disquiet heart.

She wasn't dead. William hadn't killed her.

Would wonders never cease?

Information permeated her muddled senses incrementally as she took in her surroundings. The white sheets acted as some sort of privacy partition in what she assumed was a hospital. Her nose twitched at scents unfamiliar to any hospital she'd ever visited. Something stringent and clean permeated the distinctive aroma of creosote and coal, horses, petrol, and the brine and grime of the river, all amalgamating into an atmosphere of industry.

Turning her head, she caught her breath as either the early-morning or late-afternoon sun—she couldn't be certain which —cast perfect shadows of people on the other side of the sheet.

She watched the pantomime with arrested interest.

An astonishingly tall, wide-shouldered man braced his knee against the table where another man lay. With a strong, brutal motion, he gave the patient's arm a mighty wrench.

Nora heard the shoulder go into the socket before the patient's bark of pain tugged at her heart.

A smile also tugged at the corner of her lips as she listened to a sonorous baritone soothe and encourage as the tall man made a sling and secured his patient's arm to his chest.

Years at Cambridge still never trained the Yorkshire out of Titus's voice. His vowels were as long and lush as ever.

Nora knew she had any great number of things to be agonizing over. Her life had fragmented in one catastrophic explosion, and she lay in the crater with the damage yet to be entirely assessed.

And yet, even though the pain in her shoulder became increasingly insistent, she allowed herself the sweet gift of this unguarded moment to listen to a voice she'd never expected to hear again.

Titus Conleith.

His manner was everything she remembered, both aloof and kind. But there was a gruffness to his tone that she didn't recognize, as if fatigue had paved his throat with gravel and pitch.

After finishing with his patient, his shadow drew closer, and Nora couldn't say why she feigned sleep before he approached.

Perhaps she wasn't ready to learn what he thought of her after all these years.

He paused at her bedside for a moment too long, and she simply listened to the breath he drew into his lungs and exhaled over her.

They were once again sharing the same air. She could hardly believe it.

In response, her breaths became shorter, less constant, catching as he reached down and pulled the bedclothes away from her shoulders.

Strange, that this should be happening again. That he'd brought her back from the edge of death a second time.

Had he bathed her as he had when they were younger? Did he care to?

She clenched her jaw against the pain as he ever so gently checked beneath the clean bandage that the astonishingly strong nurse had applied a few hours ago.

Her eyes cracked open of their own accord, hungry for the sight of him.

Nora had always known he'd make an even more handsome man than he'd been a lad, but she'd never guessed he'd grow even taller than he'd been at seventeen. His wide jaw and sharp chin were buttressed by a perfectly starched collar. The cream of his shirt made brilliant by a bronze vest that looked exquisitely tailored to his deep chest and long torso.

In contrast, he wore no jacket, his tie was charmingly askew, and his cheeks wanted shaving. His shadow beard was tinted more russet than dark, advertising his Irish roots.

He didn't notice her assessment of him as his gaze inspected her wound with absorbed thoroughness.

Evidently gratified by what he found, he replaced the bandage and, with utmost care, tugged the hospital gown back into place. Lingering, he pulled the bedclothes to cover her and smoothed the edge over her good arm with a large palm, as if unable to abide a wrinkle.

It was the first time anyone had touched her with deference in as long as she could remember.

"Titus." His name escaped as a rasp from a throat dry with disuse and tight with emotion.

He straightened, yanking his hand away as if she'd burned him.

Their gazes met for a moment so fraught with intensity, it would have struck her down had she not already been prone. Every word ever said and unsaid between them overflowed the filmy white chamber with a tension so thick she could have plucked entire expletives out of thin air.

In the space of a blink, all expression evaporated from his

face, and a shutter made of iron slammed down behind his eyes.

"Doctor Conleith," he corrected with careful dispassion.

With those two words, he drew the boundaries between the continents separating them, and erected fortifications that would have protected against an entire fleet of Viking invaders.

It was what she deserved, but it still devastated her.

Don't hate me. Please.

She opened her mouth, unable to truly believe they had a moment alone.

"Higgins, it seems Lady Woodhaven is awake," he clipped, effectively cutting her off.

"Is she now?" The sturdy nurse appeared at the head of her bed as if quite by magic, and leaned over to press a hand to her brow before taking a lantern from the side of her bed to shine in her eyes. Both doctor and nurse bent to check in each eye with an almost comical thoroughness.

For what, Nora couldn't begin to guess.

"Welcome back to the land of the living, Lady Woodhaven." Nurse Higgins gave an endearing, gap-toothed smile that took years from her square features as she lifted Nora's head to allow her a few sips of cool water. "Looks like you're going to pull through."

"Thank you," she whispered.

"Nora?" The wall of sheets was batted aside as if they barred the gates to a keep. Mercy, of all people, charged in like a battering ram beribboned in sapphire silk.

"Nora, *thank God.*" She made her way to the bedside, clutching at the headboard and hovering as if she wanted to do something but couldn't figure out what. "Are you in very much pain? Do you require anything? Please don't fret. Pru and Morley will be here in..." She checked the silver watch she kept on a chain in the pocket of a velvet cobalt vest. "Four minutes ago." Her dark gold brows drew together. "Odd, it's not like them to be late."

As was often the case, Felicity followed in Mercy's wake, though she hung back, clutching a book to her chest as if it could shield her from conversations with people.

"Traffic on the bridge is insufferable this time of day," she managed helpfully before flushing scarlet when she noticed Mercy, Titus, Nora, and Nurse Higgins all turned to listen to what she'd said.

As Felicity held the sheet aside with one hand, Nora was able to see past her to what she noticed was only one rather large but ramshackle room. A waiting area consisted of six chairs in a circle, one of which was just vacated by a roughshod woman who was helping the man with his arm in a sling out the door.

The proximity to the windows told her she might occupy one of two or three beds in the entire place.

She blinked back to Titus, who lingered at the foot of her bed, having made room for her sisters to stand opposite Nurse Higgins.

It distressed Nora to find him in such a dilapidated clinic. With his brilliance, he could have secured a dignified position anywhere in the Empire. He'd such dreams when they were young, such ambitions. To alleviate suffering. To fight disease. To advance scientific medicine.

Well, they were neither of them young anymore.

She'd always hoped that life had been kinder to him, because of what she'd done.

And now, it seemed, even that hope was dashed.

Hot tears stung her eyes and, for the first time since she'd awoken, she was glad he wouldn't look directly at her.

Apparently interpreting her expression incorrectly, Mercy repeated, "Are you in very much pain?" She looked imploringly up at Titus. "Should we give her something?"

Nora was in enormous pain, but it had less to do with her shoulder than the aching heart beneath it. "I-I'm all right, Mercy." She managed, with great effort, to lift her cheeks into the weak semblance of a smile. "I'd like to clear my head a little, I think."

"I agree that's best," Titus addressed Mercy rather than her, directly, as if her vivid sister could act as a conduit between them. "Though if the pain becomes untenable, I've found it can hinder healing."

"So, don't you suffer needlessly," Mercy ordered, stroking a lace glove over her hair.

Oh no. Her hair. Nora swallowed a pained groan. She couldn't bear to imagine what she looked like, and with her first love looming over her like some disheveled Adonis.

It shouldn't matter. But it did.

"Can you believe this is *the* Titus Conleith who used to work at Cresthaven?" Mercy presented him with the ease of someone who'd become well acquainted whilst she was asleep. "He saved your life not once but twice! Surely you remember, Nora? He and Felicity used to exchange books, and sometimes he'd carry our things out on picnics and shopping."

Nora's stomach turned abruptly sour at the words. Even as they'd carried on together, she'd treated him like the servant he was. He'd saddled her horses and carried her parcels, and she'd taken the assistance for granted.

"I remember everything," she whispered, hoping the hollow note in her voice didn't reveal her.

His expression never changed, though the hand that had been resting on the iron footboard of her bed now tightened.

Felicity, dressed in a more subdued blue gown than her twin, adjusted her spectacles before reaching down to brush tentative fingers over Nora's hand. "Do you remember what happened before you were...injured?"

A dreadful gravity washed her in pinpricks of pain, starting at her scalp and trickling down her spine to land in her gut. "William…"

She couldn't force any more words around the growing lump of emotion in her throat.

If her father was the architect of her misery, then William was the engineer. For over a decade, he'd hurt, manipulated, and humiliated her. He had killed five men because Nora had allowed them to touch her.

Thank God he hadn't known about Titus. *Thank God. Thank God.*

"They cremated your late husband's remains," Felicity said gently, "and I took the liberty of having them interred at the family cemetery in Shropshire, without much ado."

Nora started, then winced as the slightest movement sent a burning sort of pain through her shoulder. "How long have I been here?"

"Four nights," Mercy answered.

"We've been taking turns watching over you so Dr. Conleith can see to his other patients, but he examines you every morning and is here every evening." Felicity dared a glance up at him before her gaze darted away. "And we all meet here for tea or supper, just as Dr. Conleith does his final rounds."

Nora did her best to blink away confusion. "We all?"

Mercy gestured expansively to the clinic at large. "Felicity, Prudence, and Morley, of course. Did you know he and Dr. Conleith fought in the war together?"

"Morley did most of the fighting," Titus said with a self-effacing grimace. "I was merely a medical officer."

He was never *merely* anything.

Nora had known he'd left Cambridge for a while before returning, but she hadn't discovered why until now.

Had war crafted the boy she'd loved into this man of brutal strength and sinew? Had it hardened his gentle eyes and deepened the brackets beside his mouth?

"I'm touched," Nora whispered. "That you were all here by my side, despite..." Despite the damage her husband had wrought on the entire family.

"Of course we were!" Mercy exclaimed. "Nora, had we known what William was like. What you had to endure—"

"Mercy." Felicity seized her twin's hand, looking as if she wanted to brain her sister with the tome she still held. "Let's not speak of that now, she's only just regained consciousness."

"Right." Chagrined, Mercy dropped her hands to her sides and clutched at her skirts as if she could contain herself that way.

"Mama and Papa send their...good wishes," Felicity said with an unconvincing smile. "They'll be ever so relieved to hear that you're out of the proverbial woods."

Would they be? Nora wasn't so certain. It might have been easier for them if she and William had *both* perished on the docks.

They could bury her shame forever.

Mention of the Baron and Baroness of Cresthaven seemed to galvanize Titus into action. He pulled a notebook from a pocket hanging at the foot of her bed. "The bullet created a small tear in your axillary vein, through which you lost a great deal of blood," he informed the notes as he flipped through them with industrious fervor. "That can be blamed for your lengthy lack of consciousness. However, there have been no signs of further bleeding nor infection. I see no reason you cannot return to Cresthaven Place tomorrow to recover. I'll send notes and diagrams of my surgical repair for the attending doctor and—"

"Actually." Mercy held up a finger as if trying to get the attention of a teacher in class, though she looked nonplussed when it worked.

As if she didn't want to say what came next.

"Father mentioned... well, he thinks it's best you do not

convalesce at Cresthaven Place. Not until William's crimes are all uncovered, and the extent of the scandal is known. There was no talking him out of it. You know how he is."

After so many years, her parents' lack of concern shouldn't hurt so much.

And yet...

Nora sighed. Perhaps she'd woken up too soon, after all. "It's all right. I would like to sleep in my own bed before I have to relinquish it to whomever will become the next Viscount Woodhaven."

"Do you know who that will be?" Mercy asked with an anxious wrinkle between her brows.

"I haven't the faintest idea. William had no siblings nor cousins, and was still convinced that I'd eventually give him an heir."

A soft clack rang in the silence that followed, sounding very much like teeth crashing together. Had that vein been so prominent in Titus's forehead before?

Mercy blew a ringlet away from her eye. "I hope he's not some strident old grump with a shrew for a wife. They can't take your rooms in town, can they? I mean, you're allowed a dowager stipend, are you not?"

Nurse Higgins adopted a rather protective posture over Nora, eliciting from her the most ridiculous urge to crawl into the matronly woman's lap and sleep for days. "Now inn't the best time to be concerning her ladyship with such things, child," she gently reproached.

Sufficiently chastised, Mercy winced. "You're right, of course. Do forget all about it, Nora. I'm certain it'll work out."

Nora closed her eyes, wishing for all the world that Titus was not here to witness this. Did he know about William's crimes? About the wrongs she'd committed and the lovers she'd taken?

Likely.

She didn't care who the next Viscount Woodhaven was. She pitied him. All her husband had left him was a title tainted by scandal and weighted by untold debts.

"I—I should like to go home," she said, hating the plaintive wobble in her voice.

"That won't be possible, I'm afraid." A second masculine voice announced the arrival of Nora's recently acquired brother-in-law, Sir Carlton Morley.

He'd pulled the sheet behind Titus aside, and held it so his wife could duck around and rush to Nora before he reached out to greet Titus with a firm and familiar handshake.

Prudence, striking in a fitted day dress striped with gold and burgundy, took her place next to Nurse Higgins on Nora's uninjured side.

"There's so much to say," she whispered, kissing Nora's knuckles in a very uncommon display of affection for members of the Goode family.

Prudence had always been like that, however. Just a flower in need of rain, one who'd bloomed beneath her husband's protective, demonstrative care.

"Why can't Nora go home?" Mercy asked, cutting to the salient point as she was wont to do.

Though Titus stood a few inches taller than Morley, the Chief Inspector maintained the air of a man who commanded not only a room, but the largest and most organized police force in the civilized world. His midnight blue suit turned his glacial eyes an impossible, arresting color, and, unlike Titus, his cravat was perfect and not a single strand of fair hair would dare disobey.

The Chief Inspector was a famously contained man, but he'd demonstrated that his heart was true, and his love ran deep. He'd been prepared to die for Pru.

He'd killed for her without hesitation.

Nora wondered if he blamed her for her husband's actions.

If he suspected her of involvements in William's crimes. As it was, his sharp, angular features were softened with concern as he delivered distasteful news with care. "We obtained a warrant to search your house for evidence of your husband's cohorts, and we found it ransacked."

A sudden dizziness had her tightening her grip on Prudence's hand. "Was anyone hurt?"

"No. Needless to say, your butler's resigned his position, as have your housekeeper and several other staff. It's not safe for you to return home, Lady Woodhaven."

A sudden headache stabbed Nora behind the eye, and her shoulder throbbed in earnest now, a burning pain adding to her discomfort.

But she'd been hurt plenty of times, and had to pretend that everything was fine.

She could do it now.

"What cause have you to worry that the burglars will return?" Nora asked.

He glanced at his wife, who threw warning daggers at him with her eyes.

"Tell me," Nora demanded. "I must know."

"There…was a note left by the invaders," Prudence conveyed with palpable reluctance. "One demanding the crate that William had apparently neglected to deliver to them. They threatened to take it out of his flesh, Nora. Who is to say if they'll come for you now that he's…" She didn't say the word *dead*.

"Lady Woodhaven." Morley clutched the lapel of his coat, the only sign he had to fortify himself for the next question. "Do you know where your husband hid that money?"

"There's never *been* any money," Nora croaked, her anxiety dashing to the surface. "I'd taken to selling my jewels to pay the staff, and William squandered whatever salary he drew from the shipping company. He bragged that his newest venture was profitable, but I never saw the proof of it. I didn't believe him, all told."

She'd thought this was over. That she was finally free of him. How typical that even in death he could still threaten her safety and any chance at peace or happiness.

Morley's critical assessment was more invasive than any medical examination she'd endured, but she was too tired and soul-weary to be troubled by it. "You truly have no idea who would be after your husband?"

Nora searched the white sheet draped as a canopy above her bed for answers, noting some of the plaster from the ceiling had dislodged and peppered shadows on the fabric. No doubt, the reason the canopy was hung in the first place. "I knew he had a new venture, but he wanted to keep his where-abouts a mystery to me, and I didn't care to pry. I was stupid, I realize, but whatever took him away from the house...I encouraged it."

Her voice broke on the last word, not from tears but from fighting increasingly unrelenting pain. Her breath began to catch in spasms as a burning sensation ripped through her shoulder with gasp-inducing zings.

This was all too much.

"She's had quite enough," said Titus, accepting a cool cloth from Higgins and crowding her family away. Towering over her, he bent to wipe a sheen of sweat from her brow and upper lip.

When he brought his face close like this, she could see every striation of metallic beauty glimmering in his eyes. She could make out the variations of color in his shadow of a beard.

She could marvel at the feel of a gentle hand on her brow. How novel it was. How necessary.

"Morley, you can interrogate her some other time. She's in too much pain to be of use to you now," he ordered.

357

Nora gaped up at him. How did he know she was in pain? She'd been so careful not to let on.

Because he was a good doctor. Probably the best.

"She'll come home with us," Prudence declared. "If these cretins are after her, then she should be somewhere she's safe until Carlton has dealt with them."

Nora shook her head, her stomach curling in relief to see that Nurse Higgins had passed Titus a syringe filled with welcome oblivion. "Your house is the first place they'd look for me after Cresthaven, Pru. I won't put you and the Chief Inspector in danger."

At that, Morley let out an undignified snort. "I'm entirely capable of protecting those in my own home."

"But you cannot shirk your duties at Scotland Yard on my account," she argued. "You'll be away from home even more often if you're personally after the brigands my husband apparently stole from."

His expression was captured on the border between quizzical and offended. "I happen to know more than a few dangerous men who could keep you and my wife safe when I'm at the Yard."

She turned to the head of the Morley family. "Pru, you're with child. And until we know who my enemies are or how many—"

"She'll recover at my clinic in Knightsbridge," Titus announced before deftly sliding the needle into her arm and depressing the much-needed opiate into her vein.

Still, he refused to look her in the eye.

"You have a clinic in Knightsbridge?" Felicity asked from beside Nora, as agog as the rest of them.

Titus's chin dipped in a curt nod as Morley elucidated. "The good doctor is one of the most prolific and progressive surgeons in practice today. Hospitals and universities alike are clamoring for his expertise, but he's insisting on being a man of the people. You're lucky, Lady Woodhaven, that this new charitable venture of his was operational, or I don't know what we'd have done."

"How impressive, Dr. Conleith," Felicity marveled, staring up at him as if he'd hung the moon.

He took the needle from Nora's arm and replaced it with a cloth, holding pressure there for a moment as he crooked a lip in Felicity's direction. "I've told you to call me Titus, like in the old days."

Nora almost burst into tears at the way a touch of warmth laced his voice with velvet.

It would be what she deserved, to have to watch him fall in love with sweet, young, *darling* Felicity. They had so much in common. They were both so true of heart and she was... well she was many things now.

An invalid. An adulteress. The penniless widow of a murdering thief. Barren, ill-used, and contaminated by scandal. She'd been barely younger than Felicity was now when she'd loved Titus.

When he'd loved her, in return.

They spoke around her as the medication pulled her back down into the void, their voices urgent and quiet at the same time.

A hollow ache lodged within her that the medicine could never touch.

Why would he keep her under his roof when he could barely bring himself to look at her?

WARLORDS AND DRAGONS

*W*hat had he been thinking, insisting Nora stay beneath his roof when he could barely bring himself to look at her?

It was a question Titus asked himself every time he had to endure her presence on his examination table.

For twenty-three days, four hours and—he checked his watch—sixteen minutes, he had felt like some sort of mythic dragon with a captive maiden locked in his tower.

He didn't want to see her.

And yet, he'd become a hollow sort of fiend at the thought of never seeing her again.

Initially, he'd assumed that in the five-story Gregorian mansion he'd turned into a private surgery facility, Nora would be easy to both protect and avoid.

Stashed in his personal suite situated in the lush living quarters on the top floor, she'd have her every physical and medical need addressed by an army of staff, and she would only require his presence to see to her post-surgical care in decreasing increments until she was healed.

It was the least he could do, under the circumstances.

For his part, Titus's hours were so occupied, he barely had time to sleep, let alone think of her.

At least, that was the lie he told himself.

Using his current clinic to finance the start of five others dominated his every waking hour. He and Higgins visited at least one in each borough before the sun came up, and another at sunset, so they could spend the bulk of their time here at the Alcott Surgical Specialty Hospital.

He'd unfolded a cot in the corner of his first-floor office, and had defended the decision to Higgins's raised eyebrows thusly, "It's nearer the entrances in case of emergency, and deucedly convenient. I can't imagine why I haven't done so before."

She'd pursed her lips and rolled her eyes, wisely neglecting to mention his guest rooms upstairs.

He *didn't* have to remind her that to sleep in the same house as their guest would be scandalous and inappropriate.

To which she *didn't* reply that no one in the world knew the former Viscountess of Woodhaven was in residence, and that she couldn't possibly be the subject of more scandal than she currently was.

And he *didn't* tell her to mind her own bloody business.

Though he did employ orderlies and security on his staff, he still felt it necessary to keep an eye on things. If someone was coming for Nora, they'd have to get through him and a bevy of sharp implements first.

It was the dragon in him that made such foolhardy decisions. The same one that blazed with the instinct to wrap himself around her and breathe fire on whomever would put her in danger. He'd done so in many an exhaustion-induced dream.

But he woke to reality—and an aching back—each morning. And in said reality, he was no dragon.

And she was no maiden.

Which was why he never allowed himself to be alone with her. When Nora wandered down to the surgery as she did every evening, he made certain she was accompanied by one of her sisters, or Higgins. Titus would check her wound in this partitioned examination room, divulge the prognosis and progress, and then leave her to dress and be escorted discreetly back.

Because he couldn't trust himself to remember what sort of woman she truly was. A victim. A liar. A patient. A lover. A formative portion of his past he'd done his utmost to turn his back upon, lest he become lost to bitterness and regret.

Yes, to invite her here was to court trouble. Not only because she might be in danger, but because, despite everything, he'd come to live for these moments with her.

Moments when his fingertips found her flesh and the contact electrified him like nothing and no one else on this planet.

A doctor shouldn't feel like this, he reprimanded himself.

Shouldn't enjoy the silken strands of her hair as he pushed the midnight curls aside. Shouldn't thrill to the undoing of the intricate silk-covered buttons of her nightdress, if only to expose something as innocuous as her shoulder blade.

People were just parts. Just machines of intricate design, and he was like a machinist. A student of whatever chaotic engineer crafted such imperfect structures capable of miraculous feats of healing. He wondered sometimes that a supposedly benevolent being might build such an instable system that one tiny shift in the mechanisms and the entire thing turned on itself.

But Nora.

She'd always been something more. She wasn't simply an apparatus, she was a work of fucking art. In a world where nothing seemed to shock or thrill him, where he'd thought himself incapable of incredulity anymore. Just the sight of the improbable precision of her symmetry struck him with a sense of awe he hadn't known since he was a child discovering the newness of the entire world.

It affected him tonight just as utterly as it had done on the night he'd brought her here. Even though they'd both endured this odd routine for over three weeks, each time she appeared on his examination table elicited a strange sort of tremulous emotion. Something caught on the border of anticipation and antagonism.

Today, Mercy had kept Nora company, and was now holding a lively chat with Higgins as he examined Nora's shoulder from behind.

Titus enjoyed Mercy's company and appreciated her vivacity, especially now. She kept them from saying anything important to each other. Which was vital, because if he and Nora were alone, he might ask her why she seemed increasingly morose today.

And she might ask any one of the cryptic questions he'd seen lurking in the dark hollows of her eyes.

She might ask him what he thought of her, or how he felt. And he...hell, he couldn't answer that question in the mirror, let alone now. Furthermore, he wasn't about to unleash any sort of emotion on a woman who'd been through the trauma she had.

"Are you in pain?" he couldn't help but inquire.

"Very little," Nora replied, not even turning her head to address him.

"Is the mobility improving still?" He stabilized her shoulder with one hand, and lifted her elbow with the other, testing the movement. She winced a little, but not until they passed a threshold of motion greater than she had been previously capable.

"I see no sign of recurring inflammation and it seems the

wound itself has achieved proliferation, at least superficially. I should think we could remove your stitches tomorrow."

"That is, indeed, a relief Dr. Conleith."

They were both so serene. So polite.

It was beginning to drive him mad.

"What is proliferation?" Mercy's inquisitive voice cut through the building tension as she leaned against the wall facing both him and Nora. She'd been tracing the cheek of an articulated skeleton he'd displayed in the corner, but dropped her hand and turned her full attention upon him.

"It's the stage of healing where new tissue forms along with vessels and sinew. It's too early for comprehensive proliferation, but we are well on our way. It will take the nerves the longest to heal, in my experience. But I'd say we are completely out of the woods."

Nora merely nodded her understanding.

"That's marvelous news," Mercy declared, adjusting her slim chocolate-colored vest and fluffing her cream lace cravat. She'd obviously spent a great deal of money to adopt the appearance of a student or an intellectual, including the adornment of wire-rimmed spectacles *sans* any lenses. A castoff of Felicity's, he'd wager. However, the garnets in the comb adorning her intricate coiffure, the matching ear bobs, and the sparkle of her watch undermined the effect. As did the fact that she was obviously educated more in the feminine arts than anything else.

She was a lovely girl if one was drawn to the wholesome vigor of youth, complete with wide oceanic eyes and gestures so animated as to be considered violent in some parts of the world.

"Felicity is pretending to take a nap as herself so she can accompany Mrs. Winterton on an errand as me, so I could come here alone," she announced, her wide mouth quirking with her specific sort of mischief.

"Why alone?" Nora asked her sister. "Mrs. Winterton is not

so insufferable, as chaperones go, and seems to allow you both more freedoms than anyone they hired for Pru or me."

"Yes, well..." She darted an awkward glance to the far wall. "In light of recent events, Papa's rather put the lid on anything resembling freedom, I'm afraid. And today I'm intent upon attending a suffragist meeting."

At the mention of the scandal, Nora's bare shoulders visibly sagged, though her sister didn't seem to notice.

So that he didn't succumb to the temptation to comfort her, Titus said, "I don't know why you'd want to vote; politics is a terrible business."

Mercy's gasp conveyed a startling pitch for a surgery. "You don't *vote*?"

He shrugged. "You forget, I'm Irish and have no love for the government here. Besides, the parties are all corrupt and self-serving. In the end, they'll all send you to war to line their pockets. They'll all vote to occupy countries we have no cause to be in, whilst ignoring the immigrants and denizens of their own empire, who live in squalor and pain. Politics is a waste of my time, Miss Goode, when I have lives to save without much help from any politician."

At that, her lips twisted sardonically. "Well... if women voted, I'm certain there would be a great deal less war and a great deal more help for those in such need."

"Would that were true," he muttered. "But I don't see men allowing that to happen anytime in the near future."

Her eyes turned to chips of ice as she balled up her lace-gloved fist and punched her other palm. "Then we *make* it happen. We crush their opposition and bend their will until—"

"Careful. You're starting to sound like several warlords I know," he teased. "That's not very *merciful* of you."

Instead of taking offense, she threw her head back and laughed. "All of us are rather ironically named, it seems.

Prudence is often impulsive, Felicity is serious, I'm merciless and—" She stopped, gulping back the next words.

"And I am without honor," Nora finished without inflection.

"No!" Mercy knelt at her feet and snatched her hand. "No, no, no, that's not at all what I was—" Her features crumpled. "Oh, Nora, I *don't* think that about you. No one does."

Nora squeezed her sister's hand. "It's all right. Honor is... well it's difficult to define."

"At least none of us were named Chastity," Mercy grimaced.

Before Titus could consider her statement, Nurse Higgins charged into the examination room, saving anyone from having to reply. Her cap was uncharacteristically askew, and her cheeks as red as a ripe apple as she visibly seethed with wrath. "Mr. St. John is here again," she huffed. "He's demanding to see his wife. Has some papers she needs to sign, apparently, and when I told him she's not to be disturbed, he dispatched me to find my betters." She eyed him with mock disdain. "I suppose he means *you*."

Titus chuckled, used to the ribald banter he and Higgins enjoyed.

Elias St. John was a solicitor of no small means who'd often donated to the hospital. His wife was frequently ill and was often at the surgery being treated for a variety of ailments, from intestinal to nervous. One time, he had to operate a forearm snapped clean through.

A carriage accident, or so the police report stated.

"Inform him that Mrs. St. John is asleep. He can come back during visiting hours."

"He's threatening to take her home!" Higgins stomped her feet like a recalcitrant child.

"Impossible," he said, fighting to keep himself measured as he secured Nora's dressing. "The woman has an egregious head wound. She can barely stand without getting dizzy and falling over, nor can she feed herself through that broken jaw. I'm not releasing her until I'm certain she's out of the woods."

"If you send her back to that man, he'll kill her."

Titus's heart stopped and Mercy's eyes widened. "Nora? Did you just say…"

For the first time that evening, Nora craned her neck until her chin touched her shoulder, looking up at him with chilling certainty. "*He* did that to her."

Her words evoked that cold, bleak pain that lived alongside any other emotion regarding Nora. Twelve *years* of marriage to a man ultimately capable of attempting to take her life.

What else had she endured?

The question landed like a brick to the stomach every blasted day.

She rarely interacted with his patients, as they waited until visiting hours were over to attend her for the sake of discretion. So how could she know about Mrs. St. John's plight? Was this paranoia caused by a decade of mistreatment? Or…did she see something only a refugee of such a life could understand?

As a man who'd been to war, Titus knew that certain experiences could only be fathomed by those who'd shared them. Like Dorian Blackwell and those young lads who'd been locked in Newgate with him, or Morley and their blood-soaked battles together.

He finally looked her in the eyes, only to be unraveled by the beseeching look he found there.

"She won't survive the next time," she said with absolute conviction.

"I've thought it, meself," Higgins agreed. "There's something in that man's eyes makes me bones feel like they've been replaced by snakes."

As the surgeon, Titus rarely met his patients' families. He'd simply performed Mrs. St. John's procedures and moved on to the next patient who needed him, letting his resident doctors and the head nurse deal with kin.

"Why did no one mention this sooner?" he demanded irritably.

"What would you have done?" Higgins eyed him as if his very gender made him dubious.

"I'd go to the police. Demand an investigation. It's been illegal to hurt your wife for a handful of years now, I think." How violence against a woman had ever been protected by law aggravated him in the extreme.

Higgins actually scoffed. "Men are never convicted without another male to bear witness. Women are rarely believed. They'd only send her home to him where he'd punish her for her trouble."

"We have to do something." Nora stood, suddenly animated, clutching the bodice of her nightshift to her bosoms with her one strong hand. "Mercy, aren't you and Felicity volunteers with the Duchess of Trenwyth's Ladies' Aid Society?"

"That's right!" Mercy snapped her fingers. "She oversees that sanctuary for women. I'm certain they'd help."

Titus nodded. "I know of the Duchess; she was once a nurse at St. Margaret's."

Nora turned to him, dark eyes wild. "Do you think Mrs. St. John could be moved without her husband's knowledge? She could hide, like me, until it's safe. She could divorce him."

Titus hesitated, quickly making some calculations. "If she'll agree to it, it could be done… gently. Though, I'll have to oversee it as I worry about transport with her head wound." He scrubbed a hand over his face, trying to wipe away fatigue. "Higgins, who can we spare to send to Trenwyth's to make arrangements?"

"I can go now!" Mercy's hand shot up like she was volunteering an answer in a classroom.

"What about your meeting?" he asked.

"Hang the meeting, this is more important. I'll go straight away and return with the news."

"Be careful," Nora admonished as she received a vehement kiss from Mercy, who turned to plant one ardently on Nurse Higgins's cheek on her dash out the door.

"Precocious child," Nurse Higgins chuckled, swatting at the air. "I'll go get rid of Mr. St. John, though I'd like to dump his arse in the alley with the rest of the rubbish."

"Like hell you will go out there." Titus dropped his arm like that of a bridge gate to block her. "If you consider him a dangerous or violent man, *I'll* get rid of him. You'll stay here where it's safe and see to Lady Woodhaven."

Higgins pushed against him, but he was planted to the ground, immovable as an old oak. "Don't be daft. He'd know something was amiss if the head surgeon came out to inform him of the visiting rules."

Nora's chest heaved with what he assumed was a multitude of emotion. "Men like him do not like to make a fuss in public. He'll be back tomorrow, trying a more manipulative tactic. He'll be as charming as you've ever seen," she predicted.

Higgins looked across at Nora, eyes soft in her uncompromising features. "You would know, child, as you had a bastard like that of your own to contend with."

Nora attempted a smile, as if she couldn't stand for her pain to be visible, but was unable to disguise it properly. "I'm two and thirty, hardly a child."

Higgins nodded, accepting that Nora didn't want her pity. "We'll save Mrs. St. John. Believe you me."

"Make certain you take that new orderly with you," Titus called.

"Very well," Higgins called back. "If only because you'll be an insufferable nag if I don't."

And then they were alone.

Titus looked around as if he might find someone to save him from her.

From himself.

All he found in the white examination room was an unhelpful skeleton...and the love of his life.

He raked a hand through his hair, scratching at his scalp. What...had just happened?

Nora began to struggle to pull her simple white nightgown up from the elbow of her injured arm with her other hand.

Galvanized, Titus went to help her, brushing her trembling hand aside so he could draw the sleeve over her shoulder in a way that didn't disturb it.

He stood behind her once again, sliding exactly one million silk buttons into place. All the while, he cursed every modiste and seamstress who decided anybody could sleep in such a silly contraption.

Silently, he lamented every slip of skin that disappeared.

"I would like to do something," she murmured.

His fingers stalled. "Anything in particular?"

She shifted with a restlessness he could sense growing in his own body. "I'm not used to being useless. I always have a charity for which to raise funds or some event to organize for..."

"For..." he prompted when she let the silence stretch for too long.

"For the Viscount," she mumbled before touching her chin to her shoulder to look back at him. "I've done nothing but read and visit with my sisters while I've been recovering, but I feel well enough to be up and about. Suppose I could sit with a few patients, or help some of the women through a hard row. I don't have anything in the way of medical training, but perhaps I could provide them comfort and understanding, like Mrs. St. John, for example."

How charming and lovely, that she desired to help. He

understood her need to be useful, they were alike in that way. Compatible.

"I wouldn't be doing a very good job at keeping you safe and hidden if I paraded you around my surgery, now would I?" he asked, attempting to put her at ease without batting her idea out of the sky. "Your safety is paramount, but perhaps I can find you something to occupy your time so you don't go mad."

"You're kind." She turned to look straight ahead, and he wished he could read her expression. "Chief Inspector Morley will be here tomorrow. He sent a note saying he had news about my case..." She drifted off as he lifted her hair off of her neck and settled it down her back in a curtain of ebony silk. "Perhaps it's good news, and I'll no longer be your problem."

Was that what she was? A problem? A conundrum?

Something he had to figure out before he could sleep.

They stood like that for a moment, and Titus inhaled mightily, pulling the familiar scent into his lungs. She still used rose water, and smelled of a late-summer garden.

He became a hollow creature, only separated from the object of his yearning by the space of a breath.

And the chasm of a decade.

It was a heady torment. One he should want to be rid of.

And yet, the dragon within sought to roast Morley, as well, if he came to take her away.

He fought his curiosity as he secured her arm in the sling, enjoying the feel of her delicate limb as he arranged it against her chest before draping her cream dressing gown over her.

"Did Woodhaven...did he ever do something like that to you?" He shouldn't have asked that. He *couldn't* know the answer.

Because he couldn't kill the man twice.

INVISIBLE WOUNDS

Titus had found no evidence of broken bones whilst treating Nora, and he'd looked for it. But there were other bruises, the ones in her expression.

"I don't want to speak of William," she said, pulling away.

Of course, she didn't want to discuss it, especially not with him. He should wish her good night, then. Should let her go.

"I'll see you back to your room." It was as if his mouth and brain were currently disconnected. They would be locked in the lift together. And then they'd come to his bedroom...

Christ, he'd never be able to spend another night there without thinking of her. No matter how often he washed the linens, he'd want to roll in them like a mad hound, searching for her scent.

He knew the impulse made him pathetic. He didn't bloody care.

Usually, he'd allow a lady to be first through a door, but he checked the deserted halls of his surgery before summoning her to follow him once he gleaned that the coast was clear.

They walked in silence down the hall, past the rows of rooms wherein sleeping patients recovered from any myriad of operations from appendectomies to—God forbid—amputations.

Her slippers made no sound on the bare floors he'd ordered scrubbed twice daily. In the cream lace of her high-necked dressing gown, with her wealth of hair half unbound down her back, she resembled a ghost in the wan gaslight. A mere shade of who she'd once been.

She haunted his dreams often enough. His fantasies.

He doubted he'd be able to walk the halls of his own surgery without seeing the specter of her as she was just now. Pale and lovely. Sad yet serene.

She'd always moved with such innate grace, next to her he felt like a plodding draft horse. His heavy footsteps echoed along the empty hall as he took up entirely too much of it.

When they reached Mrs. St. John's room, she hesitated at the closed door. After looking in through the window upon the sleeping woman with naked anxiety, Nora turned to him, her expression troubled.

"Doctor Conleith..." she hesitated.

He should take back what he'd said before. Should insist she call him Titus. Everyone else in her family did.

But his name from her mouth... his breath became unsteady at the very thought.

It would be another thread of his own self-control, unraveled by her.

She shifted restlessly. "I feel compelled to thank you for—"

"You have," he interrupted brusquely. "Repeatedly."

"Not really," she contended, her gaze fixing on the bare forearms he'd crossed over his chest. "I know I've added my sentiments to my family's effusive gratitude. But in the weeks I've been here, I've not had the opportunity to express just how much I—"

"There's no need." For some reason, her gratitude rankled him. It was the last thing he wanted from her. They had any number of endless words to say to each other, and on the list he'd crafted in his mind, *thank you* didn't even make the first page. "Bullets are something of a specialty of mine, or *were...*" He drifted away, both verbally and physically as he turned toward the lift at the end of the hall.

He felt rather than heard her follow him. "You learned in Afghanistan?" she queried.

"I did."

"I always wondered why you went to war. I was told Dr. Alcott sponsored you to attend university."

It surprised him that she'd asked after him enough to have gleaned the information. The Goodes had not engaged Doctor Alcott for some time. "He did for a while, but he died of a sudden aneurysm. His family was not so keen on keeping up my education, and so I pledged my fledgling skills to Her Majesty's Army to further my experience in hopes of continuing my instruction."

"Did you suffer?" The whispered question was laced with such lamentable emotion, the fine hairs of his body vibrated with it.

"Everyone who goes to war suffers." Irked to find that the lift wasn't on the ground floor, he pulled the lever to call it down to them.

"Tell me?"

He looked at her askance. "Of my suffering?"

"If you wish. Just... tell me about you. About this." She gestured to the wide halls of his hospital. "About everything or anything."

Something hardened inside of him. Chafed and ached like an old scar in an approaching storm. "Why?"

"I've spent a decade wondering."

I've always been right here, he wanted to say. She could have found him any time.

He could only read her expression in silhouette; the glow of the gaslights situated between each doorway illuminated a woman as resolute as she was curious.

She hadn't always been like that. And, it seemed, she'd the courage to fight battles of her own these days.

Don't make a fool of yourself by doing something so pathetic as begging, Titus. Her last words fell like shards of ice on the heart she'd begun to melt. *I can no longer stand the sight of you.*

"It was a short and savage war." His intonation had taken on some of that savagery, even as he endeavored to keep his register low for the sake of the patients. "There'd been a hailstorm of bullets on either side. The battles ground men into meat, and I spent my days like a butcher, white apron and all, covered in blood. I either dug bullets or shards of shrapnel from anywhere you can imagine, or hacked mangled limbs from screaming men."

"I can't imagine," she remarked, her brow pinched with what he dared interpret as regret. "I wonder that it didn't put you off of the entire business."

"On the contrary, I returned with a burning need to not only learn but improve our understanding of the surgical arts. I did whatever I had to, to make it through university, even going so far as to use my skills for rather nefarious people."

"The Black Heart of Ben More, I gather?"

His eyebrows lifted. "You know him?"

She lifted her good shoulder in a shrug. "Oddly enough, he's a former enemy of Morley's, and I take it that they're forming something of a friendship. It is no small wonder to Prudence. She speaks of it, often."

The lift arrived with a slight squeak. The intricate and decorative metal door folded in upon itself like an accordion as he pushed it aside for her.

Nora stepped past him, the scent of roses and warm female flesh beckoning him to follow.

He kept talking, doing his utmost to avoid any fraught silences between them. "The army didn't pay enough for me to finish Cambridge, but Dorian Blackwell did. He needed a doctor in his debt to attend to his men without asking questions. I saved his eye back in the day...as well as I could. Now that he's gone mostly legitimate, I'm inclined to prevail upon his newfound generosity."

"Oh?" The question seemed to escape on a tremulous breath as he reached past her to depress the lever that would propel the lift up to the fifth floor.

As the blasted thing lurched to a start, she stumbled into him.

Reflexively, his arm went around her, pulling her to his side so she might use his sturdy form as a bulwark.

It had been a mistake, to press her soft curves against his hard angles. To fill his hands with her in the shadows.

If she wasn't a wounded woman, he might have taken the upturn of her face, the parting of her lips, as an invitation.

"I'm sorry. I'm not used to these contraptions. I'm rather uneasy to not find my feet on solid ground." She put her hand against his chest as if to push away, but it stayed there.

Right over his heart.

Could she feel it leaping behind the cage of his ribs? Hurling itself against her palm.

As if she hadn't held it since he was a lad of ten.

As if it couldn't wait to be broken again.

He released her instantly. What had they been talking about? Oh yes...

Money.

"I've sunk a fortune into this place because I couldn't stand to practice surgery in the hellholes they call hospitals here. I wanted a situation that was not only specialized, but clean, where patients had a greater chance of recovery, and it's succeeded. The infection rate is down, and the survival rate is so much higher than I even projected."

He watched the floors fall away with a glowing sort of pride in each one. "In my exuberance, I have endeavored to open many more like this. The surgery in Southwark, for example, where so many industrial accidents need seeing to. But I've overstretched, it seems. I'm often too busy performing actual procedures to raise funds. I've financed what I can… but it's rather taken on a life of its own. And there is always more need than there are those trained to fill it. I'd like to sponsor the education of young talent…"

The lift halted at the top floor, so he opened the cage and swept his hand for her to lead the way.

She didn't move. Merely looked at him with dark eyes shining in the lone dim lantern of the lift. "I'd give you my entire fortune if I had one," she said with a youthful earnestness that conjured that lively girl he'd once known.

He had to clear his throat before replying. "You are kind."

She shuffled past him, murmuring something that sounded like, "We both know I am not."

The corridors of his private residence were unnervingly silent. Not just because the plush carpeting muffled their footsteps, and velvety arabesque wallpaper dampened their acoustics. A strange expectancy emanated from the shadows in between the delicate gold sconces aligning the walls.

Their glow was dimmer than usual, gilding the atmosphere with more shadows than illuminations. Next to him, Nora was like a beacon, her gown a shock of light in the dark opulence, her hair an inky sheen around features that were the perfect paradox of soft and sharp.

Titus's heart gave an extra thump as his body responded to the proximity to her and to his bed.

Nothing could happen between them.

"Do you still like to ride?" she queried.

"Hmmm?" He wasn't certain he'd heard her correctly. Also,

the word "ride" from her mouth instinctively tightened his cock against the placket of his trousers.

It had become a meaningful word to them in their youth. One with more salacious connotations, as they often used the excuse of riding to spend amorous time together.

"Do you remember how we used to fly along Rotten Row? I miss that. If I could have anything back, it would be the horses and...those afternoons."

"I hardly have the time for such things," he answered in a tone flat enough to draw her curious attention.

"It seems we should both relearn how to enjoy ourselves."

"I enjoy what I do."

"I can tell," she said, reaching out to run her finger along a small display table as they passed it. "But I imagine you should find some recreation, just as I should find something to give my life purpose."

You could work here with me. The words leapt to his lips and he swallowed them immediately. Too much. Too soon.

Or was it too little, too late?

"Where do you think you'll go after this is over?" he asked.

She lifted her hand and caught at a strand of her hair, worrying it with deft fingers. "Well, I'm too notorious to stay in London, I think. The papers have spilled every sensational detail of my life, along with my husband's innumerable crimes. There is a dowager cottage in the country that I might prevail upon, but...I recently spent some time in Italy and grew fond of it. I think of returning often. I like the sunshine there."

"Italy?" The very word offended him. "What the devil would you do in Italy?"

Approaching the door of his chamber, she stepped aside so he could rest his hand on the latch. "Men mistreat their wives everywhere. Perhaps I can be useful in that way. It could be a way for me to make reparations for whatever damage I've done."

What would be worse? To know she lived close? Or across a continent?

He reached out and covered the hand working tangles into her hair with his own, wanting to soothe whatever anxiety caused her to fidget.

"*I* never would have hurt you, Nora." It needed to be said. He couldn't fathom the reason, but there it was.

She faced him, the lamps glimmering off a sheen of moisture in her eyes as her hand stilled beneath his. "I've never feared you for a moment."

No creature should be so soft. So inviting.

The air thickened between them and Titus didn't know how they'd come to be closer to one another. Couldn't say which one of them had stepped forward to close the gap.

"Nora?"

Her tongue darted out, glossing her lips. "Yes?"

"If you knew what I'd become? If you'd seen this place and realized what I could have eventually offered you…would you still have thrown me out that night?"

He watched her features crumple and immediately regretted the question. Even though she'd been cruel in their past. Even though she'd been so contaminated by disgrace in the eyes of society for all her supposed misdeeds.

Even though he'd never truly forgiven her…

It seemed he'd still rather tear at his own skin than cause her pain.

To his surprise, her fingers laced with his and she pressed lips as plush and smooth as petals to knuckles still rough from a youth spent in toil.

"Titus…" She swallowed twice before gathering herself to continue. "You were the brightest, best, most brilliant person I'd ever known. That I'd ever even heard of. I *always* understood you were capable of this and more. I never for a moment questioned that, unless you had the chance taken from you,

you would perform miracles. You were born to astonish the world."

Pleasure shimmered through him at her words, followed by a dart of ire. "Then...why—"

"Titus?"

At the sound of his name, so familiar on another woman's lips, he dropped Nora's hand just in time for the bedroom door to open.

Revealing Mrs. Annabelle Rhodes.

Tossing her abundant copper curls, Annabelle pressed a hand to the deep cleft of her cleavage in a gesture meant to be both enticing and astonished. "It's been a *month* of Wednesdays since you've taken me up on my...invitations."

"Annabelle," he growled.

She drew her generous bottom lip between her teeth, her green eyes already hungrily devouring him. "Since you claimed to be too busy to leave your lair, I decided to join you in it. To steal whatever moments you can spare. I've been famished for—"

"Annabelle," he forced her name through his teeth. "I did not give you a key so you could—"

As she advanced out the door, she finally noticed he wasn't alone. Her eyes narrowed as she drew her gaze up and down Nora's dressing gown.

"Titus...who *is* this?"

"I'm no one, I assure you," Nora said from beside him, turning the arm in the sling to the light. "Merely a patient."

"A patient, you say?" Annabelle planted her fists on her buxom hips. "Then what are you doing in the doorway to his bedroom this time of the evening?"

Titus opened his mouth to put Annabelle in her place, but Nora stepped in front of him. "I'm Nora," she introduced herself in an endlessly pleasant voice. So cultured. So practiced. So false. "Dr. Conleith is an old friend of the family. I've been prevailing upon his hospitality whilst visiting London, but I'll be leaving in the morning when my family arrives to collect me."

Would she?

Annabelle's features positively melted with delight, and then sobered when she realized that it was her in the scandalous position. "Oh. Well... I'm also a patient, or rather, my husband was. He died. Not for any lack of expertise on the part of—"

"I understand," Nora said, rather kindly, he thought, under the circumstances. "I'll bid you both goodnight."

"But..." Titus made to take her elbow, but she backed out of his reach. She'd been sleeping in his chamber, the door of which was filled by his current mistress.

"Until tomorrow." She smiled pleasantly and curtsied with enough grace to please the Queen, before she turned away.

But not before Titus spied the falter in her smile. The crack in her façade.

Then, with her back as straight as any royal, she glided down the corridor and disappeared into the guest room furthest away from his chamber. Shut the door.

And locked it.

WILD BEASTS AND SAVAGES

*H*ad they? Or hadn't they?

The question burned a hole into Nora's brain through the entirety of the night. Slowly. Torturously. Like the dedicated beam of sunlight a cruel child would direct through a magnifying glass at an insect.

Nora did her level best to concentrate on the conversation with Chief Inspector Morley. She knew it was important, that it had to do with her immediate future.

But how could she focus on anything else without knowing if Titus had been inside his mistress last night?

The woman hadn't stayed over—thanks be to God—but neither had she promptly taken her leave. She'd remained shut in Titus's chambers for exactly forty and seven minutes.

Long enough for a frenzied tryst, though Nora heard no evidence of pleasure.

Thank heavens for small mercies; that might have done what the bullet had failed to and finished her off entirely.

Titus had not come to her after Annabelle left, and she hadn't truly expected him to. She had no claim upon his time, let alone his heart.

Or his body.

His lovely, long-limbed, exquisitely sculpted body.

But a kiss had haunted the space between them before they'd been interrupted. Or had she conjured that through wishful thinking?

Nora *hadn't* imagined the rather unmistakable outline of his aroused sex pressing against the fitted fabric of his trousers. His physique had been as taut and strong as she remembered, and responded to the feel of her just as it once did.

With hard male need.

And his dratted mistress had been served up to him on a buxom platter, all pouty lips and giant bosoms, *apparently* famished for him.

For his cock. That was what she'd been about to say…

Had he given it to her?

"Lady Woodhaven?"

Nora blinked against the late-morning light streaming in through the parlor window, somehow blindingly bright even though the sky was a dull silver-grey. She realized she squeezed the handle of her porcelain teacup hard enough to shatter it, and set it back on the delicate saucer.

"Forgive me, Chief Inspector, I haven't been sleeping. Could you repeat the question?"

Morley cleared his throat and divested himself of his coat. Draping it across the back of the gold damask chaise, he tugged at the thighs of his trousers to perch on the edge.

He assessed her from beneath brows only slightly darker blond than the hair he kept ruthlessly short and elegant, no doubt in a ploy to soften the brutal angles of his features. If there were a more perfect man for Prudence, she'd dare the devil to find him. He was all hard jaw and starched collars, where her sister was flowing ribbons and soft smiles.

She hoped he made Pru happy. He certainly seemed to.

"I asked if *the Fauves* means anything to you." He kept his question measured, but she had the impression he evaluated every single aspect of her reaction.

She searched her memory. "A French word, isn't it? Meaning beast? Wild beast?"

"What about Raphael Sauvageau?"

She shook her head. "Was William working for him?"

"My investigation has borne out that his is the fist tightening around the black market these days. And, for a while, his men were watching your house, and mine." His expression flattened to patently grim. "It seems you were wise to go into hiding as, the deeper I dig into this brigand's machinations, the more concerned I become. His gang of degenerates call themselves the Fauves."

"Have you connected him to my—to William somehow?" She'd stopped thinking of him as her husband ages ago.

Morley rubbed at his brow as if erasing a headache. "Several nights ago I—apprehended one of his men and gleaned that cocaine is the least of Sauvageau's concerns. As he told it, a shipment of unminted gold from America went missing while in your husband's possession. Sauvageau is lying in wait, it seems, certain that much gold can't stay hidden for long. To spend it, someone must smelt it. And if it were in your possession and you sold it…your influx of fortune would become readily apparent. I imagine that's why he's watching you."

"Well I'm in no danger of a fortune, apparent or otherwise." Nora put her tea and saucer back on the tray table at her elbow, and then smoothed the skirt of her cotton frock over her knees with a wry sound. "Do you remember at the docks, before I was…" She cleared her throat. "William was frantic over a missing crate. He was going to take Prudence and me somewhere downriver."

Morley shifted with consternation, turning to look out the window toward the district over which Harrods gleamed above London's wealthy merchant class. "I'd give my eyeteeth to know where the crate is now," he muttered as if to himself. He glanced back at her, his glacial eyes softening for a moment. "We haven't spoken of that day. You must have complicated— even hostile—feelings about what happened. About me."

"Why would I, Chief Inspector?"

He blinked thrice before answering. "I killed your husband. In front of you."

Nora shut her eyes.

Not because she harbored any unpleasant feelings... but because she didn't. Morley had done what she'd fantasized about more than once. What she'd never had the courage to do.

He'd saved Prudence, and for that she'd always consider him a hero.

He apparently mistook her silence for grief. "In my experience, women often still love the husbands who hurt them. Even after they've done their worst. There's no shame in that. I don't blame you if—"

"I never loved William," she said vehemently. "*Ever*. And I will be forever grateful to you for saving my sister's life. My husband was a monster and, apparently, a killer. When I think of all he did because of me..." Emotion choked the air from her throat and tightened her muscles in such a way that set her shoulder to aching. "I only wish I'd had the courage to put an end to him sooner."

"You'd have been hanged for murder."

"Better my life than those of the innocent men he killed."

He leaned forward as if he meant to offer comfort, and then thought better of it when he caught the look of caution in her eyes.

"What he did to your...lovers, was no fault of yours." His eyes shifted away. "Tell me to mind my own business, but were you emotionally involved with any of them? Do you have... someone to turn to with your grief? I've always found Dr. Conleith to be a keen and considerate confidant—"

"Titus is the last man I'd discuss such matters with." Nora stood, pacing away from him toward the window, if only to retreat from her guilt.

"They were all kind men, even George, the philandering rake. Hadn't a mean bone in his body. But I...was with him because I knew I would never feel attachment to a man like him. Likewise, my time with the Stags of St. James was nothing more than selfish pleasure. A diversion I paid for so I wouldn't have the complication of emotion. None of them meant more to me than what we did in the darkness. Perhaps that makes me a monster, as well."

She looked at her reflection in the window, a translucent overlay against the skyline, and didn't recognize herself in it. "I mourn them. They were vital men who once *lived*, and because of my actions, they no longer do."

Morley approached her carefully, standing at her shoulder to survey the city he was sworn to protect. "As much as I'm glad I put William in the ground, I perversely understand the primitive need to kill a man for touching the woman you love. Only... most of us don't follow through on the instinct."

That he admitted his jealous nature made her smile for Pru's sake.

"But what I can't fathom," he continued, "is how you can love someone and wound them on purpose."

Titus's young face flashed before her mind's eye, his anguished expression at her long-ago cruelty wounding her a thousandfold.

"William only knew how to hurt what he loved," she said. "He didn't beat me, per se. Not with fists and rage and the hatred that I see some men unleash upon their wives. His love was obsessive. Cruel. It was as if he wanted to punish me for not loving him back."

For loving another, she didn't say.

Suddenly the tableau of the city melted away, and the years

she'd spent with a madman played like a stereograph against the grey sky. "He toyed with me endlessly. Isolated me from having friends. Made me pay for every moment I didn't spend with him, even when I took a day out with my family. He would profess his effusive love for me, threatening to kill himself if I couldn't summon warmth for him. And then, when I tried, he would see through my pantomime of affection and would tell me how easy it would be to hurt me while I slept. Would explain in graphic detail what ways he fantasized about torturing me. Terror was his weapon of choice. There were weeks I didn't sleep for fear of what he'd do, certain that this was the moment he'd finally lose what was left of his mind."

"It is unfathomable that there is no legal recourse for such behavior." Morley's voice was a tangle of frustration, the heat of his breath lightly fogging the window in front of him. "I don't wish to prod at bruises, but William mentioned that he hurt you...physically. Was that a lie?"

Nora shifted with distress, but for some reason she wanted to say it. To tell someone what the last decade had been like without worrying about their resulting emotions. Morley was a perfect recipient of such information. He wasn't a squeamish man. He dealt with the worst humanity had to offer on a daily basis. And he'd secret shadows in his eyes that had been put there by someone volatile. Though it was difficult to imagine what could strike fear into a dominant, confident man like him, she knew he understood her sense of helplessness.

"William used to tell me he would someday disfigure me, but he never so much as slapped my face. He would throw things. Break things. He tripped me a few times, once halfway down the stairs. He'd push me into the sharp side of a table or a doorframe. It was all so childish, so retributive." She swallowed a familiar rise of revulsion. "Sometimes, he would hurt me at night...when we were together. If only to elicit a response from me, he'd say. It was the guilt he felt later that disgusted me the most. The weeping. The begging of my forgiveness."

"Christ," Morley hissed, his fists tightening at his sides. "It's no wonder to me, that you sought comfort in the arms of other men."

"Comfort was always elusive," she sighed. "But sometimes I found escape."

Her surprise at his easy acceptance of her scandalous behavior caused her to study him more closely. "How very progressive of you, Chief Inspector, to be so compassionate, even when my shame is another mark on your own wife's reputation. All of England knows I paid the Stags of St. James for pleasure. Even though innumerable men openly keep mistresses and courtesans at their disposal or wile their nights away in brothels, it seems a woman's desire is not to be tolerated."

He let out a rather undignified snort, a ribbon of color peeking above his collar and crawling toward his cheeks. "I'm hardly one to throw stones, my lady, glass houses and all that. Surely you know how Prudence and I met."

As if summoned by her name on his lips, Prudence threw the parlor door wide and swept in like an errant ray of sunshine in her buttercup yellow gown. "Look who I found lurking outside of the door," she said airily, leading an obviously reluctant Titus into the room by his elbow. "He said your stitches come out today, isn't that marvelous?"

"I was waiting for your conversation with Morley to finish," he muttered.

It only took one look into his blazing eyes to know that he'd overheard *everything*.

"I wish I had more to report," Morley lamented. "Raphael Sauvageau is in the wind as far as we know, but I have my best men on it."

"I have it on good authority that even the Knight of

Shadows is searching for him," Prudence said with a conspiratorial gesture.

Morley sent his wife a quelling look. "We have no reason to believe that you're in immediate danger, as you are not spending a gangster's gold. However, it wouldn't be a terrible idea to remain here for the foreseeable future, if we might prevail upon the good doctor's generosity for a few days more." He turned to Titus with a familiar smile, one that stalled when he glimpsed his high color, tense jaw, and the dangerous gleam in his eye. "Unless…"

"Consider my generosity extended," Titus clipped, setting his medical bag on a decorative table with more force than was necessary.

Morley glanced back and forth between them for a moment, his shrewd gaze narrowing with suspicion and no little amount of concern. "Are you quite certain that—?"

"She stays." The way Titus stated the directive stirred something low in Nora's belly. He was a man of unfailing consistency, but something masculine and fierce shimmered in the air around him, even as he stood unnaturally still and contained.

For the first time she could remember, he seemed unpredictable.

It occurred to Nora to be afraid, but the fear never rose within her.

Not of him. Never of him.

Prudence went to her husband and took the arm he offered. "Best we take our leave, darling, so Nora can prepare to have her wound seen to." She bustled Morley toward the door, but not before arching a meaningful brow at Nora that said she would be asking questions about Doctor Titus Conleith at the first available moment.

"Yes, well, I'll be in touch." Morley slapped Titus's shoulder on the way out, but he didn't seem to notice.

He just stared at her without blinking, looking for all the world like a man who'd been punched out of the blue, and was shaking off the astonishment before winding up to throw his own fist.

"Do you need assistance with your buttons?" he queried through clenched teeth.

Her knees quivered, but not for the reason one might have assumed. "No. I can manage."

Nora turned away from him, back toward the window, and lifted her fingers to the buttons of her bodice. Even though she still wore her sling most of the day, he'd encouraged her to use her arm to strengthen it, including getting dressed in the morning. She'd abandoned the sling for tea with Morley, and still felt fairly well off without it.

She'd only sent for dresses that buttoned up the front and— since she'd thought it unfair to ask a lady's maid to hide away with her—generally prevailed upon one of her sisters to arrange her hair in a loose braid down her back.

As she gingerly shucked the bodice down her shoulders, she felt more exposed in her chemise and loose, low-slung corset than she had certain times when she'd been nude.

It might have been the way Titus's gaze snagged the edge of her corset, where it barely came high enough to cover her nipple. He immediately looked away, his gaze affixing to some distant point behind her as a vein appeared on his forehead.

"You'll excuse me for not attending to this earlier. I was escorting Mrs. St. John to Lady Trenwyth's." He made a terse gesture for her to sit on the chaise before him, which she did. "Higgins is still there getting her settled," he offered by way of explanation as he rummaged in his bag for a minuscule yet wickedly sharp pair of scissors.

He pulled the table in front of her forward and perched on the edge. Their knees had to mingle in between each other's in order for him to get close enough to reach her stitches.

She tried not to notice the outline of his thighs against the fabric of his trousers.

Despite his apparent ire and sharp, jerky motions, he was infinitely gentle and precise as he snipped through the stitches on her shoulder and plucked them out with clever metal tweezers.

He'd brought the scent of the city indoors with him, soot and the hint of crisp air as summer gave way to autumn. The aromas underscored other fragrances she was beginning to associate with him. Something sharp and clean, like stringent soap softened by the camphor-like essence of his aftershave.

He was fastidious with his hygiene, his teeth clean and cared for, his thick hair tamed by pomade, at least in the mornings. By this time in the afternoon, that wicked forelock, the color of burnt caramel, escaped to brush his eye, making him appear even younger than his thirty years.

Her fingers itched to smooth it out of his warm whiskey eyes. To trace the topography of his stern features with a cartographer's fervor. To rediscover terrain she'd mapped just over a decade ago. Not just with her fingers, but with her lips, as well.

She wondered if he tasted like he used to.

Her mouth watered so violently her cheeks stung with it.

"Thank you for seeing to Mrs. St. John with such alacrity." She lowered her chin, tilting her head as if she might catch his gaze.

It remained firmly upon her shoulder as he worked.

"It is my responsibility to look after my patient's wellbeing. Your gratitude isn't necessary." He discarded the last of her stitches onto a tray and stood, stepping around to stand at her back, where he expertly went to work on the exit wound.

A rebellious ire welled within her breast, overflowing until she thought she might choke on it.

What had he to be so annoyed about? He'd the perfect

chance to be rid of her, and he'd insisted she stay. She'd not embarrassed him in front of his paramour, which had been utterly well done of her, considering that she'd been tempted to scratch the woman's eyes out. So, what had ignited his remarkably long fuse?

With each stitch he pulled free, that much more of her self-containment was likewise undone, until, when he set his instruments down on the tray with a clatter, she could contain herself no longer. "I'm enjoying your hostility today. It's quite naked."

His exhale contained the long-suffering of every man who'd ever been trapped alone in a room with a confounding woman. "I'm not hostile. I'm aghast. For the past decade, I'd accepted that I'd been thrown over so you could be the woman you were portrayed as in the society papers. The ideal aristocrat. The *ton's* true beauty. Woodhaven was your cousin of some distance. Did you not realize what kind of man you were marrying? Did you understand what being a Viscountess would cost you?"

For reasons inexplicable, his questions enraged her.

"I didn't marry William to be a Viscountess. I married him because—" She couldn't say it. Even when they were angry with each other, she couldn't lay the blame at his feet. Because it didn't belong there. Not really.

She'd made the choice, even though she'd done it to save him from her father. She burned to tell him that. But what good would that cruelty do now?

"I married William because he was chosen for me. And we got on nominally well at first. He didn't show me his true self until a year had passed, and by then it was too late. He was a small, bitter man. And so, yes, I resigned myself to my fate as his wife. I endured his tortures and his spite. I advanced his position in society as hostess. I covered up his indiscretions—"

"Not without committing indiscretions of your own," he muttered.

Antagonism drove her to her feet, and she whirled to face him. "How *dare* you condemn me for that. You haven't exactly been a monk, or have you already forgotten your time alone with the shapely widow, Mrs. Annabelle Rhodes, just last night?"

His frown deepened to a scowl, but he remained silent as he gathered the paper he'd placed her stitches on and folded it, presumably for the rubbish bin.

Her eyes narrowed. "I've known a few hypocrites in my day, but I'd never imagined you were one of them."

He dropped the paper on the tray, shadows gathering on his features like ominous storm clouds. "I didn't touch Annabelle last night. I ended it with her."

Nora expelled a breath she hadn't realized she'd been holding since meeting the woman. But the information, welcome as it was, didn't douse her ire. "Well, I haven't touched a man for ages, and yet you're still obviously upset."

"Not about—that isn't what I—" He broke off with a growl, wrapping his instruments in cloth and tossing them back in his bag. "I don't condemn you for having...needs. But the Stags of St. James, Nora? You would pay *prostitutes*?" He squared his shoulders to her, his chest heaving as his volume increased. "For Christ's sake, you carried on an affair with the man who would become your sister's fiancé—"

"Only because they looked like you!"

He froze.

She clapped her hand over her mouth. But it was too late.

The truth had already escaped.

"What...are you saying?" His broad shoulders were bunched, straining against his shirtsleeves, his skin white over clenched knuckles. He was assembled like a sleek and predatory cat, his muscles gathered as if he might lunge.

Or flee.

Nora's own breath sawed in and out of her as if she'd run a league, but now that it had been said, the rest of it tumbled out of her like an avalanche of truth. "They were all tall, strong, and brutally handsome, with umber hair and...coarse hands. That's what I looked for when I selected a lover. Square, capable hands like yours, rough from working. It didn't matter what color his eyes were because I would... turn out the lights. Would make them be silent. Like we were the night we were together."

"Nora." Her name escaped him like a warning. Or a plea. His expression caught somewhere in between torment and relief. He shook his head, slowly, but she didn't know what he meant by it.

And she couldn't seem to stop herself now.

"You said *nothing* that night," she marveled, much as she'd done so many times in the years since when she'd taken the memory of their first time together to cherish. "You asked no permissions and you offered no effusions. You just knew what I wanted, and you gave it to me. We just...*existed*. And it was perfect. So, every man I paid, any lover I took, any time I found completion beneath someone's body, I—" She broke away, her jaw working to the side as she grappled with emotion too powerful to suppress any longer.

"It was all a parody. A shadow of what we'd done. Of what I wanted—yearned for—every night of my life, thereafter. I took others to my bed to erase the memory of what my husband did to me, but in my mind. In my heart. I never made love to anyone but you." She ventured forward, reaching out for him. Feeling bare and raw and exceedingly vulnerable.

"*Don't*." He held up a hand, effectively freezing her in place with her arm still outstretched. Her silent plea for comfort unheeded. "Don't you *fucking* dare," he seethed, pinning her with an accusatory glare before storming past her toward the window. "Don't take my anger from me, Nora; it's all that's kept me sane. The only thing that stopped me from blasting down the door at Cresthaven, throwing you over my shoulder, and abducting you to some place they never would have found us."

If only he would have. If only...

She turned to find his back to her, so broad and straight, the striations of his muscles visible even against the silk of his vest. But it was his reflection in the window that arrested her gaze. The agony in his eyes that broke her heart.

"God, all I can think about is the hell of your wedding night. I've never been so bloody drunk. I couldn't endure the fact that you belonged to another man, that someone *else* was inside of you."

"It was no picnic for me, either, if that helps ease your mind."

"Of course, it bloody doesn't!" he exploded, slamming his palm on a table beside him before whirling back to her. "And yet you *chose* him, Nora. After I gave you pleasure. I worshiped every inch of you until you were begging for me. I loved you, goddammit. You *know* I did. And you *chose* that...that..." He couldn't seem to land on a word foul enough to encompass her late husband.

And she couldn't blame him.

"You can't know for sure that you loved me," she whispered.

He pinned her with a glare that would have made the devil himself cower. "How could you dare doubt it?"

She shook her head, aching for him, but also realizing something for the first time. "I do not doubt that your feelings were pure. But like everyone else, you loved a construct. An image of perfection manufactured by your own desires and my fabricated behaviors. You loved your idea of who I was. Because you didn't know me, Titus. No one ever has."

He crossed his arms over his chest. "Who are you then, Nora?"

At that, she stalled. "I—I..." She could not give him a complete answer, because she didn't know it herself.

Who am I? Shouldn't someone know that by two and thirty? When everything was stripped away. The title and the artifice. The scandal and the secrets.

What was left?

"You think I didn't see through you, even then?" he challenged, visibly struggling to regain his composure. "That I didn't know exactly who and what you were. You were never faultless, but Christ, to me you were perfect. I loved you *for* your flaws, not because I was blind to them. And I never would have punished you for being who you are." He stared at the puckered skin where the bullet had pierced her, and it throbbed in response to the pain underscoring the fury she read in his expression.

"Everything he did to you. Every way he made you suffer. Holy God, Nora." He laced his fingers in his hair and pulled as if he could tear a thought out of his mind. "I would have...I would have *killed* him for you, you know that? The moment he touched you, at the first cruel word. If you would have come to me, I would have broken every oath I'd taken to do no harm, and I would have butchered the man."

He shook his head, his gaze a well of fathomless misery. "Can you imagine how it feels to know the privilege of spilling his blood went to Morley when I would have *bathed* in it, Nora? I would have smeared it on my skin like some primitive, clannish ancestor, and torn at his beating heart with my teeth—"

"No." She rushed forward, pressing her fingertips to his mouth, hot tears streaming from her eyes. "No, that isn't you. That isn't who you are."

He caught her wrist but didn't move it or toss it away. Instead he turned his cheek into her palm, the stubble of his jaw abrading her with vibrations she felt all the way up her arm. "It seems neither of us knows the other. Not anymore. But I know my mind, Nora. I always have done. I know what I am. I know what I want. And all I've *ever* wanted, was you." His eyes hardened in tandem with his voice. "And *you*..." He released her hand, visibly locking down, pulling up the ramparts and closing the gate.

"No," she cried, panicked. She wanted this. This honesty. His pain. She wanted him to lash her for what she'd done to him. If ever there was a punishment she deserved, this was it. "What? *What?* Tell me what I've done."

"You fucked them!" he roared. "You fucked *them* when I was here all along. I was *here*, Nora... I was right. Fucking. Here!"

He seized upon a crystal paperweight and wound his arm to smash it against the wall.

But he didn't.

He locked his long, talented fingers around it as if he could crush the crystal, filtering a snarl through a tight throat. After a few heaving breaths, he placed it back where it belonged.

Safe. Unbroken.

Just like she'd predicted he would. Because he was wrong about one thing.

Nora knew him.

He didn't break things or people, he repaired them. He always had. He didn't act without consideration. Even when every primitive instinct that made him so completely male, howled at him to rend and destroy.

He was better than that.

Better than any man she'd ever known.

Most certainly better than her.

"I had hoped you'd moved on," she confessed woodenly. "I didn't come to find you because I'd anticipated that you'd found a way to be happy. How could you not when you're so easy to adore? I could not add interrupting that happiness to my list of many sins. I couldn't do that to whomever loved you, any more than I could watch you love someone else. Or see the babies you might have put inside of her—"

He seized her then, tenderly, passionately, his hands bracketing her face, cradling it as if it were a precious, breakable thing, even as he delivered crushing blows with his words. "There's no one. There has never *been* anyone else. I always realized it made me pathetic. That I couldn't give the shards of my heart to someone else, knowing she'd never put it back together. Why inflict a broken man on someone undeserving? It's not her fault I'm damaged... it's *yours*."

With a low moan, his mouth descended and claimed hers, cutting off any hope of a reply.

ANSWERING THUNDER

*a*s Titus devoured her mouth, lightning struck, igniting an inferno that both humbled and terrified him.

The resulting firestorm herded every emotion toward him with all the galloping, thunderous peril of a runaway stagecoach. Desire in the lead, followed by possession, betrayal, hope, hunger, with the relentless lash of fury whipping the frenzy higher. Faster. Out of control.

The last time Titus had kissed this woman, she'd been Honoria Goode, a cossetted debutante who'd understood next to nothing about the wickedness of lust.

As shy and hesitant virgins, they'd swung like a wild pendulum between frenzied gropes and hot stolen kisses, to tender explorations requiring much encouragement and restraint. She'd been a tangle of insecurities and need, and he a machine of senseless desire tempered by blind, consuming love. Even still, she'd allowed him to lead her down the meandering paths of their mutual discoveries.

But now, it was Nora who held the reins in her elegant hands.

He'd been a fool to think he'd drive this interaction. That he'd control any part of it.

Nora had owned him from the moment he'd laid eyes on her twenty years prior, and even though he'd captured her lips, it was *her* tongue that first staked the claim.

The depths of hell he'd endured at the loss of her, of this, were matched by an indescribable height as she licked into the seam of his lips. Withdrawing, she left the taste of sweetened tea and buttery biscuits behind.

He chased the flavor into her mouth, where their tongues met and sparred for a heated moment before he coaxed her back with a gentle sucking motion. He drank in her husky moan with the thirst born of a decade in the desert.

An answering growl vibrated from somewhere so low in his chest, he wondered if it'd originated from the abyss where his heart had resided for so long.

Lured out of the dark by the woman who'd stolen it.

If I was so easy to adore, why was I so easy to discard?

He shoved the question away as their kiss became a living thing born of need and pain and pure reclamation. He learned his temper and his lust could immolate in the same blaze, and would only be doused by *her*. He suddenly didn't care if the conflagration caught and cornered them. He would gladly burn to ash, if only to be sifted through her fingers.

Those fingers shoved into his jacket, tugging it over one shoulder in a one-handed attempt to sweep it away from him.

Her left arm remained folded in front of her as if she wore her sling, and that fact drew his head up to break the kiss.

"Help me, dammit," she panted, tugging restlessly as she lifted on her toes to reclaim his mouth.

"No," he groaned.

"I can't bloody do it myself." Her expression was a lament of lust and frustration.

As he already held her jaw in his palms, he tilted her face up, urging her to look at him. "Your wound, Nora. We can't."

This close, her disappearing irises were the color of ripe black cherries, gleaming with striations of amber and ringed with honey. Her pupils dilated so large and round they almost swallowed everything else with a well of black, fathomless need.

"Undress," she ordered breathlessly. "*Now.*"

Even as he complied, shucking his jacket and discarding it on the table, he contended, "I'll hurt you—"

"I don't care." She yanked her claws down the front of his shirt, sending more than a few of his buttons clattering against the floor and rolling in chaotic directions.

"That is because you do not understand." He caught her wrist, his thumb pressing into the pulse leaping against the thin and tender skin. He could feel the blood rushing through her veins, the electric currents leaping and arcing between them. "I'm still… furious. With *him*. With you. What is between us is not…it isn't gentle. *This* isn't—"

She yanked her wrist from his grasp before stepping in to stretch her body against his, like a cat demanding affection. Her hand lowered to shape against the cock pulsing beneath his trousers, stealing any available oxygen from his lungs.

"Be as angry as you want to be, Titus," she murmured against his ear. "Unleash it. I can bear your fury, but not your distance. I can take all of you."

With her husky permission, the rest of his control crumbled.

Her mouth was already waiting when he descended upon her with all the mercy of a wild, ravenous beast. Her body jerked as he yanked at the ties of her corset and drew it off, flinging it into the ether. He no longer knew where they were or what time it was or why they should not be doing this.

Only his body existed, and hers. They could have been

Adam and Eve, every other living soul something they'd dreamed, a fabrication of their loneliness. Of their undeniable need for each other.

His lust became a ravenous, gnawing creature, hungry only to taste her. Every place she was pale and soft. Every place she was peach and delicate.

This fire between them could only be doused by a flood.

And he would make certain she was good and wet.

You'll forget them, he silently vowed. *Any other man who has had you. You'll forget them all.*

He'd always been grateful to those few women who'd been tenacious enough to entice him to enjoy the attentions they generously offered and passion they freely shared. But they'd already faded from his memory now that Nora had returned to his embrace.

His shirt only made it down to his elbows before she pushed him backward with surprising strength. He controlled his fall to the chaise, and gripped her ass as she sank with him, splitting her legs over his lap.

His hands rucked up her skirts, wading through petticoats until he found the smooth shape of her thigh, right above her knee.

This was how they would do this, the only way to protect her shoulder from discomfort or pressing up against a surface.

His body reacted with a surge of urgency and anticipation. He knew how much this woman loved to ride.

How damned good she was at it.

Beneath her thin summer chemise, the dusky tips of her breasts swayed in front of him, pebbled with arousal and need. He kissed one, then the other, breathing a hot swath through the fabric and thrilling in the delighted sounds that elicited from her throat.

Meanwhile, his hands charted a wicked path up her thighs, stopping to tease at her garters, at the little ribbons of her drawers, plucking the one that would bare her to his touch.

They each gasped in a breath as his fingers stroked through the soft intimate hair. The heated ruffles of feminine flesh were liquid silk, molten in primitive forges.

He familiarized himself with the shape of her, marveling at the differences in their textures here. Where he was velvet skin over stone and steel, she was pliant petals and softness, yielding to his touch, to his intrusion. He tested the entrance to her body and found nothing but welcoming flesh, pulsing as if to draw him deeper inside.

"Now," she groaned, bending to press tight, needful kisses to his temples, his eyes, his cheekbones and finally, his lips. "There will be time for that," she vowed. "For all of it. But I can't live another moment without you inside me."

He could have tormented her by denying her. He wanted to. To refute her control, at the very least. To display his displeasure and his dominance. He could take his time and tease her to the edges of her own capacity.

But who was he fooling? In what world could he deny her anything?

A sigh of relief caught in his throat as he freed himself from the placket of his trousers and guided his sex toward hers.

Their eyes met, and he gloried in the connection, wanting to watch her every expression.

The intimacy seemed to overwhelm her, and she leaned in to press her temple against his, even as she lifted on trembling legs to guide the crown of his cock inside her body.

He grasped the sweet curve of her backside, stabilizing her descent with his strength as he thrust up and into her.

She gasped and wriggled a few agonizing times to accommodate him, her fingers turning to claws on his shoulders, kneading like a cat.

He was the sort of man that allowed a woman time to

acquaint herself to his incursion. To kiss and cuddle and distract her from any discomfort she would feel.

But Nora didn't leave space for all of that. She made harsh, demanding, needful sounds that must have been words before they melted from her mouth.

Titus knew this language. Understood what she wanted.

He took only moments to breathe, to marvel at the magic that was sliding home. Only this moment, this need, existed. The past melted away, the future was a nebulous unknown.

She was here. Now. And all that mattered was the next hitching breath, the next caress, kiss, and thrust.

His grasp on her became covetous and unrelenting as he drove ceaselessly upwards. Titus gloried in the movements of her. The ripples of impact two people could have upon one another as they ground their flesh together until their very bones felt the force of it.

Sex for him had always been a nocturnal endeavor, and he marveled at the afternoon light gilding her pale skin, at the color decorating her chest and flaring in her cheeks. The flush of roses in her lips. The little abrasions his afternoon stubble had made against the soft skin of her mouth and cheeks.

Someday he'd leave those marks on the insides of her thighs.

The very thought brought a release threatening to gather behind his spine.

She was like a goddess above him. A Valkyrie. Battle-scarred and demanding, lifting his soul from the fray to take him to his reward.

Unable to contain his pleasure, he shifted his hand to thrum at the moist little bead where her nerves met and sang. He stroked it in soft contrast to his hard thrusts, a gentle caress against the fury and frenzy.

A ragged sound ripped from her, spurring him on, faster, deeper, harder, as she arched and trembled, her strong legs keeping perfect rhythm with him. He collected her yips and sighs like a man without hope, locking them inside of his memory.

"Come for me, Nora," he ordered.

She fell forward and he caught her waist as she bit into his shoulder, just below where the collar of his open shirt rested. She shuddered and shook, her body folding in on itself as the fingers of her right hand threaded into the hair at his nape and curled into a fist.

The pain sent a lightning bolt straight to his sex as her intimate flesh pulled and released, contracting around him like a satin vise.

He didn't want this. Not yet. Not now. He wasn't ready for it to be over.

But the more he fought it, the faster and more tempestuous the storm became. Her cries of pleasure were his ultimate undoing. The articulation of her sleek body arched like a bridge over his, undulating in a rhythmic dance. For a man so moved by the mysteries of the human body, she remained an anatomical marvel. Immaculate beauty poured over a spine of steel and a heart of stone.

Or was it glass?

One he was beginning to wonder might have been just as broken as his all along.

One who'd never stopped wanting him back.

Why? The question became the metronome to his burst of increasing speed. *Why? Why? Why?*

His climax blinded him with a flash of lightning, and his resulting roars were the answering thunder as wave after wave of clenching pleasure poured from his body into hers. He was a being of both desperation and rapture, locking her hips down against his so he might allow the gentle pulses of her sex to milk the last vestiges of his own release from him.

This would never be enough, he realized as his abdominals

clenched and released their last, his muscles twitching and trembling as they were finally relieved of their prison of pleasure. He would *never* be deep enough inside of her. Would never tire of holding her against him. Never want to be rid of her rose garden scent and husky, resonant voice.

Forever seemed suddenly insufficient.

And tomorrow wasn't yet decided.

He cupped the back of her head, pulling her down so her forehead could rest against his. They shared a few intimate breaths, allowing the storm to pass and the waves to still until they stood, each existed in a calm shaft of sunlight. He luxuriated in the feel of her exhales stirring at his overheated skin.

He thought he'd feel better. Sated and sleepy. Like a starving man after overindulging in a decadent meal.

He didn't.

Instead, he'd unlocked some sort of bottomless abyss that could only be filled by uninterrupted access to her.

Was he becoming like her husband? Obsessive and calculating?

No. He would never. But he certainly had decisions to make. About what kind of man he was, or would be.

"Nora," he exhaled her name from lungs still struggling to find their equilibrium. "If there's anything between us, I want it to be the truth, not the past. We should... talk."

"Don't," she sighed, stopping his lips before tracing their outline with a soft and languorous fingertip. "Let us talk tomorrow. Let tonight be about us. About this. Let me show you what you mean to me."

Her lips replaced her finger on his mouth, convincing him instantly as he stirred inside of her. Tomorrow. They had tomorrow.

Perhaps this long dark night he'd endured without her had been a time to forge them into what they were now. To learn of loss so they could fathom abundance. To build a foundation from the failures of their youth. Perhaps... their souls and hearts were stronger and more stalwart than they might have once been, having gained the perspective of tragedy, war, hardship, and pain.

And perhaps, if the gods were kind. If they could call the past several years a recompense for any happiness they might or might not deserve, and they could find their way to forgiveness. To understanding.

And only then could he lay claim to all her days thereafter.

AN ENEMY AT THE GATE

*E*very time Nora's shoulder twinged, she couldn't help but smile. Last night, she'd thrown Titus's cautions to the wind and overexerted it, but she wasn't about to admit it to him.

She didn't regret a single moment.

Besides, the pain wasn't unbearable, and there were other aches and twinges in more intimate places that she didn't at all mind.

She'd returned her arm to the sling like an obedient patient, and now sat at the dressing table, brushing out her hair in slow, distracted strokes.

A glow that began at her center shimmered through her in breath-stealing ripples as she assessed her appearance in the mirror.

She'd been shot. A savage gangster was after her. She was a social pariah. She'd been a widow for less than a month.

And her reflection couldn't stop smiling.

She looked younger, somehow, as if making love to Titus had erased years of misery. As if sleeping in his arms had allowed her to draw from some miraculous well of recovery.

She'd lain awake for what felt like hours after, listening to him breathe. Watching his eyes flutter with dreams. He enjoyed the slumber of a man with an unburdened conscience. There was something lovely about that. Something that'd made her feel both proud and melancholy.

It didn't matter that the day had dawned grey, nor that Titus had risen before sunrise.

She could feel him close, only a few floors below. Going about his business, saving lives and alleviating pain. She'd never begrudge him that. He loved his work, and a man with such responsibilities wasn't only worthy of her regard and her admiration, but also her respect.

How long had it been since she'd respected a man?

Besides, he'd kissed her sweetly when he'd gone, smoothing a hand over her unruly morning curls, winding one around his clever finger. "I'll return for tea?" he offered in an indulgent whisper. "We have so much to discuss."

She hadn't looked forward to anything with such relish in as long as she could remember.

They could discuss the past, of course. And then... turn their eyes to the future.

Was this hope? This glow in her chest? This soft, bubbling effervescence that made her feel as if her blood were rendered of champagne. It'd been so long since she'd felt anything of the kind, she couldn't exactly place a name on it.

The only thing she knew for certain: Titus was the cause. He was the cure to her ills and the balm to her soul.

He had the heart of a saint, the body of a god, and the appetite of a libertine.

William had grown soft and bloated in their years together, his hair thin and his middle thick. His teeth yellowed by vice and lack of consistent hygienic practices. Everything about him, from his breath to the sound of his voice, used to offend her.

Perhaps she might have felt differently had she loved him... if he'd been worthy of her regard in any respect.

Titus was as different from him as night was from day. Age had only improved upon what youth had rendered. Muscles developed through labor as a lad were kept taut with strength from training at the club with some of his compatriots from the army.

Even his scent enticed her, so sharp and clean, mixed with the cedar of his wardrobe and the spice of his aftershave. His voice had crooned wicked things into her ears with the resonance and reverence of cathedral bells, vibrating to the very soul of her.

After the tumult of their first encounter, their lovemaking had become more leisurely and deliberate, enough to where they were able to rediscover each other with inexhaustible delight.

They'd had to be creative with her shoulder, finding positions that didn't jostle her too terribly, nor could she bear weight.

Nora clamped her lips together as she remembered the way he'd gently rolled her on her side, curling his lithe, strong body against her back and lifting her leg in the air to enter her from behind.

She'd allowed herself to luxuriate in all the sensations of him. The tickle of the hair on his thighs against her backside. The corrugations of his ribs as he'd rolled and contracted.

And his clever, lovely fingers as they—

A knock sounded at the door, distracting her from her salacious reverie. Likely Felicity come to keep her company. She stood, abandoning her brush to the table, and swept down the hall, adjusting her sling as she went.

Her excitement bubbled over even before she was able to reach the door. "Felicity, darling, you'll never guess what—"

The Baron Cresthaven, her father, stood where she'd

expected to find her sister, his hands locked behind his back in his requisite regimental posture.

Though it had been only weeks since she'd seen him, he seemed older, somehow. Even though he still towered over her, he might have lost a bit of height. His beard seemed threaded with more grey and silver, and the lines at his eyes and mouth grooved deeper into his skin.

"Papa," she croaked through her surprise. She'd lived with the man for the first twenty years of her life, had seen him often thereafter, and she could still never tell if his features were indignant, or just arranged thusly.

"Honoria," he greeted with a bland sort of insouciance. As if he were disappointed to find her there, even though she could be the only person he'd come to see.

She pulled the door open wider, stepping aside. "Won't you come in?"

He walked through the entryway to Titus's private apartments, and she became immediately distraught and defensive. He was an interloper here. A tremulous anxiety caused her to feel slightly ill, his presence covering her previous good cheer like a cold, damp blanket made of scratchy wool.

Still, a little seed of hope bloomed within her. Perhaps it was finally deemed safe enough for him to visit. Or he'd news from home.

Was it too much to hope he pitied her? That he worried for her wellbeing after all that'd transpired...

She'd almost lost her life, his firstborn. Did that mean something to him?

Trailing him as he strode down the hall and into the great room arranged to make the most of the splendid views of the city, she asked, "Does Doctor Conleith know you've come? Would you like me to ring for some tea?"

"No, I won't be staying long." He blinked over at the tasteful furnishings, the damask drapes, the expensive sconces and bric-a-brac. She hated that she held her breath to hear what verdict he might pass.

He said nothing as he paused at the high-backed chair Titus favored, and put his hand on the crest, posing like a royal in a painting. He made a quick assessment of her unbound hair and the frothy gown that reminded her of the purple pansies in their gardens. "You're not wearing widow's black, Honoria."

Any hope for paternal concern evaporated like the morning fog from the Thames when sliced by shafts of sunlight through the buildings. "You don't actually expect me to mourn William, Papa; he was a murderer and a monster."

"I know very well what he was. He used my shipping company to smuggle for a gangster, if you'll remember." He exclaimed this as if it were William's worst sin of the lot, before his eyes narrowed upon her. "Still, tradition dictates you wear black. It is imperative that you're seen doing everything properly."

Deflating, she gestured to the arm bound to her body. "I'm not *seen* doing anything at all, Father. That's rather the point of being in hiding. I see no one but my sisters, Nurse Higgins, and Doctor Conleith."

"Yes... Conleith." He gave their lush surroundings another thorough inspection, as if looking for something to condemn them. To Nora's smug relief, their surroundings were every bit as fine as the furniture at Cresthaven. The rooms even larger and the amenities more tasteful and modern.

Her mother often pointed out to her father that they could relocate to some of the grander and newer houses being built in Belgravia and beyond, but Clarence Goode stubbornly held on to their Mayfair square, the one where the names were ancient and the titles as archaic as the homes.

Such things mattered more to him than anything, after money, of course. Tradition, position, reputation, followed by zealotry disguised as faith.

What an empty and terrible way to live. It was such a shame she could only come to that conclusion after the worst had happened. After she'd lost everything that *he* held dear. Her position in society, her reputation.

But what she'd found with Titus was so much more precious than that.

Passion, acceptance, a sense of wholeness, hope, and wonder. And—someday—forgiveness?

Dare she hope…love.

"That boy is taking a great risk keeping you here," her father remarked.

"Morley doesn't think so. Since Mr. Sauvageau doesn't seem to know I'm here—"

He pinned her with his most imperious glare. "I'm not referring to the gangsters, Honoria, but everyone else. Everyone who matters. Though your circumstances are *greatly* diminished and Conleith's have exponentially elevated, so much about the impossibility of your situation remains unchanged."

"*Doctor* Conleith," she dared to correct him, wanting her father to give Titus his due. "And I don't understand—"

"Of course you don't," he snorted. "*Doctor* Conleith has both made and spent an impressive and astonishing fortune on a bevy of new surgical schemes, or so I've gathered."

"I know this already—"

"He's still nobody, Honoria. He is nothing without his reputation as a surgeon and a man. He has no title to protect him, no lands to rely upon for income. His entire future is built upon the skill in his hands and the trust of his wealthy patients and patrons here."

The weight of all that was pressing upon Titus's shoulders became a heavy lead stone in her gut. Because she knew what her father's next words would be. And the truth they contained threatened to extinguish the tiny flame of hope with which she'd awoken, and plunge her into a pit of despair.

"A relationship with you could taint him. You realize that, don't you? You could ruin the success of any of his future endeavors. That's how far and completely you have fallen."

Her legs gave way as her father yanked the rug out from under them, and she landed on the velvet chair behind her.

Hard.

Cresthaven reached into the pocket of the mahogany vest that stretched over his impressive paunch and retrieved his watch to check the time.

As if he had somewhere more important to be.

"Your mother and I have discovered a way out of this debacle you've found yourself in."

At that, her temper flared. "I didn't *find* myself anywhere, Father. My husband tried to murder me. This was no fault of mine."

He waved his hand in front of his face, as if dispelling an unpleasant scent or swatting away a fly.

"This past Sunday, I was approached by the Duke of Bellingham. Apparently, his second son, Mark, is in need of a wife, and they're willing to take you on after the appropriate period of mourning. You'll be married next summer in Devon, so... enjoy this little rendezvous while you can."

"Take me on?" she echoed, aghast. "You're mad if you think I'll be impressed upon to marry again, Father; I barely *survived* the last one!"

He stepped forward, his threatening manner causing her to flinch away. Her father hadn't been a heavy-handed parent, but he'd slapped them a few times if they'd provoked him enough.

"Think of someone other than yourself for once, Honoria," he blustered, his chins vibrating with the violence of his unchecked disdain. "Mercy and Felicity are being treated abominably, shunned from society, and openly mocked. Their chances at decent marriages are effectively nil. Your mother is possibly on her deathbed with nervous conniptions, her heart growing weaker by the day. I've had to instruct the staff to hide the papers and the cordial from her. Business like mine is built on reputation, you daft girl. What do you think will happen to our wealth if our name is in tatters? You are not the only one who has suffered, but you're the only one who can reclaim some semblance of our family's honor in the wake of this disaster."

Suddenly dizzy, Nora pressed her hand to her forehead, unable to tell if she were feverish, or if her hands were abnormally cold.

She should have known. She was aware of what the *ton* did to those who fell out of favor. Nothing that her father had imparted should have been news to her.

But her sisters had never let on their distress, hadn't mentioned her mother's condition. She'd been more than happy to stay cossetted in this tower like a damaged princess, forgetting that she wasn't the only person in danger. That the ripples of her husband's actions would affect the innocent, and that she had some responsibility to amend that.

She'd never really considered that *she* could become Titus's ruin. Because he was such a strong and stalwart man. Capable and gifted and ruthless and resilient, she no more assumed she could cause him harm than a butterfly could destroy a lion.

But it was so much worse than that.

She could ruin him with her affection.

Again.

Was it some sort of curse? To have him for moments of bliss, only to have to choose between him and honor? Or to make him chose between her and ruination?

"Why would a Duke invite someone like me into his family?" she asked, kneading at her temple.

Her father's gaze darted away, sliding a dagger of unease

415

into her ribs. "He's a victim of his own scandal. Mark was kept from prison only by the hand of his father, the Duke. He's an invert, so he's being forced to go into the church... being a vicar's wife will do you some good, I think."

"An invert." She dropped her hand in surprise. "You mean, he prefers the romantic company of...men?"

"Evidently fell in love with some French actor. There are photographs." Her father shuddered. "He's reported to be nothing like William, thank God. A gentle sort of fellow, studious and dull."

Honoria instantly felt a tug of pity for Mark.

If not for Titus, such an arrangement might suit her quite well. A kind man, one who wouldn't make sexual demands of her. A quiet life in a country vicarage. She didn't so much mind the idea of men being lovers, couldn't understand why it was considered such a sin to begin with.

A click from down the hall toward the entry told her the door had been opened and shut. The sound preceded Titus's footsteps down the hall. She knew the cadence of his confident stride, and she stood suddenly. Her heart at once surged to her throat, only to take a nosedive into the pit of her belly.

This was impossible. No matter what she did, she hurt him.

If she ended it, she sliced through the tenuous bond they'd only just forged. She broke his heart again, just when he'd begun to open it.

If she stayed... she might cost him everything. His patients and his patrons. His entire life's work. Everyone she loved would suffer for that love. She was like a fragmented bomb, laying waste to all who dared to stand in her immediate vicinity.

Her father, apparently, hadn't marked Titus's approach. "I suppose you and Mark will both have to learn to be discreet with your lovers. But perhaps he'll allow you to keep your doctor on the line. Then, you won't have to cease being a whore."

Titus rounded the corner, looking every bit the gentleman doctor. Hair tidy, jaw clean-shaven, his expensive grey vest buttoned over a shirt rolled up to the elbows.

Except...

He didn't spare Nora half a glance before he marched up to the Baron, his features a black mask of wrath and retribution as he used his only slightly superior height to look down his nose.

"It is part of my personal creed to do no harm," he said in a voice measured only with darkness. "But in your case, I'm willing to make an exception."

His fist drove into her father's face with all the force of a locomotive, knocking the imposing man over.

Nora rushed forward. Though her father had fallen to his hip, he was still sitting up, holding one hand over his nose. Blood leaked through his fingers as he let loose a string of curses he could have only picked up at the docks.

Titus shook out his hand a few times, testing the mobility of his fingers before glaring down at the man he'd put on the ground.

Even though he looked as though he'd like to murder her father, he reached into his pocket and extracted a handkerchief, dangling it in the Baron's line of sight.

Lord, but he was an endlessly decent man.

Her father hesitated for a moment, but then took the offering and shoved it beneath his nose with a pained groan. "In your case, I suppose I deserved that," he said, his voice almost comically nasal and muffled by the handkerchief.

"What is *deserved* is an apology to your *daughter*." Titus looked like an avenging angel, ready to go to battle, wielding his righteous indignation. "It is your fault she is in danger. All of this was caused by the man you selected for her. Tell me,

Cresthaven, did you know the Viscount was mad before pledging her to him?"

Dammit, she just fell in love with him again.

"You can stay out of this." Her father managed to be imposing, even as he leaned his head back to stem the flow of blood from his nose. "Even now, she's as far above you as the stars are above the treetops."

"You don't think I always knew that?" Titus gestured to her, keeping his palm up as an invitation for her to take his hand.

Instinctively Nora reached for him, but then she hesitated. All the words her father said barraged her conscience like a thousand pricks from a thousand daggers.

You will ruin him. He will hate you for it.

Not as much as you'll hate yourself.

"Honoria," her father warned. "If you stay, this place will be leveled to rubble at *your* feet."

Titus loomed over him, his fist tightening once again. "Don't you dare threaten me or this institution."

"I'm not, lad. I'm simply telling you the truth."

"I'm no lad, you sanctimonious bastard. I'm a doctor, and a soldier, and a scientist. I deserve—"

"You deserve to keep what you've built and to retain the respect you've earned."

Both Titus and Nora stood there for a moment, jaws loose as they stared at the man struggling not to bleed onto the carpet.

Had he just paid Titus a compliment?

The Baron pinched the bridge of his nose with a wince, but he was a hard man, not unused to a swinging fist at the docks in his younger days. "I already told Honoria, an alliance with her could ruin everything for you. Her reputation is in tatters, man."

"My associates aren't as easily frightened off by a little scandal as yours are," Titus remonstrated.

"We both know that's not true."

Titus's eyes flicked away from Nora's questioning look, and with that, her decision was made.

And her heart was shattered.

The Baron only spoke the truth. Her love was the kiss of death, and Titus knew it.

Woodenly, she went to her father and bent to help him up with her one good hand.

"Nora. Don't." Titus reached down and lifted the Baron easily, stabilizing him on his feet before turning to her. "I don't care about all that, I never have. We can find a way to..."

"It's impossible," she murmured.

"No, it isn't. Listen to me—"

"You don't know what you're up against," her father said, checking the handkerchief to see if he'd stopped bleeding. "Her sisters are ostracized and persecuted. The press hound us at every turn, making it damned near impossible to leave the house. They camped out at the offices of my company. Two clerks quit. Poor Felicity had a tomato thrown at her the other day by one of the sisters of your dead prostitutes, Honoria. Can you imagine what that did to the bashful pigeon? She almost came undone."

Nora closed her eyes, pierced by unrelenting shame. *Her sweet sister...how could she bear it?*

She'd been a fool to hope. Last night had been nothing but a fantasy, and now her father had torn that fiction asunder with harsh but pertinent realities.

Could he not have waited? One more day. One more night?

Titus shook his head over and over, patently rejecting what she was about to do. "I can help your sisters, Nora. I have powerful allies. We can change the narrative, can influence the press. I've seen it done numerous times."

"We can change the narrative, but we can't change the

419

truth," she said, her words sounding droll and dead, even to her. "Not about me."

Titus's teeth clacked shut, and he looked as if she'd slapped him.

True to her form, instead of pulling back at the sight of his pain, she forged ahead, ready to rip herself out of his heart once and for all. "It doesn't change that William killed an Earl. That my sisters are suffering the consequences of my actions because I besmirched myself with other men. And that you will suffer, too."

He lunged forward, gripping her hands in his. "I'll survive it, Nora. I've survived worse than—"

Her father scoffed. "You can't know that, Doctor. I've seen many a businessman obliterated by reputation—"

"You've made your bloody point, Cresthaven. I advise you to not interject into this conversation again." A finger jabbed in her father's direction was all it took to press the Baron's lips together, his mottled skin blanching a little.

Despite her astonishment at her father's naked fear, Nora persisted. "I refuse to be something you survive, Titus."

"That's not what I—"

"I've made my decision." She pulled her hands from his warm grip, already grieving. Mourning. Lamenting his loss. She felt shriveled and bleak, hollowed out by pain. To walk out of here would age her another decade at least.

But she'd do it. For him.

His face hardened. His eyes becoming chips of ore, molten in the flames of his temper. "You. Decided," he bit out. "Because that's what you do, isn't it? You make the decision and I have to abide by it."

"Yes," she answered sedately.

"I don't get a say. I don't get a choice. You just run away without trusting that I might know better than him. That we might form a solution together."

"I really am sorry," she said, her throat threatening to close over the pain. She wished it would, that she could stop her breath right here and sink into oblivion. Sorry didn't begin to touch the desperate regret threatening to pull her under. "It's hopeless, Titus. I was always going to damage you one way or the other. And this is bigger than you or me. This is Mercy and Felicity. My parents. Your patients. The families devastated by both my choices and William's. If there were any other way without damaging those I love..."

He held his hand up to silence her, turning his face to the side as if he couldn't bear the sight of her. Already his knuckles were swelling, and she wanted nothing more than to kiss them. His perfect, brilliant surgeon's hands.

Ones that had saved her life twice now.

Perhaps it would have been better if he hadn't, if he'd let fate have its way with her so he wouldn't feel so tethered.

So she wouldn't feel this agony.

Perhaps they were always meant to belong to something—someone—else. She to her family's honor. He to his craft.

"You do what you have to, Nora," he said, his features cast from granite. "But don't for one *minute* think that you're protecting me. Because I'd have burned this entire place to the ground if it meant having a life with you in it."

He left in measured strides. Driven away a second time.

"That's just it," she whispered. "I'd never ask you to."

THE EVENING OF

*A*fter a week of exhausting himself with punishing amounts of work, Titus had recently discovered drinking as a simpler anesthetic than constant distraction.

After his second brown ale, the tension in his bones loosened, and the aches abated. After two or three subsequent glasses of whiskey—or gin, if he were desperate enough—he could almost convince himself that he didn't miss her.

Almost.

Her loss had always been an emptiness he couldn't seem to fill, but this time was especially cruel.

Because he couldn't even stay angry with her.

She'd thrown herself on a sword, becoming a martyr to misery out of some misguided sense of honor.

Perhaps misguided wasn't the word... she'd made some salient points, after all. Fate, it seemed, wanted them to choose between their happiness.

Or the lives of others.

But he was a scientist, goddammit. He was a man who—when presented with a conundrum—reveled in the solving of it. There had to be a way, and if she wasn't willing to find it, he would.

Perhaps at the bottom of his glass.

"Do you want another one, Morley?" he asked, raising his hand to the barkeep at the Hatchet and Crown. War veterans and officers often took their respite at this mahogany bar, therefore a man with a bleak expression and desire for solitude could find a place to drink unmolested. Men here often wallowed in their loneliness together.

As the chief inspector was a fair-skinned man, his cheeks now glowed with warmth as he pushed his glass away and fought to contain a belch. "I've had quite enough, which is still two fewer than you. I'll have to pour you into a hackney."

"I'll get him back home." Dorian yawned from where he perched on Titus's other side, and drained his stout. "I've business in that part of town anyway."

"Do I want to know what sort of business?" Morley goaded.

"You probably already do, you meddling cur." Dorian's eye patch hid his expression until he turned to flash a taunting smile at them both.

"He said he deserved it," Titus told the inside of his glass, puzzling over the same conversation for two weeks now. "What did he mean?"

"Who?" Morley and Dorian asked at the same time.

"Nora's father." Titus wondered when he'd begun to slur. He didn't even feel that inebriated. "What did the Baron mean when he said he deserved a punch from me? Why would he say that? Because he put me on the streets? What man wouldn't for deflowering his daughter?"

"Enough of this." Morley relieved him of his glass, which still had another two hefty swallows. "It's only making you maudlin. You'll be bound to the bottle if you keep it up."

Reflexively, Titus plucked the glass back and downed it in

one burning gulp, before slamming the glass onto the bar with a resounding noise. "One does well to treat an outside wound with alcohol," he contended. "But it is also an effective treatment for internal injuries."

"Sound science." Dorian shrugged into his coat.

"Yes," Titus heartily agreed. "The soundest of hypothessissiess. Hupothesi? Hypotenuse."

Suddenly his stomach lurched, and he tried to remember if he'd eaten since breakfast. He'd no appetite lately. No vigor. Everything tasted flat and beige.

"Come on, man." Dorian hauled him to his feet. "Let's get you home to bed."

"I don't sleep in my bed. It smells like roses."

He missed the glance his compatriots shared because he felt a perfectly good brood coming upon him.

"*I'm*—I should have stopped her." He swayed, looking for his hat before Morley shoved the thing into his hands. "I should have just trussed her up and thrown her in my carriage and run away to Italy. But who does that kind of thing?"

"Only the best of men," Dorian said cheekily. "So, I cannot argue the point."

Morley reached in his pockets and left a generous several coins on the bar. "Prudence says Lady Woodhaven is as bereft as you are. She hasn't accepted any kind of proposal. Not officially. There's still time to fight for her, you know."

His still, cold heart began to beat at the prospect, thrumming and stalling as if it'd forgotten how. "I'd fight the entire world for her... if she'd let me."

A youngish man with an air of danger and an overconfident swagger came toward them. Titus braced for trouble, but the lad merely handed a folded note to Blackwell, tipped his hat at the gratuity he received, and melted back into the London night.

Dorian opened the note and read quickly, his lips compressing into a tight line.

"What is it?" Morley asked, suddenly alert.

"It would seem we're going to Sheerness," he said.

"But that's...hours downriver," Titus protested, stumbling out onto cobbles shining in the pallid gaslight from a recent rain.

"Which is fortunate for you, because you'll need to sober up on the way." Dorian whistled and motioned to where his carriage waited idly a block down. "It would seem your errant lady love has hired an entire handful of personal safety guards to conduct her and her two sisters there tonight rather than wait for the train. Can you imagine why?"

Titus's heart kicked up plenty now, his hands and feet blanching cold while his ears burned, and his lungs tightened. "A town at the mouth of the Thames? I can't begin to guess—"

He broke away, as logic threaded through his whisky-soaked thoughts. He knew her. Even though they'd spent so much of their lives apart. He still knew her. Knew what drove her decisions and desires. She wanted to make amends. To free her sisters from her tainted reputation, possibly by untainting it.

"What is in Sheerness?" he demanded.

Dorian shrugged, searching his near perfect memory. "Oh, a few hotels, an estuary, a fishing and shipping port, mostly."

"Shipping, you say?" Morley clipped, cutting a look across to Titus as Dorian's carriage pulled to the curb. "If they're after what I think they are, let's hope they took a bloody army with them, because they're going to need it."

"Why do you say that?" Titus asked. "I thought she was no longer being followed."

The Chief Inspector glanced through the darkened streets as if searching for a tail. "If Blackwell knows where she's gone, there's a good chance Sauvageau does, as well. The messenger network in this city might be fast and reliable, but serves any master with coin. They know no such thing as loyalty."

Blackwell nodded grimly as he called the footman down from his carriage. "Tell Farah I'll be home in the morning... we have wild beasts to hunt tonight."

THAT AFTERNOON OF

Though her shoulder was healing nicely, the rest of Nora remained one jagged, bleeding wound. And only one doctor in the world could hope to stitch her back together.

She'd eaten more crow in the past couple of weeks than she'd prepared to, and suffered a multitude of indignities. The worst of which was clearing what was left of her things from the home that would be occupied by Adrian McKendrick, the new Viscount Woodhaven.

It wasn't that she was at all attached to the home she'd shared with William. Merely that she was convinced that by the time she married the son of a duke, she'd not have a shred of dignity to offer anyone.

It was worth it, she kept reminding herself. To once again secure Titus's future, along with—

A loud crash from below broke her reverie, and she called down the stairs to where Mercy and Felicity argued in the parlor. "Is everything all right?"

"It's splendid!" Mercy sang back. "Nothing amiss down here!"

"A vase tipped." Felicity emerged from the parlor to the hall where Nora could see her from the second floor. She was holding two larger shards of pottery and wearing a chagrined expression. "We were packing the library when a spirited debate over the superiority of romances or mysteries turned into a fencing match with the fireplace implements. Mercy cut her hand."

"Don't be cross!" Mercy's plea sounded more like a command, though she still hid out of view.

"I'll be right down." Nora checked out the window for the guards her father had hired to stand sentinel against either gangsters or reporters. She wondered if any of them knew a wit about doctoring wounds.

They stood on the walk, looking much too brutish and conspicuous for such a quiet square.

She hurried to fetch a kit of bandages and iodine from the washroom and flew downstairs to the parlor.

Felicity swept up the vase and Mercy was sitting like a child about to be scolded, her fist curled around a handkerchief.

"I'm not cross, it's only a vase," Nora said with a fond smile, holding her hand out. "Where are you hurt?"

"It's a trifle." Mercy unclenched her hand and pulled back a handkerchief, revealing a cut on her palm that still welled with blood. "When the vase fell, I lunged for it and, clumsy dolt that I am, I fell right on top of it."

"It's bleeding *so* much," Felicity said with a delicate, dyspeptic burp. "I can't look, or I'll be sick. Or faint."

"It appears worse than it is." Mercy inspected it. "So superficial, I can't imagine it'll even need stitches."

"A small mercy that," Nora murmured, dabbing a ball of cotton with the iodine and pressing it gently to the cut.

"Why?" Mercy queried. "Because the closest clinic happens to be Dr. Conleith's surgery?" She waggled expressive brows, her wide, mischievous mouth twisting in a suggestive grin. "I *still* can't believe he broke father's nose."

"I'd have given anything to have seen it," Felicity sighed.

At that, Nora shoved a bandage into Mercy's wounded hand, and promptly burst into tears.

Her sisters instantly bracketed her like two clucking bookends, their hands fluttering on her back and her arm like anxious butterflies unsure of where to land.

Nora wrestled with her runaway emotion, doing her best to rein it back in, but each bawl seemed more gasping than the last, until every breath dragged through hiccupping sobs.

Felicity crooned to her, rubbing little comforting circles against her spine as Mercy affixed a one-handed makeshift bandage on her own palm.

"You love Titus, don't you?" Felicity sighed, resting her chin on Nora's uninjured shoulder.

Nora shook her head, accepting the handkerchief Felicity handed her, and dabbing at her eyes and nose. "Don't mark this, either of you. It's been a trying time and I'm...it doesn't matter."

She took in a deep, painful breath and swallowed the ocean of tears threatening to sweep her into the tide. "What matters is that next year I'll be married to a Duke's son, Titus will be the toast of the elite scientific and surgical community, and you... you'll be the belles of the season with dowries the size of which London has not yet seen, if Father is to be believed." She smoothed the skirt of her black gown and took in several calming breaths. "There's still hope," she reminded herself.

Felicity pulled her hands back as if she were made of burning rubbish. "Hope for what?"

"For you both. For good marriages."

The twins looked quizzically at her, and then each other, before they astonished her by bursting into peals of unladylike guffaws.

"What on *earth* makes you think we want to be married?" Mercy ended a chortle with an accidental snort, which sent them both into another tumult of amusement.

Felicity wiped tears from the corner of her eyes. "I believe the idioms, *not if the entire world depended on it*, and *never in a million years* have been batted around."

Nora stared at them as if they were each two heads of a hydra. "But...you're being bullied terribly. Shunned from society. Not invited to participate in the season."

"And?" Mercy shrugged. "That leaves us time to attend lectures and meetings, and it's ever so much easier on Felicity that she doesn't have to talk to men. Or look at them. Let alone marry one, can you imagine?"

Felicity sobered at this a little, but seemed sincere when she said, "We've decided all we need is each other's company. *No* husbands. Ever."

Nora shook her head, unable to comprehend. "But... without husbands how will you afford to live?"

Mercy shrugged. "Well, Father's on the hook for our upkeep indefinitely."

Alarmed, Nora grasped her uninjured hand and forced Mercy to meet her gaze. "Father is unforgiving if you defy him like this. He'll throw you to the wolves if you're of no use to him; believe me when I tell you that."

Mercy stood, pulling her hand from Nora's frantic grasp, her eyes blazing with a sapphire zeal. "We'll become governesses then, or seamstresses. Companions or stuffy old librarians. But I'll see a cold day in hell before I see myself in a church as a bride."

Felicity put her hand on Nora's knee. "Is that why you came back, Nora? To fix our reputations?"

Choking on another sob, Nora clapped a hand over her mouth.

Mercy sighed and regained her seat at Nora's side, her curls spilling over her riotous magenta bodice. This time, she seized Nora's hand, and then thought better of it, gripping her beneath the chin like a recalcitrant child. "Stop it," she ordered with much more confidence and command than her tender years should have afforded her. "You stop martyring yourself for us or for anyone else. I'll not have it. Neither of us gives a fig if the house of Goode is sullied, and—regardless of what Father says—it's certainly no fault of yours."

"Go be happy, Nora. Please," Felicity admonished. "We'll be all right. We'll be better than that. The worst has already happened, the damage has been done. Not by you but your terrible husband."

Mercy released her so she could look over to Felicity, an identical face, if softer and more earnest. "You needn't endure any longer. You never should have done. Father is dreaming if he thinks this marriage will save everything. But one thing isn't a dream... Titus Conleith loves you. He has always loved you. And you love him, I think."

Nora shook her head, her heart bursting with love for her sisters and pain for her loss.

Of course she loved Titus. All she'd ever done was because she'd loved him.

"He hates me now, I'm certain of it," she sniffled, wiping away tears that refused to stop falling. "I left with Father when he all but begged me not to. I betrayed him again."

Felicity took off her spectacles and rubbed some fog away on her sleeve before replacing them. "According to the novels I read, if his feelings for you are powerful in either direction... that means there's hope for a happy ending yet."

"I don't know if he'll ever trust me," she lamented. "I've been so unspeakably cruel."

Mercy perked up. "What *do* they do in your novels, Felicity, when it seems all hope is lost?"

Nora plucked at a stray thread in the handkerchief. "It doesn't matter, it never ends well for the villain."

Felicity shook her head forcefully. "No, you're not the villain. You're the hero, and Titus—regardless of his apparent virility and... impressive musculature—is the heroine."

Nora looked at her askance. "How do you figure?"

"Well, you've the reputation of a rake, I gather." Felicity blushed as she said this, pressing a hand to her cheek. "And have wounds from a dark and painful past."

Mercy held her finger up to mark an idea. "You were shot at least once and stalked by diabolical fiends of the underworld."

"That's right!" agreed Felicity. "That makes you the dashing —if somewhat imperfect—hero."

Even Nora couldn't fight the tug of a smile at their antics. Bless the souls of bookworms everywhere. "So, what does the hero do to win back his heroine?"

Felicity tapped her chin. "Usually a grand gesture of some kind. The hero realizes he was utterly wrong and dreadful— sorry Nora—and he does something to make himself ridiculous for his heroine. Or he fixes all her problems and restores her honor and good name. He saves her from the villain—"

"Titus doesn't need saving from anyone except for me... that hasn't changed."

"Tosh," Mercy shoved that idea aside with a wave of her glove. "I'm sure he needs *something*; we only have to figure out what that is. What is the conflict? What would keep you two apart?"

Nora cast about for ideas, feeling too cynical to be this idealistic. And yet...

"I suppose Titus needs funding to expand his new clinics, and for that he needs financiers, investors, and wealthy patrons to his surgery. He wants to open one in every borough, so even the poor can be treated in time without having to solely rely on the underfunded and overwhelmed city hospitals."

"So, it's just a question of money." Mercy shrugged as if that were no insuperable impediment. "If you can figure out how to replace what he might lose through... well through scandalous association with a benighted—if beautiful—widow, then what's to keep you from being together?"

Nora stood, suddenly agitated by a relentless pinprick of hope in a dark abysmal sky. "It's not *merely* money, it's everything. I'm still possibly a mark for this Sauvageau person because William is haunting me with misfortune from beyond the grave."

"If only we could find that gold William took," Felicity mused. "Surely that would be enough to finance any manner of medical marvels."

Nora put a hand to her forehead and squeezed, hoping to bring forward any idea, any helpful memory. "Before he died, William was looking in shipping containers at the Southwark warehouse because it is largely unused in Father's business. The rest of the London warehouses were subsequently searched by Morley."

"What about the one in Sheerness?"

Nora turned to Mercy very slowly, her blood suddenly pulsing through her. "Say that again."

Mercy's eyes shifted restlessly or—one could say—guiltily. "Well one time, when Prudence and I were snooping through Papa's papers, I thought... I would like to figure out just how rich Father is."

"And?" Nora breathed.

"He's obscenely affluent. Perhaps wealthier than the Queen."

Felicity frowned. "I knew we were rich, but to listen to Father go on, it's as if we're on the verge of ruin at all times."

"The warehouse, Mercy," Nora redirected the conversation back to the salient topic, doing her level best not to snipe at her sisters.

"Oh, well, Father has a few warehouses closer to the mouth of the Thames. According to the papers I found, they've been for sale for months, but the rafters are rotting, so no one's been interested. He's planning on razing and liquidating the property." She put her fists on her hips. "Did you know, he has estate holdings all over, in the strangest of places. Houses we never knew existed?"

This seemed to increase Felicity's distress. "What does he do with them?"

"Who is to say?"

Nora put a hand to her heart, just below the still-healing wound that now ached when she became so tense. "It could be there," she whispered. "Morley has no jurisdiction in Sheerness."

"Should we send for him?" Felicity suggested. "For safety's sake, if nothing else."

"No, you ninny," Mercy stood as well and began to pace as she considered. "If we invite the police, they'll confiscate the gold."

"The gold has been stolen from someone..." Nora reasoned. "Even if we find it, it's not ours."

"We'd be taking from smugglers to finance medical care for the poor," Mercy remonstrated. "We're essentially Robin Hood."

Nora couldn't believe she was about to do this. "I'm not getting you two involved. You need to return home at once."

"Oh, no you don't!" Mercy wagged her finger, then winced as she jostled her wounded hand. "You're not leaving us out of this adventure. I've been reading about quests for illicit treasure my entire life and I'm finally able to go on one!"

"I do think we should hire more security...and probably shouldn't leave until after dark."

"Excellent!" Mercy swept to the front door. "I'll just ask our entourage if they have any dangerous-looking friends."

DAWN

$\mathcal{T}$itus was stone-cold sober by the time he reached Sheerness.

As they careened through the sleepy port town, dawn licked the eastern sky with silver. Clouds built a swirling mass in the distance, pregnant with an approaching storm. The ocean ebbed and surged in a murky maelstrom, as a swarming flock of dark birds waved and shifted like an ominous flag above.

When the carriage clattered up to the dilapidated warehouse at #12 Seaworthy Street—the address on Dorian's note—Titus leapt from the carriage before it even had a chance to slow down. Clutching his medical bag in one hand and a wicked iron-tipped club in the other, he realized he was more ready to use the unfamiliar weapon than the typical tools.

After suffering through the past couple of weeks, he was ready to break something.

Or someone.

The warehouse stood gaunt and bleak, hunkering alone over a vacant dock. It was as if the tightly clustered shipyard businesses to the south and north had turned their backs, leaving it to rot abandoned and alone.

Dim light flickered from a window in the corner facing the water. Along one dark alley, two passenger carriages and a cart used for hauling freight were hitched to sleepy horses. Their breaths curled from their nostrils into the chill of the morning, and Titus could almost hear the sound, so complete was the eerie silence.

Still as death.

What if they were too late?

Dread and fury threatened to overwhelm him, tunneling his vision with shades of crimson. *Nora.* His heart tattooed the syllables of her name into his ribs.

"Wait, dammit," Morley growled as his and Dorian's boots hit the ground behind Titus. "We don't know what is awaiting us in there."

"She's in there. That's all I need to know." Even as he said it, he paced at the door, desperately listening for signs of life. He looked behind him to see Morley hang a rifle over his shoulder.

"That woman is banned from entering warehouses for the rest of her natural life," the Chief Inspector muttered with no small amount of exasperation.

"Upon that, you can rely," Titus vowed, grappling back both wrath and worry in an effort to summon the strength to discover whatever horror might await them inside. "Where is the security they hired?"

"I was wondering that myself." Blackwell, a man fond of wearing long jackets even in the summer, had any number of weapons hidden on him at any given time. Whether he currently palmed a knife or a pistol remained to be seen. "Tell me you have a firearm in that bag, Doctor."

"Trust me," Titus said darkly. "I've instruments in here that would cause you nightmares."

"Good. Let us hope we don't need them."

"There's nowhere to climb," Morley grumbled, his head

tilted back to survey the drooping, dangerously sloped roof of the structure. "And no windows low enough to get to."

"The front door it is, then." Titus lifted his boot and kicked the door. The latch shattered and wood splintered as the thing exploded inward on rusted hinges.

They advanced into the gloom of the warehouse, Titus at their head, using the darkness on the street side to their advantage.

What he saw confounded him enough to freeze his feet to the floor.

The warehouse was an empty void of packed earth and mold. The air stirred with a sharp bite of pitch. Tired beams held aloft sagging rafters and a second-floor walkway was missing more boards than it boasted. A handful of shipping crates clustered at the top of a ramp that led out to the water, if freight wanted to be loaded onto smaller crafts.

A lone lantern perched on a crate and haloed three slim women, who stood abreast on the platform behind an open chest. Clad in dark colors as they were, the Goode sisters might have been hovering over a child's coffin rather than a gleaming fortune.

Titus's heart came alive at the sight of Nora, standing between her fair sisters like a midnight angel. He devoured her with his gaze, his vision blurred with exhaustion and unbridled emotion.

He released her name on a relieved breath, breaking into a jog toward her.

She shook her head, the warning in her wide eyes piercing him with caution the moment before a lone man melted from the shadows beneath the landing.

He maneuvered in front of the women and the chest with the deceptively sleek insouciance of a snake. But Titus could see that this serpent was coiled, ready to strike at the slightest provocation. He was neither bulky nor slight, tall nor short.

Though his proportions were hidden beneath, an exquisitely tailored blue suit suggested at imposing strength and ideal ratios. Dark hair gleamed almost blue in the lantern light, and a diamond winked from one ear.

Titus's fist curled around his club in readiness. Though the man appeared unarmed and unaccompanied, he knew a predator when he saw one.

This particular predator had the raw-boned, sharp-jawed elegance that would have suited the archangel for which he was named.

Raphael Sauvageau.

"The Black Heart of Ben More." The gangster bowed at the waist, adopting a smile that was dangerously close to a sneer. "It is an incomparable honor. I have been an ardent pupil of yours for many years." Though his English was perfect, his measured voice was tinged with the suggestion of a French accent.

Dorian snorted from where he stood at Titus's left shoulder, also deceptively calm as a panther about to spring. "I'd give you terrible marks. Look at you, you're here alone with no army at your back. You're obviously going to die."

"I'd rather no one die today," Morley said, belying the rifle he'd tucked into his shoulder.

Dorian expressed a sigh of consternation, adjusting his eye patch. "You've always been *such* a boor, Morley. I can't fathom how we've become allies."

The chief inspector ignored him. "Where are the security officers hired to protect these women?"

"He told them to go home!" Mercy gestured to the gangster, her features a mask of ardent disbelief. "We brought *five* useless armed brutes with us, but he somehow arrived here first. When he introduced himself and told our guards to go...well they just... *left*."

"They'd doubtless heard of me." Raphael Sauvageau's laughing, tawny eyes locked with Titus, and something like recognition flared there. "*You* are the dangerous one, Doctor," he murmured as if to himself. "One of these women belongs to you." He circled the girls, making a great show of inspecting them, not as a man, but as a beast might his next meal. "The question is, which? The bespectacled bluestocking, the mouthy minx, or..." He stopped in front of Nora, whose features remained carefully blank, her composure born of years of living with volatility. "Ah yes, the benighted beauty."

"If you touch her—" Titus lunged forward, but Dorian caught his shoulder.

"I haven't, and I don't intend to." Sauvageau put up his hands in a gesture of mock surrender as Morley drew a bead. "There's no need for all of that. It is only my brother, Gabriel, and me. We mean no one harm."

Another man stepped from behind the stacked crates to take up sentinel behind the women. He wore a long coat over shoulders half again as wide as his brother's, and a curious hood that shielded his features from view. He said nothing. He didn't need to. The way he loomed over the women spoke terrifying volumes.

Raphael kept his tone conversational, genial even. "We only needed the two of us to load our gold into the cart and we will be on our way."

"Horseshit," Dorian spat. "Surely your savages are close by."

"*Fauves*, not savages." Raphael's eyes gleamed with a dangerous ire. "We are untamed but elegant beasts. We aren't like the brutes and bullies here. We are teaching men to find their own sovereignty. To create their own class in a system that would repress them."

Morley made a distinctly British sound of disgust before he muttered, "Bloody French, even their gangsters are *vogue*."

"Monegasque," Raphael corrected. "Half English, actually, but that isn't what you need to worry about... *your* current problem, is that I stand between you and your women, and you stand between me and the door through which I need to carry my gold. Fortunately for all of us, these challenges are easily resolved."

Morley cocked his rifle. "You've balls of brass. I'll give you that. But you're insane if you think you're walking out of here with that gold."

"Say I don't." An edge leaked into the gangster's voice, turning his consonants lethally sharp. "Like you, Dorian Blackwell, I have a long memory. I do not forget what is taken from me, and I always take what I'm owed…would it do for any of you to wallow in wonder over when I'll chose to collect on the debt? Because there *will* be a reckoning. I am just as relentless as any of you. Dare I say more so." He plucked at a loose fiber from Nora's sleeve, and only the delicate flare of her nostrils advertised her panic. "No one in this room would be safe."

This time no one stopped Titus when he advanced. "I will end you, Sauvageau."

The pile of muscle behind the girls unsheathed a knife. He did nothing with it, but each woman tensed at the sound, the twins reaching for their elder sister.

On anyone else, Sauvageau's smile would have been disarming. "Correct me if I'm wrong, Doctor, but did you not take an oath to do no harm?"

Titus wasn't a doctor right now. He was a man. A man come to claim his woman, to snatch her out of the jaws of a monster.

And then throttle her with his bare hands.

"I'm a surgeon," he hissed. "Which means I know *exactly* how to carve into you until your voice would give out from the screaming."

Raphael glanced back at Nora with an impressed expression. "I do believe he loves you."

She stared at him, her heart shining in her eyes. "I love him."

Titus almost dropped the implements in his hands. To hear

the words from her mouth for the first time stole his breath. But the fear that they could be her last words filled him with a dread he'd not known possible.

"And so we find ourselves at an impasse." The gangster clapped his hands together. "Kill me and take my gold, and start a gang war the likes of which this city has not seen. Let me go and take my gold, then look over your shoulders until I come for it... and for you. Leave now and give me back my gold. And be done with the entire business." He opened his arms like a benevolent king before turning to Nora. "The Fauves have no dealings with you or yours, and the Chief Inspector saved me from having to kill your husband for stealing from me in the first place." He glanced at Titus. "Did you a favor, I think."

"But—but what about the clinics?" Felicity's panicked question echoed through the room like the ricochet of a bullet. When the gangster turned to her, Felicity gasped, putting her hand to her mouth as she visibly began to shake. Behind her lenses, her clear, blue eyes went owlish and round as wells of tears gathered in spikes in her lashes.

"What's this you say?" Raphael glided toward her with a serpentine grace, and she took several steps backward, tripping on the hem of her gown.

Gabriel caught her shoulders with lightning reflexes. The wicked knife still in his hands, the flat of the blade resting against her arm.

She looked at it and whimpered, going slack like a frightened bunny in the enormous man's grip. Her skin blanched a ghostly shade and her breath started to sob into her throat as if she couldn't gulp enough air.

Raphael held out a hand, but paused when she shrank away. "*You* needn't fear me, child. What do you mean about the clinics?"

"I—I can't...I—I..." Felicity broke off, beginning to hyperventilate in earnest.

"Back away, sir." Mercy lunged forward and slapped Raphael's hand aside. "She cannot breathe when she is frightened!" She yanked her sister toward her and, to Titus's astonishment, the silent and mysteriously hooded Gabriel released Felicity from his grip and retreated toward the water, sheathing the knife immediately.

Something about his posture told Titus that he was not... unaffected by the encounter.

Strange.

For his part, Raphael gazed down at the hand that'd been slapped away as if truly seeing it for the first time, and then up at Mercy with an arrested expression.

As if sensing danger, Nora stepped forward, thrusting herself between Sauvageau and her younger sisters. "You asked when we arrived, why we'd chosen now to come for the gold you'd lost."

"Not lost," Raphael corrected. "It was taken."

She flicked a glance at Titus, looked away, and then back as if she couldn't help herself. She stared at him, though she answered the gangster. "The reason we thought to...recover the gold was to give it to Dr. Conleith, so he could properly operate and finance the surgeries he's building in the city."

Titus was only paces from her now, but he couldn't reach her, not without the risk of Sauvageau doing something dangerous. "Nora... what the devil?"

Sauvageau rested his elbow on his folded forearm, crooking his finger against his chin. "I've seen these surgeries in the city. I thought they were called Alcott's."

"Doctor Preston Alcott was a mentor of mine," Titus explained, hoping to take the focus from Nora. "One who has passed."

Sauvageau nodded. "Conleith is a bit too Irish for current

times, I suppose." He looked Titus up and down. "You're young for such a celebrated surgeon."

"No older than you, I'd wager."

"Touché." A dark brow lifted. "I assume you didn't send your ravishing lover and her entourage to procure you this gold."

"I'd never," Titus vowed before sending Nora a hard look. "She'd insisted she didn't know where it was."

"She only learned of this warehouse last night," Mercy rushed to explain, whilst still rubbing a hand over Felicity's back as she glared imperiously at Sauvageau. "This was *supposed* to be her grand gesture, and *you* are ruining it."

Raphael's dark eyes lit with amusement even as he said, "I've ruined a great many things, and people, Miss Goode, but this is the first time a grand gesture has fallen victim to my name."

Titus was as irate as he was confused. "Grand gesture? Nora, what is she on about?"

Nora rubbed at her eyes as though to wipe away tears, but they remained curiously dry.

Mercy fielded the question before she could summon an explanation. "We—Felicity and I—told Nora that we didn't give a fig about husbands, or our reputations, and so she doesn't have to marry the Duke's son. We thought that if we could retrieve the money you needed for your clinics, then you might forgive her for leaving you...even if it *was* partly to save you." She tossed her golden curls. "Again."

"*Mercy,*" Nora hissed.

Everyone in the room fell away until, in Titus's vision, there was only her, dressed in raven black, her pale skin gilded by lamplight. "Is this true?"

She glanced around at their audience and drew a steadying breath as she drifted to the edge of the platform. "I thought..." She hesitated. Swallowed. Once. Twice. "I *knew* that if you loved me, you stood to lose everything, and I couldn't live with that. But I imagined that if… if I could give you the fortune you stood to lose, we could possibly see a way to—to be together."

His anger welled to the surface. "You could see a way. *You* could see a way, Nora, because the path has always been clear to me. I told you that."

She shook her head, her eyes fathomless wells of regret. "I realize you think that now. But I've seen what the loss of fortune does to a man. It drove my husband to the very depths of madness. To do unspeakable things and to ally himself with criminal dregs."

"You wound me, my lady." Sauvageau covered his heart as if she'd pierced it. "After I've worked so hard to fashion myself as the criminal elite."

She went on as if he wasn't even there. "William hated me in the end… did you know that? That a man can love and hate at the same time? It is an ugly thing, Titus. I couldn't have born that from you. It would have destroyed me to watch the light leave your eyes. To see those who respect you turn their backs. To watch as doors are slammed in your face and friends desert you. You might think that you're strong enough to survive that, and maybe you are… but I'm not. This city needs you. The world needs what you're going to discover. The miracles you'll perform."

Titus suddenly wished he could sit down. It all made a bit more sense now. This entire time he'd expected her to trust him. To understand what he wanted and what he meant for them and to believe that he could bring it all to pass. However, in doing so, he'd forgotten that the men in Nora's life were forever making decisions for her. And she'd been tossed about on that turbulent sea like a boat with torn sails and no anchor.

What cause had she to believe in anyone?

"Nora, I—"

A heartrending sob broke through the noise, and they all

turned to see Felicity bravely holding both hands over her mouth, now, as hot tears streamed from her eyes.

Raphael, who seemed to have made a point to remain close by, handed Felicity a handkerchief as the soft-hearted girl wept.

She stared at it for a moment, as if it might bite her, then reached out and took it.

The gangster's face softened in miraculous increments. "You must be possessed of a heart as cold as mine, Miss Goode, to remain unmoved by their plight."

She sniffled and dabbed at her eyes, her lashes wiping at the fog of her spectacles. "I just... I thought I'd arranged a happy ending..."

His mercurial noise might have been a chuckle. "You are a clever girl. You don't really believe there is such a thing as a happy ending, do you?"

"Of course I do." She emitted a hiccupping sigh before taking several hitching breaths. "I believe that sometimes the stars can align. That one change of heart can change the course of fate. That forgiveness and love are possible, even against the most terrible odds...even for someone like you."

Raphael snorted and started to retort. Then, as if he heard a summons no one else did, he turned to the shadowy corner of the room where the hooded figure stood. "Permit me to confer with my brother a moment." He strode to Gabriel, where they held court in rapid, quiet French.

After several bombastic and crude gestures, he returned, wearing a carefully blank look. It was impossible to tell if he'd won or lost.

"Gabriel and I have come to a conclusion," he announced from between clenched teeth. "It seems we wish to make a charitable donation, enough to build a handful of hospitals."

"Oh come off it," Dorian Blackwell called from the dark. "*No one* is *that* altruistic."

"I do not disagree. Consider it a payment, Doctor Titus

Conleith, for a surgery you will perform in the future. Buy the best instruments. Attend the most important lectures and instructional theaters on the reconstruction of bones and skin. And pray that your skills are what they are reputed to be when next we darken your doorstep."

Before Titus could ask more, the man clicked his boots and bowed. "We'll be in touch." Curiously, he paused to pluck his handkerchief from Felicity's lax fingers, and smirked over at Mercy's dumbstruck expression. "Surely *that* fulfills the requisites for a grand gesture."

She merely gawked at him, slack-jawed, and uncharacteristically speechless.

Instead of waiting for an answer, he turned to the silent figure in the corner, and they strode into the darkness.

After a pregnant moment, Dorian gathered himself and strode toward the door. "I'm going after them."

"Don't." Morley held him back.

"But, Titus can't serve as surgeon to *two* gangsters. It just isn't done."

Morley eyed him with a hound-like petulance. "I thought you were legitimate."

"I am... mostly." Dorian sucked his teeth. "Even so, that upstart bastard irks me."

"Only because he reminds you of yourself not so long ago before you *supposedly* reformed."

Titus could do nothing but stare at Nora as their banter faded into the background.

She loved him. She'd just said so. She did all this... for him.

For his forgiveness. For a chance.

A latent growl worked its way from deep in his chest and burst forth as he dropped his weapon and bag, lunged for her, and swept her into his arms.

"*Titus,*" she gasped, flailing for a moment before locking her arms around his neck to secure herself as he marched toward Blackwell's carriage. "What the devil are you doing?"

"Something I should have done ages ago," he gritted out.

Felicity rushed after them, but Morley seized her elbow and redirected her. "We'll take another coach," he said, exchanging a knowing look with Blackwell.

Titus nodded at the driver, who jumped down and opened the door so he could unceremoniously plunk Nora down on the luxurious seat and follow her inside.

THE LONG ROAD

$\mathcal{N}$ora did her best to head off a lecture. "You don't have to condescend to me about the foolishness of this endeavor, but I couldn't have known our hired security would go running at the first sight of trouble," she began as Titus tucked his long legs into the coach and shut them in together, creating a tight oasis of luxurious cobalt.

"Are you hurt?" he asked in a carefully bland and measured voice.

The question warmed her. "I'm all right. They never touched me."

"Good." Instead of uncoiling at her answer, his jaw locked together as if to keep from roaring. "Now what in *God's* name do you think you were trying to—"

She put up a staying hand. "I know you're angry—"

"You can't *begin* to imagine what I'm feeling right now." He broke off, a muscle working furiously just below his temple as he simply stared at her, his eyes glinting with an emotion she was truly incapable of defining.

Nevertheless, Nora absorbed his features with all the appreciation of a prisoner glimpsing the light of day for the first time in years. His golden eyes were haunted by shades, and deeper grooves sprouted from their edges. Ashen skin stretched more tightly over his dramatic cheekbones, and a few days' growth of beard widened his jaw from masculine to dangerous. His clothes were rumpled and he smelled of whiskey.

He looked truly awful.

He was the most beautiful man alive.

And he'd come for her. It was all she could do not to grin in the face of his temper. To beam with a light she was afraid could not last.

"What did they mean?" he rumbled in a voice edged with lethal calm. "Mercy said you saved me... again."

Nora allowed guilt to pull her gaze down to where their knees almost touched. "Mercy says a lot of things."

"And your father, he said he deserved my anger...why?"

A little tremor coursed through her. She'd promised herself to never burden him with this truth, but perhaps she'd been mistaken. "I think... you know why."

"I want to hear it from you."

Nora collapsed back on the seat, letting her head fall against the damask velvet as she affixed her stare somewhere above his unruly hair. "I married William all those years ago because... Papa threatened you if I didn't."

His fists curled on his thighs, and his every muscle bunched, but Nora forced herself to continue.

"He vowed that he'd make certain no school would accept you and no household would employ you. That he might have you thrown in prison or worse. He went so far as to threaten to put me in an institution, as well. It all seemed so hopeless, and you had such dreams, such ambition and promise. I—I loved you too much to condemn you to that. I didn't think sacrificing a girl you'd only been attached to for three months would be so bad as losing everything you ever—"

"Three months," he echoed, the syllables drawn out carefully as he leaned forward. "Three months? *You* only loved *me* for three months. I loved you since the moment I laid eyes on you."

That snapped her gaze back to his solemn features. "Impossible. You were ten when we met."

"And you were the dream I didn't dare to allow myself to hope for, even then."

Defeat followed quickly on the elation he'd evoked with those words. Nora dropped her head in her hands and hid, so she didn't have to look at the mess she'd made of everything. "And now...I'm a nightmare."

His knees hit the floor of the carriage, and he reached for her wrists. Pulling her hands away from her eyes, he slid his fingers over her jaw until he held her face cupped in his palms. He looked down at her as if she were a revelation, his gaze suddenly tender, though his features remained taut with an agonizing emotion. "My entire life I've been certain that I loved you considerably more than you would ever love me, and I'd made my peace with that. But... God, Nora, if I'd only known—"

Those two words. *If only*. They'd driven her mad before.

She shook her head, new tears sliding down her burning cheeks and landing in his palms. "I *died* the day you left. I've done so many things in my life I regret, but hurting you that night has always been my most egregious sin. I never even cared if my subsequent actions doomed me to hell, because hell is living in a world where you were close and yet impossible to reach. And now I fear that even with all I've been through, nothing's changed. I am still ruined."

"Not to me." His grip tightened, his thumb silencing her as he traced the outline of her lips. "Listen, Nora. I am merely a doctor, but as you see, I have powerful friends. Your father couldn't *wish* to have a circle of influence like mine. The Chief Inspector. Dorian Blackwell and his wife, the Countess Northwalk. The Duke and Duchess of Trenwyth. The Earl and Countess of Southbourne... I could go on—"

"Don't you understand," she interrupted. "These are the people I could drive away with the scandal attached to my name."

To her utter astonishment, a rumble of mirth vibrated from him. "You don't know these people, but you will. And they'll support you. They'll dare the rest of the *ton* to shame you. And even if they did, Nora, we'd keep other society. This is a whole wide city full of people. Hang everyone but you and me."

For some humiliating reason, this only made her weep harder.

He thumbed away her tears, only to have them replaced with new ones. "You said something to me that has been weighing on my conscience..."

"What's that?" she sniffed, trying to regain control of herself.

"That you don't know who you are. That you don't feel that you are deserving, but *I* know you, Nora. Every man in your life has made you feel unworthy but, darling, you are kind and self-sacrificing. You've always made yourself responsible for others in your care. Your family, your bastard of a husband, your sisters. I could lift that burden from you. I could care for you, so that you might turn your kindness elsewhere. You can find whatever purpose suits you. And I'll be right beside you, if you'll let me."

Overwhelmed, Nora gripped his arms, intent upon pulling him away, but she couldn't bring herself to do it. Not when he was right in front of her, kneeling between her knees, saying the words that filled the empty well of her soul. "I...don't—I can't believe this is happening."

"Why not?"

"Because every time I've dared myself to hope, it's been ripped from me... and I allowed it. I facilitated it. When I think of the time we've lost, of all the things I could have said and done differently..." She laid her palms on his chest, searching for the thrum of his heart and finding it there, strong and steady. "I realize it was irresponsible to come for the gold, but I wanted to do *something* to fix what I'd broken. I was desperate and reckless..."

He broke her words off with a searing kiss, his lips a warm and reassuring pressure against hers, parting her lips so she could taste the salt of her tears. He kept the kiss gentle and voluptuous, his tongue slick and soft against hers, making no demands. Asking nothing. Just offering. Coaxing.

He pulled back before the kiss could deepen any further, though the pace of his heart had quickened beneath her palm.

"God, I love you," he breathed against her mouth, the hands bracketing her face roaming to cup her head and smooth down her neck. "I didn't need a grand gesture or a crate of gold any more than you need ask my forgiveness. I'm not angry, I should never have been angry. Medicine is my calling, but *you* are my life. Nora." He kissed her temples, "Nora..." her eyelids and brow, "my lovely Nora." He smoothed his lips over her cheek until he returned to her mouth. "You are the greatest treasure. The sparkle beneath a grey sky. You are the beauty no one else can compare to."

"How blind you are," she said wryly, expecting any moment to wake from a dream.

He pulled back to spear her with a look full of so much affection, she nearly expired from the dizzy optimism it evoked. "I can only see you. Here. Right in front of me. We decide our futures now. You and I. Nora, will you marry me?"

She gripped his shoulders, suddenly frantic. "Yes. Today. *Right* now. Before anything happens to stop it."

He chuckled, fondly caressing her hair. "Nothing will happen. Nothing will take you from my arms. Never again. Not if you come to me with your worries and burdens. Not if you let me in to help you. I want to protect you. I want that to be my right and privilege. The whole world could collapse tomorrow and all I'd want is to experience it with you. Would you promise to let me?"

Ardent emotion robbed her of her words, so she simply nodded, her fingers curling in his lapels to draw him down for another luxurious, whisky-flavored kiss. One that deepened and heated as his fingers ventured possessively over her skin.

Nora sighed into his mouth, releasing with the breath a tremulous marvel at the machinations of the day. She'd been heartsick only last night. And now her love was in her arms.

She couldn't bear to think of the dismal years and treacherous road they'd had to take to find each other.

But as his fingers began to caress their way up the silk of her stockings, she was very glad, indeed, of the long road back home.

EPILOGUE

SIX MONTHS LATER

Titus applauded with the exuberance of the crowd as his beaming wife handed a pair of scissors to the Duchess of Trenwyth. Once the ribbon was cut and a picture taken for the press, the citizens of Southwark were treated to refreshments and libations, even a few happening by on their way from work.

Though the venture was his, Titus was more than content to step away from the hubbub around the attractive and wildly popular duke and duchess. He allowed the press of people to crowd him out, until he found himself leaning against a stoop across the street, hovering by an alley.

This was a year of dreams realized, and he selfishly wanted a moment to savor it.

Many souls gathered to see that Alcott's Southwark Surgery had expanded to a proper clinic with gleaming instruments and a brand-new surgical theater with a staff of three noted physicians and six capable nurses.

Similar surgeries in Whitechapel, South Bank, Lambeth, Greenwich, and Hampstead were under construction. In thanks not only to an influx of, admittedly, ill-gotten gold, but also the patronage of several philanthropists and Titus's own profits from Knightsbridge.

And in the center of it all, was Nora.

At first, of course, their marriage had been met with a chaos of scandal, most of which they avoided with a honeymoon in Italy, France, and a lovely yachting trip to Greece.

Upon their return, the Duchess of Trenwyth and her influential Ladies' Aid Society clutched Nora to their collective bosoms and began a full-scale society campaign the likes of which even the Prime Minister would be proud.

He and Nora had taken up riding again in Italy, and had purchased several mounts to keep in the city. They'd escape the office for a bracing gallop, and he'd watch her hair fly out behind her, her lips parted in the smile that graced her mouth more readily these days. Her sister Prudence promised to join her just as soon as she could climb on a horse after her and Morley's child arrived.

With the Duchess of Trenwyth at Nora's side when he could not be, trotting through the park was again a friendly venture. She'd become more of a celebrity than a pariah, and her narrative had all the salacious notes of Lady Godiva, a rebel rather than a ruined woman.

There were naysayers and gossips, of course. And her father and mother had all but publicly disowned her, but Nora met the pain of it with her head held high and her heart open. On top of her philanthropic endeavors, she worked by his side, providing comfort to the sick and protection to women, coordinating escapes in some cases and empathetic advice in others.

She was happy with their life—with him—or so she kept insisting as they lay entwined each night, slick and exhausted and no less ecstatic for it.

And he was glad, even though happiness didn't even come close to describing what he felt.

He was...complete.

Life wasn't perfect; in fact, chaos and calamity commanded most of his days. Suffering and death were part of a surgeon's existence. But no matter the misery he was subjected to, she was the soothing caress that had become the balm to his soul.

They laughed together. Teased and tormented each other. Spent lively meals with friends and made plans to travel and take holidays.

It was a life many men could only dream of... and here he was living it.

A smile tugged at the corner of his lips and a wash of awareness warmed his skin, alerting him that she was nearby before she melted from the crowd.

A vision in a frothy scarlet gown with a matching black hat, she drew the eye of every man in her vicinity as she glided toward him with a radiant smile.

"It's a bracing burden to have such a lovely wife, but I suppose it is a cross I must bear," he purred as she melted into his side and tipped her head to rest her temple against his shoulder.

"Why do you think I came searching for you?" She beamed up at him, black cherry eyes twinkling with mirth. "The ladies of Southwark were beginning to gather in this direction, I had to come and stake my claim. They'll be fabricating all sorts of ills to have you examine them."

"You're patently ridiculous." He dropped an adoring kiss into her hair. "We should leave," he whispered. "I'm already bored of this."

She laughed, knowing they both would stay for the duration, and collapse in a depleted heap at the end of the day. It was a game of theirs, to plan their social escapes. One they'd started to play when the anxiety of a gathering would overwhelm her in the early days of her return to society.

She scanned the crowd milling about. "All we'd have to do is melt into this alley. Where should we go, husband? Should we ride in the park?"

"I'd love a ride," he growled against her ear. "But we might get arrested for indecency if we do it in the park."

She swatted his chest, then froze.

"What is it?" he asked, instantly on alert.

Instead of answering, she tugged on his sleeve, gesturing with her gaze, across the way to the fringes of the gathering.

A hooded figure stood staring right at them, his preternatural stillness seeming to make him invisible to those who teemed around him.

Gabriel Sauvageau.

Titus stared back, not in challenge but in acceptance. He dipped his chin in greeting.

Gabriel did the same before melting into the crowd and disappearing into an alley.

"What do you think he wanted?" she asked. "We've not seen or heard from the Fauves since Sheerness. But I worry about them sometimes… about what they'll ask you to do."

Titus shook his head, still staring at the corner around which the man had disappeared. "They didn't have to leave the gold. I don't care who needs medical attention, I would give it to them. It's my responsibility to treat a wound. Doesn't matter what sort of person they are, that's for better men than I to judge."

"There *is* no better man than you," Nora said, rising on her toes to press a soft kiss to his cheek so she could whisper in his ear. "You stitched my life back together when I thought no one could…and *that*, dear husband, is why I will always love you."

DANCING WITH DANGER

CHAPTER 1

LONDON, 1881

*A*n incomparable idiot.

It was the only description for the man blocking Mercy Goode from the murder scene *she'd* discovered her own self.

And yet he had the *audacity* to sneer down at her in that condescending way menial men did when granted a little bit of authority. His shiny badge declared him Constable M. Jenkins. A tall but scrawny bit of bones scraped together between comically overgrown muttonchops.

"If you don't vacate the premises now, I'll see you sleeping behind bars tonight, and make no mistake about that." He narrowed beady eyes and loomed in an attempt to intimidate her.

Mercy glared right back. Since she was entirely too short for a proper loom, she bared her teeth to do him one better in the foul expression department.

An errant bee had more capacity to terrify her than this blighter with his ridiculous feathery mustache. From the moment he'd arrived, he'd tried to get rid of her, and *that* she would not abide.

"See here!" Mercy poked him in the chest. "*I'm* the one who found the body thus murdered and sent for Scotland Yard. Therefore, I'm a valuable witness at best and a possible suspect at the very least. If you advise me to leave before a detective inspector arrives, he'll be furious. You could lose your position, which..." She trailed off, scanning the man up and down for any possible signs of capability. "If you want my opinion, might do both you and the London Metropolitan Police a favor."

The slack-jawed halfwit blinked in mute amazement, his dull brain taking an inordinate amount of time to process her statement.

Mercy used his dumbstruck torpor to sweep around him and slide into the stately, feminine solarium where the corpse sat propped in a high-backed burgundy velvet chair.

Poor Mathilde.

Swallowing a lump of regret so large it threatened to choke her, Mercy's hands curled into fists. Mathilde had known she was in danger. They'd discussed it at length when the scandalous socialite—bruised, battered, and quite drunk—had come seeking shelter at the Duchess of Trenwyth's Lady's Aid Society. The Duchess, along with Mercy's twin, Felicity, had hatched a plan to secretly smuggle the woman out of the country as soon as humanly possible.

Evidently, not soon enough.

If only they had made other arrangements.

If only Mercy had skipped her weekly appointment last evening and insisted on squiring Mathilde away under the cover of night, instead of allowing the sweet—but unreliable— woman to decide upon the circumstances.

When she wanted to dissolve into frustrated tears, Mercy only allowed herself to indulge in a hitch of labored breath before she bit into the flesh of her cheek. It was imperative she contain herself. She could not show weakness.

Not here.

Not in front of a man who would whip her with it. Who would make her wait somewhere else until she controlled her "feminine hysterics."

The very idea was intolerable.

"I'm so sorry I failed you," she whispered to the unnaturally still body. Her fingers itched to brush back one errant lock of what was otherwise a perfect brunette coiffure.

Mathilde had been a beautiful woman in the prime of her thirties. Scandalous, sultry, and... scared.

They'd only ever met in person but thrice. And yet, Mercy felt this tragedy as if a dear friend had passed.

"I vow I will not rest until they find who did this to you," she whispered.

At those words, a strange, feverish chill washed down her spine and prickled along her nerve endings. She was suddenly bathed in awareness of someone nearby.

Watching.

Glancing about, she only found Jenkins, apparently roused from his stupefied confusion at her feint around his blockade.

Perhaps it was time for her to rethink her position regarding ghosts.

She'd been categorically opposed to the idea of the supernatural in almost every respect.

Until now.

Certainly Jenkins didn't carry such an aura of malice.

Even though she'd made him cross.

"Oi!" He stormed into the room after her, his expression morphing from one of surprise to suspicion. "The detective inspector isn't but a moment away, so don't you dare touch anything."

"I know better than to disturb a murder scene," Mercy announced with a droll sniff.

"What makes you reckon she was murdered?" he asked, eyeing her with rank skepticism. "The lady could have very well died in her sleep. You know something you're not telling?"

Despite her distress and remorse, Mercy felt a surge of relish at being able to finally trot her extensive knowledge on the matters of murder in the presence of an arrogant dolt.

"Prepare your notepad, dear Constable, and I shall elucidate." She pinned her hands behind her back in a regimental posture. One her brilliant brothers-in-law often adopted when lecturing her about being more judicious.

Not that such homilies were effectual in her case.

But the men in her family appeared especially important and erudite while standing thusly, and even though she didn't usually listen, it was certain that most people who were unacquainted with their soft hearts and darkest secrets would be inclined to do so.

"Do you see the slight edema there at her neck?" She motioned to the open throat of Mathilde's high-necked gown, where the once-porcelain skin was now tinged a blue-grey. "This suggests asphyxiation, but there are no ligature marks, nor is there bruising." She bent closer, inspecting the wound. "But a distressing bit of an interruption in the cords of her muscle, just there, leads me to believe that when your coroner arrives, he'll find that her neck has been quite broken."

Mercy exhaled a shaking breath, grasping onto her composure with both hands. If this dullard could keep his wits about him when faced with such a tragedy, then she was equally determined to.

"She wouldn't have died instantly." Her throat rasped over traitorous emotion. "Likely, she'd have been paralyzed, but able to talk and scream until the pressure crushed her trachea." Her fingers reached for her own neck in sympathy, her bones heavy with guilt and her heart surging with an ardent vow to retaliate. "Her name was Mathilde Archambeau. That's A-R-C-H—"

She glanced over at Jenkins. "Why are you not writing this down?"

"Because we know exactly who this woman is," said a stolid voice from the doorway. "And we have already surmised who is responsible for her death."

Mercy whirled to find an average, if incredibly sturdy, man in a billycock hat and matching grey morning suit. He strode into the solarium with his coat lackadaisically draped over one arm. A square chin framed a nose that could have been unflatteringly likened to a potato. Eyes spaced too close together gleamed with improper interest as he conducted a thorough and disrespectful examination of Mercy's person.

He was at least fifteen years her senior and wore a wedding band on his left finger.

Marriage didn't stop men from ogling her, Mercy had found. Most possessed a weakness for a young slim woman with pale ringlets and a passably attractive face.

That was all they saw when they looked at her with the same desire she witnessed now. Her smooth, unblemished youth. Her diminutive shape and sparkling blue eyes.

She could disarm just about anyone with her winsome charms.

Until she opened her mouth.

Then their desire melted into anything from dismay to disgust.

As Mercy's father often said, she'd make a perfect wife, if only someone could relieve her of her wits and her willfulness.

Or at least her tongue.

Her charms, as it happened, were only skin-deep.

Ah well, c'est la vie.

Fingers the size of breakfast sausages curled around her gloved hands as the newcomer bowed over her knuckles. "I'm Detective Inspector Martin Trout, at your service, Miss..."

Trout. A more apropos surname was never given.

"You know who did this?" Mercy plucked her hand away, blithely stepping around his subtle press for an introduction. "You know who murdered Mathilde?"

"That's a relief. I was beginning to think it was *her*." Constable Jenkins gestured toward Mercy, his brass buttons catching on the afternoon light streaming in through the windows from the back gardens.

One such window, Mercy noted, was open.

In February?

When even the fire blazing in the hearth wasn't enough to ward off the moist chill in the room.

"Don't be ridiculous, Jenkins," Detective Inspector Trout said, sidling closer to Mercy. "Our division is very familiar with this household. Mrs. Archambeau was unquestionably killed by her ham-fisted husband, Gregoire."

Mercy deflated instantly. So much for the police being any help. "No, Detective Inspector, that is where you are wrong. It had to have been someone else."

"Wrong?" The man echoed the word as if he'd never heard it before as shadows passed over his ruddy features.

Mercy nodded. "Mathilde and I had someone follow Gregoire onto a ferry to France where he was to conduct business for a week at least. You see, while he was away, she was going to leave him, due to the aforementioned mistreatment of her." At this, Mercy's brows drew together as she speared the man with her most imperious glare. "Which begs the question, Detective Inspector Trout, if you were aware that Mr. Archambeau was a cruel man, why didn't you arrest him or at least take measures to keep poor Mathilde safe?"

Ah, there it was. The dulling of his desire.

All semblance of approbation drained from Trout's murky eyes, replaced by instant antipathy. "Mathilde Archambeau is a notorious drunkard and recently made a cuckold of her husband on a number of occasions," he informed her stiffly.

"Yes," Mercy clipped, "Mathilde admitted to me that she drank, among other things, to dull the anxiety and misery of living with such a man as Mr. Archambeau..." Stalling, she also recalled the rapturous expression on the woman's features when she'd confided that she'd taken a lover recently. One who'd coaxed such pleasure from her body, she'd become addicted to that, as well.

If only Mercy hadn't been too embarrassed—and too stimulated—to ask the man's name.

For, surely, *he* was a suspect.

"Certainly, Mathilde's indiscretions didn't warrant violence against her. Indeed, she didn't deserve this terrible fate," she said.

"I don't know about that." Trout gave a tight, one-shouldered shrug and twisted his lips into something acerbic and ugly as he glanced down at the departed. "Were I to catch my missus with anyone, I don't imagine the outcome would be much different. She'd be lucky to escape with a sound hiding, and *he'd* be certain to end up in the Thames."

This, from a man who'd undressed her with his eyes, only moments before.

Mercy decided to take a different approach.

It was that or lose her temper.

"Look over here." She hurried to the window and swiped at the ledge, the silk of her white glove coming away dirty with mud from the garden. "I entered the Archambeau household through the front door, as would Gregoire, if he'd come home early. Someone very obviously climbed in this window recently. Someone strong and limber, to have scaled up to the third-floor terrace in last night's rain. Strong enough to say... snap a woman's neck with his bare hands." She moved the drapes out of the way, uncovering one large footprint in the arabesque carpet. "I deduce that if you find the man who wears a military

Brogan boot with such a definitive heel, you'll find Mathilde's murderer."

She couldn't say that she expected an ovation or anything, but the grim consternation on both the lawmen's faces threatened to steal some of the wind from her sails. "Confirm Gregoire's absence from the country if you must—no one would fault you for being thorough—but also it's your duty to examine and investigate any other evidence, and this is certainly compelling." She looked at Trout pointedly. "Do you happen to know the name of her lover? Maybe he—"

Trout moved with astonishing speed for a man of his girth and was in front of her in an instant. Those large sausage fingers of his spanned her wrist in a bruising grip and yanked her away from the window. "Time for you to leave."

"Unhand me, sir!" Mercy demanded.

He dragged her toward the door, speaking through clenched teeth. "Regardless of her supposed wealth, Mathilde Archambeau was a degenerate who associated with students, theater folk, socialists, and suffragists. Her husband is little better. I do not know to which group you belong, but I'll tell you this... you'll be hard-pressed to find a detective who will spend extra precious time and energy on behalf of a drunken immigrant slag. Her death means there is one less *nasty* woman in my borough—"

Mercy's hand connected with the detective's cheek before she realized she'd meant to slap him. Her palm stung, even beneath her glove, and she'd barely time to close her fingers around it before her blow was answered with a backhand to the jaw.

The force was such that her neck gave an audible crack when it wrenched to the side. She would rather have died than allow a cry to escape, but the pain was so acute, so startling, she couldn't hold in the whimper.

Jenkins stepped toward them. The frown of concern

twisting his mustache blurred as hot, unwanted tears muddled Mercy's vision.

"Inspector, is such brutality necessary—"

"Shut up, Jenkins, and get me the shackles. I'm arresting this harpy for accosting an officer of—"

The sound of splintering wood froze all in the room into a momentary tableau of shock as the door on the far wall shattered beneath an overwhelming force.

Mercy's pulse slammed in her veins as recognition seized her with a queer and instantaneous paralysis.

The last—well, the only—time she'd seen the newcomer, his gait had been lazy and arrogant. His movements loose-limbed and careless, as if he'd conquer the world when he bothered to get around to it.

He had made it abundantly clear to her in the past that he did nothing lest it pleased him.

And what he took pleasure in at this moment, was violence.

All semblance of charm and leisure had been replaced by a body coiled with the tension of steel cables and grey eyes glinting with all the lethality of gunmetal.

He was across the room in a blink, lunging like a viper.

He struck. Struck again.

Blood flew and bone crunched.

Suddenly, Trout was no longer grasping her but crumpled in a moaning puddle at her feet.

When Jenkins reached for his cudgel, the interloper only had to whirl and point a long finger in his direction to cause the lawman anxious hesitation. "If you raise that weapon against me, *mon ami*, I swear in front of God—and this beautiful woman—that I will take it and deliver the most humiliating beating you've ever received."

His voice like a saber, smooth and wickedly sharp, was tinged with the barest hint of a French accent. It slid into her ear with that same vague sensation of malevolence she'd experienced only moments ago, raising every hair on her body.

Some primitive instinct roared to life in his presence, one that warned her of imminent peril.

"The last man who raised a weapon against me...will never walk again." He stood with his back to her, squared against the indecisive constable. Lean muscle flexed rigid beneath his exquisitely tailored suit as vibrations of aggression and intimidation rolled off his wide shoulders in waves and stole whatever courage poor Jenkins possessed.

The policeman returned trembling fingers to his sides as he, no doubt, recognized how close he stood to death.

Because the man in front of him was possessed of one of the most identifiable names in the empire.

A notorious libertine.

A flagrant and lawless fortune hunter.

A gangster bequeathed with all the masculine beauty of Eros himself.

He turned back to her, brushing an errant ebony forelock of hair out of his eyes to aid in his unrepentant assessment.

What Mercy read in his gaze stupefied her further.

Where before there had been intellect, charisma, and cunning, only ferocity resided now. Ferocity and...something that looked confoundingly like concern.

His evaluation was a tangible thing. It caressed her in places she'd given no man license to touch.

Least of all him.

His scan of her body started at the hem of her dress and left no part of her untouched until he met her eyes.

And then, right in front of her, the ferocity dissipated, replaced by that signature insouciance he was so famous for.

It was said he'd smile like a Cheshire cat whilst disemboweling his enemies.

Mercy didn't doubt it in the least.

He lifted his knuckles to brush against her still-smarting cheek, and she flinched away.

Not because she feared him—

But because she wasn't ready to find out what the sensation of his touch would do to her. When his very presence set her nerves alight with such volatile, visceral thrums of awareness, how could she bear the pressure of his skin?

He obviously misinterpreted her retreat as a muscle flexed in his jaw. "I will relieve him of the hand he struck you with, *mademoiselle.*"

He said this as if offering to shine her shoe.

A siren broke the moment as the thunder of horse hooves clattered into the cobbled courtyard. Voices shouted and the very rafters shook with the force of a veritable army of police.

The arrival of his comrades injected the sputtering constable with fresh nerve.

"No one will believe this," Jenkins marveled. "I'll be the man who arrested *the* Raphael Sauvageau, Lord of the Fauves, and hanged him for murder.

CHAPTER 2

*M*ercy had often been described as fearless.

Indeed, she did little to disavow people of the notion. In her home, fear was used by her authoritarian parents to coerce and control. She witnessed how it plagued Felicity, her twin. How it granted her domineering father power over people he had no right to possess.

And so, she'd decided from a very young age that she would fear as little as possible and therefore maintain as much power as she could.

Oddly enough, an ironic phobia had developed in the wake of her declaration of personal sovereignty.

She couldn't stand to be caged.

In fact, the confines of the prisoner transport wagon made her fingers curl with the need to claw at the locks, the walls, the very flesh that immured her soul to her body.

The shiver that had previously run through her had now become a quake so intense, her bones threatened to rattle together.

Though the iron and wood interior of their cage was intolerably frigid, a sheen of sweat perceptibly bloomed at her hairline and some of it gathered to trickle between her breasts. The sway of the coach on dubious springs felt to her like a rowboat on the open ocean during a sea gale.

It was making her green at the gills.

Well, if her breakfast were to make a reappearance, she'd be certain to direct it at the shackled man taking up more than his share of space, not to mention entirely too much of the fetid air.

She refused to acknowledge Raphael Sauvageau as she lunged at the door, kicking out at it with all her might. The irons securing her wrists in front of her were attached to a bar above the long bench by a chain that set her teeth on edge with the most grating rattle.

As the carriage lurched over a bump, the chains were the only reason she didn't end up on the floor in a heap of petticoats and sprawling limbs.

Mercy hadn't gone easily into confinement. She'd writhed and scratched and spit like an angry tomcat being forced into a bath. It'd taken four constables to subdue her.

Behind her, the damnable gangster had sauntered toward his imprisonment as if he were on a lazy stroll, looking so much like he preferred his hands to be manacled behind him so he didn't have to hold them there on his own.

His calm was patently infuriating. And if she were speaking to him at the moment, she'd make certain he knew it.

"Let me out, you knob-headed ignoramus!" she shouted through the bars, gripping them and shaking, as if it would do any good. "It shouldn't be a crime to slap a man for being a discourteous toad, especially when he gave as good as he got!"

She ignored a sound emanating from the man locked inside with her, unable to tell if it was mirth or wrath.

The uniformed officers around Mathilde's tidy row house disappeared as the conveyance rounded a corner.

In one final fit of pique, Mercy slammed her palm against

the door with a satisfying clang before heaving herself onto the bench in a huff.

"I can't be here," she said to no one. Particularly *not* to the only other occupant of the coach. "My father is a baron and a commissioner, and my brother-in-law is the Chief Inspector at Scotland Yard. I'll never hear the end of it." She tugged at her tight manacles, twisting her slim wrists this way and that. "Oh, blast and bloody bother!"

This time, the rumble of amusement was unmistakable, drawing her notice.

"Really, I must beg you to refrain from saying such things," Raphael Sauvageau intoned in a voice that threatened to curl her toes.

He lazed on the bench across from her as if it were as comfortable as a throne, legs sprawled open at the knees and expensive jacket undone. The threads of his trousers molded to long, powerful thighs, calling attention to an indecent bulge at their apex.

"I'll say what I like, you—you—" If she wasn't doing her best to avoid looking at it—at *him*—she would surely have delivered a most clever and scathing remark.

"Do not misunderstand me, *mon chaton*, I have no wish to censure you. It is only that I find your attempts at profanity relentlessly adorable and distracting. It is torture to be unable to do anything about it." Beneath his charcoal suit, he lifted a helpless shoulder made no less broad for the captivity of his arms behind his back.

"The only thing you can do is to sod right off," she snipped. "They're going to put you to death, how can you be so calm?"

That Gallic shrug again. "I have many reasons not to panic, not the least of which is that I don't want to give them the satisfaction of knowing they ruffled my feathers." He raised one dark, expressive eyebrow at her.

Mercy felt her frown turn into a scowl. Every person in a

five-city-block radius categorically understood the current state of her feathers. They hadn't been merely ruffled. But plucked.

Fit to be tied, she was.

Drat.

Mercy sagged back and let her head fall against the wall, squeezing her eyes shut.

She didn't want to look at him.

What was he about calling her adorable? Had he meant it as a slight? A condescending jab at her youth? She was only all of twenty, but she was well educated. Well read.

Not to mention...one just didn't go around calling people adorable, did one? Not unless they were your nine-year-old niece or something equally perturbing.

She was a *woman*.

And some part of her wanted him to know that. To acknowledge it.

Raphael Sauvageau was pure, unmitigated male. His voice deep. His manner predatory. His gaze unapologetically lustful.

When he spoke, his voice purred against her skin.

And yet, he could seduce a woman without saying a word. Make her aware of all the deep, empty places she ignored.

He was wickedly, no, *ruthlessly* attractive. Roguish and virile with sharp bones that cut a portrait of indolent cruelty.

That was why she refused to open her eyes, because sometimes, looking at him made her brain turn to a puddle of useless, feminine liquid that threatened to leak out her ears, leaving her with no wits at all.

With no logic. No reason to resist...

Regardless of her attempt to ignore him, she could feel his eyes upon her like the gaze of some ancient divinity. Pulling at her sinew and bone. Sucking at her veins as if he could drink her in.

What *was* he?

How many women were charred in the combustible heat of such a gaze?

She didn't want to know.

Furthermore, she refused to be one of them.

Their first and only previous encounter had been the summer before. She'd gone with her eldest sister, Honoria—whom they called Nora—and Felicity in search of a missing fortune to save the man Nora had loved her entire life.

When they'd found the fortune in gold, they'd also found Raphael Sauvageau, the half-Monégasque, half-English leader of the fearsome Fauves—a French word meaning "wild beasts." He and his brother, Gabriel, laid claim to the gold that had been stolen by Nora's criminally atrocious first husband, the Viscount Woodhaven.

Their meeting had been fraught with intensity and the suggestion of threat.

Mercy and Raphael had sparred verbally, and she'd gone away with the feeling that he'd enjoyed it.

Or perhaps that she had.

Mercy's brothers-in-law, Chief Inspector Carlton Morley and Dr. Titus Conleith, had found out and come for the sisters, confronting the Sauvageau brothers.

Instead of a war breaking out between the men, Raphael and Gabriel had relinquished their gold to Titus and Honoria, which had been a substantial amount, with a promise to return for some mysterious future medical procedure.

According to Titus, he'd not heard from the Sauvageau brothers in the months since.

None of them had.

And yet, the rogue had often intruded, unbidden and unwanted, into Mercy's thoughts. She'd remember how he looked in the dim light of the lone lantern the night they'd met. All lean muscle and vibrating intimidation subdued by a veneer of cunning, charisma and undeniable intelligence.

He lurked always in the periphery of her silent moments. Like a serpent in the shadows, deceptively calm, coiled to strike.

He was an invasion. A trespasser. And he didn't even know it.

Or maybe he did.

Maybe...he'd done it on purpose. Some sort of serpentine mesmerism that had nothing to do with her unruly thoughts and desires, and everything to do with his villainy.

Yes, that must be it.

The fault was his, obviously.

Had he worked the same sort of magic on Mathilde?

That thought sobered her enough to redirect her panic into rage.

"May the devil fetch you if you hurt Mathilde." Though her eyes remained closed, she injected as much virulence into her words as she could summon.

"He'll fetch me regardless, but I... cared for her."

Despite herself, the veracity in his voice drew Mercy's lids open so she could study him for other signs of deceit.

His expression was drawn and serious.

Lethally so.

Daylight slanted in through the bars, making his eyes glint like polished steel. Motes of dust frenzied in his atmosphere as if drawing energy from the electric force of his presence. A thin ring of gold glinted in his left ear, and sharp cheekbones underscored an arrogant brow.

He'd look stern but for his mouth, which was not so severe. It bowed with a fullness she might have called feminine if the rest of his face wasn't so brutally cast.

Mercy hadn't realized she'd been staring at his lips, gripped with a queer sort of fascination, until they parted and he spoke.

"You were quite impressive back there."

"What?" Mercy shook her head dumbly. Had he just complimented her? Had they just been through the same scene? She'd never been less impressed with herself in her entire life.

Would that she could have been like him. Smooth and unaffected. Infuriatingly self-assured.

And yet...he'd only been that way after breaking the nose of the officer that had struck her, and possibly his jaw.

Lord but she'd never seen a man move like that before.

"I listened to your deductions," he explained.

"From where you were hiding in the closet?" she quipped, rather unwisely.

Something flickered in his eyes, and yet again she was left to guess if she'd angered or amused him.

"From where I was hiding in the closet," he said with a droll sigh as he shifted, seeming to find a more comfortable position for his bound hands. "You're obviously cleverer than the detectives. How do you know so much about murder scenes?"

Mercy warned herself not to preen. She stomped on the lush warmth threatening to spread from her chest at his encouragement, and thrust her nose in the air, perhaps a little too high. "I am one of only three female members of the Detective Eddard Sharpe Society of Homicidal Mystery Analysis. As penned by the noted novelist J. Francis Morgan, whom I suspect is a woman."

"Why do you suspect that?" His lip twitched, as if he also battled to suppress his own expression.

"Because men tend to write female characters terribly, don't they? But J. Francis Morgan is a master of character and often, the mystery is even solved by a woman rather than Detective Sharpe. His heroines are not needlessly weak or stupid or simpering. They're strong. Dangerous. Powerful. Sometimes even villainous and complicated. That is good literature, I say. Because it's true to life."

He'd ceased fighting his smile and allowed his lip to quirk up in a half-smile as he regarded her from beneath his dark brow. "Mathilde's murderer now has one more person they'd do well to fear in you."

She leveled him a sour look. "Does that mean you fear me?"

He tilted toward her. Suddenly—distressingly—grave. "You terrify me, Mercy Goode."

She had to swallow twice before she could deliver her question without sounding as breathless as she felt.

"Did you do it?" She leaned forward, bracing her elbows on her knees as she examined his features thoroughly. "Did you kill Mathilde Archambeau?"

"No." He looked her in the eye as he said this. Unblinking. Unwavering. "She was dead when I arrived."

The ache in his voice tugged at her and, she was ashamed to admit, uncoiled something complicated from around her guts. Something dark and unfamiliar.

Surely not jealousy.

Not for a dead woman.

Not because of a man like him.

"Why didn't you call for the police, then?" she demanded.

He flexed his shackled arms, leveling her a droll look of his own. "I'm one of the most wanted men in the empire."

Berating her own stupidity, she winced, causing the welt on her cheek where she'd been struck to throb. Testing the wound gingerly, she sighed, grateful her fingers were cold against the sore, swelling flesh.

"What were you doing there in the first place?" she queried impatiently.

He didn't answer.

Instead, his gaze affixed on the spot where her fingers explored her own cheek. Every twitch of discomfort she made seemed to turn his eyes a darker shade of grey, as if a storm gathered within them.

"I will break every bone below that man's elbow for the

pain he caused you." Shards of gravel paved a voice that had only just been smooth as silk.

"I abhor violence," Mercy lied, if only to condemn him.

If only to escape the very visceral vibrations that shimmered through her at the ferocity in his tone.

She drew her fingers from her face and folded them as primly in her lap as her manacles would allow.

He snorted with disbelief. "Is that why you read the macabre mysteries of Detective Eddard Sharpe? They are always deliciously brutal. Which is your favorite?"

She set her jaw stubbornly against a little thrill at the idea of discussing the books with him, but refused to be drawn in. He was a criminal and a condemned man.

A foe. Not a friend.

"I shouldn't think a man such as yourself took the time to read...or even knew how." She was acting the spoiled baron's daughter, but she thought it might make that illumination behind his gaze dull. That blaze of interest. The heat that hadn't waned during their conversation, but grew in strength and brilliance.

He simply stared at her expectantly until she found herself blurting, "My favorite is *The Legacy of Lord Lennox*."

His eyebrow lifted again. "If I'm not mistaken, it's the most violent of the series. A man gets sawed into pieces and his bits are delivered to his family members. One of whom is the murderer."

"That's different," she huffed, refusing to be impressed. Refusing to picture the man in front of her lazing about some chaise longue, his limbs slack and his shirt undone as his eyes traced rows of delectable words.

Did he nibble at his cheek as he read? Or perhaps thread those elegant fingers through his hair...

She snorted at her own absurdity. "Fiction. Entertainment safely contained in the jacket of a book."

"In my experience, reality is ever so much more fantastic than fiction. And nothing is so dangerous as the written word. It is how power is usurped and ideas are spread. Literature is the most dangerous weapon a man can use. After all, it has been written that the pen is mightier than—"

"Are you afraid of the noose?" she interrupted him abruptly, for if he finished quoting Edward Bulwer-Lytton, she might do something ridiculous.

Like kiss him.

He shocked her with that effortless rumble she was coming to recognize as his chuckle. "I'm not going to hang, *mon chaton*."

"Stop calling me that," she spat. "If you are half of what they say you are, if you've committed half the crimes you've been credited with, I don't see how you can escape execution."

Raphael leaned forward, the light across his eyes following the shape of his brow, gleaming off the ebony of his hair and then settling on his shoulders like Apollo's own mantle as he brought their faces flush.

Mercy had to force herself not to lean back.

Somehow that felt like a retreat.

"What things do they say I am?" he murmured.

She ticked them off on her fingers as she answered around a dry tongue, pretending his proximity didn't distress her. "A hedonist. A libertine. A profligate. Scoundrel. Gangster."

"Ah, for once, *they* are right," he admitted wryly.

"A murderer?"

Cool air kissed her neck, but what caused her to shiver was the tantalizing heat of his breath as he bent even closer. "I have helped men to the next world, *mon chaton*. But I've never hurt a woman. I did not kill your friend."

"Then I ask you again. What were you doing there? Were you Mathilde's lover?"

A muted clang caused them both to jump, and Mercy let out

a little cry of surprise as the back of the carriage dipped slightly.

She couldn't say if it was the movement or her own instinct that shifted her body closer to his warmth.

To his strength.

Even though he smirked down at her with no little amount of masculine smugness, his gaze searched hers for something.

For permission?

An inner voice warned her that if she opened her mouth, it would be granted.

She lunged away then, scooting to the far edge of the bench in time for the door to swing open.

While they were still moving?

A mountain of a man in a dark coat and a hood slid inside and closed the door behind him. He turned his head toward her, but in the dim coach, she couldn't make out anything that resembled a face.

Only a dark abyss was visible in the oval of shadow left by his low hood and his collar.

He stared at her from the darkness, though.

Nay, examined her like one might scrutinize an insect before crushing it beneath his shoe.

With wicked claws he scored that instinct that lived in every human. The one that screamed a warning into her soul that she was not safe.

Her bones veritably crawled beneath her skin to escape him.

If Raphael was dangerous, this man was...well, he defied description.

"What took you so long, Gabriel?" Raphael hissed. "Ten minutes more and it would have been too late."

Raphael's brother said nothing. He studied her for the space of two more discomfiting blinks and then gave her his massive back, bending toward his brother.

She'd been dismissed.

It would have offended her, were she not so relieved. It was as if she'd disappointed him, somehow.

As if he'd been looking for someone else.

He produced thin metal instruments from his coat and deftly—for a man with hands as large as his—went to work at the lock on his brother's manacles.

Mercy could count on one hand the times she'd been rendered speechless.

Gabriel Sauvageau had picked the padlock of a police vehicle and slid inside *while it was moving* without raising the alarm or even alerting the drivers.

How was this done?

While he worked to free his brother, he muttered in barely perceptible French, his voice a rasping whisper that hinted at a baritone as dark, deep, and smooth as moonlight over marble.

The very devil might have a voice like that.

Mercy had always been a terrible student. She wiggled too much, her brain pinging from one thing to the next until so many of her thoughts threatened to tumble everywhere like a litter of unruly puppies.

But she'd retained a rudimentary understanding of French.

And if she wasn't mistaken, Gabriel had said something to the effect that they'd rescheduled a meeting at the zoo to the following Wednesday at...three o'clock?

"You're being unspeakably rude," she admonished them, hoping to hide that she comprehended their conversation.

Well... sort of comprehended it.

Raphael had the decency to look chagrined. "In this case, I must beg your forgiveness, *mon chaton*, as my brother speaks very little English."

"Why do you call her *your kitten*?" Gabriel asked in French.

"Because I like her claws." Raphael replied with a look at his brother that ended any further discussion on the subject.

Gabriel freed one hand and went to work on the opposite wrist. "What happened with Mathilde?"

Raphael flicked her a glance and narrowed his eyes as if assessing how much she understood.

A certain level of fluency was expected from educated women of her class.

Mercy found something fascinating on her own manacles, refusing to look up at him.

After a pregnant pause, he said. "We will discuss it later. Where do we meet Marco?"

"By the Loo."

Mercy searched her French vocabulary for the word loo and found nothing. Did they mean the washrooms? She wrinkled her nose. Did they say that for her benefit? To throw her off maybe? The toilets were not a very fitting location for highbrow clandestine intrigue to take place.

But then, who was she to tell criminals where to convene?

"We have to go, we're almost to the bridge." Gabriel freed his brother's other wrist.

"You go. I'll lock up." Raphael motioned for the padlock, which Gabriel tossed to him before sliding out the door just as smoothly and silently as he'd arrived.

The springs depressed just slightly when the cart was alleviated of his weight. The Goliath of a man stepped off the tall carriage with the same grace a dancer would stride away from a curb onto the cobbles.

The ceiling of the cart was too short for Raphael to stand, so he stooped toward her as he reached his long, muscled arms out to the side in the stretch of a free man.

"Here." Mercy lifted her wrists. "Release me!"

Instead of taking her manacles, he gathered the hands she offered into his large, rough palms, his thumb running over wrists made raw by her struggles.

And just like that, they were no longer in a cage. No longer was she shackled by iron...but instead a velvet rope wound its way around her limbs, cording and knotting her to him.

She felt at once vulnerable and invincible.

Safe and in peril.

The fresh, expensive scent of him overpowered the staler odors of the carriage. His eyes were mesmerizing, taking up the entirety of her vision, forcing everything else to fall away.

Forgotten.

He moved with such swiftness, and yet when his lips sealed to hers, the press of it was astonishing in its gentility. His neck corded with tension, his shoulders bunched, and his grip tightened.

But his mouth. Oh, his mouth. It sampled her with a series of light strokes, restraining his ardent passion with well-practiced skill.

Mercy forever displayed the wrong reactions to stimuli. This time was no different.

Any space in her temper for anger or aggression was overtaken by an abject exhilaration. An undeniable excitement that bordered on impatience.

Though it was increasingly cold, they built their own fire, igniting something between them that had a portent of inevitability.

An inarticulate sound vibrated from somewhere deep within him, quickening her heart and rushing the blood through her veins with an injection of heat.

She surged closer, her fingers gripping his collar as the kiss deepened of its own accord. She couldn't tell whose mouth opened first, but their tongues met and danced.

Sparred.

In this moment, they had their own language. One that was as lilting and lyrical as any that existed. It was guttural and tonal and it gathered responses from her she never thought herself capable of making.

She knew there was more. More of this wild storm building between them. More of this man she wanted to explore.

More of the world she wanted to see.

Wanted him to show her. To teach her.

Dangerous. A voice warned from somewhere far, far away. Someplace buried so deep in her psyche, she might have forgotten it even existed.

Her reason. Her wit.

He'd interred it beneath the avalanche of desire tumbling through her, tossing her end over end until she couldn't decide which way was up.

Danger. You're in danger.

The warning was closer now, more urgent. Enough to draw her back, breaking the seal of their lips.

She only had a moment of gratification at a similar haze unfocusing his stormy eyes before the clouds parted and he blinked down at her with an expression both alert and regretful.

"Forgive me," he whispered, releasing the lock on her shackles and letting them fall to the floor.

She looked down at them in mute astonishment, not having even noticed he'd been working on them.

By the time she'd registered that he moved, he'd slid out the door and pulled it shut and secured the padlock just as she lunged for him.

"Wait!" she cried, wrapping her fingers around the bars. "You're going to let me rot in jail while you go free?"

Now that they were in a busier part of the city, she could hear the astonished gasps and exclamations of the passersby.

He hung from the carriage by one hand at the hinges of the door and one foot on the ledge as he grinned into the cart through the barred window.

"I know who your family is, Mercy Goode, you'll be back

home in time for tea." His eyes were no longer glinting, but ablaze with silver light.

Rage surged inside of her, fueled by the heat still thrumming and throbbing through her.

"You know nothing about my family, you merciless cad," she hissed. "You're lucky I'm locked in here or I'd—"

"You'd do something reckless, no doubt, like follow me..." He said this with a confounding sort of fondness. "And that's too dangerous. Even for you."

Frustrated. *Furious.* Mercy shook the iron bars once again, then shoved her hand through them, attempting to claw at his eyes.

He leaned back just in time, the thick locks of his hair fluttering in the draft coming off the roof of the moving coach as he barked out a laugh.

God, he was handsome when he smiled. Especially when his lips were glossed and a bit swollen from kissing.

She could cheerfully murder him.

Swinging back, he brought his face close to the bars, his eyes drilling into hers with that dizzying change they made from mirth to sobriety. "If we see each other again, Mercy Goode..." he warned in a voice made of sex and honey.

"Be ready for me to taste the rest of you."

CHAPTER 3

The reasons the jailers took a wide-eyed second glance at Felicity Goode were threefold.

The first being that she was exceptionally lovely today in a lavender gown threaded with violet ribbons and a matching velvet pelisse. The latter, cinched too tightly at the waist, accentuated the dramatic indent of her figure, and created a lovely backdrop for her cascade of flaxen hair beneath her smart hat.

The second was that the stunning midnight-haired woman on Felicity's arm was the wife of their most revered and respected Chief Inspector, Sir Carlton Morley.

Prudence, their second eldest sister.

This would be the first time these men might have seen her lately about, as she'd been kept frightfully busy doting on her infant twins, Caroline and Charlotte.

She was still apple-cheeked from pregnancy, her glowing dark eyes happy, if half-lidded by the sort of exhaustion only known to new mothers. She'd wrapped herself in burgundy velvet to make up for the pallor of her complexion.

And third, Felicity was the unmistakable mirror of Mercy,

who stood facing her from the other side of the dingy iron bars. Their resemblance was uncanny.

Most twins had a hint of identifiable difference. A freckle here, a jutting tooth or a divergent shade of hair.

For Mercy, to look at Felicity was to look in a mirror. Even their parents had an impossible time telling them apart.

Which, in Mercy's opinion, spoke volumes about them as parents.

More out of blindness than concern, Felicity squinted into the cell where Mercy had been blessedly alone for the better part of two hours. Though she'd terrible vision, she was urged to not wear her spectacles in public, as they were considered unflattering. This time, however, Mercy knew she'd eschewed her spectacles for a different reason.

One that was Mercy's own fault.

"Imagine, if you will, my surprise when a constable came round the house to inform Mama and Papa that *I'd* been arrested," Felicity huffed.

"Please don't be cross with me," Mercy begged her twin, wincing with shame. "I knew that if I gave them your name, someone would be more likely to come fetch me. Everyone likes you better."

"That isn't at all true," Prudence protested, tossing her curls with a saucy snap of her lithe neck. "You are both our beloved treasures. Now wait here whilst I fetch Sgt. Treadwell to unlock this cell so I can take you home and murder you in private. You're bloody lucky my husband is in court today." With an impish smirk she swept away, the train falling in gathers from her bustle, swishing with her efficient strides over the well-worn wood.

"Thank you, darling!" Mercy called after her, wrapping her fingers around the cold iron bars. The sooner she had her freedom the better.

She hadn't taken a full breath in hours.

Felicity, eyes wide with rapt incredulity, laced her fingers over Mercy's until they knotted around the bars together in a complicated grip. "Are you all right?"

Mercy nodded, though her beloved sister's affection was nearly her undoing. "Are Mama and Papa furious?"

At that, Felicity brightened a bit. "Actually, I received a postcard today in lieu of their arrival. They've decided to extend their stay on the Riviera another month, perhaps two. Perhaps if we can whisk you out of here without a scandal, they'll never have to know."

"You couldn't have brought me happier news!" Mercy blustered in relief. The Baron and Baroness Cresthaven, their parents, were two of the most pious, pinched-faced fuddy-duddies to ever hold a title. Any time they spent away from the house was like a ray of sunshine on a frigid, grey day in late winter.

Like this one, for example.

"Did you *really* strike an inspector?" Felicity whispered, glancing around to see if anyone stood nearby.

"Martin Trout." Mercy spat the words as if they tasted of his namesake. "He told me Mathilde *deserved* what her husband did. I *barely* swatted him." Mercy rolled her eyes as righteous indignation tightened her rib cage. "And he repaid me tenfold."

Tilting her head to display her bruising cheek, she enjoyed Felicity's clucking and tutting over the wound, now that she didn't have any handsome, smirking men to keep her chin up for.

"I have a poultice of parsley, arnica, and comfrey that will rid you of the bruise in half the time it would take to heal on its own," her twin promised. "Titus even had me make some for him to disseminate to his patients. Wasn't that wonderful of him?"

Mercy's forehead wrinkled at the breathlessness in her sister's voice when Dr. Titus Conleith's name was spoken. He'd been a coal boy in their household when they were small, then a stable hand, and a footman as he'd grown into a man.

Though he was a few years younger, he'd loved their eldest sister, Nora, with a singular passion since the day he'd met her.

And, Mercy suspected, Felicity had loved him with the strength of a little girl's hero worship.

Titus was handsome in that rough-hewn, somber kind of way. Studious, deferential and ruthlessly clever. He was a man of unflinching principle and a fathomless well of patience. The very picture of a gentleman with the shoulders of a war hero and a reputation of the most respected surgeon in Blighty.

But to Felicity, he was the boy who'd squirreled away books for her to read and didn't poke fun when she used to pronounce her R's as W's.

"I hardly want to believe Mathilde is dead." Felicity's features crumpled with sorrow.

Mercy answered with a nod, gripping her sister's fingers tighter.

It was Felicity who'd met Mathilde first. She volunteered at the hospital sometimes, reading to the infirmed and holding new babies. Helping Titus mix tinctures or taking stock of the pharmacy.

She was as much a liability at the hospital as she was an assistance, since she fainted dead away at the sight of blood. No one had the heart to suggest she go elsewhere, for fear it would make her feel unwanted.

Felicity had spent the crux of her life being told that, as the fourth and last daughter in a string of disappointing female births, she'd been the reason her mother could have no more children.

And there would be no heir.

However, when Gregoire Archambeau had fractured Mathilde's wrist, landing her in the hospital, it had been

Felicity who had coaxed the woman into seeking help with the Lady's Aid Society where Mercy volunteered her time.

The twins had decided then and there that they were genius to split their attentions thusly. To be able to provide women and their children comprehensive help both medical, emotional, financial, and even offer protection and relocation if necessary.

Felicity put a white-gloved hand to her heart as if the news of Mathilde's death had pierced it. "Did she...did she do it herself? Or was it an accident brought on by too much drink and—and such?"

They both knew what *and such* stood for. The cocaine and opium Mathilde had become a slave to.

"She was *murdered*," Mercy revealed with a grave frown.

Felicity gasped. "It couldn't have been Gregoire; I watched him mount the gangplank to the ferry and he didn't disembark again. He'll be in France by now."

"I know." Mercy pursed her lips. Lips that still tasted of Raphael, even hours later. Lips she kept pressing her fingertips to, remembering the pressure of a startling—*searing* kiss.

No. She couldn't let that indiscretion derail her. She had a murder to solve. Even Detective Eddard Sharpe didn't allow the sultry Miss Georgina Crenshaw to distract him in the middle of a case.

"You...found Mathilde's dead body?" Felicity sniffed as if holding in a torrent of emotion. "Are you all right? Was there blood? Did she suffer?"

Mercy wanted to spare her sister the answers to her rapid-fire questions, but her twin always knew when she was lying. "No blood. But yes, her death was... a violent one. Someone throttled her, and broke her neck."

Felicity released her hand to slide her fingers to her own neck. "Do you think it was her lover? Did you ever find out who he was?"

"You'll never guess," Mercy said, admittedly gorging a bit on the drama of it all.

"Tell me."

"Raphael Sauvageau." The name tasted lush on her tongue.

Just as he had.

Her sister blanched as pale as startled milk.

Felicity was, no doubt, remembering the night at the docks when she'd stumbled into Gabriel Sauvageau's arms. The man had been wearing a wicked mask and brandished a long, sinister blade.

He'd not cut her. In fact, he'd not hurt her in the least.

But they couldn't be certain he *wouldn't* have, had the night gone differently.

"What's this about Raphael Sauvageau?" Pru asked, approaching with a knobby, bent officer whose age dictated that the largest responsibility he could handle was the keys.

"Found with the dead body, he was," the sergeant rasped, shaking his finger at the door as if the man in question stood there. "You're lucky he didn't slit your throat before he escaped the prison cart. Or worse." He eyed Mercy with a grandfatherly warning.

"He was *arrested* with you?" Pru gasped.

"And he *escaped*?" Felicity cried at the same time.

"In the wind, that one. Unlikely we'll ever catch him again." Sgt. Treadwell attempted to thread the key into the lock three times before the tremors in his liver-spotted hand would allow it.

Mercy waited until they'd thanked the officer, who released her with a stern word and told her that Trout had dropped all charges when he learned who her family was.

No doubt, the inspector didn't want to be the man who'd struck Chief Inspector Carlton Morley's sister-in-law.

The *she struck me first* argument didn't hold much water.

Once they'd bundled into the coach, Mercy regaled them

with the horrors of the afternoon as quickly as she could, knowing that once she got home, she'd have to spend at least an hour in the bath to scrub the day away.

She told them about everything.

Everything...but the kiss.

Their eyes were both big and round as the full moon when she finished her tale, and no one spoke for a full half minute.

It was Felicity who broke the silence. "Do you think the Fauves supplied Mathilde with all the...medicines she took?"

"Who else?" Mercy surmised. "They're brigands and we know they've smuggled cocaine before. Let us not forget the inconsiderate bastards didn't spring me from the prison cart. They left me there!"

"Yes, their most heinous crime, indeed." Pru chuffed out a little laugh as she studied Mercy with a quick, level look. "Did he truly break Trout's nose?"

"Possibly his jaw...and a few fingers." Mercy wondered how a man's features could be both savage and eerily blank all at once as he methodically put Trout in his place. "Sauvageau threatened to break every bone below the man's elbow."

"Did he?" Pru's lips quirked in a faint smile. "It sounds to me like he fancies you."

"I agree." Felicity nodded.

"Fancies me?" Mercy huffed, sliding her palms against one another, wishing they'd not taken her gloves on such a cold day. "Over the corpse of his freshly murdered lover? I don't care if he is the handsomest rake in the empire, I'd not consider such a thing in this lifetime."

Felicity chewed on the inside of her cheek, her eyes looking at some distant spot outside the window. "So, his brother leapt onto the carriage, picked the padlock, and sprang him without the drivers knowing? That sounds rather...Well, it's a bit extraordinary, isn't it? Like something out of an adventure novel."

"Extraordinarily infuriating is what it was." Mercy swatted Felicity's knee. "Or did you forget the part where they *left me there*? It's not funny!"

"I'm not laughing," Pru said from behind her hand as her shoulders shook with mirth.

"It was rather inconsiderate of them," Felicity rushed to concede. "No doubt they left you because they knew you'd be safe in police custody, whereas they were likely off to do something diabolical and undoubtedly dangerous."

Mercy didn't tell them that he'd said as much.

"I imagine they didn't want you following them." Felicity brushed aside the curtain of the coach to check on their progress through the city.

"I wouldn't have had to follow them," Mercy said mulishly. "I know exactly where they will be."

"Where's that?" Felicity asked.

"The loo at the zoo."

"Pardon?"

"I heard them talking, and while my French isn't perfect—"

"Your French is atrocious," Prudence teased.

Mercy ignored her. "They said they were going to meet someone named Marco in front of the loo at the London Zoo."

"They're not going to meet at the toilet." Felicity remained distracted until she realized she'd said something out loud and then snapped her lips shut.

Mercy lunged, seizing her shoulders and shaking them. "What? Felicity, what do you know?"

Her sister gulped. "What will you do if I tell you?"

"What Detective Sharpe would do. Obviously."

"That's what I was afraid you'd say."

Prudence cut in, resting a motherly hand on Mercy's arm. "This isn't a storybook caper, Mercy, these men are lethal. You should tell Morley where they'll be. He'll find out about them for you."

"I will," Mercy vowed. "Tell me what you know, and I'll tell you where they'll be."

Felicity gulped, squinting at her for a different reason than her blindness. This time, it was true suspicion. "In French, the word spelled l-o-u-p is pronounced *loo*."

"And?" Mercy pressed.

"It means wolf."

Mercy's heart sped. "There you have it. They'll be at the wolf exhibit at the zoo at three o'clock."

Prudence reached into her vest and pulled out a dainty watch. "It's half five. We've missed them."

For once in her life, Mercy kept her mouth shut.

She'd also kept her promise. She'd told them where Raphael Sauvageau could be found.

Just not exactly *when*.

CHAPTER 4

A WEEK LATER

It turned out to be a beautiful day to plan a war.

Raphael Sauvageau loitered by the den of wolves at the London Zoo, idly watching across the way as two delighted children were given rides on the back of a sardonic-looking camel.

The morning had been blustery and grey. Stinging rain blown sideways by errant gusts pelted citizens who were brave or foolish enough to venture out. After luncheon, the rain disappeared as if someone had turned off a spigot in the sky, and celestial pillars of light pierced the late February clouds with the shafts of spring.

By three o'clock, the brick and cobbles of London glittered with gemlike droplets of golden light, and the city came to life, people bustling back into the streets.

The animals kept by the Zoological Society of London were likewise pleased with the changing weather. Zebras frolicked in their pastures and a giraffe licked a treat from out of the hands of a passing boy, who promptly burst into tears.

Adjacent to the zoo, the London elite flooded Regent's Park, eager to bask in the rare warmth and to hunt for any hint of emerging buds on the winter-bare flora.

Raphael watched the skeletons of the trees with grim detachment.

Knowing he would not live long enough to see them blossom.

What would *she* look like in the spring, surrounded by blooms shamelessly baring their colors for her? The most vibrant lily couldn't compete with the shade of her lips once they'd been plumped and pinkened by his kiss. The bluebell would wither in contrast to the hue of her eyes.

She was unlike anything or anyone he'd ever before encountered.

Mercy.

Even her name was a phenomenon he'd never known.

A concept he didn't understand.

It surprised him how powerfully he longed to explore her. Desired her to show him Mercy. In any form.

Her delectable form.

Indulging in a faint sigh, Raphael turned to see Marco Villeneuve saunter toward him, adjusting the diamond-encrusted cufflinks on his shirtsleeves.

A tittering group of schoolgirls in beribboned hats passed by, accompanied by their chaperone, a middle-aged woman with a sour face and cheeks drawn down by years of disappointment.

The handsome Spaniard touched the rim of his hat, and the ladies giggled.

When Raphael did the same, they sighed.

When he winked, two of them stumbled.

"You are shameless, *hermano*," Marco drawled, drawing closer and clasping his hand in fond greeting. Were they in their own countries, they'd greet with a kiss on each cheek.

Raphael scoffed. "Shame is a futile emotion crafted to plague those fragile enough to care what others think of them."

"Indeed." Marco leaned his shoulder against the wrought iron gate of the wolf enclosure and flashed his cocksure grin. Though his suit was of the finest craftsmanship, his chocolate-colored hair hung longer than was proper beneath his hat. It lent his tall, rangy form an untamed element that added to the dangerous allure he weaponized against women.

Intelligent females saw through him before he was able to break their hearts.

The others, well...they went away more cynical and suspicious of handsome rogues.

Marco slid his whiskey-colored gaze to the wolf enclosure and studied the five creatures as they paced and panted, eyeing the men as if to invite them in rather than warn them away.

They were of a kind, these beasts.

Raphael hated to see them caged.

One wolf, a dark, scruffy fellow with a blaze of white on his wide chest, climbed the hill that had been artfully arranged with boulders and soil to appear as if made by the chaos of nature. As the beast approached a lounging grey wolf, he flattened his ears and made a feral sound, yellow eyes snapping with ferocity.

The grey wolf bolted upright, relinquished his position, and slunk away, head and tail low as he found a new spot to rest.

The alpha sat above all.

"Well, *Jefe*, everything has been arranged as you instructed." Marco extracted a box of matches and lit a cigarette with a long draw before releasing the smoke on a heavy exhale. "Lord Longueville will be attending the Midwinter Masque, and will be likely to bring his generals from the High Street Butchers. You, Gabriel, and I will be present, of course, though I wonder if we should invite a third party to witness our conversation with Longueville. Word will spread that the battle for control of supplying vice to the *ton* is about to commence."

"I do not disagree." Raphael was careful not to let his complicated emotions show on his countenance. He was stirring trouble.

The lethal kind.

"I thought this was *loco*—I still do—but it might actually be crazy enough to work." Marco puffed out a breath filled with smoke and wonder before he glanced up. Whatever he read in Raphael's expression caused him to amend. "I should know better than to doubt you, *Jefe*."

Raphael waved his hand, absolving him of all that. "We Fauves do not follow without question. We are predators, not sheep, and we must be cunning. Question everything."

"As you say." Marco's head dipped in deference.

The hierarchy of the Fauves was not unlike those of the wolves. Intricate, subtle, and yet, brutally uncomplicated. There were no figureheads. No pomp or ceremony. There was the uncontestable leader of the pack. The alpha and his subordinates.

He was the one who led the hunters to their prey. And he was the one who took first blood. He claimed the greatest bounty before the rest of the pack fell upon it like scavengers.

But as the leader, it was incumbent upon him to provide, to remain uncontested. Or, if he was challenged, he must meet it with all the dominant ferocity of any king of beasts.

He had to win. Every time. To prove he was fit to lead.

That he was a man to be followed.

The mantle threatened to smother him sometimes.

But what else could he do? What else did he know?

Nothing.

This was all he was. All he had. A legacy of vice and villainy and a lifetime of lies. He was a man whose past was nothing but shifting shadows and secrets, and his future was—

An endless wasteland coated with the same.

Battles and blood, until one day a lesser beast would challenge him...and tear his throat out.

He'd have to.

Raphael was not the sort of man to submit to the sovereignty of another.

"Are you second-guessing the plan?" Marco queried, peering up from beneath the lowered brim of the hat. "If this goes awry, there will be blood."

"There's always blood," he quipped. "This will be no different."

Blood. Both red and blue.

He was playing a dangerous game, pitting his enemies and allies against each other.

A game where there would be victors, but no one truly won.

"No second thoughts," he clarified. "All has been prepared except—"

A flash of light struck him blind for a moment and he winced, blinking rapidly. When he opened his eyes again, it was gone, leaving a disorienting shadow in his vision as if he'd glanced directly at the sun.

Once his vision cleared, he found the culprit immediately upon searching over Marco's shoulder.

The sun had reflected off binoculars peeking over a shoulder-high hedge.

No, not binoculars. A shiny gold pair of opera glasses.

Gold, like the lovely ringlets surrounding said item. A charming coiffure held in place by butterfly combs and garnished with baby's breath.

Detective Eddard Sharpe would be proud of this intrepid investigator. He was often quoted in his books as saying that when a necessary implement was not readily at hand, a true investigator improvised.

Opera glasses of all things. Raphael couldn't fight the tremor of a smile softening the corners of his lips.

Christ, but Mercy Goode could not be more endearing.

She'd, no doubt, donned her taupe, high-necked coat in the hopes of blending with the crowd. However, the light color actually caused her to stand out amongst people swathed in grey or black wool jackets against what had once been intemperate weather.

Who wore beige to the zoo on a wet day?

Of course, she'd understood the conversation he and Gabriel had in her presence. Gentle ladies were taught French, weren't they?

Marco, realizing that Raphael's notice had been directed elsewhere, glanced behind him to find the culprit. "What is it?"

"Nothing," Raphael said, shifting his gaze to the side. "I saw someone I recognized."

"Not the police, I hope. They are searching for you in every nook and shadow of the city."

"Which is why I'm hiding in the sunlight."

Marco chuckled and tapped his temple. "Always a step ahead, *Jefe*. That's why you're in charge."

Raphael put a hand on Marco's solid shoulder, only half meaning the fond gesture as he drew the gangster toward the lion's den—in the opposite direction of the curious girl. "I'm avoiding a woman," he explained as he ducked them behind a shed and then quickly changed their direction.

"Say no more." Marco winked conspiratorially and kept up with nimble strides.

Raphael got to business as he led Marco toward a back gate. "I had you meet me here because Dorian Blackwell is said to be fond of taking his children to Regent's Park in the late afternoon. Sometimes they come to the zoo, sometimes not, but I need you to find him and invite him and his most trusted men to the masquerade."

Marco's eyes widened. "Dorian Blackwell? The Blackheart of Ben More? He and his men ruled this city not so long ago, but everyone says he's reformed since he married a Countess. Retired, even."

Raphael inclined his head. "I think he would be interested in a market share of this product. He still holds enviable economic influence, from the dregs of the underworld all the way to Parliament."

Marco's eyes flashed with greed. It was something Raphael knew he could always rely upon...a man's own self-interest.

"Consider it done." Marco crushed his cigarette beneath his bootheel and strode toward the zoo's gate, one hand on the lapel of his dandy plaid suit. He held said gate open to a fine elderly couple who thanked him with wide smiles.

They'd miss their valuables later.

Raphael doubled back toward the wolf exhibit.

Flattening his back against the reptile enclosure, he peered around the corner to find exactly what he thought he would.

Mercy Goode standing before the wolves, forehead wrinkled and plump lips tightened into a recalcitrant frown.

He'd lost her and she resented him for it.

Poor thing. He wanted to tell her it didn't detract from her considerable detective skills. He was a professional criminal, and she little more than an inquisitive girl.

She had no chance of capturing him.

It surprised him to find that his hand had found its way inside his suit coat, to rest over his chest.

She made the muscles around his lungs squeeze at the same time his heart seemed to double in size and radiate a confounding warmth.

Kissing her in the carriage had been a mistake.

And yet, when he searched what passed for his conscience, he couldn't find it in himself to regret it.

Since the first moment he'd laid eyes on her, he'd been transfixed.

Beguiled.

No one that bold and brash should have such innocent eyes.

She was a force of nature, like a firestorm or an earthquake. Something that left the terrain forever altered in her wake.

She was unforgettable. Indescribable. Delectable.

How could he go to war without tasting that for himself?

Especially when she'd looked at him in *that* way. With the heavy-lidded gaze of a woman who wanted to be kissed but was too proud to ask and too untried to take what she wanted.

Raphael bit into his fist. He couldn't tell which was a more exquisite hell. Wanting to taste her? Or having sampled her flavor, knowing that a more sublime pleasure awaited the man who unlocked the passion roiling beneath the barely contained surface of her propriety.

Knowing, without a doubt, that he could release her like a volcano, and watch as she erupted into ecstasy.

He should go. He had so much to do, to prepare for.

He needed to be rid of her. For both of their sakes.

Visibly deflated, Mercy stowed her opera glasses in the velvet pouch hanging from her wrist and turned to contemplate the wolves.

They'd come alive at her approach, panting and pacing, some of them making wild, hungry sounds.

Raphael knew exactly how they felt.

His feet carried him toward her as if moving without his consent. There was no stopping this, he was propelled —*compelled*—by her mere presence. She was, indeed, like the sun, and he was merely a helpless body trapped in her orbit.

How could he leave when she appeared so glum? How could he be the cause of such a frown?

He'd done some terrible things, but her displeasure would bother him all day.

So intent was she upon her disappointment, she didn't mark his approach until he spoke. "I always pity them, the predators," he murmured as he drew abreast of her, standing close enough that their shoulders nearly touched.

Other than a lift of her bosom with a sharp intake of breath, she made no move to acknowledge him.

Raphael leaned against the iron bars of the enclosure, watching the alpha pace back and forth. Staring deep into eyes that seemed so ancient and feral, compared to this so-called civilized place.

His chest ached for them both. "I wonder what it would be like to be as they are. Creatures of instinct and insatiable hunger...caged but longing to roam free."

Mercy tilted her chin to level him a sharp look, scoffing gently. "I am a woman. I don't have to wonder such things. I already know."

A pensive sound escaped him on a huff of breath. "It has never been a mystery why men keep women caged by so many unseen confines," he said. "Their laws. Their clothing. Societal expectations...And through doing this, men have devised the most fiendish jailers."

"Yes, you men have fashioned yourselves as most cunning oppressors," she agreed with an arch bitterness in her voice. "Congratulations."

"No," he purred, turning toward her. Inching closer. "Women's greatest enemy is other women. If you ever stopped competing for the favor of your oppressors and rose up against us, instead, we men wouldn't stand a chance."

At this, she shifted, her sharp chin dipping so she could study him from beneath the veil of her lashes. "You speak as though you're an expert on the subject of my sex."

"Women are too complicated and varied for one man to become an expert," he said, rather modestly, he thought, congratulating himself.

Her eyes narrowed further, reminding him of a cat irked by the attentions of a tiresome human. "Is it women who are complicated? Or men who are just too simple or fatuous to figure out what should be painfully obvious?"

He held his hands up in a gesture of surrender. "You're right, of course. Let us not say complicated. Let us say...intricate. Comprised of so many parts both fragile and indestructible. Mechanisms of emotion and logic, trivialities and also infinite wisdom."

He motioned to the wolves. "We men are the beasts. Quarrelsome and querulous creatures of instinct and desire."

"Is that why you call your gang *the Fauves*? The wild beasts. Because you are encouraging such animalistic behavior?"

Raphael nodded, wondering why it sounded wrong when she said it, why it pricked him with defensiveness. "My father invented the name and our creed. We were beasts before we fashioned ourselves men, and built our own cages of law and order. But once, we had the morality of a wolf. The ferocity of a bear. Cunning and speed of a viper."

"A viper." She held up her finger as if to tap an idea out of the sky. "That is what you are."

He contemplated the word. "I've been called worse."

"Worse than a snake?"

He lifted a shoulder and loosened it again. "I don't mind snakes so much. They're clever creatures... They're only villainized because of the one who tempted Eve."

She swatted the air in front of her as if batting his words away. "I find that story patently ridiculous."

"Do you?"

She rolled her eyes and tossed her head like a skittish mare. "We haven't the time for me to count the ways."

"I'd still love to hear you do so," he murmured, finding that he wanted very much, indeed, to know what she thought about anything. Everything. He found her relentlessly entertaining. "Another time, perhaps."

"I'm not planning on spending an inordinate amount of time in your presence." Gathering her skirt, she shifted away from him as if she needed space.

Distance he didn't want to give.

"You're angry with me," he prodded.

"Have you forgotten that you escaped the law and *left* me to face it? What sort of nefarious reprobate does that?"

"I knew you'd done nothing wrong, and that your family would close ranks and protect you. In my defense, I had business only a nefarious reprobate could conduct. Since you are not one, I couldn't very well be responsible for your safety."

Her chin jutted at a stubborn angle. "I'm an investigator, not an idiot. I wouldn't do anything unduly perilous. Also," she glared at him as if she could bore through his middle with the blue fire in her eyes, "you kissed me, you impolite blackguard! Without my permission, I might add."

"Ah, for that I *would* ask your forgiveness, Miss Goode..." His mouth softened and curled up at the memory. "If you had not kissed me back."

"I *never*!" She pushed away from the wolf enclosure and stomped toward the gate, her skirts swishing angrily.

"I know what animal *you* are," he teased, ambling after her with his hands shoved in his pockets.

So he did not give in to the impulse to reach for her.

"I am no other creature than woman."

"You are a fox," he corrected. "Playful. Clever...cautious and elusive. Yes. You, Mercy Goode, are a vixen."

"What I *am* is growing tired of your company," she snapped.

"Might I remind you that you were the one who followed me here?"

She whirled on him, her little nostrils flaring and her eyes sparking with azure storms. "I—that—I mean—" She pressed her lips into a frustrated hyphen before gathering her response. "Don't you dare for one *minute* feel flattered. I was investigating you. To see if you were doing anything despicable. I didn't come for *you*, but to gather information that would help Mathilde."

Oh, that he could make her *come* for him.

Raphael drank her in. She was lovely when she was angry. Her Cupid's bow mouth pursed and white at the edges with strain, her snapping gaze electric with color, and her little fists balled with fury.

She was so young. Perhaps too young for his thirty years. She glowed with an inner incandescence that didn't belong to this grey country. He wanted to sweep her away to a villa along the cerulean coast of his homeland. To strip her bare while white gauzy curtains danced in the sea breeze. He would let the sun kiss every inch of her pale skin just before his lips trailed in its wake.

"I want you to leave justice for Mathilde to me," he said, curling the fingers in his pockets into fists, so he didn't give in to the urge to sweep her hair away from the curve of her neck. "I will avenge her."

It would be among the last things he did.

"Avenge her?" Her eyes narrowed and she took a step closer, her ire at him thrown over for a clue. "Are you saying you know who is responsible for her death?"

"I have an idea."

"Who then?" she demanded.

She would never drag it out of him. Would never be drawn into his world. She was everything good and light and worthy. She was a beacon, one that both attracted him and warned him away.

Raphael changed tactics, taking a threatening step toward her. "You've already done something perilous. You came here. To find me... Alone."

He should have expected anything other than a retreat from her. "As you can see, sir, we are *not* alone." She gestured to the throngs of people, some passersby paying them a bit of curious attention.

"*We* are not alone," he conceded, drawing her hand into his to brush a kiss against the knuckles of her gloves. "But if you are with me...you are in danger."

"From whom?" She glanced about them dramatically, as if searching for the danger of which he spoke.

Surely some primitive instinct within her had to realize how close he was to—

"I'm perfectly safe," she said in a tone more convincing than confident. As if she were trying to persuade herself. "My—my brother-in-law, Chief Inspector Carlton Morley, is nearby."

"No, he isn't," Raphael tutted, advancing on her with measured steps. Forcing her to retreat in small increments. "I know Morley, he's as decisive as he is honorable, which means he'd have me in chains before I could do this."

Raphael seized her by the elbow and swung her into a deeply shadowed alleyway between two enclosures, with all the deftness of a man twirling his partner in a waltz.

He ducked them into the alcove of a door and slanted his mouth over hers, desperate to taste her before she could take in enough breath to protest.

509

CHAPTER 5

*B*ut she didn't.

She didn't struggle or fight.

The first time he'd kissed her, he'd taken her by surprise. She'd been unerringly sweet and obviously untried.

And still she'd captivated and aroused him more than the most skilled of courtesans.

She was artless. Guileless. And in her presence, he was something he'd never been before.

Helpless.

She didn't remain still or soft in his arms. She didn't become rigid nor limp with fear nor anger.

She went wild.

Her fingers were claws in the lapels of his jacket. At the taut muscles of his back. Then suddenly scoring his scalp as she turned his impulsive seduction into a battlefield. Her lips pulled tight against her teeth. Her tongue went on the offensive, thrusting into his mouth and tangling with his.

God, he'd only meant to pilfer a sip of her. Sample her particular confection of flavor and savor it.

But *she* devoured *him*.

Raphael's blood pounded in a deafening roar, screaming through his veins with a victorious thrill. His entire body was consumed with the taste of her, like a crisp, sparkling Alsatian summer wine, both tart and sweet, with a sultry bite.

She intoxicated him.

Her ferocity called to something inside of him.

Because he knew it for what it was. Both an attack and a defense. He'd cornered her, and so she would make certain she was in control by claiming the kiss.

And he didn't want that.

What he wanted was her to enjoy it.

Bracketing her face with his hands, Raphael brushed tender thumbs over the downy curve of her cheekbones as he fought back the savage lust that hardened his body. He longed to take her. To possess and invade her, to thrust into her with the same abandon she showed now.

Images tormented him. Of her bent over things, tied to other things, writhing at the wickedness he could wreak upon her.

It tantalized him to the brink of madness.

And yet.

Some foreign sort of affection welled within him. While his body was hard, inside his rib cage, something loosened.

Softened.

This was not a moment to conquer.

But to seduce.

He brushed his thumbs to where their lips met, and nudged at the corner of her mouth, drawing it open and slack. He broke the seal, unhooking their tongues. Instead, he dragged his slick lips over hers in languid, gliding motions. Once. And again. Coaxing her to respond.

She reacted just how he'd hoped, her arms more embracing than clutching. Her hands kneading rather than clawing.

God, he could live to make this kitten purr.

Had there ever been a woman so perfectly rendered for kissing?

Her curves were more pronounced next to the hard planes of his own body, her breasts straining against his chest, her hips flaring dramatically when his hands charted the indent of her waist to rest there.

Somewhere in the distance, a lion roared. A child squealed.

The sounds broke her of whatever thrall he might have held.

Small hands flattened against his chest before she gave a mighty shove.

Raphael allowed it, retreating several steps.

Glowering in his direction, she wiped at her lips with the back her gloves, as if scrubbing the taste of him away. "You must stop doing that," she commanded. "It's—It's—"

"Delicious?" he supplied helpfully.

"Disgusting," she spat.

"You did not seem disgusted to me," he taunted. "What I think you are, is afraid."

"I am *not* afraid of you." She circled him like he might be a predator about to attack, inching toward the entrance to their intimate alley.

Raphael tried not to examine why he felt the small distance between them in the very essence of himself. The pads of his fingers, the fine hairs of his body. They seemed tuned to her by some magnetic force, drawing him forward.

"Are you afraid you'll like me?" he challenged. "That you'll want more?"

"N-no." Her eyes darted this way and that as she took two more steps backwards.

"Why are you retreating, then?"

She froze. Blinked. Then squared her shoulders, drawing herself up to her full—if less than impressive—height.

"I'm not retreating, I'm—I'm leaving. There's a difference."

Spinning on her bootheel, she hurried until she reached the end of the alley, and flounced around the corner.

When Raphael caught up, she was strolling toward the entrance, quite obviously doing her level best to keep her footsteps steady so not to appear as though she fled.

He should let her go.

He should turn around and put her behind him. Focus on the task at hand and not give in to the strange and unmistakable lure.

It was as if she had his heart affixed to a spool of string like a kite, and he trailed after her—above her—in quivering anticipation of the moment she would pull him out of the wind.

No good could come of this. He...should...just...

"I'll squire you out." The offer slipped from his lips before he could pull it back.

She rewarded his chivalry with a sharp glare. "I hardly need a squire, and don't require your company."

"Evidently not, but in order to quit the zoo, I also need use of the gate."

"There's the other entrance." She pointed toward the back where he'd left Marco.

"Alas, this one is the one I prefer." He offered a gesture of regret that conveyed *there's nothing to be done*, and sauntered after her.

She made an exceedingly unladylike sound of exasperation and quickened her pace. "Just keep your hands and your lips to yourself."

Raphael lengthened his strides, having no issue keeping up with her. He breathed in the frigid air tinged with her singular scent, and didn't even lament the clouds as they drifted toward the sun in a threatening manner.

Even at the bitter end of winter, when all tended to be grey and gloomy, she smelled of sweet herbs and sunshine, evoking memories of sipping pastis on sun-drenched verandas of the Mediterranean.

The shadows could not touch her. The grey couldn't dim her, no matter how it might try.

And he was a moth mesmerized by her flame.

A vendor called to her, holding out paper wrapped around candied nuts.

"No, thank you," she said as she bustled on by.

He trotted to catch up. "You're a lady of taste, surely you can spare a coin for—"

Raphael maneuvered himself closer and it only took a censuring look to send the man scampering in the other direction.

"Unbelievable," she muttered beneath an irate breath.

"You're welcome." He flashed her a winsome smile as if he'd not caught the sarcasm in her voice, and clasped his hands behind his back to make himself seem more casual.

She whirled on him, thrusting a finger at his chest. "What is the matter with you? Do you enjoy throwing your strength and malice into the faces of those less powerful? Do you prefer it when people fear you? Does it lend you some perverted sort of thrill?"

"Of course not," he defended, running the tip of his tongue over lips that still tasted of her. "I get my perverted thrills elsewhere."

"Bah!" She threw her hands up in an ironically violent gesture of defeat and stomped away, abandoning all pretense of composure.

Thoroughly amused, Raphael fell into step with her. "I shouldn't like *you* to fear me," he explained.

"As I said, I do not, but you just intimidated that poor man back there."

"I didn't want him to hassle you."

"No, of course not, when you're doing such an excellent job of it."

He sighed, hating that he felt the need to explain himself to her as he had no one else in his entire lifetime. "Fear isn't something I find enticing, merely...useful."

"Useful?" She wrinkled her forehead in puzzlement as if she couldn't fathom how or why anyone would use such an awful, powerful phenomenon. "You mean, in your criminal enterprise?"

"Yes."

"You make men fear you so that you may control them." She said this with conviction, as if she had experience in the matter.

Keeping his hands distinctly clasped behind him—so as not to give in to the overpowering urge to once again pull her against his body—Raphael surprised himself by telling her the truth. "There is a difference between leading men and controlling them. Again, I *prefer* people not fear me."

"But you *just* said you use—"

"It does me no good to incite terror of *me*, per se," he clarified. "If I have an enemy, I find out what they already fear and turn it on them. I figure how to sow it among their own ranks until the right eye doesn't trust what the left eye sees. I can make it so the heart and the brain fear each other, and then the muscles and blood don't know whom to obey. When men fear what they used to love, that fear often turns to hate. And then they rip out their own hearts. They pluck out their own eyes... They devour themselves."

"That's..." To his abject astonishment, she was quiet for five entire steps before conjuring a word. "Diabolical."

"That, *mon chaton*, is when I strike. When they are blind. When they'll never see me coming."

"Oh." She looked off into the distance, melancholy sitting strangely on her face. As if it didn't belong. "I do not think

Mathilde ever saw her killer coming. At least... I hope she did not. That she wasn't afraid."

Lanced by the selfsame ardent hope, Raphael asked, "Why did you come seek me out when I'm wanted for Mathilde's murder?"

"Because I...I don't think you killed her."

"You would not have kissed me back if you did."

"I did *not* kiss—"

He interrupted her protestation. "What makes you think I am innocent?"

"I don't have to tell you," she said, still stubbornly refusing to look at him.

"Please."

The soft word caused a hitch in her step. Perhaps she heard the desperation in it. The earnest grief he'd been keeping at bay.

Sighing, she relented. "For one, your shoes were impeccable and expensive, and the boot that left the mud on the window was grooved like that of a Brogan. A man's military boot, but this one was higher, like a woman's. I can make no sense of it."

"I could have changed shoes." He played the devil's advocate.

"Unlikely." She pursed her lips, chewing on the bottom one with a pensive frown. "Also, her neck was snapped in a motion that signified her murderer was left-handed, and I've noticed your right hand is your dominant one. And besides... I credit you with more intelligence than to stay at a crime scene long enough for the body to cool."

Raphael did his best not to preen. She was a woman who didn't give much credit. It was strange how much even a tiny compliment like that seemed to stir him.

"Who told you we were lovers?" he puzzled aloud. "Mathilde wasn't the type of woman who revealed her secrets, not with Gregoire as a husband."

At the question, she looked over at him, and the concern he read in her eyes almost caused him to stumble. "Don't be cross with her. She didn't use your name. Merely revealed to me that you were young, dark, dangerous, powerful, and that you were—"

She broke off, her gaze skittering away.

The color darkening her cheeks, still flushed from his kiss, intrigued him. "I was, what?"

"It doesn't matter. It has nothing to do with the case."

"I'd still like to know. If it was something Mathilde thought of me."

At that, she conceded. "She intimated that you were...rather skilled."

He snorted his disbelief. "Mathilde didn't use such banal terms as 'rather skilled.'"

"All right," she hissed. "She told me you were capable of passion she'd never known a man to possess. That you knew a woman's body as if you'd created it for your own skill. She said that no lover had ever made her perform such wicked acts. Had never made her want to."

Raphael flashed her his most charming smile. "Well, Mathilde was many things, but she wasn't a liar."

"No. She wasn't." For once, there was something they agreed upon. "You revealed yourself by being there the moment her husband traveled away."

"So I did," he said, just realizing it, himself.

"Did you love her?"

She seemed as surprised to ask the question as he was to hear it, and he had to cast about his heart for an answer.

For the truth.

"I was...fond of Mathilde. But there is only one person alive that I can profess to love."

"Yourself?"

Her clipped answer surprised a bark of laughter out of him.

"You know me better than you ought to for only having met me twice before."

"A detective is trained to make keen observations about people." She tapped the spot beneath her eye with her fingertip, indulging in a satisfied smile.

"A shame none of the detectives they sent after me were women."

"You'd be caught by now, no doubt."

"I imagine you are right."

She lifted her hand to her eyes, shading them from the quickly dissipating sun. "I've observed something else."

"What is that?"

"We are being followed."

CHAPTER 6

Mercy suddenly wanted Raphael Sauvageau to live up to his name.

He was just so unnervingly cool and infuriatingly collected. All loose limbs and unaffected insouciance, even as he checked their periphery for a threat.

As if finding one wouldn't at all ruin his day.

If this man had as much sway over fear as he claimed, then what was it that could send him into histrionics?

Everyone feared something.

You terrify me, Mercy Goode.

Surely, he'd been joking.

He gave their surroundings a surreptitious examination. "Does the man following us have a billycock hat and a grey morning suit with the paper tucked under his left arm?" His lips barely moved as he peered off into the opposite direction of the man in question.

A lance of trepidation speared her gut. "You've spotted him, too?"

Turning, he lifted his hand in a wave at their voyeur.

Mercy almost slapped it out of the air before he informed her, "His name is Clayton Honeycutt. He's one of my Fauves."

"You're being followed by your own men?" she asked in disbelief, blinking over at their shadow, who nodded in greeting.

"We tend to trail each other. To go very few places alone. Our backs are never exposed, and it keeps us honest—well—at least among our own."

Something about the way he said this caused her to examine him more closely. He was being wry...and yet...a tightness appeared at the corner of his mouth that hadn't been there before.

"You have a good eye," he praised. "An admirable instinct for such things. Not many people can pick us out of a crowd like this."

Mercy tried to hide that his words pleased her, and found it impossible.

So delighted was she, in fact, that she neglected her defenses against him for a rare, vulnerable moment. Forgot that his masculinity was honed to a razor's edge, wielded with masterful ease. That his musculature was well-thewed and sculpted like that of a lean predator, one that relied on his speed and stamina as well as his strength.

One that moved about the world with nothing to fear.

And everything to claim as his own.

It became increasingly hard to believe that such a charismatic man, radiating a sort of godlike beauty, walked among mortals like her.

She forgot that she'd promised not to be charmed by him. Not even intrigued.

Let alone enthralled.

Her moment of weakness was all he needed.

His glittering grey gaze, like the silver tip of an arrow, found a chink in her armor and skewered her right through.

He looked at her as no man ever had. As if his eyes only ever sought after her. As if they only knew her, and no one else. No other woman.

And that was a dangerous lie.

One he hadn't exactly told her, and yet she found herself wanting to believe it.

She needed to quit his company, before she let something more dangerous than a kiss happen...

Before she initiated it.

Marching forward, she kept her eyes on the gate, needing to think of something—anything—other than the kiss he stole from her.

The tender sweep of his lips across hers.

"I don't think Mathilde loved you either," she said, half to consider the notion, and half to whip him with it.

"Pardon?" His voice held an edge she didn't want to look over and identify just now.

"Well, when she wanted to escape her brutal husband, she came to the Lady's Aid Society...rather than to you. Why do you think that is, Mr. Sauvageau?"

"I couldn't rightly say..." He sounded pensive. Troubled. And Mercy was glad to hear it, because it made this man seem human.

"Did she tell you she was leaving?" Mercy ventured. "Did she ask you to go with her?"

He was silent for a beat longer than she expected an honest man to be. "No. I knew Gregoire was going back to France, but I was not privy to Mathilde's plans to leave him, even though I'd demanded she do so many times."

"Would you have gone with her if she asked?" Mercy slowed her march. Suddenly the gate was getting too close, and she didn't feel as though she could breathe until she heard his answer.

Which was patently absurd.

"No," he said again, his tone measured with a chemist's precision. "Mathilde knew me too well to ask."

She could think of nothing in reply to that, so she drifted silently forward for a while. Usually, the beavers and waterfowl in the gardens would charm and distract her, but today her notice was captured by a different sort of beast.

It was he who broke the silence. "Mathilde had a ball to attend the night after next, she'd have considered it the greatest tragedy to miss it."

"Indeed." Mathilde had informed Mercy of the Midwinter Masquerade being held at Madame Duvernay's. All of the *demi-monde* would attend. Famous actresses and courtesans. Women who were kept by dukes and royalty. Mediums and occultists, writers and scholars, indeed, artists of all renown and modality.

These had been her people, and Mathilde had wanted to say goodbye before she left forever. She was most adamant about it, in fact, making furtive explanations about people who she might see.

Might her murderer have tried to stop her from attending?

"What will you do now, Miss Goode?"

His question broke her reverie. "Nothing's changed. I intend to find Mathilde's murderer, of course. Don't think I've forgotten that you mentioned you might have an idea of who it could be."

His eyes shifted, as if sifting through the truths to give her.

"There's no need for you to find a lie," she prompted. "You can tell me what you know. You can *trust* me."

His assessment of her was slow, but not languorous nor seductive as it had once been. This time, it was full of questions she couldn't define, and a cynical sort of sadness that slid through her ribs to tug at her heart.

"A man achieves what I have by trusting only that other

people will betray him. In my world, naïveté is the chief cause of untimely death."

"How awful that must be." She grimaced with distaste. "Why anyone would join a world like that is beyond me."

"Some of us have no choice," he murmured, his eyes fixing to a far-off point. "Indeed, it is the belief of the Fauves that the entire world is just such a savage place. We merely chose to accept the fact, and then grant ourselves the greatest chance of survival in this jungle man has crafted for us."

Mercy considered this. Considered *him*. For the first time, she imagined that she peeled back the years from his sardonic beauty. Erased the cynical set to his mouth and the ever-present tension in his shoulders. She relieved him of the mantle of menace and the threat of violence, to uncover who he might have been once upon a time.

A boy. Carefree and mischievous. Precocious and witty with that disarming dimple in his left cheek.

What sort of variables formulated by the Fates created this man who stood before her?

What choices had he made?

What choices were made for him?

"How do you know, then, if anyone is ever giving you correct information?" she wondered aloud.

He pondered this. "Oftentimes, if they owe me, or if our interests align, that can make an ally for a time."

"Well, there we are then!" she exclaimed, clapping her hands together once. "I suppose I owe you for the gold you gave Nora and Titus, so—"

He shook his head in denial, and the sun shone blue off his ebony hair. "That was a payment for services about to be rendered. And I forfeited that to your sister and her husband, not to you."

"What about a transaction, then," she offered. "Surely that's a language you understand."

At that, his eyes flared with interest. "I'm listening."

"You tell me what I want to know, and then I'll tell you what information I have. A fair trade, wouldn't you say?"

His expression flattened. "Not the transaction I was hoping for, but... I suppose it'll do."

"Excellent." She offered her hand for a shake to seal their deal.

He took it, looking a bit bemused.

Even through her glove, she was suffused with the potency of his touch. Something as innocuous as a handshake with this man felt wicked.

Not wrong, per se.

Illicit.

She was aware of every tactile sensation. Of the rasp the very whorls his finger pads made on the silk. Of the restrained strength in his grip. The way he lingered over the gesture, as reticent as she to let go.

Clearing her throat, Mercy plucked her hand away and reached into her reticule, pulling out a notepad. "You first. Who do you suspect wanted Mathilde dead?"

Raphael's voice altered as he spoke, too heavy and low to be easily heard over the squeals of happy children, the sounds of unhappy animals, and the chatter of the London elite. "Mathilde was a woman of glorious highs and devastating lows. She often indulged in...substances to help her manage these riotous moods of hers. I knew this could be destructive, but I could not bring myself to admonish her for seeking to control her suffering."

"Did you provide her with these substances?" Mercy asked, careful to keep the judgment from her voice.

"Sometimes." He looked out over the heads of the crowd, as if searching the past. "She had spells when she seemed as though her energy would never cease. She did reckless, devastating things. Initiated brawls in public. Seduced other

524

women's husbands. She even stole from me once to sell to her friends in the *demimonde*. I'll admit I have killed for that, but I would never hurt a woman, least of all, her."

He couldn't even trust his own lover. The thought made Mercy desperately melancholy, even as he continued.

"After these spells, she'd sleep for an entire week, as if her very soul was weary." He blew out a sigh, as if fighting a bit of that weariness himself. "She and Gregoire relocated here from France to escape a scandal there," he continued. "Though she refused to give me details, I gathered that she was wanted for a theft from the Duchesse de la Cour. I have often wondered if she sought me out because she thought I could protect her. From her enemies...from herself."

He paused, and she thought she saw a very human emotion soften his chiseled features.

Regret.

"The Duchesse is visiting a cousin here in London, which causes me to wonder if she's reaped her revenge on Mathilde." His somber eyes found hers. "That is the lead I intend to follow."

Mercy tapped her pencil against the pad, biting at her cheek in thought. "Mathilde did say she had to conduct some final business before she left...do you think the Duchesse will be at this masquerade you mentioned?"

"I cannot say. I intend to find out before then." He rubbed a hand over his jaw, which seemed to be less smooth as the afternoon wore on. "It is your turn to relinquish information."

"What would you like to know?"

"What was the destination of her escape?"

That was an easy question to answer. "We were taking a train to the coast, and from there she was going to disembark to America."

Raphael nodded, a bleak smile haunting his lips. "She often spoke of seeing the Brooklyn Bridge. Of taking a train all the way to the Pacific Ocean." His face hardened and he turned to her. "You will not go after this murderer."

She bristled. "You cannot issue me orders as if—"

He sliced a hand through the air to cut off her protestations. "Has it occurred to you, Miss Goode, that this killer might think nothing of slaughtering *you* and degrading your pretty corpse before leaving it in the gutter, should you get in his way?"

"Of course it has," she sniped, doing her best to seem undeterred by his graphic warning. "I'm not planning on getting in his way, only finding him out. Then I'll turn the evidence over to the authorities. That is what an intrepid investigator does."

He shook his head the entire time she spoke, all semblance of charm and charisma replaced by a solemn determination.

"It's too dangerous," he insisted, leaning on every syllable for undue emphasis. "Leave it alone, Miss Goode. Leave it to me. You go back to your balls, your books, your seamstresses and your suitors. Live a long and privileged life for those of us who—"

"Ha!" She poked him in the chest and then shook her hand when her finger crumpled against steely muscle. "I'll thank you to note that I have no suitors at present, nor do I desire one, and I'd rather attend the dentist than a ball. So, do not presume you have the measure of me, sir."

He regarded her with resolute skepticism. "You mean for me to believe you don't love dressing in silks and having rich men trip all over themselves to offer for you?" He rolled his eyes. "Do go on, Miss Goode."

"I've plenty of interest and no offers." She crossed her arms over her chest, daring him to laugh.

Instead, he gave a dry snort. "Next you'll be telling me about blizzards in the Sahara."

"Don't be cruel," she admonished him. "It's patently obvious why no man would want me."

His smirk disappeared when he looked at her, replaced by a start of disbelief. "You're being serious."

"Deadly."

"I rarely find myself at the disadvantage of not knowing what someone in the *ton* finds patently obvious, as you put it... but I can't bring myself to imagine to what you are referring. I should think you have to beat the suitors away with a club."

Mercy squelched a threatening glow of pleasure at his words. His discombobulation seemed genuine, but he was a notorious charmer.

She refused to fall for it.

"It's not one thing," she explained, suddenly feeling itchy and defensive. Irate that she had to spell it out for him. "It's everything. It's *me*. I'm incapable of feeding the ego of a man with the insincere laughter or empty compliments they seem to require. I do not easily suffer fools, which means I have not ingratiated myself to many other debutantes or mothers of single noblemen. I read too much. I talk too much, which subsequently reveals that I am possessed of too many opinions." She began to count the reasons on the fingers of her hand. "I am political. Willful. Argumentative. Self-indulgent. All the things men abhor in a woman."

"Weak men," he murmured, a spark igniting in his gaze. "Perhaps you need someone other than the dandies of your class to tame you."

"Tame me?" His wicked suggestion aroused her, which irritated her in the extreme. "Don't make me laugh. I cannot abide the whims of any man, be he dandy or dominant. I do not desire to keep a household. I do not want to be known as Lady So-and-so, this man's wife. I want to be me. My *own* person." She paused in her passionate speech, amending it without hesitation. "Except for Felicity, of course. I couldn't live a life apart from her. We shared a womb. She's the other half of me. She possesses all the fragility and gentility I do not...and she suffers—"

Suddenly she froze. Realizing she'd revealed more to this man than any other. That she'd been on a tirade that must have dried up any interest he might have had.

And why should that matter?

"Suffers what?" he asked.

"Nothing. You needn't worry about her."

"Tell me," he prodded, and when she looked up into his arrested expression, she could believe that he really wanted to know.

That she hadn't frightened him away.

"Felicity...she has these conniptions. Spells, you might call them."

"Like Mathilde?" he queried.

She shook her head. "No. She is easily startled. Constantly trepidatious and worried. She has a hard time breathing, but not in the way of asthmatics. Her heart races and she will sometimes be sick or faint. She does faint an alarming amount. It's as if she stole all my fear for herself so I could be as I am. Brash and bold. We are a mirror of each other. And her reflection is so fragile. So gentle..." Mercy blinked at a stinging in her eyes. "Well, anyway, I would never leave her alone, and a husband would invariably ask me to. He wouldn't want for competition of my affections."

She looked up to find Raphael regarding her with infinite tenderness. His eyes were not opaque or full of secrets. They were open. Challenging.

Burning.

No. He was not mysterious, this man. He wore his darkness. Advertised his sins. Pinned his emotions to his suit like a badge of honor.

"I don't want to go without ravishing you at least once."

Comprehension of his words didn't quite land at first. "Go where? Wait... What?"

He stepped closer, his expression intent. "I desire you like I have no other woman. I would take as many nights as you would offer, but I'll settle for just one."

Mercy blinked at him, certain she misunderstood his meaning. He was casual but serious. Relaxed, but intense. Surely, he wasn't asking if she would—

"Would you let me fuck you, Mercy Goode?"

Her mouth went slack, and she lost whatever substance held her bones together. She wished for a chair, a couch, a bench. Anything upon which to sink.

She looked around at the people. The families. This place that was so bustling and wholesome. Where propositions like his simply didn't belong.

Oh my. Mercy wanted to check her burning face for fever, but she didn't dare.

What was she right now? Upset? Insulted?

Enticed?

His eyes were searingly tender as he searched her face for an answer. "You are not slapping me. Or screaming at me. So, am I to imagine you are considering it?"

"You—were Mathilde's lover." And she was only deceased for a day's time.

At that, his features became impossibly kinder, his gaze containing admiration. "I have touched no other woman since the night I gifted your sister with my gold."

"But that was...months ago," she marveled, doing her best to remember that she could not believe a word from his mouth.

He shrugged. "So it was."

"Mathilde made it seem as though she'd been with you not so long ago."

His eyebrows lifted. "Did she say that? That she and I had been lovers *recently?*"

"Come to think of it... no." She examined her reaction to that.

Her heart felt one thing.

Her body another.

His muscles remained lax, even though he allowed her to witness the uncontested hope radiating from him. "I assure you, Miss Goode, Mathilde and I did not share an understanding of any kind. Not in *that* way. There was nothing like romance between us, do you understand? I am doing her memory no disservice by propositioning you. I will be working harder to find her killer than the police. She will be avenged; you have my word. But I will be too distracted by my obsession with your lips to be of much use, unless you yield to me."

Swallowing around a sandpaper tongue, Mercy could only blink up at him.

For once in her life, she had nothing to say.

Because she was captured in the culmination of her eternal struggle.

The one between what she *should* do.

And what she wanted to do.

She might die an old maid, but she certainly didn't plan on being a virgin.

Suddenly, everything Mathilde told her about him spun through her mind, sped through her blood, and landed in her loins.

The rapture he was capable of imparting. The pleasure. The desire. The stamina.

The sin.

He stepped closer, watching the war play out on her face, and spoke to tip the scales in his favor. "If you are to never take a husband, at least let me give you the knowledge of what to expect from a lover. Though I pity the man who next attempts to follow me."

The sheer arrogance in his claim should have turned her off of him instantly.

And yet, he said this with an odd sort of darkness. Like he pitied her next lover because he was already considering doing him violence.

"Let me have you tonight." His whisper sizzled through her.

"T-tonight?" she gasped out.

He made a gesture both helpless and sanguine. "I am a man for whom tomorrow is never a certainty, and so I live every night as if it were my last."

"How wondrous and terrible to not worry for tomorrow," she murmured.

"Wonderous and terrible. That is my existence in two words."

One of the wolves howled in the distance, a wild, mournful sound so foreign in the city.

Mercy turned toward it, needing not to look at him for a moment.

To catch her breath.

Was she truly considering this madness?

His breath was a warm caress against her ear as the clean masculine scent of him enveloped her. "Tonight, *mon chaton*," he purred from behind her, his finger skimming her shoulder blades so lightly. "Let me stroke you until you are exhausted with pleasure. Demand what you want from me, I do not mind. Let me teach you what you deserve to know. What you should always expect. What your body is capable of."

Yes.

Mercy couldn't say the word, so she nodded.

She felt rather than saw him smile, even as he stepped back, granting her some space so she could finally breathe.

Pressing her fingers to her lips, she couldn't stop thinking about his tongue. Inside her mouth, it'd been warm and slick and tasted like depravity.

She'd been surprised it wasn't forked, devil that he was.

How would it be on other parts of her?

All her life, she'd hated the story of the serpent in the Garden of Eden. The allegory for temptation in the face of consequences.

She'd never understood why Eve bit into the apple.

Not until this very moment.

Not until this man with shining hazel eyes and a voice made of velvet and vice, tempted her beyond reason.

Trying to string her thoughts together, she stammered, "How would we...? Where will we? I mean..."

Her questions never found him she realized, as she turned back to clarify.

He'd disappeared.

CHAPTER 7

*M*ercy had often thought that for such a fair-complected man, Chief Inspector Carlton Morley was a bit of a dark horse.

Even as he paced the plush Persian carpets of her parents' solarium, his every movement was measured and controlled.

Carefully contained.

He was more compelling than handsome, she thought. His brow stern and the set of his jaw arrogant.

No, authoritarian. That was it.

A man who expected to be obeyed without question, likely because he was in charge of the entire London Metropolitan Police.

Which was why his choice of wife was so confounding. Her elder sister Prudence was ironically impetuous. But, Mercy supposed, her habitual *imprudence* accompanied a beauty of demeanor only matched by that of her soul, so it was impossible not to love her.

At least, in Morley's case.

They were ridiculously—disgustingly—happy.

For her part, Mercy couldn't begin to imagine being in love with a fellow who rarely relaxed and was always right.

And not in the way that most men *assumed* they were always right based on little more than their hubris and trumped-up opinions.

Morley was unfailingly well-informed and infuriatingly correct, more often than not. When he spoke, people leaned in to mark him because he was possessed of both power and practicality.

And that, Mercy was given to understand, was a rare combination of virtues.

Objectively, she supposed she understood why Prudence found him attractive, what with his corona of elegantly styled pale hair and eyes so cold and blue they might have been chipped from a glacier.

They only melted for Pru and the twins, becoming liquid and warm.

Mercy liked to watch the transformation her sister brought about in him, how his wide shoulders peeled away from his ears and every part of him seemed to exhale.

With his family, he could be charming. Cavalier, even.

He was protective and useful, honorable to a fault, and Mercy knew that beneath the furrow of disapproval on his brow was a wrinkle of worry for her. He watched them with the passionate overprotectiveness belonging to a man who'd once lost his own sister to tragedy.

It was why Mercy would suffer his warnings and lectures.

Because she knew that behind the bluster was a brother.

One who cared.

The Goode sisters were unused to compassionate men in their lives, having a staunch, religious father who maintained two demeanors where his family was concerned.

Critical or indifferent.

His greatest disappointment was not having a son, and he

used his daughters like pawns in medieval land disputes, leveraging their reputations, fortunes, and beauty to garner him more prestige and power.

It entertained Mercy to an endless degree how often he'd been thwarted.

First by Pru, whose fiancé, the Earl of Sutherland, had been murdered moments before they were to walk down the aisle. She'd been arrested for the deed by Morley himself, and then rescued from the hangman's rope by a hasty marriage to the selfsame Chief Inspector.

Honoria—Nora—had done everything she'd been expected to, including marrying Lord William Mosby, Viscount Woodhaven.

That man was the most disastrous thing to happen to the Goode family. He abused Nora terribly, squandered all their money, and used their father's shipping company to smuggle illegal goods for none other than the Sauvageau brothers and their Fauves. Ultimately, he stole a crate of gold from the Sauvageaus and made dangerous enemies of them. His escape was foiled when he'd taken Pru hostage and Morley put a bullet through his temple.

My, but last year had been eventful.

Mercy wished for her sister now, wondering how much longer it would take for Pru to return from feeding Charlotte and Caroline.

Morley was like a pendulum of paternal disapproval moving back and forth in front of her as he lectured her about...well, about something or other.

The sermon had begun on the subject of her poking around murder scenes where she didn't belong, but she'd lost him some ten minutes back when he'd moved on to her arrest.

Here's why you shouldn't slap detectives and all that such nonsense.

She was generally inclined to answer back, at least to

defend herself, but he'd already mentioned that Detective Trout had been dismissed for his heavy-handed retaliation against her.

Or would be, after he was released from the hospital due to the beating Raphael had inflicted. Now Morley was down one detective—albeit a mediocre one—during a crime wave.

That's where he'd lost Mercy's attention.

Her mind drifted from how "the entire situation could have been avoided if she'd not ventured where she ought not to have been in the first place." Et cetera and so forth.

No, drifted was the wrong word, it evoked the idea of aimlessness.

Her thoughts only ever went in one direction these days.

They were steered, propelled.

Captivated.

Would you let me fuck you, Mercy Goode?

The wicked proposition was a constant, obsessive echo in her mind.

It thrummed through her in Raphael's velvet voice, snaking its way into her veins and coiling deep in her loins.

Those words from any other man would have repelled her. She was someone who demanded deference. Someone who expected to be treated with the respect due her station. Not only as a gentleman's daughter, but as a woman—nay—a human being.

But, somehow, Raphael Sauvageau managed to make the profane query sound like a prayer.

A plea.

It was as though he'd asked, *Would you let me worship you?*

Because of the veneration in his eyes. The reverence that impossibly lived alongside the depravity in his gaze.

The pleasure in his promise.

He hadn't asked, *Would you fuck me?* The unspoken question

being, would you pleasure me? Would you slake *my* hunger and fulfill *my* desires?

No. He'd offered to stroke her. To pleasure her. To teach her what to expect from a lover.

As if he would relish in providing her delight.

Mercy knew enough about lust to have felt the evidence of his desire against her skirts in the alcove where they'd kissed.

He'd been hard. He could have taken her right there.

His singular paradox of wildness and restraint called forth her own undeniable passions.

She'd not relented to his proposition because he'd wanted her.

But because she'd desired to take what he offered.

He was no sort of man to be allowed within miles of her heart, but her body?

His body?

Now there was a hard, rugged terrain she yearned to explore.

Mercy had to duck her head lest Morley read the wicked turn of her thoughts. She could feel her excitement burning hot in her cheeks, the tips of her ears, and...lower. Deep within.

Tonight.

She fought a spurt of panic. She still didn't know when. Or where. Or how. Or... when.

Would he dare come to Cresthaven? Would he send a message for a clandestine rendezvous somewhere?

What if he didn't?

She gasped in a breath. What if he changed his mind and didn't contact her at all?

What if she waited for him like a breathless ninny and he went off to some other strumpet, laughing at the thought of her pathetic virginal eagerness?

He was a degenerate, after all. A professional swindler.

She couldn't have imagined the intensity of his need, could

she? Surely, she'd have seen through any sort of artifice on his part.

Unless he was a better deceiver than she was an observer.

Perish that thought.

The sound of Raphael's name, a foul word on Morley's tongue, brought her surging toward the surface from the murky depths of her ponderings.

"Who? What?"

Morley's brows, a shade darker than his hair, pulled low over his deep-set eyes. "Have you been listening to me?"

"Yes?" Mercy's eyes moved this way and that as she searched her empty memory for evidence against her lie. What had he just said?

He frowned with his entire face. "Is that a question?"

"No?"

"*Mercy*."

"You were...disparaging the leader of the Fauves, yes?"

He rolled his eyes and lifted his hands in a gesture of resignation. "I said, I do not like that you were alone with Raphael Sauvageau."

At that, she straightened in her seat, her spine suddenly crafted from a steel rod.

"Alone?" she parroted, her voice two octaves higher than usual. "Where did you ever hear such a thing? Utter lies. There were people everywhere. We were *not* alone."

Except for when he'd kissed her.

Had someone spied their moment in the alcove?

"In the police carriage, Mercy, do try to keep up."

"Ohhh." She relaxed back with a relieved little laugh that ended on a sigh. "Well, yes, there was that time."

"To think you were locked up with him, right after he'd done Trout such violence..." His electric eyes bored into hers. "After he mercilessly executed Mathilde Archambeau. I promise you, Mercy, heads will roll for this. You should not have been subject to his company. You're lucky he didn't do you harm in his escape."

"You don't need to worry about that." Mercy waved away his concern. "Mr. Sauvageau didn't kill Mathilde."

With an aggrieved sigh, Morley sunk to her mother's hideous pink velvet chair, and leaned forward, resting his elbows on his knees and letting his hands hang between them. "And just how did the blighter manage to convince you of that?"

"He didn't," she informed him archly. "I deduced it."

"Deduced?"

"Yes. Deduced. A verb. It means to arrive at a logical conclusion by—"

"I know what it bloody means, Mercy, I'm simply trying to imagine how you could possibly have inferred evidence that my investigators had not."

Doing her best to keep her animation to a minimum, Mercy informed him about the open window, the boot print, the angle of poor Mathilde's neck and Raphael's right-handedness. She even drew diagrams, which—to Morley's credit—he studied very carefully before he looked up to regard her with new appreciation.

"I'm going to have to consult the coroner's report, but if all is as you say, I think Raphael Sauvageau owes you a debt of gratitude."

Nothing could have dimmed the brilliance of Mercy's smile. Not only because her investigative skills had assisted in exonerating an innocent man—well, perhaps *innocent* was not an apropos word to use in reference to Raphael Sauvageau—but also because she'd have the pleasure of informing said gangster later that night.

Probably.

If he showed up.

"I'm given to understand that Mathilde had an enemy in the

Duchesse de la Cour over a theft back in France," she continued, holding up a finger as if to tap an idea out of the sky. "Perhaps the Duchesse and Mathilde's dastardly husband, Gregoire, were in cahoots."

"Cahoots," Morley chuckled.

"What?"

"No one uses that word."

"I use that word." Detective Eddard Sharpe used that word.

"You'd have made an excellent detective," he said with gentle fondness.

"Thank you." She primly smoothed her skirts over her thighs and rested her gloved hands on her knees. It was high time someone recognized that.

Someone other than Raphael, that is. He'd been the first to compliment her on her sleuthing skills.

Sucking in a deep breath, Morley heaved himself to his feet with the vital exhaustion of a new father and the responsibility of the entire city's safety on his shoulders. "We'll look into it."

"When?" she inquired.

"When we're able." He ran a palm down his face and glanced at the door through which his wife had disappeared a quarter hour past. "I should go find Pru."

"When will you tell me what you find?" Mercy stood as well, thinking she needed to bathe before tonight. "The coroner will have his autopsy done tomorrow maybe, the day after next?"

"I report to you now, do I?" Morley regarded her with a sardonic glare.

"I promised Mathilde I'd find her murderer."

His arch look softened. "And that is lovely of you, Mercy, but women like Mathilde—who keep the company she kept, and indulge in the vices she enjoyed—they often find themselves in dangerous situations. And they just as often meet such an ignoble end at the hands of men who leave no evidence for us to follow."

"There is evidence, Morley, there's the boot print."

"Which is compelling, but not absolute. Any number of men could have left that print, and it'll be difficult to use something like that to convict in court."

Mercy scowled at him. "You're acting as though you're preparing me for her murder to never be solved."

"That's exactly what I'm doing."

His answer paralyzed her. Morley got to where he was by nabbing and convicting more murderers than anyone in the history of Scotland Yard.

"How could you say that?" she accused.

His gesture was cajoling as he placed a warm hand on her forearm. "We are stretched so thin, Mercy. I'm endeavoring to hire more officers, but detectives are difficult to come by. There is a rise in gang violence because the substances of the streets have spilled into the solariums of the wealthy and powerful. I'm putting down migrant riots and trade strikes. We're in the middle of a crime wave, and I'm doing my utmost to keep hundreds of women and children who are still alive, that way."

"What are you saying?" Aghast, she stepped out of his reach. "That the murder of one measly drunken socialite doesn't merit investigation? Do you agree with Trout when he said Mathilde isn't worth the trouble it would take to find her justice?"

"Of course not." Morley ran frustrated fingers through his hair, tugging as if to pull a solution out of it. "I'm saying an investigation like this is rarely simple and almost never timely. We will do what we can for Mrs. Archambeau, you have my word. In fact, this is just the sort of case the Knight of Shadows takes interest in, eh?"

He gave her a friendly nudge to the shoulder.

Mercy nodded, more to get rid of him than anything.

"Let this go, Mercy. Let justice take its course."

The Knight of Shadows was an effective vigilante, to be sure, but no one knew how to contact him. He was a man. He did what he liked.

Oh, she'd let justice take its course...

Because justice, as everyone knew, was a woman.

CHAPTER 8

"*H*ow did this happen?"

Raphael knew to expect the question, but he never ceased to flinch upon its asking.

Because it produced a maelstrom of emotion he couldn't escape.

Guilt. Shame. Pain. Hatred.

Most of *all*, hatred.

Less toward the men who had done this to his brother, than the one who had brokered it.

He still seethed.

Grappled rage into submission as he watched Dr. Titus Conleith palpate his brother's ruined face for the final examination before tomorrow's reconstructive surgery.

Raphael detested everything about hospitals, though this one was nicer than most.

The glaring awful whiteness of them, the smell of solutions and cleansers. Of shit and blood and food and death. Even the neatness of them rankled. Rows of beds full of misery. Nurses dressed in smart uniforms, their hair held in severe knots beneath starched caps.

It made him all the more determined to die whilst young and healthy.

Gabriel was the only soul alive that could get him through these doors.

If his brother could suffer such indignities, the least Raphael could do was be there.

He only had to watch.

They had visited Dr. Conleith several times in the past handful of weeks, and never once had the surgeon savant made the dreaded query.

How did this happen?

How did Gabriel come to be without a large portion of his nose? How was it that his ocular bone had split so completely as to cave in, leaving him unable to properly open his left eye? How had the skin of his cheek ripped all the way through, from the corner of his mouth to his temple, only to be stitched together by a drunken hack?

"Violence." Sitting on the surgeon's examination table, Gabriel gave the same short answer he always did. The truth, and yet...

Not all of it. Not even close.

The memory—*memories* were Raphael's absolute worst.

And it hadn't even happened to him.

The violence.

Dr. Conleith reached for the stark-white-bulbed lamp, pulling it closer to Gabriel's face. It illuminated the macabre smile crafted by the tight, uneven line of the scar branching from the corner of his mouth to his hairline.

Raphael could barely stand to look at it, even after all these years.

He wanted to strike the handsome doctor for pointing such glaring lights on the ancient wounds when he knew how it distressed his brother. His fingers itched to bloody the stern brow that furrowed with pity as he bent over Gabriel's expressionless, long-suffering face.

It was the tension bulging his brother's muscles and the trickle of sweat running from his shorn scalp into the back of his collar that brought out the instinct to break the doctor's strong jaw as it flexed and released, as if chewing on a thought.

Must it be so light in here?

They visited under the cover of night so as not to be so thusly exposed.

As if he could instinctively sense the rage simmering right beneath Raphael's skin, the doctor glanced over to where he lingered by an articulated skeleton, holding the wall up with his shoulder.

To Conleith's credit, he didn't seem cowed by the brothers Sauvageau in the least. "I ask not out of morbid curiosity, but occupational necessity," he explained with his very professional brand of patience. "It appears to me that some of these wounds sustained subsequent trauma, which makes my job a great deal more difficult."

Subsequent trauma, what a gentle way to put it.

Neither he nor Gabriel answered.

Dr. Conleith rubbed at his close-cropped beard, one with a more russet hue than his tidy brown hair. "Answer me this, then. In regard to the ocular cavity, this was done by an instrument, I suspect?"

"It was."

"Blunt or sharp-edged?"

"Sharp." Gabriel's words were often difficult to mark. His voice hailed from lower in a chest deeper than most men could boast. Protected by dense ribs and muscles built upon what seemed to be other muscle, the register was often so low as to be lost.

The reason they often created the fiction that Gabriel couldn't speak or understand English was twofold. One, because people spoke more freely around someone who might not mark them.

And the other, because speaking caused Gabriel discomfort.

The stitching done to his mouth and cheek had been of such terrible design, it'd taken the ability to part his lips very well without fear of tearing the wound anew.

"So sharp, but not as sharp as the instrument that tore the cheek open, is that correct?" The doctor used his thumbs to lift the lip up toward the exposed nasal cavity.

Gabriel, a man who'd undergone more pain than even Raphael could imagine, gave a grunt of discomfort.

Raphael pushed away from the wall, taking a threatening step toward the doctor, who'd turned his back.

His brother held out a staying hand, planting Raphael's feet to the floor.

"I'm sorry for any discomfort," the doctor said gently as he released Gabriel's face and stepped away to wash his hands. "I was testing the elasticity of the skin."

"It was lumber."

Conleith turned around, his hands frozen with suds, as if he'd not heard Gabriel correctly. "Pardon?"

Raphael's mouth dropped open in astonishment. They never spoke of it. To anyone.

Ever.

"Long and square cut." Gabriel stretched his arms out wide to show the length of the wood that had caved his face in. "The kind used to build houses. Does that...change anything? Will you still be able to operate?"

Though Gabriel was his elder brother, larger in every respect, Raphael felt such a swell of protectiveness, he swallowed around a gather of emotion lodged in his throat, threatening to cut off his breath. Not even when they'd been young had he spoken with such uncertainty. With such hope and dread laced into one inquiry.

"Of course." The doctor answered in his quick and clipped tone. "Without question." He turned back to the sink to finish scrubbing his hands.

From his vantage, Raphael watched the doctor work diligently to school the aching compassion out of his expression.

It was appreciated.

Conleith obviously knew enough about men to realize that those who led a life such as theirs equated compassion with pity.

Pity was an insult.

And insults were answered.

Must have learned that in the Afghan war, where he'd earned his hard-won reputation by reportedly stitching together men even more broken than his brother.

Though that was hard to believe.

"Explain to me, Doctor, why you must put Gabriel through more than one procedure. This wouldn't be to make it seem as if the fortune we allowed you and your wife to keep was worth the trouble... "

The seams of the midnight-blue shirt strained over Gabriel's shoulder as he lifted his arm to jam a finger in Raphael's direction. "Do not intimidate the doctor," he commanded in their heavily accented French.

Raphael made a rude gesture and answered him in kind. "Does he look intimidated to you?"

The man was in no danger, and not only because he was the only surgeon who could perform such procedures in this country, but because he was married to Mercy's beloved eldest sister.

The idea of doing anything to cause her pain produced an ache in his own body.

"It's a valid question." Conleith strode to the skeleton held upon a post next to Raphael, whose nose looked alarmingly like his brother's. "Since your wounds have been healed for years, I'll need to re-break some of the bone in your cheek and then use a panel of sorts to sculpt it back together per a foundational technique pioneered by the Italian doctor, Gasparo Tagliacozzi." He showed on the skull where the break would occur and where the panel would be fitted. "I certainly have reason to hope that this will help with the terrible headaches you're plagued with. However, the procedure is new and complicated and could take several hours. I shouldn't like you to be anesthetized much longer than that, the risk of you not...regaining consciousness is too high."

Gabriel's chin dipped once. "I understand."

"Subsequently, Dr. Karl Ferdinand von Gräfe has shown me how to take skin from another part of your body, and not only shape you an entirely new nose, but also cut open your badly healed scar tissue and graft it so you will be able to speak and chew more easily."

"Where will the skin be taken from?" Gabriel attempting to furrow his brow was a terrible thing to behold.

More ghastly than normal, in any case.

The doctor hesitated. "Usually from the arm, but because of your tattoos, we'll have to take it from your back."

"All right, Doctor." His brother stood, and it still surprised Raphael to note that Conleith was every bit as tall as the towering gangster, if only three fourths as wide.

Not that Titus Conleith was a diminutive man. Indeed, he was strenuously fit, but Gabriel should have been named Goliath. Or Ajax.

As he'd the proportions not often seen on a mortal.

"Tomorrow night, then." Rather than offering his hand, Gabriel nodded to the doctor, who seemed to understand that he'd rather dispense with the pleasantries.

He turned away from any sort of audience as he affixed the black mask over his features. It stayed put by way of a strap that encircled the shorn crown of his head like the band of a hat, and settled down over the left side of his features with a frightening, if familiar, prosthetic shape of a man's face.

It always reminded Raphael of someone attempting to break free of a black marble statue.

After, Gabriel donned his long black coat, drawing up the hood to hide as much of himself as possible.

The observant doctor bustled around, rolling his shirt-sleeves down his forearms and affixing the cufflinks to allow them the semblance of privacy. "I like my patients to bathe and scrub as clean as possible and also to forgo meals the day of a procedure, if possible," he said. "Sometimes the anesthetic can cause nausea, and I shouldn't like you to aspirate whilst asleep."

With these last few words, he opened the door to their private room—a courtesy not afforded to many patients, no doubt—and escorted them out the door and into the night.

Both brothers enjoyed a simultaneous inhale of crisp February air as they melted into the familiar darkness of the streets.

They'd always been creatures of the shadows.

But perhaps not for much longer.

"For a moment there, I thought you were going to tell him about the pits," Raphael prompted. "About everything."

It wasn't cold enough to lift his collar to shield him, but Gabriel did it anyway as he ignored any mention of the pits. "The two procedures will set everything back. We'll need to make other arrangements."

"I'm not worried." Raphael lifted his shoulder and watched the billow of his breath break as he walked into it. "What are a few more days? No one will be looking for us."

Since Raphael couldn't read his brother's expressions, he'd learned to pick up on other cues, some as subtle as mere vibrations in the air between them.

The set of his boulder-sized shoulders, the number of times he cracked his knuckles, as he was wont to do when brooding.

"I still don't know if we can pull this off without bodies to confirm our deaths."

Raphael elbowed his brother, feinting at shoving him into a gas lamppost. "Find me a body that could pass for yours, and I'll gleefully murder him and enjoy pretending it's you."

Gabriel didn't even pretend to be amused. "It is hard for me, knowing I will not be awake to oversee things."

Clutching at his heart, Raphael acted as though he'd been skewered. "Your lack of trust wounds me, brother. Fatally, I expect. I should not have to fake my death."

"Keep your voice down," Gabriel snarled, searching the empty night for interlopers.

The Fauves didn't haunt this part of town.

Sobering, Raphael rested his palm on Gabriel's shoulder, the one from which the real mantle of leadership rested.

As the face of the Fauves, Raphael was an effective figure-head. Sleek and elegant, dangerously charismatic, cunning, and collected.

And, admittedly, not difficult to look at.

But few knew that he was the tip of the blade wielded by his brother.

Gabriel wasn't just muscle, as most suspected, he was might.

He was master.

Because of the rules by which they'd always lived.

The rules they now carefully planned to leave behind.

"I have it well in hand, brother." Raphael squeezed the tense muscle before releasing it, wishing he could say more.

Wishing he had more time with the only person he loved in this world.

Gabriel's chest expanded with another measured breath. "Tell me again."

"Once you are recovered enough to travel, you will retrieve your new papers from Frank Walters and go to the Indies. I have transferred our enormous fortune to St. John's Bank in

Switzerland, where I will retrieve it. After, we will meet in Antigua and from there go to America using our new identities."

"You'll telegraph the villa if something goes awry," Gabriel reminded him unnecessarily.

"That goes without saying, even though you've said it twenty times too many."

A grunt from his brother was as close as he ever came to a laugh.

"The extra days will serve us well," Raphael continued. "It gives me time to make the arrangements to have Mathilde's ashes go with us. We can spread them from the Brooklyn Bridge. She'd like that, I think."

Gabriel's gait changed, which was how Raphael knew he was about to say something that made him uncomfortable. "I know she was difficult... but I am sorry Mathilde is gone."

"As am I."

They fell silent as they stopped at the back-garden gate of the mansion no one knew they occupied. Their fountain tinkled in the background, mingling with the sounds of an approaching couple.

Raphael thought back to the day when his father had told them that the only way to escape their destiny was death.

Well...turned out the bastard had been right.

As the couple approached, the man deftly moved his lady to the opposite side of the walk, placing himself between Gabriel's bulk and her body.

Though they were in the part of the West End that was well patrolled, and where street ruffians rarely dared to venture, it was Gabriel's bulk and general air of menace that ignited the man's protective instinct.

Besides that move, the pair paid them little mind as they swished by, chattering as if nothing could touch them in the infatuated world they'd created.

Raphael would not have even marked them, if not for his brother.

Gabriel watched them with undue intensity. His fingers twitched as the man ran his hand along the woman's face.

Shifting uncomfortably, Raphael second-guessed his own plans for the evening.

All he'd desired in the hours since he'd left Mercy's side, was to return to it. Once the sun had gone down, he'd been nearly vibrating out of his skin with anticipation.

Walking around half hard at the thought of having her, hoping no one would notice.

Especially his brother, who had never so much as touched a woman.

He'd been born and bred a machine of violence. And nothing more.

Where would Gabriel fit in this world when they were through? He knew nothing else.

He *was* nothing else.

Raphael thumped Gabriel's chest to catch his attention. "Don't be worried, yeah? The doctor said that big dolts like you don't die in surgery often."

"I'm not nervous."

"Then what is wrong with you?"

His neck swiveled back to the woman. "Nothing."

Raphael took in a gigantic breath, bracing himself for extreme disappointment. He wanted Mercy with an ache he'd never known, but on an evening as momentous as this, he should be there for his brother.

"Do you want company?" he asked. "Let's get a round, yeah?"

"Not tonight." Gabriel fished his pipe out of his pocket and packed it with an expensive tobacco he was fond of. "I'm going to check a few things."

That brought Raphael to attention. "What things?"

"Never you mind."

Raphael rolled his eyes. There was no talking to him when he was like this. "Well, I'll be off then."

He pointed his shoes in the direction of Cresthaven Place.

"What are you about tonight?" Gabriel asked, as if it had only just occurred to him to do so.

"Never *you* mind." Raphael threw the answer over his shoulder.

"Raphael Thierry Sauvageau." His brother's glare was an uncomfortable prickle along his spine, so he turned to face it.

"I'm *going* for a woman, if you must know, you insufferable nag." They'd always japed and jibed and poked at each other. Gabriel knew he had women. That he was somewhat a lothario, but they never really discussed it.

It had always seemed insensitive to do so.

Tonight, it felt especially so.

He put out a hand. "Gabriel, I'm sorry. I—"

"Don't be." The words were released into the night like a puff of smoke over gravel.

Impatience warred with guilt in Raphael's chest. "Why don't you just put on an entire mask and pay some strumpet to at least suck your—"

"*Go*, Rafe."

He put his hands up. Feeling both awful and relieved.

Were he making any other decision regarding his own future, he'd have insisted they abide.

Were his life expected to be any longer than a couple of nights... he'd have spent it all gladly with his brother.

But Gabriel had been right about one thing. The men of the underworld—and the officers of the law—would never believe them truly dead without a body to identify.

And that body would be his.

Gabriel had never lived a life before, and Raphael had devoured whatever he could from his own existence.

Now, he'd the opportunity to give his brother a second chance.

But first...Raphael would taste a bit of heaven before hell claimed his restless soul.

Mercy Goode would be the name on his lips. Nay, the taste lingering on his tongue when he met his death at the Midwinter Masquerade.

CHAPTER 9

It wasn't a noise that woke Mercy.

But her body.

It came alive, rousing her from restless, wicked dreams. Banishing them from memory the moment her eyes flew open.

And found Raphael Sauvageau silhouetted against her window.

The wispy white drapes stirred around him, reaching as if disturbed by a shade, or by the very potency of his atmosphere as he stood.

Watching her.

The light of the lone lamp she'd left burning painted shadows on his face, casting one single expression in both stark and savage relief.

Hunger.

She remained burrowed to the neck beneath her plush blue blankets, shivering not only with cold, but with vulnerability.

One look from him threatened to strip her bare. Expose her in ways she'd not prepared for.

He'd come for his pound of flesh.

He'd come to claim her.

Mercy cast about for something erudite and worldly to say, some greeting that a temptress, a lover, would tantalize him with.

"Erm—hullo."

Well...Shelley she was not.

"I was going to let you sleep." His voice rumbled into the air of her room with a foreign vibration, splashing against her nerves with all the threat of thunder in the great distance.

A man had never entered this room, certainly not at night.

"I wasn't sleeping." She yawned against the back of her knuckles.

"Oh?" He drifted inside, shutting the window behind him. Locking them in together.

"Do you often snore whilst awake?"

"I don't snore," she protested.

A smile toyed with the corner of his mouth, though he didn't argue the point. "Forgive me for being tardy. I had urgent business with my brother to attend, and it took longer than I hoped. An eternity, in fact. When I knew you were here. Waiting."

"You weren't tardy, as I didn't know when to expect you." She would have shrugged if she were not curled on her side, swaddled in a pile of blankets. "If I'm honest, I expected a messenger at first. I thought it would be tidier to meet somewhere other than Cresthaven, where we might be discovered."

He conducted a quick study of her room, the rich blue accents contrasting with clean white walls gentled by gilded paintings and tapestries. "Here is as safe as any place. Your parents are not in residence and your sister is in the next room fast asleep."

Should she be disconcerted or impressed that he knew that? "Might someone be roused if...if we make noise?"

His eyes flared as he approached her bed, but he made no

move to join her upon it. Instead, he crossed his arms and propped his shoulder on her tall bedpost.

If he was dangerously handsome in the sunlight, at night he was utterly fatal.

The darkness embraced him as a creature of its own. Blessed him with satirical beauty and fiendish grace.

He was a demon in a bespoke suit.

"You are so open," he noted. "So straightforward and bold. There isn't a hint of coyness or artifice about you."

A defensiveness welled in her chest. "I don't know how to be coy and I don't have time for artifice. Besides, why are women expected to be shy or tentative? Why must the fact that I am bold or inquisitive be revolutionary?"

"I was admiring, not admonishing. I find everything about you refreshing. Alluring."

"Oh... well... thank you." Mercy chewed on her lip, trying to figure out a way for them to *not* say anything further. The longer men spoke with her, the more likely she was to drive them away.

"Why don't you undress and get in?" she ventured, tucking back a section of the covers.

He made a sound of disbelief deep in his throat. "You want me to undress here? In front of you?" He uncrossed his arms and lowered them to his sides, regarding her with a wicked scrutiny. "Are you a voyeur, Mercy Goode?"

"I don't know what I am," she answered honestly. "But you can't get in bed with your shoes on. Nor can we—accomplish our aim—while you're dressed, I expect."

"Accomplish our aim?" His mouth flattened with chagrin. "Is that what we're calling it?"

The tips of her ears began to burn again, she ducked her head under the covers. "Don't make me say the word while I'm looking at you."

His chuckle was like the purr of a tiger and washed her in

prickles of awareness, pebbling the tips of her nipples. "How can you do the deed if you cannot speak the word?"

He made an excellent point, though she'd die before telling him so. "Fornicate," she spat from beneath the coverlet. "Now could you take off your clothes and join me please?"

This time his laughter was genuine and rich. She shivered with pleasure at being the one to have produced it.

Even if it was at her expense.

She peeked out at him.

Bucking away from the bedpost, he blinked at her from beneath dark, suggestive lashes. "Oftentimes, lovers undress each other."

"Oh..." She struggled into a seated position, clutching the sheets to her unbound breasts. "Well, I undressed myself so you wouldn't have to."

Raphael closed his eyes for a moment and brought his fist to his mouth where his teeth sank into a knuckle.

Suddenly uncertain, Mercy asked, "Should I not have done? Do you want me to put my nightdress back on so you can be the one—?"

"No!" He cleared his throat. Inhaled. Exhaled. And tried again. "No... I will undress and join you there. Keep the damned covers on or I'll not be able to contain myself."

"I shouldn't think you're here to contain yourself, rather the opposite," she teased.

"For a woman's first time, a man should *always* contain himself." He said this as if lecturing himself.

She didn't know enough about it to disagree with him.

The sight of Raphael's deft fingers undoing the knot at his collar did something wicked to her insides. All her boldness deserted her as he undid the buttons of his shirt and vest, shucking them down his shoulders.

Mercy's eyes widened at the sight of his tattoos. Black ink danced and swirled over his tawny skin, rising over broad, round shoulders and circled down one corded arm. They were a chaotic array of blasphemies. A religious icon inked adjacent to a naked woman in a suggestive pose. A raven perched on a skull. Other beasts interspersed with pagan symbols and words or verse in his native language.

One thing became instantly obvious. He was the art...the depictions were merely decorations.

The disks of his chest were smooth, unfettered by hair or adornment, and sloped down to the slight corrugations of his ribs and the deep etchings of abdominal muscles.

The only hair she could see, aside from his head, was a dark line disappearing into his trousers.

He undressed without hurrying, watching her watch him.

Touching her, all of her, without touching her at all.

His hands rested at the placket of buttons beneath which the barrel of a bulge nudged to be uncovered.

Mercy almost swallowed her tongue. Should she be anxious?

Was she?

Raphael paused long enough for her to take in a breath. "Have you ever seen a naked man before?"

She forced herself to drag her eyes back to his. "Of course, I have."

His dark brow arched as darker questions emerged upon a growl. "When? Who?"

"Well... there's David, of course, and various other statuary. I mean, Achilles is right there in Hyde Park for all to see."

He seemed to relax, and when he looked at her, his eyes swam with limitless tenderness.

"There was also a medical text Felicity and I found in Titus's office. We studied that *most* thoroughly. I know all there is to know about the male anatomy...medically speaking."

A soft catch in his throat could have been a laugh, but he schooled his features admirably.

"But never...in the flesh?" he clarified.

That word. *Flesh.* It made her tingle.

She didn't *want* to be untried. Couldn't bring herself to admit her inexperience in front of a man who likely knew all there was regarding what they were about to do.

And so, to retreat from answering an uncomfortable question that would leave her open to his derision, she found herself babbling.

Starting a conversation.

At a time like *this*.

And actively hating herself as she did so.

"I wanted to tell you...I exonerated you to Chief Inspector Morley. Scotland Yard is no longer after you—well—for Mathilde's murder, at least."

"Oh?" His hands remained hooked in his waistband and made no move at all.

"He seemed convinced as I that you didn't do it."

"I suppose I owe you my gratitude, Detective Goode." He smiled down at her.

"I showed him the sort of boots that left the print and... I drew diagrams." *Stop talking, you ninny,* she ordered herself. Or he'll never undo his trousers. "I was thinking perhaps tomorrow night we could both go to the Midwinter Masquerade, see who we can question regarding Mathilde."

Lord, but she was bungling this.

She should have guessed that she would.

His hands fell away from his trousers. "You're not going to the masquerade."

"I don't recall asking your permission."

"I don't recall mentioning to you where it was being held."

For once, she bit her tongue.

Mathilde had informed her where it was being held, but *he* needn't know that.

"Mercy." He went to the bed and sat on it, taking one of her hands and allowing the other to keep her modesty, such as it was. "Women like you don't belong at the Midwinter Masquerade. You'd regret it if you went."

"I'm not an idiot. You needn't threaten me."

"I'm warning you. It's not a savory affair. Surely you know that."

"Everyone knows that," she said with a droll look. "Are you going to be there?"

"If I were to attend, I might not be around long enough to make certain you're safe."

"Why not?"

For the first time, he couldn't seem to meet her gaze. "If you find anything else out about the case, do not follow up on it yourself. Go to the authorities. To Morley."

"But—"

"Please?"

She sighed...wondering if this man had ever begged another human being in his entire life.

She phrased her reply with the utmost care. "I will go to Morley with anything additional I learn about the case." *After the Midnight Masquerade*, she amended silently. She was no retiring debutante who needed her delicate sensibilities protected along with her reputation. She knew better than to be alone with any of the reprobates who would surely attend. But it was the last plan Mathilde had ever made. She owed it to the woman to seek the truth there.

He raised her hand to his lips, kissing the back of her knuckles. "I consider it a personal favor."

"You're going to leave tonight," she realized aloud. Of course, that's what he'd been referring to when he said he would not be around. They weren't proper lovers. This was no affair of the heart. He'd made certain to let her know that, even during his proposition.

Would you let me fuck you, Mercy Goode?

He said nothing about caring or cuddling.

Staying.

He would fuck her and then... What? Thank her promptly and dress?

Even sitting, he towered like some Roman god, skin like honey poured over steel.

And frozen with an aghast expression on his face.

"Not that I'm expecting you to stay," she rushed on in one breath, attempting to appear nonchalant. "I am aware that such liaisons are conducted without much ceremony or expectation, and I wanted you to be comfortable knowing that you'll get none from me. We shall...do what it is we're here to do and take what—several minutes at least? Though I've heard it can be as brief as—"

He'd covered his mouth with his hand, but he couldn't hide the shake in his shoulders or the creases of mirth at the corner of his eyes.

"You're laughing," she accused, incensed. "Is this funny to you?"

"Don't be irate with me, *mon chaton*. I scoff only at the idea of a brief encounter between us."

She knew she looked churlish, but she was trying to decide whether she believed him or not.

His eyes became pools of liquid desire. "With you I intend to take my time. I will make it last until the tolling of the bells warn of the dawn."

Her thighs quivered. "Oh. Well...I'll admit that I prefer that. It seems silly for you to come all this way if you're only going to take all of a few minutes."

"The home I share with Gabriel is not so far." He gestured to the west. "But I would have dragged myself through Siberia in winter to be here tonight."

At this, she smiled, feeling uncharacteristically shy by his unabashed appreciation of her.

"I'm glad," she murmured. "That we desire each other with equal fervor."

Oh, *now* what had she said that was funny?

"Darling," he managed over his mirth. "If you wanted me like I wanted you, we'd be on our second time by now."

"Oh. Well..." Not to be outdone in the surprise seduction, she dropped her sheets and let them pool in a white cloud at her waist.

The laughter died with a groan in his throat.

He didn't just look at her. He consumed the sight of her with an ardent fervor.

"You are stunning, Mercy," he marveled. "Exceptional. You never cease to astonish me."

"What do I do that is so surprising?" she wondered aloud.

"Most women would at least make modest, maidenly protestations. Force me to coax them to reveal themselves to me."

"Most women are trained to act like simpering fools," she scoffed. "Is that what you want from me?" She pressed the back of her hand to her forehead, enjoying that he watched how her breasts lifted with the gesture. "Oh, do allow me a moment to swoon here in virginal protestation so I might feel less guilty for succumbing to the seduction of this large and dangerous rogue who is intent upon ravishing my pure and virtuous person. I am an innocent, harmless girl caught in his dastardly web—"

His unexpected touch at her throat seized her breath there.

Her heart skipped a beat, then two, paralyzed as his strong fingers trailed to the back of her neck, pressing deeper against the tight, quivering muscles there.

"In my experience, women are generally arousing or amusing, I'm delighted that you are both."

"I amuse you?"

"You transfix me, Mercy. You captivate me."

With deft and clever circles, he found the tender knots in her back and undid them with steady, circling pressure.

He did this to relax her, and it was working.

And...not working.

The strength in his hands was both potent and restrained. She found the dichotomy endlessly erotic.

Hypnotic, even.

Her blood thickened. Slowed to a heavy languor as if warm honey drenched her veins with sweet, treacle sensuality.

Probably she should compliment him, as well. He certainly deserved it.

"You also...intrigue...*Oh*, that feels so good," she groaned and closed her eyes in bliss as he found a tender spot and curled his relentless fingers into it.

"Just you wait, *mon chaton*," he promised against her ear. "Do not be too easily satisfied. I like a challenge."

She couldn't summon the words with which to reply. Not only because of what his diabolical fingers did to her, or the way his words made her heart quiver instead of beat.

But because a wave of aching emotion tumbled over her, swamping her with unidentifiable yearning. Not just for the carnal sensations his touch evoked, but for this affection between them.

This physical touch that was not demanding nor expectant.

Unhurried. Deliberate. Both intimate and innocuous all at once.

She sighed as he released her tresses from their pins, lock by spiraling lock, testing the weight and coil of the curl as if he'd never before threaded fingers through a woman's hair.

Or never would again.

After a while, he said, "Though you jested before, there is truth in what you said. One you must consider carefully. I am a large and dangerous man... My web is one of deceit and blood."

"I knew that already. I'm not blind."

"No." He leaned forward, brushing the ghost of a kiss against each of her eyelids. "You have excellent, beautiful eyes. You see what most do not."

"Your flattery will get you nowhere, you cad." She reached out, shocked when her hand encountered the warm flesh of his chest.

Shocked that she kept it there, searching for the beat of a heart she could never claim.

"I'm already where I want to be." The earnestness of his expression unstitched her as he reached his own palm out, and pressed it to where her own heart hurled itself against the cage of her chest.

"What do you feel when I touch you?" His voice washed her in a pleasant glow, the question putting her at ease. "When you touch me?"

"Butterflies," she answered honestly, placing her other hand over where wings made a riot in her belly.

He tilted his head, his hand moving lower, not to her breast quite yet, but almost. "Butterflies? Don't they erupt when you are afraid?"

"I'm not afraid," she lied.

"What are you?"

"Excited."

"Excitement is often born of fear."

But was fear also this delicious? She wondered.

Her silence seemed to consternate him. "Is that why you relented to my wicked proposition? Am I your one chance to dance with danger?" His hand stilled as he gazed at her. "Will you regret saying yes to me when this is over?"

"Certainly not." Her eyes flew open and she drew back, an offended frown tugging at the corners of her lips. "I said yes because you're the one man who makes me feel more alive by just walking into a room. I said yes because I was categorically certain I'd regret it if I refused this opportunity for pleasure."

His eyes gleamed like those of a night-hunting predator beneath a moonless sky.

She'd the sense she'd just disconcerted him.

Oh dear, had she been too honest again?

This time, when his fingers dug into the back of her neck, it was to drag her forward and slant his lips over hers.

She melted into him like wax beneath a flame, surrendering and puddling in the fire he ignited.

Dragging his tongue against hers, he licked and tasted, his breath coming in rasping pants. Feral, guttural noises vibrated across her lips, into her mouth, and down to the very core of her.

His hands wandered, the skin rough and the movements gentle.

He seemed to understand her impatience. To craft it, mirror it, and then ignore it, drawing out some delicious distraction with a swirl of his tongue or a barely-there nip of his teeth.

She could kiss him forever, but it wasn't enough. She desired him closer. Over her, beneath her. Beside her.

Inside her.

He wanted her, too, dammit, so why didn't he just—?

As if he'd heard her thoughts, he was suddenly above her. Settling his weight between her parted thighs, he kept the sheet and his trousers between them.

His lean hips kicked forward, introducing her to the hard length of his arousal as he fed the fire of their kiss until it threatened to scorch her.

Mercy couldn't tell if he'd uttered the ragged moan or she had.

Dangerous thoughts filtered through her consciousness as he caressed her in places she hadn't expected. He drew knuckles across her jaw, and she imagined devotion in his touch. He feathered caresses across her clavicles and ghosted his palms down bare shoulders.

She might have found a pledge whispered on the pants of his breath.

Impossible.

Even in the darkness, she could sense the pace of his heart, hammering with a tempo as furious and drastic as her own.

He dragged his lips from hers after a moment, making a moist trail with his mouth up the line of her jaw.

It wasn't his lust that amazed her, it was his tenderness. His lips quested across her hairline, temple, and down the nape of her neck. He took in deep drags of breath, as if he could lock the scent of her inside of him.

"Mine." His head dipped low enough, the word caressed her throat, chased by lips that stopped to sample the tender skin and tease the sensitive nerves there.

Her entire being trembled in expectant anticipation of his touch, of the shivery whisper of his warm breath a moment before his lips followed.

"You are an incomparable beauty." He said this like an accusation, before his mouth found her breast and began an erotic assault upon it that left her utterly defenseless. He deprived her of air, of thought, of any sort of reason as he held her immobile beneath him. Some of his tenderness seemed to abandon him now, as he licked and nipped at her with intensifying aggression.

Her body bloomed for it. She knew what making love entailed. The mechanics of the act, at least. But she'd been truly unprepared for this instinctive urgency.

This assault of sensation.

How did anyone bear it?

She barely noticed his shift in weight until the slide of the sheet became a torturous shiver down her body as he drew it away from her.

He stretched on his side next to her, freeing his hand to explore the skin he'd uncovered with carnal strokes.

When he turned to look at what he'd exposed to the lamp-light, Mercy seized each side of his jaw with both hands and imprisoned his mouth to hers.

She'd thought she was ready to be naked.

But not to be revealed.

He didn't protest as she plunged her tongue into his mouth, tasting his need, sweeping in the rhythm of her growing desire.

A clever finger traced inside her thigh, petted through soft intimate hair, dashing erotic sparkles of sensation over her entire body.

Her breath froze as he delved into bare, wet flesh. Her pulse didn't just run, it fled, escaping her as he slid unhurried explorations through sensitized ruffles of feminine skin.

He broke the seal of their lips, moaning something in French she was too mindless to translate.

She melted—liquified—beneath his expert touch. She marveled at the slippery warmth of her own body's response to him. Wondered if she should be ashamed. Or embarrassed.

Too entranced to bother with either.

She felt drugged with some throbbing intoxicant. It dragged her into a miasma of pleasure and threatened to drown her beneath turbulent, ocean-deep waves of sensation.

Languid explorations tightened to circles around the place where a shimmer of heat threatened to become a firestorm. His increasingly urgent breaths crashed against her mouth as he lingered upon the threat of a kiss, but kept his mouth enticingly elusive.

She clutched at him, with her fingers and with—Oh, God— the spasming intimate muscles of her sex as he drew a teasing circle around the entrance to her body.

A gasp closed her throat as he nudged gently there, and she stilled, not realizing until this very moment just how desperately she desired him inside of her.

"I want to taste you," he growled. "Would you let me?"

"Yes," she said impatiently, tugging at his shoulders to bring their lips back together. "Yes, of course. *Please.*"

His chuckle was demonic. "I like it when you beg."

"I was *not* beggi—where are you going?"

He prowled down her body, wide shoulders rolling like a great cat as he did so. His nose and lips stopped to sample at her scent, and then nibble at soft and tender parts of her.

Her clavicles.

The undersides of her breasts.

The gently rounded plane of her belly.

"You're clever, Inspector Goode, I'm sure you have some clue as to where I'm headed."

The very thought made her nearly apoplectic, but she dug her fingers into the sheets so as not to stop him out of sheer humiliation.

"I thought you meant to kiss me," she clarified.

His laugh would have made the devil shudder. "Oh, but I *do*. I mean to kiss you thoroughly."

"But...but..." *There?* She squeezed her thighs shut as his lips trailed the short downy distance from her belly button to the triangle of dark gold hair below.

"Everywhere." His hands nudged her wobbly legs open, and she nearly gave in to the instinct to protest.

She'd heard of the French being more wicked than the average lover, but this was beyond the pale. Wasn't it? Or at least unhygienic...

Did he really mean to—?

Crisp air feathered across the wet heat between her parted legs. His fingers, firm and competent, pinned her thighs all the way open, utterly exposing her to him.

"Look at you," he whispered, his words landing *there*. Against her most intimate parts. "Magnificent. I should have expected..."

Expected what? She wanted to ask.

Would have asked.

Had he not done exactly what he promised, and kissed her.

The shock of his hot wet mouth against her warm wet sex... She never could have imagined the contrast of it. The pure illicit pleasure it evoked.

She felt those lips everywhere.

Or perhaps her entire world simply faded to only contain what his mouth currently did to her.

All she knew was the heat of his breath.

The slick velvet of his tongue.

The gentle coaxing of his lips.

Mercy looked down the topography of her body as if such an act needed a witness.

Their eyes locked, and she thought of the serpent again— especially as his tongue flicked and slithered in gentle pulses over her most sensitive flesh.

The light burnished him in stark relief, his shoulders so corded and wide against the thin white skin of her limbs. His arms, so densely muscled, held her a willing hostage as he consumed her like a condemned man might his final meal.

The peaks of her breasts were drawn into tight, aching beads, and without thought, she cupped one. Hoping to warm it, to soothe some strange throbbing there.

The groan he emitted vibrated through her loins and drew a surge of bliss into a threatening crest. His lips never left her sex, sealed to her with a rhythmic suction that created subtle, shadowed hollows in his cheeks.

It was the bliss on his features that transfixed her. The rhythmic undulations of his hips against the counterpane where he sprawled. The deep sounds of pleasure she felt in her very bones.

He enjoyed this.

A storm built below his mouth. Swirling in the movements of his tongue.

The thunder was no longer in the distance.

No, it was inside of her. Rolling and pulsing and deeply erotic.

Tears stung her lids. She was suddenly unprepared for something so profound. So powerful it threatened to tear her away from herself.

So inevitable, she knew she could not fight it.

That it would not stop.

"Raphael?" She whimpered his name for the first time.

His gaze found hers, his pupils so dilated his eyes looked demon black.

"What is—? I don't—I'm—I'm—" Through a sort of feverish delirium, she couldn't bring herself to finish the sentences she desperately needed him to hear.

What is going to happen?

I don't know what to do.

I'm lost.

He didn't stop. He didn't hesitate, slow, or even pause.

But his eyes contained a sincere sort of understanding, and he released her thigh to slide his hand—palm up—across the sheet at her side.

She grasped at his offer of salvation the very instant she was pitched over the cliff.

And she'd never been more grateful for anything as she was for the curl of his strong fingers around hers.

Mercy dangled between solid ground and air for an intense and breathless eternity before plummeting into a writhing, delirious, free fall of ecstasy.

The strokes of his tongue became lashes of lightning-hot pleasure bolting through her blood, suffusing her with electric charges that ebbed for a moment of answering thunder. She needn't have worried about making noise, as she couldn't produce a single sound as the storm tore the breath from her lungs.

She writhed and thrashed with uninhibited euphoria. One moment grinding into it, and the next retreating from it.

As if by magic, Raphael seemed to realize when it became too much, when the pleasure threatened to shatter her on the rocks below.

The strokes gentled then, becoming cajoling and reverent, like a prayer or some such profane thing. He drew out the last spasms from her core with sinuous skill until she utterly collapsed.

Even though he'd destroyed her with pleasure, Raphael still picked over the wreckage of her body with thorough, searching little nips and licks. Reanimating her boneless, corpse-like torpor with little twitches and trembles of aftershocks.

When she made a helpless, plaintive noise, he finally relented, pulling away with a wet and depraved sound.

Releasing her hand, he rolled away and stood, wiping the slick leavings of her from his lips with the back of his hand as he kicked off his shoes.

She wanted to clutch at him, to call him back, and felt so pathetic for the impulse, she forced herself to quell it immediately.

The pleasure had affected her, of course it had, but what she'd not expected was how emotionally penetrating the experience would be. How vulnerable and ridiculous it would leave her.

She had to tread carefully here. This man took lovers, he did not commit to them. He was dangerous and deviant and dreadfully unpredictable.

He'd leave her.

He'd take her, then he'd leave her.

Remember that, she told herself, even as she devoured the sight of him looming above her bed.

Silent as a reaper, and no less lethal.

His nostrils flared and his eyes gleamed. Breaths sawed in and out of him like the bellows of a furnace.

She was about to learn what it was to lie with a man.

Not to make love. He'd been very careful never to use those words.

To fuck.

That's what they were doing here.

He would teach her the delicate indignities of the carnal act. She would know why men used the words they did to describe the deed. Thrusting. Riding. Pounding. Claiming.

She would know the softness and the violence of it.

Wordlessly, his gaze seared down at her as his hands fell to the placket of his trousers, deftly undoing them and the garment beneath before letting it all fall from his lean hips.

Mercy stared at his naked form in breathless awe.

He was something more than gorgeous. A chiseled effigy of immaculate masculinity. Too perfect. Too large and vital for one woman.

He'd warned her.

True to form, she'd refused to listen.

And, as usual, she would have to reap the consequences.

One of which might be her very first broken heart.

CHAPTER 10

R aphael never sampled the substances his father—and now he—sold. Because he'd seen time and again what physical attachment did to a person.

How ruinous it became.

But as Mercy rose from the cobalt velvet swirls of her bed covers, like Calypso from the sea, he knew he was lost.

She might have been stripped to the skin, but she'd left him exposed and raw, down to the very essence of what made him a mortal.

A man.

Her flavor was ambrosia.

Her body an altar to the bacchanalian gods.

Her skin pale and soft or—in some places—peach and succulent.

That flesh called for him to reach for her now, but something in her eyes caused him to hesitate. A new expression she wore, both marvel and melancholy.

Withstanding her perusal was an exquisite torture.

But he'd been tortured before.

He'd survive it.

Better that she become used to the sight of him first, to the idea of his body, before he fell upon her like the lustful beast tearing through his veins.

Though she seemed uncertain, she was the one to rise to her knees and reach out.

To close the gap between them.

Her questing hands branded fingertip-sized trails of fire over his shoulders, down his pectorals and across the ticklish spokes of his ribs.

He didn't dare move. Her innocent exploration of him was a most elegant agony, one he wasn't certain he ever wanted to escape.

She didn't take much time, impatient minx that she was. Didn't linger over his tattoos or his muscles, or the parts of him that were not foreign to her.

They both had arms, nipples, a stomach.

There was certainly a difference in shape between them, but not one that seemed to unduly concern her.

She looked him right in the eyes as slim, cool fingers wrapped around the girth of his throbbing sex, forcing a tight gasp from his constricting throat.

Heat collected behind his spine and pulled the pendulous weight beneath his cock tight into his body with the gathering spasms of release.

Groaning, he seized her hand.

"What's wrong?" she asked, eyes wide with concern. "Did I hurt you?"

He brought her knuckles to his mouth and kissed each precious one. "Quite the opposite. Your touch threatens to end this moment too quickly."

"I don't mind," she cajoled.

"*I* do." Affronted, he pulled her close for a searching kiss.

Didn't she understand that he needed this night to last forever?

Not only because he didn't have many nights left, but because even though he was a man who always claimed what he went after, he rarely went after what he truly wanted.

Somehow, this young, untried woman seemed to know what it was that he *needed*. Intrinsically answering questions he hadn't yet thought to ask.

Her fingers slid into his hair, both soothing him and setting the nerves there alight with sensation. He'd needed her touch, craved it, and yet a sense of guilt kept him from seeking it.

Tonight was his to give. To teach. To soothe and comfort. A woman's first time took patience and skill and reserve that only a knave would abandon.

His ferocious and terrible instinct would have him pin her to the bed while he remained standing so he could press her knees by her head and watch himself fuck and fuck and *fuck* her until they collapsed with thirst and exhaustion.

He wanted to feed her from his hand and bathe her so he could bend her over and do it again. He wanted her to tie him up and ride his mouth. His cock.

He wanted her in every depraved way a man could take a woman.

And the simple ones too...

Mercy Goode was inherently a carnal woman, given to impish mischief and endless curiosity. She wouldn't be content with basic, gentle lovemaking for long.

She'd want more.

And he'd be gone before long.

Holy Christ, she'd find someone else.

Possessive instinct surged, and suddenly she was in the circle of his arms, her lithe body clenched against his with such strength, he lifted her knees from the bed.

A turbulent rage rose beneath his lust, churning opaque

emotions from where he'd forced them to lie dormant like the bed of sludge beneath a lake of ice.

Why now?

When decisions had been made, and his fate sealed. When he'd vowed to atone for all the wrong he'd never wanted to do...

The right woman barged into his life and turned his entire world upside down.

Made him question everything he thought he knew about himself.

Made him yearn for things that were patently impossible.

Made his blood froth and churn with torrents of need, and his heart trip and kick with boyish, frivolous emotions.

Like hope, for example.

Or whatever this odd amalgamation of impossible softness and desperate intensity could be called.

Was there a word for it?

For yearning more insatiable than lust? Hunger more excruciating than deprivation?

Pain more insidious than the shattering of bone?

The three languages he spoke fluently offered up nothing. Though, the feel of the naked woman molded to him might have addled his brain somewhat.

Her response to the imprisonment of his arms was unfettered and open and fearless, just like her.

Pressing herself to him, she scored his scalp with her nails, rolled her body in sinuous undulations, as if the entire ravenous intensification of their encounter had been *her* bloody idea.

In fact, she tugged at him with surprising strength for such a delicate creature, pulling him back to the bed and nearly climbing him like a falling tree as he lay her back on the counterpane.

Her thighs fell open beneath his weight, her long legs

locking around his waist.

The delicate heat of her sex singed him with need.

"I'm ready," she sighed, her voice still husky from her climax and her lashes fanning long shadows against her flushed cheek.

He bloody wasn't.

Or—rather—he *was*. Too ready. Too hungry. He wanted to shove into her like a brute. To rut like a stag and submit her like a stallion. If only he could crawl inside of her, somehow, to join with her in a way that would leave a part of him locked within her.

Christ, was this why people procreated?

Something about that thought sobered him a little. Enough to let him pull back and gaze down into her lovely face.

Her hair was a riot of precious metals in the lamplight. The strands at her nape a deep bronze, and those at her temple light as mercury. The tresses fanned out around her creamy shoulders in waves of corn silk and spun gold.

Eyes shining like brilliant sapphires, she flicked her little pink tongue across lips red and swollen from the abrasion of his kisses, as if savoring the taste of him there.

Or the flavor of her own desire.

The gesture nearly undid him.

Her pert nose flared with heavy gasps that fell against his face in sweet-scented puffs. Their shared breaths felt more intimate than the most immoral acts he'd ever committed.

Finally, he settled his hips into the cradle of hers, grunting as the crown of his cock slid against the wet cove of her body.

Her gaze showed no uncertainty and it lanced him all the way through. He'd done nothing in his entire benighted life to deserve such trust.

And yet. There it was.

"I'm sorry if I hurt you," he whispered, kissing her with a conciliatory tug of his lips.

"I forgive you," she whispered, squirming her hips in gasp-inducing impatience. "But only if you hurry."

If only all demands were so easy to satisfy.

If only all hurts were so easily forgiven.

Setting his jaw, Raphael nudged forward.

Initially her body gave, welcoming the plump crown of him with a slick kiss. When he encountered hindrance, he cursed viciously, stalling his progression.

"I'm sorry," she gasped, her features tight with concentration.

"No, *mon chaton*." He dropped kisses onto her cheekbones, her eyelids, the wisps of curls at her temples. "No. *I* am sorry. Tell me to stop." It would be a feat even Hercules might have failed, but he'd do it.

"You're trembling," she remarked, smoothing her palms over his shoulders shaking with the burden of his restraint.

"I—I can't bring myself to hurt you."

"I'm not in pain. Just...pressure." She wriggled against him again, testing the barrier.

Jesus. Fuck.

He couldn't do this. Not with her. Not *to* her.

When he made to withdraw, she gripped at him with sharp claws, her nails creating delicious little crescents of pain on his back.

"Do it," she commanded, her features becoming a mask of determination before she buried her face against his neck. "Do it. Now."

He could do nothing but obey.

With a surge of his hips, he impaled her.

Her teeth sank into the meat of his shoulder and she gave a whimper that gutted him.

Gathering her close, he curled around her as they each shuddered and surrendered to the feel of him seated inside to the hilt.

KERRIGAN BYRNE

Their breaths synchronized, as the tight clutch of her molded around him. Eventually the pulsing muscles milked at his cock, seeming to pull him even deeper, like a fist of wet silk.

He could come like this. Deep inside of her. Without moving anything.

The Fauve that he was desired just that. He could simply bathe her womb in his seed, thinking it could take root.

How could it not when he was so deliciously deep?

Never. An insidious inner voice reminded him. You promised to *never.*

A hasty breath created a movement where they were joined. And the noise she made stirred him.

A sigh of curious delight.

Encouraged, he rolled his hips slightly and she responded each time with tiny sounds in her throat. Little mewls, like that a kitten would make.

His kitten.

Mon chaton.

Then she said the most dangerous words one could utter to a man like him.

"More. I want more."

It was all he needed.

He gave it to her, in long, deliberate—if careful—thrusts. He fed her his length once. And again. And again. Wedging himself impossibly deeper each time.

Her arms clutched at him, her lush mouth opening in a silent quest for a kiss, but he denied her.

He had to watch, to see the play of emotion run across her face. To observe what he wrought inside of her. The astonishment and the acceptance. The heat and the hunger. The shuddering surrender.

Raphael knew the moment she'd become a prisoner to her pleasure. It pulled her away from him. Unfocused her eyes and brought her entire concentration inward. He knew what his languorous strokes built, that the angle of their hips created friction not only inside but against the engorged knot of sensation that was the button to every woman's desire.

Sweat bloomed between them, creating a damp, erotic slide of flesh against flesh. It was as if they had fused into one, that he'd become buried so deep inside her body, that he might have reason to hope to lodge himself in her heart, as well.

Their limbs tangled in untidy knots, mirroring his emotions.

Perhaps if he entwined them so thoroughly, there would be no unraveling them.

This.

This was the danger of addiction.

When something took you away from yourself. When it became as essential as air or water. Oblivion merged into sensation and colors fused into high-relief and time lost all meaning. Perhaps the future was a memory. Or the past was a lie.

Or there was only this.

This moment. This joy. This act. This emotion.

This woman.

He'd not expected her to come again. Not her first time.

But when her spine arched and her sex spasmed around him in delicious contractions, something like panic surged as his own climax gathered through his veins.

It sped toward him, an avalanche bent on annihilation. He already knew how powerful it would be and still couldn't leap out of the way.

It would ruin him. Shatter him.

He barely pulled out in time.

Burying a roar in the velvet of her quilt, he let his cock slide between their bodies as his release ripped him apart. It was a cataclysm of pleasure, something so mind-altering he knew the moment defined him.

Because there was the resolute man he'd been before he tasted the heaven that was the embrace of Mercy Goode.

And the tragedy of everything that was about to happen next.

CHAPTER 11

$\mathcal{M}$ercy thought that relinquishing her virginity would make her feel older, somehow. More experienced and womanly. Perhaps even wise, now that she'd been initiated into the society of secret smiles shared by Nora and Pru, her two married sisters.

Instead, she felt very young and vulnerable as she complacently allowed Raphael to wipe away the slick leavings of their joining from her belly and between her thighs.

She stared at the shoes he'd discarded in haste. The ones he'd wear to leave her.

Would he put them on? Was it time for him to go now?

Now that she was cold and oddly small and lonely in her massive bed.

Mercy took a moment to admire the masculine shape of his backside as he turned away from her and ministered to his own hygiene.

She wished she were a sculptor. A painter. Any sort of artist that could capture him in a rendering.

For memories had a tendency to fade, and she wanted to appreciate his beauty every day.

He returned to her, and her heart lifted as he slid into the bed and gathered her against him. Settling on his back, he arranged her boneless limbs over his muscled form like a marionette before spreading her curls across his chest so he could stroke her hair with lazy fingers.

She nuzzled into him as he yawned with such ferocity his jaw cracked and his limbs shuddered with it.

As elegant and sinister as he was with his fine suits and caustic conversation, Mercy discovered she rather liked him like this.

Silky hair mussed by her fingers in the throes of pleasure, hazel eyes at half-mast and a drowsy curve softening his hard mouth. Even his jaw had relaxed, the cords beneath his ears and next to his temple released.

The damp chill of the late-winter night lurked just outside of where their cobalt coverlet and gold lamp ensconced them in a decadence of warmth and flesh and velvet.

Though he'd pulled the blanket to their waists, she could still consider their differences with idle curiosity. Decide what she liked and what she had to accustom herself to...

If that were an option.

The steely muscle beneath his marble-smooth skin mesmerized her as she let her fingers wander the peaks and valleys of his geography. She appreciated all that he was, the dusky hue to his skin. The warm fragrance of him, like cotton and salt.

Crisp hair on his leg tickled the inside of her thigh, and she drew her appendage over the abrading stuff, letting it scratch away the irksome itch.

His breath evened. Moving from the chest beneath her cheek down to his stomach. The hammer of his heart slowed to a thump, and he was silent for so long she thought he might have fallen asleep.

She lifted her head to check and found him staring—

unblinking—into the middle distance as his fingers toyed with her hair.

"Is something troubling you?" she asked, pretending not to be anxious as she perched her head on her palm.

He was not quick to reply. "I don't know if it's the darkness of the hour or of the situation, but I can only think it is a cruelty of fate that I found you."

"Well...there's a thing to say." A frown tugged at her mouth, at her heart, and she pushed back from him, offended in the extreme. "When I was feeling just the opposite. Thinking how fortunate I was to have spent such a time with you. To have enjoyed myself so thoroughly. Did I..um... Have I misunderstood your seemingly enthusiastic responses?"

"No, no, sweet Mercy, that is not what I meant." He cupped her chin, cradling it as if it were made of spun glass. "It is cruel to have a night like this, knowing I cannot have another. It tinged this incomparable pleasure with exquisite pain."

"We *could* do it again." She brightened, his words a balm for her bruised heart, even as she lamented the idea of losing him. "My parents have extended their stay on the continent another month. And even after they arrive home, I could finagle a way to occasionally meet you at the Savoy or—"

He shook his head, his eyes abysmal wells of bleak despair. "*Mon coeur*, you mustn't care for me. You mustn't become attached."

Mon coeur. My heart. How could he call her something like that and then insist there was nothing further between them?

Was the endearment just a sweet and flippant nothing to him?

She cocked her head. "Do you care for nothing? For no one?"

He drew in a long breath through his nose. "It has been my secret all these years. I have gained so much because I didn't care if I lost it. I risk everything when I take a gamble, and I have not lost for so long...until now."

"What do you mean?"

He speared her with a gaze so intense she felt as if it punctured her all the way through. "I told you I only love one person on this earth, and I referred to Gabriel, but...I am in danger of falling for you, Mercy Goode."

She blinked at the immediacy of his confession. He hadn't said love, though the word lingered on the periphery of their conversation. "I've heard it said that men in bed are often men in love. You do not know me enough to fall—"

He coiled at the waist, levering to a sitting position so as to bracket her cheeks with his hands, capturing her face in a gentle prison so he might bore the truth of his words into her. "I want you to know that I have been unable to stop thinking about you since the moment we met. That is something—"

"Yes," she clipped. "That is something I've heard before. Is it not easier to imagine that you are infatuated with my youth and beauty than with me?"

"I cannot contest that you are the loveliest creature, but your sister is equally handsome and stirs me not at all. It is not only this chemistry between us that draws me to you. It is everything. Your entire bold, adventurous, domineering, warrior's spirit. It is the life that spills from you, that radiates like a star in the middle of your own solar system. You don't just tempt me, you *fascinate* me—obsess me—and no one has managed to do that in a very long time."

"Then..." She cast her gaze down and schooled the longing from her voice. "Why not continue this while we are inclined to do so?"

"Because the moment I care for something...someone...it gives them power over me."

"Your enemies?"

"Yes, but I was referring to...my men."

At that, she sat up straighter, folding her legs beneath the sheets to face him fully. "I don't understand."

His face softened and his gaze touched every part of her face, as if committing it to memory. "That is because you are not part of this brutal world in which I exist, and I would not have it touch you. I will—die first."

Mercy's brows crimped as she did her utmost to puzzle him out. One thing missing from the mysteries of Eddard Sharpe was this vagary of fate. The villains were dastardly characters motivated by hatred, greed, or any number of ugly impulses belonging to man.

Rarely—never—were they noble or tender with predispositions toward generosity and kindness.

This man, this wicked, rakish criminal was possessed of a conscience. A code.

And yet...

"Why did you become a Fauve?" she asked, knowing she tread on dangerous ground. "Furthermore, why lead them if they would so easily turn on you? What sort of life is that?"

"It's the life Gabriel and I inherited," he answered simply, as if he'd resigned himself to such a disappointment long ago.

"Inherited?" she echoed.

"From *le Bourreau*." He muttered the name as if it tasted of ashes in his mouth. "The Executioner."

He slumped against her headboard, the covers sliding around his lean waist. Broad shoulders rolled forward a little as if Atlas himself could not have contained such a burden. His eyes unfocused slightly, as he looked into the past.

"HE WAS AN ENGLISHMAN WHO MARRIED A MONÉGASQUE GIRL— my mother—leveraged by the debts her father owed him," he explained in a voice devoid of emotion. "He kept her—us—in a villa in Monaco where he ruled the underworld there. Gaming establishments, brothels, and smuggling ships..." His fists curled in her bedclothes as his eyes glittered with a hatred so cold and absolute, she shivered with it.

"Fighting rings."

Mercy covered his taut fist with her hand, and it unclenched beneath the pressure until he turned it to thread his fingers with hers.

"Your father, he...died?" she asked gently.

His jaw worked to the side in a show of gall. "My mother went first, suffered terribly from the syphilis he gave her, and he lingered—too long—disintegrating until parts of his body rotted away, to match the soul beneath."

Mercy hadn't been faced with such animosity before, not really. Her relationship with her father was either cold or contentious, but all they felt for each other was a rather mild form of duty and disappointment.

Raphael hated his father with a rage-induced loathing she'd not known him capable of.

It frightened her.

"Did he...was he...awful to you?" she queried.

His expression was carefully impassive. "He was horrible to everyone. I was no exception."

"You should have been." Mercy ventured closer to him, wanting to provide him comfort but feeling ill-equipped to do so. "You were his son."

"His second son."

"Did you resent that?"

"Never," he answered darkly. "I was glad to be a small, rather undeveloped boy even after fourteen or so. I was lucky that he ignored me. That he thought me too pathetic to much notice."

"Why would you be glad of that?" she asked, thinking she already knew she didn't want the answer.

"Gabriel was always so extraordinarily big and strong and

as savage as my father had crafted him to be. He was heir apparent to the Lord of Louts. And the prince to those who called themselves the Fauves. And still, when my father needed money, he threw Gabriel to the pits."

"Is...that why he wears a mask?"

Raphael nodded, swallowing once. Twice.

"My brother always protected me from my father and now, you understand, it is my job to protect him."

"I understand," she murmured. And she did. It never mattered what kind of man he'd wanted to be. Because he was who his father made him. "So, like the monarchy, when the king of the Fauves dies, his sons inherit?"

"Only if they are worthy. If they can command the respect of the men."

"What if you didn't want to be a part of it anymore? What if you gave the mantle over to another?"

He dragged a finger over her cheek, his gaze gentle and resigned. "Would that I could, *mon chaton*, but men in our world can only escape by dying. There are too many secrets between us, too much at stake. These men are often criminals because they have no one to trust, nowhere to turn for protection from poverty and despair. That sort of desperation turns a man into a beast. Men like my father turn those beasts into soldiers. Gives them a code. A family to die for. To kill for. A way to advance. And, like in the wilds, the pack will turn upon you if you show weakness. If they can no longer rely upon you to provide."

To be held captive by power, she could barely imagine it. "So...if you were not born into this life, you would not have chosen it?"

"Never."

"What would you have done instead?"

"I would have been a ship's captain," he answered without thought.

"Oh?"

He glanced at her astonished expression with a wry twist of his lips. "It's the only part of my position I truly enjoy. When we transport overseas, I've taken to the mechanics and running of the ship itself...not that it matters now."

"Of course, it matters." She squeezed his hand. "It's significant to me."

He snorted. "Why? Because you can now imagine a different reality in which I am a good man?"

"You laugh, but I'm not entirely convinced you're a bad one."

A rueful sound escaped him as he drew a knuckle down the curve of her shoulder, following it all the way to her elbow. "Believe me, I am."

"Well, ironically enough, I'm not a good girl, either."

That cleared some of the ice from his gaze. "Yes, you are."

"Shows what you know!" she said. "I'm forever disappointing everyone. Making mischief, saying the wrong things, wanting what I ought not to...fighting to change the world."

"Please don't ever stop," he whispered, his fingers digging into her waist to nudge her closer. "Instead, change the world to suit you, Mercy Goode; if anyone could, it'd be you." He lowered his head to nudge at her nose with his own. "I—I only wish I could be here to see it."

She blinked. "Tell me where you are going."

"Nowhere." He tossed her a charming, brilliant smile and seized her, rolling them over until she was straddling his torso with her hands braced over his glorious chest. "At least not tonight."

CHAPTER 12

*R*aphael just paid an enormous fortune for a lie.

But no world existed where Gabriel would allow for his real plans to come to fruition, so he kept up pretenses for his brother's sake.

The man in question studied his identification papers with precise and methodical sweeps of his eyes, as if committing even the fine print to memory.

"When I wake, I'll be Gareth Severand." Gabriel tested the words in his graveled voice and winced as if they tasted strange in his mouth.

Dr. Titus Conleith leaned a hip against his desk where they'd gathered in his hospital office. "I was told by Frank Walters—who sends his regards along with your new identities —that keeping names somewhat similar in cadence and lettering helps one assimilate and identify easier."

While Gabriel folded his limbs into one of the chairs across from the desk, Raphael turned to pacing. The room was as warm and masculine as its master. The overstuffed furniture and landscape canvasses seemed incongruous with the sterile environs of the rest of the hospital.

This was where Conleith took people to tell them that they or their loved ones were going to die, Raphael suspected.

And in a way, that's exactly what he was telling them now.

Gabriel and Raphael Sauvageau would be essentially deceased after tonight.

Once Gabriel went under the knife, Raphael was supposed to set a plan in motion to implode the Fauves from the inside.

"You've barely glanced at your papers, Rafe," Gabriel prompted, lifting his chin to peek over at his identification.

Raphael screwed on a sardonic smile. "That's Remy Severand to you."

Titus studied them from beneath his somber brow, his sharp bronze eyes always seeming to conduct an examination, even when one wasn't his patient. "Have you decided where you're going to land when this is all said and done?" he asked. "Not Monaco, surely."

"Too much past there to have a future." Gabriel shook his head adamantly, adjusting his mask as if eager to be rid of the thing. "Perhaps someday we'll return to Normandy or France, but I think for the time being, we'll lose ourselves in the West."

Raphael nodded in agreement.

Titus bucked his hip away from his desk and reached for the white coat draped over his elegant chair. "I think it's marvelous you get a fresh start away from your tainted legacy. I'm a firm believer in second chances." He punched his arms into the coat and reached the door in a few long-legged strides. "I'm going to go make certain the surgical theater is prepared. I'll leave you two to say your goodbyes before the procedure. It'll be...lengthy."

Say your goodbyes. The doctor had no idea how final that sounded.

Because it was.

Raphael didn't want to say goodbye. He hated them.

It was why—even though every fiber that stitched his body

together had felt adhered to the heaven that was Mercy Goode's bed—he'd peeled himself away to vanish before dawn illuminated her cherubic face.

Because he might have given in to the insatiable urge to have her once more.

Or the impossible desire to stay.

As Gabriel took another moment to study the papers in his hands, Raphael studied him.

He'd a patchwork body, that was for certain. His ruined face wasn't the only place he carried scars. His arms and chest had become a canvas of tattoos decorating a physique that was a monument to power.

And to violence.

But nothing felled his brother.

Nothing.

That wasn't about to change. Gabriel had survived so many things that would have crushed most other men.

He'd likewise survive Raphael's loss. He would keep his word and go to America to spread Mathilde's ashes.

Then, he'd live the life they both craved.

The one Gabriel deserved.

"I'd like a final smoke before I go under the knife." Gabriel stood, reaching into his jacket pocket.

It occurred to Raphael, not for the first time, that his brother looked almost amusingly incongruous in such finery. His neck didn't like a collar and his jaw always wanted shaving, even after a razor had been taken to it. Though his mask was meticulously crafted, it made for a sinister, unsightly spectacle.

Better that than the terror beneath.

Raphael followed his brother outside, watching Gabriel's ritual of pulling the hood low against any kind of weather for the last time. When he woke—when he healed—he'd have a face he could show to the world.

Raphael wished he'd be able to see it.

Gabriel rested his shoulders against the grey stone of the hospital, bending his knee to prop the sole of his boot on the wall. A passerby might imagine that the towering man held up the building, rather than the other way around.

This was harder than Raphael had expected. He wanted to stay. He wanted to run. He wanted for the thousandth time...a life that hadn't been fucked before he was even born. "Do you want me to stay until you're asleep?" He asked the question with a demonstrative fondness he wasn't prone to.

If Gabriel noticed, he didn't say. "Nah. You've work to do." He poked the tamper into the bowl of his pipe. The instrument looked comically tiny in his hands, something like a child's toy. "Besides, that was always my responsibility."

Their gazes locked.

Yes, Gabriel had always stood watch over him. Had taken the wrath of their father upon his gigantic shoulders. When they were boys, Raphael's nightmares would plague him, and Gabriel would sit up with him, both a sentinel against and savior from the nightmares in the dark.

The day he'd become so disfigured, it had been Raphael's turn in the pits. He'd been so young and scrawny.

Terrified.

Gabriel had shoved him in a locker and taken his place in the ring.

This was why Raphael would die for him...

"Have you ever thought what we'll do...after this?" Gabriel's pensive question interrupted his reverie.

Raphael blinked against the drizzle and a little confusion. "Do?"

Gabriel made an impatient gesture. "You know, in America, or wherever we settle. What will we *do* with ourselves?" He struck a match against the rough edge of the stone and cupped his hand over the flame as he touched it to the fragrant tobacco in his pipe.

"Live like kings, that's what you'll do. There's fortune enough that your children's children's children won't have to worry. You'll do whatever you bloody well please."

Gabriel sank deeper into his hood as Honoria Goode dashed by, one arm shielding her lovely hat with a newspaper, and the other hand lifting her skirts as she nearly skipped up the stairs to the hospital to avoid the rain.

Even she didn't know what her husband was about to do. Conleith had agreed it was safer.

Raphael's eyes followed Mercy's eldest sister, his eyes hungry for any sort of reminder of her. She and Honoria were as different in coloring as night was from day. The elder two Goode sisters had midnight hair and large dark eyes, but her jaw was crafted with the same sharp lines and stubborn angles. Her shape formed with the same delicate perfection.

Raphael licked his lips, thinking he could still find hints of Mercy's incomparable flavor on them.

"Children..." Gabriel exhaled the word on a long puff of smoke. "I've never allowed myself to think of something like that. Even if I'd ever been able to convince a woman to— Well, I'd never thought to maintain our legacy. I suppose I'd hoped our father's seed would die with us, perhaps his violence would, too."

Raphael feigned his usual irreverent mirth. "Likely not, I've probably got a million bastards out running around some-where. Find you a handsome hazel-eyed tramp and I've prob-ably boffed his mother."

"I know you better." Gabriel's solemnity wiped the smile from Raphael's face.

Because he was right.

Raphael was as careful as he could be, even in his conquests. He'd never wanted to sire a child, to assign the poor thing a bastard's status.

A bastard that would have become an orphan.

He'd always known he'd make a shit father.

"Why are you asking about the future, anyhow?" he clipped, stealing the pipe from his brother and taking an uncharacteristically long inhale.

He'd never been much of a smoker, but it certainly couldn't hurt to start on today of all days.

His last day.

"Couldn't tell you." Gabriel scanned the bustle of the streets. Streets they'd claimed to own, corners upon which they'd done business for ages. "Who am I, if not a fighter? Who are we, if not criminals, thieves, and smugglers? I'm going to wake up with this name, Gareth, and it tastes wrong in my mouth. Maybe it wouldn't...if I had a purpose."

"Well, you'll have a few bloody weeks to brood on it in the hospital while your face is gooping back together...I wouldn't worry about it. Things won't change so much."

Gabriel retrieved the pipe from him and took another draw. "You don't know that."

"I know you'll have all this gold to spend, and don't worry, I'm pretty sure you'll still be dog-fuckingly ugly, so that will at least be familiar." Raphael punched him in the shoulder.

Usually, a bit of banter cheered his brother, but not today. "The doctor said there would still be scars."

"Sure, but you'll have a fucking nose, won't you? Besides." He waggled dark brows. "Posh birds who crave a bit of rough will ask to kiss your scars, see if they don't."

Gabriel shook his head and shoved him back. "Get on with you, now."

Raphael knew his brother couldn't smile. The scars wouldn't allow it. But he remembered what Gabriel's mirth looked like.

And that was enough. He superimposed the memory over what was left of his brother's face.

Inside, he felt exactly how Gabriel looked. Destroyed by lashes, slashes...

And scars.

"Gabriel, if anything should happen—that is—if it takes me too long to get to the Indies, go to America without me. I'm having Mathilde's ashes sent to—"

Gabriel perked at that. "You're leaving almost a month ahead of me, of course you'll get there first."

"Of course, but you never know...plans go awry."

Pushing himself off the wall, Gabriel towered over him, staring down hard from his one good eye. "Are you thinking of staying for *her*? Because it's not possible. It's too dangerous for them both."

"I don't know what you're talking about." Raphael had to turn away. What a shit time to realize he was terrible at lying to his brother.

He wasn't going to stay.

He was going where no one could follow. Going to find his father in hell and be part of the bevy of demons tormenting the bastard for eternity.

"I saw you last night." Gabriel's low murmur whipped his head around.

"Pardon?"

"Sneaking into Cresthaven." His brother picked a sliver of tobacco from his tongue.

"Are you following me?"

"No."

Raphael narrowed one eye at him. "Then what were *you* doing at Cresthaven?"

It was Gabriel's turn to look away. "I had business nearby."

"No, you bloody didn't."

"It doesn't matter." Gabriel made a dismissive gesture. "It said on the police records that Felicity Goode was in the police wagon with you, but that wasn't her. It was her twin."

Raphael didn't have to feign indignance this time. "How can you tell them apart? You've spent all of five seconds in their company."

"Felicity doesn't speak like Mercy." Gabriel's voice changed in a way that sparked a dark and painful knowledge in Raphael's gut. There was a reverence there. Something that echoed in his own hollowed-out soul. "She doesn't move so sharply through the world. So decisively. Her steps are...careful. Her words are soft."

Raphael narrowed his eyes at his brother. It couldn't be... "You were at Cresthaven last night watching Felicity Goode? For *shame*, you voyeur!" He nudged at him with an elbow.

"I *am* ashamed." Gabriel refused to be mollified. "I can't help but wonder if I feature in any of her nightmares."

"I'm certain she's forgotten you even exist," Raphael said over a derisive noise.

That didn't seem to make it better.

"This isn't...guilt, is it, brother?" he accused. "You like her. You *want* her."

Gabriel had looked at women before, but he'd never watched them. Not like this. He seemed to have come to terms early in life with the fact that his face condemned him to the life of a monk.

"Two brothers tempted by two sisters." Gabriel made a grunt that might have been humor or grief. "It's all rather Shakespearean, isn't it? One of the tragedies, in our case."

"I'd never love Mercy Goode," Raphael claimed, wondering why he still felt as though he were lying to his brother. "It wouldn't be safe for her. But...I didn't want to leave without..." He couldn't seem to finish his sentence.

"You're not being cruel to her, are you? Didn't leave her with promises that will break her heart?"

That Gabriel even cared surprised him more than he could express.

Ultimately, he shook his head. "No. She is in no need of entanglements. That woman has made it abundantly clear, a man would only get in her way."

Gabriel nodded, taking a deep breath of the crisp air, turning his face to the sky to let the rain plink against his mask.

"Don't worry about Mercy and Felicity Goode," Raphael advised, though whether to Gabriel or himself, he couldn't quite figure. "They have a fierce bond, unshakable trust, and a future together."

"As do we, *brother*. As do we." Gabriel turned to him and clasped his shoulder in a rare show of fraternal affection. "Enjoy your last few weeks as the handsome one, Rafe. Or should I say, Remy? I'll see you in Antigua."

Raphael could only bring himself to nod.

Turning, Gabriel conquered the steps to the grand building with an almost jubilant jog, taking two at a time.

The next words were lost to the soft sound of the rain as it pattered against the cobbles of the streets that would become his grave.

"Goodbye, *mon frere. Vive la vie*."

Live life.

CHAPTER 13

*M*ercy resolutely *did not* think of Raphael all the next day.

She awoke to find he'd vanished like the night mist off the Thames when the sun burned it away. If not for the whisper of heat and the musk of his aftershave haunting his side of the bed, one might have thought last night nothing but a fever dream.

She rolled over and buried her face in the pillow he'd so unceremoniously abandoned. Intimate muscles ached and protested in a way that was both wicked and dispiriting.

He was gone.

Of course, he would be. She'd expected it. Accepted it. And refused to feel any sort of ridiculous melancholy about it.

Except...had he even kissed her goodbye? Did she sleep through it?

Or had he simply slithered away like a wary thief in the shadows, grateful to be spared any inconvenient or emotional farewells?

Not that he'd have had to suffer such nonsense.

They'd both understood that they were lovers for one night only.

And, Holy Moses, did they ever make the most of their evening.

She'd had him three times in three different ways, though he'd sent her rocketing into the stars a total of five.

Dear God, but was he insatiable. She'd had to beg for respite, and only *then* did he wrap his large, warm body around her and lull her to sleep with his even breaths stirring her hair.

She refused to be sentimental about it, dammit. She wasn't one of those ridiculous women who took to their beds when neglected by a man.

It was only that...she'd felt like a treasure lying wrapped in his embrace. Something coveted and rare.

It'd been rather lovely.

Different.

It wasn't that she *needed* to feel that way, of course. She'd come to terms with the fact that she was a thorn in the collective side of the world at large.

Forever too much or not enough.

It was just that, the sensation of fitting so perfectly against his hips, her head resting in the deep groove of his chest. The way the tempo of their hearts seemed to harmonize with the effortless synchronization of their breath.

For the moment in between waking and the oblivion of sleep, she'd felt like a part of him.

Rather than *apart* from the world.

Perhaps because she was untried in the ways of intimacy. Affection wasn't something their family encouraged. Or even condoned.

That had to be it.

Raphael's disappearance wasn't the architect of this strange sense of attachment and loss. This empty sort of yearning that hollowed out the space behind her breast.

It was simply that she was untried and unaccustomed to such an arrangement, and needed to amend her reaction to it, lest she become some simpering ninny and do something atrocious.

Like cry over Raphael Sauvageau.

How many tears had fallen for the rake? Likely enough to fill the Atlantic.

Hers would *not* be added to the tide.

She had work to do. A murderer to find. And no mere man would get in the way of her mission. All she had to do was be unwavering in her relinquishment of him. Not allow him to permeate her other incredibly weighty thoughts and important tasks.

He would, no doubt, attend the masquerade that evening, but it was best she avoid him as he'd made it clear in no uncertain terms that he didn't want her there.

Well...she wasn't one to be ordered about.

She would take a weapon. Would stay in safe and crowded areas with plenty of witnesses.

And she'd solve the murder before him, by Jove.

See if she didn't.

That decided, she did a marvelous job of *not* thinking about him all day.

She didn't think of him as she lingered over breakfast and read the newspapers in bed. Because such an activity would surely *not* be enjoyable with a companion. It wouldn't do to imagine all sorts of amusing opinions he might have about things. Or wonder if he'd maybe share a nibble of her toast. A man his size probably had quite the appetite of a morning...

Did he prefer tea or coffee?

It didn't matter, she forcefully reminded herself. It didn't bear consideration.

She *did not* think of him when she soaked in the bath and

scrubbed the memory of his clever—no, *masterful*—fingers and mouth from her skin.

He'd been inside of her. Joined with her.

What a novel thing that a human could connect with another in such a way...that they were made to do just this. To delight in it.

Did everyone fit together so perfectly? Was their pleasure so overcoming and instinctual?

She wanted to find out, but something told her that to do so with another man would find her disappointed.

Better not to wonder. Not to dwell.

Did he feel altered somehow by their night together? Like it merited some sort of distinction. Like a change in the very map of the stars?

Why would he? Why would anyone?

She *did not* think of him when she viciously chopped the heads off their hothouse flowers for her maid to arrange in her hair.

Nor when she selected a dagger to strap to her leg.

She wasn't angry. She wasn't hurt.

She didn't miss him.

She didn't even *know* him.

Unlike Detective Eddard Sharpe, Mercy had not mastered the art of infiltration and disguise.

Not yet, in any case.

So, she was incandescently glad when Felicity insisted upon accompanying her to the Midwinter Masquerade. Social functions were not her sister's forte, as such, but Felicity's attachment and sense of obligation to Mathilde's memory was no less intense than her own.

They dressed in identical sapphire gowns and donned masks the color of the moon on an overcast evening, intricately decorated with gems and filigree.

Once again forgoing her spectacles proved to make the night interesting for Felicity.

Mercy might have told her sister about her night with Raphael, if she'd been allowing herself to think of it.

But she wasn't.

* * *

MERCY REMEMBERED HER FATHER ONCE READING FROM THE Bible about a den of iniquity. The phrase haunted her now as she watched the spectacle that was the Midwinter Masquerade. It made the sedate balls she attended appear like absolute child's play.

Killgore Keep was a grand old Plantagenet fortress that'd been renovated over the years by obscenely wealthy owners. It hunkered next to a quaint canal complete with a Tudor-era mill and extensive grounds. Amelia Trent, the widow of Captain Rupert Trent, a long-dead hero of the now defunct East India Company, was the first woman to own the keep. She spent her late husband's ill-begotten fortune as a patroness for artists of all kinds, and a rumored haven for the darker, more deviant side of the bohemian set. Mrs. Trent was famous for her bacchanalian fêtes, and her February spectacle was said to be a bombastic balm for the late-winter gloom.

Mathilde had procured Mercy an invitation, as they were to abscond that very evening.

Mercy made certain to impress herself upon the footman as she arrived so that when Felicity followed a quarter hour after, he'd assume he was merely allowing her reentry.

The ruse worked splendidly, and after she and her sister met for a moment in an alcove to work their stratagem, they broke apart, doing their best not to be seen together.

In such a massive manse, stuffed to the brim with the

celebrities of the *demimonde*, it wasn't difficult to remain obscure.

Not only did they need to find the Duchesse de la Cour, they also endeavored to ascertain if there was a chance Gregoire had found out about Mathilde's lover. The Archambeaus' innermost circle of friends might have known about Mathilde's infidelity, and Mercy had a list of names to approach. Even though Gregoire himself had left the country, there was a possibility he'd found the money to pay for his wife's demise.

After an hour or so of idle but probing conversation—and not so idle eavesdropping—Mercy found herself both perplexed and concerned. There were not merely artists, actresses, naughty nobles in attendance, but a rather disproportionate congregation of rough-looking and incongruously well-dressed men.

Some were part of the joviality, drinking and dancing beneath the massive crystal chandeliers, or playing chance in one of the many illegal game rooms. Others tucked themselves in corners or alcoves, locked in conversations.

Or illicit embraces.

People sniffed powders from snuff boxes and smoked pungent substances from hookahs, pipes, and elegant cigarette holders.

Mercy was aware of an expectancy hovering over the gathering.

As if something violent waltzed in their midst, waiting for the right moment to unleash unholy chaos. She thought it must be why people celebrated and laughed uncommonly loud, in an attempt to drown out the low din of their disquiet.

Did they not see certain men placed strategically around the manse? Adjacent to the revelry but taking no part of it.

Like sentinels.

Waiting.

Were these men all Fauves, perhaps? If so...how did they gain entry?

And where was their leader?

Mercy lurked just out of sight of the ballroom where she peeked in to find that Felicity had been escorted to the dance floor and might have been floating on a cloud in the arms of an elegant man with a roguish mask.

Her sister was not the easiest of conversationalists, but she'd always been an extraordinary dancer. Fluid and graceful and astonishingly comfortable.

It was the only time she forgot to be afraid, Mercy supposed. The music would sweep her away, and she knew the steps so well, her perfection was artless. She didn't have to look at her partner, nor did she have to talk to them if she didn't want to.

She positively glowed, and Mercy wasn't the only person to appreciate that.

Her sister really failed to notice how often men stared at her.

Or maybe she did realize, and that's what made her so afraid all the time.

Too often, the notice of a man was a dangerous thing.

One figure in particular stood half in the shadow of the grand staircase, his features shrouded by a lupine mask. Something in the way he stood, so absolutely still surrounded by chaos.

Like a mountain besieged by storms.

"Your sister is a beautiful dancer."

Goosebumps erupted all over Mercy's body at the seductive murmur, tinged with a French accent, that slid like a blade into her ear.

Partly because she'd been so intent on the shade of the wolf, it distressed her that someone could have crept so close. And partly, because she'd not heard that sort of sensual appreciation in the voice of a *woman*.

Whirling, she found herself staring into the gentle leonine eyes of a statuesque lady with a wealth of russet hair. She'd the regal bearing of a queen, though the elegant hands in her crimson gloves trembled slightly.

"I did not think you would come. Not after Mathilde—" She broke off, swallowing twice before continuing. "I suppose I must introduce myself. My name is Amelie Beauchamp, Duchesse de la Cour. Which one of the Misses Goode are you? The kind-hearted Felicity, or the delightful Mercy?"

"I can't speak to delightful, but I am Mercy Goode." Bewildered, she took the woman's extended hand and gave the ghost of a curtsy. For a villainess, the Duchesse certainly did have a dulcet voice. One only made for gentle solariums and sedate rose gardens, not such turmoil as this.

"I have heard you are asking after Mathilde tonight." The Duchesse watched her carefully from behind a mask the color of burgundy wine and gold. "Am I to presume that you are searching for the architect of her demise?"

"Her *murderer*, yes." Even though the woman apparently kept a tight rein on her composure, she thought she saw a reaction to the word.

Not a flinch, per se. But something close to it.

As the waltz ended, the two women took a moment to study each other while the shift in dance partners caused a din above which it was difficult to converse.

The Duchesse de la Cour was an incredibly elegant figure. Though uncommonly tall, her undeniable presence had less to do with her stature than the fine set of her jaw, the fullness of her lips, the sense of both wisdom and fragility emanating from her.

Could this woman bedecked in rubies and silk and swathed in an atmosphere of gracious courtesy be capable of murder?

Mercy didn't have to look to see that her sister had appeared at her elbow. She could always tell when Felicity was near with a satisfying sort of click, like that when a puzzle piece found its place.

One could only call the Duchesse's smile fond as she welcomed Felicity into their midst. "In her letters to me, Mathilde did not exaggerate your uncommon resemblance. I feel as if I know you two merely from your antics."

"Letters?" Taken aback, Mercy said the word with more emphasis than it called for. "I was under the impression Mathilde came here to *escape* you. Or at least the scandal you caused."

The Duchesse gave their surroundings a furtive glance. She gestured to a cozy cluster of furniture arranged in a shadowed corner by a billiard table that had evidently been abandoned in the middle of a game.

They drifted to it, the Duchesse sweeping a glass of champagne from a passing footman on her way.

Mercy sat with her back to the corner, noting the Duchesse did the same.

She wasn't certain who the other woman was keeping an eye out for, but in Mercy's case, it was certainly *not* Raphael.

Not in the least.

"Tell me, Your Grace, have you come to collect whatever it was Mathilde allegedly stole from you?" she asked, spearing the woman with a look she imagined an inquisitor might employ.

"*Mercy,*" Felicity admonished in a whisper as she settled herself across from them on a high-backed chair. "Perhaps we shouldn't be antagonistic just now."

"It's all right." The Duchesse tipped her glass of wine back and drained half of it in two bracing swallows. After taking a moment to compose herself, she said, "There *was* a scandal with Mathilde and me...and it had to do with treasure, but not jewels or trinkets. Something infinitely more priceless." She cast Mercy a meaningful look. "Is it not said that the heart is worth more than any fortune?"

"Love?" Mercy's eyes peeled wide with sudden comprehension at the same time her sister gasped.

She regarded the Duchesse, recalling what Mathilde had said about her lover. Dark. Handsome. Mysterious. Foreign. Sensual...

The woman was all of these things.

Long lashes swept down behind her mask. "I am sorry if I have shocked you, I almost thought Mathilde might have confided in you about me, as you were to bring her to me. I can't imagine what you must be thinking." The Duchesse finished her wine with a morose sigh.

"I'm thinking you were both going to leave your husbands and run away together."

"You would be right," she nodded. "The ship you were going to conduct her to belongs to me. I am the Duc de la Cour's second wife, and he has taken to his deathbed, as they say. I can't think that it's soon enough." Her bitterness was not at all concealed by her mask.

"My stepson, Armand, has made my life untenable, and so I have taken the money that is mine and had arranged for Mathilde and me to sail to foreign ports indefinitely. I was going to help her set aside the medicines she took...the vices that were killing her slowly. We were each other's safe harbor. Our lives were to be a grand adventure...and someone took that from us." Her eyes went from a whiskey-gold to a fiery amber as her features hardened behind her mask. "I am here to find out who it was."

"So am I," Mercy said with fierce determination, making another scan of the room, wondering if her killer was part of the revelry. "I wish Mathilde would have told me about you, Your Grace, it would be easier to believe your story. To be certain you had nothing to do with her death."

Felicity kicked her ankle.

"I understand," the Duchesse said around another melancholy sigh. "It is hard for us—*was* hard for us—as you might imagine. And because of where she came from...Mathilde did not trust easily."

"Of course it was difficult; people are not very understanding, are they?" Leaning over, Felicity placed her cobalt glove over that of the Duchesse. Sapphires over rubies. "I am sorry you lost your love."

Mercy allowed Felicity's endlessly romantic heart to soften her own toward the idea of the woman's innocence.

The Duchesse gave Felicity's fingers a grateful squeeze, then snatched her hand away. "Please do not be kind to me," she pled in a watery voice. "Not yet. I will have time to shatter into pieces of grief, but first she must be avenged."

Visibly grappling for her composure, Her Grace followed Mercy's gaze out toward the crowd. The revelers had taken on a fantastical quality, like a painted tableau or a moving picture. Vibrant, silken butterflies too frenetic to land.

Mercy put a thoughtful finger to the divot in her chin. "Do you wonder if your stepson has found out about the two of you and disapproved enough to be remonstrative?"

The Duchesse shook her head most violently. "Armand would never get his hands dirty, though he might have hired it done, a local ruffian, no doubt. I was trying to find out when..." She trailed off as something caught her attention.

It wasn't at all difficult to follow her gaze to exactly what had seized the Duchesse's notice.

Raphael Sauvageau demanded the consideration of any room he entered.

It was as if he claimed every plot of ground he trod upon, and dared someone to take it from him.

Mercy told herself that her heart only leapt because of the circumstance.

Not the man. Nor the sight of him in formal attire, his shoulders straight and jaw sharp.

Lucifer himself couldn't have been more devilishly handsome nor shrewd and savage than he, striding at the head of a handful of men who were nigh on nipping at his heels, as if his word, alone, held them on a short leash.

He approached a group of lads playing billiards. All of them, Mercy noted, were not fellows who easily wore white-tie finery, and yet each sported crimson carnations in their buttonholes.

"Do you know him?" Mercy asked the Duchesse.

"Who doesn't?" she replied ruefully. "I know he is playing a dangerous game tonight. That there are men here baying for his blood."

"What do you mean?" Mercy asked, unable to tear her eyes away from him.

The Duchesse shifted in her seat. "I overheard a conversation only moments ago between a man named Marco Villenueve and a Lord Longueville. Apparently, Mr. Sauvageau, he—how to say this?—he retracted a deal and blamed it on someone...a butcher?"

"The Butcher of High Street?" Felicity supplied with owl-wide eyes.

"Yes, yes, that's the one." The Duchesse nodded. "Everyone who stood around him looked as though they would have murdered him on the spot if they weren't in the public domain. He'd admitted to taking their money and sending it to Russia." She placed a hand at the base of her throat. "Russia, in this day and age? Madness."

Mercy suddenly understood what she was looking at. A tense conversation between the High Street Butchers—a particularly organized rival gang—and the King of the Fauves.

Her lover.

She tried superimposing the man who'd occupied her bed

and body last night over the man who stood across the increasingly crowded billiards room.

He'd been rumpled and randy or, at times, tender and tentative. Touching her as if she were as delicate as one of the carnation petals he now plucked from the buttonhole of his enemy and crushed beneath his shoe.

What the devil was he thinking? That was tantamount to a public challenge to men like them, even *she* knew that.

Wars had been started over less insult.

"Lord Longueville is a dastardly man," Felicity offered, turning so she could covertly peek over her shoulder in the guise of a stretch. "I heard Father once called him a pustulant boil on the arse of the empire. He is said to have lost his fortune, and thereby became this Butcher of High Street. Why, I wonder, is Mr. Sauvageau challenging him?"

"It makes no sense. He's generally considered to be a suave and politic fellow..." The Duchesse trailed off again, her eyes narrowing on him. "I heard the men talking about moving against him the moment he leaves tonight. More will be outside the courtyard of his estate in wait for his Gabriel, who is a notorious recluse. I don't know him well, but I feel an odd sense of duty to warn him."

Felicity scrutinized the Duchesse. "Why would you feel a duty to—"

"I'll do it." Mercy stood so quickly, she became a bit lightheaded, whether from the heat of the crowded manse or the sudden pounding of her heart, she couldn't be sure.

She blinked away the sensation before all but yanking Felicity out of her seat.

"You and the Duchesse should go for the authorities without alerting anyone. I think there will be violence here tonight."

"Erm..." Felicity gulped and looked at the floor, her face flushing behind her mask.

"What is it?"

"Don't be angry."

A pang of anxiety thrummed deep in her stomach. "*Felicity.*"

"I engaged an errand boy before we left, and sent a note to Morley the moment we arrived."

"*What?*" She forced the word out through clenched teeth.

Felicity put her hands up as if to ward off a blow. Or a gunshot. "I know you didn't want that, but, Mercy, it was fool-hardy for us to walk into such a situation without anyone knowing where we are. The moment we arrived I sensed danger, and who better to turn to than our reasonable and protective brother-in-law?"

"Felicity, you have no idea what you've done." Mercy threw her hands in the air. "Morley is still obligated to take Raphael into custody."

"Raphael? Why would you be worried about..." Felicity cocked her head in a very sparrow-like gesture. "You say his name as if you're acquainted. Mercy, are the two of you...involved?"

Oh Lord. She was entirely unprepared to answer a question of that scope. "No! Well... Yes. That is—I—we—"

"*Mon Dieu.*" The Duchesse covered her mouth. "You're in love with him."

"I never!" The protest rang false, even to her own ears.

She felt rather than saw the Duchesse lift a dubious eyebrow from behind her mask. "Lovers, then?"

Mercy's lips slammed together. She couldn't bring herself to deny it. To lie. And yet, how could she explain? If he was involved with Mathilde, then would the poor grieving Duchesse have her heart broken all over again to hear of it?

"You *made love* to the man arrested for Mathilde's murder?" It was Felicity's eyes that carried the gravest of wounds. "And worse, you didn't tell me?"

It was the first secret ever kept between them.

Mercy took her twin's hand. "I met him in front of the wolf exhibit yesterday and he asked if he could come to me... I—I couldn't resist him. And also, I couldn't bring myself to talk about it. Not when things are so complicated. But I promise you I'm not being sentimental when I tell you that I know he's innocent of this crime. I have evidence."

Felicity pulled her hand away. "But he's guilty of a thousand other crimes! Or don't you remember the night he might have *killed* us for the gold Nora's late husband stole from him?"

"He gave that to Titus and Nora's hospital," Mercy pointed out.

"It was no gift. He said he'd collect on the balance, remember? I think of that every day. What sort of debt Honoria and Titus might find themselves beholden to? When will he come for our sister?"

"He won't." Mercy's defense of him sounded pallid and desperate, even to her own ears. "He wants out of the Fauves. The gang was his father's, and he was born to this life, but his plan is to leave it all behind."

To leave her behind.

She turned to the Duchesse. "I suspect that has something to do with his reckless behavior tonight. I think...I think he might be trying to destroy what his father built."

"Mercy, you're speaking madness!" Felicity shook her a little.

"No...she's not," the Duchesse shocked them both into silence with her words. "Gabriel and Raphael Sauvageau's father was known as *le Bourreau*. The executioner. He was said to have been an Englishman of some renown, though no one knew his identity. He was infamous in Monaco and France, indeed, all over the Mediterranean. I know that he used his family awfully, and broke his eldest son in the fighting pits."

Felicity wrapped her arms around her middle, shaking her head in disbelief. "How do you know all this?"

Mercy wondered that as well.

The Duchesse's chin gave a tremulous wobble. "Because *le Bourreau* hurt Mathilde. Showed her...unnatural affections when she was just a girl, even though she was the daughter of his wife's sister, Patrice."

Mercy gasped in horror for poor Mathilde. "You mean..."

"Yes, Mathilde and Raphael are—*were* cousins. This is why I feel some duty toward him. He is a ruthless man, to be sure, but he was kind to her. Even when kindness was never a part of that awful dynasty."

Cousins.

Not lovers.

That was why Raphael had come to see Mathilde on the day she died. Why he was so fond of her without professing any romantic relationships.

It was why he was so intent upon finding her killer.

Because they were family.

She turned back to the billiards table to find that he'd disappeared, though their men were still at each other's throats.

Damn but that was an irritating skill of his. Slithering away just when she needed to talk to him.

"I have to find him. To warn him. Whatever he has planned tonight, he has to stop it."

Felicity grabbed for her as she fled away, but missed. "Mercy, no!"

"You were right, Felicity, to send for Morley. You must go find him now. Must tell him there is a war brewing in this very house that might spill onto the streets of London, and then go home where it's safe."

With that, Mercy turned and plunged through a crowd of drunken crowing lads, intent upon searching every room in the house until he turned up.

Oh, when she caught up with him, he'd have more than a few things to answer for. Just how did he plan on finding

Mathilde's killer when he was busy stirring discontent between dangerous people?

Didn't he understand he was putting himself in undue danger?

Just as she was elbowing through the crowd at the doorway to the ballroom, a strong hand seized said elbow and yanked her toward the dance floor.

One minute she was walking. The next she was waltzing, and the transition had been so seamlessly elegant and effortless, it could only have been perpetrated by one arrogant rake.

"What the everlasting *fuck* are you doing here?" Raphael snarled against her ear, even as he encircled her in an embrace that could only be considered protective.

Mercy hated that dancing in his arms was about as exhilarating as flying. That she thrilled at every press of his thigh against hers and every subtle flex of his arm or his shoulder as he led her through the steps to the dizzying waltz.

She tried not to notice that his nostrils flared when he was angry, and beneath a mask that seemed to be made of dark serpentine scales, each furious breath was rather endearing.

"What do you think?" She tossed her head with brash irreverence, daring him to dress her down. "I'm looking for Mathilde's murderer! Which is what you should be doing instead of—"

"I thought we agreed you'd leave that to me." His fingers almost bit into her back as he pulled her indecently close to avoid being clobbered by a drunken couple.

"You *assumed* I'd leave it to you," she bit back, finding herself reluctant to regain a proper distance, regardless of her ire. "I *agreed* to take my further findings to the police, which I will now that I have further findings. I didn't before, and so no agreement between us was breached."

He opened his mouth to reply, and she beat him to it, cutting off any incoming homilies.

"Listen to this." She squeezed the mound of his coiled bicep in her excitement. "I spoke to the Duchesse de la Cour, who claims she wasn't after Mathilde but about to run away with her. They were lovers, if you'll believe it."

He didn't miss a step, but remained silent for an entire refrain of music, as if he didn't know which part of their conversation to address first.

"Mathilde...with a woman? I always thought it was Marco..." he muttered.

"Who?"

"My second in command who was placed by my father before his death. He's the one most likely to turn on me when —" He paused. "It doesn't matter. I do know that Mathilde procured most of her vice from Marco. Often those arrangements are...physical. I know she'd angered him lately, and I intended to wrest a confession from him tonight."

She glowered up at his impossibly handsome, aggravating face. "And you kept that tidbit of information from me? How dare you!"

The look he sent back to her threatened to immolate her on the spot.

Not because it was angry.

Quite the opposite. It was possibly the most tender, honest gaze she'd ever received in her lifetime. "I would die before I put you in the path of a man like Marco Villenueve... The Good Book says never to cast your pearls before swine."

"Yes, well, it also says never to eat shellfish, and I had a cracking huge lobster last night."

He barked out a harsh, caustic laugh that did nothing to soften the pinched lines of worry casting his features into stark and savage relief. "I don't know whether to be delighted or infuriated with you."

"While you make up your mind, hear this," she plunged ahead. "The Duchesse thinks possibly a member of her ducal family might have hired an assassin once they found out about their plans to leave together. So, you see, you can't start a gang war right now because we're so close to finding your cousin's killer, Raphael." She paused for a moment to glare up at him. "By the by, don't for *one minute* think you've gotten away with implying that you two were—"

She made a plaintive squeak as he spun her off the floor with such force, they stumbled toward a hall beneath the grand stairs, parting the crowd, unconcerned with another drunken couple stumbling around.

"Where are we going?" she huffed, trying to dig her heels in as he dragged her toward a simple, unadorned entry that branched from the main room.

"I'm getting you out of here safely...so I can throttle you in peace," he said from between teeth that his coiled jaw wouldn't allow to separate. "Goddammit, Mercy, you have no idea what you've done."

CHAPTER 14

*M*ercy wriggled, jerked, and flopped about, but was unable to break Raphael's relentless grip as he tirelessly dragged her up a dark set of spiraling stairs and into a deserted passageway. "How dare you manhandle me, you ignominious arse!"

"I've been called worse," he muttered as he pinned her to his side with one arm, to test several door handles. Finding one unlocked, he shoved her inside and followed in, slamming the door shut.

"Oh, no you don't! I am not about to be tossed into some—" Just where were they?

Mercy paused to look around their dim surroundings, noting the two small, bare, if neatly made beds, open trunks, and matching spare-looking wardrobes. Unused maids' chambers, it seemed. Which would explain why the entire part of the house was abandoned, overcome as the staff would be during such an affair as this. They'd be below stairs where the kitchens were located, along with the male servants' quarters.

Raphael slid the lock on the door and blocked it with all six feet of hard, infuriated male.

The only light filtered in through the thin windows above the beds, provided by several lanterns in the garden. It slanted over him at just such an angle, casting half his features in light and the other half in shadow.

As if the two battled over him.

Mercy stood fast, planting her feet shoulder-width apart so as not to advertise how the very sight of him made her weak in the knees. "I don't know what you think you're doing but I demand—"

"I'm saving you from your own recklessness!"

Mercy was certain the look in his eyes might have caused any number of men to tremble, to surrender. But she would not be cowed.

And God help her, she refused to surrender.

Not again.

"Don't be absurd," she scoffed. "If anything, *I'm* saving *you*. I can't believe you told Lord Longueville, one of the worst men alive, that you took his money. Do you know his enemies disappear in the night? He's in league with the High Street Butchers! Not only will he be after you, but so will that rather dodgy fellow—Marco was it—that works for you. The Duchesse said they were baying for your blood. Not to mention the police are—"

He lunged forward, as if to seize her, but at the last moment, he snatched his arms back, his fists clenched so tightly the creases turned white. "I wasn't supposed to be saved tonight, you *magnificent* fool."

"What?"

She'd seen those stark, savage hazel eyes turn every possible color depending on the light. His emotion. His intention.

But never like this. Flashing with twin lightning bolts in the half dark. Then gathering with thunderous grey clouds.

A storm approached, and it was about to break over them both.

"You think I didn't know *exactly* what I was doing?" He sliced the air between them with the flat of his hand. "I know that the Butchers and Lord Longueville are working together. I know they approached Marco, and that Marco failed to tell me, which means he's already mounted a mutiny of the Fauves against me. The Fauves would have dumped my body at the bloody door of Buckingham Palace and Longueville and his Butchers would have strung me from Hangman's Dock. Either way these streets were to be my grave tonight."

"Wait..." Everything inside her went unnaturally still. She stood in the eye of the storm, searching him for the truth. "You're *serious*," she realized with a jolt. "You were intending to perish tonight? To actually die? As in...not exist any longer?"

She waited for him to deny it. Which he would, certainly. Any moment now.

The expression on his face stole her hope before he even formulated a reply.

"My plan calls for a martyr," he explained in a tone devoid of emotion. "The Fauves still loyal to me will seek vengeance against Marco and his traitors. The Butchers will, no doubt, take advantage of the chaos and rise up to swallow the battling factions whole. The Blackheart of Ben More and Morley won't allow for such pandemonium, and I've anonymously provided enough evidence to search Longueville's estate, where they'll find what they need to stretch his neck. And I'll be goddamned if you're here to be any part of it. There *is* a war coming, Mercy, and you need to get out before it starts."

She scowled at him. "You're mad!"

Threading fingers through his hair, he snarled, "What I am, is desperate."

"I meant you're insane if you think I'm leaving you now. Someone has to keep you from killing yourself, you bleeding idiot."

He seemed to search the night for something, anything, to

convince her. "What about the Duchesse and Mathilde? Who will crack the case after I am gone?"

Crossing her arms, she raked him with her most imperious glare. "You're going nowhere, Raphael Sauvageau, I'll not allow it."

"You can't stop me, Mercy. It's already done," he insisted.

"That doesn't mean it can't be undone!"

Seizing her, he bent so their eyes were close, his boring the reflection of the moon into her very soul with palpable agony. "You think I want this? It's the only way out. The only way *Gabriel lives*. When my corpse is found, so too will be Gabriel's mask. Dr. Conleith is hard at work this very evening, sorting out his injured face. The Fauves will assume we are both gone, and my brother can finally live with his new identity."

Titus was in on this? Did Nora know?

"No." She wrenched away, whirling so she didn't have to face him. "I don't accept this."

"Wouldn't you give your life for your sister?"

His question landed like a dagger in her back.

"Of course, I would! But there has to be some other way. Can you not have a new identity as well?"

"I'm too well known. I've too much money, infamy, and the men beneath me happen to be wealthy enough to search for ages, because as much as I've hated it, I'm damn good at what I do."

She could feel him getting closer, and wished her knees didn't go weak at his proximity.

"The world is only getting smaller, Mercy, and I would be found eventually. I have contacts in every port. I've either swindled or smuggled for half the known world, and to truly go into hiding, we'd have to find some place off a map, where the only thing to do is make our own swill and buggar local livestock. I'm not going to live like that. And I don't want that for my brother. He's already suffered enough. And..."

He broke off and they were both silent as footsteps plodded by. Someone opened a door to the next room and rustled around in it before heading back the other way, muttering about apron straps and extra mending.

"*And what?*" Mercy demanded when they were again safely alone.

"I've lived enough for two lifetimes."

"No, you haven't. No!" She shoved at him. "I'll not allow it, you selfish bastard."

"Calm down, someone will hear you." He gently encircled her shoulders with soothing fingers, but she jerked away.

"I will not calm down!" She paced a few feet toward the bare walls and then spun back to him "Why did you kiss me then, if you were just going to do this? Why make love to me? Why the devil would you make me...make me care for you?"

His features collapsed then. Broke open like a shattered glass. "I kissed you, Mercy, because I knew your taste would be better than any last meal I could devise. I made love to you because I *am* a selfish bastard, and I wanted a glimpse of what heaven would be like before I join the ranks of the damned. I thought you knew better than to care. That you understood I don't deserve it."

Mercy didn't realize what was welling inside of her until her hand flung out and struck him on the cheek.

God, that was satisfying.

The pain.

The blank look of shock on the beautiful bastard's face.

Heat swirled inside her. A conflagration of rage fed by helplessness and...and something else. Something so profound and breathtaking it threatened to turn her to ash.

She wanted to scream at the idea of his loss. His death. This vital, tender, brilliant villain. This man who would dismantle his father's tainted legacy for the love of his brother.

Who would give his life.

She slapped him again. Harder this time. Apparently unable to control herself at the tragic thought of his demise.

His head flinched ever so slightly to the side, but he said nothing. Did nothing. Took her fury on the chin while those bleak, abysmal, exquisite eyes threatened to destroy her with the agony she read in their depths.

She pulled her hand back once more, the sting from her previous strike having yet to fade. Words tumbled into her throat, but she couldn't seem to speak them. Not to the face of the man who was the specter of every wicked dream she'd dared to remember.

The answer to every question she'd not known to ask.

The only reason she'd consider abandoning her vow to remain alone.

That thought stole her breath as she stared at him in mute wonder.

He'd the body of a man, and the soul of a beast. An animal's primitive instinct. And it summoned something so ancient and powerful from the deepest parts of her. Something needful and violent, carnal and famished. He teased and tantalized her. Amused and antagonized her.

And the entire time he was planning his own death.

She had meant to slap him again, she really had. To strike the very idea out of his head.

It was impossible to discern who lunged first.

His muscles twitched, hers responded, or the other way around, it wasn't relevant in the end.

When their bodies crashed together like waves finding their own shore, all that mattered was that their lips finally met. Savored. Punished. Pleaded.

Devoured. Consumed.

Her fingers bracketed the rough skin of his jaw, a lovely tactile dichotomy to the smoothness of his lips.

Like silk and sand.

The kiss did not douse the flames of fury within her, merely fed them, fanned them, sent the heat licking its way over her flesh until it landed deep inside her womb.

Her snarl of demand somehow escaped as a whimper of need.

She was dimly aware of a sense of weightlessness and a rush of air before she found herself pinned on her back to a mattress.

Above her, Raphael's teeth bared and his eyes glinted with a dangerous hunger. He caught her wrists and effortlessly held them in one large hand, securing them above her head.

He descended on her then, a low growl erupting from him as he dragged his mouth everywhere. Her jaw, her neck, the angle of her clavicle before returning to her lips to start a different trail.

Vibrations of heat and hunger shook her to her very bones as a terrific heaviness gathered in her loins. She found herself astonished that a kiss might convey more than words. She felt the unrequited need, the loveless lifetime of desolation.

He was not gentle as he'd been the night before. The tender, skillful lover had been replaced by this savage, cruel beast. He used his teeth, nipping at tender skin and then smoothing it over with the hot velvet of his tongue.

Even though he was heavy enough to crush her, some fervency rose within her, telling her she'd never get close enough. No matter how deep he went.

She opened her legs, intent upon locking her ankles around his back, clinging to him like the pathetic barnacle he'd made of her. She pressed up against him, grinding at the turgid barrel of his erection through the damnable barrier of their clothing.

His brutal sound was her only warning before she found herself shoved face down on the mattress. Rough hands pulled her hips up and back, and the whisper of fabric foreshadowed the crisp air hitting the warm skin of her upper thighs as he shoved her skirts above her back.

Her drawers gave nothing but a sigh of protest as he ripped them, and the raw sound he made as his fingers found the backs of her garters released a flood of desire from the very core of her.

He split her with his finger, testing the flesh already slick and eager.

Willing.

Her fingers twisted in the rough wool blanket beneath her, she arched her back toward a sudden, intense onslaught of need.

His hand gripped her bare hip and after a few jerking motions, he was there. The blunt head of his cock kissing the folds guarding her sex.

He stilled then, his grip on the flesh of her hip bruising as the only sound in the night was the rasp of his panting breaths.

"Damn you," he finally snarled. "Damn you for..."

For what?

She never had the chance to ask.

He drove inside her with one searing, merciless thrust. Penetrating not just her body, but searing her very soul.

There was a momentary sharp pain as flesh still tender from the previous night struggled to contain him once again.

Biting her lip, Mercy forced herself not to gasp, because she wanted this. Needed it. Craved the violence of this storm between them. She threw her head back and pressed her body toward him. Taking him impossibly deeper. Until the bones of his hips met the soft flesh of her ass.

With a low, appreciative sound, he set a rhythm as relentless as he was. His cock parting her, filling her, injecting her with currents of lightning-quick pleasure as he drove so deep, she thought at times he caressed her womb.

She could feel his heartbeat inside of her as her intimate

muscles gripped and goaded him with lugubrious tension, unwilling to release him each time he withdrew.

He gripped her dress, holding it like the reins of a horse as he drove deep and hard, bucking her forward with the force of his thrusts. He held her captive as he undid her completely.

Mercy said his name. Then she screamed it.

Bending over her, his hand reached around and covered her mouth.

She could taste her own slick desire on his skin, and she bit into the rough pads of his fingers as he crippled her with release. Relentless spasms uncoiled within her, thundering through her veins with such astounding force she couldn't help but bear down against the overwhelming bliss.

An inhuman sound tore from him, then another, as his impressive muscles locked into a jerking tempo.

His cock swelled impossibly larger inside of her the moment before a rushing jet of warmth bathed her womb, heightening her own climax until stars danced in her periphery, threatening to steal her consciousness.

And why not? He was a consummate thief, after all.

She'd never offered him her heart.

But he'd taken it all the same.

CHAPTER 15

Damn her.

Damn her for making him feel more alive than he ever had, on the night he was supposed to die. For teaching him what hope felt like. For making him wonder what a future might be.

Damn her for changing everything. His plans. His mind.

His heart.

What was happening? He'd been a man of absolute resolve and relentless, one-minded orientation until *this* whirlwind of a woman touched down in his life.

She challenged everything he'd known to be true.

It was more impossible between them now than it had ever been. His machinations were a runaway train charging down a steep mountain.

Chased by an avalanche.

There was no stopping it.

Time was of the essence, and yet he couldn't bring himself to bloody withdraw from the velvet warmth of her body, even long after the earth-shattering climax had passed.

How could he leave the world she inhabited? It'd somehow become impossible. Unthinkable.

Because she cared. She'd admitted it with those lustrous blue eyes gone dark with anger tempered only by desire. Anger precipitated by the pain of his loss.

Other than his brother, he couldn't think of another person alive that would mourn him.

Until Mercy.

She was the one to pull away and detach, bringing him plummeting back to reality with a jarring crash.

She rolled to her back and he turned away, righting himself as he allowed her the privacy to do the same.

"Well, I hope that settles things," she said after a moment of rustling fabric, her crisp tone rasping over the afterglow of satisfied lust.

He wished he felt the same.

Things were more unsettled than ever.

And his need for her would never be satisfied. Not if he lived another hundred years.

Gathering his fortitude, he turned back to her in time to see that she'd tidied herself with her ruined undergarments and stood, balling them up in her grasp.

"These are for the rubbish." She set about looking for a bin. Finding one, she dropped them inside before catching her reflection in the mirror and smoothing her hair back into place.

Was there ever a woman more precious? This force of nature in a petite, golden package. His fierce vixen. Not merely gorgeous but adventurous. Stimulating. Magnificent.

He was used to making a stir wherever he went, but if she were ever to throw off the mantle of civility thrust upon her by her family, by society, her rank...

She'd eclipse him with a brilliance to shame the sun.

629

He'd never wanted anything more than to witness such a thing.

Sweet Christ, they'd never even taken off their masks.

And now she'd be moving around the earth with those flimsy garters holding up her sheer stockings and no drawers.

The very idea was enough to make him ready to have her again.

Mayhem erupted beneath them. Cries and whistles screeched over the sounds of doors splintering open and the clatter of wagons thundering up the drive.

"What the bloody devil?" He raced to the door and opened it, glancing down the hall to see if the ruckus had reached their deserted corner of the manse.

A few footsteps thundered down the narrow stairs, but only the skirts of frightened maids appeared before they dashed by.

"Oh, dear."

Closing the door, he turned to the woman who'd uttered the words, with slow, deliberate movements.

She offered him a smile of chagrin. "That...sounds like Morley and his men."

Raphael hurled a few choice French curses into the night, and she held her hands up as if to block them from landing on her.

"Before you get angry with me, I wasn't the one who summoned the police. That was Felicity. She did it without my consent and, believe you me, no one was more cross about that than I. But in the end, it's a good thing because—"

"Felicity?" He advanced toward her, his heart thundering in his ears. "Tell me she's not downstairs in *that*."

Mercy shook her head. "As soon as we realized what you were about—and how many dangerous men were here—I sent her to meet Morley. He'd surely have made certain she was safe."

"Good." He seized her, planted a quick, hard kiss to her

bruised lips. "I'll clear you a path to him, but you must stay here."

"And *you* must be joking." She wrenched away from him and strode toward the door. "I'm not hiding up here when the Duchesse is caught up in the bedlam."

He caught her elbow. "Any number of those men are not above taking hostages to escape the police. There are innocent people threaded throughout a labyrinth of warring factions. And, as you said, most of them are out for my blood. How am I supposed to concentrate on the task at hand if you're in danger?"

"I'm not harmless, I'll have you know." Her jaw thrust forward as she reached into her sleeve and produced an impressive-looking knife. "Do you really think I'd trust a suicidal gangster to set things to right? Not bloody likely, I'll take my chances down there, thank you."

"But—"

She gave her golden curls a saucy toss. "No one knows of our...connection. So if someone comes for your throat, I'll simply step aside and let them have at you, and it'd be what you deserve."

As she flounced away, one knee-weakening truth became unerringly obvious.

He was in trouble.

No.

He...was in love.

To him, the emotion hadn't been definable. He'd never truly stopped to ponder it. Just accepted that he felt something like it for his brother. Had done so once for his mother.

Not that his emotions for Mercy were anything filial. Indeed, he hated to admit they might be stronger even in so short a time.

He'd known he'd loved Gabriel because his brother meant

more than himself. Because he'd die for him. Kill for him. His loyalty was absolute and unquestioned.

But for Mercy?

He'd burn the entire world to the ground if she asked him. He'd accomplish any Herculean task. Sail to the ends of the world to fetch a trinket she liked.

He not only loved her enough to stay if it were possible.

He loved her enough to let her go if it meant keeping her safe.

The realization galvanized him forward as she wrenched the door open and plunged into the hall.

He hovered behind her like the very wrath of God, brandishing his own sharp dagger as they spiraled back down the stairs. Raphael searched for another way out, but the only entrance and exit to this specific tower dumped them right toward the main hall of the keep.

Damn these old fortresses.

He lunged around her as they struggled through the short corridor toward the great hall, gathering her free hand in his. "You'll stay glued to me, Mercy, or so help me God!"

To his surprise and utter relief, she nodded in compliance.

Keeping her latched between him and the wall, Raphael shoved past bodies who'd begun to flee down whichever hall they could find, not knowing they raced toward a dead end.

An acrid smell itched at his nose, smoke and something bitter.

He snatched a panicked footman clean off his feet. "What's going on out there?" he demanded.

"Madness!" The gawky lad's voice squeaked with the fear of a man barely out of his teenage years. "Someone spied the Bobbies and before we knew it, a tussle broke out right on the ballroom floor. Men at each other's throats. Never seen anything like it. Someone tossed over an oil lamp and now the drapes in the gaming den have caught. Best we run, man."

Cursing, Raphael released him and shouldered his way to the end of the hall.

He took a quick toll of the anarchy when they broke onto the landing that wrapped around the great room's second story, at eye level with the ostentatious chandelier.

Morley's men spilled into the courtyard like blue-coated rats. Some doing their best to contain the tide of panicked partygoers, funneling them out to safety.

Others brandished an asp to meet the blows of gangster cudgels.

Longueville was nowhere to be found, and without him and Raphael to maintain the temperature on the simmering tension between the Fauves and the Butchers, it had boiled over into this potentially lethal catastrophe.

It wasn't supposed to have happened this way. Only the leaders and their closest comrades were to meet here and witness his challenge.

Then they'd gather their men to come after him in the night.

That was how things were done in their world. They were no street-rat ruffians, their wars were waged in the dark so there were no witnesses.

Away from the public and the police.

But Longueville had blatantly brought an army to a masquerade, willing to crush revelers if necessary.

The rules of engagement had been thoroughly breached.

Two staircases led down to the ballroom floor, one on the east wall and the other on the west.

Raphael and Mercy weaved through abandoned card games and a fortune teller's upended table toward the west staircase as a fight began to spill up the east side toward the second floor.

"The Duchesse was in the billiard's room when last I saw her!" Mercy called over the din. "There!" She pointed to a large solarium now crammed with people trying to escape the smoke beginning to seep up through the three open archways.

Raphael nodded, his eyes lasering everything else away but a bold figure who'd led the police charge into the courtyard. He already had two Butchers in irons and was dragging them roughly toward a police cart very much like the one in which Raphael had first kissed Mercy.

Chief Inspector Morley.

He'd get Mercy to him before returning for the Duchesse.

Her safety was paramount to anything else.

Cursing every fucking god in existence, Raphael tucked Mercy deeper against his side, readied his weapon, and waded into the fray. He was careful to keep his dagger away from drunken, panicked courtesans, artists, and actresses as they shoved and fled.

Keeping to the outskirts, he hoped to avoid the increasing intensity of the violence in the great room. Once on the main floor, he had no qualms about using his elbows, fists, or his blade to quell any who came close. Who thought to claim bragging rights by landing a blow against Raphael Sauvageau.

He had one eye on the brawl and the other on the exit that remained infuriatingly distant, when he felt Mercy lunge behind them.

Raphael whirled just in time to see her blade embedded in the chest of one of his own men, who'd apparently thought to attack from behind.

They thought to stab him in the back. Thinking, no doubt, that he wouldn't see it coming, this coup against the rules of conflict.

Because he'd taught them the code and abided by it.

But Marco...he didn't have a code. He would conduct his villainy out in the open, if only to amass the notoriety the Sauvageau brothers had taken a lifetime to procure.

Raphael would see him in hell, but first...

Gaining ground, he stopped an attacker with a swift elbow to the throat. He threw his dagger at another man who had a running start. It embedded in his eye, dropping him instantly.

Now Raphael was weaponless, but it didn't matter, he only had five paces to the door and sharp fucking knuckles.

Anyone in his way had a death wish. The peal of a woman's scream rose above the din, the desperation in the sound seeming to slow time itself.

"Felicity! She didn't leave in time!"

Raphael had to employ both hands to stop Mercy from lunging through the brawl toward the far staircase.

Where Marco Villeneuve fought against the crowd of tussling men, his arm around the waist of a struggling, petite woman Mercy's exact likeness in feature and formal gown.

Felicity's mask had been torn away and her hair ruined by the cruel hand threaded through it, using the pain of his grasp to subdue her.

Tears streamed down cheeks frozen in a heart-wrenching mask of panic that Raphael could never even imagine painted on Mercy's resolute features.

"We have to get to her!" Mercy cried, her own expression more temper than terror.

Felicity spotted them across the crowd, and the sight seemed to inject her with courage. As close as they were to the fire, Felicity's struggles produced violent coughs that interrupted her sobs. However, she landed a lucky blow with her elbow into Marco's sharp jaw.

Stunned, Marco released her.

Only to spin her around and deliver a merciless blow with the back of his hand.

Felicity dropped beneath the fray, disappearing from view.

An inhuman roar brought Raphael's notice to the top of the stairs.

What he saw slackened his limbs with shock.

Mercy chose that moment to lunge so frantically toward her sister, and he almost lost his grip. "Let me go!" she screamed. "I will murder that man!"

"You won't have to," he said, strengthening his grip on her, pointing to the top of the stairs.

Gabriel was unmistakable, even in a lupine mask Raphael had never seen before. He charged down the stairs toward Marco. What men were not tossed over the banister became little better than smears on the wall.

To Marco's credit, he stood against the oncoming juggernaut, pulling a knife from his belt.

A shot from the direction of the door brought time to an absolute standstill. Everyone screamed and the collective crowd ducked, subsequently checking themselves for wounds.

"Are you struck?" Raphael grasped Mercy, gripped with horror. "Dammit, are you all right?"

"I'm unharmed," she said, her voice shaking and small.

Raphael checked the entry for the shooter but could identify none.

When he looked back toward the stairs to find that Gabriel had disappeared in the thickening smoke, he felt as though the bullet had found his own chest.

Marco was reaching down to collect Felicity, who'd yet to recover from his blow.

Raphael wheezed out his brother's name just in time to watch him rise from behind the banister like the very specter of the black-swathed reaper.

Gabriel and Marco both lashed out at the same time, one with his blade, the other with nothing more than a scarred fist the size of a sledgehammer.

Gabriel's punch connected with an audibly satisfying crunch of bone, though Marco's knife barely missed the eye he'd aimed it for.

By the time the traitorous Spaniard finished rolling arse-over-end to land in a twisted heap, Gabriel had stooped to retrieve Felicity from where she'd been draped unconscious on the stairs.

Raphael's eyes burned, his throat closed over with emotion.

Not with relief.

With horror.

Horror that echoed in the gasps and exclamations of the congregation before leaping out of Gabriel's way as he carried the young Baron's daughter like a bolt of cobalt cloth.

Marco's knife had missed his brother's flesh, but it'd cut his mask away.

Exposing his face to everyone.

Gabriel kept his chin held high, relentlessly marched forward, using his monstrous appearance to part the sea of people still ebbing toward the door.

Raphael surged forward, shoving through the crowd, knowing he'd get Mercy to safety.

Trusting his brother to save Felicity.

He could see through the doors ahead that Morley had tossed his prisoners into the police wagon. Just in time to catch a sobbing woman with a bloodied nose as she collapsed.

Raphael had half-expected the Chief Inspector to have fired the shot, as he was a famous marksman, but there was no way he could have done it.

He was simply too far away.

Just as they were about to break free of the castle's threshold, a figure lunged from around the corner and kicked out at Mercy's legs.

She gave a sharp cry of pain, and went sprawling onto her hands and knees.

Striking like a venomous cobra, Raphael had the man's throat in a vice grip before anyone could react. "You'll die for that," he vowed, reaching down with his other hand to lift Mercy off the ground.

"So says the dead man walking." Even over the deafening chaos, the unmistakable click of a pistol washed Raphael's veins in ice.

"Think you can knock me down and get away with it?" sneered former Detective Inspector Martin Trout, his face still a tapestry of purple and yellow healing bruises. "Unhand me, or I pull the trigger."

Raphael's hands ached for the feel of Trout's thin bones breaking beneath them. He would pick his teeth with this man. Would make him choke to death on his own genitals for daring to touch her.

Something inside ignited, engulfing those pushing for escape in a billow of smoke.

The crowd rushed the door with renewed vigor. Bodies flowed around them as if they were stones in a rushing river, heavy enough to not be swept up in the current, but in danger of being swallowed by it.

If Raphael moved, Mercy might be trampled.

She gasped his name and tugged at his sleeve, having yet to regain her feet. The pain she valiantly tried to hide from her voice lanced through his chest. "Raphael, his boots!"

Raphael looked down to see the barrel of the gun aimed not as his middle, but Mercy's head. And below even that.

Were Brogan boots with an uncommonly tall heel.

Like one a detective of dubious height might buy to enhance his stature.

The soles of which had left muddy footprints beneath Mathilde Archambeau's window when he crept in to murder her.

"It was you!" Mercy snarled, a fierce woman even on her knees. "You cretinous pig."

Raphael released the man's neck with the greatest reluctance, knowing a fear he'd never imagined possible at the sight of a pistol about to kiss the temple of his woman.

"Just a hired gun, so to speak," Trout corrected, oozing with antipathy and malevolence. "Spoiled French aristocrats pay better than the English government to punish their scandalous stepmothers. Better, even, than the High Street Butchers."

"If you shoot now, you'll be found out." Raphael nodded in Morley's direction. "You can't murder the Chief Inspector's sister-in-law when he's right across the courtyard."

Trout grinned. "This is all laid at your feet, and people see what we tell them to see, which is the King of the Fauves killing a Baron's daughter and me wrestling the gun from you to put you down. I'll emerge from the fire a bloody hero. Your fucking brother-in-law will likely pin the medal on my jacket himself." His finger caressed the trigger. "I thought that woman on the stairs was you," he spat. "Don't worry, I won't miss a second time."

CHAPTER 16

From Mercy's perspective, Raphael moved with such incredible speed, the rest of the world slowed in comparison.

One moment she was staring down the barrel of the instrument of her death.

And the next, he'd seized the pistol by said barrel, wrenched it toward his own middle, and twisted it out of Trout's hands before another shot could be fired.

He didn't shoot the man, as she thought a generally unscrupulous gangster such as he might do.

Rather—with his demonic features made even more so by his mask—the violence he perpetrated on Trout with the butt of the pistol no doubt left the man wishing for death.

If he didn't succumb to it.

She wasn't sure a man could survive such a savage beating.

She wasn't sure she cared.

A crimson mask blocked her view just as she was coming to liken the odious detective's face to the ground meat inside sausage casings.

"Are you hurt?" The Duchesse pulled at her elbow, lifting her to her feet.

Mercy stared at her dumbly. Was she hurt? The opposite, it seemed. She felt no pain whatsoever. She couldn't feel her fingers or her lips. Perhaps she gestured in the negative, but she couldn't tell.

"That man was hired by Armand to kill Mathilde," Mercy said in a rather matter-of-fact way.

The woman's kind eyes hardened. "That is exactly Armand's way. He often turns to the corrupt officials to do his bidding." She ripped off her mask, whirled, and spat on him, stepping on his neck with the sharp heel of her bejeweled boot.

"You break her neck, I break yours."

And she did.

Dimly, Mercy was aware of Raphael's strong arms sweeping her away, of following a burgundy gown back into a burning building.

"Felicity!" She dug in her heels, searching the increasingly smoke-clogged room for her sister.

In all the chaos, she hadn't witnessed her sister's escape, and considering who was carrying Felicity, it wasn't likely she'd have missed it. He was head and shoulders taller than most men.

"Many of us took pleasure barges and gondolas to get here," the Duchesse said over her shoulder. "I directed your sister and Gabriel to the tunnel beneath the keep that will take us to the canal where my boat is waiting."

That roused Mercy from her stupor better than anything else she could imagine might do. *Felicity.* Her guileless sister was a stranger to violence. So sweet-natured and timid was she, no one ever even entertained the notion of striking her.

They hurried by torchlight through the thousand-year-old tunnel toward the sound of water lapping at the stone docks. Voices ahead of them advertised that others had come this way in search of their boats, and what that meant for her sister, Mercy couldn't imagine.

A strange birdlike whistle from the dark caused Raphael to tense and freeze beside her.

Veering to the left, Raphael went toward an alcove that branched off the main causeway; Mercy and the Duchesse followed quickly on his heels.

They found Gabriel sitting with his back against the stones, hood pulled low over his face, those startling, abysmal shadows swallowing the horror of his features from view.

Cradled in his massive arms, Felicity looked like a child rather than a woman of twenty.

His fingers hovered over the place above her cheekbone where a raw mark formed.

Pale lashes cast shadows over her cheeks, and Mercy made a raw sound of relief to see them tremble.

She rushed to her sister, sinking down next to the giant of a man to take her cold, limp hand. "Felicity, can you hear me?"

"She woke." The graveled voice came from the void behind the hood. "She opened her eyes, said your name, and...and looked at me..."

A bleak note underscored his words with abject desolation.

"She faints when she's..." Mercy cut off, realizing the man had spoken in perfect English.

"When she's terrified," he finished.

Raphael had mentioned before that Gabriel did not speak English. No doubt, it was a truth they hid from the world.

"I don't have her smelling salts." She tapped Felicity on the uninjured cheek. "Darling, can you come around? Do you hear me?"

"Some cold water from the canal, maybe?" the Duchesse suggested, tearing the hem of her dress. "I'll soak this and put it against her neck, that might do the trick."

A resourceful woman, the Duchesse.

Raphael loomed over them, both a comforting presence and a frightening specter of wrath splattered by the blood of his enemy.

He glared daggers down at his brother. "Why are you not being carved into by Dr. Conleith right now?"

The face in the shadow of the hood didn't lift, but shifted away from her, answering in French. "Because, *mon frere*, I went to the surgeon's table thinking of what you said when we parted. The precise words you used when you spoke of the future. Never once did you refer to us. Only to me. Then I realized, you were making the biggest mistake of your life. Sacrificing yourself for a monster like me."

"You wouldn't be a monster anymore, you bastard, *that's* what we paid a fucking fortune to Conleith for!"

"Changing my face doesn't change who I am. What I've done..."

"I wanted you to have a fucking chance!" Raphael exploded, snatching a rock from the ground and hurling it into the darkness. "And after this debacle they'll hunt us to the ends of the earth."

"No, they won't." Morley melted from the shadows as if they gave way for him.

Mercy had never been so conflicted to see someone in her entire life. On one hand, she was so utterly glad he had come.

On the other, she feared what he might do.

As usual, his chiseled face was cast in stone. Imperturbable. Inaccessible.

Only Pru seemed to be able to read him. To reach him.

"I'm prepared to say you were both lost in the fire," Morley offered crisply. "Consider your deaths official. That is less paperwork for me, anyhow. But may God help you if you're caught in London again, for I won't."

Raphael turned to him, attempting to wipe some of the

blood from his cheek with his sleeve. "Why do this, when our capture would be a boon?"

"Because," Morley's pale gaze snapped to Mercy, and she might have read fondness beneath the censure. "Because you were right about the boots, Detective Goode, and had I listened to you earlier, so much of this might have been avoided."

The Duchesse rejoined them, a wet cloth in her hand. She regarded the addition of the Chief Inspector with a dubious look.

Morley did little but nod, saying for her benefit, "I highly doubt the coroner will be able to determine which killed Inspector Trout. The wounds to his face or to his neck. In my opinion, he can be added to this rubbish heap of a night. I should like to avoid an international incident, besides." He gave the Duchesse a starched bow of deference.

"*Merci*," she replied.

Morley turned to gaze down at Felicity, his expression troubled to find her in the arms of one of the largest, most brutal men in Christendom. "Fainted, did she?"

Mercy nodded. "I'm afraid so." She brushed her hand over the little curls at her sister's temple, wondering if hers felt so downy soft. "Marco Villenueve terrorized her. He...he struck her."

"When we find him, I'll fucking kill him," Morley said darkly, surprising even her with his vehemence.

At that, Gabriel's neck snapped up, revealing some of his ruined lip to the torchlight.

It was Raphael who spoke, however. "I assumed he was killed in the fall down the stairs. He was a crumpled heap of bones."

Morley shook his head. "No one has been able to locate him, alas, he's quite disappeared."

A prickling at the back of Mercy's neck told her that to

stand near Gabriel was possibly the most dangerous place to be at the moment.

Fury rolled off his shoulders in palpable waves.

And yet, he unfurled to stand without even jostling his burden, limping slightly as he offered Felicity into Morley's care. "It is *your* face she should see when she wakes," he said.

Morley took Felicity, eliciting a groan from the woman. "There we are. You're all right."

"You're bleeding." Mercy pointed to a pool that'd gathered where Gabriel had sat against the wall, the liquid gleaming like spilled ink in the firelight.

Gabriel only rolled his shoulder in a rather Gallic shrug, until Raphael checked the pool for himself, and found drops of blood along the path his brother had tread.

"Where are you hurt?" he demanded, clutching at his brother's coat.

"It's nothing," the man growled, reverting back to his native tongue.

"That amount of blood is not nothing, you fucking lunatic, now tell me. I'm taking you to the hospital."

"Stop fussing, little brother." Gabriel shrugged him off. "The hospital is where I'm headed anyway...it'll just be another scar."

"We'll accompany you," Raphael offered, jerking back a little when his brother held up a hand against him.

"No," he said fiercely. "I have my carriage. The plan hasn't changed, Raphael, so you must go. And if you do something impetuous and get yourself killed, I'll follow you into the afterlife and make your eternity a living hell."

"Brothers." The Duchesse made an amused sound that no one seemed to mark.

"I will meet you." Gabriel thrust a finger at his brother. "London isn't safe for you to show your face anymore."

Raphael stormed forward in protest. "But how can I—"

"*Ca suffit*, Raphael!" he snarled, causing everyone to start.

That's enough. His enormous shoulders sagged, and he placed a hand against the wall as if he needed it to hold him up for a moment. "Just let this be easy for once. Let me not have to fight. I'm so fucking *tired* of fighting. Just...go. So I can follow. *Vive la vie.*"

Live life.

Mercy held her breath as she watched Raphael do the same, she watched the war wage within him. Love and worry for his brother, the need to survive...

Finally, he nodded. *"Vive la vie."*

The leviathan paused for an imperceptible moment and Mercy thought his gaze might have shifted back to Felicity.

It was impossible not to have soft feelings for her sister, even for a man as hard as he.

Finally, he strode away so straight and tall, one might not even notice the drops of blood he left behind.

The shadows seemed to welcome him as one of their own, and Mercy stared into them long after his shape had disappeared.

Not because of the man who'd slid into their embrace, but because of the man behind her. The one whose embrace she craved the very most.

The one who was leaving.

Suddenly she wished the world would disappear, so she could give him a proper goodbye.

"Raphael." It was the Duchesse who said his name. "Gabriel told me that you two have Mathilde's ashes. That you have booked tickets to take her to places that were special. Places that we—she and I—were planning to visit together."

Needing to see him, Mercy turned and found his eyes upon her even as he replied to the Duchesse. "That was...on our itinerary, yes."

She stepped forward, a proud woman unused to asking for favors. "It seems providential, don't you think, that she and I were planning on taking my ship around the world. That we were going to lose ourselves, or perhaps find ourselves in foreign ports. If you are in need of losing yourself as well...I think Mathilde would have been happy for us to keep each other company and remember her."

"Duchesse," he said carefully. "I am honored...I..."

"I think you may call me Amelie. I would prefer to put my days as a Duchesse behind me." She pulled off her mask as if freeing herself from a mantle borne too long. Flicking a coy gaze at Mercy, she said, "I will go to my little boat to have the staff ready it. We will be prepared to stop and gather anything or...anyone you may wish to take with you before we board my ship."

"*Merci*," Raphael breathed, looking a little dazed.

Above them, in the keep, Mercy was aware of an inferno eating at a piece of precious history.

And it felt like a candle compared to what burned in her bosom as she looked at him.

"This is your chance at freedom." She summoned a smile from somewhere, pasting it onto her stiff and brittle lips. "I have...much to thank you for."

She glanced to Morley, who stood looking rather uncomfortable, though whether from their conversation or the weight of the woman in his arms, it was difficult to tell.

"Well." She smoothed down her dress, soiled by the extraordinary events of the night. "If you ever do come back to London, I can't promise I'll still be at Cresthaven. But you can find me Thursdays at the Eddard Sharpe Society. I hope you'll...that we'll...see each other."

Dammit, was she going to cry? Not in front of him. Anything but that.

Why did her heart have to choose *now* to break?

Why did saying goodbye seem like the worst thing that would ever happen to her?

Raphael reached for her, the backs of his knuckles brushing away a tear she'd not been aware had escaped.

"You look so bereft, I might weep," he murmured, his eyes crinkling with a smile that hadn't yet made it to his mouth. "It's as though you thought you were not invited along."

She blinked one. Twice. Her heart forgetting to beat as she analyzed his words.

"Are you asking me to...go? As in...with you?" Surely, she'd misheard.

"No." He stepped closer. Never had she seen such emotion in his eyes. Such unmistakable meaning. "I'm asking for so much more than that. I'm asking for *everything*."

She drew back, pressing her hand to her forehead. "This can't be real. You were just about to—to allow yourself to be killed not an hour ago and now you're...you're...what?"

Not *proposing*, surely.

"The only reason I contemplated leaving this world, Mercy, is to save the one person who has ever loved me. I thought no reality existed where I'd get to hope for a life that could offer a woman like you." He gathered her hands, lifting each knuckle to drag beneath a worshipful kiss. "I don't want to leave this world if you're a part of it. Because you're a part of *me*, whether you love me back or not."

She choked on her own breath and spasmed in a flurry of coughs. "I'm sorry. Did you say...love?"

"I said love." He nodded, unabashedly. "I give you my heart, used and damaged as it might be. I offer you my soul, black as it is. My money, which is an obscene amount." He grinned impishly, producing that bloody dimple.

Lord, but he didn't play fair.

"My body is yours in every way. My protection. My trust." He cupped her chin in his hand, and it humiliated her to find that more tears pooled in the grooves of his palm. "I would give my life, if only for a moment beneath the sun that is your smile.

Your grace. Your passion. Come with me, Mercy. Let me prove that I can deserve you."

She sniffed, so overwhelmed she felt as if she might simply float across the water like one of the gondolas. Desire so overwhelming swept her breath out of her lungs. This was what she wanted. This man. This life.

She opened her mouth as her heart sank. "I...I *can't* leave Felicity."

"Go," urged a weak voice.

She whirled to find her sister on her feet, leaning heavily on Morley, who had been astonishingly silent and stoic through the entire ordeal.

"What did you say?" Her blood was still for a full moment, while the person she held most dear looked her in the eyes with steady resolution.

And not a little bit melancholy.

"I cannot be your other half forever. You always needed more than that."

"Felicity! You can't think—"

When Mercy would have gone to her, Felicity stopped her with one gesture. "He *loves* you. And I'll be all right. I have Morley, Pru, Nora, and Titus, and it's not like you'll be gone forever. Perhaps I'll visit you in exotic places?"

Was she truly contemplating this madness? "But our parents...I can't leave you to face them in the wake of such a decision."

"I'll deal with them," Morley sighed, running an exhausted hand over his face. "Prudence will have my neck in a noose for this."

Suddenly her heart was pounding. Throbbing. Threatening to gallop away like a herd of stampeding horses.

"Surely you're not agreeing to this, Morley." She gestured at Raphael, not trusting herself to look at him. "Have you forgotten he's a thief? A ne'er-do-well? A profligate libertine

I've known all of five minutes?"

"A lesser man would be wounded." Raphael placed a hand over his heart as if she'd pierced it.

"I was once all of those things." Morley stared hard at the man who offered his heart to her. "I believe we do not have to be what our circumstances would have made for us. We can forge our own path. We can choose to be better."

"All I want to be is worthy of her," Raphael said with such vehemence, she found new tears pricking at the corner of her eyes.

Morley nodded his approval. "London could be made safe for you... It would take some doing. Some time to change the narrative, to see where the balance of power shifts when all is said and done. Longueville will need seeing to. Leave that to me."

"Everyone's gone mad," Mercy realized.

Including her. Because she was actually contemplating this. Leaving her home. Her twin. Her other beloved sisters and nieces and brothers-in-law.

For the journey she'd always yearned for.

To share with a man who was beginning to mean everything to her.

Felicity drifted forward and enfolded her in an embrace, her body trembling with valiantly unshed tears. "You're miserable here, Mercy. We all know it. Our parents will return, and you'll be locked in a battle that will only end in a disastrous marriage or with you disavowed. You've always talked of independence. A grand adventure. This might be your one chance to claim it."

"What will you do? Might you come with us?" Mercy offered.

Felicity shook her head. "Mercy, for once, stop worrying about me. I'm grown, perhaps it's time I step away from your shadow. I'll toddle along. It'll be fine, just...promise me you'll write. All the time."

Mercy must have nodded, because Felicity kissed her, then turned to take Raphael's hand. "And you promise to make her happy?"

He pressed a fond kiss to her knuckles. "It's all I want, *petite sœur.*"

"She's not easy."

"I'm still right here, I'll have you know," Mercy said with no little indignation.

Raphael flashed his most charming, cocksure grin. "I'm looking forward to the challenge."

Mercy dashed away every tear, not knowing if she was infatuated or infuriated. "You're getting ahead of yourselves. I haven't even agreed to go anywhere!"

Felicity and Raphael shared a knowing smile that lit her temper. "What did I tell you?"

Raphael winked and let out a long-suffering sigh.

"Unbelievable!" Throwing up her hands, Mercy marched a few paces away, if only to try to chase her unruly emotions.

"*Mon chaton.*" Raphael caught her, and the feel of his strong fingers threading with hers stunned her to stillness.

Not just rooting her feet to the ground but weaving something undeniable through the pads of her fingers, threading up the veins in her arm, and pouring into her heart. From there, it pulsed into the rest of her with every beat.

It was him. His name. His face.

The love that shined there when she turned back to find them alone beneath the earth.

"I can't explain it, after only knowing you such a short time," he said with the earnestness of a youth shining on the face of a brutal man who'd never been blessed with a childhood. "But I know I've always been some sort of empty vessel, and I think I understand why my entire life I've never felt whole." He pressed his hand to her heart, the palm warm as he seemed to savor what he found there. "I am not me. I am we. *Us.* That feels complete. My heart only seems to beat when you are near. I stand before you. No. I kneel at your feet."

He hit his knees, pressing his forehead to her fingers as if paying tribute to a goddess. "I am a man stripped of pride and wit. Of everything that gave me power. This is what I offer you. A new start. I'm asking—I'm begging—not for your forgiveness. Not for your mercy. But for *you.* Mercy. *For you.* Will you be mine? Will you let me call myself yours?"

She studied his face for a hint of artifice, and what she found there broke open something inside of her that exploded into incandescent sparks of the purest exhilaration. Life with this man. Discovery. Travel. Adventure. Pleasure.

Love.

Wasn't that worth any sort of risk?

A sliver of doubt dimmed his smile. "I know you didn't want to be the property of man, Mercy. And I'd never ask that of you. You own me heart and soul, but I don't think I'd love you this passionately, if you could truly be possessed—"

"Stop." She seized him and pulled him to his feet. "Stop. I cannot take any more joy or it'll split me apart. Of course, I'm going with you. Of course, I'm yours. I was yours the moment you kissed me, you dolt. Now do it again before I change my mind."

With a smile brilliant enough to illuminate the night, he swept her in his arms and claimed her mouth, sealing their bargain with a kiss that was impossible to maintain through their unrelenting smiles.

"Come," he urged, linking his arms with hers. "Let us leave all this chaos behind."

They walked hand in hand through the shadows of the dark night, knowing that their brilliant future lay just on the other side.

EPILOGUE

*R*aphael broke through the surface of the warm waters off the Antiguan coast with a mighty surge of his limbs. The sun felt like the very smile of God on his face, and he wiped the ocean from his eyes to be greeted by a view that never ceased to strike him with pure wonder.

The gleaming white sands and the indescribably clear blue water provided the perfect backdrop for a tangle of vibrant vegetation and exotic trees. The opulent Villa de la Sol was part Spanish cathedral, part Persian palace, resplendent in the noonday brilliance.

But what made this place paradise, was the goddess draped in a hammock beneath a tasseled umbrella.

The sight of her humbled him into stillness, and Raphael treaded water, taking advantage of a rare moment to observe his wife unaware.

He woke every morning anxious to make certain he hadn't dreamed his good fortune. Mercy Goode had consented to make an honest man of him at sea—provided they omitted the part about her obeying or submitting to her husband.

When asked what word might replace the original, she'd studied him for a moment, then decided "adore."

They'd been true to their word. They loved, cherished, honored and most assuredly *adored* each other.

She nestled in a pool of thin white skirts; her bare leg draped over the side of her hammock. In her hand was *The Affair of the Benighted Bride*, the latest adventure of Detective Eddard Sharpe. The gentle ocean breeze teased locks of her unbound hair, only shades darker than the sand she kicked at with her toe, encouraging a gentle sway.

She glanced up as the Duchesse—Amelie—filled her dainty glass with a juice made from the local guava fruit she'd mixed with champagne.

The women toasted each other, and Amelie must have said something witty because Mercy tossed her curls back, exposing her elegant throat as she laughed with unrestricted abandon.

A wave of joy threatened to drown him.

Christ, he worshiped her with such uninhibited devotion, he became jealous of the sun's own caress on her skin.

Raphael disrupted a school of tiny, colorful fish as he displaced the water with powerful strokes. He swam until he could use his feet against the sand to propel him through a tide that tried its utmost to hinder his advance.

By the time he'd reached the beach upon which the women reclined, the two were locked in an animated discussion, gesturing wildly.

"... And that is why women belong on the bench and in juries." She waved her book. "J. Francis Morgan is plainly saying that surely such a gross miscarriage of justice would not have occurred should a woman have had ought to do with the case. She would have seen through the ruse right away. Why must it be a man's world when they do a right proper job of cocking it up?"

Raphael kept wisely silent on the subject as he made his approach.

Amelie wrapped her arms around her bent legs and rested her chin on her knees. "Women know that it isn't a man's world. Not completely. We simply have a more subtle influence. We change things when men are not looking, thinking they are important to play at war and conquest."

"But they do more damage than we can repair," Mercy said with vicious passion. "I don't want my influence to be subtle. I want to change things while they watch. While they weep."

"I've no doubt you will." Raphael retrieved a towel from the small stand he'd driven into the sand, upon which his clothing hung.

"You, my love, are merciless."

"And *you* are not the first person to tell me that."

As he applied the towel to his skin, Amelie finished her drink in two impressive swallows and pushed to her feet. "If you will excuse me, those of us with red in our hair are wise to get out of the sun after noonday," she said with a languorous stretch. "Besides, I need to pack if we are to leave for the States, where we will no longer be allowed to lounge about in the half-nude, more is the pity."

She flashed them both a cheeky wink before lifting a hem that had been cut like a riding kit. Flowing and feminine, but certainly more trouser than skirt.

Raphael bid her adieu before draping the towel over his head and scrubbing as much of the ocean water from his scalp as he could.

"For a life on the lam, I say we're surviving rather well," he remarked before drying his face and neck.

"I dare say I'm enjoying my time as an exile," his wife replied blithely. "And I certainly have no complaints regarding the view."

He surfaced from beneath the towel to find her eyes making a lazy, appreciative journey up his torso.

His body responded to the heat in her gaze, though he decided to allow her a respite as she'd declined to join him in the water due to the arrival of her monthly courses and complaints of fatigue.

Still, he joined her on the hammock, his weight forcing her to roll toward him, allowing him to gather her close and fuse their mouths for a deep kiss that tasted of passion, guava, and a hint of brine.

"Tell me, wife, about what sparked your indignance at your novel?"

She opened her mouth, then closed it with a befuddled expression. "I'll have to reread the passage now. You've made it quite impossible to pay attention."

He drew a finger down the line of her nose. "I'm learning your attention is often difficult to pin down."

She turned her head to the side, playfully avoiding his next kiss. "That's ridiculous. You don't know the first thing about—" She seized his bicep. "Raphael. *Look*. There's a dolphin!" Pointing in her excitement, she leaned so far forward, the hammock would have been unsettled had he not been there to steady it. "An entire family of them. Oh! I've never seen such a thing."

He draped her across his chest, his amusement at her over-wrought delight spilling over as laughter.

He decided to forgo taunting her with an *I told you so*.

They settled back to sway, and watched gleaming grey sea creatures frolic and leap, seeming to mimic their joy.

Lingering long after the dolphins disappeared, Raphael coiled one of her curls around his finger, enjoying the waves, the breeze, and the closeness between them.

"I don't think I've ever been happier than this moment," he murmured, pressing his lips to her temple. "I wish I could bottle this feeling like a scent. That I could wear it on my skin always. Escape back here whenever life is bleak."

She pushed up, bracing her hands on his chest as she leveled him a sober look. "You know, the more I love you, the angrier I am with you. To think that you almost missed this. That you might have died..."

"I concocted that scheme before I met you because I'd never truly felt alive." He dropped his forehead against hers. "You changed all that."

Her lip quirked. "I suppose I'll have to forgive you eventually."

"You could punish me first, if you like," he suggested with a naughty wink. "A hundred tongue lashings. Or real lashings, if that's what you prefer."

She gave him a half-hearted shove before settling down against him once more. "I'm excited for the life we're going to live together, and I'm happy to see America, though I'm not looking forward to donning my corset again."

He chuffed, before a familiar anxiety lanced through him. "Do you ever get homesick for England?"

Staring into the distance, she replied, "I miss my sisters. I worry for Felicity. But I know we'll go back, eventually. I'm in no great hurry."

He caught her hand. "We'll go back. We'll go anywhere you are happy," he vowed.

She caught both of his wrists and pulled them around her. "I'm happy right here. In your arms. I can miss England sometimes, but I'm incapable of being homesick."

"Oh?" His lips found the shell of her ear and stopped for a nibble. "Why is that?"

"Because, husband, my home is wherever you are."

ALSO BY KERRIGAN BYRNE

A GOODE GIRLS ROMANCE

Seducing a Stranger

Courting Trouble

Dancing With Danger

Tempting Fate

Crying Wolfe

Making Merry

THE BUSINESS OF BLOOD SERIES

The Business of Blood

A Treacherous Trade

A Vocation of Violence

VICTORIAN REBELS

The Highwayman

The Hunter

The Highlander

The Duke

The Scot Beds His Wife

The Duke With the Dragon Tattoo

The Earl on the Train

THE MACLAUCHLAN BERSERKERS

Highland Secret

Highland Shadow

Highland Stranger

To Seduce a Highlander

ABOUT THE AUTHOR

Kerrigan Byrne is the USA Today Bestselling and award winning author of several novels in both the romance and mystery genre.

She lives on the Olympic Peninsula in Washington with her two Rottweiler mix rescues and one very clingy cat. When she's not writing and researching, you'll find her on the beach, kayaking, or on land eating, drinking, shopping, and attending live comedy, ballet, or too many movies.

Kerrigan loves to hear from her readers! To contact her or learn more about her books, please visit her site or find her on most social media platforms: www.kerriganbyrne.com